ORBS OF WISDOM

DRAGON GATE, BOOK 6

LINDSAY BUROKER

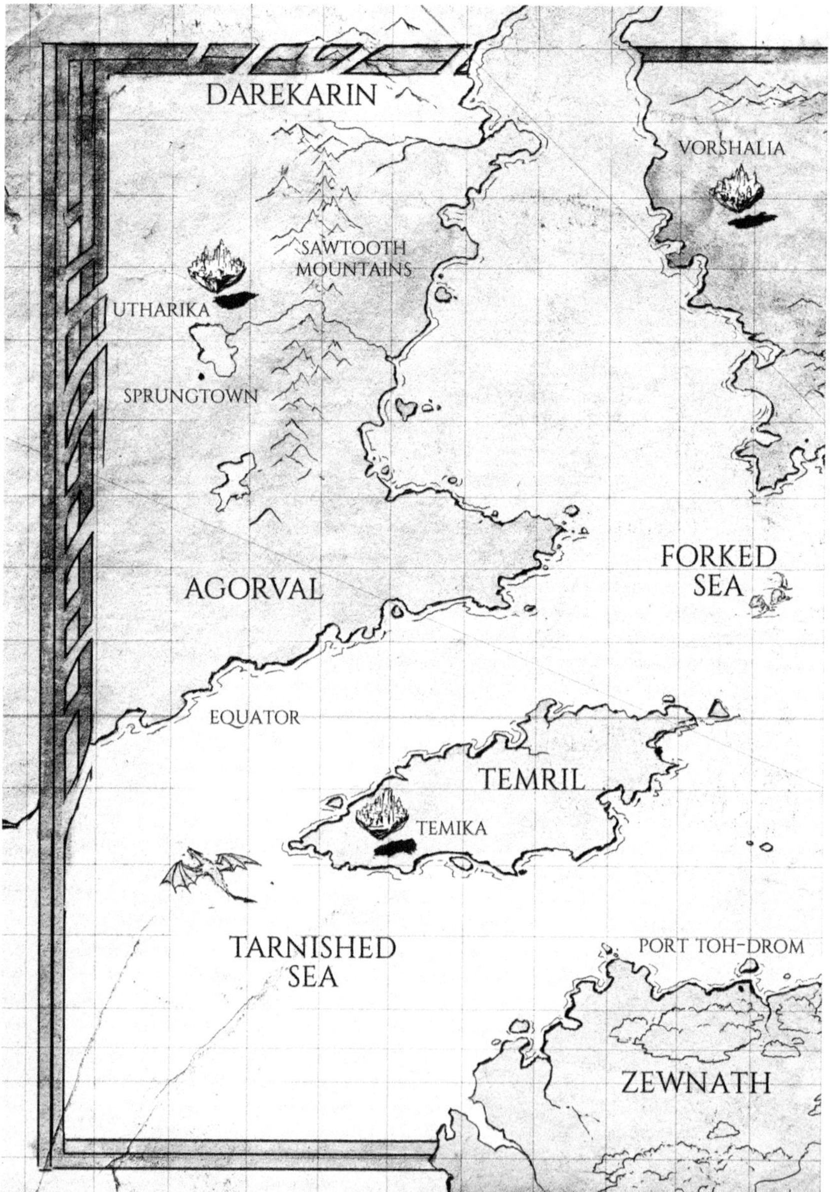
DAREKARIN
VORSHALIA
SAWTOOTH
MOUNTAINS
UTHARIKA
SPRUNGTOWN
AGORVAL
FORKED
SEA
EQUATOR
TEMRIL
TEMIKA
TARNISHED
SEA
PORT TOH-DROM
ZEWNATH

DYVAR
JUTOKOR ISLANDS
VOR
WORTLAND
ABKORI
WORTAR
BAKORA
ZARLESH
AMURI
DRAGON PERCH
PERCHVER
ZAR
BLUE BAY
AR ISLANDS
ARIKA
TORVIL

FOREWORD

The final book in the series is here!

Please let me thank all those who helped along the way: Shelley Holloway, my editor. Sarah Engelke and Cindy Wilkinson, my beta readers. Jeff Brown, my cover illustrator. Vivienne Leheny, my audiobook narrator. And finally, Willow and Cutter, the dog supervisors and support staff.

Thank you, dear reader, for following along with the books. This is a big one. I hope you enjoy it!

1

SHIKARI FLEW FROM THE TOP OF A FOUNTAIN TO THE CROWN OF A statue to the roof of an abandoned market stall, pausing to perch there and peer curiously around the sky city. More than a few mages and servants gaped at his passing, and alarmed squawks and gasps preceded Jakstor Freedar and Lord Malek as they strode through Utharika with the dragonling, heading for a part of the city that Jak hadn't seen before.

A crafter carrying an armload of weapons spotted Shikari, yelled, and ran into a building. On a whisper of magic, the door slammed shut behind the man.

Among a population of mages, one might have expected bravery and composure in the face of such a young dragon—after all, when Shikari stood on all fours, his head wasn't much higher than Jak's—but the citizens didn't want anything to do with him.

Given that it had only been a day since brown-and-gray mottled adult dragons had attempted to tear down the barrier and knock Utharika from its floating position a thousand feet above the ground, that was perhaps understandable. Still, blue-scaled

Shikari was friendly and curious, and anyone with a hint of perception should have been able to see that.

A *thwack* came from behind Jak, followed by a clatter as a post broke and ceramic pots clunked onto the street. A terrene woman wearing a mageband screamed and ran into an alley.

Jak looked in time to see Shikari spring away from the crushed stall and broken pottery. He looked sheepishly at it.

I did not realize the roofs of human dwellings were so frail, Shikari spoke telepathically into Jak's mind.

I didn't realize you'd gotten so heavy, and that's a vendor's stall, not a dwelling. I don't think the building codes for them are as strict. Jak eyed Malek, afraid he would call the dragonling a menace, though he'd barely seemed to notice. As a zidarr, supreme mage and warrior, Malek was usually the epitome of focus and alertness, but his eyes had been haunted and distracted since Mother had revealed that she and King Uthari were afflicted with the same parasite that had turned most of the dragons into aggressive, unbalanced monsters. *Can you fix it with your magic, Shikari?*

The last thing Jak wanted was to cause a terrene human difficulty in making ends meet. As if invading dragons weren't bad enough, that woman—the artisan who'd crafted the pots?—already took a great risk selling her wares in a city of mages.

Certainly.

Shikari straightened, his wings spreading wide and his tail thrusting out behind him. His yellow reptilian eyes closed to slits as he regarded the mangled stall and shattered pottery. Jak sensed magical power emanating from the dragonling as broken ceramic and shards of wood lifted into the air.

The pieces of wood fitted themselves back together, re-forming the stall, with Shikari using magic to reinforce the posts and roof so it wouldn't collapse again under the weight of future dragon visitors. He melted the ceramic in order to re-form it, but instead of recreating the original pots, dragon-shaped pitchers and drinkware, with curving tails creating handles, soon occupied the shelves.

With his handiwork complete, Shikari strutted toward Malek and Jak, his head held high.

"Uhm," Jak said. "I don't think those are going to sell right now. Half the kingdom is on fire, thanks to dragon attacks."

Once we rid my kind of the parasite, dragons will help humans as they did long ago.

"At which point, it will be trendy to have dragon-shaped earthenware?" Jak asked.

Certainly.

"We're almost to the street the Rivlen family lives on," Malek said, continuing on. "We would have been there already if someone hadn't scared away the magecart driver."

"All Shikari did was hop on," Jak said. "He didn't roar or menace anyone."

"After he hopped on, he started chewing on the upholstery and the driver's clothing."

"Well, if you're going to wear something with beads dangling on fringes, you can't be surprised if animals and curious dragons are attracted. I bet people's house cats swat at those beads all the time."

"Your dragon is slightly larger and more intimidating than a house cat."

Shikari lifted his head even higher. It had taken his roar weeks to develop from a squeak to something substantial, so he had to be pleased to be called intimidating.

"We won't be able to stay long," Malek said, turning at a corner and walking under an ostentatious archway with towers to each side, the architectural details gilded. Even the cobblestones of the wide boulevard appeared gilded. They glinted in the morning sun. "The portal has been loaded onto the gateship, and as soon as our supplies are on board as well, Uthari wants us to leave."

"Trust me, I'm eager to leave and find a way to fix Mother." Jak didn't mention Uthari, though he supposed he should hope for the king to be healed before he turned into more of an aggressive monster than he already was. It was possible the symptoms of the parasite would present differently in humans than dragons, but Jak couldn't imagine any infestation would *improve* Uthari's personality.

"Yes. Had the engineer not ordered parts that weren't available in the city, we could already be flying south." Malek gazed off in that direction.

"I wish we could check on Captain Rivlen before going through the portal, but the Glacier Islands aren't remotely on the way to Zewnath." As a cartography student, Jak well knew that they—and the huge dragon-steel fortress the dragons had reputedly built—were fifteen hundred miles south of their destination in the Zewnath jungle.

Malek slanted him a long look. "Neither she nor any of her fleet have been heard from since her brief report, in which she informed Uthari's servant of the existence of the floating fortress. I don't know what you're planning on telling her parents, but it is possible that she and the other officers on those ships are dead."

"She's alive. I'm planning to tell her father that she's an amazing officer, a powerful mage, and an honor to her family. *Someone* needs to say those things to him." Jak admitted that a nineteen-year-old *wild one,* who'd only been a mage for a couple of months and who Uthari would prefer to be dead, might not be the best person to convince the senior Rivlen that his daughter was a boon to the family. But she'd been haunted by a lifetime of her father not believing her good enough. Jak didn't know if he could change that, or make a difference in the way her father interacted with her, but since he was here in Utharika, he felt compelled to try.

Malek was polite enough not to point out that it was none of Jak's business, but it had to have crossed his mind.

Would Rivlen's father let Jak in to talk to him? He ought to be willing to invite in Uthari's right-hand man, Lord Malek. That was the main reason Jak had asked Malek to come along. That and because he'd worried random mages in the street might try to flay him and Shikari if they didn't have someone known and respected to vouch for them.

"This is it." Malek stopped on the right side of the street in front of gilded doors that towered more than fifteen feet high in the middle of an equally tall stone wall. He rested his hand on a dome embedded in the framework. It glowed, buzzing a soft query. "Lord Malek and Jak Freedar to see Admiral Dayum and Meyari Rivlen."

Jak blushed, embarrassed that Malek knew the names of Rivlen's parents—or had thought to look them up—and he hadn't. Admittedly, this was Malek's city and Malek's world. Jak was a guest. Technically, he was still a prisoner.

The doors swung open, and Shikari bounded ahead of them into a courtyard with a three-story fountain looming in the middle, encircled by a pool the size of some ponds back in Sprungtown. Large orange-and-white fish flitted around in the water. Koi. The pond on the university campus held a school of them.

Not surprisingly, they caught Shikari's attention. He galloped across the flagstones and leaped into the pool as the front door of the house opened.

A stern-faced man with a trimmed gray beard and mustache scowled out at him. A buxom dark-haired woman at his side let out a startled shriek before he frowned at her, and she fell silent, though she did lift a hand to her mouth as she stared at the dragonling wading around in her fountain.

"There's no need for histrionics, Meyari," the man said. Was he

Rivlen's father? "It is but a young dragon, and I am certain Lord Malek has it under control."

He would be less certain of that if he'd seen the incident with the vending stall.

As Malek strode forward, the man bowed toward him, and his wife pressed her hands together in front of her chest and bobbed her head.

"Lord Malek," she said. "You honor us with your presence in our home."

"Enough, Meyari," the man said. "This will be a discussion between powerful men." He tilted his head back toward the marble foyer visible in the shade behind them.

"Powerful men?" Jak mouthed.

Would that include him? He was the reason Malek had come.

Meyari hesitated, then bowed her head again and backed away, though Jak sensed her taking up a position behind a column in the foyer instead of disappearing into the house.

"How may I serve you and the king?" the man asked Malek, not glancing at Jak or acknowledging his existence in any way.

Already, Jak had no trouble imagining him neglecting his daughter. He peered back toward Meyari, worried she was treated just as badly. He sensed that she had power but not nearly as much as her husband, whose aura nearly rivaled Malek's.

"Admiral Dayum Rivlen." Malek inclined his head.

Dayum must have been retired, else he would have been preparing to leave with the fleet.

"I am not here to request your service," Malek continued, "though it's possible it will be needed if dragons return."

"I assisted with the defense of the city yesterday." Dayum glanced at Shikari, who was mucking around in the water and had already eaten two of the koi. Dayum was probably wondering if he needed to defend his fountain as well.

"Excellent. I accompanied young Jak, who requested to visit

your home. He wishes a few words with you before we leave the city." Malek extended a hand toward him.

Was that all the introduction Jak would get? Nothing about what a talented student and eager pupil he was or how he was distinguishing himself as a mage and a human being and would be a fine suitor for Dayum's daughter?

Jak hadn't intended to mention his relationship with Rivlen and told himself the introduction was fine. Malek had gotten him through the door. The rest was up to him.

Jak removed his hat and bowed to the man. "Admiral Rivlen, I'm Jak Freedar, and I've had the opportunity to work with your daughter of late."

Dayum scowled at him. Jak didn't know if he'd already managed to offend the man with his words, or if being so young and presuming to speak to a retired admiral was offensive in and of itself.

"Ask them if she's all right," came a soft call from the column.

Dayum turned his scowl over his shoulder toward his wife, but whatever response he gave was telepathic.

"What do you want?" he asked Jak aloud.

"Just to let you know that your daughter is an amazing officer. She's extremely brave in battle, leading her people from the front, and she smites her enemies with her powerful magic. It's all very impressive. You should be proud of her."

Dayum's scowl only deepened. "What are you, some infatuated servant?" He didn't scowl at Malek, but he did look to Malek in confusion. For an explanation?

"No, Admiral. I'm a cartographer." Until he earned his degree, Jak was a cartography *student*, but there was no need for extreme precision. "I've also studied dragons. King Uthari, uhm, picked me up to help the fleet in what has become a trying time."

Jak dared not lie with Malek standing next to them, but Uthari's people—specifically Malek—*had* picked him up. Admittedly, Uthari had been more interested in his mother than in Jak, but...

"Jak is an academic advisor," Malek said when Dayum looked to him again.

Jak had to wrestle down the urge to hug Malek and thank him for not saying, *Jak is our prisoner*. One didn't hug zidarr in public.

"He doesn't look old enough to advise anyone on anything."

"I'm older than I look." Jak put his hat on and stood straight. "And I know that your daughter cares about your opinion and wants you to be proud of her." He hoped Rivlen wouldn't hear about this and consider it meddling instead of an earnest attempt to help her. "And you should be. If you'd seen her in battle, fighting dragons from the forecastle of her ship, you would know how heroic she is."

"Uh huh," was all Dayum said. "You're not going to ask me for permission to marry her, are you? Whose family did you say you're from?"

"No, my lord. Er, Admiral. My lord Admiral."

The man sighed.

"I merely wanted to let you know that she's a good mage and officer, and I'm sure that with her help, we'll be able to rid Torvil of the dragon threat."

Is she alive? Meyari asked into Jak's mind.

He hesitated. *I haven't heard from her recently, but I believe in my heart that she is. She's a very capable mage and warrior.*

Worry emanated from Meyari, and he feared his answer hadn't been as comforting as he'd wished.

Splashes came from the fountain behind Jak, and something splatted down on the flagstones.

There is much food here, Shikari informed him. *Take this opportunity to gorge yourself.*

When Dayum's scowl deepened, Jak wasn't surprised to glance

back and find a koi flopping on the flagstones. He picked up his gift from Shikari and ran it back to the fountain.

Those are pets, Shikari. Please stop eating them.

Shikari lifted his head, another koi sticking out of his maw, its tail flapping wildly. *Pet food?*

No, just pets.

"Boy, you will rid my fountain of that oversized reptile," Dayum said. "What is he doing to my fish?"

Dayum lifted his arm, and Shikari floated out of the fountain.

"He's a growing dragon and gets hungry." Jak stepped in front of his charge, hoping to keep Dayum from using more magic—and Shikari from retaliating. He rested a hand on the dragonling's head, also hoping to keep him from jumping back in the water. The koi in Shikari's mouth disappeared as he swallowed.

"Dayum," came his wife's plaintive call. "Please ask Lord Malek for details."

Jak's answer must not have been enough for her.

The admiral sighed again and looked at Malek, though he kept sending dark glances at Shikari. "We've heard about the fortress and that part of the fleet is missing, including our daughter's ship. Are there any updates?"

"Not at this time," Malek said. "The rest of the fleet is heading south to deal with the threat."

Shikari stepped closer to the fountain, a longing look in his eyes, and Jak shifted to block him. "We'll get you something from a market on the way back to the ship," he whispered.

"I see," Dayum replied to Malek. "We will look forward to updates."

Malek inclined his head once more and stepped back.

Fearing the meeting was over and he hadn't accomplished anything, Jak blurted, "I'm sure Rivlen is alive and leading her people well, Admiral. You'll see when we get back. I know she'll be instrumental in dealing with the dragon threat."

Dayum's eyes narrowed. "You'll address my daughter as *Captain* Rivlen, boy, and I suggest you turn your lust toward the serving wenches, before you irk the wrong person and find yourself deader than my prize fish."

Dayum stepped back into the foyer, and the door thumped shut.

Jak slumped in defeat.

Malek pointed toward the courtyard exit. "I've received a report that the gateship will be ready to depart shortly."

"That didn't go as well as I'd hoped," Jak admitted, falling in beside Malek and making sure Shikari came along.

"Since you are not known to the admiral, and you haven't a reputation that precedes you, it's unlikely your praise of his daughter will have meant much."

"Yeah," Jak said glumly. "I wish *you* had praised her."

Admittedly, the retired admiral hadn't seemed dazzled by Malek's deadly zidarr-ness either. During his years of service, he'd likely worked with numerous zidarr.

"He did not ask for my opinion. It would also be difficult for me to offer glowing praise right now, given that Rivlen hasn't served Uthari with her entire heart and soul." Malek slanted Jak a long look.

Jak had a feeling Uthari had found out that Rivlen hadn't done all she could to keep Jak from building the kerzor and sticking it in Tonovan's head. And that he'd told Malek all about it.

"Don't take this the wrong way, my lord," Jak said circumspectly, "but you seem to have made some choices lately that would suggest you're not heart-and-soul Uthari's loyal zidarr anymore either, at least when it comes to certain professors."

Given that the Zidarr Code forbade relationships, Jak had been surprised to realize his mother and Malek were spending time together as more than friends.

Malek appeared more morose than offended by the statement. "I would not give myself glowing praise now either."

Jak? his mother's voice sounded in his head. *The gateship is ready to go.*

I know. We're coming.

He quickened his pace. With his mother's health on the line, and the future of humanity at risk, they dared not delay.

~

Between the portal standing upright and lashed to the narrow deck and Jak's increasingly large dragon sprawled in front of it, Malek marveled that the gateship hadn't tipped over and plummeted to the ground far below. Neither dragon nor portal weighed a great deal, but having the ancient artifact that the ship was meant to fly *through* balanced on top of it was asking for trouble.

If they ran into any storms, Malek would have to use magic to protect the vessel and its load from the wind. How the gateship would navigate underwater, he didn't yet know, but Lieutenant Vinjo had been banging and clinking at the portholes and spreading what smelled like pine pitch over the seams since well before dawn.

You are prepared to leave? Uthari asked from the deck of the *Soaring Eagle*, one of twelve mageships being readied for their own journey.

A full day and night had passed since Captain Rivlen's report about the fortress. The lack of updates since then suggested the *Star Flyer* and the two mageships that had flown south with it had been destroyed. Either there had been no survivors, or the domejirs had been too damaged for communication. Both scenarios were grim, and Malek felt like he was shirking a duty by not going with the fleet to face the dragons and their new fortress. But he had another assignment.

I am, Your Majesty. Are you certain you don't wish to accompany us? Malek gestured to the deck of the long, narrow vessel, though he expected Uthari to reject the offer. Uthari wouldn't find Shikari an appealing shipmate, and Malek couldn't imagine his liege riding on something so pedestrian and lacking in comforts. He was surprised Uthari wasn't taking his yacht this time, though it was possible he didn't want it damaged—or destroyed—by dragons. *If Jadora is successful in finding a way to get rid of the parasites in your bodies, she would be able to deliver the treatment much more quickly if you were with us.*

Thus far, neither Uthari nor Jadora appeared changed by their microscopic invaders. The parasites were, Malek reminded himself, a different species from the bacteria he'd been infested with on Nargnoth, but the similarities were enough to prompt him to make comparisons. When he'd been exposed, less than a day had passed before he'd started losing his composure.

I am aware, but with Tonovan gone, I must lead the fleet myself. Even across the distance between the two ships, it was impossible to miss the coolness in Uthari's gaze. *Watch your back on this mission, Malek. You may believe those two care for you, but you travel with vipers.*

Malek didn't argue, but he knew he had nothing to fear from Jak or Jadora. He'd seen their thoughts before they'd developed the ability to hide them, and they hadn't changed as much as one might have expected from people quickly developing great power.

Jak's actions had been predictable. Had Malek been with him on the *Star Flyer*, he believed he would have anticipated the creation of the kerzor and stopped it. It was hard, however, for Malek to mourn Tonovan's passing. His only regret about not being there to stop Jak was that Jak was now in trouble with Uthari. Malek might have invited Uthari to come along with them, but he was relieved his king wouldn't, else he might have sought another way to ensure control over Jak. Since his plan to infect Shikari with that parasite had failed...

I know you believe you have their loyalty, Malek, Uthari continued when he didn't answer, *but people change once they develop power, and you haven't truly known them that long. As I said, watch your back.*

I will, Your Majesty.

And rest assured that I would not be upset if that engineer does not return. Uthari curled a lip at Vinjo's back.

Vinjo was hanging from scaffolding on the hull of the gateship while he applied what Malek dearly hoped was something more effective than pitch. There *was* some magic about the dark substance but not enough that he was confident in its ability to repel thousands of pounds of pressure of water.

I am certain you can navigate that craft without him, Uthari added.

I am not certain I could navigate it underwater without him, Malek said dryly.

You underestimate yourself.

Malek inclined his head politely, though, in this instance, he didn't agree. The dragon-steel weapons and the portal had been sharing visions, but he didn't know what exactly awaited them on the water world. All he knew was that they'd yet to go through the portal without encountering dangerous enemies, and he expected nothing less this time. It would be better to leave navigating the ship to someone else so he could focus on defense.

The hatch creaked open, and Lieutenant Sasko climbed out. She glanced at Malek before heading to the railing, probably guided to the correct spot by her sense of smell. Pitch was pungent.

Wrinkling her nose, she leaned over to address Vinjo. "Are you ready to go? Professor Freedar is antsy to depart."

Shikari roared, though he appeared to be directing the noise at a flapping flag on another ship rather than the mercenary.

"And so is Jak's dragon," Sasko added.

Vinjo peered up, spatters of pitch making his hair stick together in clumps, and waved a brush. A hint of magic in his bucket kept the pitch from hardening while he worked. "Yes. I can complete my enhancements along the way."

"Are you sure *enhancements* is the right word for smearing black gunk on the side of the ship?"

"If the desired result is a waterproof craft, certainly."

"It was more aesthetically pleasing before."

"Also more pleasing to water molecules seeking entrance. Will you help me up, good Lieutenant?" Vinjo smiled at her.

Not certain how a terrene human was supposed to help up someone she couldn't reach, Malek used his power to levitate the engineer onto the deck. "Go directly to navigation without flirting, and launch the craft."

Vinjo gaped at him. "I wasn't *flirting*, Lord Zidarr."

"I require that he wash his hair before he flirts with me," Sasko said. With typical mercenary irreverence, she didn't add an honorific.

Malek thought about correcting her, especially since Uthari was still watching, but instead used his magic to usher them both toward the hatch. No doubt Jadora would call him pompous for insisting people call him *lord*. Perhaps the idea should have made him aware of how much he'd changed for her, but he only smiled. For some people, it was worth changing a little.

After Vinjo and Sasko disappeared below, the hatch clanging shut behind them, Malek caught Uthari's frown and wiped the smile from his face.

Is there anything else, Your Majesty? Malek asked preemptively.

We will keep in touch via the dome-jir. Uthari squinted. *I understand that craft has one now.*

Oh? Malek couldn't sense one.

Check the drawers. The officers on board that Rivlen sent along weren't as powerful as I would have wished—or that I requested she send to guard the boy—but they're not entirely incapable. One reported that the engineer made a dome-jir. They've confiscated it from him twice now, but he keeps getting it back and hiding it in niches camouflaged by magic. Find it and take control of it so he can't report to his king or any of Zaruk's fleet.

I will do that immediately.

Punish him if he attempts to betray us in any way.

Yes, Your Majesty.

Malek didn't point out that Vinjo was their prisoner, whom they'd captured and forced to work for them, so it would have been understandable if he *had* attempted to report in to his superiors. If anything, Vinjo was betraying his people by working for Uthari. But Malek doubted his liege wanted to listen to such semantics now.

As the gateship glided away from the docks, some of the mageships were also departing. Malek had hoped for a head start, wanting to complete his mission on the other world and return in time to help Uthari battle the dragons at their fortress.

Once you've visited those orbs and learned how to destroy the parasite, Uthari said, *continue south to join us in the Glacier Islands. I suspect the dragons have been preparing for us and that we'll need all the help we can get. It's unfortunate that so few of the other kings have answered my summons and agreed to send ships to join us. As we travel, I'll try again to gather allies for this. The other rulers are shortsighted if they don't realize the threat this fortress represents and that we must address it instead of waiting for the dragons to finish what they plan and come to destroy us.*

Yes, Your Majesty. Malek politely did not point out that Uthari might have had more luck making alliances if he hadn't ordered Tonovan to kill King Temrok. Surely, the rest of the rulers were wary of him now. It wouldn't surprise Malek to learn that the other rulers were now planning how they would take over the Uth Kingdom if Uthari and his fleet fell in battle.

Malek lifted his head. He would do his best to make sure that did *not* happen.

To aid you in your journey, Uthari said, *there's a gift I recently acquired in your cabin. I have the matching one. With Thanok's luck, they'll help us achieve victory.*

Yes, Your Majesty.

Uthari dismissed him, and Malek, curious about the gift, went below.

Lying on the bunk in his cabin was a beautiful dragon-steel longsword, a weapon similar in length and heft to the lesser-dragon-steel blade he'd carried for years.

Malek wrapped his hand around the hilt, testing it with a few swipes, and was about to thank Uthari when he noticed the sigil of Darekarin, King Darekar's kingdom, fused in silver onto the dragon steel. Malek recalled that the king had wielded twin dragon-steel longswords when he had, in his younger days, led his fleets into battle.

Without a doubt, he knew his *gift* had been stolen. There was no way a king would trade away such a rare and valuable weapon.

Malek wanted to believe that Uthari had a grand plan and knew what he was doing, but he worried his king was making enemies in a time when they badly needed allies.

2

TEZI WOKE TO HER HEAD THROBBING AND SAND PLASTERING THE SIDE of her face and even her tongue. When she blinked open her eyes, she found it also crusting her lashes and lodged in her nostrils. She gulped in air to blow the gritty stuff out of her nose and dragged a damp sleeve over her eyes, but her clothing was as sandy as everything else, and all she did was irritate them. Worse, the movement broke open a scab that had formed—how long had she been unconscious?—and warm blood trickled from her hairline.

Damp and sore, Tezi winced at something jabbing her in the hip. She lifted her head to peer blearily around, squinting at the light as pain reverberated inside her skull. Afternoon sun gleamed in the sky above the beach, but she shivered. It wasn't a warm sun, not like in the jungles of Zewnath or the hot desert of Zar.

Her neck protested as she turned her head, looking up and down the beach for people. She couldn't have been the only survivor of the wreck.

The last thing she remembered was being on the deck of the *Star Flyer* and using her axe to protect the other mercenaries from mental attacks from dragons before they destroyed the ship, and it crashed into the sea.

"The axe!" she blurted, patting around, terrified she'd lost it and that it was forever gone, sunken to the bottom of the sea.

But it was embedded in the sand under her. The haft was what had been jabbing her in the hip.

Relieved, she pulled the axe out and brushed off the sand, amazed that she'd managed to keep hold of it when she'd been unconscious in the water.

As she cleaned it off, the double-headed blade flashed blue. Maybe it had helped her keep it in her grip. The semi-sentient weapon probably hadn't wanted to be lost to the sea any more than she had.

Using it for support, Tezi pushed herself to her feet. Blackness encroached on her vision, and she wobbled. As she took steadying breaths, struggling for her equilibrium, she peered out to the sea, searching for sign of the wrecked ships and her Thorn Company colleagues.

She was in a cove and couldn't see far to the east and west, but the utter lack of life or even wreckage from the ships worried her. Was it possible everyone had died far out at sea and the axe had somehow saved her?

It flashed blue again. A yes? She envisioned herself in the water, one hand around the haft as it used its magic to pull her through the waves to shore.

"There you are," came an exasperated call from the trees above the beach.

Recognizing the voice, Tezi spun with relief.

Captain Rivlen, her usually impeccable uniform grimy with rips and stains, and her boots laced with seaweed, stepped out of the trees. Her hair was pulled back in a bun, but it was a sloppy one, especially compared to her typical style, with sand and pieces of grass lacing the dark strands.

"Captain Rivlen," Tezi called, her voice raspy, sand still coating her tongue. She spat to force it out, but her mouth was so dry that she didn't succeed. "Has Thorn Company made it? Where is everyone?"

"Some are in the next cove over." Rivlen pointed to the east. "We haven't accounted for everyone yet. All three ships were completely destroyed. I'm sorry, but it's likely not all of your people made it. Not all of mine did."

Tezi didn't think Rivlen had as close a relationship to her own officers as Tezi did to Thorn Company, but she nodded in sympathy. It was hard losing anyone, and Rivlen had been the ship's commander, so she would feel responsible.

"How did you find me?" Tezi wondered as she shambled up the beach.

Rivlen waved at her axe.

Of course. As a mage, she was able to sense dragon steel.

"I almost didn't," Rivlen said. "I don't know how you ended up miles from the rest of us."

"I think the axe helped me. I was knocked out." Tezi probed a gash above her temple as she eyed the sky. The battle had been before midnight the night before, so she'd been unconscious for a long time.

"I wouldn't be surprised. Come on. We need that axe."

Tezi wobbled and must have looked too bedraggled to walk on her own, for Rivlen reached out an arm to offer support.

"Sorry," Rivlen said, "I'm a lousy healer, but a couple of the officers who made it are decent. They'll fix you up when we get over there."

"It's all right." Tezi willed strength into her knees, but she did accept the help and leaned on Rivlen as they headed toward the trees. Not surprisingly, she didn't see anything resembling a path and wondered if it would be easier to walk on the beach, but the sand ended on the way out to a rocky point, and the jumbled and jagged boulders didn't appear accommodating. "Thanks for coming for me, ma'am. I'll pretend it's because you would be crushed if I were lost, not because you need my axe."

"The axe led me to you, but I'm collecting *all* the people who were shipwrecked on the beach. It's my duty as the captain."

"So you *would* be crushed." Tezi managed a smile, though everything hurt and her lips were cracked and dry, so it was hard to maintain.

"Yes, my life would lose all meaning without you in it." The words were dry and sarcastic, but Rivlen thumped her on the back as they walked. "I'm hoping that axe will make cutting down trees feasible. We need to build at least one mageship, even if it's as crude as that druid raft was. It'll be hard though. Very little has washed up on the beach and nothing as handy as toolboxes. We're using our magic to knock over trees for wood, but few of us are proving as handy as that engineer. Too bad I had to send him back to Uth."

Tezi could well imagine the overpowered mages heaving over trees, roots and all, with their magic and then staring in confusion at them as they tried to figure out how to craft them into a ship. The engineers like Vinjo were adept at using their magic to build, but most of Rivlen's officers had been chosen for their ability to throw fireballs at enemies rather than because they had useful survival skills.

"You don't think your people will come to rescue us?" Tezi asked.

"It's possible, but they don't know that we're alive or exactly where we are." Rivlen ducked under a branch draped with moss, then helped Tezi over a log. "The dome-jir is broken, and Uth is too far away for any of us to reach people there telepathically. My engineer is trying to fix the communications device, but he's better with ship's engines apparently. Another reason Vinjo would have been useful. He can take two paperclips and turn them into a power supply."

"He did seem versatile."

"The fleet will also be busy figuring out how to deal with those dragons and their new fortress. Searching for us will be a low priority."

"Meaning it could be a long time before someone comes looking for us." Tezi's stomach growled.

She had a feeling little food had washed up on the beach, and she didn't see any fruit dangling from branches in the forest. This might be a part of Zewnath, a shoreline down at the southern end of the continent, but the more temperate climate didn't lend itself to trees filled with bananas, coconuts, and mangos. Unless mages were more useful at hunting than they were at most things, they might be lucky to find a few berries and catch fish.

"Yes," Rivlen said. "Which is why we're going to build a ship of our own and get back in the sky."

A falcon screeched from the forest, taunting them for their lack of natural aerial abilities.

Tezi's teeth chattered as they walked, and she wished the sun were warmer—and that her clothes were drier. Damp and crusted with salt and sand, they chafed with each step.

"You doing all right?" Rivlen asked her.

"Just missing the jungle heat."

"Here." Rivlen held out her hand. For the axe?

Tezi gave it to her, assuming Rivlen meant to offer some helpful magic that would have been impossible while Tezi was protected by the weapon's power. Only as she released it and Rivlen's fingers wrapped around the haft did Tezi realize she no longer worried that Rivlen would take the axe from her. She wasn't Tonovan—that was certain—but she was a mage and *had* expressed interest in the dragon-steel weapon. Hundreds of people had, and more than one had schemed to get it from Tezi.

But Rivlen had her own dragon-steel dagger now, assuming she'd managed to retain it. And she wasn't a jerk.

Warmth flowed into Tezi, relaxing her tense muscles, and a hot wind swirled around her, gradually drying her clothes. It riffled through her hair, and seaweed she hadn't known was tangled in her blonde locks blew to the ground.

Once Tezi was dry, Rivlen handed back the axe.

"Huh," Tezi said as she accepted it.

Rivlen raised her eyebrows. "You thought I'd keep it?"

"I didn't actually. I just realized... I guess I trust you."

"I've earned the trust of a nineteen-year-old terrene mercenary coated in sand? Finally, my career aspiration to be embraced by the common man has been achieved."

Tezi squinted at her. "I'm not sure *why* I trust you."

"Because I'm honest."

"Snarkily honest."

"Nobody wants sappy honesty." Rivlen led them down a recently made path of crushed foliage and snapped branches, the forest ending as they approached another beach. Evidence of the torn-up trees she'd mentioned lay in knee-high grass waving in the sea breeze. A future lumberyard, at least the mage version.

The rumble of the surf kept Tezi from hearing voices as they neared the beach, but as soon as she spotted the brown uniforms of Thorn Company, she hurried ahead, hoping more of the mercenaries had survived than Rivlen had implied. Tezi hoped *everyone* had survived.

A smile stretched her cracked lips when she spotted Dr. Fret sitting beside patients propped against driftwood logs. There was Corporal Basher, grousing about something, judging by her jerky hand gestures. Probably that her cigars had been lost or ruined by the water. And there were Corporals Lady and Arrow.

Tezi longed to see Captain Ferroki but remembered she'd gone over to the druid raft a few hours before the battle. Sent to scout the fortress because of its camouflaging magic, that vessel had been farther ahead.

Was there any chance Ferroki and the druids had made it? Tezi feared not. The last she'd heard, they'd been discovered and had been warning Rivlen to turn the fleet around.

Her smile faltered as she realized there were only about two dozen Thorn Company uniforms. Ferroki, Sasko, and Tinder hadn't been aboard the *Star Flyer*, but everyone else in the unit had been. That meant they might have lost more than half the company.

Tezi glanced toward the forest as Rivlen strode toward a cluster of mages and hoped to see more brown uniforms among the trees, the mercenaries sent to forage perhaps. But if any of her people were out there, they were too far away to see.

"Tezi." Fret rose to give her a hug. "I'm glad you made it."

Her eyes were bloodshot and moist, and her voice quavered. Tezi swallowed, certain that meant she'd lost some patients.

"And you even managed to keep that beast of a weapon." Fret smiled, but it faltered almost as soon as it appeared. "We have a lot of missing people. Words, Barizon, Striker, and..." Her voice grew tight, and she rasped the last words. "I think we lost the captain too. And Sorath. They were with the druids, and..."

"I know." With tears seeping from Tezi's eyes, she returned Fret's hug.

After all they'd been through, the company surviving battle after battle relatively unscathed, it didn't seem right that so many had been lost in a shipwreck. Yes, that ship had been wrecked because it had been destroyed by a dragon, not due to natural causes, but Tezi had begun to believe the company could make it through those dragon battles, that they would keep finding a way to survive.

"I'm still hopeful that more will wash up on the beach alive, but..." Fret gestured toward the heartless sea, the waves crashing against a rocky promontory a reminder that they'd beaten the odds to have even this many survive.

Tezi continued to believe the axe had saved her, that she otherwise never would have woken.

"I hope Tinder is safe," Fret whispered. "And Lieutenant Sasko."

"I'm sure they are," Tezi said, though she wasn't sure at all. They'd been heading to Utharika, and the king had no love for mercenaries. "They didn't have anything to do with the kerzor and Tonovan's death," she added, hoping that would indeed save them from Uthari's wrath.

"I don't know if the company will survive this. Without the captain to keep us together and with Sasko on the other side of the world… Maybe it won't even matter, not if we can't beat the dragons. I'm afraid we're doomed, Tezi." Fret shook her head, her eyes haunted. "Doomed."

Normally, Tezi would have dismissed Fret's words since she was perpetually pessimistic. In this case, it was hard to argue with her.

"Corporal Tezi," came a familiar voice from a campfire someone had started. Fish cooked over it on a spit made from branches.

"Hello, Yelotta." Tezi forced a smile, though Yelotta was her least favorite of the three recruits she'd been assigned, mostly because she'd been making snide comments about Tezi's abilities with the axe and her leadership skills in general. Tezi wouldn't let herself wish that Yelotta hadn't made it and someone she cared more about had, but the thought did cross her mind.

"Mursa died." Yelotta surprised her by flinging her arms around Tezi. "Before we even crashed. I saw one of the dragons get her."

"I'm sorry." Tezi returned the hug. "What about Hevlina?"

"I don't know." Yelotta shook her head as she buried her face in

Tezi's shoulder. "I didn't see her die, but she didn't make it to the beach either."

Tezi slumped. Even if she'd barely gotten to know the three recruits, she hated that two of them had been lost. Ferroki had assigned her the new mercenaries to command, to guide and mold into Thorn Company soldiers.

Though Tezi didn't think she could have done anything more than she had to protect them, she couldn't help but feel she'd failed. She'd failed to keep them alive, and she'd failed the captain.

"All of my old company is gone too. Nobody that was in the back of the *Star Flyer* made it off. That dragon smashed it and—" Yelotta broke off with a sob, releasing Tezi and limping to a log where she slumped down in the sand.

Tezi didn't know if she should go after her or say something more. But what could she say? What comfort could she give? She knew death was a part of being a mercenary, but she'd never expected to lose so many comrades at once. Nor had she expected to have to deal with losing people in her command so soon.

She looked to Dr. Fret, hoping for advice, but she was bandaging someone's arm. Tezi went and sat on the log by Yelotta and rested a hand on her back. She doubted it comforted the woman at all, but it seemed like the right thing to do. Maybe one day, this would all get easier, and she would intuitively *know* the right things to do as a commander.

"Dragon!" someone called from the promontory at one end of the beach.

Tezi's stomach twisted as she peered out to sea and glimpsed the winged figure in the distance. It was flying parallel to the beach instead of toward them, but that didn't reassure her. It might have been sent to scout the landmass nearest its fortress to make sure there weren't any threats in the area.

As Tezi looked over the bedraggled and injured mercenaries

and mages on the beach, she didn't think they represented a threat. But what if the dragon felt differently?

Being back in the kitchen of the gateship and using the compact space for a laboratory didn't bring back fond memories for Jadora. Tonovan had attacked her in that room. She'd watched Malek wrestle for his sanity in it. And she'd struggled to make headway on defeating the death-darter bacteria there.

In the end, all she'd done was sedate Malek, Tonovan, and the others; it had been the knowledge and power that the ancient dragon Zelonsera had given Jadora that had allowed her to eradicate the bacteria. It hadn't been her education, brilliance, or intuition that had granted that victory. It had been a cheat.

And this time, there was nobody with knowledge of how to defeat the dragon parasite for her to lean on. Unless she found something illuminating within the Orbs of Wisdom, she would have only her own intelligence and personal experience to rely upon.

Oh, Uthari's people had filled the laboratory with equipment and books, to the point that there was barely room for two people to stand, but Jadora doubted the answers were within them. Nonetheless, she was scouring tomes, seeking inspiration as she struggled to focus. Awareness of the parasite multiplying within her made it difficult.

How much time did she have? For how long would her thoughts remain coherent? For how long would she remain... herself?

Jadora willed those fears away and pulled out the slides with the blood samples she'd taken back in Utharika. She'd kept hers and Uthari's, since they'd tested positive for the parasite, but she'd also kept Malek's. He'd tested negative, but he'd been standing right next to her and Uthari—trying to defend her from the zidarr Gorsith and also Uthari himself.

It was possible it had been chance that he hadn't been infected, and that it didn't mean anything significant, but it was also possible... that it did.

She slid his sample back under the microscope but fresh blood would have been better. With a few small vials, she could run more tests. Maybe it was possible that something in the ancient magic Uthari had once applied to Malek to turn him into a zidarr had altered his blood and inadvertently done something to make him less palatable to that particular parasite.

Malek? Jadora reached out telepathically, sensing him up on deck.

Earlier, he'd been communicating with Uthari, but the gate-ship and the fleet had since parted ways. Malek was, however, still up there. Musing about the future? Making sure the wind didn't knock the portal off the deck? She snorted, finding that scenario likely. Magical straps and braces or not, it was precariously perched.

Yes?

If you would be willing to oblige, I need something from you.

My presence in your cabin to satisfy your womanly needs?

Jadora smiled at his playful mood. When she'd first met Malek, she wouldn't have guessed he was *capable* of play. She still hadn't gotten a laugh out of him, but he smiled from time to time.

Samples of your blood, actually, and in the lab.

That doesn't make me as eager to hurry to your side.

No? Jadora asked, though she already sensed him coming down the ladder. *What if I promise you a kiss?*

You've convinced me.

As for the other, my womanly needs always enjoy your presence, but it might not be wise to give in to them.

It's never been wise. Malek opened the hatch and stepped into the lab. After eyeing the looming stacks of equipment and books, he stepped over to the counter to join her. "But we jointly agreed to cast wisdom to the wind, did we not?"

"I'm not sure I agreed to anything. I was merely moved to ardor by your presence and lost control of my faculties."

"All three times?"

"Your kisses are ardor-inspiring."

"Are they? Fascinating." He smiled and kissed her.

As much as Jadora wanted to lean into him and enjoy it, especially now that they'd flown away from Uthari, she drew back and rested a hand on his chest. "It's possible the parasite can be transmitted through, ah, bodily fluids."

"Like saliva?"

"And other things." She glanced down, blushed, and looked back up at his chest instead of meeting his eyes. "There's much I don't know about this parasite yet. Does it *need* those motes to travel from host to host, or can it float a certain distance on a cough or a sneeze? The motes may have been developed because dragons are separated when they fly and don't mingle closely together in communities regularly. It's possible there is more than one way the parasite is shared."

"I see." Malek lifted a hand and stroked her cheek but didn't try to kiss her again.

That made tears threaten to moisten her eyes. She *wanted* him to kiss her and vice versa. When her time remaining might be limited, she hated to waste it. She also hated the thought of never being with him again.

Sniffing and trying not to cry in front of him, Jadora leaned against his chest and wrapped her arms around him. She would risk a hug.

"This is an interesting method of taking blood samples," Malek said gently, returning the hug.

"I find that pre-injection hugs make my patients less likely to develop hard feelings toward me."

"I see." He kissed her forehead, then stepped back, removed his jacket, and pushed up his sleeve.

Yes, best to get straight to business. It wasn't as if they had an abundance of time.

Jadora had already prepared syringes and nodded as she reached for a needle. "I'll test you again for the parasite, and then I also want to see if there's anything peculiar in your blood."

One of his eyebrows arched. "Should I be offended that you think there might be?"

"You don't know exactly what the zidarr magic did to you, right? It could have altered your blood and made you less appealing to parasites."

"Not to *all* parasites. The ones the death darters injected me with enjoyed my blood and body tremendously."

"I remember." Jadora slid a needle into a prominent vein inside his elbow, his lean, muscular frame making it easy to target. "You may have gotten lucky this time, but if it turns out that something about you was repellent to the dragon parasites... that could be a big clue to help me solve this."

"Ah." Malek tilted his head as she filled small vials with his blood. "The knowledge the dragon gave you doesn't include anything about zidarr magic?"

"No. We haven't run into zidarr on other worlds—though the guardians on Nargnoth seemed comparable in power—so it's possible that it's something our mages' ancestors developed here on Torvil after the dragons disappeared. Uthari mentioned some rituals and old magic..." Jadora eyed Malek warily, wondering how much he knew about Uthari's past. Given that the old wizard's past went back centuries, it might not be a lot, but Uthari might also have shared some of those details with his loyal zidarr. "He told me he used one type of magic to extend his life by taking life from others. Before he had his machine and concoction of chemicals created."

"I'm not aware of how that magic works, but I know there are old rituals that are frowned upon by modern mages. The zidarr ritual is shrouded in secrecy, and even we know little about the mechanics." Malek spread a hand on his chest. "The knowledge and original writings are passed down from fathers to sons among the ruling class. When a mage becomes king or queen by force, he or she sometimes has to pay, bribe, or otherwise coerce one of the existing rulers for some of that information. All rulers want their own zidarr, of course."

"Of course." As she prepared a slide, Jadora smiled at his matter-of-fact statement, which he probably didn't consider pompous in the least. "I've seen some of the differences the magic made in you. Your increased stamina, stronger-than-typical musculature, and I'd guess your skeleton is stronger than average too, since you're able to jump down from great heights. Your ligaments and cartilage must also be impressive in order for your joints to endure that force."

"Nobody has called my ligaments impressive before. Or contemplated them analytically, as far as I'm aware."

"You know I'm a special woman." Jadora placed her slide under the microscope.

"I do know this."

Malek opened a drawer and drew out an oval-shaped object with a magical signature. It was the nullification device that could put the portal into hibernation. She'd noticed it when she'd been unpacking laboratory equipment and assumed Uthari had sent it along in case they needed it.

"There's still no sign of the parasite swimming around. That's good." Jadora bit her lip and focused her magical awareness on the sample, hoping her senses might detect something that was invisible to her eyes, even with magnification. Magic, after all, didn't show up in any visible or tangible way. At least as far as she knew. Perhaps someday, she might run experiments to see if she could identify and measure it with modern equipment.

"You wish to quantify magic?" Malek asked in an amused tone, returning the device to the drawer without commenting on it.

"Are you reading my mind?" She hadn't thought that other mages could do that anymore.

"No. You're muttering, and I'm listening. Zidarr have superior hearing, you know."

"Superior hearing *and* superior ligaments. It's a wonder I was able to keep from flinging myself at you for as long as I did."

"*I* thought so."

She smiled at him but only briefly before returning to the sample. A part of her wished she could expose him to the parasites again to see if, given a second chance, they would infect him. But if they did, he would be in the same dreadful situation as she. Unfortunately, she didn't think they would be enticed by having a drop of his blood inserted into one of their growth dishes. They didn't *consume* blood, as far as she could tell, but merely thrived inside their hosts, sharing the same nutrients that the dragons—and now humans—derived from their food.

"I don't get the sense that your blood is magical," Jadora said.

"I don't believe it is. The changes I endured during the zidarr ritual were one-time and permanent. It was a painful experience. I remember strange magic infusing me and altering me, altering the way I would grow musculature and repair bone and such going forward."

"I'm sorry you had to endure that pain."

"It was a small price to pay for my vengeance."

Jadora remembered the story he'd shared of his mother's death and how King Werok, King Zaruk's predecessor, could have saved her but didn't. His first mission after his zidarr training had been to kill the man.

Sometimes, she forgot that he'd trained to be not only a warrior but an assassin. She preferred honorable Malek, not skulking-through-the-night-and-slitting-throats Malek. How many missions like that had Uthari sent him on over the years? Shaping him into a killer eager to obey his whims?

Jadora almost wouldn't mind dying to the parasite if it meant Uthari would also die, and Malek would no longer be beholden to him and his plans. His first kill might have been for the sake of his own vengeance, but she had a hard time believing the rest of them had been. Malek didn't seem like a vengeful man to her, not unless he was pushed far. Nor did he take pleasure in killing.

She shook her head. It would be better *not* to die. Once this mess with the dragons and the parasites was resolved, she and Jak—and perhaps Shikari—could find another way to deal with Uthari.

Jadora twisted the knob on the microscope. "I wish this had stronger magnification. It's possible there's more going on in your blood than I'm able to see."

"That's the best microscope Uthari's men were able to find in the city."

"It's mundane though. Perhaps with magic, greater magnification might be achieved."

"I can see if the engineer has ideas," Malek said.

"I would appreciate that, though perhaps I should be the one to ask him. You're not the best at making polite requests."

"Zidarr give orders. They don't make requests."

"That must be why you're so dreadful at it." Jadora leaned back from the microscope and smiled at him so he would know she was teasing.

"It's true I've had little practice." Malek returned her smile but only briefly. His eyes were grave as he met her gaze. "There's something I wish to ask you before..." He turned his palm toward the ceiling.

"Before I start to change?" she guessed.

"I hope you won't, but yes."

Jadora also hoped she wouldn't, that the parasite wouldn't have as dramatic an effect on human hosts as on dragons. It was possible they had only infected her because Shikari had been protected, and she and Uthari had been the only viable options. She worried about getting near Shikari now and was glad he was too large to fit belowdecks anymore. If she *did* get close to him, the parasite might be able to jump from her to him.

"What are your wishes, should you become unable to be reasoned with?" Malek asked.

She opened her mouth, about to ask *wishes for what*, but she realized what he meant. Back when he'd been infested and on the verge of losing control of himself, he'd asked Jak to slit his throat. He'd said he would prefer death to being sedated indefinitely or going mad and harming others. Jak had been unwilling to assist him in that, just as Jadora would have been. Fortunately, it hadn't been necessary, but the memory of his request haunted her.

If she grew dangerous to others, would she want her own death? With her new power, it was possible she *could* be dangerous if she lost control. Before, it would have been easy for Malek or even a terrene guard to keep her locked up, but now...

She stared bleakly at the counter as she imagined a crazy version of herself attacking Malek.

"My wish is for Jak to be safe," she said quietly. "I'd like to finish the work I promised Zelonsera I would do, but if that's not possible... I suppose it doesn't matter what happens to me. But I would appreciate it if you would keep an eye out for Jak when... *if* I'm gone."

"I will protect him."

"Thank you."

"Do you have wishes pertaining to yourself? Sedation until a solution can be found?"

Jadora blew out a slow breath. "If I don't find the solution, I'm not sure who else would be able to."

His eyebrow rose again. "It's possible I'm not the only arrogant one in this room."

She snorted. "I only feel that way because of the knowledge Zelonsera put in my head, not my own intelligence or academic background."

"Are you sure?" He smiled gently.

"Well, I did admit I think I'm special."

"Yes."

Jadora closed her eyes and leaned against him. "Did Uthari say anything about this? Does he want me, ah, taken care of if I become… trouble?"

"He did not. Logically, if he mandated sedation for you, he would have had to give the same order in regard to himself."

She doubted *sedation* would have been what Uthari had in mind if he decided she was a threat. "I trust you to do what you believe is right in the moment, Malek. As long as I know Jak is taken care of, I can accept whatever happens to me."

He wrapped his arms around her again.

"I don't want anything to happen to you," he said quietly. "Especially since…"

"What?" She tilted her head back to meet his eyes.

"Perhaps I shouldn't say anything."

"You're going to tease me and then refuse to expand?"

"I don't know if I should get your—*our*—hopes up."

"Tell me."

"Or you'll use magical coercion on me?" Now, both of his eyebrows went up.

She hadn't been trying to do that, had she? No, she was positive she hadn't. "I'll poke you with needles."

"Again?"

"Yes. Perhaps in the backside instead of the arm."

"That would be dreadful. All right. Uthari said if we can rid the world of the dragons and fix the problem with the parasite, he'll let me retire and be with you."

Jadora stared at him for a moment before she could whisper, *"Retire?"*

Had Uthari said what Malek wanted to hear to ensure maximum effort and compliance from him? Or was it possible the wizard had spoken such words and meant them?

Intense longing filled her as she imagined returning to her work at the university with Malek at her side, maybe even with him as her *husband.* Could she do that if it meant Uthari was still ruling from his sky city and terrene humans were still enslaved?

"That is what he said, and, as far as I'm aware, Uthari doesn't have a history of lying to me. He rarely tells me his machinations in detail, but when he tells me he will do something, he does."

"It's hard for me to imagine you retired, but I wouldn't object to having a life with you."

"I'm glad I'm not that objectionable," he said.

"You know what I mean." Jadora swatted him on the chest. "I love you Malek. And I would love to be with you and for you to be the honorable, noble man you're meant to be, not someone who has to work with people like Tonovan and carry out morally questionable tasks for your king."

"There's much to do before such a future could come to pass, but the thought of being with you, and it being sanctioned by my king, makes me want to succeed more than ever."

"I'll do my best to make sure we do."

Malek started to kiss her on the mouth, but he must have remembered her warning about bodily fluids, for he shifted to touching his lips to her cheek. Since she'd been the one to warn him, she couldn't rightfully be disappointed, but she longed to share another full-on kiss and more with him.

"I'll speak to Vinjo about possible modifications to your microscope," Malek said, stepping back.

"You'll make it a polite request?"

"Certainly." He bowed to her and walked out, leaving her alone with samples of blood to study and mulling to do.

As he'd said, now more than ever, they had a reason to succeed.

3

As the gateship flew southward, Lieutenant Sasko paced in the tiny cabin she shared with Sergeant Tinder, chewing on her thumbnail and absently stepping around her roommate's head on each pass. Tinder was face down, with her boots up on the bottom bunk and her back straight as she performed decline push-ups.

Maybe Sasko should have been exercising too, but she was busy worrying.

Nobody had filled her in on anything—Vinjo was the only mage on board who regularly spoke with her, but he didn't know much either. It was only thanks to overheard conversations between the four red-uniformed officers who had been detached from the *Star Flyer* to guard the gateship that she'd heard rumors. And the rumors weren't good. They spoke of a floating fortress the dragons had built above the Glacier Islands and said the *Star Flyer* hadn't been heard from since reporting that they were approaching it.

As far as Sasko knew, all of Thorn Company, save herself and Tinder, were still on the *Star Flyer*. Or they *had* been on the *Star Flyer*. What if it had been destroyed?

Mages could speak via their magical communications devices to each other all over the world. It was a bad sign that nobody had heard from Captain Rivlen.

Sasko tried to remain calm, reminding herself that there could have been updates that she hadn't heard about yet. It was possible Captain Ferroki, Dr. Fret, Corporal Basher, Corporal Tezi, and all the others were fine. Maybe Captain Rivlen had spied on the fortress from a distance, then wisely hightailed it back to Zewnath or somewhere else to find more allies and regroup.

"No need to panic or worry about the future until we know more," Sasko muttered as she passed Tinder's head again. "Or wonder if you're still a *lieutenant* if you only have one troop."

"What are you talking about?" Tinder paused, her arms quivering until she locked her elbows.

"I'm reminding myself that we're lowly mercenaries who are usually the last to be briefed, especially in the world of mages. Just because we haven't heard anything about Thorn Company and the *Star Flyer* doesn't mean they're not fine."

"Who are you calling *lowly,* Lieutenant?"

"You. Your head is level with my knee."

The hatch opened before Tinder could rebut, and Vinjo slipped inside, closing it quickly and putting his back to it. Pitch still clumped his hair together in tufts. Sasko wondered if shampoo would get it out, or if the substance would require a more creative solution. His face glistened with sweat, but she didn't think that was acidic enough to break down magically enhanced glues.

"Have you been working hard," Sasko asked him as Tinder stood up, "or are those beads of sweat due to nerves?"

"I heard Lord Malek is looking for me," Vinjo whispered.

"If he's looking for you on this little ship, he's going to find you."

Vinjo glanced at something on his wrist. One of his stealth devices.

"He'll find you even if you turn that on. You smell like a forest." Sasko sniffed him. "A sweaty, panicked forest."

"The mages from the *Star Flyer* said there'll be no more *shenanigans* now that he's on board. He's going to torture me when he finds out I was the reason Zaruk's ships attacked us. That's what they said. After he scrapes every piece of information out of my mind." Vinjo licked his lips. "Sasko, I *know* things."

"But are they things anyone cares about?" Sasko hadn't interacted much with Lord Malek, but her impression of him was that he was aloof and distant rather than cruel and self-absorbed, like most of the other zidarr. She could deal with aloof and distant. She preferred her mages that way.

"Sasko. I know all about—" his eyes widened, and he sprang away from the hatch, almost smashing into her as he swung to face it, "—things," he finished in a whisper.

The hatch opened, revealing Malek standing in the corridor.

Despite his tangible fear—and tangible sweat dripping down the side of his face—Vinjo spread an arm and stood protectively in front of Sasko.

"That's not necessary," she murmured. "I don't know anything about anything."

Malek gazed blandly in at them. Or maybe that was an aloof, distant gaze. He barely glanced at Sasko and Tinder before stepping inside and focusing on Vinjo.

Sasko shifted uneasily. Malek didn't sneer or step on mercenaries who didn't move out of the way in time, not like so many of the mages, but he *did* radiate power and supreme competence. Even if Tezi lent her that dragon-steel axe, Sasko wouldn't want to face him in battle.

"You've created a dome-jir for this ship," Malek said.

"Uhm," Vinjo uttered.

"And hidden it, cloaking it with magic."

"Uhhhmm."

Sasko, who knew about that incident, didn't say anything, but when Malek looked at her, squinting slightly, she suspected he read every pertinent thought in her mind.

"You will retrieve it and bring it to me," Malek told Vinjo. "I will be in charge of communications on this journey and choose whom to contact and whom *not* to contact."

"I understand. I'll get it right away." Vinjo started to lower his arm and step toward the hatch, but he paused and looked back at Sasko, as if afraid to leave her unprotected. Tinder, whom Vinjo was less concerned about, folded her arms over her chest and leaned against the wall.

"The mercenaries are not in danger from me," Malek said. "*They* have not been contacting zidarr from enemy kingdoms."

"Right." Vinjo darted around Malek and into the corridor.

"Lord Malek?" Sasko asked. "Have you heard anything about the *Star Flyer* and Thorn Company? We've only gotten rumors, and... they were concerning rumors."

"We haven't received any updates since yesterday when Captain Rivlen reported the druids' encounter with a dragon-steel fortress and that the *Star Flyer* was about to be attacked. Uthari and others have attempted to make contact, but they weren't able to connect with the dome-jirs on her ship or the two that accompanied it. They've probably all been destroyed."

"The dome-jirs or the ships?" Tinder exchanged a worried look with Sasko.

"Dome-jirs aren't easily destroyed," Malek said. "Unless someone targeted them specifically, it's likely the ships were also destroyed."

His tone was matter-of-fact, and if he cared about the lost officers—and mercenaries—he didn't show it, though when Sasko slumped against Tinder for support, he did soften his voice and add, "It's always possible that some people survived. Uthari is leading the rest of the fleet to the Glacier Islands, and I'm sure they'll check the area and try to find the wrecked ships."

"But it'll take them days to get there, won't it?" Sasko imagined the Thorn Company women clinging to wreckage as sharks—and dragons—circled.

"A couple of days, yes."

"And it's possible *they'll* be wrecked by dragons too." Sasko rubbed her face and wiped away the moisture threatening to leak from her eyes. She didn't want to cry in front of a zidarr.

But it was difficult. Usually, she wasn't the most pessimistic person in the company—Dr. Fret held that position—but it was hard to feel hope at that moment.

"It is," Malek said. "If we're successful on our mission, we'll continue south and help the fleet."

Sasko managed to keep from blurting *what can we do,* though the words sprang to mind. Yes, Malek was a powerful zidarr, but there would be lots of powerful mages on those ships, and she hadn't yet seen evidence that much besides the dragon-steel weapons bothered the dragons, and Sasko and Tinder didn't have those. The little gateship didn't even have cannons.

The hatch opened again, and a clunk preceded Vinjo stepping inside. Some tool or device had fallen from the pile of doodads balanced in his arms. Sasko recognized the spherical orange dome-jir among them, though it only glowed when it was in use. She also recognized Vinjo's stealth device and a few other gadgets she'd seen before but didn't know the function of.

"This is everything I have, Lord Malek. That I've built, I mean."

Malek eyed the clutter, then, without moving, used his power to levitate the dome-jir out of the mess. Something else clunked to the deck.

Malek also took the stealth device, and Sasko grimaced. For

Vinjo's sake, she would have preferred it if he'd been able to keep that, though they wouldn't be useful against dragons.

"What do the rest of your gadgets do?" Malek asked.

"This is a vegetable peeler. This loosens screws that are too tight. This jumpstarts a flagging power supply. That can I dropped is engine lubricant that's self-lubricating. This—"

"Never mind," Malek said. "I wouldn't want to take away your ability to self-lubricate."

"I hear men find that handy," Tinder said.

Sasko elbowed her. "This isn't the time for inappropriate humor."

"Come on, Lieutenant. You ought to know that with mercs, it's *always* the time for inappropriate humor. Better to laugh in the face of death, depression, and certain doom than weep and give in to defeat."

Sasko, who was still struggling to keep tears from falling, shook her head.

"The zidarr agrees." Tinder pointed at Malek.

As far as Sasko could tell, Malek's aloof face hadn't changed.

"I don't think zidarr laugh," Sasko murmured.

"I saw his eyes twinkle," Tinder whispered back.

"Maybe lubricant flew up and got in them."

"That is possible."

Eye twinkles notwithstanding, Malek ignored them. As Vinjo turned back toward the corridor, Malek reached out and put a hand on his shoulder.

Vinjo didn't flinch, but he did jerk to a halt and regard that hand with supreme wariness. Sasko did too. Ever since she'd overheard Vinjo communicating with his zidarr brother, she'd worried there would be repercussions, that Uthari's people wouldn't be pleased. And Malek was as high up among *Uthari's people* as one could get.

"Is the ship now prepared for underwater travel?" Malek asked.

"I'm still working on some tweaks, my lord," Vinjo said, "but it'll be air- and watertight by the time we get to the pool. I'm also building ballast tanks attached to the outside that will let us rise and sink in the water by alternating how full they are of water or air. The challenging part is reinforcing the hull sufficiently to withstand the great pressure that we could encounter if we're attempting to sail—er, swim—deep underwater. Nobody's been able to tell me how far below the surface we'll be going, so I can't make any calculations regarding the necessary hull strength. The ship is made out of wood, which... isn't ideal. I've reinforced it with some magic, but we'll all want to create a barrier around it as we go through, and hope we're not crushed the instant we come out of the portal underwater."

Sasko blinked. She'd learned they were heading to another world to look for information on the dragon parasite, but this was the first she'd heard of challenges beyond the usual threats of human-eating monsters. As if she hadn't had enough to worry about.

"I can magically reinforce the hull or erect a barrier to withstand great force," Malek said.

"We'll also have to limit the length of our journey, due to air constraints. This ship isn't large and therefore can't hold a lot of air to start with. If we're forced to stay underwater for more than a few hours... especially with this many people on board..."

"Would it be better to leave most of the people behind?" Malek looked at the mercenaries.

"Oh, may I volunteer for that?" Tinder lifted her hand, then glanced at Sasko, gripped her hand, and lifted it as well. "We can stay by the pool in the jungle and watch for enemies."

"The kinds of enemies that come out of the portal and can eat entire crews of mageships?" Sasko asked.

"I was thinking more like wolves and panthers that might wander in from the jungle," Tinder admitted, lowering their hands.

Sasko well remembered battling those awful flying worms and the giant armored creatures that had come through. She might prefer the risk of an underwater journey on another world. Even better would be if she and Tinder could somehow bypass both options and help people look for Thorn Company.

She would, however, hate to leave Vinjo. He didn't have any allies here.

"We'll figure out who's necessary for the trip when we arrive," Malek said. "Vinjo, I am pleased that you are continuing to work on this ship on our behalf. I know King Uthari didn't give you a choice, but you could have sabotaged the vessel or tried harder to get away." Malek squeezed his shoulder and released him.

Vinjo's jaw sagged in shock.

"If we survive all this," Malek continued, "I'll attempt to get you back to your homeland."

"Will King Uthari allow that, my lord?" Vinjo whispered, hope entering his eyes.

"He said he would prefer that you not return with us from this mission." Judging by the dryness in Malek's tone, Uthari had been implying Vinjo should *die*, not be taken home to Zar. "Were you back in your desert kingdom, you would clearly not be able to return with us."

"Are you... interpreting your king's orders creatively, my lord?" Vinjo gaped at Malek as if he'd sprouted dragon scales. "I didn't think zidarr could do that."

"We're not all monsters," Malek said quietly.

"My brother is moderately monstrous."

"I've heard brothers are often like that."

Vinjo snorted. "It's true that it started before his zidarr training. He used to break my projects and steal my tools."

Malek picked up the can that had dropped and balanced it atop Vinjo's pile.

"Thank you, my lord." Vinjo started toward the corridor again, but Malek held up a hand.

"One more thing. Do you have on board the materials that Jak used to create a kerzor?"

The relief that had been spreading across Vinjo's face vanished. "I don't know anything about that, my lord."

Sasko winced. Even if she hadn't known better, she would have been able to tell Vinjo was lying.

"I want the materials destroyed," Malek said.

"The... materials I don't know anything about?"

"Yes."

"Some of them have other uses. *All* of them do. That's why I had them."

Not only was he a poor liar, but he was an inconsistent one.

"Destroy one then," Malek said. "A crucial component."

"My understanding is that Shikari was the crucial component."

"You can't destroy him," Malek said, dry again.

"I'll, uhm, see what I can do, my lord."

"Good." Malek lowered his hand.

Vinjo sprang free, as if he were a rabbit that had been trapped in a cage. He dropped his can of lubricant again as he ran toward engineering and didn't return to pick it up.

"Will he be punished, Lord Malek?" Sasko asked warily, wanting to protest if the answer was *yes. Jak* had made the kerzor. It had probably been his idea from the beginning.

"Not if he doesn't cross me. He's been useful, and he's been punished enough." Malek looked at Sasko and Tinder. "If your company no longer exists, after we're done, I'll ensure that you're paid and also drop you off back in Zar."

Malek stepped out of the cabin, closing the hatch behind him.

Sasko sank down on the bottom bunk, the words *if your company no longer exists* echoing in her mind.

Maybe she should have been glad that Malek was being reasonable, but she could only dwell on the fact that all of her friends, everyone save Tinder, might be dead. What would she do if the company was no more? Was there any point in mulling it over while dragons were terrorizing the world?

"No," she whispered.

~

Colonel Sorath's back, hip, and stump ached, his pickaxe attachment abrasive from salt drying on it after he'd been dumped in the sea. Worse than all that was the pain coming from the front of his shoulder, where dragon talons had pierced him all the way through, barely missing his lungs. Yoshartov had carried him for miles that way, and Sorath had blacked out before they'd arrived at the fortress. The half-dried blood from the wound made his torn tunic stick to his mangled flesh.

Now, he sat slumped against a hard blue-black wall while trying not to move. He alternated between being comforted that Ferroki was beside him, as wounded as he but still breathing, and chagrined that he hadn't kept her from ending up in the same dreadful place as he had.

They weren't the only ones imprisoned in the fortress. Dozens of bedraggled people shared the cylindrical-shaped chamber the dragons had dropped them in from above. The only entrance was up there, a round door that opened in segments and was thirty feet above the floor. It had been closed since they'd been dropped off, leaving them trapped as surely as if they'd been in shackles.

A faint magical light and warmth came from the walls. Sorath didn't know if the dragons had deliberately built the chamber that way, to keep their human prisoners from freezing, or if it was a byproduct of building a structure from dragon steel.

They hadn't seen Yoshartov since he'd dropped them off, and Sorath had no idea what had befallen the druids. Had they all drowned—or been killed—after the dragons ripped apart their raft?

He didn't see any of the green-haired magic users among the prisoners. These people had already been in the chamber when Sorath and Ferroki had been deposited. They had a variety of hair and skin coloring and wore clothing from around the world. Most murmured—and cursed—to themselves in Dhoran, but Sorath caught a few other languages; some he didn't recognize at all. He and Ferroki weren't the only ones dealing with wounds, and one man had died while in the chamber. Someone had draped a shirt over his eyes before the others moved away from the body.

"If the dragons truly want servants," Sorath muttered, "they're not treating us well."

He would rather die than serve a dragon—or anyone powerful who thought far too highly of him or herself—but as long as they were alive, there was hope. Sorath didn't know how he and Ferroki could escape from this—it wasn't as if the dragons had boats waiting below the fortress so that human guests could come and go—but if he could find a way to sabotage the floating structure and ruin their plans to take over Torvil… that would be worth his life.

Ferroki stirred in response to his voice. "Given the relationship you have with that one-eyed dragon, I was hoping for better accommodations and care." She winced as she touched the puckered skin around one of the talon gouges visible through her ripped tunic.

"You were? The fact that we trade insults every time we fight didn't lead me to believe he would give us a four-poster bed, a feast, and bath servants."

"I was fantasizing about medical treatment, fresh water, and something to eat." Ferroki lowered her hand. "Bath servants don't feature in many of my dreams."

"No? You must never have known the joy of having someone else scrub your backside and fluff your nether regions dry." In truth, Sorath had only experienced that once, at a resort in the Mountains of Dakshar. His old commander had taken the officers there to celebrate a victory. That had been more than twenty years earlier, and the details were fuzzy in his mind, but the nether-region fluffing had imprinted itself.

"That is not an experience I've had, no, but if we get out of this and my wounds heal, I'd be amenable to letting you scrub my backside. I'm less certain about fluffing."

"If we get out of this, I'll scrub anything you like." Sorath managed a smile and lifted his arm, enduring the pain that movement elicited so he could gently wrap it around her shoulders. "And I'll let you scrub anything of mine that *you'd* like."

"I think you'd let me do that whether we get out of here or not."

"I suppose that's true. Usually, I prefer privacy, but if you produced a brush or a sponge..."

A screech came from above, and the smiles they'd been sharing dropped. The round door in the ceiling opened, and a dragon landed at its edge, furling its wings as its talons wrapped around the frame. Sunlight and blue sky were visible above it, but icy air whispered inside and curled about the prisoners.

"Speaking of a lack of privacy," Sorath muttered as the brown-and-gray dragon peered downward.

People huddled and looked away, as if by avoiding eye contact they might keep from attracting its notice.

Sorath stared defiantly up at their reptilian captor, though he doubted it would speak with them. This wasn't Yoshartov. Sorath had no idea if the one-eyed dragon was in the fortress, or if he had been sent to look for more dragon steel.

We grow weary of eating only fish, the dragon announced into their minds, causing people to huddle even tighter to each other and against the walls. As usual, it didn't speak in Dhoran, but Sorath understood the words nonetheless. *It is time to dine on the flesh of those who would see us dead.*

Sorath released Ferroki and stood, wishing he'd managed to keep Grunk's dragon-steel dagger, but Yoshartov had plucked it from his grip. It was probably lying in a courtyard with the other dragon steel that had been collected, waiting to be melted down and crafted into who knew what addition to the fortress. A princess tower, perhaps.

More likely, a weapons turret. Sorath shuddered at the memory of that thick red beam shooting out from below the fortress and blowing the druids' raft to pieces. The druids' magically *protected* raft. It could have withstood fireballs and several assaults from dragons, but the beam weapon from the fortress had been too much.

Take only a few and leave some for later, another voice sounded telepathically in Sorath's mind. *Delicacies have to be savored.* The voice descended into cackles.

"They're all mad," Ferroki muttered.

"I think so too." Sorath was about to add that everyone knew humans tasted horrible, but a whisper of magical energy surrounded him, then hefted him into the air.

His stomach dropped as his body rose toward the opening. He'd been chosen for dinner.

Several other people cried out as they rose alongside him.

"Sorath!" Ferroki yelled from the ground, her hand outstretched toward him.

"I'll go down fighting," he promised her, though he knew she didn't want him to go down at all.

Sorath shook his head, fear and fury mingling and making him want to lash out. When he'd chosen the mercenary life, he'd always known he would die eventually, taken down by some enemy, but this hardly seemed fair.

"If you intend to kill us," he yelled at the dragon lifting them, "give us weapons. Let us fight for our lives and die in battle instead of ignobly, trapped by your magic."

You already fought and lost, human. Now it is time for us to dine. The dragon sprang from the top of the chamber and flew over the mile-wide floating fortress, bypassing spires with what looked like nests atop them as he headed to an open courtyard framed by several towers. Three other dragons waited, their scales all the same mottled brown and gray.

Hungry reptilian eyes peered up at Sorath and the other humans floating toward them. The dragons' maws parted, as if they were gazing at a platter of freshly baked pastries being delivered, and saliva dripped from their jaws.

Sorath balled his fist, wanting to punch something, but only intangible magic held him aloft.

What are you doing with my servant? a new voice cried. A *familiar* voice. Yoshartov.

For the first time ever, Sorath felt hope at the sound of that voice. But his captor slung him and the others down in the courtyard in the middle of the dragons, and he didn't know if that hope was premature. He didn't even see Yoshartov.

Growls and snarls came from the waiting dragons. They didn't lick their lips—dragons didn't *have* lips—but their tongues darted out between their teeth, and one bent low to sniff Sorath.

He crouched, fist and pickaxe raised, determined to go down fighting. If nothing else, he would take out a few of those fangs.

But as the maw inched closer, power wrapped around Sorath again.

Frustrated, he yelled, "Cowards!" thinking the dragon meant to keep him from swinging as it levitated him into its mouth.

He didn't sail toward that waiting maw. He levitated upward as Yoshartov flew toward him, his single yellow eye squinting.

No dragon shall eat my servant! Yoshartov cried.

Save the others too, Sorath thought, hoping the dragon was reading his mind. *Please. I'm sure they'll make good servants.*

Anything to save their lives...

But it was too late.

The other dragons ignored Yoshartov, springing on the humans in the courtyard that he *hadn't* lifted into the air. Screams drove daggers into Sorath's heart, and he shook with rage as the dragons tore their prisoners to pieces.

Yoshartov flew closer, clasped Sorath in his talons—this time, he didn't pierce Sorath's flesh—and flew toward the cylindrical prison tower.

Though the lingering cries of people who hadn't yet been killed horrified him, Sorath realized he had little time to come up with something before he was deposited back in the chamber. "If you put me back, they'll try to collect me to eat later. Don't you have quarters or someplace where you can stash us?"

You wish to serve me now, Colonel?

"The alternative isn't that appealing, so I guess."

I knew you would come to see what an honor it is to be chosen by a dragon such as myself.

"No doubt."

Yoshartov banked to head in a different direction.

"Wait," Sorath blurted. "Ferroki wishes to serve you as well." Realizing the dragon might not know her name, Sorath imagined her in his mind.

Your mate? Yes, of course. Female humans are excellent servants. Very nurturing and caring.

That didn't describe any of the Thorn Company women, except perhaps Dr. Fret, but Sorath nodded in agreement. "Yes."

Whatever got Ferroki out of that prison with him.

A few seconds later, she floated into view. Yoshartov flew over and grasped her in another set of talons before banking and flying toward the back of the fortress. He passed several nests on pedestals, dozing dragons curled up in some of them, then furled his wings to dive for a tunnel opening. They flew inside, Sorath's legs almost hitting the ground, then glided past alcoves and toward a trio of caves with barriers shimmering at the front of each. One of those barriers dropped, and Yoshartov flew in and landed, depositing Sorath and Ferroki on twigs, leaves, and other nesting material that must have been flown in from Zewnath.

I must attend a meeting, but you will wait for me here. Later, I will instruct you on serving me. Yoshartov flew back out, the shimmering barrier returning.

Though he had no doubt they were still prisoners, Sorath left the nest and prodded the barrier with his pick. It buzzed angrily, and an electrical charge went through his appendage and up his arm. He jerked back, shaking out the numbing pain.

Once more, he wished for Grunk's dagger. It would have popped the magical barrier with ease.

"Did you see those glowing tendrils and spheres in a chamber between the alcoves in the tunnel?" Ferroki waved back to indicate the way they'd come.

"No." Sorath had been looking at the nests and their occupants instead of into the alcoves.

"I only got a quick look as we flew past an area with a bunch of magical things in it. I wondered if it might be the control center for the fortress, like the engine room on a mageship."

"A place where, if the magical devices inside were destroyed, the entire structure might blow up and fall in the sea?" Sorath asked.

“I believe we’re over an island, but essentially.”

“Let’s hope that whatever serving Yoshartov entails, it’ll provide the opportunity to explore the fortress and find its weaknesses. As long as this place is intact and full of dragons, our people are going to be in trouble.” That was especially true if the dragons were only in Stage One of their plan. If they managed to get the portal and bring *more* of their kind into the world... Sorath shuddered at the thought.

“Our people are already in trouble,” Ferroki said grimly. “And even if we’re walking around *serving* your one-eyed dragon, that won’t mean we’re safe. It didn’t look like the other dragons care much if certain humans have been claimed by their brethren.”

“Dear Ferroki. You didn’t think you’d be safe accompanying me anywhere, did you?” Sorath smiled sadly and hugged her.

“I suppose not.” She leaned against his chest. “Clearly, I was foolish to join you on that raft.”

“*Clearly*.”

4

RIVLEN STRUGGLED NOT TO FEEL INDIGNATION AS SHE USED HER power to snare fish from the cove and fling them onto the sand, but her stomach was growling, and it was her duty as fleet commander to make sure her people were taken care of. Some of the mercenaries were gathering the fish she caught and carrying them to campfires burning farther up the beach.

Never had Rivlen thought she would have to use her abilities for pure survival. At least the dragon they'd seen earlier hadn't come to investigate their beach.

Other mages, those more capable of crafting, were attempting to turn the trees they'd felled into lumber that could be used for a ship. For a *raft*, she amended. Without tools and a skilled shipwright, there was little hope of building something more sophisticated.

"As long as it gets us to..." To where? Rivlen didn't know where her goal should be. They were a long way from home, but what allies did they have below the equator? The only druid she'd had a hint of a relationship with, Kywatha, was likely dead.

Even if Rivlen could talk other druids into helping, her fleet had been shipwrecked more than a thousand miles from the jungle pool, the only place she knew for certain their people lived. The only reason she was aware of their distance from that place was because of the one thing besides the dragon-steel dagger that she'd managed to salvage from the *Star Flyer* before it had gone down.

Rivlen pulled out the spherical map device that Jak had made and thumbed it open again. An image of Zewnath floated into the air above it.

When he'd first given it to her, she hadn't realized it showed one's current location. A tiny red spot marked their cove far to the south and slightly to the east of the mountains and the pool.

Rivlen closed the device and pressed the cool metal sphere to her forehead, wishing that Jak were there with her. He would have lightened her mood by saying something goofy about her using magic to catch fish. Then his dragon would have eaten half of what she hauled out.

"Are you all right, Captain Rivlen?" one of the mercenaries asked, a short woman who was plucking up fish. Her brown uniform was decorated with colorful yarn trim, and Rivlen recalled that she was the knitting doctor.

"Yes." Rivlen slipped the sphere back into her pocket, careful to button the flap so it wouldn't fall out. "I'm just... missing someone."

"I understand completely." The woman—Dr. Fret, that was her name—smiled, but it was a sad smile, and worry lurked in her eyes.

"You have someone back home?"

"On the gateship, actually. She was, uhm, sent away."

"Lieutenant Sasko?" Rivlen had thought Sasko had feelings for that engineer. Or did Fret mean... Rivlen curled a lip. "Not that mouthy sergeant."

"Sergeant Tinder." Fret's smile grew more fond than sad. "She has a big heart under her mouth."

"Huh. Well, *they're* probably fine. They didn't shipwreck."

"Yes, ma'am. And, uhm, Jak is probably fine too."

Rivlen stifled a grimace. She hadn't realized her relationship with Jak was common knowledge, but she could hardly be surprised. Secrets were hard to keep on a ship with hundreds of people.

Unfortunately, Rivlen couldn't agree with the doctor. The mercenaries didn't know the full tale of the kerzor and General Tonovan's death—and how angry Uthari had been about it all. Rivlen feared she'd sent Jak off to his death.

"I hope so," was all she said.

"Captain," one of her lieutenants called from the trees as he waved urgently for her. "We have company."

Expecting animals, Rivlen jogged up the beach, but her senses soon told her that he meant *human* company. Druid company, she wagered. Who else with power lived on this benighted continent?

Two wolves came into view first, blue-eyed creatures that emanated magic. But as Rivlen approached the trees, she spotted green-haired druids with thong necklaces holding clumps of gems and feathers. Instead of woven-grass vests and tunics, these men and women wore sewn hides for clothing. Many carried bows and spears, as if they preferred such crude weapons to using their magic.

It was amazing that such an unsophisticated people could produce power to rival that of trained mages, but Rivlen sensed some of them had strong auras. She instinctively double-checked her defenses. If these druids had heard from the druids who'd battled against mages at the portal, they might be predisposed to dislike Uthari's people. They might even be disgruntled that the fleet had ended up stranded on their beach.

"As if we had a choice," she muttered.

"Ma'am?" Lieutenant Varsk asked.

"Keep an eye on them." Rivlen strode toward the newcomers, her hand resting on the hilt of the dagger, but she didn't draw the weapon. *I am Captain Rivlen of the* Star Flyer. Of what *had been* the *Star Flyer*, she thought but didn't project telepathically. *We were stranded here by dragons. Do you have a communications device that I may use to let my superiors know where we are? I'm sure you don't want us in your land, and we're not eager to stay.*

The druids exchanged looks with each other. The group numbered more than thirty, but Rivlen couldn't tell who was in charge. They might not understand Dhoran, but they should have grasped her meaning even if the words were foreign.

Without speaking, several druids skirted her and the lieutenant and walked toward the beach. Rivlen tightened her grip on the dagger hilt.

Watch out, she warned the mercenaries and mages on the beach. Thus far, the druids hadn't done anything aggressive, but that didn't mean much. One of their ubiquitous stone monuments might be lurking in the trees, waiting to launch green beams to blow up stranded troops.

Rivlen picked out one of the older druids and spoke telepathically directly to her. *If you have a communications device or a way to get in touch with people on other continents, I would like to use it. Once we're rescued, I can arrange payment or something else in trade.*

The woman gazed at her. *What do you offer in trade, mage? Your people know only how to plunder, not give.*

Not as much as dragons plunder. We were working together with some druids when they attacked. Do you know Kywatha?

She is known to us. The druid looked toward Rivlen's pocket. *What bauble do you carry? It is not a weapon.*

No, it's not. Rivlen pressed a hand protectively over the pocket that held Jak's device. *It's a map, nothing more.*

Its magic is intriguing. If you give it to me, I will take you to our tunnels and a device that allows communication to other continents.

Rivlen scowled at the woman. What could possibly be *intriguing* about the magic of Jak's device? To her, it felt like many other magical tools, including the engines and energy supplies that powered the gateship. She wouldn't be surprised if Jak had added some of his own flair to the device, but if Vinjo had taught him crafting, it should have a signature similar to the engineer's work.

I would let you look *at it in exchange for the use of your communications device,* Rivlen replied, *but I can't give it away. It was a gift from a friend.*

That and the dragon-steel weapons I sense are all that you have that are of interest to me. I am positive that you will not give us those. *Your kind crave powerful weapons like bears crave honey.*

Exasperated, Rivlen looked at the beach, trying to think of something else she could trade. But shipwreck survivors weren't known to have vast stores of wealth and treasure, and her people were no exception. If they had been, she wouldn't have been using her magic to scrounge fish.

It crossed her mind to call all her officers together to *force* the druids to take them to the tunnels and their device, but their numbers were about equal, and she wasn't positive her injured and bedraggled people would win. There could also be more druids in the forest, or one of the monuments she'd envisioned.

"Look!" one of the mercenaries called.

The druids had passed their group and were gazing out to sea, toward a boat that had appeared, rising and falling with the cresting of the waves. Not a boat, Rivlen decided, but another raft. Maybe a catamaran. It had a mast and sail, but the complexity didn't go much beyond that. It *was,* however, magical, and she suspected it had been made by the same shipbuilders who'd crafted the crude flying raft. Or was it possible that some of the druids had survived the dragon attack and cobbled the catamaran together out of their destroyed vessel?

Now, we shall find out what happened out there, the druid woman said, squinting at Rivlen.

Squinting *suspiciously* at Rivlen? Why? Did she not believe that dragons had attacked her fleet? Maybe Kywatha hadn't had time to report the floating fortress to her people.

Dragons are what happened, Rivlen said as the catamaran bobbed closer, magic guiding it through the waves toward their cove.

We shall see.

One of the wolves growled as it watched Rivlen.

She checked her defenses again and told her people, *Be careful. We may have to fight them.*

The weary looks the mages and mercenaries sent in her direction weren't encouraging.

As the catamaran drifted closer, Rivlen could sense druids, but she couldn't tell from a distance if any of them had familiar auras. There were also darker-skinned people who might have been roamers, some of the roamers who'd been on the raft. But was Kywatha among the survivors? She was the only druid Rivlen had interacted with and whom she believed would tell the truth to her people.

The druids on the beach used their power to bring the craft more quickly into the cove. Most of the occupants were injured and lying down, and they barely reacted. There were fewer people on board than there had been on that raft. Fewer than half.

Rivlen straightened when she sensed a familiar aura. Kywatha. She was among those lying down, and her aura was fainter than Rivlen remembered. Due to injury?

Kywatha? Rivlen reached out. *Are you awake? Your grumpy people don't want to help us. I need to get a report back to my superiors so we can get as many mages in the world as possible down here to fight those dragons. If we don't, your continent is closest to the fortress and might be in the most trouble.*

She should have mentioned that to the woman with the wolf. That might have swayed her more than offers of compensation.

When Kywatha didn't answer—she had to be unconscious—Rivlen turned to speak again with the leader. But the woman was frowning at her and spoke first.

Many of our kin died in the same battle that saw your ship destroyed. If we learn that you were duplicitous or turned on them...

Rivlen lifted her chin. *We did not. And we are not your enemies. As I'm sure they will tell you, there are dozens of dragons with a new fortress out there now. They are our mutual enemies.*

The woman's squint only deepened, and her gaze descended to Rivlen's chest. No, to the red uniform jacket she wore. *You are one of Uthari's officers. You brought that portal to our land and killed many of our people.*

I followed orders, and that was weeks ago. Things have changed. Talk to Kywatha when she wakes up. She'll tell you what happened. We've been working together since the dragons came.

The woman looked toward the catamaran as magic drew it up on the beach, those on board so weary that few stood up or climbed off. *If she wakes up, I will. In the meantime, do not attempt to leave the area.*

The druid strode toward the catamaran, leaving one of the wolves behind to glower at Rivlen.

"Where exactly does she think we would go?" Rivlen shook her head, again lamenting that she'd lost her ship and was stranded on this Thanok-forsaken continent. There was a war to be fought for the freedom of humanity, and she was stuck on a beach, defending herself against moody druids.

Jak sat on the deck, leaning against Shikari's side, as the gateship left Agorval behind and flew south over the Forked Sea. Between the portal and the dragonling, there wasn't much room, but nobody else was up there, so he liked it.

He was practicing making fireballs, though he wondered if there was a more useful type of magic he should be working on. Something that would be more effective against dragons.

As his scaled friend sunned himself, it occurred to Jak that he had a resource—maybe even *two* resources—to consult. Would Shikari or the portal give up any secrets about dragon weaknesses? Did the great creatures *have* any weaknesses?

Jak thought of the fable of the mouse that defeated a lion by sticking a thorn in its paw. Lions, however, couldn't use magic to wrap impervious shields around themselves.

Portal? May I ask you a question?

A vision popped into Jak's mind, the underwater world with the three Orbs of Wisdom mounted on pedestals. A sense of glee emanated from the portal.

Yes, we're on the way there.

More glee came from it, though a hint of wariness followed, and the vision changed to show the Zewnath jungle with mottled dragons flying over it. A hunting party? Or a patrol that was monitoring the area?

The trees dwindled to show the pool where the portal had once been set up. A dragon perched on the cliff overlooking the waterfall.

It's guarded? Jak asked.

The next feeling the portal emanated was uncertainty.

You don't know but think it might be?

Agreement.

They're looking for you too, aren't they? Jak hadn't been with his mother during the dragons' first attempt to steal the portal, but it had been clear when they'd attacked Uthari's castle that they'd wanted it.

Glumness.

This ship has some camouflaging magic protecting it. It worked to somewhat hide us from the dragons on Nargnoth. Do you think it'll work against the dragons here?

The portal showed Jak an image of itself riding on the deck, as it was now, while emanating radiance and pulsing blue light.

Well, don't do that. People on the other side of the world will sense you if you're lit up like a sun.

It's telling you that its power is a beacon, whether it wishes it or not, Shikari put in.

Are you spying on my conversation? Jak asked.

Shikari thumped him in the back with his tail. *You're right beside me.*

I guess if I wanted privacy, I should have sat on the other end of the deck.

Then you couldn't lean on me and use me for a backrest.

Yes, but I also wouldn't get whapped in the back with a tail.

Dragons have a saying about enduring scales in their teeth to enjoy the deliciousness of fish.

You can remove scales, you know. Jak pantomimed scraping them off with a knife.

Have you seen many dragons carrying such tools?

You have talons and magic. I'm not going to pity you for lacking fingers and thumbs for making utensils.

Dragons are mighty and have no need to be pitied.

Except for the woeful scales between their teeth. Maybe if we put that device of Vinjo's on the portal to nullify its power, the dragons wouldn't be able to sense it through our camouflage. Jak switched back to directing his words at the artifact. *We could keep you hidden until we're at the pool and ready to activate you.*

Uncertainty again emanated from the portal. Uncertainty and

distaste. For some reason, Jak thought of the face Malek made whenever he referenced his experience with the kerzor.

I'm sure you don't like it—does it steal your awareness of the world? —but if it kept the dragons from noticing you and our ship, wouldn't that be good?

The reluctance that followed didn't suggest to Jak that he ought to run down and get the device. He was a little surprised that the portal had let Uthari put it on back in the castle. Maybe Uthari had used magic to hide his actions. Or maybe the portal had been distracted by all the other threats around.

The hatch opened, and Malek climbed out.

"Are you working on your fireballs?" He looked at the empty air in front of Jak. "Or lounging in the sun against your dragon?"

"If the latter, it's dangerous lounging. Shikari thwacks you with his tail on a regular basis."

The tail came up, as if to demonstrate, and Jak grimaced and lifted his hands. Instead of whapping him, Shikari stuck the tip in Jak's ear.

"That's an odd dragon," Malek said.

"I think of him as quirky." Jak removed the tail. "And *so* much better than the mottled ones. He doesn't want to maul and eat humans. That's a predilection I like in a dragon."

"We should work on your magic while we have time."

"I'm ready." Jak had almost asked Malek for a lesson earlier, but he'd been with Mother. Not helping her with anything, as far as Jak had been able to tell when he'd peeked into the lab, but gazing sadly at her. Since Jak was also worried about the parasite and how quickly it would advance inside her, he understood the feeling perfectly. "I was about to ask Shikari and the portal if dragons have any secret weaknesses that less powerful beings might exploit."

What you should ask is why he brought that loathsome dragon-steel collar and chain along. Does he plan to imprison me again if I'm not suitably obedient? Shikari regarded Malek warily.

Uh, I hadn't realized he had *brought it along.* Jak closed his eyes and used his senses to examine the gateship from bow to stern. So much magic infused the craft that it was hard to pick out individual items. The auras of the portal, Mother, and Malek also tended to blot out other things, but eventually he *did* sense a pile of dragon steel in one of the cabins.

"Why did you bring that collar along, Malek?" Jak asked. "Did Uthari order it?"

"He had it placed on the ship when we were loading it."

"So you can force Shikari to be obedient?" Jak grimaced. "He objects to that."

If he tries to collar me, I will do more than whack him with my tail. Shikari showed off his fangs. They were growing impressively long and sharp. *He will not find it pleasant.*

"In case Shikari is infested and becomes aggressive," Malek said. "With your mother now carrying the parasite, it seems possible that it will try to jump from her to him."

"She's staying in the ship, and Shikari doesn't fit in the ship."

"Even so, there's not much between them." Malek waved toward the hatch. "And she mentioned that it might be possible that the parasite could pass from person to person through... other methods."

Jak raised his eyebrows at Malek's uncharacteristic pause but didn't ask for details. "If that's true, we should all be tested for it often."

"Yes."

Jak hated the thought of Shikari being infested, but he also would hate seeing him chained. Was that *truly* why Uthari had ordered the collar sent along? Jak trusted Malek to be honest with him, but he didn't trust Uthari at all. And since this ship now had a dome-jir, Uthari could send orders to Malek long after they were out of telepathic range.

Dragon steel is our weakness, Shikari said. *You know this. Your weapons made from it can cut through our barriers and our scales.*

I was hoping for more of a weakness, especially since I don't have a dragon-steel weapon.

Shikari sniffed. *Perhaps your blacksmith should have been crafting swords instead of chains.*

I agree.

"I don't suppose you also brought along some of Mother's acid concoction that can mold dragon steel?" Jak asked Malek. "Then we could turn the links of that chain into daggers. Or spears. That's what the warriors on Nargnoth used, though I don't think the tips were made from dragon steel, were they?"

"No." Malek tilted his head thoughtfully. "We never did find out what their spears were made of that pierced a dragon's barriers and scales."

"I wonder if Mother knows, now that she has Zelonsera's knowledge." The spears hadn't been more effective than dragon steel—and probably not *as* effective—but Jak was curious. Maybe there were other things out there that could be used against dragons. Until they figured out the parasite problem, they needed all the advantages they could get. *Mother?*

Yes? She sounded weary. Had she slept at all the night before or been up working? Or was the infestation making her tired?

We're trying to think of things that would be more useful than fireballs against dragons. Did Zelonsera share with you what the warriors on Nargnoth did to their spears to allow them to penetrate a dragon's defenses? I remember they didn't feel very magical to my senses. It was a faint signature.

Mother was silent for a moment, and he imagined her sifting through all the knowledge she'd been given, like a student flipping through a card catalog in the library, seeking the right title.

Yes. They caught death darters and dried and crushed them, then turned the powder into a paste and dipped their spear tips in it.

Powdered bug guts are their secret weapon?

As you'll recall, the death darters themselves were magical.

Yeah. Jak rubbed the back of his head, remembering how the bugs had flown through his and Malek's barriers without trouble, the same way Shikari had sauntered through Tonovan's barrier. If not for that skull cap he'd been wearing, he also would have been stung at the base of the skull and infected with the bacteria in their venom. *The death darters weren't able to sting Shikari, though. I remember they were trying, but their stingers didn't pierce his scales. Why would it be different with spears?*

Maybe the death darters weren't what was magical. Maybe it was the bacteria they carried inside them.

So, when the natives crushed them, it actually would have been some of the bacteria that they tipped their spears with rather than anything special about the bug guts?

It's possible. The dragons were largely indifferent to the death darters, so Zelonsera didn't share a lot of knowledge on the science.

I suppose it's not important, Jak said. *We're going to a new world, not Nargnoth, so it's not like we could pop in and capture some of those bugs. And we already have dragon steel. That seems more effective than the bug guts. Or the bacteria-within-the-bug-guts.*

It is interesting though. The bacteria from the death darters might be rivals of a sort to the unicellular flagellate eukaryotes from the dragons. Natural competitors and enemies.

I didn't realize bacteria went to war with each other.

Mother chuckled into his mind. *Oh, yes. All organisms compete for resources, and many have means of keeping those competitors away. For example, it's very common for fungi to effectively attack bacteria and vice versa. Some of our medicines are based on that. I wonder...*

Yes?

Malek, who was waiting for an answer on the spears, lifted his eyebrows. Jak shared what Mother had told him and added, "She got distracted, and I'm not sure what else she was going to say."

"If there were a trace of the death-darter bacteria in my blood," Malek said, "I would wonder if that was why the motes didn't try to enter my body, but I believe Jadora eradicated it completely. I've used my senses to check myself many times to ensure there's no sign of microscopic invaders."

I'm going to run some new tests on Malek's blood, Mother said, as if she'd been listening to him speak. Maybe she'd simply been thinking along the same lines.

He says there's no bacteria left in him. He's certain of it.

I don't think there is either, but maybe...

Jak waited to see if she would share more, but she didn't.

"Mother's working on something," he told Malek.

"Good. In the meantime, we will practice our magic."

"Fireballs?" Jak sighed.

"Perhaps the ability to compress air into a weapon. I managed to punch through a dragon's defenses briefly that way in a battle the other day. It's possible it was only because it was distracted, but I was under its belly, so it might have been a less-protected spot. Either way, it will give you versatility."

"I do strive to be versatile. Women like that."

"Do they?" he asked in amusement.

Malek probably thought Jak didn't have the experience to know—the last time they'd trained together, it had been before Jak had spent the night with Rivlen. As he recalled, Malek hadn't thought he had a shot with her. He had the urge to tell Malek that she'd realized his value and that they'd had a wonderful time together, but he bit his tongue before blurting anything out. He shouldn't feel the need to brag—or defend his experience—to anyone else.

What he *should* be worrying about was whether Rivlen was still alive. The fact that nobody had been able to make contact with her was troubling. Jak had called out to other mages across great distances before. Maybe, since he had a close relationship with her, he could do so now.

Closing his eyes, Jak imagined her face and her location somewhere in the south, then reached out, willing his voice to travel thousands of miles to her. *Rivlen? Are you alive out there?*

He held his breath as he waited for an answer, but if she was alive and heard him, she didn't answer.

That didn't mean she was dead, he assured himself. She was just too far away. He'd never communicated with anyone across that many thousands of miles. Maybe by the time they reached the pool in Zewnath, he would be close enough.

If she was still alive.

5

As night fell and the new druids helped heal the survivors who had drifted in that afternoon, Tezi alternated between checking the horizon for dragons and watching Rivlen for cues. She and a couple of her lieutenants stood at the head of the beach, a druid to either side of them.

The mages had been communicating telepathically, so Tezi didn't know for *certain* that Rivlen was a prisoner, but Thorn Company hadn't been allowed to leave the beach. The druid leader Kywatha was lying unconscious on the catamaran while a healer frowned and muttered over her.

"It's not good," Corporal Basher said, walking up to Thorn Company. She'd been gathering intelligence from the survivors.

Yelotta jumped, as if she'd been deep in thought and startled by the words. Deep in mourning perhaps. She'd stuck close to Tezi all day, her gaze haunted.

"The captain?" Dr. Fret asked.

Basher shook her head. "The roamer I talked to said Sorath had a magical mark on him that the dragons were able to use to find him through the camouflage on their raft. He threw himself overboard to sacrifice himself and keep the dragons from paying attention to the raft, but it didn't matter. They destroyed it anyway. Someone saw Captain Ferroki get knocked overboard with him, and the roamers are sure they're both dead. All except a crazy blind lady who keeps saying Sorath will ride a one-eyed dragon into the battle and help ensure their people's freedom."

"Those dragons don't seem amenable to being ridden," someone murmured.

"No kidding," Basher said. "That seer woman is a loon. I can't believe she survived all that."

"How did any of them?" Tezi asked, trying not to dwell on the notion that Sorath and Ferroki might be gone forever. It didn't sound like anyone had seen them killed. Maybe there was still hope that they'd survived. Somehow.

"I guess the druids used their magic to create protected air pockets for themselves and dove underwater while the dragons were casting fire at the destroyed wreckage of their raft," Basher said. "The dragons eventually gave up, probably deciding it wasn't worth getting wet to dive into the water and get them. Or they figured the druids would die and the sharks would get them."

"They must have gotten word out to other druids before the crash." Dr. Fret nodded toward the stone-faced men and women keeping an eye on their camp. "And avoided being eaten until that boat got out to them."

"Why couldn't the *captain* have avoided being eaten?" someone asked, her voice choking.

Others sniffed and lifted their hands to wipe tears, and Tezi felt her own chin quiver. She wanted to stay strong, especially with Yelotta beside her, needing someone to lead her, but it was hard with the others sinking down in the sand and giving in to their grief.

"Who's in charge now?" someone whispered. "We lost our senior sergeants too."

"I don't know," someone else said. "Does it matter anymore? We never should have been out here. What are mundane mercenaries supposed to do against dragons? This was a suicide mission from the start."

Murmurs of agreement and remorse swept through the mercenaries.

"No," Tezi heard herself say. Before she could think better of it, she moved to stand in front of the women. "We can make a difference. We *have* made a difference." She held up her axe. "We have one weapon that can kill them, and we'll get more. And we'll get off this continent and find a way to fight the dragons. We *have* to. If the captain truly is dead, we can't let her sacrifice be in vain. She and Colonel Sorath would have wanted us to help save the world."

She meant the words to have a rallying effect, but the mercenaries either ignored her or watched her with slumped shoulders and defeat in their eyes.

"Those weapons don't grow on trees, kid," someone said, forgetting she was a corporal now, or not caring. "Tinder lost the one she had, and it's only a matter of time before you lose that one."

"No, it's not. I—" Tezi halted as her axe-head flared blue, and a vision swept over her.

In it, she was back in the jungle, the portal on the ground and stars swirling in its center, as if someone had departed through it —or someone was about to *come* through it.

Confused, Tezi sank to one knee and leaned on the axe for support. Was this a memory? It couldn't be the future. The portal had been taken with Uthari's fleet when they left. It would be in their sky city by now.

Unless... What if Uthari had ordered it brought back to Zewnath for some reason? Or what if the dragons had stolen it? And *they'd* set it up? So more of their kind could come through to this world?

The idea was horrifying. With only forty dragons, their forces had already proven too strong for ships full of mages to defeat.

In the vision, Tezi climbed atop the portal and lifted the axe, shaking it at a dragon swooping down from above. A single mage-ship was also visible in the sky—the long and narrow gateship.

The dragon swept past it, talons outstretched as it reached for the portal. To snatch it up and fly away with it?

Tezi leaped from atop the portal and swung her axe toward its head. Just before the axe blade would have smashed into its eye—its *one* eye—the dragon rolled to the side. Its wing clipped the portal, and a talon grazed Tezi as gravity caught up with her and she fell. She landed painfully, but the dragon also crashed down, rolling sideways and ending up in a stream, water flying everywhere and spattering her cheek.

The vision faded as the Tezi in it was rising to her feet and readying the axe again.

"What?" she blurted, shaking her axe haft. "You can't stop it now. What happens next?"

She grew aware of the sand underneath her and the mercenaries gaping at her as she yelled at her axe. A young man with wild green hair, tattoos, and abrasions on his cheeks and hands also peered at her. Though Tezi hadn't expected to see him again, she recognized him.

"Hello, Grunk." Tezi tried to smile at him, but seeing the druid without Sorath—and knowing Sorath might have died—made it more of a wince. "I'm glad you survived."

He froze, almost looking like a startled animal in the wilds, then gave her a jerky bow. She'd never seen the druids bow and wondered if he did it because he thought it was what she expected for a greeting. He startled her by following it with drawing his dagger, but he didn't point the weapon at her, instead turning and slashing at the air, as if he were sparring with an invisible opponent.

When he finished, he turned back and bowed again. *You came for me on the evil mageship,* he spoke into her mind. *I will protect you now.*

"Er." Tezi didn't think she *needed* a protector, but she didn't want to seem unappreciative. "Thank you."

For a third time, Grunk bowed, then sheathed his dagger. It was one of several blades either hanging from his belt or strapped to his thigh or tucked in a boot sheath.

Tezi glanced toward the local druids standing guard, most of them frowning at the mages, making sure nobody did anything aggressive. "Can you tell them what happened, Grunk? That we were aligned with Kywatha and the other druids against the dragons, not opposing them? I think there's some confusion about that."

Grunk gazed sadly at the druids around the beach and started to shake his head, but he glanced at her, then squared his shoulders. *I do not fit in well with them, and many think I am not sane, but I will try.*

Since Grunk had licked blood off his knives the first time they'd met, Tezi had no trouble envisioning the druids believing him crazy. Even now, there was a feral aspect to him, in the way he crouched, the way his hands never strayed far from his weapons, and the perpetual wariness and suspicion in his eyes.

"Thank you," she said.

"Tezi?" Rivlen's voice came from behind her as Grunk walked away.

"I had a vision, ma'am." Tezi turned to face her and was about to explain, but two druids stood right behind Rivlen like bodyguards. Or *prison* guards.

"Of us getting off this beach and contributing to the war?" Rivlen asked wistfully.

"Actually, yes. At least, I was doing... something. Fighting a one-eyed dragon back by the..." Tezi hesitated to talk about the portal with the druids there. Their people had fought so hard to have the ancient artifact taken down, and, in her vision, it had been in use in the center of their continent again. "Back somewhere important," she finished.

Shouts came from the catamaran. The two druids with Rivlen looked in that direction as someone helped Kywatha to a sitting position. Rivlen's guards jogged toward the craft, leaving her alone with Tezi and the mercenaries.

"Good," Rivlen said. "I hope she tells them what's what. They've been accusing me of turning on their people. Like *we're* the ones who told the dragons to come get them."

"Up until a couple of weeks ago, you *were* trying to kill their people," Tezi pointed out.

Rivlen scowled at her. "Up until a couple of weeks ago, there weren't dozens of dragons in the world to worry about. What else was in your vision?"

Tezi summed it up for her.

"I've seen that one-eyed dragon," Rivlen said. "It was trying to kill Colonel Sorath while others were fighting us. Back in the battle where you lopped off a tail."

Only the very tip of a tail, alas.

"Why would Uthari have sent that gateship back with the portal?" Rivlen asked. "Is there something on another world that could help us with our problem?"

Tezi could only shrug. "I know less than you do, ma'am."

"I think we both know less than that axe."

"It's only selectively chatty about what it knows though."

"No kidding." Rivlen pushed a hand through her hair, almost knocking her bun loose. "Come on. Let's see if Kywatha can tell these people that we're to be trusted and that we need to get to a dome-jir."

Tezi trailed Rivlen to the catamaran, where Kywatha now sat up, her dark-green hair plastered to her shoulders and a vacant look in her eyes. When her gaze passed over Tezi and Rivlen, there wasn't any sign of recognition in it. Was she dazed from a strike to the head?

Most of the survivors appeared dazed. Grunk was one of the few who'd walked away from the raft. Tezi didn't see the elder druids who'd been in charge of the raft along with Kywatha. Maybe they hadn't made it. She guessed only about a quarter of those who'd been on the raft were present, with as many roamers as druids among the survivors. Tezi doubted the blind seer would have any sway over the druids.

"Kywatha," Rivlen said, waving to get her attention. "Will you tell your people that we're allies?"

Kywatha, who'd always seemed quick-witted and powerful during Tezi's brief encounters with her, focused blankly on Rivlen. "I don't remember you."

Rivlen blinked. "It hasn't even been two days since we discussed plans together."

"I… don't remember anything." Kywatha's fingers twitched toward her temple, as if she could draw out her memories, but she only shook her head in frustration.

"Slavemasters' hell," Rivlen muttered.

The two druids who'd been guarding her returned to her side and pointed spears at her. *Tell your people to surrender their weapons. You are our prisoners.*

Tezi tensed, doubting Rivlen would accept that.

Grunk waved at the druid leader, and it looked like he said something telepathically to her, but she frowned and gestured for him to move off to the side. She might have said something disparaging, as well, for Grunk's face fell before he skulked off.

The mages spread across the beach must have heard the telepathic command, for they backed away from the druids. Instead of surrendering their weapons, they raised them, their faces tense. Tezi's axe buzzed in warning as the mages created defensive barriers around themselves. The druids did the same, clustering together to face Rivlen's officers.

Rivlen drew her dagger but ordered her people to hold.

There are more of us in the forest and in the tunnels, the druid woman told them. *If you fight, you will not win.*

Don't underestimate us. Rivlen eyed her, perhaps thinking of springing on her first if a skirmish started.

"We should be fighting the dragons," Tezi said, though she didn't know if the druids understood her language when telepathy wasn't used, "not each other. Ask the druids who were with Kywatha." She tilted her axe toward Grunk and then toward the other survivors near the raft. "And the *roamers*. Can't you see what happened in their minds? They were all there. They know it was the dragons and not us that took down their raft."

Ask that one. Rivlen pointed her dagger at the blind roamer woman. *She knows a lot.*

Roamers cannot speak for druids nor know what happened via telepathic links. Despite her words, the druid leader eyed the seer.

"Read my mind," the old woman said, raising a staff tipped with lesser dragon steel. "I see that our people will work together. We *must* work together. It is our only hope to successfully stand against the dragons."

Long seconds passed as the leader stared at the seer—reading her mind?—and the mages and druids glowered at each other, barriers up and weapons raised.

As Tezi gripped her axe, she glanced at Thorn Company, wondering if she should run across the beach to try to protect as many of her people as she could. Most of the mercenaries had retained their swords and magelock rifles, but she doubted the firearms had charges or would do anything against such powerful foes. More likely, they would be wounded by magic flying about in a battle.

We will all enter the tunnels together, the druid leader finally said.

Will some of us enter as prisoners? Rivlen hadn't yet lowered her dagger.

If you do not come with us, you will remain here indefinitely. Your people are too busy to look for you, if they even know you live.

The druids headed up the beach and into the forest without looking back, some helping the injured people from the catamaran who couldn't walk on their own, the amnesiac Kywatha among them. After conferring briefly, the roamers walked after the druids. Rivlen glowered at the druid leader's back as her officers looked to her, waiting for orders.

"The jungle is in that direction," Tezi offered, lifting her axe to remind Rivlen of her vision.

Rivlen snorted. "About a thousand miles in that direction."

"Maybe they have a way to get us there more quickly than walking."

"I doubt these people are going to want to help us reach that pool in the jungle, especially if the portal is being returned to it." Despite the words, Rivlen sighed, pointed her dagger after the druids, and ordered her people to follow them. She clearly didn't want to go, but what choice did they have?

~

Jadora attempted to push away her weariness as Vinjo tinkered with her microscope. Delicate magic flowed from his fingers as he hummed to himself.

She grabbed a towel from the sink and dabbed her face and eyes, wondering if the warm flush to her skin signaled fatigue or... something else. Her body creating a fever to fight off invading organisms that were spreading through her system like a fleet of mageships sent to conquer an enemy kingdom?

"How small are the things you're trying to look at?" Vinjo straightened and faced her—sort of. He looked past her shoulder as he tapped nervously at a wrench dangling from his belt.

At least he wasn't looking at her chest and telling her what a good family he was from. She hadn't forgotten her encounters with Uthari's officers, mages stirred to libidinous thoughts by her aura. As far as she'd noticed, Vinjo only had eyes for Lieutenant Sasko.

"I need to see proteins," Jadora said. "Antibodies specifically."

"What kind of bodies?"

Vinjo, she reminded herself, was an engineer, not a biologist. "Antibodies. They're Y-shaped proteins created by the immune system to locate and neutralize pathogenic bacteria and viruses that have invaded the body."

"Oh. They sound lovely."

"They're what allow you to fight off illness, so I agree." Jadora didn't know if Malek's immune system had created antibodies in an attempt to destroy the death-darter bacteria, but it seemed his body would have mounted a response, even if it hadn't been effective. "I may also be looking for some other markers that could have been left behind after the bacteria were eradicated. I'm not sure exactly what, but if there's something in Malek's blood now, something the dragon parasite doesn't like, I want to be able to see it." She wished she knew if she was wasting her time, if Malek truly was immune to the parasite. "So, basically, I want as much magnification as you can give me."

"I see. Yes." Vinjo turned back but bumped a vial with his elbow, causing it to roll off the counter.

Jadora used her magic to catch it before it could hit the floor, then floated it back up as Vinjo belatedly grasped for it.

"Sorry," he blurted. "I'm really sorry. I'm a little—" He glanced warily at her before bending back over the microscope, his fingers drumming the counter.

"Nervous?" Jadora didn't know why. It wasn't as if she were a zidarr.

Even if Malek had been present, she didn't think he'd done anything to drive fear into Vinjo's heart either. They'd barely interacted.

"You're very powerful now," he said. "Like my grandmother."

Jadora blinked. "I'm not that old."

She supposed Jak was old enough to sire children, but she hoped he didn't have any plans for that, as she wasn't ready to be a grandmother. She had too many problems to solve, and she still thought of herself as young—all right, maybe middle-aged. That image of herself might be hard to maintain with grandchildren toddling underfoot.

Snorting, she shook her head. This was *not* important to contemplate right now.

"She used to berate me a lot," Vinjo said as he fiddled with the microscope. "She liked my brother, because he was powerful and could hurl fireballs around before he was potty-trained."

"Truly?" Jadora hadn't thought mage powers manifested themselves at such a young age.

"Well, it seemed like it. He was the one all of our relatives approved of and doted on, all except my mother. She likes me. I make her useful things."

"Like magically enhanced microscopes?"

"Last year, I made her an automatic dough kneader."

"I can see where that would be useful."

"Yes. She likes to bake bread and cookies. I miss her cookies, especially the powdered-sugar snowballs. We live in the desert, and I asked about snow when I was a kid, and she had a recipe from the north for snowball cookies and made them. They're so good. Do you think Sasko will make me cookies one day?"

"I don't know what her hobbies are, but I think she'd be more likely to polish your sword for you."

Only after Vinjo's head jerked up and he bumped another vial did Jadora realize her unintended innuendo. Vinjo's eyebrows rose hopefully, but he seemed to realize she hadn't intended to be suggestive.

"I don't have a sword," he said.

"Maybe a wrench."

"I'm not sure she would polish that either. She did *hold* my tools for me." He smiled. "Maybe I can retire from the military, invent all kinds of useful things, and then she can help me sell them, and we can *pay* someone to make us snowballs."

"That could be a logical plan." Jadora's fingers twitched toward the microscope as she wondered if he'd finished his modifications. "Or your mother might enjoy making some for both of you."

"I don't know. I think my family is... not happy with me now." Vinjo sighed and pushed the microscope toward her. "I think that's as good as I can make it under these circumstances." He waved about to indicate the gateship and its limited supplies and tools.

"Thank you, Vinjo."

"Maybe, if you find my work useful, you could recommend to Sasko that she... well, we'd started getting intimate the other day, before we were interrupted by a mage walking in. I thought she might come visit me that night, so we could go back to what we'd been doing, but she didn't. And she didn't come *last* night either. I thought about going to her, but would that be too forward? She's a tough and independent warrior woman. I'm not positive she craves sex the way I— uhm, some others do. But maybe you could suggest to her that if she came to my cabin, I'd lock the door magically and ensure *nobody* could disturb us."

"Perhaps you could suggest that to her yourself." Jadora picked up the slide she'd made earlier and slipped it under the microscope.

"You don't think that would be pushy? I'm not sure she likes assertive men. The *mages* are assertive, and she thinks they're jerks."

"Just tell her how you feel and what you want to do. If she doesn't agree, she'll let you know."

"If *you* talked to her... you're powerful now."

"I hope you're not asking me to use magic to influence her."

"No, no. *I* could do that." He hurried to add, "but I *wouldn't,*" when Jadora frowned at him. "You're powerful and motherly now, so she'd naturally see your wisdom and agree with what you said."

"I doubt she agrees with anyone except her captain."

Vinjo tapped his lip thoughtfully. "Maybe you're right. Maybe *she's* who I should ask. Captain Ferroki is the one who first suggested Sasko spend time with me, after all. I hope we get to see her again soon."

"I'm sure we will," Jadora said, though she didn't know if the rest of the Thorn Company mercenaries were alive. She took Vinjo's arm to guide him to the door. "In the meantime, have a nice long chat with Sasko, all right? It could be that she's interested but doesn't want to be intimate on a crowded ship."

"Oh, do you think?" Vinjo muttered thoughtfully to himself as Jadora nudged him into the corridor.

"We're getting close to Zewnath," someone called from navigation as she shut the door.

Nerves fluttered in Jadora's belly. It wouldn't be long until they reached the pool and could set up the portal.

She bent over the microscope again, sucking in an impressed breath at the details of a cell that came into view. Things that she'd never seen before and couldn't name. She supposed her biology books wouldn't cover such minuscule cell components.

Wait, Uthari had provided her with microbiology books from the Utharika library. Perhaps the authors of those, mages who'd surely used their power to enhance microscopes before, would have provided some insight. She knew that some of the world's scientific understanding came from what mages could detect with magic, things far smaller than regular humans could spot with mundane microscopes.

Hours passed as she read, looked at the slides, and took notes. Eventually, the door opened again.

She was on the verge of telling Vinjo to talk to Sasko on his own before her senses identified Malek as the person walking in. He closed the door behind him and didn't speak, merely waiting for her to reach a stopping point. Oh, but she'd found so much that hadn't been visible before, and it was hard to tear herself away. There were tiny proteins of *all* kinds. The mage texts had diagrams, but she hadn't been able to see them for herself before.

"Vinjo was successful with his modifications?" Malek asked.

"Yes, and I've found something fascinating." Jadora wiped sweat from her upper lip, refusing to acknowledge that she felt flushed and warm. Maybe it had nothing to do with parasites and was due to their flight south to a warmer climate.

"So I assumed when you kept looking in the microscope instead of at me."

"You're not offended, are you?"

"That you find microscopic material fascinating and me only moderately interesting? No."

"You're fascinating too."

Malek issued a skeptical grunt and joined her at the counter.

"This is your blood, after all." She telepathically shared with him an image of the protein she'd found.

"Ah, good. Then I won't be jealous of your assiduous contemplation of it."

Jadora swapped in a slide containing a drop of her own blood. She'd already looked at it countless times, but she wanted to confirm something new that she'd noticed. "That particular protein is not present in my blood, and it's not in any of the texts I've gone through with common protein structures diagrammed.

There are thousands, if not tens of thousands of different kinds, and it's not like the texts have everything in there, but I'm intrigued that this particular protein shows up all *over* in your sample. It stuck out because I can *sense* it now that I'm looking at it."

She looked at him to make sure he grasped the significance.

"Are you suggesting it's magical?" Malek asked.

"I am. Very faintly. And I mean *very*. I didn't sense it before, and it's the barest hint of a signature, as you'd expect from something so tiny, but I can't help but wonder if it's something that was left behind by the death-darter bacteria. As I said, it's not in my blood sample." She pulled out the slide of her own blood and then examined her other blood samples. "It's not in Jak's or Uthari's either."

Malek peered into the microscope. "I'm not sure what I'm looking at, but I don't sense anything."

Jadora frowned, certain it wasn't her imagination that she felt a hint of magic. Standing a couple of feet away, she couldn't sense anything on the slide, but when she'd been close and peering right at the proteins, she had.

"You are more powerful than I now." Malek leaned back from the microscope. "It *is* possible that you can detect fainter magical signatures than I can. I assume it's not typical for human proteins to have such."

"No. There's nothing in the books about animals, plants, or insects having magical proteins, cells, blood, or anything else in their bodies, but these texts were written by mage scientists from Torvil, people who never traveled through the portals and took samples on other worlds."

"Hm."

"I still have samples of the bacteria from the death darters. I'll check to see if I can find the protein in them. I also want to look at more people's blood to see if anyone else has this." Jadora grabbed syringes and empty vials, then patted Malek on the arm. "I'll be right back."

She jogged to the ship's small navigation cabin and took blood samples from Vinjo and a mage in the co-pilot's seat peering down at greenery below. On the way back, she grabbed another mage walking out of the latrine. "I need your blood. For science."

"Er?" He looked like he might have protested but must have decided against it—maybe her aura swayed him—for he didn't move when she took his arm and pushed up his uniform sleeve.

Without explaining, Jadora returned to the laboratory and made fresh slides. Malek watched without commenting, merely waiting to hear whatever she shared with him.

Neither Vinjo nor the other two mages had the protein.

Jadora still had the magically sealed dishes in which she'd grown samples of the death-darter bacteria as well as the dragon parasite. All along, she'd assumed she would have to study them to find the answer. Being careful not to let any of the death-darter bacteria escape into the air, she made a slide with them. Malek waited patiently as she examined it.

"They have it," she whispered. "As well as other microscopic structures that faintly pluck at my senses."

"I'm also able to sense that the bacteria are magical, but they are a collective blob to me." He smiled ruefully. "I am not able to pick out individual microscopic components."

Jadora considered him thoughtfully. "This isn't that surprising of a find, and I don't know if it has anything to do with you not being infected by the dragon parasite. We still don't know if that was chance or if they found you, for some reason—" she eyed his slide, "—an unappealing host."

"Are you still growing samples of the parasite?" His gaze drifted down the counter to her backpack, to where the dishes of the various strains of bacteria were growing.

"I am. I have several dishes along."

"Would it be useful if you attempted to intentionally infest me with it? To see if I'm immune?"

Jadora shook her head. "I'm not doing that."

"I asked if it would be useful," he said dryly, "not if you would do it."

"Well, you wouldn't know how to do it, so the latter matters a lot."

His eyebrows rose. In a challenge?

Malek could probably figure out which samples were which and how to inject himself with them.

"Would it be useful?" he asked quietly. "To prove if these proteins make me immune? Or at least not an ideal host?"

"Yes, but let me isolate some of them and insert them into one of the dishes with the dragon parasite. I'll see what happens there first."

"That will take time, won't it?"

"Yes, but it's the logical next step. We can't rush this. If you're *not* immune to the dragon parasite and I intentionally infested you with it..." Jadora wiped away the beads of sweat on her upper lip again. "You don't want this. Trust me."

"I appreciate that you care for me and don't want to risk my life, but it would be worth risking one person to save many. Or a whole race. Don't you agree?"

"Quit being so reasonable, Malek," she snapped, more out of frustration—and fear at the thought of losing him—than because he was wrong. More calmly, she said, "Let's do it in my sample dishes first and see what happens."

"Very well."

"Even if it turns out that a protein left behind by the death-darter bacteria *did* keep the dragon parasite from choosing you, it wouldn't be as simple as isolating them and injecting them in a person. They wouldn't multiply. They're a result of the bacteria having multiplied and swept through the body. And we know what happens when *that* happens."

"Yes," he said grimly. "Keep studying this. If it leads to a solution, that will be excellent, but I will assume it won't and will continue as planned with the mission. We'll reach the pool and be able to set up the portal soon."

"Good. I'll keep working as we travel on the other world to the orbs."

Malek frowned, watching as she wiped sweat, this time from her brow.

"You might not have much time," he said quietly.

"I'll hurry." She smiled, hugged him briefly, then stepped back. "If you'll allow me to return to it."

"Of course. Let me know if you decide it would be useful to experiment on me." He looked toward her backpack.

A lurch of fear took her. What if he decided to wait until she slept and inject himself, regardless of her desires?

"I will, but don't do anything rash. There's still time." She hoped that was true.

"Very well," Malek said again. He inclined his head, as if promising to respect her wishes, but he glanced once more at her backpack before walking out.

6

Rivlen strode at the head of a loose formation, her lieutenants and the rest of the mages and mercenaries walking behind her. They watched her for clues as she followed the druids through a wide earthen tunnel, the sides emanating soft green light.

The passageway was similar to ones she'd been in near the pool, and she imagined popping up through a manhole into the lush humid jungle, but she reminded herself they were a thousand miles from that spot. Her people wouldn't be there waiting for her either. If the druids didn't have a dome-jir that she could use to contact her superiors, this was a waste of time. One, unfortunately, she had little choice about.

With half her people injured, Rivlen hadn't wanted to start a battle. Besides, it was pointless to fight other humans right now. She had to convince the druids to help her—to help all mages—against the dragons.

But the druids weren't talking with her. They strode ahead, conferring with each other and glancing back seldom.

Rivlen kept wondering if she'd made a mistake in letting the druids lead them away from the beach and their efforts to build a mageship that could fly them home. But they'd had no shipwrights, and she hadn't known if her officers would be able to craft anything sufficient for the task.

During the walk, Rivlen glanced back and spotted a green-haired druid about Tezi's age walking right behind her shoulder. With her axe in hand, Tezi didn't appear worried by his close proximity, but he had a feral, dangerous look about him. Rivlen vaguely remembered him from the raft, when she'd visited to confer with Kywatha, and realized he might be the druid prisoner who'd escaped Tonovan's brig during the dragon battle at the portal. He'd been *in* that brig because he'd helped kill numerous mages and mercenaries to rescue another druid. What did he want with Tezi?

Rivlen snorted. The same thing most men wanted with her probably. Her axe and her body.

Though Tezi could handle herself, Rivlen dropped back to walk at her side near the head of the mercenaries. The roamers were farther back, those who'd been well enough to travel. Some of them and the druids had remained behind to be tended on the beach by healers.

"Do you know where they're taking us, ma'am?" Tezi asked.

"They haven't told me anything. Hopefully to a dome-jir." Rivlen switched to telepathy to ask. *I assume you're aware of that druid kid walking behind your right shoulder?*

Yes, ma'am. That's Grunk.

He looks wild and dangerous. Rivlen didn't sense a powerful aura from the druid, but he gripped a knife as he watched her, his tangled thatch of green hair dangling in his eyes.

Yes, ma'am. He said he's going to protect me.

Rivlen was about to ask if Tezi *wanted* a protector, but another druid appeared, jogging down the tunnel toward them from the opposite direction. He stopped and whispered to the leader who'd spoken to Rivlen. A ripple of dismay went through the group, and they shared concerned glances with each other.

She tried to intercept their thoughts or a few of their telepathic words, but they guarded their minds as well as trained mages.

Frowning, the druid leader looked back, immediately spotting Rivlen and scowling at her.

"What now?" Rivlen grumbled.

The leader waved for her to approach. At least Rivlen wouldn't be kept in the dark.

Tezi followed her, telling her people that she would find out what was going on. With their captain and lieutenant gone, Rivlen didn't know which of the mercenaries was in charge. She doubted it was their newest corporal, but the others appeared too beaten down to object to Tezi stepping up.

When Rivlen and Tezi joined the group, the druids were still conferring, using a mix of telepathy and words spoken in their language. Since they didn't include Rivlen in the conversation, she had to wait, shifting impatiently from foot to foot.

The roamer seer, perhaps an elected leader of their people, squeezed past others to also join the group.

"The portal is returning," she said, lifting her staff.

The druid leader looked sharply at her.

"I have seen it in a vision. It returns to the pool."

The newcomer nodded grimly, but it was the leader who addressed them.

Our northern kin sent a message, she told Rivlen and the roamer seer, *that they sensed its powerful aura once more flying over Zewnath, and that all druids must be on the alert.* Her eyes narrowed as she focused solely on Rivlen. *We thought your people learned their lesson after unleashing all those dragons, but now they bring it back? Why? To open it again?*

Rivlen wanted to object to the druid's certainty that *her* people were bringing the portal, but Tezi had said she'd seen the gateship near it in her vision. That might mean the rest of Uthari's fleet was with it. Rivlen turned her protest into a statement the druids might find more palatable. *If you have a dome-jir that I can use, I can contact my people and find out what's going on with the portal.*

The druid leader snarled like a bobcat defending its cubs. *What's* going on *does not matter. That it's being returned to the place where it can be opened does. Already, there are more dragons in the world than we can handle. What if* more *come through?*

Rivlen spread her arms. *I would fight to stop that.*

The leader's eyes narrowed even further. *You would battle against your own people and help the druids gain control of the portal?*

That's not what I said.

Our people would bury it deep in the earth so it couldn't be used again.

Let me use a dome-jir, Rivlen said. *If you received word from your northern kin, you must have such a communication device.*

No. We will not go back to the settlement. We must gather our people, board the yuvarslith *and hurry to the mountain pool. We must stop the portal from being opened again. You and your people will come with us. If you will not side with us in this, you will mark yourself an enemy, and we will destroy you.*

The leader spun, shouting words to her people, and strode off up the tunnel, almost at a jog. The rest of the druids, including the one who'd delivered the message, ran to catch up.

Had there not been more druids in the rear, prodding the roamers, mercenaries, and mages along, Rivlen might have been tempted to head back to the beach. But if the druids were going to that pool, and Uthari's mageships were carrying the portal and also heading there, it would be Rivlen's chance to reunite with the fleet.

As much as she dreaded being reprimanded for having lost her ship, her duty dictated that she do her best to report in. And she would.

"What's a you-var-slith?" Tezi whispered, having apparently heard the telepathic conversation. "Do you know?"

Rivlen shook her head, but the druid Grunk raised a hand. He didn't speak aloud or telepathically to Rivlen, but he must have given Tezi a message.

"He says it's an underground... wagon." Tezi raised her eyebrows at Grunk.

The druid pantomimed a chain.

"A number of magical wagons linked together," Tezi added. "They travel fast."

"It'll have to be *extremely* fast," Rivlen said, "if it's going to get us to that pool before a mageship that's already on the way."

Grunk nodded firmly and waved for Tezi to continue onward.

Rivlen looked wistfully back the way they'd come, but the druids in the rear were ushering her people forward. So far, she'd deemed it best to avoid battle, but as she followed the leader down the tunnel, she wondered if that would continue to be an option.

The druids wanted her to fight to keep the portal from being used, but her loyalty was to her own people, no matter how dubious a scheme they might have concocted.

Be prepared to turn against them if we have to, Rivlen told Tezi telepathically.

The druids? Tezi glanced back at Grunk.

Yeah. Your protector might become your assassin if Uthari is the one who brought the portal back.

Tezi's forehead furrowed. *Do you think that likely? Or did the dragons maybe steal it? They were collecting dragon steel the last we heard.*

You're the one who saw the gateship in a vision.

It could have been chasing after the portal rather than putting it to use.

We'll find out soon, Rivlen said. *Tell your people to be ready. You're still working for Uthari.*

Tezi's forehead furrow deepened, and she didn't reply.

Would the mercenaries decide they'd had enough of *working for Uthari*?

Rivlen supposed she didn't need them—it was only Tezi with her axe who was useful—but she felt compelled to hold the remnants of her little fleet together, inasmuch as she could. After her earlier failures, having to admit the mercenaries had chosen to switch sides, or disappear into the jungle, wouldn't go over well with Uthari. Already, she dreaded what he would say when she reported in. She hoped *he* wasn't the one bringing the portal to the pool.

~

On the deck of the gateship, Jak gripped the railing and gazed at the dark jungle below. Before nightfall, they'd passed over Port Toh-drom, the citizens out doing repairs on their city. Jak hadn't witnessed the one-eyed dragon's attack on it, but he'd heard about it, and he'd glimpsed the rubble that was all that remained of the tower where Yidar had once tried to kill him and his mother. It was strange how long ago that seemed, but it had only been at the beginning of the summer.

Back home, north of the equator, autumn had begun. Jak hadn't set foot on the ground when he'd been back in Uth, so he hadn't seen the trees changing colors, except from far above. A twinge of nostalgia plucked at him, longing for his home and a much simpler time, one when wizards hadn't known he existed and dragons hadn't flown through the sky, attacking towns and cities.

The hatch clunked open, and Jak looked curiously toward it, not sensing anyone with a magical aura. That left only Tinder and Sasko, and they hadn't talked much with him on the trip. He knew Tinder a little from their adventure on Vran, but he hadn't had many opportunities to speak with the Thorn Company second-in-command.

As Sasko stuck her head out, Jak resolved to have a conversation or two with her before they traveled through the portal. He had no idea if the mercenaries were still being paid, or if the rest of their company had survived. Sasko and Tinder might resent being dragged along again on another mission without being asked if they wanted to come.

"Hello, Lieutenant." Jak lifted a hand.

Shikari thwapped his tail against the deck in what might have been a greeting. It could also have been a warning to Sasko not to accidentally step on it in the dark.

"Do you have a minute?" Sasko rounded the tail, eyeing it warily, and joined Jak at the railing.

"Yes." He removed his hat and wiped moisture from his brow. The sunset hadn't alleviated the jungle heat much.

"Lord Malek said not to disturb you if you're conjuring fireballs."

"It's as humid as a greenhouse in summer. All I'm conjuring right now is armpit sweat."

"Gross."

"Is it? As a mercenary, you're not accustomed to such things?"

"I am, but it's still gross. I wanted to ask you... Well, you're a mage now, right?"

"I'm learning to be one," Jak said. "If there's a final exam or test for some kind of certificate, I haven't heard about it yet. I understand that there's a lifetime of study involved."

As Sasko took a moment to digest that, he wondered if he'd put her off with his modesty. Maybe she didn't think he was qualified to answer whatever question she had. Or maybe he'd traumatized her with talk of his moist armpits.

"What are you wondering?" he prompted.

"From what I've heard, mages have to be close to speak telepathically to each other, but some powerful mages—or is it wizards?—can reach out over greater distances."

"That's right. Wizard is just a title that mages give other mages that are extremely powerful. And likely have a kingdom."

"Are you able to reach out to Captain Rivlen or any of the Thorn Company mercenaries? Anyone from the three ships that went south with the druid raft? I'd like to know if the company is still alive."

"Ah." Jak wondered why she hadn't asked Malek since he could speak across greater distances than Jak and was a far more powerful mage, but maybe Sasko found Malek intimidating.

Earlier, he'd been up on the deck, finding a place between the portal and the dragon where he could practice his sword exercises. Shikari hadn't thwapped his tail at *him*.

"I'll try to reach out to Rivlen." Jak didn't mention that he'd already tried exactly that several times—and failed.

He gripped the railing, closed his eyes, and, after checking the area for dragons, attempted to project his words to the south. Since he didn't know where she might be, he had to fling them out broadly and hope to reach her.

Rivlen? Are you able to hear me?

Only the familiar silence responded to him. He took a deep breath and tried to project his words even farther.

Rivlen? I'm worried about you.

This time, he thought he sensed the barest hint of... something. It wasn't a response, and he was too far away to sense anyone's aura, but something brushed his awareness. Rivlen? Someone—or something—else?

If you don't answer me, I'll be quite put out. I might send Shikari to find you and wreak havoc on your ship. Jak tried to send an image of the dragonling romping across the deck of the *Star Flyer* with latrine paper draped over his back and horns.

The ship is gone.

The response was so faint that Jak barely heard it, and it was hard to tell who'd sent the message. *Rivlen?*

The dragons succeeded in destroying the Star Flyer *and the other ships in the fleet. The druid raft too. We were wrecked on the southern end of Zewnath, and now we're in druid tunnels, possibly prisoners.*

It *was* Rivlen. Her news wasn't good—not in the least—but she was alive, so there was hope.

Jak's fingers tightened around the railing. *Is there a way I can help? I can barely hear you.*

All he could tell was that her words originated far to the south —which made sense based on what she'd said—and that they were muffled. Maybe that was because she was in druid tunnels. He remembered that some of them had insulating qualities and that he'd struggled in the past to communicate with people through their earthen ceilings.

I can barely hear you too. Where are you?

Flying south over the northern part of Zewnath.

A long pause followed, and he repeated the words in case they hadn't reached her.

Do you have the portal?

Yes. How did you know? Jak couldn't imagine her sensing it from that far away.

The druids *know. Druids from all over the continent. Their people are escorting us and trying to reach the pool in time to keep it from being erected again. Is that where you're heading?*

Yes. We need to go to another world to get information from artifacts called the Orbs of Wisdom. Jak didn't think he'd mentioned them to Rivlen before. *We have to go. Mother has been infected with the dragon parasite. And so has Uthari. We have to find a cure now, more than ever.*

"Is anything happening?" someone asked while Jak was waiting for a response—Tinder.

She'd joined Sasko up on deck. He'd been too busy concentrating to notice.

"I'm not sure," Sasko whispered to her. "After telling me about his armpit sweat, he started trying to find Rivlen telepathically."

"Gross."

"That's what I said."

"Is it true that he's sleeping with Captain Rivlen?" Tinder asked. "I heard rumors."

"She might like sweaty armpits."

"I'm *right* here," Jak said. "And concentrating, if you don't mind. Rivlen is alive, and I'm trying to talk to her."

"Good. Is Captain Ferroki alive?" Sasko asked. "And the others?"

"Dr. Fret?" Tinder put in.

"I'll ask."

Does that mean Uthari is going to go mad like the dragons? Rivlen asked after digesting the news. *And turn mottled?*

We don't know yet what the effects will be on humans, and I'm more concerned about my mother than Uthari.

I guess now that she's so powerful, we don't want either of them to go mad.

Jak's concerns about his mother had little to do with her power, but he didn't say that. It was a valid thing to worry about. He rubbed his forehead. *Tinder and Sasko want to know about Thorn Company. Especially Ferroki and Fret. Did they make it? Are they with you? Are you* really *a prisoner?*

After all the times Jak had seen Rivlen in battle, it was hard to imagine her being bested, even by powerful druids. *She* was powerful too. But if her people had been shipwrecked and injured, that could explain it.

The druids think we are. I didn't order our people to fight them, since we lost our dome-jirs and needed to get off that beach anyway, but, Jak, if you're setting up the portal because Uthari ordered it... Are you? Or did you steal it and go off on some scheme?

Jak thought about objecting to the notion that he was a thief and a schemer, but after he'd stuck a kerzor in Tonovan's head and been responsible for his death, it wasn't that farfetched for Rivlen to believe that. Besides, he *had* been thinking about stealing the portal. Only the fact that Uthari had been infected and changed his mind about letting them take it back to the pool had made theft unnecessary.

Uthari ordered it, Jak said. *Malek is here with us.*

Then we're going to have to fight the druids together, Rivlen said grimly. *Possibly a* lot *of them. They wanted us to help them fight to keep the portal from being erected again, but obviously I can't order my officers to turn against Uthari.*

Or me, right?

Fret is alive, and so is Tezi, Rivlen said, not responding to his question. *Some of the others are too, but the mercenaries lost people. So did I. The other captains, for starters. As strange as it seems, I'm in command of what was our fleet now.*

That's not strange.

I've been failing Uthari all month.

Yeah, but he's... Jak reminded himself that she was a loyal officer in Uthari's fleet. *Difficult to please.*

No kidding. According to the druids, Sorath and Ferroki didn't make it. The druids lost a lot of people too, and Kywatha is an amnesiac now.

Jak's shoulders slumped.

"It's bad news, isn't it?" Sasko murmured.

Jak nodded and shared what he'd learned.

How far are you from the pool? Rivlen asked.

We ought to be there sometime tomorrow. Are you flying there on a mageship? Do you know if there are druids already there?

We got on a magical underground train of floating wagons, and we're zipping through wide tunnels fast enough to make my stomach queasy. Dr. Fret just puked over the side and spattered vomit on roamers in the wagon behind her.

Thanks for that graphic update. Jak supposed he couldn't talk when he'd been speaking of armpit sweat earlier.

I assumed Sergeant Tinder is who wanted to know about Fret and that she would want to know how hale the doctor is.

Is she injured?

Only sick from the motion, I think. And the roamers cursing at her.

I don't suppose you could sabotage that wagon train and keep it from arriving? As much as Jak would love to see Rivlen again, he didn't want to see legions of armed druids waiting at the pool to attack them and try to wrest the portal away.

I don't know enough about engineering to tinker with the magic powering them and do something subtle. And I assume they'll notice if I light the wagons on fire. Then we'll have to fight them in these forsaken tunnels. If we get to the pool, we can help you. Is Uthari there too? The fleet?

Uhm. Jak looked around at the small gateship, the night sky devoid of the running lights of any other vessels. *It's me, Malek, Mother, Vinjo, the two mercenaries, and the four mages you sent along.*

That's all you've got to battle legions of druids?

I'd prefer not to battle legions of anything. That's why I asked about sabotage.

Rivlen groaned into his mind. *You better hope the camouflage on the ship is still working. Though I'm not sure how you'll set up the portal. They're going to sense that as soon as you get close. No, wait. They* already *sensed it through the camouflage.*

Jak grimaced. He'd been afraid of that. It must have been when they'd flown past Port Toh-drom. He'd sensed druids among the citizens, doing repairs to the monument in the city square.

I'll try to hide it. Jak would have to use Uthari's device, regardless of the portal's wishes.

Good luck. After a hesitation, Rivlen added, *I'm glad you're well. I worried that Uthari would kill you.*

He wanted to, I think. But his plans went awry when he infested himself and Mother. Jak explained how that had happened, wanting Rivlen to know that the predicament they were in was Uthari's fault. Even though he understood that her career meant much to her, and she was trying to please her aloof father, he wanted her to realize that Uthari was horrible and shouldn't be followed.

Ugh, was all she said.

Jak couldn't tell if the single word conveyed deep and profound realization or not. *I'm glad you're well too. I miss you. And, uhm, I miss being with you. Last night, I dreamed of you. I mean us.*

Entangled in the sheets in the throes of energetic passion?

Something like that. I would like to have throes with you again.

I have no doubt, she replied dryly.

Jak supposed he wouldn't get mushy sentimentality from Rivlen. She might have a vulnerable inner core that he'd glimpsed a few times, but her hardened exterior dominated.

I managed to keep your map, she said.

I'm glad. It touched him that she'd prioritized that. He knew she cared, even if she didn't say it.

If you can survive the druids, I'll happily make a date to engage in throes with you.

I'll look forward to it. I—

Humans! a snarling voice broke in.

Jak jumped a foot and reflexively swept out with his senses.

We hear you speaking, humans.

Though Jak couldn't sense any dragons nearby, that voice could only belong to one of them. One patrolling over Zewnath somewhere between him and Rivlen? He was mortified that the creature might have overheard their conversation about throes.

You are bringing the gate to us. Excellent.

That's not the plan, Jak said.

Maybe he shouldn't have said anything. Rivlen had fallen silent.

A mad cackle sounded in his mind, a throaty gargling like

nothing he'd heard Shikari utter. *What you plan does not matter. We will take it, just as we will take this world.*

Jak pulled back his awareness, not wanting the dragon to be able to follow the trail to him. Maybe he was naive to believe it didn't already know precisely where he was.

"Something wrong, Jak?" Tinder asked.

"You went as pale as Tezi," Sasko said. "Without the cute freckles."

"A dragon just threatened to come take the portal," he said.

They swore.

"We'll tell Malek," Sasko said and headed for the hatch.

Jak nodded, though he could reach out to Malek telepathically and did. *We have a problem.*

Another one? came Malek's prompt reply.

Jak sensed him in navigation with Vinjo. *Two, actually. Problems like to come in hordes.*

Go ahead.

I was able to contact Rivlen—can you report to Uthari that she's alive and being escorted to the pool by some possibly hostile druids?

The pool where we're taking the portal? Malek asked. *Will they attack?*

It sounds like that's their plan, but there's also a dragon out there. Somehow, he heard me talking to Rivlen, and he butted in with threats. Jak summed up the rest of his conversation, leaving out talk of throes.

I'll see if Vinjo can get any more speed out of the ship, Malek said. *If a great number of druids show up, we won't be able to best them in a battle, and a dragon... Perhaps if it's alone, we may have a chance, but they've been showing up in twos and threes.*

Yeah, and we're closer to their fortress now. They could show up in tens and twenties.

If that happens, we'll all be dead.

I'm going to try to put Vinjo's device on the portal to nullify it, and hopefully its aura, until we're ready to use it.

We should have put it on from the beginning.

When I suggested that to the portal, it objected.

Is it going to object now?

Jak imagined creeping up to the portal with the device, only to have it send him flying overboard with a branch of red lightning to the chest. *I hope not.*

7

Sorath and Ferroki sat side by side in the dark den where Yoshartov had deposited them, shivering through their torn clothing, their wounds throbbing. Earlier, Sorath had prowled the confines of the space, seeking a way out or a weapon that could be used against the dragons, but there was nothing save fronds bunched together in a nest. A lot of fronds for a *large* nest.

Given how far they were from the mainland—or any islands capable of growing vegetation—Sorath couldn't imagine how Yoshartov had gotten them there. Magic, he supposed, and envisioned the dragon uprooting numerous trees and floating them hundreds of miles across the sea.

"How are we going to get out of here and figure out a way to sabotage and destroy this place?" Sorath murmured, staring up at the blue-black dragon-steel ceiling of the den.

"The answer lies with our new master, I believe," Ferroki said.

Sorath's mouth twisted at the word *master*. "We're *not* servants."

The flap of wings sounded in the wide tunnel outside the den, and Yoshartov came into view. The barrier vanished, and he landed in their chamber, wings furling to his sides. A net of squirming freshly caught fish dangled from his maw.

Servants, I've brought food for you to prepare for me, Yoshartov announced in their minds, then shook out the net. His wet bounty flopped down, two- and three-foot long toothfish and icefish and other species Sorath didn't recognize.

"Prepare?" Ferroki glanced at Sorath. "Jak's dragon eats everything he catches raw, if not still alive and squirming."

Sorath, disgruntled at being called a servant and expected to prepare food, only glowered.

I have observed that humans put salt and spices on their foods, Yoshartov said. *I am curious about their culinary practices and the cuisines of this world, and I wish to consume spiced food to see if I enjoy it. You shall prepare these fish properly for me, in the human way.*

"Do you want them cooked?" Ferroki asked. "And is there a kitchen in your fortress?"

A what?

"A place for preparing food."

"Yes." Sorath said, pushing his annoyance to the side. This could be an opportunity to get out of the den. "We'll need spices and a kitchen to prepare the fish in, and you'll also need to heal us. We're far too gravely wounded to wield the implements of food preparation."

Yoshartov cocked his head, as if puzzled by everything, and Sorath, trusting the dragon was reading his mind, envisioned himself in a fancy chef's kitchen with a knife in one hand and a huge pot dangling from his pickaxe while he made vigorous scaling and cutting gestures that would require a person to have an uninjured torso and arms.

It is more difficult for me to read your minds when you are surrounded by our metal, but you must dance to prepare the foods, yes? This is a human ritual?

"Dance?" Ferroki mouthed, but she quickly nodded in agreement.

"Yes. And we need to have access to the spices you wish to taste. Perhaps you can take us to Port Toh-drom to shop in their market. I *know* you know where that city is." Sorath envisioned the tower that Yoshartov had destroyed to get to the tiny bit of dragon steel inside, though he didn't know if the dragon would catch the memory.

Sorath couldn't be sad about that. If Yoshartov was struggling to read their minds, that was a good thing. Maybe it meant he and Ferroki could more successfully plot an escape—or the destruction of the fortress.

My servants may not leave. I might lose them!

"That would be tragic," Sorath muttered.

He noticed that Yoshartov rarely said *we* to refer to himself, as many of the other dragons did, and wondered if it meant he'd retained more of his sense of self. Maybe it simply meant he was more self-centered than the rest.

"At the least, we must have a kitchen or a special area where we can cook over flames and dispose of refuse," Ferroki said. "You don't want fish scales and guts all over your lair, do you?"

Humans do not consume the guts?

Ferroki curled her upper lip. "Not generally, no."

Fascinating. Dragons do not prepare food, so we do not have what you call kitchens. But refuse... Yes, we have a place where that can be disposed of. I will take you there.

"Don't forget to heal us," Sorath said. "For the dancing ritual."

Ah, yes, of course. My servants should *be fit, the better to serve me.*

"Exactly," Sorath said.

Yoshartov cocked his head again and studied them both. Soon, a warm tingle flowed into Sorath. Beside him, Ferroki gasped. Was the dragon healing them both at once?

The tingling magic exhilarated but also weakened Sorath, as if it were drawing upon his own energy, and he sank to his knees. Ferroki dropped down beside him, groaned, and leaned against his shoulder. He wrapped an arm around her, the gesture less painful than it had been earlier.

When the tingling and warmth faded, the pain did as well. Sorath pushed his shirt aside and found pink scar tissue where the talon puncture wound had been earlier. The lumps on his head and the aching inside his skull had disappeared.

"Thank you, Yoshartov," he made himself say, even though the dragon had been responsible for the wounds to start with.

"You are a very kind master." Ferroki smiled at Yoshartov.

Sorath had never seen her flatter anyone, not even King Uthari, but he couldn't blame her for trying to get on their captor's good side.

Yes. I am a benevolent dragon. One of the flopping fish rolled onto his talon, and Yoshartov squashed it under his foot, ending its life with a decisive prong through the head.

"Indeed," was all Ferroki said.

"You're better at playing the role of humble servant than I am," Sorath murmured.

"I've had a lot of practice as a mercenary leader working for mages. I'm surprised you haven't."

"Those mages would have preferred I kiss their butts, but I always struggled to swallow my pride and do that." Sorath sighed. "It's probably what led to them resenting me and the annihilation of my company."

"It's not wrong to have pride."

"In this world, it is."

Magical energy swept under Ferroki and Sorath, levitating them into the air. Yoshartov backed out of the den and flew into the tunnel with them floating after him.

This time, when they passed a chamber full of spheres, cylinders, and pumps, Sorath took special note of the glowing magical devices inside, as well as the tendrils that disappeared into the walls and floors—to spread power to different parts of the fortress? As Ferroki had said, it reminded him of the engine room of a mageship. He wondered if early human mages had borrowed their engineering knowledge from the dragons that had once visited the ancient world.

Too quickly, they floated past the chamber. Sorath vowed to find a way back to it, though he was positive they would need a dragon-steel weapon to sabotage the devices.

If they somehow found a way, maybe the entire fortress would fall out of the sky, bounce off the glacier underneath it, land in the sea, and sink to the bottom. The thought made him smile. Such damage might not be irreparable for dragons, but it ought to delay their world-domination plans. Especially if it came at an inopportune time. Such as when others were attacking.

Had any of the druids or Captain Rivlen's people survived their visit to the fortress? Sorath hoped that word had gotten out to the rest of the world, and that all the mages and druids of Torvil were working together to prepare an assault. If they were still oblivious to the fortress and what the dragons planned... then it wouldn't matter what Sorath and Ferroki did here.

Yoshartov flew them into a busier part of the fortress, into the courtyard where some dragons had dined earlier. Sorath grimaced at the memory.

Dragons were flying about or lounging in nests on perches overlooking the courtyard. On the far side, Yoshartov took them through a short tunnel and into one of several windowless towers before setting them down. The high-ceilinged chamber stank of charcoal, and burned pieces of bone were scattered across a soot-covered floor.

Sorath stared. Those were human bones. This was a crematorium, not a kitchen.

Refuse is taken to this place and incinerated. Fish guts can easily be destroyed. You will work here.

A moist flop sounded behind them. Sorath spun in time to see all the fish plopping onto the floor.

"We'll need a knife, a fire, and spices," Ferroki said.

"A *dragon-steel* knife would be perfect for gutting fish," Sorath added.

You wish me to arm you with a weapon capable of harming a dragon? Do you think I'm a fool?

"Sadly not enough of one."

"Do you, the mighty Yoshartov, fear one small human warrior with a dragon-steel blade?" Ferroki asked.

I do not *fear the human colonel. I have battled him numerous times, and he is incapable of besting me.*

Sorath clenched his jaw, wishing he could deny it, but it was better for Ferroki's argument that it was the truth.

"Then please bring us a blade suitable for this task, mighty Yoshartov." Ferroki spread her hand toward the pile of fish that rose to their waists. "We lack the fearsome attributes of a dragon, so we cannot use tooth or talon." She lifted her trimmed fingernails to demonstrate their lack of talon-ness.

Were I to bring such a blade, Colonel Sorath would attempt to slay me with it. Even though he is not my equal, and I do not fear my servant, I wish a meal, not a battle. Yoshartov flapped his tail down, causing charred pieces of bone to skitter across the sooty floor.

"Colonel Sorath will give you his word that he won't attack you," Ferroki said.

"What?" Sorath asked.

Yoshartov lowered his head on his long neck and peered into Sorath's eyes. *Is this true, servant?*

Servant. Sorath ground his already clenched teeth.

Ferroki looked at him and nodded, no doubt thinking that their plan was to sabotage the fortress, not worry about one dragon. Still, Sorath would attack any of them if an opportunity presented itself and he thought he could win. The only way to save the world was to eliminate the dragon threat, one way or another.

But Yoshartov was staring expectantly at him, so Sorath didn't say that. He tried not to even *think* it.

"If you bring me a blade to scale the fish, I promise not to attack you with it today."

For three days, my wily servant. Yoshartov's yellow eye gleamed. *And you promise to make a most succulent meal.*

"If you bring spices, we will," Ferroki said.

Yes. I will do this. After the colonel gives his word.

Sorath sighed. "If you bring me a dragon-steel blade, we'll prepare your meal, and I promise not to attack you for three days."

Excellent. I will tell the female I am attempting to impress that we will have fine and exotic local cuisine tonight. Yoshartov sprang into the air, flapped his wings, and left them alone in the tower.

"He's trying to *impress* someone?" Sorath asked.

"That explains why he wants something special. Look." A clatter sounded as a blue-black dagger skidded along the floor and into their chamber, as if it were a puck the dragon had struck with a stick—or his tail.

"That's *my* blade," Sorath grumbled. "Technically, it's Grunk's blade. I had to promise to cook and restrain from killing that dragon to get something back that already belonged to us."

Ferroki patted Sorath on the shoulder as he plucked it off the ground. "It's a victory nonetheless. If they put another barrier across the exit, this should be able to pop it."

"Yes, but do you know how to prepare exotic local cuisine?" Sorath had been an officer for a long time. He had a few vague memories of cooking lizard steaks over fires while camping in the deserts of Zar, but they hadn't been fancy. Or heavily *spiced.* Mercenaries weren't fussy.

"I know how to gut fish, but Corporals Dashi and Arrow do most of the cooking for the company." Ferroki's face grew wistful, and she gazed toward the wall, though there were no windows for them to look out. "I hope they're still alive."

"I hope all your people are," Sorath said, though he feared they weren't and that he and Ferroki might be on their own when it came to completing their mission. "I also hope we can bumble our way into preparing a meal a dragon will consider sumptuous."

"What kinds of spices will he find, I wonder," Ferroki said with a faint smile.

Sorath imagined the dragon levitating crates stolen from some poor merchant's shop all the way from Port Toh-drom to the fortress, bottles of oregano and turmeric tumbling free along the way. "I don't know, but let's hope dragon palates aren't that discerning."

"From what I've seen Jak's dragon eat, they can't possibly be." Ferroki nodded toward the exit to the tower. "I don't think he put a barrier across it to keep us from roaming."

A dragon flew through the courtyard, its yellow eyes squinting at them through the tunnel before it disappeared from view.

"Even if he had, as you pointed out, the dagger would be able to pop it." Sorath made a pricking motion with the tip of the weapon. "We may be able to wander back to that engine room and take a look." A *destructive* look.

No sooner had he said the words than another dragon plopped down in a nest that looked straight into their tower. Sorath didn't know if Yoshartov had sent it to stand—sit—guard, or if that was coincidentally where it had chosen to rest, but they wouldn't be able to leave the tower without walking in front of its snout.

"Later," Ferroki murmured.

Sorath nodded. With Yoshartov presumably already gone to hunt for spices, it wouldn't be a good idea to roam anyway. If they were caught out, one of the crazy dragons that wasn't interested in servants might eat them, the same as it had noshed down the owners of the bones that were scattered on the floor.

"Besides," Ferroki said with forced cheer. "You have fish to prepare. You did promise."

"So I did."

The parasites in the magically sealed dish were ignoring the protein.

Jadora had hoped for more of a reaction, that they would destroy it or move away from it or do *something* to indicate that they found it unappealing. Maybe she would put some of the living death-darter bacteria into the dish with them. Even though she'd had samples of both along for some time, she hadn't thought to try that yet.

Jak opened the door, and she applied a fresh seal to the dishes, double-checking to make sure nothing had escaped. He walked to the drawer to retrieve the nullification device for the portal.

Jadora wiped sweat from her brow and watched him with concern. "Will the portal allow you to put that on it?"

"I'm about to find out. If it strikes me with lightning and knocks me overboard, I may need you or Malek to peel my blistered and broken body out of the treetops."

Jadora leaned away from the microscope, digging her knuckles into a knot in her lower back. "I'll come up with you. I need a break."

"Will it be safe for you to be close to Shikari?"

She winced. She'd forgotten he was up there. "No."

So much for her break.

"I can ask him to fly around. He's working on improving his aerial skills anyway." Jak held up the device. "I'd like you there in case the portal gets uppity."

Jadora nodded. "I'd like to be there too."

Some fresh air might help her weariness. The little laboratory had come to feel hot and stifling.

"Have you found anything useful yet?" Jak asked.

"I'm running some tests. So far, the results are inconclusive, but I'm hesitant to jump ahead to experimenting on someone to try to prove hypotheses."

"Someone?" Jak raised his eyebrows as he ran his thumb over the flat side of the oval-shaped device. "Like yourself?"

"I'd be open to experimenting on myself at this point." She smiled faintly. How much worse could things get for her?

Jak didn't return the smile, instead frowning as he scrutinized her. "You don't look well."

"You're supposed to lie to your mother and tell her how beautiful she is, even if she's ill."

"Isn't that more of the job of your..." Jak waved toward the navigation cabin—toward Malek?

He seemed to have accepted that they now had a physical relationship, but maybe he wasn't comfortable speaking about it. She supposed few children, no matter how old they got, wanted to hear about their mother's sex life.

"I'll accept compliments on my appearance from either of you." Normally, her *appearance* was the furthest thing from her mind, and she much preferred compliments on her academic prowess, but she wanted to pretend her physical body wasn't deteriorating under the effects of the parasite.

"Then you look stunning. And, er, sweaty. Do you have a fever?"

"Yes."

"Should you lie down and rest?" Jak looked toward the microscope and the pages and pages of notes strewn about the counter.

"Probably."

"Will you?"

"No."

"If our roles were reversed, I think you would give me a stern lecture and force me to go to bed."

"We don't have time for rest."

Shaking his head, Jak headed for the ladder. Jadora followed closely after him. She did need a break, but she also worried about what would happen if the portal didn't *want* that thing affixed again. She didn't know how Uthari had managed to put it on back in his castle.

Presumably, when Vinjo had first sneaked aboard the *Star Flyer* and placed it, the portal hadn't known what it was or that it should defend itself, but now... now it knew perfectly well. It liked Jak, but she sensed he'd only been half-joking when he mentioned the possibility of lightning strikes.

On deck, the air was muggy and not as refreshing as Jadora had hoped. Shikari stood beside the portal, using his magic to sweep large flying insects into his maw.

"Are those enough to fill his belly?" Jadora decided the dragonling had grown again in the short time since they'd left the castle. She stayed back, waiting for Jak to suggest to Shikari that it was time for flying practice.

"An appetizer," Jak said.

Shikari looked back at them, swished his tail, and sprang into the air.

The last time Jadora had seen him fly, Shikari had looked more like a drunken bumblebee than one of the elegant adult dragons, but he'd improved as he'd grown, his wings lengthening and widening. With a few powerful flaps, he cruised away from the mageship, his blue scales gleaming iridescent in the morning sunlight.

"Don't go far," Jak called. "Other dragons could show up at any time. With friends."

I do not sense other dragons yet, Shikari spoke into their minds, *but if they fly close, I will roar ferociously and warn them to stay away from the humans that I protect.*

"The humans he protects?" Jadora asked. "Is that us?"

"I believe so, but I don't think he's ready to fight other dragons yet. Or even large birds with sharp talons and beaks."

I could annihilate a bird, Shikari announced.

Jadora had only heard Shikari speak telepathically a couple of times, and it was still surprising to her that a creature who'd so recently hatched from an egg had grown so quickly and had such a mature mind.

Shikari twirled in the air, then dove, startling a flock of roosting birds out of a tree. He didn't give chase, instead tucking his wings and diving all the way to the jungle floor, disappearing from their view as the leaves and branches camouflaged him. But he soon reappeared with an animal he'd captured in his maw. Some kind of cat-sized jungle rodent with a long gray tail. Shikari roared, inasmuch as one could with a mouthful of rodent, and tossed it high in the air, then flew up, spun a circle, and caught it before it could fall.

"Maybe mature wasn't the correct adjective," she murmured.

"I've observed that young dragons like to play with their food," Jak said as Shikari tossed the rodent again.

Jadora was fairly certain he'd put it out of its misery with the first chomp of his jaws. Now he was just... entertaining himself. "You did something similar," she said.

Shikari had the rodent by the tail and shook it about several times, flicking it and catching it once more, and finally gobbling it down.

"I hope you didn't serve me a lot of meals with the tails still attached." Jak fingered the device and looked toward the portal.

A sense of protest emanated from the artifact.

Jak grimaced. Jadora had been afraid of that.

"Another dragon and a bunch of druids sensed your arrival in

Zewnath," Jak told the portal. "If we don't put this on you, our enemies will be able to track your aura right to us. If the dragon beats us in a fight, it'll capture you and take you to its fortress."

The sense of protest grew stronger, along with an image of the portal glowing blue and erect next to the pool.

"I understand that you don't wish to be put into hibernation, but it's only for a short time." Jak stepped toward the portal. "We'll take off the device and activate you as soon as we reach the pool. We need to fly through you to reach the orbs, remember?"

I sense a dragon coming. Shikari flapped his wings hard and flew swiftly back to the mageship. *Two dragons.*

Jadora didn't sense the creatures yet, but she trusted that Shikari was correct.

Nodding firmly, Jak lifted the device. "I have to do this, portal. I promise I'll take it off again soon."

As long as the dragons didn't destroy them all...

Jak stretched the device toward the portal but paused. Waiting for consent? Jadora didn't know if he would get that. It might have to be enough that it hadn't zapped or electrocuted him. Yet.

Right after she had the thought, a sense of reluctant trust emanated from the portal. Trust for Jak?

As if that had been what he waited for, Jak nodded again and placed the device, pressing it to the side of the portal. As if it were magnetic, it stuck where he placed it.

Jadora sensed the aura of the portal fading from her awareness as it entered a state of hibernation. A moment later, the dragons came within range of her senses, and she winced. Had they waited too long?

The hatch opened, and Malek climbed out, his main-gauche and a new dragon-steel longsword in hand. He strode over to stand next to Jadora.

"You left your laboratory," he said.

"Isn't that allowed?" She smiled wearily and leaned against his side.

"It will be easier for us to protect you if you stay below."

"You may remember that I'm not without means of protecting myself these days." Jadora wiggled her fingers, though her last encounter with a dragon hadn't gone well. "Besides, the dragons have shown that they're capable of extracting me from within a well-defended mageship."

"I remember," Malek said grimly.

"Can we do anything extra to camouflage the ship?" Jak asked.

"I'm attempting to add my ability to magically hide things to the camouflaging strands of energy that Vinjo wove into the hull," Malek said. "We'll see if it's sufficient."

"Before I attached the device, the portal reminded me that it's fought dragons before and driven them off," Jak said.

Maybe *that* had been why he'd paused before placing the device.

"I know, and it's possible that we, with its help, would be victorious against two dragons, but there may be more out there, just out of our range. Also, we *can't* crash in the jungle. We have to get to the pool, place the portal, and complete our mission." Malek looked at Jadora and opened his mouth, as if to say more, but he closed it again.

She hoped he wouldn't mention how tired she looked. She knew. She was living inside her body.

He merely shook his head sadly and stood protectively beside her with his weapons drawn. Jadora smiled when she realized Shikari had landed beside Jak and held a similar position, though she doubted he had the power to drive off an adult dragon yet. Even though he'd grown much larger, he was still small compared to the others, and he didn't have experience battling them. Back at Uthari's castle, they'd almost lost Shikari.

Mindful of the parasite within her, Jadora moved to the far end of the deck from the dragonling. Malek stuck close to her.

The hatch opened again, and Sasko poked her head out. "Vinjo said a dragon is coming."

"*Two* dragons are coming," Malek said.

"Do you want us up here to help?"

"No."

"Unless Vinjo has some of those grenades that spit acid paint all over dragons," Jak said.

Jadora arched her eyebrows, not having seen such things used.

"I'll check," Sasko said. "Those were Tinder's grenades that he modified, but nobody thought to resupply us with fresh grenades before this trip."

"Because you never left the ship or requested supplies," Malek said.

"Leaving the ship in a mage enclave seemed like a bad idea," Sasko muttered and ducked below again.

"She couldn't have wanted grenades very badly," Malek said.

"Your city *is* intimidating." Jadora squeezed his arm.

Malek grunted.

Jadora pointed to the south as the dragons flew into view over the treetops, their mottled brown-and-gray bodies absorbing sunlight rather than gleaming in it, the way Shikari did.

They weren't flying directly toward the ship, rather curving left and right. Searching for it?

"What are the odds that they'll fly by without noticing us?" Jadora whispered.

The dragons had to know roughly where to look, for they were heading in the right direction.

Malek held a finger to his lips. The ship started descending toward the trees. Jadora twitched, believing something had gone wrong or that the dragons had somehow sabotaged the steering, but Malek nodded to himself. Had he ordered Vinjo to navigate the vessel lower? So it would be less noticeable to normal vision as well as magical senses?

Nobody spoke as the dragons flew closer and the ship slowed and sank between the trunks of trees rising hundreds of feet from the jungle floor. Vines and leaves rustled in a soft breeze, some brushing the side of the hull. The dragons flew closer.

We know you are near, humans. And we know you have our gate.

The ship stilled, hovering between the branches, the sky partially visible through the leaves. Earlier, birds had been chirping and insects buzzing, but nothing stirred now.

It belongs to our kind, not you thieves. We will take it and place it in our lair so that we may use it.

Jadora didn't reply that they wouldn't be able to use it from the Glacier Islands, but the thought came to mind. Though, even as she considered it, she wondered if it was the truth.

They hadn't *tried* to use the portal anywhere except by the jungle pool, the place to which it had guided them, because it had been set up there before. Since she, Jak, and Malek had visited the first world, and they'd developed their hypothesis that the portal had to be within view of whatever its anchor constellation was to operate, Jadora hadn't thought to question if it might work from anywhere on Torvil that the Dragon's Tail constellation could be seen. If so, it might operate from many places in the Southern Hemisphere.

That's the one that spoke to me earlier, Jak whispered into their minds as the first dragon flew past above them, its brown-and-gray belly briefly visible through the leaves.

A moment later, the second flew past a hundred yards to the west. Thanks to a gap between the trees, Jadora glimpsed its head as it cruised past.

And that's the one-eyed dragon that kept picking fights with Sorath, Jak added. *He's been involved in collecting dragon steel all along.*

He's not getting our *dragon steel,* Malek said.

Humans, do not hide and delay us, the one-eyed dragon said. *You interrupt my quest for spices.*

"For what?" Jadora mouthed, not daring to speak the words loudly with the dragons so close.

Malek and Jak shared her bewildered look.

I must impress the great queen dragon Vexahnali, so that I may gain rank among our kind, but you interrupt my quest. The one-eyed dragon roared into their minds.

Silence, you fool, the other dragon said. *Just find the gate.*

Their words grew more distant as the dragons flew farther away, and Jadora started to believe the camouflage had worked, that they'd successfully hidden themselves and the portal, but the dragons banked and turned around, continuing their search. Continuing their search *nearby*.

They may sense the dragon-steel chain and collar, Jadora realized. *And your new sword, Malek. When did you get that?*

A gift from Uthari. It should be useful in battles.

Of that, Jadora had no doubt. But all the dragon steel on the ship might mean they were more likely to end up in one of those battles sooner than they wished.

The dragons flew past again, off to the east this time.

We may have to fight them, Malek said. *They're going to search until they find us.*

I only sense two of them, so far. Jak looked at the device affixed to the portal.

If they did need to fight, they would need to remove it and get the portal's help.

Their winged enemies banked to come closer again. The one-eyed dragon was flying straight toward them, and Jadora feared he'd sensed them and knew exactly where they were.

Shikari crouched, his muscles bunching as he prepared to spring at their foes, though he glanced at Jak and the portal a few times, as if he would prefer to hide behind them, as he'd done when he'd been little.

The two dragons halted abruptly, and Shikari didn't need to spring, at least not yet. They found perches and landed. Though Jadora couldn't see them through the canopy, she imagined the treetops bowing under their weight.

The one-eyed dragon roared, then sprang into the air again. He led the other dragon away, heading south from their position.

"What happened?" Jak whispered. "They were so close to finding us. Did another dragon call them away?"

"Maybe," Malek said. "It's also possible the druids arrived at the pool. We're not that far away from it now."

"Why would the dragons be worried about the druids?" Jak asked.

"They may believe we're taking the portal there to meet them and figure it's a good place to ambush us." Malek frowned. "They wouldn't be wrong."

"A few minutes ago, I was considering something. What if we don't need to be in that exact spot to activate the portal?" Jadora explained her hypothesis that anywhere on Zewnath with clear visibility of that constellation might work. Anywhere in the Southern Hemisphere, for that matter.

"If that's true," Jak said slowly, "they would be able to use it from their fortress over the Glacier Islands."

"Yes."

"They could place it there and call forth dozens more dragons," Jak said, "bringing them right into their lair. Readying an army to finish what they've started and completely raze every civilization on Torvil."

Malek lifted a hand. "They don't have it yet. We'll focus on keeping it from them."

"A good way may be to find some other clearing in the jungle and use it from there," Jadora said.

"*No*," Jak protested.

Jadora and Malek lifted their eyebrows.

"Rivlen is heading to the pool," Jak said. "And the mercenaries too. They're all prisoners of the druids. We need to help them."

"Our mission must take precedence over rescuing fleet officers," Malek said. "Once we find a cure, we can return. I've already reported to Uthari that they're alive. Once the dragons are dealt with, he will send a ship to get them."

"They may not have that much time. And Rivlen isn't just a fleet officer. She's… important."

"If we don't show up with the portal," Jadora said, "she and the others might not be in danger from the druids."

"They will be. They are. She said the druids who have them think they're enemies. They weren't there when our peoples decided to work with each other, and Kywatha was injured and has amnesia. Please." Jak stretched imploring hands toward Malek rather than Jadora. "We have to help them. They wouldn't even be in trouble if the druids hadn't sensed us. I should have put that device on the portal from the start, whether it wanted it or not."

Malek sighed. "Very well. We need to leave behind some strong mages to defend the portal and keep it open while we're gone. Rivlen would be more ideal than the mediocre mages we have along."

"Thank you," Jak said.

The ship slowly rose and started south again. Malek looked at Jadora, as if to say something, but he frowned at… her neck? And then his gaze fell to her waist. Or maybe he was looking at her hand?

She lifted it, worried some of the motes might be floating about her, lured out by the proximity of Shikari. But her heart stuttered at what she saw, an odd patch of gray on her otherwise olive-toned skin.

"Dirt," she muttered, though she knew before she touched it that it wasn't.

Even so, she rubbed it with her hand, as if it were a smudge that might come off. But no. Her skin was turning gray. Just as the dragons had turned from beautiful blue to dull gray-and-brown.

She looked up, meeting Malek's eyes, but she had no idea what to say. He was also speechless, his eyes full of dread. He understood the implications as well as she.

She closed her eyes. How long until her personality changed? Until she went as mad as those dragons?

8

Chill earthy air swept past Tezi's face, tugging at her braid, as she and the other mercenaries rode in one of several floating wagons that sped through wide tunnels. In the rearmost wagon, a spherical yellow energy ball powered a magical engine that drove the train. Tezi hadn't the faintest notion of how quickly they were traveling, and the druids hadn't been updating them, so she had no idea when they would arrive.

Rivlen stood in the wagon ahead of Tezi's, her head bent toward her two lieutenants, but whatever their conversation was about, it was telepathic.

"Do you know what's going on?" Dr. Fret asked, joining Tezi. The green glow that emanated from the tunnel sides showed the bags under her eyes and bruises on her jaw and temple.

Tezi knew she had to look as rough, but Fret had also been tending the injured, setting bones and stitching gashes, and she hadn't slept much. The wagon ride was smooth, if stomach-turning when they went around bends, but a greenish tint to Fret's bronze skin suggested she didn't care for it. Earlier, she'd been one of several to be sick over the side, drawing an irritated comment from the druid leader about leaving detritus in their tunnel. As if they couldn't incinerate vomit with their magic.

"Not really," Tezi said. "All I know is the druids found out someone is taking the portal back to the pool, and they want to head them off to keep it from being used again."

"Someone?" Fret raised her eyebrows.

"I don't think they know who yet." Thanks to her vision, Tezi had suspicions, but even she didn't know for certain.

Rivlen looked back at them. *Jak, Jadora, and Malek are on the gateship*, she said telepathically. *I don't know if the druids know yet how many ships they'll face, so keep that information to yourself.*

Tezi hadn't planned to blab anything to them, and she didn't mention it to Fret, since the druids would be able to read her mind.

We're debating if it would be possible to sabotage these wagons, Rivlen continued, *to keep the druids from reaching the pool, but it sounds like some of their people are already there. It may be better to turn on them when we get there.*

Turn on them? Even if Tezi didn't care for these new druids, she'd gotten along decently with Kywatha and her people, and had hoped a new alliance might be struck. *Don't we need to work together and focus on the dragon threat?*

Yes, but they don't realize that. Rivlen shook her head. *They're worried about the portal being opened and more dragons coming through in their backyard.*

Maybe we should try to help Kywatha regain her memory so she can explain our alliance to them.

They're better healers than I. If they can't do it, I wouldn't be able to either. Sabotage is more in my skillset.

A faint creak came from the wagons, and they slowed down, the wind that had been battering Tezi's face and clothes fading.

We may be out of time, she said.

Damn it. We can't be there already, can we? Rivlen looked up at the ceiling, where roots dangled through the earth. Before, there'd been nothing but rock up there. That had to mean they were close to the surface. *I don't sense the portal. I do sense...*

"What?" Tezi asked silently and aloud.

Fret looked at her.

"Rivlen senses trouble," Tezi explained.

"She confides in you?"

"Sometimes. We have an understanding of sorts." Tezi had once mentioned to Captain Ferroki that she, like Rivlen, had wanted to kill Tonovan, but she'd never told Fret or any of the other mercenaries. With the general now dead, it didn't seem important to explain.

Fret's forehead furrowed. "Be careful. She may command us to throw ourselves into battle again, and after we've lost so many, that's not a good idea. We should try to get out of the jungle. Especially if the captain is gone." Fret blinked moist eyes and shook her head.

"I think our fate is tied to hers, ma'am," Tezi said as the wagons slowed further, a hint of light visible ahead. "Without Uthari's people, we'll be stuck in the jungle indefinitely."

There are dragons out there, Rivlen told Tezi. *Be ready to fight.*

Yes, ma'am.

Fighting dragons, no matter how deadly, would be better than turning on the druids. After all, the dragons were their true enemies.

The wagons floated toward the light, and Tezi could soon make out vines draping the tunnel exit. A draft brought hints of foliage and flowers to her nose, the lush jungle scents she remembered from the pool rather than the ferns and pines of the temperate shoreline where they'd shipwrecked.

A rumble sounded in the distance. The roar of a dragon? Or the waterfall by the pool?

A few druids climbed out of the wagons while others remained in them.

Rivlen hopped down and looked back at Tezi. *Bring your axe. We may need it.*

"Stay here, ma'am," Tezi told Fret. She glanced back, spotted Yelotta and others looking curiously at her, and thought about asking some of the mercenaries to join her, but until they had weapons capable of harming dragons, there was little point.

Tezi jogged and caught up with Rivlen before she reached the vines. As the roar faded, she realized it hadn't been a waterfall.

The druids peered through the vines and into the jungle, a dense stand of trees ensuring the wagon train wouldn't continue, not unless there was another tunnel nearby. Drooping branches held leaves such a deep green that they were almost blue.

"I think we're about five miles from the pool," Rivlen whispered, her eyes toward the sky, though little of it was visible through the canopy. "I remember seeing those weepy-looking trees when we were flying south of it, searching for the druid headquarters."

Tezi almost pointed out that the trees might grow in many places, but one of the druids pointed upward, and she glimpsed the brown-and-gray scales of a dragon that was flying past. Keeping her mouth shut sounded like a good idea.

Rivlen frowned at Tezi's axe and then at the dragon-steel dagger on her belt. The dragons would be able to sense the magical metal. They might have sensed it hours ago and been flying along above the tunnels, waiting for the weapons to appear above the surface.

"Are they here for us?" Tezi asked.

"They may be. Or for the portal. Though I can't sense it." Rivlen looked toward the druids. The female leader and an elder had their eyes closed as they frowned toward the jungle.

Be ready to fight, the druid leader said telepathically. *I believe they want—*

The druids lifted their hands, forming a barrier in front of the tunnel. Rivlen and several others crouched and drew their weapons. Branches broke and leaves were ripped from the trees as an invisible wave of power washed through the jungle.

The druids grunted, their faces twisting with concentration, but the barrier must have held, for nothing reached them. Or so Tezi thought. Then the roof of the tunnel a hundred feet behind the wagons quaked. Clumps of dirt rained down, and the ground trembled in sympathy.

"Extend the barrier," Rivlen barked. Her face was as tense with concentration as those of the druids, so Tezi assumed she was helping.

We can't, the leader replied. *Not without risking weakening that which is directly around us.*

That which is protecting *us,* another druid added.

A dragon soared by above the trees and roared. The earthen roof quaked again, and trees were ripped up by the roots. Between one eye blink and the next, a huge portion of the tunnel ceiling tumbled downward. Rocks, dirt, and half a tree fell through, crushing the rearmost wagon.

Fortunately, the mercenaries and roamers had scrambled out of the train when the roof first started quaking, and nobody was hurt, but sunlight poured through the hole, revealing rubble filling the tunnel. The wagons couldn't navigate around all that; they were trapped.

"We need to lower our barrier long enough to attack," Rivlen said. "They'll wear us down if we—" She halted with a grimace of concentration. Staving off another attack?

One of the druids groaned and sagged against the tunnel wall.

Tezi gripped her axe, wishing she could help. This reminded her of the last battle with the dragons when none of them had flown close enough for her to fight. They'd destroyed the ships from a distance, relying purely on their magical power. Power that she couldn't fight.

"We need dragon-steel projectile weapons," she grumbled.

Rivlen gave her a sharp look. "In one of our chats, Jak mentioned the natives on Nargnoth had spears that could pierce dragon barriers."

"Dragon-steel spears?"

"I think it was something else, but we *could* make dragon-steel spears. Uthari's smith is capable of crafting with the metal now."

"I know." Tezi remembered the dragon-steel cell bars that had trapped Grunk and looked back, not surprised to find him standing silently, only a few feet behind her.

He nodded gravely to her, two daggers in his hands.

"We ought to be able to do better than spears." Rivlen's gaze snagged on one of the mercenaries—no, on the magelock pistol belted at her waist. "Something designed to fire magical charges wouldn't work, but maybe a black-powder weapon could shoot dragon-steel bullets."

"It would be a tremendous waste if bullets flew wide and couldn't be found," Tezi said, though she found herself nodding, approving of the idea of dragon-steel bullets. Then she and the other mercenaries could help without getting as close as they needed to with an axe or dagger. "We still don't have that much dragon steel, right?"

"We could find stray bullets by their magical signatures, but, ideally, we'd give them to sharpshooters who'd be unlikely to miss."

Another roar sounded, followed by a fresh attack. The druids cursed as they struggled to keep their barrier up, and more of the tunnel crumbled behind them.

"Too bad Uthari's blacksmith is probably back in Utharika." Rivlen wiped sweat from her brow.

The next wave of power ripped through the trees out front, tearing them from their roots and toppling them toward the tunnel entrance. Several druids grunted as they landed on their already beleaguered barrier.

We have to fight back somehow, one of the druids said. *If we don't, they'll wear us down eventually. We have no monuments or great artifacts nearby to call upon to help us.*

I'm aware, the leader replied.

Where is the gate that our kind made? one of the dragons boomed. *We will destroy you if you keep hiding it from us.*

"They don't know where it is, either?" Rivlen grumbled.

Seconds later, she and several of the other magic users gasped.

Grunk gripped Tezi's shoulder and waved for her to come farther back into the tunnel. *The barrier is down,* he warned.

"Then I should go out and fight." Tezi pulled away from him and lifted her axe.

There are two. It is too many for one axe.

"Rivlen has a dagger."

Rivlen yelled a frustrated battle cry and strode between the vines so she could target their enemies. With a snarl, she sent a fireball hurtling up into the sky.

Though Grunk tried to pull Tezi back again, she resisted and stepped outside to join Rivlen.

The dragons had knocked down all the trees near the tunnel, and large green-blue leaves and broken branches littered the ground. One creature flew close, talons flexing, but it didn't come within range of Tezi's axe. Rivlen's fireball struck its armored side and bounced off, doing no damage.

Several of the druids found the energy to attack, but without the barrier, they were vulnerable themselves. The dragons blasted magic at the tunnel, and several druids and mages were hurled back. A wagon also flew backward, people shouting, "Look out!" as it crashed into the ceiling of the tunnel, then landed on another wagon.

Tezi waved her axe in frustration, wishing she had dragon-steel bullets at that very moment. The dragon flew back and forth not twenty feet above the ground.

One of their foes launched a huge wall of fire. Heat and light preceded it, and the druids scrambled to get another barrier up. Tezi winced as the flames washed over her, even though her weapon protected her. Rivlen roared and launched a wall of fire of her own.

Humans are no match for dragons! Give us the gate. Do you hide it in that warren?

"Why do they think *we* have it?" came Basher's frustrated call from where she crouched beside a destroyed wagon.

"Good question," Rivlen muttered. "Wait, I sense it." She lowered her arms and frowned. "It wasn't there a second ago, but now I sense it right—"

A branch of red lightning came from the north, the source not visible through the treetops.

"There," Rivlen finished as the lightning bolt struck one of the dragons.

That looked like the red lightning that the portal shot out. Thus far, Tezi had only seen Jak and Uthari convince it to attack, and it had punished Uthari the last time he presumed to order it to do so. That had to mean Jak was there.

A ragged cheer went up from the druids and mages.

The dragon was as startled as Rivlen had been, and it either didn't have its defenses up on that side of its body or the powerful lightning tore them away. It had been flying around as it hurled magic, but now it crashed to the ground, not twenty feet from the tunnel entrance.

Seeing her chance, Tezi risked sprinting toward the creature with her axe.

"Look out, Tezi!" Fret called. "There's lightning all over the place. You'll be struck."

"Jak won't let it hit me," Tezi called back as she ran, certain of her assessment. If she could keep one dragon from escaping and flying back to its fortress, she had to try.

The one-eyed dragon was still airborne. It screeched as the red lightning bolts struck it, but it didn't crash. It flapped its wings and flew over the tunnel, disappearing from view.

As Tezi reached the downed dragon, it shook its head, smashed its tail into the undergrowth and rose to its feet. It turned toward her, its fang-filled maw opening, and she almost froze. But she was already committed. She rushed not toward its head but toward its less dangerous hindquarters. As she swung her axe, the dragon whirled, pulling its back end away from her slash and darting its deadly snout toward her.

Afraid she couldn't dodge quickly enough, Tezi hefted the blade upward, hoping to strike the dragon under the jaw and keep it from biting her. A fireball roared over her head as her axe swung close enough to pierce its barrier, dropping its defenses. The spinning inferno would have roasted Tezi if not for her blade. The flames struck the dragon in its open mouth, prompting it to jerk its head back while snapping its jaws shut.

While it was distracted, Tezi ran under its head and slammed the axe into its chest as hard as she could. The blade sliced through its scales and sank several inches into thick muscle. What would have sliced a human in half barely bothered the dragon, but it did spring back, lifting a foreleg to attack her.

Talons flashed as they swiped toward her face, but Tezi threw herself back in a roll and jumped to her feet several yards away. Though Rivlen had hurled another fireball at the dragon, it had its defenses back up, and the flames bounced uselessly away. With its roar echoing through the jungle, the creature sprang at Tezi.

She leaped to the side to avoid its snapping jaws, but its neck whipped to follow her, and she feared she'd been arrogant in believing she could best another dragon. Even injured, it was too fast for her, and she hadn't been able to take it from behind.

Not giving up, she swung the axe at its jaws again, trying to keep its fangs from piercing her. Hot saliva smacked her cheek.

The air flashed red, and as dragon steel met fang, another lightning bolt slammed into the creature. The axe cleaved off a chunk of tooth before the dragon stiffened, its long neck growing rod-like as the lightning arced all around it. More fireballs slammed into it, both from above and from the tunnel entrance. The green balls of energy the druids favored followed, pummeling the dragon from all sides.

Tezi was tempted to leap in and try for a killing blow with the axe, but if the weapon slipped from her hand—or was stuck in the creature's side—she would be vulnerable to the deadly magic coursing past her. Besides, with the powerful lightning disabling the dragon, she didn't think the mages and druids needed her help.

Backing away, she glanced toward the sky, wondering if the others might have also kept the one-eyed dragon from escaping, but it was nowhere in sight.

From the distance, it did deliver parting words into their minds. *I see that you've brought our gate. You couldn't fight and hide it at the same time. I shall return for it!*

The dragon Tezi had been battling flopped to the ground, its eyes glazed, its tongue lolling out between one chipped fang and another. The red lightning faded, though Tezi still couldn't see the source. All through the battle, it had come from beyond the trees, shooting over them and somehow bending to strike at the dragon on the ground.

"You going to keep that for a souvenir?" Rivlen pointed at the piece of fang on the ground, her forehead bathed in sweat after expending so much effort summoning her magic.

Tezi wiped her own brow. Her battle had been short, but in the humid jungle, it didn't take much to break a sweat.

"Do you think it's lucky?" Tezi asked.

"It's lucky you didn't get your skull crushed by it."

"Does that mean I didn't look like a swift and agile warrior?"

"You did fine, but dragons like to munch even swift and agile warriors." Rivlen looked up as the ship that Tezi had expected all along came into view, though it was fuzzy around the edges and oddly hard to see. Then she remembered that it had magical camouflage; someone must have enhanced it or added to it, for it took a moment before she could focus on the familiar faces at the railing. They were dwarfed by the great round portal balanced on the deck behind them.

Rivlen lifted a hand and beamed a surprisingly warm—and relieved?—smile up at Jak. Shikari's large snout poked through the railing, nostrils twitching as he peered down at the gathering.

Tezi also started to wave, but the grim-faced Malek stood beside Jak. She never knew where Thorn Company stood with him.

Further, the druids filed out of the tunnel and looked up at the gateship, their faces equally grim. *More* than grim. They radiated displeasure as they looked not at Malek and Jak but at the portal, the sun behind it casting an elongated shadow over the torn-up land.

If they try to place that in our jungle again, the druid leader said, raising her arms as she scowled at Malek, *we* will *fight them.*

Sasko, Tinder, and Vinjo climbed up the ladder to the deck of the gateship where Malek, Jak, and Shikari were at the railing, looking down at a large gathering. From the navigation cabin, Sasko had seen the druids, Captain Rivlen, and Tezi fighting in front of a tunnel, but numerous Thorn Company women had come out as well now too. Sasko grinned with relief and waved at the familiar faces.

Earlier, she and Tinder had asked if Malek wanted them on deck for the dragon battle, but he'd told them to stay out of the way, that they wouldn't be able to help. After her encounters with dragons, Sasko hadn't been able to disagree. Fortunately, the portal had hurled lightning bolts at their winged enemies, and the battle had ended quickly.

She was surprised Jak hadn't unleashed the portal at the dragons when they'd first encountered them, but it sounded like everyone believed there were more in the area—or that could quickly come into the area—and that the portal could only fight so many. In addition, if they *lost* the portal, their mission would fail before it even began.

A few roamers and mages were looking at the dead dragon on the ground, but the druids were glaring up at Malek and the gateship. Malek glared back at them. Sasko realized they weren't the same druids she'd met before, save for a familiar green-haired kid standing beside Tezi. She'd seen that druid hanging around with Colonel Sorath.

But Sorath wasn't there. And neither was Captain Ferroki.

Even though Sasko was pleased to see Dr. Fret, Corporal Basher, and a couple dozen other Thorn Company women, emotion tightened her throat as she realized the rumors might be true; the captain might be dead. Many others were missing as well.

"Is that Fret?" Tinder whispered, elbowing Sasko aside and almost tripping over Shikari in her rush to reach the railing. "Fret!" she called into the silence that had fallen after the battle.

Dr. Fret was hanging back in the mouth of the vine-draped tunnel, peering uncertainly at the druids and the dead dragon, but she smiled at Tinder and lifted a hand.

"I need to go down there." Tinder poked Jak in the shoulder. "Or she needs to come up here. I haven't seen her in *ages*."

"Uhm." Jak glanced at her but pointed at one of the female druids. "Can you wait a moment? That woman and Malek are exchanging telepathic threats. And Rivlen is trying to mediate, though she's frustrated and may start hurling fireballs at those who won't listen to her."

"I've observed that's typically how mages mediate." Sasko drew Tinder back since she seemed oblivious to Jak's words and kept poking him. At least she wasn't poking Malek.

"Not *all* mages," Vinjo murmured.

"You hurl wrenches instead of fireballs, I know," Sasko said.

"My dear warrior woman, I thought you knew me better than that. You don't *hurl* wrenches. You lovingly caress them. You hurl grenades."

"I can agree with that."

Malek frowned back at them, and Sasko shut her mouth. If it was as tense as Jak had hinted at, this wasn't the appropriate time for banter.

"Can this ship handle the weight of bringing fifty more people aboard?" Malek asked Vinjo.

"Uh, it's already got a large load." Vinjo waved at the portal. "We're lucky dragon steel isn't as heavy as other metals."

"We don't want to bring all of them with us on our journey anyway, right?" Jak asked, though he didn't take his gaze from Rivlen.

They might already have levitated her up to the gateship, except there were a couple dozen mage officers with her that she was likely in charge of. Sasko didn't see the captains from the other ships that had been with the *Star Flyer*.

If Malek tried to bring the mages with them while leaving Thorn Company, Sasko would protest vehemently. Tinder already appeared ready to fling herself into the trees and climb down their trunks to reunite with Fret.

"We do not," Malek said, "but we can't leave our officers in the jungle."

"Or our mercenaries," Sasko said.

Shikari flapped his tail against the deck. Sasko didn't know if that meant he agreed that they shouldn't leave their allies, or he was impatient and wanted to go hunt.

More of our people are gathering at the waterfall, the druid leader said, now speaking into all of their minds. *We will not allow you to erect the ancient gateway again. It's already been proven that horrible monsters, including dragons, are eager to invade our world and will do so as soon as they have an opportunity. We cannot allow more problems to come to Torvil.*

We need to take one more trip through it, Malek replied, also sharing his telepathic words with everyone. *We will remove it as soon as we've completed our mission.*

Our mission is to go to another world that may hold the answer to how to change the dragons back to the benevolent creatures they once were, Jak added, gesturing animatedly. *We may be able to figure out how to remove all threats here on Torvil and have dragons as friendly allies again.*

Malek looked over at him, but Sasko couldn't tell if he objected to him butting in or not.

We cannot take the risk of more powerful enemies entering our world, the druid leader said. *We will not allow you to erect it for even a short time. If you show up at the pool with it, our people will destroy your ship.*

"But we helped you," Vinjo blurted, pointing down at the dead dragon.

"Yeah," Tinder said, even though neither she nor Sasko had done anything. "If not for the portal and Lord Malek, you would have gotten your butts blown up by dragons. Look at your squished tunnel." She waved toward sinkholes in the earth with trees fallen into them.

"They don't understand you," Jak whispered. "Those druids are from the south, and I don't think they have someone who speaks Dhoran."

Guard the pool if you wish, Malek told the druids, sounding like he was giving up on negotiations.

Frowning, Jak glanced toward Shikari. He must have telepathically told him something for the dragonling flew down and landed in front of the druids. They exchanged alarmed glances and raised a barrier around themselves.

Sasko shook her head. Thorn Company was stuck *behind* that barrier.

Shikari ignored their defenses, instead prancing around between the druids and the dead dragon. He leaped, did a somersault in the sky, and fluttered his wings to land lightly again. His thick blue tail swished in the air, looking more like it belonged to a cat on the hunt than a fearsome dragon.

This is Shikari, Jak announced telepathically to everyone. *As you can see, he's a good, friendly, and delightful young dragon.*

The druids eyed the antics warily and kept their defenses up. Maybe they didn't see tail swishing as delightful.

Rivlen and Tezi, who were still near their fallen enemy with their weapons out, stepped back to avoid being trampled or swatted with a wing. The look that Rivlen tilted up to Jak suggested she thought Shikari might apply a little restraint if he was going to pass himself off as an ally.

He's also smart and helpful, Jak continued. *He likes humans and wants to end the threat from the tainted dragons, not only on Torvil but all throughout the portal network. He is what dragons could be if we're able to complete this mission. A parasite currently infests all of the mottled brown-and-gray dragons—all those attempting to destroy or enslave our civilization. But if the parasite can be eradicated, our enemies could return to their natural state. They could become allies. Shikari is what dragons* should *be.*

Shikari faced the dead dragon, lowered his forelegs to the ground, and roared at it, tail swishing again. The druids only exchanged more wary glances.

"I'm not sure showing the druids how silly he is will sway them," Malek told Jak.

"Well, he's only a few months old. What can they expect? He hasn't chewed on any of their footwear yet. They should be pleased."

"Perhaps highlight how he's capable of helping people."

"Right." Jak looked down at Shikari, and the dragonling looked back—another telepathic exchange? The dragon roared up at him.

"I can't tell if that was a noise of agreement or disagreement," Sasko muttered.

"I don't think the druids can either," Tinder said.

But Jak smiled and spread his arms as he looked down at the druid leader. *To show how helpful he is and that he wants to be friends with humans, Shikari is willing to use his power to heal any injured among you. Are there any who need assistance?*

"*Thorn Company* probably needs assistance," Sasko said.

"We'll help them too," Jak said, taking his eyes from the druid leader.

She was looking back at him, holding his gaze. Considering his offer?

Sasko was surprised Malek was willing to let Jak take the lead in the negotiations, but Jak *was* the one with a dragon.

The druid leader turned and waved toward someone in the mouth of the tunnel, the vines still dangling down and hiding many of the people inside. A male with spiky green hair escorted a familiar woman out. Kywatha, the druid who'd been leading the raft before it had been destroyed.

Sasko stared intently at her. The last she'd heard, Ferroki and

Sorath had been on that raft. If *Kywatha* had survived, wasn't it possible they had?

Our cousin was injured in the shipwreck and lost her memory. The druid leader looked at Jak and also Shikari. *If this dragon is capable of healing her and returning her knowledge of who she is and what has passed, we would be grateful.*

"Is *grateful* the same as letting us carry out our mission?" Tinder muttered.

"I don't know," Sasko said.

Shikari turned from the dead dragon he'd been roaring at and ambled closer to the druids. He sat on his haunches and faced Kywatha, who gazed uncertainly at him, no sign of recognition in her eyes. Shikari cocked his head like a dog hearing a strange sound.

"He says dragons don't get amnesia, so he's not familiar with that particular brain injury," Jak said quietly, "but he'll try."

Malek nodded. "We'll continue our mission regardless of what they say, but it'll be easier if they don't fight us."

Shikari's tail swished in the upturned soil as he concentrated on Kywatha. She swayed on her feet, and the male druid tightened his grip to support her.

"I'm going to get our people up here while the druids are distracted," Malek said.

"How *many* people?" Vinjo asked, but nobody answered him.

The mage officers, their red uniforms dirty and torn, levitated toward the deck of the mageship. Captain Rivlen sheathed her dagger—was that a dragon-steel weapon she'd managed to acquire?—and held her hand out toward Tezi, accepting the axe before floating herself up. Once she relinquished her weapon, someone was able to levitate Tezi up as well.

"Uh oh," Vinjo said.

"The rest of Thorn Company too." Tinder had noticed that

Malek was ignoring the mercenaries, and she rushed forward and gripped his arm.

He looked coolly at her.

"They're useful and valuable even if they don't have dragon steel," Tinder assured him, tightening her grip.

Sasko grasped Tinder's arms, trying to pry her fingers off Malek, lest he grow irritated and use his magic on her, but she was also worried Thorn Company would be left behind. Summoning all the politeness she could manage, Sasko said, "Our mercenaries too, please, Lord Zidarr. We can't leave them here."

"We should take the roamers too," Jak said. "And help them get back to their people."

"The ship can't hold so many," Vinjo said.

Malek gazed at Tinder and Sasko, and Sasko was positive he cared nothing for the roamers or Thorn Company, but he looked at Jak, then sighed and levitated the mercenaries toward the ship.

"Vinjo," Malek said. "Go down to the engine room and coax more power from your devices to ensure the ship stays aloft. If necessary, I will use *my* power to levitate it, but if we end up going some distance, that will grow difficult to sustain."

"Professor Jadora could help too, couldn't she?" Sasko asked.

From what she'd heard, Jadora had been given so much power that levitating a ship—or even a city—ought to be doable.

"She is... not feeling well." Malek exchanged a grave look with Jak.

Uh oh, had that parasite she'd taken on made her sick? Sasko had only heard bits and snatches about what had happened in Uthari's throne room, but she'd gotten the gist.

"We could also use a druid guide," Malek murmured.

Rivlen had landed on the deck near them, and she pointed down at the wild-haired young man that had been standing near Tezi. "That one knows the area."

Malek nodded. He must have recognized the druid too. Sasko

was certain he'd attacked the mercenaries at the pool weeks earlier, and helped a druid prisoner escape, but maybe that had all been forgotten or forgiven. They had larger problems now, after all.

A soft gasp came from the druids nearest Kywatha. She'd slumped against the male holding her upright and would have dropped to the ground if not for him.

I fixed her, Shikari spoke into their minds, startling Sasko since he'd never spoken before that she'd heard. *I fixed her. I* am *a helpful dragon.* Shikari spun a circle, then leaped into the air, flapping his wings, before settling back down.

The druids murmured uncertainly. With her eyes rolled back in her head, Kywatha didn't appear that *fixed*.

The druid leader stepped up to her and rested a hand on her shoulder, peering intently at her.

"I believe he did repair the damage to her brain," Malek said.

"Shikari has lots of experience with brains." Jak grinned at him.

Malek touched his temple, appearing more haunted than pleased at whatever memory came to his mind.

Down below, the druids settled Kywatha into a cross-legged position on the ground, still gripping her shoulders to support her. The woman appeared exhausted, but her eyes were open. She gazed blearily around and nodded to herself. Surprisingly, she held Rivlen's gaze. It wasn't a warm look, but she did seem to recognize Rivlen.

Her memories have been returned, the druid leader stated. *She is weary from the healing and must rest.*

But you can see the potential in Shikari, right? Jak asked.

The druid leader looked at him but didn't answer the question. *You may take your people*, she told Malek—half of them were already onboard, so it would have been late for her to object to that—*and we will not attack you as you fly away, but you must leave our continent and never return. We hope your young dragon* will *be an ally to humans, and that this parasite you speak of, if it exists, can be thwarted, but we cannot allow you to open the ancient gateway again. Do not bring it back to Zewnath, or we will destroy it and fight you.*

Jak and Malek looked at Kywatha—hoping she would naysay the leader?—but she'd dropped her head wearily into her hand and didn't seem that cognizant yet. Even if she'd regained her memories, she might not outrank this new druid leader or be able to talk her into changing her mind.

The frame of the gateship creaked as more and more people landed on the deck, and it started to sink toward the treetops.

"Vinjo," Malek said. "The engine room."

"Yes, my lord."

As he hurried below, Malek closed his eyes, and the ship stabilized and lifted back above the treetops.

"I'll get the roamers," Jak offered.

Malek opened one eyelid to give him a flat look but didn't reject the offer. As Thorn Company landed on the deck and roamers started being lifted aboard, Sasko and Tinder ended up mashed against the railing. Tinder left her to squeeze past people, reach Fret, and give her a hug powerful enough to crush walnuts —or doctors. But Fret endured it and hugged her back, giving her a kiss.

Feeling claustrophobic, Sasko was tempted to go below with Vinjo, but with the captain gone, it was her duty to lead Thorn Company. She maneuvered toward Tezi and Basher to get an update, almost running into Rivlen, who was making her way toward Jak and Malek.

"Are we heading toward the pool?" Sasko asked quietly, wondering if she would yet end up having to fight.

Malek might not have believed that she and Tinder could be helpful against a dragon, but she suspected he would be happy to throw them into a battle against druids.

"No," Malek said.

Sasko blinked and glanced at the portal. "We came all the way down here, and now you're leaving?"

While *she* didn't think getting in a fight with all those druids would be a good idea, she had a hard time believing Malek would give up on his mission—or allow the druids to cow him. But the ship was already on the move, heading north, as if to leave Zewnath and fly back to Uth.

"My mother believes we might not need to be in that exact spot on the continent to operate the portal," Jak said before hugging Rivlen.

Even though Sasko had heard they had a relationship now, she expected the aloof captain to push him away or stiffly endure the embrace, but she must have missed him, for she returned the hug fiercely. Until Shikari, who was flying laps around the ship, cruised past over them, letting his tail droop so it whacked Jak on the back of the head.

"Does your dragon not approve of romance?" Rivlen asked, drawing back and frowning at Shikari as he banked to fly in another circle.

"Oh, he doesn't mind it," Jak said. "He often whaps me with his tail to show affection."

"Uh huh. There's a welt affectionately rising on the back of your head now."

"I don't think so. My head is hard."

"I have noticed that," Rivlen said dryly.

Malek lifted a hand toward the young druid, his shaggy green hair hanging in his eyes. On the ground, the kid had been sticking close to Tezi, but once he'd landed on the deck, he hadn't been willing to squeeze through the crowd to get close to her. He crouched in the bow of the ship with a dagger out, baring his teeth and growling at anyone who didn't give him space. Those teeth were filed to points.

"*That's* the druid you picked to be a guide?" Sasko asked.

"He's from the area," Jak said. "And, uhm, friendly to Tezi."

"A lot of men that age are friendly to Tezi." Sasko noticed roamers and mage officers of *all* ages looking at Tezi, maybe admiring that she'd leaped into battle with the dragon, or maybe admiring that she remained beautiful despite the grime and torn clothing.

Malek gestured again and must have telepathically commanded the druid to join them. The kid only crouched lower, shook his head, and growled in his direction.

Malek's eyes narrowed. He had to be using his magic to ensure the ship stayed aloft, but that didn't keep him from being able to levitate the druid into the air again.

Snarling, the kid swiped about with his dagger as he floated over the heads of the passengers. People eyed him warily, even powerful mages, and stepped back inasmuch as they could on the crowded deck.

"I don't think he likes being manhandled," Jak said.

"Too bad," Malek said. "That one-eyed dragon escaped, and with their telepathic range, he's likely alerted their entire fortress that we and the portal are here. We won't have much time."

Jak grimaced. "How quickly do you think we can reach the orbs once we set up the portal and go through?"

"It's impossible to know. They may be close to the portal on that world or not. All we know, if the visions prove true, is that they're underwater."

The ship creaked again under the weight of so many passengers.

"Maybe we should have tested it underwater on the way here," Jak said.

"Our engineer wasn't yet done applying his magical pitch." Malek looked back toward the tunnel, it and the druids now out of view, and used his power to alter the path of the gateship, veering it toward the mountains.

The druid kid landed in front of him, his arms pinned by magic at his sides so he couldn't lash out with his dagger. Even so, Sasko took a step back from him. His chest heaved as he fought Malek's magic, and there was an animal-like wildness to his eyes. A *rabid*-animal-like wildness.

"You are from the area," Malek said, holding Grunk's gaze, unfazed by his madness. "We need a place large enough to hide the portal from dragons or mageships flying by but where it can face the southern sky and the Dragon's Tail constellation. Ideally, it will be some distance away from the pool where it was set up before."

The druid snarled at him.

"This is Grunk, Lord Malek." Tezi lifted a hand toward him and patted the air, a soothing gesture.

The druid—Grunk—glanced at her but was in no mood to be soothed. He bared his pointed teeth at Malek, fearless in the face of the powerful zidarr. Or maybe too mad to realize how easily Malek could snuff out his life?

Sasko knew she should round up Thorn Company—some were already gravitating toward her—and get an update on everything, but she felt compelled to see what happened with the druid boy.

"We should be kind to him," Jak whispered to Malek. "I'm sure he can telepathically reach out to the other druids and..." Jak lowered his voice even further, "let them know we're not exactly complying with their wishes."

"I'm not being *un*kind to him," Malek stated.

Jak eyed Grunk's pinned arms, the druid's muscles straining against the magic that kept them against his body.

"He's a danger to those around him," Malek said. "I can't free him unless he settles down."

"I'll help if you can release him." Tezi took a step toward the seething druid, even as everyone else kept edging back inasmuch as they could in the crowd.

"Get him to calm down, and I'll release him," Malek said, his eyes boring into Grunk's. Was he trying to read the druid's mind to find his hiding place for the portal?

Sasko had no idea how good the druid's mental defenses were or if Malek could easily peel them away.

"Grunk." Tezi rested a hand on his shoulder, stepping close enough to draw his eye, though he kept spearing Malek with glares. "Will you assist them? I believe it could end up helping save the world."

The druids wish them to go, *not hide that thing,* Grunk replied telepathically.

"We have a mission," Jak said, "one that can indeed help the world. *If* we're able to complete it."

Sasko doubted the druid cared much about saving the world—he seemed like a prisoner in his own crazy head—but he settled somewhat under Tezi's light grasp.

"And if we're able to return afterward," Jak added in a quieter tone, glancing back in the direction of the tunnel and the druids.

"You will be," Rivlen said. "Lord Malek, if you set the portal where you wish and go through it, I and the rest of the remaining mages will guard it while you're gone and ensure it stays open." She lifted her chin and radiated self-confidence.

Rivlen might believe she could stave off druids and dragons, but Sasko was less certain. Oh, she'd seen Rivlen hurl walls of fire and knew she was powerful, but the dragons were far more than powerful. And the druids en masse were strong opponents too.

Jak squeezed Rivlen's hand and smiled at her.

Malek noticed their handclasp but didn't comment on it.

"Go below, Captain," was all he said. "I'll come down shortly and get a report from you to send along to King Uthari."

Rivlen's face was always cool and professional, and it didn't change much at the dismissal, but a hint of something flashed in her eyes. Not fear, exactly, but... concern?

"Yes, my lord." She bowed and walked past numerous people toward the hatch.

Malek focused on Grunk once more, though he didn't ask any more questions. Grunk's eyes narrowed, and he curled his lip, showing off his teeth again.

"There's a large cave in the mountains that might work for our needs," Malek said—extracting the information from Grunk's mind? He nodded, and the gateship shifted slightly again. "If we can avoid dragons and druids, we'll make our trip tonight."

"Shikari will let us know if dragons are coming," Jak said.

Shikari had disappeared below the canopy, but as Jak peered off to the port side, he burst into the air, covered with mud, leaves, and broken vines.

Malek arched his eyebrows.

"I guess he found a mud hole to cool off in," Jak said.

"Like a pig in a wallow?" Malek asked.

"Maybe, but that won't keep him from alerting us. As you know, he's a very helpful dragon."

Shikari twirled in the air, mud droplets smacking people on the deck.

Malek wiped brown moisture from his face. "Indeed."

9

"OUR DRAGON HASN'T RETURNED WITH HIS SPICES," SORATH remarked.

"Or to incinerate our waste," Ferroki said.

Sorath and Ferroki stood, surrounded by fish heads, tails, scales, and guts. Their raw fish fillets were ready to be seasoned and cooked, but their dragon captor had neglected to start a fire before leaving. Nor was there a table or counter, so the limp fillets lay on the floor near the wall. Ferroki had attempted to clean the area before resting them there, but soot permeated the tower, so that had been a challenge.

"There aren't any flies around, fortunately, but it's starting to smell a little ripe in here." Ferroki wrinkled her nose.

It was a cute nose wrinkle, and if they'd been in a setting with slightly more ambiance, Sorath might have kissed her. Now that his wounds had been healed, he felt invigorated and ready for action. That action should involve sabotaging the fortress, he supposed, and not putting moves on a woman.

"We could ask that dragon to incinerate our debris." Ferroki pointed at the one in the nest in the courtyard, the nest that happened to look into their tower.

"I don't want to talk to any of the dragons if we don't have to." Sorath waved in the direction that screams had come from earlier. He had a feeling that more of the captured humans had been turned into dragon meals. "I suggest we wait." He lowered his voice. "Unless our guard disappears, in which case, it might behoove us to try to get back to that room full of magical devices and destroy them."

He raised the dragon-steel dagger Yoshartov had returned.

"Attempting to destroy the devices that keep the fortress floating a thousand feet in the air," Ferroki said, "might not be the best plan when we're inside of it."

"I know, but..." Sorath let his chin droop to his chest. "I don't want to commit suicide, but, if nothing changes, I think it's only a matter of time before they kill us. Better to strike a mighty blow against them before they do. If not, and if we end up being eaten by dragons, we'll die full of regrets." He frowned, thinking of all the regrets he'd had before the dragons had even arrived in their world. "*More* regrets," he grumbled.

Ferroki rested a hand on his arm above his pickaxe. "I know. I'll help in any way I can, even if I don't look forward to plummeting to my death while inside a flying fortress."

"I think it only floats, not flies."

"Oh? Our wizards create sky cities that float. I would have expected more from dragons."

"I was considering earlier that it's likely our people stole the technology from the dragons."

"Probably."

Sorath sheathed the dagger so he could clasp her hand and rubbed her skin with his thumb as he gazed into her eyes. "One of my regrets, should we be chomped to death in a dragon's maw, is that we never got to be together."

"If there weren't people screaming in the background and a dragon peering in our tower, I'd suggest we remedy that while there's still time, but the evidence that we're in an incineration chamber is off-putting." Ferroki looked around the sooty floor, gaze lingering on the charred pieces of bone they'd attempted to brush into a pile off to one side.

"Doesn't put you in the mood, huh?" Sorath thought *he* could have managed to bestir his libido, but he'd often observed that women liked more ambiance.

"Not exactly." Ferroki brought her gaze back to him. "But how about this? If you figure out a way to get us out of this fortress with our lives, we'll find a secluded spot, and I'll do my best to make sure there's at least one thing you won't have to regret."

"Oh?"

"Oh." She nodded and smiled.

"I may have to rethink my plan to nobly go down with the fortress."

"I should think so." Ferroki rose on her tiptoes and kissed him.

Sorath slid an arm around her, careful not to bump her with his pick, and returned the kiss, hardly caring if a dragon was ogling them or not. He was on the verge of trying to convince her that the tower *did* have sufficient ambiance for more than kissing when she drew back and peered past his shoulder.

"The dragon is gone," she whispered.

Sorath released her and crept through the short tunnel toward the entrance to the courtyard, drawing the dagger again. A hint of a buzz suggested Yoshartov or the other dragon had placed a barrier to keep them inside, but maybe it hadn't realized they had a dragon-steel blade. Sorath stuck it out ahead as he approached, and a faint pop reverberated through him.

In the entrance, he paused to peer around the courtyard at the other towers and corridors accessible from it. There weren't any dragons in sight, and a couple of tower-top nests were empty.

"Are they having a meeting somewhere, or is this a trap meant to lure us out?" Sorath had a hard time believing the dragons cared enough about him and Ferroki—or any of their human prisoners—to lay a trap for them.

"I would guess a meeting." Ferroki whispered. "Or they're doing some improvements to their fortress." She pointed at the tallest tower visible, one close to what had been the front of the fortress when they'd approached on the druid raft. Two dragons perched atop it, one levitating a large red sphere in through the sole window near the top.

"What do you think that is?" Sorath asked.

"A weapon?"

"The beam didn't come from up high. It shot out of that tail-like thing we saw hanging down from the bottom of the fortress," he said, considering the window. It would have a good view of the sea to the north, the direction human fleets would likely come from. *He* would put a weapon there. "That sphere is the exact color that the beam was."

He remembered it well. The moment when it had shot from the fortress to annihilate the druid raft was etched in his mind.

"Maybe they're moving it to a more defensible area."

"That could be," Sorath said as the sphere disappeared inside. The dragon stuck its head in after it. To mount it in front of the opening? "If that *is* the beam weapon, maybe we should sabotage it. If Uthari's fleet—or anyone's fleet—decides to attack the fortress, they would appreciate it being inoperable."

"Definitely. And if Thorn Company is with them, *I* would appreciate it being inoperable."

Sorath nodded, though he hoped Thorn Company, whatever remained of it, wouldn't be brought down here again. Aside from Tezi with the axe, there was nothing the mercenaries could do against dragons. Even the druids hadn't been effective against them, not against so many.

Their work completed, the two dragons left the tower, flying toward the rear of the fortress.

"This could be our chance." Ferroki nodded toward the empty courtyard.

"Do we go to the weapon or chamber with the power devices? They're going to know as soon as we sabotage something with a magical aura, so we may only get one try. If we crash the fortress, the weapon will probably be inoperable."

"True, but let me bring you back to the conundrum of how *we'll* escape before it plummets a thousand feet onto a glacier and kills us," Ferroki said.

A screech came from the sky, and another dragon appeared. They leaned back into the shadows of the tunnel, Sorath hoping they hadn't missed their opportunity to escape.

The dragon flew over the courtyard but didn't look down. It landed in a nest atop the tower with the sphere and settled in, its tail drooping over the side. The dragon faced out to sea rather than toward them, but...

"That might make it more challenging to reach the weapon," Sorath whispered.

"Yes." Ferroki shook her head sadly and pointed toward the tunnel on the other side of the courtyard that led back to the cave and dens—and power chamber. "If we're quiet, we might still be able to make it back there."

Sorath nodded, eyed the dragon in the nest, then led the way. They followed the wall of the courtyard, using the contours of the fortress to stay out of view of the dragon, but there was no roof to cover them if another flew past overhead, so they hurried.

"I wish there were a way to communicate with our people," Ferroki whispered as they entered the tunnel on the far side.

"Yes," Sorath said, though, if Thorn Company had been destroyed in the attack, maybe it was best that she not know.

He understood what it was like to lose one's entire unit. It could make a person suicidal—it *had* made him suicidal. He wouldn't wish that fate on anyone, least of all Ferroki.

They made it to the cave opening and hurried inside, but clacks and grunts came from the depths ahead. They weren't alone. Before, there hadn't been a dragon in the power chamber, but would that remain the case?

Grip tightening around the dagger hilt, Sorath crept forward, ready to fight if he had to, but he would prefer to enact his sabotage first. He wanted to achieve something here, not simply die.

Yellow-orange light emanated from the power chamber, but just beyond it was the entrance to an alcove. Or a *den*. Snapping sounds came from within. The crunching of bone?

A grunt and moist chewing noises followed another crunch, and Sorath envisioned a dragon inside, curled in its nest while eating a meal. Whatever it was dining on wasn't fish, not with bones that crunched like that.

The memory of the humans trapped in another tower came to mind, and fury made him clench his fingers around the dagger hilt. Were the dragons plucking their prisoners out one by one to dine on?

The idea of these monsters ever becoming allies to humans was impossible to imagine. They were nothing like Jak's Shikari. In that moment, all Sorath wanted was to leap around the corner and plunge the dagger in the dining dragon's eye.

His tense shoulders must have hinted of that desire, for Ferroki put a hand on his back, then pointed to the power chamber. Since they could enter it without passing the other alcove, they had to try. No matter how badly Sorath wanted to slay the dragon ahead, he had to be reasonable and admit it was unlikely he would succeed. He made his legs turn into the chamber.

Inside, with the light from more than a dozen glowing devices washing over them, Sorath felt exposed. There were no dragons in this chamber, but the crunches and lip-smacking noises continued, a reminder that an enemy was close. The dragon-steel walls might camouflage the aura from the dagger, but if their scaled enemy had a good nose, they had to worry about it catching their scents.

Sorath stepped over power tendrils and led Ferroki past several devices so they would be hidden from view. They put their backs to the far wall and considered the spheres, cylinders, and quirky shapes that had no name. One tall device that reminded him of a pump had moving parts, but most rested on the floor or floated in the air, some with tendrils snaking out of them and others not.

While Sorath debated which device appeared critical and should be attacked first, Ferroki pointed at a corner where four thick tendrils disappeared into the floor. Did she want him to try cutting them?

With the dragon so close, he didn't dare speak aloud, even a whisper. He pointed at the pump device and raised his eyebrows as he made a stabbing motion. Ferroki shrugged, glanced at the spot on the floor, then shrugged again. Sorath envied the mages their ability to speak telepathically with each other.

"I'm going to try that first," he mouthed and headed for the pump.

Sorath pressed the tip of the dagger into a seam. The device glowed brighter and sent sparks into the air. Barely restraining a curse, he stepped back, lifting his pickaxe limb to protect his face. The dagger might protect him from magic, but if that was pure electricity, he didn't know if he would be safe.

When the sparks died down, he pressed the dagger to the device again. Turning his face away, he leaned into it, attempting to cut the device without making noise. It was probably foolish to believe they could accomplish this without alerting that dragon, but he had to try.

More sparks flared, one landing on his sleeve and singeing

through to his skin. Again, he jerked back. Even though the device had responded, the dagger hadn't made a dent.

He tried another seam, but the device was sturdier than it looked. Frustrated, he leaned more of his weight against the blade, shoving hard and enduring the hot sparks that landed on him.

We smell you, humans, a voice spoke into Sorath's mind. The crunching noises had stopped. *How did you escape your prison?*

Sorath scowled at the device. He hadn't even scratched it.

The sounds of talons clacking on metal came from the tunnel outside. Knowing they were about to be caught, Sorath gave up on silence and on the pump device. He spun and hacked at a glowing orange sphere behind him, determined to drive the dagger into it. But this device didn't break either. A jolt streaked up his arm, and he almost lost his grip on the weapon.

The talons clacked to a stop outside the chamber, and a mottled brown-and-gray snout came into view above the pump, blood dripping from its fangs.

Sorath sprang behind a cylinder as tall as he, hoping the dragon would hesitate to attack him if he was close to the magical devices. It wouldn't want to risk damaging the very things that kept its fortress aloft, would it?

What menace are you humans hoping to accomplish? The dragon sounded more amused than furious. *Whatever it is, you will fail. Your kind are puny. We will make you our next meal, though you are scarcely worthy of being eaten by a mighty dragon.*

Sorath hacked at another sphere. Once more, it didn't break. Feeling betrayed, he scowled at the dagger. If he hadn't used it to pop that barrier, he would have believed Yoshartov had tricked him, that it wasn't a dragon-steel blade after all.

A cry of pain came from the back of the alcove. Ferroki.

Abruptly, Sorath realized she wasn't protected the way he was.

Come to me, my next meal. The dragon chuckled into their minds.

Sorath sprinted for the back, intending to grab her and extend the dagger's protection, but she wasn't there.

"Sorath!" she blurted from above the devices.

Arms flailing, she was floating toward the maw of the waiting dragon.

~

Rivlen paced in the long corridor of the gateship, the only corridor it had. She hadn't been inside the compact vessel often and didn't presume to step into any of the cabins—the ones with open doors all had gear on the bunks anyway. She sensed Jadora in a cabin—or, if memory served, that might be the kitchen—near navigation, but the door was closed, and Rivlen didn't open it, assuming she'd remained below to work on important scientific things.

The overhead hatch opened, and Jak dropped down the ladder, blinking in surprise at finding her in the corridor. He should have sensed her aura, but with so many mages now on board, maybe hers was mingling with all of theirs. For that matter, Jadora's aura was so powerful that it overshadowed almost everyone else's.

"Is Lord Malek coming down?" Rivlen asked him.

Malek had been terse with her, and she worried it was because Uthari was displeased with her. She had little doubt that the king had told his faithful zidarr everything about her role in Tonovan's death and letting Jak create the kerzor. By now, Malek had likely learned that she'd lost the *Star Flyer* as well as the rest of her little fleet. Since he'd flown often on the *Star Flyer* before she'd been given command of it, he probably had fond memories of the ship.

"Ah, I don't know. I think he's flying us to a cave." Jak raised his eyebrows. "I was hoping you'd be more interested in *me* coming down to see you."

Rivlen rubbed her face. "I'm not *un*interested in you. I just have... concerns."

"Well, *I've* had concerns about you. For days, I didn't know if you were alive." Jak clasped her hands. "So I'd like to hug you and kiss you now if that's all right." His brows rose higher, and he smiled warmly at her.

"It's all right," Rivlen said, though she would be a distracted romantic partner until she found out if Malek had any messages for her—or disappointment in her that he wanted to express.

"Good." Jak stepped closer, but the hatch opened again, and someone else came down the ladder, one of her officers leading two roamers.

"Where's the lavatory on this needle of a ship?" the officer asked, grabbing his crotch like a toddler. "We were in that tunnel *forever*."

"I think the druids just piss in them," one of the roamers said in accented Dhoran.

"That's uncouth."

"I heard they can use magic to incinerate their messes."

"I prefer to use my magic to incinerate my *enemies*. The lav?" The officer looked at Jak and Rivlen, though he frowned in confusion at their clasped hands.

Rivlen drew hers back, catching a flash of disappointment in Jak's eyes, but he stepped back so the men could squeeze past as he pointed toward the head at the rear of the ship.

"Perhaps we could talk somewhere private," Rivlen said, not wanting to disappoint Jak.

He brightened. "I have a cabin."

"Do you share it with your mother or your dragon?"

"No. Shikari doesn't fit down here anymore, and Mother is... busy." Worry creased Jak's brow as he looked toward the kitchen, but he clasped Rivlen's hand again and led her to his small cabin. "Was your experience harrowing?" he asked as she shut the door behind them. "Do you need love and support instead of hugs and kisses?"

He gazed earnestly at her, his aura wrapping around her like a cloak, warm, gentle, and appealing.

By Shylezar, she *did* need support. And love? They hadn't used that word with each other, but it didn't surprise her that Jak would feel strongly toward someone he'd slept with—or spent time at all with. He probably loved his dragon too.

She smiled. "I'm amenable to both."

"Good." His face grew more serious, the face of a man instead of a boy, and he lifted his hands to the sides of her face to kiss her, the warmth of his touch mingling with the warmth of his aura.

It hadn't been that long since she'd seen him last, but he seemed to have grown stronger—more powerful. Maybe he'd been practicing with Malek, bringing out more of his abilities.

Rivlen kissed him back, glad to be with someone who *wasn't* irked with or disappointed in her. She slid her arms around him, stepping closer, pressing her body against his. How long until they reached their destination and Malek came down to get a report? And could she and Jak manage to keep their emotions—their magic—from flaring and announcing to everyone on the ship that they were making love?

The thought of Malek walking in on them naked made her rest a hand against Jak's chest, intending to push him back, but she paused. As soon as they reached that cave, Jak and Malek would place the portal and fly off to another world, one that might be dangerous. She'd volunteered to protect the portal and keep it open so they could come back, but what if something happened to them there? What if Jak died, and she didn't see him again?

She growled and curled her fingers, grabbing Jak's shirt. Instead of pushing him away, she pulled him closer.

She sensed his pleasure, his enthusiasm, but then a hint of confusion, and he paused, breaking the kiss and looking down.

"Something in your pocket is poking me."

"You don't recognize it?" Rivlen pulled out his map device, though it could have been her sheathed dragon-steel dagger he'd noticed. She suspected he would be more pleased to see the former and know she hadn't lost it.

Jak grinned again. "You really did keep it through being attacked by dragons, shipwrecked, and captured by druids?"

"I did, but for the record, the druids did not *capture* us. I agreed that we would go along with them in the hope that I'd get to use a dome-jir at some point and report in to Uthari." Rivlen grimaced, reminded that she would eventually have to do that. No doubt, this ship had a dome-jir.

"I'm touched that you didn't lose it." His grin broadened.

She tried to return the gesture, but she sensed Malek's aura in the corridor outside. Had they arrived at their destination already? Or had he come down to question her?

"You seem distracted. Is my goofy grin not alluring?" Jak tried unsuccessfully to squelch it as he radiated pleasure at her.

"Your *power* is alluring," Rivlen said, still basking in the warmth of his aura. "And then you open your mouth."

"And it gets even *better*?" His eyes crinkled.

"You *are* goofy."

"Goofily alluring, though, right?" He wrapped his hand around hers, the map device still in her grip, and sent a zing of his magic through her. "I've missed you, Rivlen."

Gooseflesh rose all over her body as his power zipped along her nerves. Anticipation fluttered in her stomach as she remembered the last time they'd made love, in the cell of the *Star Flyer*, after he'd defeated Tonovan.

You can call me Xeva.

Jak gazed solemnly into her eyes. *Do you let many people do that?*

No.

Thank you for trusting me, he said, as if he understood the significance even more than she did. Maybe he did.

She pulled him close again, wanting to have him touching her physically and with his magic, giving her exactly what she wanted and more. What she needed and craved after the last few harrowing days.

But a knock on the door made them part. Their eyes remained locked, and Rivlen wished she dared send their visitor away. But it was Malek. And he would want his report so he could send it along to Uthari.

Jak straightened his shirt and cleared his throat. "Yes?" he called, no doubt hoping Malek wanted to ask a question and would go away if he received an answer.

Rivlen snorted, certain that wasn't the case.

I must contact Uthari before we leave, Malek spoke telepathically to them, politely *not* barging in. *I require a report from Captain Rivlen. She's arrived sans a great deal of her crew. And her ship.*

Rivlen winced. Malek's telepathic tone was as flat as his spoken one usually was, but she felt condemnation, whether he intended it or not. *I'm ready to report.*

"I'm not," Jak muttered, but he took another step back as the door opened.

Malek stood in the frame, eyeing them, as if not certain if he should step farther in. Maybe he'd expected them to be writhing naked on the bunk. Admittedly, given a few more minutes, they might have ended up there.

Perhaps Jak was thinking the same thing, for his cheeks flushed a deep pink. "We were reacquainting ourselves with each other," he blurted. "Did you know we'd, er, acquainted?"

Rivlen winced again, less out of shame for her career failures than at Jak's unnecessary burbling. She was positive Malek didn't care, other than to perhaps think she was unprofessional for forming a relationship with Jak, who, the last she'd heard, was at the top of Uthari's list of people he was irritated with. But Malek didn't feel that way about Jak, did he? He'd been standing side-by-side with him when they'd flown in to help with the dragon battle.

Maybe she shouldn't read too much into that. Jak could command the portal to attack. Maybe that was the only reason Malek hadn't had him in chains in his cabin.

"I gathered from your visit to see Admiral Dayum Rivlen that you hoped for some kind of acquaintance," Malek murmured, then gestured for Jak to step out.

"You went to see my *father*?" Rivlen gaped at Jak. "*Why*? And what did you *say*?"

"I wanted to let him know that you're an amazing commander and person, because you are, and he should acknowledge it. He shouldn't want some *zidarr* when he's got a wonderful daughter who's a powerful mage and whom any family would love to claim as their own."

Now *her* cheeks flamed red. What a thing to claim with Malek, Malek who knew she'd lost her ship and let Tonovan be killed on her watch, standing right there. By the power of all the ancient dragon gods, save her from the adoration of young men.

"Jak," Rivlen groaned. "I'm sure he wasn't impressed with you *or* your words. He's..."

"Difficult? Yes, I noticed. I think your mother might have liked me though. At the least, she seemed curious about me."

Rivlen shook her head, not sure whether to be mortified at his attempt at intervention—or whatever it had been—or touched that he'd cared enough to want to talk her father into... whatever he'd been envisioning.

"Jak," Malek said. "Leave us. I'll have the captain's report without commentary."

Jak took a step toward the door, but a thought must have struck him, for he halted abruptly. "You're not going to punish her, are you? Or interrogate her?" He stepped protectively in front of Rivlen. "Did Uthari order that?"

"What are you *doing*?" Rivlen asked, not wanting his protection. If Uthari *had* ordered Malek to punish or interrogate her, she would deserve it.

"Defending you from cruel and unfair judgment and persecution," Jak whispered over his shoulder.

Malek lifted his eyes toward the ceiling. "Go wipe the mud off your dragon, Jak."

A hint of magical compulsion accompanied the words. For a moment, Jak gritted his teeth and fought it, but Malek's eyes narrowed, and Jak walked jerkily out.

Jak's power might be growing, but he was still no match for a zidarr, and Rivlen doubted he wanted to get into a true battle of wills—or magic—with Malek.

The door clanged shut, and Rivlen sensed Jak going up on deck, but he called telepathically back to her, *Let me know if you need help.*

What are you going to do? Challenge Malek to a duel?

If we need to protect you, Shikari will help me.

I can fight my own battles, Jak.

I know, but I don't want to see you hurt.

Which was why, she was certain, he'd gone to see her father. She shook her head. *I knew what my duty was when I signed up to be an officer.* She hesitated, not wanting to brush him off, even if he was being a little obtuse. *But thank you for caring.*

You're welcome.

Malek clasped his hands behind his back. "When you're ready, Captain."

"Yes, my lord. And I'm sorry about..." Rivlen waved to indicate Jak.

Malek only nodded curtly. "What happened after you parted ways with the fleet and traveled to Temril?"

Erg, he wanted everything all the way back to then? That included Jak's making of the kerzor and Tonovan's death. She'd reported those incidents to Uthari over the dome-jir, but Malek probably wanted to get the information in person. That way, he could more easily watch her face and gauge her honesty.

Rivlen took a deep breath and started from the beginning. Her only hope was that in telling Malek, Uthari's right-hand man, she might not be required to report everything again later directly to the king. At least Malek liked Jak, she was fairly certain, and might not judge her as harshly for having developed feelings of her own for him. He *definitely* liked Jak's mother.

Afraid to tell anything but the whole truth, Rivlen looked at his collarbones and recited everything that had happened. She didn't make excuses or embellish, but she *did* point out that Tonovan had been an ass in Temril and that his actions had prompted King Temrok's assassin to stow away and ultimately kill him. Jak might have made Tonovan vulnerable, but he hadn't sliced the general's throat himself.

Though she wanted to, she didn't omit that she'd spent the night with Jak, or that she'd gotten an inkling of what he intended with the kerzor. She admitted her failures, including that she'd lost the *Star Flyer* and the other ships between southern Zewnath and the dragon fortress in the Glacier Islands. They'd been against impossible odds there, and she hoped Malek and Uthari understood that, but she again didn't make excuses, simply stating the number of dragons and that they hadn't been able to defeat them or escape.

"Oh," she blurted at the end, reminded of the idea she and Tezi had come up with. "It occurred to us that if Uthari's blacksmith is still with him that he might be able to make dragon-steel bullets that could be fired from a black-powder weapon."

Maybe if their idea proved useful, Uthari wouldn't be as aggravated with her.

Malek nodded. "Homgor mentioned the possibility."

"Oh?" Rivlen struggled to keep the disappointment off her face; she'd hoped it had been an original idea. A *useful* original idea.

"Uthari doesn't think bullets will do much to harm a dragon, even if they pierce their scales, since they're so small."

"They'd at least bring down their barriers temporarily, wouldn't they?" Rivlen thought of the times she'd fought beside Tezi, an axe wave enough to pop a dragon's defenses, even when she didn't reach scale and blood.

"If such a small amount of dragon steel is sufficient for the task, yes."

"Then everyone with riflemen could use magic to attack and take advantage. If one could fire rapidly, one might be able to *keep* a dragon's defenses down for the duration of a battle."

Malek nodded. "I'll mention it to Uthari. It's worth exploring, and I believe he's got the blacksmith on his ship."

"His ship, my lord? The king isn't remaining in Utharika?" Rivlen had started to feel relieved that Malek had said he would share her idea, but if Uthari was on a ship, it could only mean one thing. He and his fleet were heading down to the fortress. That meant the odds were good that she would end up having to report to him in person after all. She barely stifled a grimace.

"He's gathering as many allies as he can and going to face the dragons."

"But your mission is different, right? Isn't it to find something to get rid of the parasite?"

"It is."

"Doesn't Uthari believe that his success in confronting the dragons at their own fortress would be contingent on you succeeding?"

"I don't know if he does. He has a more personal reason for wishing my mission to succeed."

It took Rivlen a moment to realize what he meant, until she remembered Jak had said Uthari had managed to infest himself with the parasites, as well as Jadora. That would definitely give him a *personal* reason to want a cure found.

"If we're able to work quickly and learn what we need to eradicate the parasites," Malek continued, "it's possible we'll make it back in time to give him what he needs to finally defeat the dragons. That's where you come in."

"My lord?"

"The druids are going to soon realize we didn't leave the continent with the portal. And the dragons will be back to look for it too."

Rivlen nodded, certain a *cave* would do little to hide its aura or keep powerful beings from sensing it and finding it.

"If they're allowed to take it while we're in the other world..." Malek spread his palm toward the ceiling.

"You won't be able to come back."

Jak wouldn't be able to come back.

"Correct," Malek said. "I'm leaving all but essential people here. I want you to be in charge of them—and of keeping the portal open."

Rivlen swallowed, daunted. Even though she'd volunteered to do exactly that, she couldn't help but notice she kept being given impossible missions.

"Yes, my lord," she made herself say.

"King Uthari isn't pleased with some of the decisions you've made of late, and he's extremely irked about Tonovan's death."

"I know."

"Perhaps, if you're instrumental in our success on this mission..." Malek turned his palm upward again. "Let's just say that he is now extremely interested in seeing it succeed, in having a solution to the parasite found."

"I understand." All along, Rivlen had believed that there was merit in Jak and Jadora's idea to cure their powerful enemies rather than having to fight and kill them all—and likely be killed themselves—so she nodded.

"There's a device that can set the portal into hibernation, nullify its power and much of its aura."

"Is that why I didn't sense it until you got close?" Rivlen asked. "I assumed it was because this ship is camouflaged."

"It is, and that was part of it, but the dragons were able to sense it, regardless, except when the device that Vinjo made was attached to it. Of course, the portal can't be used as a weapon as long as it's in hibernation, but I'm not positive anyone except Jak and Jadora can convince it to shoot lightning at dragons. The portal wants a solution to heal its kin, not to annihilate them."

"Its kin?"

"We've learned that souls of dragons live within the portals, that they long ago locked themselves into the artifacts when they realized there was no way to avoid being overrun with the parasites. That's why they seem to be intelligent."

"Will the portal *let* us put that device on it?"

"Jak will ask it to, so let's hope. He did say it was reluctant to let even him put it to sleep, but as long as it believes it'll be wakened again, it may allow it."

Hope. May. This didn't sound promising, but what choice did Rivlen have? Someone had to stay behind and keep the portal from being taken. If it was, Jak and the others might never be able to return.

Malek dipped into a pocket in his jacket and pulled out two watches on chains. They appeared hastily made from scrap parts, and Rivlen suspected Vinjo's work, though she didn't sense any magic about them. Malek placed one in her hand.

"These are synchronized and set to the time in Port Toh-drom. Assuming you're able to place the device on the portal, each night at midnight, remove it for fifteen minutes. We'll attempt to come through at that time. That will limit the amount of time enemies will be able to sense its aura."

"I understand."

"Start tonight. I doubt we'll be able to find what we need and return so quickly, but it's possible."

"Yes, my lord." Rivlen wrapped her fingers around the watch, glad he was trusting her with this, even if she was daunted. "And you said I'm still in charge of the mage officers?"

"And the mercenaries and the roamers. Use them in battle if they can help."

"Is this— ah, have you reported in to King Uthari about our survival yet?" She didn't know when he would have had time.

"Not yet, but I will before we leave this world."

"What if he… doesn't agree that I should be in charge?" Rivlen didn't know who else Uthari would appoint, since they'd lost the captains of the two other ships, and there weren't other troops in the area to draw upon, but if he was angry with her, he might put a random lieutenant in charge and remove her from duty altogether.

"I believe he'll accept my decision in the matter. He's otherwise distracted right now." Malek nodded to her and opened the door. "I'll make my report to him, and we'll leave shortly."

"Yes, my lord."

Rivlen didn't know how she would keep the druids and the dragons from finding them—even if the portal's aura was diminished, their enemies could sense her, her mages, and their dragon-steel weapons if they got close—but she would do her best. No, she would do more than that. If she had to, she would die to keep the portal open so Jak and the others could come back.

10

SORATH SPRINTED AROUND THE MAGICAL DEVICES, HURRYING TO reach the dragon before Ferroki did. Under its power, she levitated near the ceiling and toward its open maw, helpless to escape. Blood from its last meal dripped from its fangs.

Roaring in fury, Sorath leaped for the dragon, reaching it before Ferroki. As he slashed with the dagger at what he hoped was a vulnerable snout, the magical grip released her. She twisted in the air and landed in a crouch.

The dagger popped the barrier around their enemy, and its slitted reptilian eyes narrowed in surprise. It mustn't have expected a human prisoner to be armed with a dragon-steel weapon.

Sorath plunged the blade into the side of the dragon's snout before it recovered and reared back. A wave of power blasted toward him, but the dagger protected him, and it barely whispered past. But Ferroki lacked that protection.

"Look out!" Sorath cried.

Before he could grab her, she skidded back and crashed into one of the devices. Cursing, Sorath lunged for the dragon again, but it had lifted its head, and he couldn't reach it. The creature's maw opened, and it snapped at Sorath, its fangs far longer than his simple dagger.

Do not attack my servants! a voice boomed in his head.

Sorath and the dragon halted. Fangs still on display, it turned toward the tunnel outside the power chamber.

Recognizing Yoshartov's voice, Sorath took the opportunity to run over and help Ferroki to her feet.

"Are we saved?" she asked, grimacing and touching the back of her head.

"I don't know. He's not going to be happy we were wandering around either."

Your servants are roaming our fortress as if they're residents, not food, the other dragon said.

Another set of talons clacked on the metal floor, and Sorath glimpsed Yoshartov beyond the other dragon's bulk.

They are preparing me food, Yoshartov said.

In the power-control cave?

Yoshartov's head came into view, snaking past the other dragon's chest as he peered through the entrance at Sorath and Ferroki.

"We were looking for a fire," Sorath said, "to cook the fish fillets over."

A fire? the enemy dragon boomed. *They were trying to damage our devices with that little knife.*

"We thought smacking the knife against them might create sparks—" and it *had*, "—to start a fire." Sorath casually leaned an elbow against a floating sphere while Ferroki gave him a they're-not-going-to-buy-that look.

The servant Colonel Sorath still believes I'm a fool, Yoshartov said, gazing at them with his single eye.

Everybody thinks you're a fool, the other dragon snapped. *Get your verminous humans out of the control cave, or we'll devour them whole.*

Sorath wondered if the dragons realized they alternated between referring to themselves as *I* and *we*. Only Yoshartov mostly stuck with *I*.

He peered at the other dragon. *Your snout is bleeding, Gavorstoffle.*

I cut it on a knife.

My servant poked you. Yoshartov opened his maw, tongue lolling out between his fangs.

Was that a laugh?

I will complain to the queen about your servant. He should not have *a knife.*

He will make me fish. I have brought spices!

You are an idiot. The queen will have you punished.

Go tattle to her then. Yoshartov looked at Sorath again. *Follow, servants. You are not permitted here. You could have been eaten by a cranky dragon with a bloody snout.*

The other dragon grunted—or maybe that was an indignant huff—and stalked out of view.

After making sure Ferroki hadn't been badly injured, Sorath followed Yoshartov out of the room. He couldn't help but cast a long look back at the magical devices, but there was little point in plotting ways to stay—or return—until they figured out how to destroy them.

Your puny weapons will not disturb our powerful magical fortress, Yoshartov said as he led them back toward the courtyard.

"Apparently," Sorath muttered.

"Will this dragon queen punish you?" Ferroki asked.

Yoshartov looked back at them. *Not if I please her sufficiently with your exotic meal of spiced human cuisine.*

"A *queen* is who you're trying to woo?" Sorath asked.

I am not seeking to woo *her, only improve my position in the clan.*

For her, I carried so very much dragon steel to build this fortress. If she commands me to find more, I shall tear up ten worlds in search of it.

"I think your dragon is in love, Sorath," Ferroki murmured.

"Apparently," he said again, having no greater words and not positive that Yoshartov didn't have *wooing* in mind.

As they crossed the courtyard, the scents from a pungent mix of spices tickled Sorath's nostrils. Maybe the dragon *had* brought entire bags of the stuff back.

He stumbled to a halt when they entered the fish-preparation tower—he preferred to think of it as that rather than the crematorium or incineration chamber—and found a broken wooden vendor's cart on the floor, everything from salt crystals to saffron to peppercorns spilling out from it.

"You brought a whole cart?" Sorath asked as Ferroki sneezed.

I assumed you would need many spices to make superior cuisine satisfactory for a dragon of my stature.

"What happened to the vendor?" Sorath asked grimly, hoping a man's mangled body wasn't inside the smashed cart.

He fled into the jungle when I landed atop his cart.

"Huh, I wonder why."

My magnificence can be startling.

"And your giant fangs and talons."

You are a quirky servant, Colonel. Begin the preparations. Soon, I will take to the queen a delicious human dish. Yoshartov flicked a talon, and a fire started near one wall. Then he backed out of the tower, saying, *I will return*, before flying off.

Sorath rubbed the back of his neck. "I'm not sure where to start."

Ferroki sneezed again. "I suggest we make the best fish we're capable of and then find a place to hide."

"Hide?"

"Just a hunch, but I don't think the queen is going to be that enamored with Yoshartov's gift. That other dragon's report, that we were trying to sabotage their fortress, may be far more interesting to her."

Sorath grimaced. "Maybe we should hide *instead* of preparing food."

"I would agree, but you did promise we would make him fish." Ferroki managed a faint smile, though she looked like she was fighting off more sneezes. "Servants shouldn't lie to their masters."

"Hilarious."

"As I always strive to be," she said in a deadpan voice.

Jak and Rivlen stood on the lumpy ground of a cave, its large mouth open to the south, the Dragon's Tail constellation coming into view as the night sky darkened. Malek had given them the task of levitating the portal off the gateship and setting it up inside.

Using his geyser imagery, Jak attempted to contribute at least half the power required to move it. With Rivlen at his side, he wanted to make sure she sensed he was doing his fair share—and that he'd improved as a mage since he'd first levitated her from the deck of a ship. It was possible he tried too hard, for, when his geyser erupted upward in his mind, the portal hefted fifty feet into the air instead of sedately floating over the railing of the ship.

Rivlen gave him a sidelong look. "More isn't always better, you know."

"Sorry."

As Jak lessened the amount of power he was using to let the portal sink toward the ground, Shikari flew out of the trees, tucked his wings, and glided through it. He looped up and over it, then went through twice more. On the third time threading the needle, he misjudged how quickly it was falling and clipped a wing, but he recovered quickly and settled on the ground at the mouth of the cave.

"Are you showing off how much your flying skills have improved, Shikari?" Perhaps Jak wasn't the only one seeking to impress others.

Shikari roared at the jungle, and buzzing insects and nocturnal birds fell silent.

"I'm told more isn't always better," Jak informed the dragonling.

Rivlen snorted.

I am practicing, Shikari told him. *Soon, you will be able to ride on my back, and we will go through the ancient gateway to other worlds together.*

Make sure to fly a little lower when I'm on your back. Jak envisioned clunking his head as Shikari arrowed through the portal too close to the frame.

Shikari waved his tail in the air. *Humans who ride dragons must learn to duck when appropriate.*

I'll keep that in mind.

Shikari roared again.

"He's perky tonight," Rivlen observed.

"He's excited that I'm going to find what we need to save his people." Jak wished he could take Shikari along, but he didn't fit inside the gateship, and if they came out underwater, he wouldn't be able to breathe. Jak would have to leave him behind to help Rivlen defend the portal.

"Our people too, I hope," she murmured.

"That's the goal." Jak looked toward the side of the ship that held Mother's laboratory. It lacked portholes, so he couldn't see her working in there, but he sensed that she was.

She hadn't come out in hours, even for the dragon battle, and he worried about her. What if that mottled gray splotch on her hand was spreading? What if her personality was changing?

The portal clipped the mouth of the cave, and he returned his focus to it, mumbling, "Sorry."

And here he'd been teasing Shikari about his aim.

Guided by Rivlen's more experienced touch, they eased the portal inside, seeking a place to set it down, but the ground was uneven. Before, the portal had used its magic to dig itself into the dirt by the pool, but solid rock might be more of a challenge for it to manipulate.

"Hold that." Rivlen pointed at the portal.

Jak summoned more power as he felt her pull away. Before he could ask what she was doing, orange flames filled the air in the cave, heat washing over them. She focused her fire on the lumpy rock under the portal, and Jak looked away, the brightness and heat almost too much. The smell of scorched earth wafted to his nostrils, and he wrinkled his nose. When the flames died out, the floor of the cave was charred but flat.

"I didn't know you could incinerate rocks," Jak said.

"With enough heat, you can incinerate almost anything."

Be careful how much power you use, Malek spoke into their minds from the navigation cabin in the gateship, where he was using the dome-jir to let Uthari know they were about to leave. *We're only about twenty miles from where we left the druids. Those with keen senses may be able to detect large usages of power, even from that distance.*

Yes, my lord, Rivlen replied.

Jak didn't think their power usage could equal the omnipresent aura of the portal, but he didn't argue. He was in a good mood. He'd been reunited with Rivlen, however temporarily, and he was about to leave on the mission he'd wanted to go on for weeks. No, this was the mission he'd *always* wanted to go on, even before he'd known about the parasite. To turn dragons from foe to friend.

With the cave floor flattened, the portal settled easily, but it didn't flare with power that would prompt it to stand upright of its own accord. It had done that when they'd first put it down by the pool.

Can you activate yourself from here? Jak asked it.

If this didn't work, they would have to return to that pool, and he suspected druids were there waiting—guarding the spot.

The portal put an image in his mind of the pool with a sense of uncertainty—a question.

It would be dangerous for us to go there, Jak said. *But look—the constellation is in the sky. Can't you work from here?*

The portal showed him the pool again, this time with a sense of *home.*

"What's going on?" Rivlen asked. "Shouldn't it be able to stand up by itself now?"

If we put you there, the druids will take you and bury you, or the dragons will steal you to use.

After a contemplative moment, the portal flared blue, the symbols on the inside lighting up. A soft thud sounded as it settled onto the charred rock.

"It can stand. We'll find out if it can operate." Jak touched his hat, the dragon-steel medallion nestled in the band slightly warm to his touch. Back on Nargnoth, he'd been able to activate the portal without the key, but he would do it the normal way tonight, to give them the best chance of everything working. Of success. "As soon as we're ready."

He didn't know if Malek had finished his report yet, and not all of the roamers and mercenaries had been lowered from the deck to the ground. None of them had appeared enthused when they'd been told they would spend more time in the jungle and have to scrounge for food since the gateship hadn't brought enough for more than its crew, but Malek had said the fleet would be there eventually to help.

That information had mollified the mages, but Jak doubted

Rivlen looked forward to Uthari arriving. He hoped the king was too busy worrying about the dragons and his own predicament to punish Rivlen for her failings. Jak felt a little silly for having believed Malek might do that on Uthari's behalf, but he feared Malek was still Uthari's man and obedient to his wishes.

"How long do you think we have until your crew is ready?" Rivlen looked toward the back of the cave, then smiled at Jak. Was that a *sultry* smile?

"I'm not sure, but Shikari could keep anyone from coming back and disturbing us if we wanted to explore back there. And we probably should, to make sure there aren't any threats."

"Undoubtedly. That's common sense." Rivlen stepped closer to him, brushing her shoulder against his. "I was touched that you wanted to defend me from Malek. If he didn't like you, it would have been highly foolish of you to stand up against a zidarr, but it touched me nonetheless."

"I'm glad you were touched." Jak glanced toward the mouth of the cave to make sure nobody was paying attention to them, but with Shikari there, occasionally roaring at the nightlife, the mages and mercenaries didn't seem that inclined to climb up the slope and walk in. He shifted closer to Rivlen and slid his arms around her waist. "I *like* seeing you touched."

"I like it when you do the touching."

"I like that too." Jak kissed her and thought about suggesting they might have time to enjoy each other's company before they had to part ways. But concerns about the mission and what might happen if he didn't succeed sauntered through his mind. He also worried about what would happen to Rivlen while they were gone since the portal had already proven to be a target and she'd promised to guard it. He broke the kiss and looked into her eyes. "If you're attacked while we're gone, stick close to Shikari, all right? I know he's still young and goofy, but he's powerful too.

He'll watch out for you. And, if you can, will you watch out for him too?"

"Does that mean catching him fish and bugs?"

"He can do that for himself now, though I'm sure he wouldn't object if you dropped scintillating morsels in his mouth."

"Scintillating morsels of bugs?" Rivlen pantomimed what might have been plucking wings off insects.

"Any meat, fish, or insect should do. He's not picky."

"So I've noticed." She smiled and squeezed his hands. "I'll keep an eye on him, but you'd better come back. I'm positive he would pine terribly if you died."

"Only he would?"

"I might be a little disappointed to lose you." One of her hands dropped, straying to the pocket where she carried his map device.

It meant a lot to Jak that she'd managed to keep it while being attacked and shipwrecked. There couldn't have been time for her to grab many things before the *Star Flyer* had gone down—he'd seen how few belongings the survivors had with them. But she'd made sure to get that.

His throat tightened, and he didn't trust his voice to utter a response to her words, so he only stepped forward and hugged her, closing his eyes as he rested his head against hers. She returned the embrace, relaxing in his arms and emanating contentment.

He thought about saying he loved her, but he didn't know if they were ready for that. She had, however, given him permission to use her name, her name that he hadn't heard anyone else use. That seemed as significant as promises of love.

"Don't get yourself killed out there," she murmured quietly.

"I'll do my best."

"Good."

11

MALEK ATTEMPTED TO FOCUS ON HIS LIEGE'S WORDS AS HE STOOD IN navigation with his arms folded over his chest, the dome-jir glowing orange on the console and Uthari's head and shoulders floating above it. But he found himself using his senses to check on Jadora. Since they'd noticed that patch of gray on her hand, she'd disappeared into her laboratory and hadn't come out. And now, as Malek gazed at Uthari's face, he could pick out a patch of gray above his eyebrow.

"I've gathered a few mageships from the Ar Islands," Uthari was saying, "and I've left a message for King Wortalia, but Jutok, Dy, Zaruk, and Vorsha's successor refuse to join us. They don't even sound like they're preparing fleets of their own to take to face the dragons in the Glacier Islands. It's possible they are and didn't tell me, but I wouldn't be surprised if they're waiting to see how *we* do before committing their troops. No doubt they want us to whittle down the enemy forces while suffering devastating losses ourselves." Uthari sneered. He even *growled*.

Usually, Uthari retained his calm, even in stressful situations, but he'd radiated irritation throughout their communication, and sweat beaded on his forehead. Malek wondered how long it would be before Jadora grew more agitated, quicker to anger. Maybe it had already happened, but she was aware of it, and that was why she had secluded herself.

He'd almost gone in to check on her in person, instead of sweeping his senses over her from afar, but he didn't want to disturb her if she was absorbed in her research. And perhaps, a tiny, cowardly part of himself didn't want to see her devolve in front of his eyes, not when he could do nothing to help her.

"Are you paying attention, Malek?" Uthari snapped.

"Yes, Your Majesty."

"As soon as I gather more ships, I'll head south. You will leave Captain Rivlen and the other officers who survived the shipwreck behind when you travel through the portal?"

"Yes, Your Majesty." At the beginning of their conversation, Malek had reported everything Rivlen had shared with him. "Someone capable needs to protect the portal so that it's not stolen while we're gone. The dragons are aware that it's back in the Southern Hemisphere."

"Rivlen may be *capable*, but of late, she's been extremely unreliable, shirking her duty to sleep with that devious *boy*. I never should have promoted someone so young so quickly."

Malek didn't comment, nor did he look toward the cave where the portal was set up. The task had been complete for some minutes, but Jak and Rivlen had disappeared into the depths of the cave, leaving the dragon to stand guard. Uthari would not approve of their continued dalliance if he found out.

"I'll bring Gorsith to your position once I reach the area," Uthari said. "He will be better capable of leading the mage officers and ensuring the dragons and druids don't get the portal."

"Yes, Your Majesty." Malek was surprised Uthari hadn't left Gorsith in Utharika, but perhaps he believed that if they were unsuccessful in destroying the fortress, there would be no point in worrying about the sky city's defenses—about *any* city's defenses.

"I also want Rivlen punished," Uthari said. "Back when she left Temril, I offered her a chance to redeem herself, but she sent weaklings along to guard the boy, intentionally defying my orders. Were we not growing short on powerful commanders, I would demote her, if not cast her out of the fleet completely."

"What kind of punishment?" Malek asked flatly, not interested in doling out pain, especially not when time was of the essence. Malek didn't disagree that Rivlen hadn't been completely faithful in following Uthari's orders, but *he* hadn't been either. It would be hypocritical of him to punish her for crimes he'd also been guilty of.

"Pain. Enough to make her regret crossing us and ensure she won't do so again."

"You don't think it would be better to dangle a reward than make her resent us?" Malek heard a door open in the corridor and sensed Jadora step out.

She was in time to hear Uthari's enraged, "You reward people who excel and perform well, not who sleep with untrustworthy boys who never should have been allowed to live." Uthari's eyes closed to slits. "I insist you punish her, Malek. I'd order you to punish the boy for Tonovan's death, but you've already made it clear you won't do that." He bared his teeth, reminding Malek of the mad druid Grunk instead of the unflappable king he'd known for thirty years.

Malek thought of the promise Uthari had made, that if Malek succeeded in finding the solution to the parasite and ridding the world of the dragon threat, Uthari would let him retire, let him start a new life with Jadora. Did Uthari remember that? Or was he losing his mind as well as his ability to be reasonable?

"You *pause*, Malek?" Uthari demanded. "What is she to you that you would protect her?"

"Nothing," Malek said, though Rivlen was something to Jak, and Malek didn't want to see Jak hurt. Nor did he want to have to hurt Jak if he stood up for Rivlen against him. "But it would be unwise of me to punish her when I wish her to defend the portal with her life while we're gone."

"I already told you I'll bring Gorsith."

"You are close?"

"We'll be there in a few days."

"We must leave tonight, Your Majesty. I don't have to tell you that time is of the essence."

"No, you don't." Uthari leaned forward. "But I don't have my general at my side in this, and I want *someone* punished for his death. Malek, I command you. Punish Rivlen or punish the boy. They'll both know the consequences of crossing us and think twice about doing it in the future. I *order* you to do this, Malek. Do not defy me. Not if you want the reward you deserve."

"I will do what I believe is best, Your Majesty," Malek said, and waved his hand to end the communication.

He didn't want to endure further railing from Uthari—nor did he want to see more evidence that Uthari was losing himself, that the parasite was advancing and affecting his personality as it did so. Soon, Uthari might no longer be the man Malek had known for so long. Worse, as he fell apart, he might become a threat to all those around him.

"You won't do it," Jadora whispered from the hatchway.

"No." Malek turned slowly, afraid to see how the parasite was affecting her, but he couldn't ignore her or turn his back on her. Never that.

"Good." Jadora stepped into the cabin and rested a hand on his chest. "Thank you."

She didn't yet have any patches of gray skin on her face, but the spot on her hand had spread to her wrist and disappeared under her sleeve. Her cheeks were flushed, her skin moist with sweat. She wasn't snapping or baring her teeth at him, but there was a hint of something different in her eyes, as they locked on to his. A wildness or maybe even a savageness that was out of place on the face of his rational professor.

"You haven't defied him before," she whispered, her gaze intent as her fingers curled to grip his shirt.

"He's not himself."

"But you wouldn't punish Jak even if he was," she said with certainty.

"No," Malek agreed, aware of her hand against his chest, the warmth of her body, the power of her aura, and the way she licked her lips and looked him up and down. It sent a flush of heat through him, desire pushing away thoughts of their mission.

"You're not his man anymore," she whispered. Pleased?

Malek didn't nod, for his instinct was to deny it, to deny that he'd changed and to state that he was still loyal to the man who'd trained him and whom he'd served for so long. But he didn't speak the denial, and he realized he wasn't sure it was true. In choosing to disobey Uthari, had he made a more significant choice than he'd realized? Severed a relationship?

He didn't want to think so, but he knew *Uthari* now doubted his loyalty. Once he was cured, maybe Uthari wouldn't remember that. Maybe all would be forgiven. But if it wasn't, would Malek beg for Uthari's forgiveness? Or would he walk away with Jadora? Jadora, who was looking him hungrily up and down, her touch invigorating him, prompting him to step closer, to rest his hand on her hip.

"You're not yourself anymore either," he said softly.

"I know. I can feel parts of me slipping away, my focus becoming elusive, and... some inhibitions fading." She rubbed him through his shirt, then raked her fingernails across his chest, the sensation arousing. "But nothing has changed how I feel about you. You protected my son, and I want you."

His fledgling desire flared from flame to fire, and Malek growled, running his hand up her side. She arched her chest toward him, her head falling back, the curve of her neck tempting him.

He lowered his head to kiss it as he pulled her tight against him, her aura intoxicating. She groaned and pushed her hands around to his back, then up into his hair, nails scraping along his scalp.

As he kissed her, her touch spreading heat through him like wildfire, Malek wondered if she'd forgotten her insistence that they not exchange *fluids*, and that she wouldn't risk experimenting on him. If she had, he wouldn't bring it up. He'd *wanted* her to experiment on him, anything to further their understanding of the parasite. And he wanted *her*, one more time before they risked their lives traveling to the underwater world. He wanted her *many* more times, the gods willing.

All along, she'd been helping him, even when they should have been enemies, captor and captive. She'd been more straightforward with him than Uthari had been. And she hadn't ever tried to manipulate him, dangling a reward before him to ensure good behavior—or punishing him for bad.

With passion he'd never thought someone like him would feel, Malek pushed the door shut and pressed Jadora against it as she clung to him, letting her emotions flow over him. When they'd made love before, she'd been reserved, not letting her mental defenses down fully, but now her adoration and desire for him washed brazenly over him, and he understood what all those kings feared, why they forbade their zidarr from growing attached to others. He loved Jadora and wanted to protect her and make her happy, more than he did his king.

"Malek," Jadora breathed, panting in between kisses. "I want you. We shouldn't, but—"

"Yes," he growled. "We should."

And they did.

Sasko held Vinjo's bucket of magical pitch as he swabbed the stuff over the deck boards, filling in the gaps. Earlier, he hadn't been able to completely coat the area, due to the portal perched there, but Jak and Rivlen had levitated it into the cave. A blue glow had emanated from it earlier, suggesting it was set up and ready to use.

"Just as soon as I'm done here," Vinjo said.

"Are you reading my thoughts again, Vinjo?" Sasko peered through the railing to the jungle below where Tinder was already down with the mages, roamers, and other mercenaries. Malek had instructed them to set up a camp and obey Captain Rivlen until he returned.

Thorn Company and the mages had obediently started building shelters, but the roamers had drifted away and were having a meeting. Debating if they should risk a long jungle trek to get back to their people? They'd gathered around the blind seer woman, but Sasko was too far away to hear their words.

"I'm sorry," Vinjo said, "but your thoughts ooze right out of your head and all over me."

"Uh huh. Do you really think that pitch is going to protect the ship and allow it to operate underwater?"

"It'll depend on how *deep* underwater. I understand there's no way to know that until we arrive." Vinjo scowled at the deck.

"If you end up really deep, and it's too much for the ship to withstand... will you have time to turn around and come back?"

"I hope so." Vinjo flexed his back and rotated his arm, his shoulder probably aching after all the pitch he'd brushed on these past days. "I would think that Malek would be able to magically protect the ship for that long."

"But you don't know, do you?" Sasko shook her head sadly and rested a hand on his back. A part of her was relieved that Malek had told her and Tinder to stay behind with the rest of Thorn Company, but she would worry about Vinjo while he was gone. What if he didn't come back? She knelt beside him and rubbed his shoulders, in case it would help with his sore arm.

"No. It's too bad the dragon can't come along. His magic is getting powerful."

"Jak's leaving him?"

"He won't fit in the ship, and he can't fly after us if we're going to come out underwater. Dragons can't hold their breath forever, I understand."

"I guess it's good that he'll be here to help us," Sasko said. "Assuming Rivlen can convince him to do so. Malek ordered me to pull out the dragon-steel chain and collar, so maybe someone's supposed to leash him if he doesn't obey."

"That wouldn't likely go well."

"It might not be for that. Maybe they have a smith coming and want to melt down the dragon steel—*acid* it down, as I understand it—to make weapons. Tezi and Rivlen were talking about the possibility of dragon-steel bullets earlier."

"Hm. I wonder if I could snag a couple of links from that chain." Vinjo tapped his chin. "The dragon-steel weapons protect those who carry them from magic, right? What if I affixed some of it to the hull? Maybe it would protect the whole *ship* from magic."

"I didn't think magic was what you were worried about encountering." Sasko waved at the pitch bucket.

"Who knows what threats we'll run into on another world? More than water, I'm certain. I'm going to ask if I can try. If that blacksmith were here, I'd be tempted to ask him to armor the whole ship with dragon steel."

"I don't think there's that much in that collar and chain."

"It would be a thin armoring. Mm, Sasko? You rubbing me is magnificent."

A groan wafted up from the mageship. For a second, Sasko thought Vinjo was making the noise, showing how much he appreciated her shoulder massage, but it had come from inside.

"What was that?" Sasko asked.

She'd thought only Jadora and Malek were left inside the vessel. They weren't the types to emit such noises... were they? Another groan came through the hull, followed by a passionate cry of *yes*.

"Someone else may be getting rubbed magnificently," Vinjo said.

Sasko started to shake her head, as it was hard to imagine those two losing their equanimity, even in the throes of passion, if that was what was going on. Maybe one of Rivlen's mages had remained aboard and hooked up with one of the mercenaries.

"It's not a bad idea to enjoy joint rubbing," Vinjo said, looking over his shoulder, "before parting ways to go off on dangerous missions."

"Is that so?"

"Very so." He gave her a lopsided smile, but it grew serious as he gazed at her. He reached across his shoulder to clasp one of her hands, using his magic to send a warm sensual tingle up her arm. It flowed through her body to her core, everything tightening along the way in anticipation of pleasure.

Abruptly, thoughts of enjoying *joint rubbing* grew very appealing.

"Would you be interested?" he asked softly. "I know I'm not as powerful as a zidarr or as muscled as a mercenary, but I've been told I have a talented touch." Even as he spoke, he showed her, and she caught herself leaning against him, wanting more than the gentle teases with his magic.

"Told by women?" she whispered. "Or told by your engines?"

"They don't usually talk to me, but I'm *sure* they approve of my touch."

"Are you? Seems cocky."

"Is there any chance you like that in a man?"

"I do, actually. Self-confidence is sexy." Sasko closed her eyes as another wave of magic flowed through her, sparking along her nerves like nothing she'd felt before.

Vinjo shifted to his knees, turning to face her, to lift a hand to her cheek. "You don't mind this?"

Mind? She was about to tear off her clothes so she could plaster herself to him. "No. Keep going." She leaned close and kissed him, hoping to encourage more touches.

It didn't take much to encourage him. He wrapped his arms around her, sliding his hands under her uniform top, even as he continued stroking her with his magic. *I wasn't sure if you wanted it —me. Ever since we got caught in navigation together, you've been ... I didn't know if that mage made you hate mages like me.*

I've hated mages for a long time, but you're not like them. I've just been hesitant to pull you into my cabin since there have been so many people around, and I share that cabin with Tinder.

Well, we're alone on this deck right now...

Never mind the hundred people milling below the ship and the groaning coming from navigation.

They can't see *us, and they're all busy.*

Sasko doubted everyone was *that* busy, the navigation-cabin occupants excepted, but this might be their last chance. Besides, with Vinjo using his power to ignite her passions instead of simply torquing engine parts, she had no interest in pushing away his advances. No, she found herself kissing him, touching and stroking him, wanting to give him something to remember her by and a reason to come back.

I want to be with you, Vinjo spoke into her mind, as they kissed, too breathless to speak aloud. *You keep standing with me, and you don't mind that I'm quirky. I want to be with you tonight and always.*

He unbuttoned her top, and she leaned into his warm hands, a soft groan of her own escaping her lips as he explored her body. *I had a vision of us together*, she admitted. *In the future, after all this is over.*

Magnificent.

My vision or my breasts?

Both. He grinned and lavished his attention on her, and she tugged his tunic over his head. The homemade grass trousers he'd been wearing for weeks fell off of their own accord, or maybe at a tug of the drawstring from his versatile magic. *I want to be with you in the future, even if I have to become a girl mercenary.*

I might not be as interested in you if you become a girl.

No? Even if my touch is magical?

Maybe, if the world gets fixed, it wouldn't need as many mercenaries, female or otherwise. Sasko went back to kissing him and stroking his naked body as he pulled her down on the deck with him. She decided not to mention that *toddlers* had been a part of her vision. He might not be ready for that, and she didn't want to do or say anything to deter him from his assiduous attention to pleasing her.

I'll always need a strong warrior woman, he said.

This *strong warrior woman, I hope.*

That would be my preference, yes. No other would hold my wrenches, brushes, screwdrivers, hammers, and— He gasped as she held something else of his, and she grinned mischievously.

I believe I love you, Lieutenant Sasko.

I'm glad.

12

As the ship lowered down, preparing to fly into the cave and through the portal, Jadora tried not to look at or touch the new splotch of gray on her arm. There was a fresh one on her leg as well, the spots rough like sandpaper under her fingers.

Soon, her whole body would be that unappealing sickly color. Malek wouldn't want to touch her then.

She shook her head, telling herself that being *touched* wasn't her priority, but some lusty, savage part of her had forgotten that and taken over when she'd seen Malek in the navigation cabin earlier. They shouldn't have had sex; the day before, she'd *told* him it was a bad idea since the parasites might be transmitted that way, but her common sense had fallen out of her head for some reason. During that hour with him, she'd experienced hunger and lust such as she'd never known. Even afterward, she'd had to force herself to return to her laboratory to work instead of pulling him to the deck for more.

All Jadora could believe was that it was a side effect of the parasite that she hadn't anticipated. Uthari had been more aggressive and short-tempered, as far as she'd been able to determine from eavesdropping on his conversation with Malek, but she… she'd lost her rational mind, succumbing to primitive instincts that wanted her to have sex.

She was surprised Malek had allowed it, that he'd forgotten what she'd said about the possible danger to him. Or maybe—she jerked her head up to stare at the wall without seeing it—he *hadn't* forgotten.

Had he *wanted* to risk being infected? To see if he was immune to the parasite?

If he wasn't, they would both be compromised, leaving Jak and Vinjo—the only other people who were going along—to figure out the Orbs of Wisdom and a cure for the parasite on their own. But maybe Malek believed she could figure it out if she had proof that he was immune. Maybe he had that faith in her.

"Oh, Malek," she whispered, then plucked up one of her syringes.

If she had inadvertently transmitted it to him, it was too soon for the parasite to appear in his bloodstream, but she would later take another sample from him. She slipped the syringe into her pocket and went to navigation to watch their approach and brace herself for what might be a rough arrival on the other side.

Vinjo sat in the pilot's seat, his hair more mussed than usual and his shirt askew. In the other seat, Jak sat, nibbling his nails as the gateship paused in front of the portal. Malek stood behind him like a statue, gazing intently at it.

Everyone was waiting to see if the portal would work from within the cave.

Vinjo leaned forward and blew a kiss through the porthole. Sasko stood out there with his pitch bucket, and she saluted him with the brush.

"Last-minute sealing?" Jadora guessed.

"No, the sealing is all done, but she affixed something to the bottom of the ship." Vinjo looked back at her. "I was able to unfasten the last link in the dragon-steel chain attached to the collar."

"And you... glued it to the hull?"

"Yes, for luck."

"That's a rare and valuable item to risk losing—for luck."

"So I said," Malek murmured.

"Not only luck," Vinjo said. "I'm hoping that having it on the hull will protect the ship from magic, the same way holding a weapon protects its wielder."

"Ah," Jadora said. "That makes sense."

"And we won't lose it. My magical pitch concoction dries quickly and could hold an elephant by his nose hairs. *Trunk* hairs."

"An interesting image," Jadora said.

The portal flared to life, and nobody replied to her. Stars swirled within it, forming a constellation visible from the world they would visit.

Jak thrust a triumphant fist in the air. "It works here. Good."

Jadora nodded. She'd believed it would, but she hadn't been certain.

"Maybe good." Malek shifted his gaze from the portal to her. "If we can use it here, it's possible the dragons can use it from their fortress."

"I know," Jadora said grimly.

Malek lifted an arm toward her, and she stepped closer, drawn toward him. Always drawn toward him.

"We'll have to hope the others can keep them from getting it," she added.

"Yes." Malek kissed her temple and shifted her so that her back was to his chest, and they could watch the ship's approach to the portal together.

She might have been self-conscious about the embrace with her son scant feet away, but Jak was waving to Shikari and Rivlen, both of whom stood next to Sasko in the cave, and he didn't notice them.

I know what you did earlier, Jadora thought to Malek.

Satisfy all of your womanly urges?

Besides *that.*

Ah. How long until you can use the syringe in your pocket to sample my blood and see if the parasite entered my body?

Jadora looked over her shoulder at him. *I didn't think you could read my mind anymore*, she said, though she remembered letting her emotions and thoughts out when they'd been making love.

I usually can't. But I know you. He touched the exact pocket she had the syringe in and smiled.

It might take a day or more, but I'll check in a few hours. And it's nice to be known.

Yes.

He might have said more, but Vinjo pointed to the portal, where the stars had settled, their destination hanging in the middle.

"We're going through," he said.

Vinjo guided the ship into the portal, and the last thing Jadora was aware of was Malek's hard chest against her back and him kissing her on the cheek.

Her senses buzzed as they traveled between worlds, an indeterminate amount of time passing before they flew out on the far side. Or they *should* have flown out. The ship halted abruptly, as if it had crashed into a wall, and she didn't know if they'd cleared the portal. Nor did she know what would happen if they were stuck halfway through it when the magical passageway closed.

The mage lamps that kept the interior of the vessel illuminated flickered, threatening to go out.

Vinjo swore and pushed the lever that should have propelled the gateship forward. It shuddered but didn't continue. Outside, weak blue light flashed, highlighting thick gray-blue vines pressed against the porthole, strange squiggly growths on all sides of them like nothing Jadora had seen before.

Were they underwater? Jadora couldn't tell through the vines.

A groan came from the engine room in the rear, but the ship only shuddered again.

Before Jadora reached out with her senses, she was aware of magic all around them and more magic off in the distance.

The framework of the ship creaked. A few of the vines shifted.

"Are they *alive?*" Vinjo squeaked.

"I think it's a plant," Jak said, leaning forward.

Something similar to a suction cup appeared right in front of him, stretching and flexing against the glass of the porthole, and he jerked back.

The interior lights flickered again, then went out completely.

Jadora sensed Malek draw upon his power. The gray-blue vines snapped, and the ship surged ahead with a lurch.

Off balance, Jadora grabbed Jak's seat to keep from pitching back against Malek, but he was like a rock, solid and immobile, and kept his protective arms wrapped around her.

Vinjo slowed the ship immediately, probably not wanting to push them farther forward until they knew what they were dealing with. With the vines broken away, Jadora could tell they *were* in water. Dark water, though a faint blue from what had to be the portal behind them provided a hint of light.

The way ahead was as dark as the interior of the ship, and Jadora shivered, glad for Malek's arms around her. She might have power now, but that didn't keep her instincts from warning her of danger—and making her feel uneasy.

Some of the vines remained attached to the ship, including the one sprouting the suction cup. It kept flexing against the porthole in front of Jak, reminding Jadora of a mouth.

"Could someone make that go away?" Vinjo flicked his fingers at it. "It might puncture a hole, and then we'll be in a lot of trouble."

More creaking came from the hull around them, as if to suggest they were *already* in trouble.

Jadora summoned her power to stir the water outside, creating a current that pushed the vines away from the vessel.

The creaks faded, as if the ship were pleased to be free of them, but Jadora could sense Malek using his magic to reinforce the hull and suspected he was the reason the noise stopped.

"Will you turn us around?" Jak asked. "I sense the portal, but it doesn't feel… right."

Jadora checked it herself and agreed with the vague assessment. Its aura was weaker than she was accustomed to sensing from the portals, almost as if it were in a state of partial hibernation.

"I'll try," Vinjo said. "We strained the power supply, and the controls are sluggish underwater. Despite my modifications, don't forget I built this ship for propulsion through *air*, not water."

"You're doing fine." Jak smiled at him. "It's a good ship. I'm glad you made it."

Appearing heartened by the praise, Vinjo tapped controls on the console. Something clanked ominously in the back, and the ship jerked as it rotated, but it *did* turn.

Jak swore as the portal came into view. *Partial* view. A huge mass of those vines covered it and spread out along the sea bottom, or maybe it was a lake floor. Since water itself wasn't magical, Jadora couldn't sense it and tell how many miles it stretched, nor how far above them the surface was. She couldn't even tell if they were in fresh or saltwater, not without going out for samples. And, oh, how she would love samples. Samples of the water, of that plant, and of everything else interesting they encountered while they were here.

"I'm not sure it's a plant." Malek pointed at a massive heart-shaped blob from which the vines appeared to emerge. Many of them ran toward the portal, but others spread across the ground, running off into the darkness in all directions.

"I'm not sure it's not," Jadora said.

"It's magical," Vinjo offered. "I can sense it."

"Whatever it is," Jak said, "it's doing something to the portal."

Jadora nodded. The ancient artifact still glowed blue from being activated by their arrival, but it was a fainter blue than usual, and, even as they watched, it flickered, much as their lights had.

"Feeding on its power," Jadora guessed.

Jak looked at her in alarm. "If it siphons off all the portal's power, will that keep us from going back? Will it *kill* that portal? And the dragon soul within?"

Jadora riffled though the knowledge Zelonsera had left her, but the dragons either hadn't encountered the vine entity before, or she hadn't deemed it important enough to include in what she'd shared. Jadora knew that when the dragons had visited this world before the time of the parasite, the Orbs of Wisdom hadn't been underwater. Something had happened in the ten thousand years since to flood this area.

And flood it deeply.

"I wonder how far underwater we are." Jadora stepped away from Malek to peer up as much as she could through the porthole. The fact that no sunlight filtered down to them—no light at all—suggested they were deep. Of course, it could be nighttime up there, and then there would be no light to permeate the water.

"The vines were difficult to break," Malek said. "Thick and strong with magic enhancing them. That creature must have developed to thrive under pressure in deep water."

"But you *did* break them," Jak said. "I bet if we worked together, we could clear more away from the portal. To make sure we can go back when we need to. You can't even see the symbols right now, not with vines and suction cups covering them."

"It's probably been like this for a long time." Jadora suspected it had taken the entity years if not decades to grow such an extensive network of vines. "And the portal still operates."

"*Barely,*" Jak said. "It could be on the verge of running out of energy and going dead forever."

"The magic that powers the portals has kept them operational for thousands of years." Jadora was reluctant to intentionally harm anything, whether plant, animal, or something altogether different. "It's possible their magic can power them for all of eternity."

The portal's blue glow disappeared, leaving the water and the interior of the ship in darkness. Alarm surged through Jadora before she remembered that always happened. After travelers successfully passed through the portal, its glow disappeared, and it returned to looking like little more than a monolithic blue-black ring.

She could still sense its power, the aura all the portals emitted, though as she'd noticed before, this one was emanating less. Reluctantly, she admitted Jak's fear wasn't groundless.

"Their magic can power the portals for thousands of years *if* they haven't had killer plants sucking away their energy." Jak rose to his feet and gripped the console. "I'm going to do something."

Jadora lifted a hand. "I don't think that's wise."

Jak frowned. "What if we have to leave this world in a hurry because we run into trouble, and we find the vines have grown back over the portal, even more than Malek can break?"

"I am sufficiently powerful to handle *vines*," Malek said.

"Are you sure?" Jak asked. "Like you said, they're magical and really strong. And what if you're exhausted from a battle? Or from keeping this ship together for days?" Jak pointed at the portal. "How about we cut those away, and that's all? We wouldn't be killing anything, especially if that's a plant." His eyes brightened. "It would be *pruning*."

"It's possible the portal is its primary source of energy—the way the sun provides energy for plants on the surface. Also, let me remind you that we don't know if it's a plant. How would you like it if someone pruned your leg off?" Jadora understood that her son felt protective toward the dragons and the portals—after all, they communicated with him—but it was a bad idea to start *pruning* things they didn't understand on a world they'd never visited before and knew nothing about.

Malek looked thoughtfully at her. Or was that pensively? "We were able to break the vines impeding the ship without repercussions."

Maybe he agreed with Jak's point that he might be exhausted by the time they returned this way—too exhausted to fight a magical plant.

Abruptly, she remembered the choice he'd made. That *they'd* made. It was possible she'd infected him with the parasite, and he worried about the state he might be in when they came back this way.

So far, the parasite hadn't seemed to affect her power or ability to sense magic, but she couldn't deny that it affected her in other ways. Her cheeks warmed as she remembered the lust that had roiled through her and how she'd thrown herself at Malek.

It was also possible that *she* wouldn't be in a state to help on the return trip. Which would leave only Jak and Vinjo.

"If we are going to prune it," she said, "let's do as little as possible, in the hope that we don't upset it."

"I'll do it," Jak said. "Then it'll only be mad at me."

"I don't think that'll matter when we're in the same ship as you," Vinjo muttered. "If you give me some time, I could make a tool that would do the pruning."

Malek shook his head. "We had better not waste much time

here. You mentioned that we have a limited amount of oxygen, correct? Unless we're able to go up to the surface and replenish it?"

"We'll have to do that if we're going to stay long," Vinjo said, "because, yes, we have a limited amount of time."

"Go ahead, Jak," Malek said. "I'll help you."

Jadora sensed Jak mull for a moment, trying to find a mental trick to help him cut the vines. Malek aided him, guiding him and teaching him.

Once more, she felt warmth toward him, gratefulness that he was willing to defy Uthari and refrain from hurting her son—or letting him be hurt by harming someone close to him. She leaned back and squeezed Malek's hand.

"I don't think it likes that." Vinjo pointed to the heart-shaped core of the entity.

Was it throbbing? It hadn't been doing that before.

Jadora opened her mouth to suggest they pause, but great swaths of cut vines floated away from the portal. Jak and Malek's work.

The portal glowed blue again, and she sensed emotion from it. Relief? Gratitude?

Malek and Jak cut away more vines. Maybe it was worth irritating the entity if they could help the portal. After all, on other worlds, Jak had succeeded in communicating with the portals and gaining information from them. Since Jadora had no idea in which direction the orbs lay, or if they were even in this body of water, information would be useful.

The heart-shaped entity throbbed faster. Vines along the sea floor rippled, drawing back from the portal.

"We might want to move out of the area," Jadora said. "In case it's intelligent enough to know we're responsible."

"An intelligent plant?" Vinjo sounded skeptical, but he did grip the controls to turn them around.

"We haven't confirmed that it's a plant," she reminded him.

Why couldn't anyone remember that? "Even if it is, it's magical. Who knows what its capabilities are?"

"True."

"I wish I could get a sample of it," she murmured. As far as she knew, there weren't any magical plants or animals on Torvil. If they all survived this and accomplished her mission, she would love to study specimens from this place.

Malek slanted her a knowing look, but all he said was, "The portal is free. Vinjo, take—"

Vinjo squawked in surprise as a thick vine lined with suction cups thudded against the porthole, instantly attaching.

"—us away from here," Malek finished.

With a surge of power, he knocked the vine away, but three more vines thudded against the porthole to replace it.

More thuds sounded from the sides of the ship, as if every vine on the sea floor was reaching up to grip them. When Jadora examined the area outside with her senses, she realized they were.

"So much for a piece of dragon steel helping the ship," Jak said.

"They're not using magic against us," Vinjo said. "They're physically attacking."

Malek shifted from knocking the vines away to creating a protective barrier around the ship. He started with it kissing the hull, then expanded it outward, pushing away the vines gripping the exterior.

Vinjo attempted to send the ship surging forward, but they blocked the way ahead. The vines had risen up like a dense forest, too thick to penetrate.

"Can we go up?" Jak asked uncertainly.

"They're above us too." Jadora sensed them curving over the deck of the ship, pressing against Malek's barrier from above. "And behind now," she added quietly.

The forest of vines that had sprawled across the sea floor now rose up in every direction like prison bars. Prison bars so dense that they could no longer see the portal or the heart-shaped entity that was likely the brains controlling them.

Vinjo urged the engine to greater power, even funneling some of his own magic back through the ship to infuse it, but all they managed to do was ram the nose of the gateship against the vines.

He slumped back in his chair. "We're trapped."

~

Tezi stood in the mouth of the cave, the blue glow from the portal having faded several minutes earlier. It didn't look like the gateship would turn around and come right back. She hoped it hadn't been destroyed as soon as it arrived.

Rivlen walked past Shikari, who was growling at something in the foliage on the hillside below, and joined her in the mouth of the cave. She held a gray oval-shaped device in her hand.

"What's that?" Tezi asked.

"Something Vinjo made that can put the portal into a dormant state and hopefully make it harder for druids and dragons to detect from a distance." Rivlen pantomimed sticking it on the side of the artifact, though she hadn't yet approached it.

"Will the portal still operate if it's on there?"

"No."

"Then how will our people come back?"

"I'm to remove it for fifteen minutes at midnight every night until... well, Malek didn't specify how long. Until they come back."

And if they weren't able to come back, what then? Would Rivlen have to stay here indefinitely, hoping they one day would?

"I'm going to wait a little bit before putting it on." Rivlen lowered her arm and looked toward a flat area in the trees where the mages, mercenaries, and roamers had set up a rudimentary camp. They lacked tools and supplies to do much more than cut branches, make lean-tos, and spread fronds over them.

"Good idea." Tezi pointed at Shikari, whose tail was swishing in agitation as he kept growling. Had a belligerent raccoon wandered out of the jungle? Or was there some danger they ought to prepare for? More dragons? "What's bothering him?"

"That dragon-steel chain and collar is in the brush down there. Malek dumped it over the side of the gateship earlier."

Tezi blinked. "Dumped? Isn't dragon steel too valuable for that?"

"He doesn't intend to leave it in the jungle, but if Lord Homgor the blacksmith is with Uthari's fleet and they fly this way, he might be able to turn it into bullets. Assuming he has along some of the acid concoction he uses to manipulate dragon steel."

"Is Uthari's fleet *supposed* to fly this way?" And would Uthari be with it? Tezi grimaced, having no interest in seeing the wizard, not when she'd assisted Sorath in killing one of his zidarr.

"I hope not," Rivlen muttered. "But if the fleet does come, Uthari will find a professionally set up camp and mage officers ready to go into battle against the dragons. Mercenaries ready too." Rivlen slanted her a look.

"Thorn Company is always ready for that," Tezi said, though most of her comrades had been dejected since the captain had died and they'd lost so many people in the shipwreck. Things were a little better now that Sasko and Tinder were back, but Tezi wondered if the company would stick together after this long mission ended and they were free to seek other employment.

The thought of Thorn Company disbanding saddened Tezi, but she didn't know if she could envision it continuing on with the captain gone. As her second-in-command, Sasko had to be prepared to take over, but her heart didn't seem to be in the mercenary life of late. She'd had the same weary slump to her shoulders as the others since she'd rejoined the company, and she'd given Lieutenant Vinjo a long kiss before he'd departed on the gateship.

Tezi vowed to do her best to raise people's spirits and help out. She hadn't been a mercenary for that long, and she wasn't ready to quit.

Rivlen must have decided that enough time had passed, for she walked back into the cave and slowly approached the portal. The wary glances she gave it made Tezi think she worried about it striking her with lightning. Maybe that was a legitimate concern. It might not *want* to be put in hibernation.

When Rivlen was two steps away, it flared blue, its light reflecting off flecks of quartz in the side of the cave. She hesitated.

"Jak said you would allow me to do this." Rivlen lifted the device above her head, as if showing it to the portal. "For your own good and so the dragons don't get you. I'll be back at midnight to remove it. Every night until our people return."

The light slowly faded. Maybe it was Tezi's imagination, but the portal seemed to emit a telepathic sigh as it went dark.

Though still wary, Rivlen affixed the device. The portal didn't object further.

"Is there anything else we can do to camouflage it?" Tezi asked as Rivlen returned to her side. She would never know exactly how magic worked, but she had a feeling the portal's aura intensified whenever it used its magic, such as to establish a gateway to another world—or to flash blue in discontent.

"I don't know," Rivlen said.

"Throw fronds over it?"

"I'm sure that'll fool dragons."

A growl wafted up from Shikari, who was poking at the dragon-steel chain now.

"Do we need to figure out a way to hide that too? All dragon steel has an aura that those with power can detect, right?" Tezi touched her axe.

"It does, but these items aren't as noticeable as the portal. I don't think the dragons will be able to detect them from halfway across the continent. I usually have to be pretty close to sense them."

"But you're not a dragon."

"Fortunately." Rivlen eyed Shikari.

He gave the chain a final swat, then ambled up the slope toward them. He sat on his haunches facing them, and Tezi was surprised to realize how much he'd grown. His head was above hers now.

"Are you going to want us to hunt for you now that Jak is gone?" Rivlen asked him.

Tezi remembered Rivlen and Jak using their magic to catch insects on Vran. Shikari had been parrot-sized and ridden on Jak's shoulder then.

I am growing and am mighty now, Shikari announced. *I can catch my own food.*

Even though Tezi had known Shikari was capable of communication now, having him speak telepathically to her still startled her.

"That's good. Maybe you can help us hunt down some food too. The supplies the gateship left us with were scant, especially for so many people." Rivlen waved toward a couple of campfires where mages and mercenaries were roasting whatever animals they'd coaxed out of the jungle and onto their spits. "We're not much better off now than when we were shipwrecked on the beach."

"There's less sand in my crevices now." A creek meandered down from the mountains near the cave, and Tezi had found a moment to scrub those crevices earlier.

Food isn't the most important thing now, but I do like it. Shikari's maw opened, revealing his pointed fangs.

"We all do," Rivlen said.

You are Jak's mate, yes? Shikari focused on her. *And you lead here while he is gone?*

"I lead when he's here too," Rivlen said dryly. "And we're friends, yes."

Friends who had sex in caves, Tezi thought to herself, fairly certain that had happened earlier.

Perhaps Shikari had the same thought, for he gazed into the depths of the cave behind the portal. In the dark of night, it was hard to tell if Rivlen's cheeks turned pink, but she did glance back, huff, and fold her arms over her chest.

You call him Jak? Rivlen asked, perhaps deflecting the mate talk. *Not Father? He's basically been raising you.*

He does not have wings or scales and can't fly. He would be a funny father for a dragon.

He's kind of a funny mate too, Rivlen said but smiled fondly. Maybe even longingly, for she cast another look at the portal.

He is my ghesivalar.

And that means what?

Shikari swished his tail thoughtfully. *Companion? There is not a human word. But he will ride me soon. I am almost big enough for it, and we will fly into battle together and protect each other always.* Shikari looked toward the starry sky to the south. *I sense dragons.*

"Too bad Jak isn't here now," Tezi said. "If they fly close, you're going to get that opportunity for battle soon."

I sense multiple dragons, Shikari said. *If we fight so many, we will lose. We must be sneaky to avoid their notice and keep them from taking the portal. That would mean Jak could never come back.*

"That's why I put that device on it. To nullify its aura so the dragons won't notice it. Though I may have waited too long." Rivlen looked in the direction Shikari was peering.

The dragonling's tail swished again. *The device does help the portal to be less noticeable, but the dragons saw it earlier, and we have not gone far. They know it is still in the area, especially since you are here with other dragon steel.*

"What do you propose?" Tezi asked curiously.

A plan. Sneakiness.

"Such as?" Rivlen asked.

I do not know. I am only young. I have not fought many battles, but I know there must be plans.

"I've heard that," Rivlen said, her tone dry again. "Do you know how many dragons are coming?"

I have sensed four so far. It is possible there are others that haven't yet come into range of my senses.

"Four. Great." Rivlen rubbed her forehead. "I wish we'd been able to talk those druids into helping."

The female I healed will lead her people to help once she has recovered.

"She told you that?"

No, but it is true. She was grateful to me.

"She'd better be, but if she didn't say she would help, I wouldn't count on it."

"How can we drive them off? If they see that chain and collar, would they worry about us imprisoning them?" Tezi pointed at the dark shape lying on the slope.

"We're not capturing any dragons," Rivlen said. "We want them dead and not a further threat."

Shikari gazed sadly at her. *I do not wish dragons dead but to be rid of the parasite and returned to their pleasant and fun nature. Dragons are supposed to be fun. I want some of my kind to play with me.*

Before Rivlen could answer, Sasko and Dr. Fret approached with meat on skewers. Shikari's snout lifted in the air, nostrils twitching.

Tezi's stomach rumbled, and she was tempted to twitch her nostrils too.

"Is that for us?" Rivlen asked. "It would be a good idea to fill our bellies. We're going to have another battle to endure soon unless we can figure out a way to camouflage the whole camp."

"Kywatha figured out how to camouflage their raft, didn't she?" Tezi asked. "By studying Vinjo's work?"

"Another reason it would be useful to have her here instead of napping in a medic's tent somewhere."

"We actually brought these for Shikari," Dr. Fret said. "We want to make sure Jak's dragon is taken care of while he's gone." She offered a skewer of meat to him.

"*Jak's dragon* is a mighty hunter capable of finding his own food now," Rivlen said. "He said so."

He had, but that didn't keep Shikari from plucking the skewer out of Fret's hands. As his tail swished contentedly, he chomped down the cubes *and* the wooden stick on which they were threaded.

"We're brainstorming with Shikari to come up with plans." Tezi accepted a skewer for herself, nodding her thanks to Fret and Sasko.

Another went to Rivlen and the rest to Shikari.

"Is he a strategic mastermind?" Sasko asked.

"A lot more than I was at three months old," Rivlen said, surprising Tezi with the compliment. "He says there are four dragons coming. I want to get everyone in the cave. We'll make a stand there and hope we can reinforce the roof better than the druids and I managed in the tunnel earlier."

"Can't the portal fight off the dragons?" Sasko asked. "It blasted eight of them when they attacked Utharika."

"*Eight*?" Rivlen glanced back at it.

Sasko shrugged. "It helped anyway. Uthari and Malek and some other powerful mages were there, but I saw its lightning bolts do a lot of damage."

"It's hibernating at the moment." Rivlen was still eyeing it.

"Can't we wake it up?" Dr. Fret asked.

"Yes, but then the dragons will find it more easily."

"Don't they more or less know where it is?" Sasko asked.

"Not exactly, and the concern is that it won't attack dragons without Jak here to ask it to do so," Rivlen said.

I could ask it. Shikari showed them his fangs again, bits of wooden skewer stuck between them. *But it doesn't want to kill dragons. It also wants dragons to be fun again.*

"That's problematic," Rivlen said.

"Fun dragons are problematic?" Fret asked.

"Not-dead ones are," Rivlen grumbled.

If the portal doesn't fight the dragons hard enough, Shikari said, *they could capture it and take it away.*

"Yeah," Rivlen said. "That's what we're trying to avoid."

"Won't it be easier for them to take it if that device is on there, forcing it to hibernate?" Tezi asked.

Best would be to trick them, Shikari said. *Sneakily.*

"I'm still waiting to hear how we can do that," Rivlen said.

Shikari stared toward the south again, his tail going rigid. *They speak to me. They know I am here and want to kill me or make me one of them.*

"We won't let them take you," Rivlen said.

Shikari turned in the other direction, though the trees obscured much of the northern sky. *Others come.*

"Dragons?"

Tezi grimaced, her heart sinking.

Humans. Mages. On many ships.

"Oh? I can't sense them yet, though I can detect the dragons now. They're about ten miles away, I believe." Rivlen waved to the south, then raised her voice to call, "Put out the campfires."

Tezi suspected their dragon-steel weapons would be greater beacons than a few cook fires, but she didn't say so.

"Do the humans belong to our fleet, Shikari?" Rivlen asked. "Can you tell?"

The mage king who fought the dragons at the floating city is there.

"Uthari." Rivlen should have been relieved that help was on the way, but she winced.

I will be sneaky and speak to them, Shikari said.

"Uh, speak to who?" Rivlen asked.

Shikari turned back toward the southern sky, and Tezi had a feeling he meant the dragons, not the fleet of mages.

"Is that smart when we're trying to hide from them?" Tezi asked.

Rivlen spread her arms.

Long moments passed with Shikari gazing to the south. He didn't report how his communication was going, and they could only guess from the way his tail swished or paused, then finally flapped against the rocks in irritation.

"I can sense the fleet," Rivlen reported quietly. "I think they're at the pool. I'm going to risk reaching out to them. The dragons are still coming. Not directly at us—I think they're heading toward the pool too—but they'll figure out where we are soon enough." She touched her dragon-steel dagger and waved at the collar and chain.

Tezi crouched, resting the head of her axe on the ground between her legs. She tried to will energy into her limbs, but it was late, and it had been a long day. As soon as the dragons came into view, she would revive, with fear and anticipation surging through her veins, but that knowledge didn't keep her from hoping Thorn Company could avoid another battle. As long as the dragons didn't come, they couldn't get the portal, and the way would remain open for Jak and the others to return—hopefully with a solution. The world desperately needed a solution.

"The dragons are turning away," Rivlen said with wonder in her voice. "What happened?"

Brow creasing, she looked at Shikari.

His tail went up, and he lifted his head, his yellow eyes

appearing smug. *I told them Jak's mate would call upon the portal to help in a great battle and also has plans to make the confrontation last as long as possible to keep the dragons busy here, while fleets that flew around the bottom of the world sneak up on the floating lair from the pole with great numbers and dragon-steel weapons.*

"And they believed you?" Rivlen asked.

I said it in a sneaky and clever way. Also, this other fleet approaches, so that helped them believe. Unless they are being sneaky with me, *they are going back to defend their lair.*

Tezi wasn't sure whether to wish she'd heard the conversation —and the dragons attempting to out-sneaky each other—or not.

"They do appear to be flying away," Rivlen said. "Off to the south."

"That's good," Sasko said.

"They'll be back," Fret said certainly.

"Because of the portal?" Sasko asked.

"Because nothing good ever happens anymore."

"Uthari and the fleet are approaching." Rivlen strode down the hill to the camp to wait for their arrival.

Fret nodded. "That falls under the category of *nothing good*."

Shikari bumped Sasko in the shoulder. *Do you have more toasted meat cubes?*

"I'll see what I can find," Sasko said.

She and Fret headed to where the campfires had been doused. That left Tezi alone with the dragonling as the first black-hulled mageship floated into view. She didn't know whether to be glad for their arrival or not.

13

SORATH WOKE WITH A START TO THE SOUND OF TALONS ON THE dragon-steel floor. It was a sound he suspected he would hear in his dreams—in his nightmares—for the rest of his life.

Ferroki must have heard it too, for she rose to a crouch, glancing at the magical fire that still burned and the fish fillets they'd done their best to cook without utensils. At one point, Sorath had used his dagger as a skewer to rotate the heavily spiced food over the flames. They'd lacked a plate to put the finished product on, so the charred fish now sat in small piles on the sooty floor. Sorath couldn't imagine anyone eating the fillets, much less giving them to a queen to win her favor, but he wasn't a dragon. Maybe the dragons would find the charcoal-coated food delicious.

Yoshartov entered the tower. *The meal has been prepared, my servants?*

"It has." Ferroki bowed politely to him.

Sorath fondled the dagger and tried to gauge how much time had passed since he'd sworn he wouldn't attack Yoshartov for three days.

Excellent. I will share it with the queen.

All the fillets floated into the air.

"You might want to warm them a bit with your magic," Ferroki suggested. "We finished cooking them a while ago. We didn't realize you would disappear for so long."

I had to endure a lecture. Sometimes, it is difficult being a dragon.

Sorath grunted. Right.

The other dragons were not pleased that my servants attempted to cause trouble. You must stay here from now on, or I may not be able to protect you.

"Make sure to talk to the queen about her interests and passions," Ferroki suggested. "Compliment her on things she strives to excel at. Don't just talk about her beauty."

You advise me on improving my position in dragon society? Yoshartov sounded amused.

"On impressing a female," Ferroki said. "As the captain of an all-female mercenary company, I know a little about how they think."

I do not know what she is passionate about.

"Find out. Trust me."

Hm.

After the fillets floated out of the tower ahead of Yoshartov, he turned to leave, giving them a view of a bloody gouge in his flank.

That hadn't been there before. Had the dragon who'd wanted to eat Ferroki attacked Yoshartov? Or had another dragon?

Let us all hope that the queen enjoys partaking in this exotic human cuisine. Yoshartov and the fillets disappeared from view.

"What happens if she hates exotic human cuisine?" Ferroki asked.

A distant scream came from another part of the fortress. A *human* scream.

"I have a hunch," Sorath said, wishing for the tenth time that there was some way he could save those people's lives. But he and Ferroki were in danger of suffering the same fate. "The cooks might be punished. Were you truly giving him advice on impressing a woman? Er, a female dragon?"

"He's the closest thing to an ally we have here."

"I'm not sure someone counts as an ally if they believe you're their servant." Sorath tapped the hilt of the dagger.

"Better than believing you're his dinner."

"True. I guess I'll wish him the best in his pursuits. If he and the queen are both distracted, that'll be two fewer dragons we have to worry about." Sorath eyed the exit to the courtyard, tempted to sneak out again, but if they didn't have a way to damage the magical machinery that kept the fortress in the sky, there wasn't a point. "I wonder if the beam weapon is made from the same material as the devices in the control room."

"Control cave." Ferroki smiled slightly. "I don't think dragons have rooms."

"Just nests and caves, yes. Maybe we should sneak over to the tower with the weapon in it and see if it's vulnerable to aggressive prodding." He held up the dagger.

"I believe the word you're looking for is stabbing."

"Vigorous and aggressive stabbing, yes."

"I'm game to try, but it will probably be as impervious as everything else here."

"I know, but we can't sit here and do nothing." Sorath half-expected Ferroki to point out it would be smarter to do exactly that, that they would be more likely to live if they did what Yoshartov wished and stayed out of trouble.

But she said, "I know," and touched his arm and gazed sadly at him. "I'm afraid we don't have the tools necessary for sabotage, but I'm willing to try again."

With appreciation and tenderness welling up in his chest, Sorath drew her into a hug. "If we get out of this, will you take a break from being a mercenary captain long enough to go on leave with me?"

"Yes."

"I appreciate how prompt your response was."

"I've been fantasizing about a break for a while. The whole company needs one."

"I was envisioning *private* leave involving just the two of us."

"And aggressive prodding?" Her eyes crinkled as she looked at his face.

"Gentle but firm and *pleasing* prodding, I should think."

"Sounds romantic."

"It will be."

"Then I won't invite the whole company along."

"Good. I'm not an exhibitionist." Sorath rested his chin on her head and closed his eyes. "That's why I would prefer to attempt my sabotage without any dragons walking in on me." He wondered if he might have found a way to destroy the devices in the control cave if he'd had more time. "What were you pointing at on the floor when we were in there?"

"There were fine lines around where those tendrils disappeared under it. I think there was a panel or door there. You've seen the infrastructure of the sky cities, the underground access tunnels and shafts for the workers who maintain the system."

"Yes. But dragons would be too large to use shafts. Wouldn't they have to design something else?"

"They could be large shafts."

He snorted.

"Or they could access them with their magic and not need to go inside. They could also send human servants to work on things in tight spaces."

"Let's investigate the weapons tower first, and then, if we're not caught, we can try to get back to the control room. *Cave*."

Ferroki nodded. "This time, before you start your aggressive prodding, maybe we should look for a switch or lever that might simply turn off the weapon."

"I don't know if magical devices work that way. Besides, if the dragons could easily flick it back on, turning it off wouldn't do much."

"I suppose. What if we heaved it out the window?"

"I'm game to try."

"Me too." Ferroki clasped his hand and extended her other arm toward the courtyard, as if she were inviting him to dinner instead of to sneak into tremendous danger if not to their deaths.

"You're a fabulous woman. Would you like me to inquire about your passions and compliment you on your captaining skills?"

"Obviously."

~

Jak stared at the impenetrable forest of gray-blue vines surrounding the ship, even trapping them from above, keeping them from rising toward the surface—wherever that was. For the moment, Malek and Mother had a diamond-hard barrier up around the ship that the vines couldn't penetrate. But Jak sensed them squeezing it, trying to get through, and he didn't know if Malek and Mother could keep it up indefinitely.

As powerful as they were, the plant or animal or whatever it was also had power. Each of those vines emanated magic, and even more came from the heart-shaped core of the entity. And why wouldn't it be magically strong? It had been siphoning power off the portal for who knew how long.

"Jak," Mother said, "let's keep cutting the vines away—it can't have an infinite amount of appendages to throw at us—while Malek keeps up the barrier."

A creak came from the frame of the ship.

"Don't forget enhancing the hull," Vinjo said. "My root pitch is effective at keeping the water out, but the water *pressure* is another concern. I think we're really deep."

"I'm aware," Malek said tightly as he focused on applying his magic in multiple directions at once.

That was something Jak hadn't yet learned how to do. "I will, but let me try to talk to the portal first. It kind of woke up when we cut away the vines plastered to it."

Mother nodded. "I sensed that it was relieved."

"Yes. Exactly. Maybe it can help us get away."

"Wouldn't it have done that itself if it could?" Vinjo asked.

"Well, it doesn't have *legs*." Jak shrugged. "Maybe it used its power to keep the entity away for a long time but, over thousands of years, got tired."

"Ask it where the orbs are too," Mother said. "None of the visions we've received have included maps."

"Right." Jak wished they'd been able to bring Shikari along, but he'd admitted he didn't have any knowledge of this place since it had changed a great deal since dragons last visited.

Jak reached out to the portal, hoping it would speak with him. He'd had varying degrees of success on different worlds, with some of the souls that inhabited the ancient artifacts being helpful and others being aloof.

The weakness of this portal concerned him, and he tried not to think about its power extinguishing forever while he and the others were here, trapping them on this world. After all, the portal had survived that power-sucking plant for a long time. Or so he suspected. It was possible the thing had sprouted up recently and, with all that delicious portal power fueling it, spread its vines and taken over the area quickly.

Mighty soul in the portal? Jak asked politely. *We're trying to help free dragons from the parasite that's altered them, so we can return them to what they once were. Will you help us? Can you direct us to the Orbs of Wisdom? We seek their knowledge.*

A spark of interest came from the portal but not a message.

Jak didn't expect a map or a string of instructions—only the portal on Nargnoth had spoken to him and only once—but the others had communicated images with him. Was this one capable of that?

He summoned his magic and attempted to reach out to it with more than telepathic words. Though nobody had taught him how to meld his consciousness with another's, that was what he wanted to do, to sense what it sensed and understand what it understood. He felt it accept his link, accept him. It was almost easy. Maybe the portal no longer had the power to fight off strangers? To defend itself?

Sadness greeted him. Sadness and a morose belief that the end was near.

Jak swore under his breath. Did the portal believe it was dying? *Was* it dying?

Don't give up. We'll help you. Do you want us to completely destroy this entity? Has it been preying on you?

The time of the water creatures has come, a sorrowful voice whispered in his mind, distant and weak. *The time of the dragons has passed.*

No. There are lots of dragons alive and waiting to be healed. And we're going to do it.

"Jak?" Malek prompted. "Are you making any progress?"

"I'm trying to give the portal hope and a will to live."

"See if you can give the plant less of a will to live while you're at it."

Focused on the portal, Jak bypassed words and shared through imagery what they'd learned and what they intended to do. *Please,* he finished, *which direction to the Orbs of Wisdom? Do you know?*

They are of the Old World, and they are dying, just as I am. The portal shared an image of another gray-blue entity, its vines stretching through ancient underwater ruins and up pedestals to curl around the flickering orbs that rested on them.

"No," Jak blurted.

"That doesn't sound good," Vinjo muttered.

Fear coursed through Jak's veins, the fear that they were too late, that this world and all remnants of the dragons on it were lost. Would they even be able to tap the symbol and open a passageway home?

The portal shared another image, one of their ship facing it and of Jak swimming up to it to insert the key and tapping the symbol that led back to Torvil. The portal tried to muster the power to form a connection, but the stars it formed in the center flickered and went out. Regret accompanied the image.

Jak rubbed his face with a shaky hand. *Are you sharing a vision of what* might *happen or what you're certain* will *happen?*

He didn't know how the magical network worked but had a hunch that most of the power for creating a passageway came from the portal at the origin point, not the destination point. If that was true, it might mean people could arrive in this world... but never leave. Dear Shylezar, what if the dragons had known that and *that* was why they hadn't visited this world to consult the Orbs of Wisdom themselves?

The portal didn't speak, only sharing another feeling of regret. An apology.

"Kill the plant," Jak rasped, terrified it was too late. What if the portal couldn't recover?

"That's what the portal wants?" Mother asked.

"It's *killing* the portal." He turned imploring eyes toward her but only for a moment before closing his own. *He* would kill the thing.

As Malek had shown him when slicing through the vines earlier, Jak imagined great flows of water flooding valleys as they poured down from mountains on the map of his mind. They tore through vegetation, leaving nothing but scattered stalks in the water's wake. After a moment's hesitation, his mother joined in, sending such tremendous power into him to aid him that he would have sunk to his knees if he hadn't been seated. Even Malek helped, diverting some of his magic from his other tasks.

Working together, they cut through the vines around their ship without too much trouble, but the heart-shaped core of the entity was another matter. They sent tremendous power into it, attempting to funnel great currents of water to blast it, so much that its walls or flesh or whatever it had burst under the pressure.

But it had magic of its own and resisted them, pulsing faster, sending out repellent currents that battered their ship. Malek's barrier protected it, remaining wrapped around their vessel, but the currents affected it, and they bobbed, being pushed back from the portal and the entity.

Mother growled, channeling even more of her strength into destroying the thing. So much power came from her that it almost overwhelmed Jak. It was like standing next to the sun.

Finally, the heart of the entity blew up. The water muted what might have been an epic explosion above the surface, but pieces of gray-blue flesh still sailed outward in a thousand directions. Some of them reached all the way to the ship, splatting against the porthole and sticking, a dark ichor oozing out and turning the water around it inky black.

"Ew," Vinjo said.

With a weak sigh, Mother fainted.

She would have collapsed on the deck but Malek caught her, alarm widening his dark eyes.

"Mother?" Jak spun out of his seat.

An ominous creak came from the framework of the ship.

"Lord Malek," Vinjo blurted. "You dropped the—"

Once again, Malek reinforced the hull of the ship, but he also swept Mother into his arms.

Her eyes had rolled back in her head, and she barely appeared to be breathing. Jak reached out with a trembling hand, touching her shoulder. A fresh splotch of gray marred her cheek, a reminder of the parasite advancing within her blood.

"Mother?" Jak whispered.

"She used too much power. I'll take her to a bunk. Vinjo, get the ship away from the area before something comes to feast on the dead entity. Jak, find out which way we need to go." Malek turned with Mother in his arms and left navigation.

Worried for her, Jak wanted to follow, but he had to obey Malek's orders. Vinjo didn't yet know where to steer the gateship, and they couldn't waste time sailing in the wrong direction.

Portal? Jak looked back toward it, though it had gone dark. Everything had. Only a sphere of yellow light that Vinjo had conjured illuminated the navigation cabin. Outside, all was darker than midnight. *We'll try to save the Orbs of Wisdom, but we need to reach them. Which way?*

It is too late, came the portal's whisper.

It might not be. We have to check, regardless. Which way? Please. Can you share a map with me? Or at least point us in the right direction?

Long seconds passed. Jak didn't know if the portal was ignoring him, trying to remember, or didn't know.

He was about to prompt it again when not a map but a view of the world from high above entered his mind. It was as if he were a dragon, soaring thousands of feet in the air.

From that vantage point above the world, Jak witnessed volcanic peaks wafting sulfurous smoke into the air, making the sky reddish gray instead of blue. They jutted up from water that had risen all around them, lapping at their rocky gray sides, nothing growing on the craggy slopes. In the distance, a greater land mass was visible, something at a high enough elevation that it remained above the flood waters, but it was as gray and devoid of vegetation as the sides of the volcanos.

Dread knotted in Jak's stomach as he realized this world must have suffered some cataclysmic event. Numerous volcanoes erupting or an asteroid striking the planet? He didn't know, but he worried the air up there might not be breathable, which meant that when the gateship ran out of oxygen, they might not be able to replenish it.

"As if we didn't have enough to worry about," Jak muttered.

Vinjo turned forlorn eyes toward him.

In the portal's vision, two green dots of light appeared above the water, floating between the volcanos.

I am here, the portal told Jak, making one dot flare brighter. Then it dulled and the second one brightened. It was located near the base of one of the volcanos. *The ancient city of Jaragon lies there. Be careful if you go. The* dak'shaa *were drawn by the magical artifacts left there. There are many of them.*

Is that the, uh, entity we fought?

Yes.

When that one started feeding off your power, why didn't you destroy it? Jak asked.

It had been so long since anyone visited here and used me that I saw little point. I assumed my kind were dead, and I was forgotten. My continued existence... did not matter.

Well, it does *matter. We're going to fix the dragons and we'll come back here and put you somewhere that you can be used again.*

I haven't the power to send you back to your world, the portal said, confirming what Jak had feared.

We'll figure something out. Don't worry about us. If only that weren't bravado. *That city doesn't look that far away. We'll reach it, and we'll find a solution.* Jak tried to make himself believe that. He had to, or there was no point in continuing on.

The portal didn't answer, only emanating that sense of regret again as the overhead view faded from Jak's mind.

"That way," Jak told Vinjo after he oriented himself. He pointed away from the portal, into the lightless depths ahead.

The framework creaked again, and Vinjo eyed the ceiling with concern. Jak hoped the orbs weren't located any deeper underwater than their current elevation. If they had to go farther down, even with Malek's magical reinforcement, the ship might be crushed by the water pressure.

Trusting him, Vinjo nodded and navigated their craft in the indicated direction.

Jak went back to check on his mother while wondering how much he should tell her and Malek. The last thing he wanted was for *them* to believe this mission was hopeless and that they were doomed.

But what if it was and they were?

14

NO FEWER THAN TEN BLACK-HULLED FLEET SHIPS FLOATED OVER THE camp, coming to a stop as the auras of the dragons faded from Rivlen's senses. She squinted at Shikari, wondering if he truly had been responsible for driving them off. Or convincing them that a threat loomed back at their fortress.

Rivlen had no reason to think the dragonling would lie to her, but she struggled to believe the equivalent of a little kid had managed to outsmart a bunch of adult dragons.

Admittedly, he'd pointed out something the dragons already knew, that the portal was powerful and could hurt them with its lightning strikes. It was likely the dragons *didn't* know that Jak, the only person who'd convinced the portal to strike—without incurring its wrath—wasn't there.

The one I do not like is here, Shikari announced.

He was in the mouth of the cave, either hiding or guarding the portal—or both.

Uthari? Rivlen guessed, not sure if the dragonling had addressed her specifically or spoken to the camp as a whole, but she doubted he had included anyone on the mageships.

That one attempted to infect me with parasites. He is evil.

He doesn't like people getting in the way of his plans.

Because he is evil. Mate of Jak, you must know this. Anyone who wishes those parasites to infest more dragons cannot be trusted. Dragons should be pristine and free of influence. He was not even infested himself when he chose to fling the parasites at me, so they cannot be blamed for his evil acts.

Rivlen shook her head, refusing to speak poorly of Uthari, especially when he had arrived and might have a way to catch her words, no matter how pinpoint she attempted to make them.

Now might be a good time for you to go for a hunt, she allowed herself to say, Jak's request that she watch out for his charge coming to mind. That dragon-steel chain was still on the hillside, and she would hate to see Uthari order someone to wrap it around Shikari. *Then he won't be able to try to infect you again.*

Would it not be cowardly for me to leave you to face him?

No. He's my... I work for him. I'll be fine.

Shikari gazed down at her from the cave mouth. Had he not realized that? Rivlen reminded herself that he was young and probably hadn't been that cognizant of things until recently.

I will go hunt.

Good. Take your time, and enjoy yourself. I assume the fleet will continue on shortly to deal with the fortress.

That is good. My clever ruse will only work if a threat to the dragons does indeed show up. If they realize nobody is coming for them...

They'll return for the portal. I know.

Shikari launched himself from the mouth of the cave, the whisper of flapping wings announcing his route. He stayed low, finding a way through the trees so that he wouldn't have to rise up above the canopy—so the crews of the mageships wouldn't see him.

They likely *noticed* him, with their senses if not their eyes, but, hopefully, they weren't here for Jak's dragon.

Rivlen eyed the mageship she sensed Uthari riding on. He was inside, but she expected him to come out on deck to speak to her eventually. Speak to or reprimand her.

It wasn't Uthari who stepped into view on deck but the zidarr Gorsith. His aura crackled around him, almost as powerful as Uthari's and Malek's, and when he gripped the railing to look down at the camp, his gaze went straight to Rivlen.

She raised her eyebrows in silent inquiry, eyeing the scar tissue at his throat. She'd seen the zidarr around Utharika and knew he was older and more experienced than Yidar had been, but she couldn't remember ever speaking with him and knew little about his personality. Until now, he'd remained back in the sky city, left behind to protect it while Uthari and the others were dealing with the portal. Given how many dragons lurked in the fortress, it wasn't surprising that Uthari had brought another powerful zidarr to help.

Who killed the dragon back at that tunnel, Captain? Gorsith waved in the direction that Rivlen had last seen the druids.

Many had a hand in that, my lord, Rivlen replied.

So, not you? Gorsith quirked an eyebrow.

I launched fire at it when a mercenary cut through its defenses with a dragon-steel weapon. Rivlen didn't mention Tezi by name, not wanting to draw attention to her. Though the dragon-steel chain lay in the camp, waiting for the blacksmith to turn it into something more useful, her axe was still a valuable weapon, one a zidarr—or king—might decide to take from her.

Not you, then.

Rivlen clenched her teeth, wishing she'd cut down the dragon's barrier with her dagger, but she'd been busy trying to keep the other dragon from crushing all the people left in the tunnel. *Not me alone, no.*

King Uthari thinks you have potential to be a great and powerful leader. Gorsith arched the single eyebrow again. *But if that were true, you would have managed to save more of our people, and you would have chosen mages over mercenaries and roamers to pull from the shipwreck.* He looked disdainfully at those in the camp behind Rivlen.

We crashed. It wasn't a matter of having a choice about who to save. Some made it to shore, and some didn't. Is there something I can do for you, my lord?

Gorsith's gaze returned to hers. *Our king does not know if he can trust you.*

He can.

He's tasked me with testing you.

Unease knotted in Rivlen's gut. *What kind of testing*?

Gorsith hopped onto the railing and jumped down, dropping thirty feet before landing in a deep crouch, no hint of magic softening his fall. He had those enhanced zidarr bones and muscles, so it was probably like hopping off a stump for him. When he straightened, he locked his eyes on Rivlen and strode toward her.

Set the dragon steel aside. Gorsith pointed at the dagger in her belt sheath.

So you can effectively use your magic on me?

Set it aside, or I will physically take it from you. He rested a hand on the sword hanging from his belt. *You know my training and that I'm capable of it.*

I do. Rivlen thought about fighting him anyway, but she was loath to lose a battle when so many witnesses—men and women she commanded—stood nearby.

Reluctantly, she drew the dagger, set it on the ground, and stepped away from it.

King Uthari has insisted you be punished for your failures of late, Gorsith told her. *Though he didn't detail them for me, I got the gist. I'm surprised he didn't task Malek with punishing you, but perhaps this is too lowly a task for him. I understand he's off on another important mission.*

Rivlen couldn't tell if Gorsith was bitter about that, about being left behind on punishment duty while the favored zidarr was sent off. Yidar would have resented it, but he'd been young and ambitious. Perhaps Gorsith, who appeared to be in his mid-thirties, was a more wholehearted devotee of the zidarr lifestyle and craved nothing except to please his master.

Did he task you *with punishing me*? Rivlen lifted her chin. For weeks, she'd been anticipating this. As much as it might hurt, it would be a relief to have it over with. *Why doesn't he come punish me himself?*

Gorsith stopped a few feet away from her, his defenses up. In case she attacked him? As if she would dare with Uthari and twelve mageships full of powerful magic users up there. Dozens of officers had come to the railing to watch, and she ground her already clenched teeth. If she deserved punishment, so be it, but she would have preferred the courtesy of having it done in private, not in front of people she might one day have to lead.

She also sensed the mercenaries and mages on the ground falling silent as they watched her and Gorsith, though neither of them had said anything aloud.

Gorsith cocked his head. *He is not himself and has said he must conserve his energy.*

Because he's infected with a parasite.

Apparently. This is not a task I relish, but I serve him and will obey. Will you fight me? He appeared indifferent to whether she would or not.

With all those mages up there to help? I'd be a fool to do so.

They will not interfere.

Do what you need to do, Lord Gorsith, and let us get this over with. Rivlen wondered how punishment was supposed to be a test. If she survived it, would she be considered worthy to continue serving Uthari? If it killed her or she ran screaming into the jungle, he would know she wasn't?

Very well.

Rivlen braced herself and couldn't keep from drawing her defenses around her. Maybe she shouldn't have put up a barrier, should have instead laid herself bare and knelt for punishment, but she couldn't bring herself to be so meek.

Gorsith only nodded, as if he'd expected nothing else. Without any other movement, he drew upon his magic to attack her barrier.

Clenching her fists, she fought him, fought to keep it up and the pain away. When she'd been a girl, she'd applied for the zidarr training, wanting to become one of them, but she'd been deemed inadequate. Not powerful enough. Not someone with enough potential. Since then, her father had barely spoken to her. She wished she could show that she was more powerful than a zidarr, but already she trembled from the effort required.

As Gorsith applied tremendous force, reminding her of the times Tonovan had ripped away her defenses, she willed every ounce of power into maintaining the barrier. Maybe this time, she would prove the stronger. Maybe *that* was the test.

But she wasn't able to hold up under Gorsith's power. Like a hurricane gale battering a straw hut on a beach, he tore away her defenses strand by strand, leaving her straining and panting as she struggled to keep him from getting all the way through, from ripping into her core.

Sweat beaded on her forehead and dripped down her spine. Hours seemed to pass, though she knew it was only seconds as Gorsith stood calmly, his hands behind his back, focused on her but not straining the way she was. Finally, he batted away the last of her defenses and drove a dagger of pain into her mind.

Her knees gave out as agony tore into her brain and spread through her entire body. She couldn't hold back her scream, a tormented cry that she feared the dragons heard all the way in their fortress.

"Stop hurting her!" Tezi called from the camp, the words barely penetrating Rivlen's awareness. The pain consuming her made it hard to focus on anything else, but she glanced in that direction and tried to raise a hand to tell her to stay out of it. The last thing she wanted was Tezi on the ground being tortured alongside her.

Several of Rivlen's mage officers were restraining Tezi, physically since their magic wouldn't work. They hadn't succeeded in taking the axe from her, but they were keeping her from lifting her arms to wield it. Others used their power to keep the mercenaries from helping Tezi—or Rivlen.

Had she not been in so much pain, Rivlen would have been touched that they wanted to help her. Her own people clearly wouldn't interfere.

Gorsith twisted the mental knife that was embedded in Rivlen's brain, creating further waves of agony. As he did so, she grew aware of another presence in her mind. Uthari. Of course he was watching.

No, he was doing more than that. He was sifting through her thoughts and memories while she was too distracted by the pain to hide anything.

When they'd spoken via the dome-jir, he hadn't been able to read her mind, but now that they were close together, he had access to everything. The feelings she'd developed for Jak, how she'd had a hunch about the kerzor but hadn't acted, how she'd taken him to bed, and how she'd failed to send powerful mages along to guard him on his way to Utharika.

If he'd escaped or killed me, it would have been your fault, Uthari spoke into her mind.

I'm sorry, Your Majesty. Rivlen panted, barely able to gather her thoughts with Gorsith continuing to torment her—obeying Uthari's wishes that he do so. *It was foolish of me to let myself care about him.*

Yes. I am afflicted with this parasite because of him and his mother. They are not loyal to our kind. That he arranged Tonovan's death should have shown you that. A wave of fury washed over her, coming from Uthari instead of Gorsith, though he hadn't stopped hurting her, and she gasped and writhed, wondering if her heart would give out under the assault.

I made a mistake. I'm sorry. I just— Rivlen wanted to beg Uthari to stop, to make *Gorsith* stop, but as much as she hurt, she couldn't bring herself to plead with him. *Give me another chance to prove myself. I'll be useful against the dragons.*

Gorsith twisted the mental knife again, and she gasped, falling onto her hands and knees. In another moment, she would be curled in a ball on the ground.

She pushed back at him, needing a moment to breathe, to think. She needed to be coherent to deal with Uthari, not in so much damn pain. With a blast of her own fury, she drew on all her reserves, imagining Jak there funneling more power into her, and managed to knock Gorsith back a step. For a blissful moment, the pain went away, but he only scowled and reasserted himself, using more power than ever to press her to the ground and make her vulnerable for Uthari.

You do have potential, Uthari said, surprisingly sounding the faintest bit pleased by her defiance, her brief success against Gorsith. *It wasn't that lack that kept me from choosing you to become a zidarr. It was that all of my other zidarr were male, and I was well aware how distracting a female can be to young men. And even some older men.* An image of Malek popped into her mind. *Should you help me defeat the dragons, I'll inform your father thus, that it wasn't a lack on your part. And if you choose to be loyal to me over your boy lover, I'll reward you even further.*

Gorsith was reapplying himself assiduously, finding new ways to hurt her, and Rivlen struggled to form words in her mind.

This is the test, Captain, Uthari continued. *Not if you can survive punishment—of that I have no doubt—but if it will make you resentful or if you agree that you were wrong and that you wish to go forward as my loyal officer, someone I can trust fully.*

I do, Your Majesty. I've always wanted that. I just... She'd *also* wanted Jak, someone who supported her unconditionally and believed in her. Why couldn't she have both?

Though she hadn't shared the thought telepathically, Uthari saw it anyway. *Because he is a traitor to his talents and what he had the potential to be. You must choose. Loyalty to your king and your people and your* family, *or to a scheming boy?*

Rivlen could feel him peering into her mind, examining her like a specimen on one of Jadora's slides. She couldn't help but wonder if he was implying that her family would be in danger if she chose incorrectly. Her father was powerful and could take care of himself, but her mother...

I choose you, Your Majesty, she whispered into his mind with a silent apology to Jak, wherever he was.

Good. Gorsith will finish your punishment, and then you will report to me.

Dear Shylezar, it wasn't over yet? How much would she have to endure? Hours? Days?

Yes, Your Majesty, she made herself say.

A splash of water against her back startled her. The pain halted abruptly.

"Stop hurting her," Tezi said, this time from right behind Rivlen.

She growled at Gorsith, her axe raised, as if to strike him. Tinder and Sasko crouched beside her with swords and empty canteens—they must have tried to startle Gorsith by flinging water at him.

Puzzled, Rivlen glanced back. Several of the mercenaries had been knocked to the ground, but the druid kid Grunk was distracting the mages who'd earlier gripped Tezi. He darted in and out, slashing at them with a blue-black blade.

Where had he gotten—

Damn it, that was *her* dragon-steel dagger. Or at least the one she'd been carrying since taking it from Tonovan's cabin. Grunk had picked it up from the ground while she'd been distracted.

"If you attack me," Gorsith said calmly, eyeing Tezi and ignoring Sasko and Tinder completely, "it will be the last action you ever take."

"We all need to work together to deal with the dragons," Tezi said, her eyes blazing fearlessly as she stared at him, "not waste our time and power attacking each other. You two are on the same *side*."

"She is being punished, per our king's orders," Gorsith said, "not attacked."

"Well, knock it off."

Gorsith's eyes narrowed, and he crouched, prepared to spring at Tezi. With a zidarr's extensive weapons training, he wouldn't need magic to defeat her.

That is enough punishment, Uthari's voice rang in Rivlen's mind. He must have spoken to Gorsith as well, for the zidarr straightened instead of lunging at Tezi. *Captain Rivlen, you will report to me so that we can further discuss the matter.*

Rivlen kept from grimacing—barely. What if *discuss the matter* was another way to say that he would punish her or *test* her further?

With her body hurting all over, and the worst headache she'd ever had pulsing in her skull, she didn't know if she could survive more of that. Nor did she want to be questioned further about Jak. She already felt like she'd betrayed him by choosing Uthari and her career—and her family—over him. Jak would understand, but knowing that only made it worse.

And someone get that dagger from that crazy druid, Uthari added.

Grunk continued to dart in and out among the mages, keeping them busy, and he'd landed a couple of slashes with the blade. Two officers gripped bleeding cuts on their arms as they glowered at the kid.

Yes, Your Majesty. I'll do it. Rivlen shouldn't have let him get the dagger in the first place.

With her entire body trembling in the aftermath of the punishment—the torture—she struggled to rise. Sasko and Tezi, keeping an eye on Gorsith, offered her a hand up and support when she swayed. Once again, Rivlen observed that the mercenaries were willing to help her when her own people weren't.

Maybe she'd brought that upon herself. Her officers might not know all the details, but they knew that if she was being punished, it was because she'd gone astray somewhere.

Tezi remained facing Gorsith, her axe in her hands, while Sasko helped Rivlen toward the camp.

Return the dagger to me, Rivlen spoke into Grunk's mind.

He paused and looked at her, though he kept glancing warily at the mages he'd been skirmishing with. They looked like they would spring at him as soon as he relinquished the dragon-steel weapon.

I'll keep them from retaliating, she added, though she wondered if she could with Gorsith looking on.

He might join in with the mages in attacking the kid, and he'd already proven he was more powerful than she. She twisted her mouth bitterly, tired of having to deal with people who fell into that category.

Promise? Grunk crouched, one hand guarding the dagger, and met her eyes.

Did she? Could she?

I'll do my best.

His face scrunched up skeptically.

"Please give it back to her, Grunk," Tezi said. "I'm sure she appreciates you helping us, but it's hers."

Rivlen didn't comment on any appreciation she might or might not feel. With Gorsith and so many mages watching, she dared not suggest that she liked the mercenaries coming to her aid against them.

Tezi's words swayed Grunk where Rivlen's hadn't. He shook his head, as if he was sure it was a bad idea, but he came forward and offered the hilt of the dagger to Rivlen.

"Thank you," she said.

No sooner had Grunk stepped back and out of reach than five mages, including the two he'd cut, attacked him with magic.

"Stop them," Tezi blurted, rushing forward with her axe.

Furious, Rivlen lashed out at the mages with a mental attack.

You will not make a liar out of me, she said, dredging up more power than she'd thought she had left to push them back.

With the comforting dragon-steel dagger in her hand again, her magic flowed out of her with great force. Maybe it was born from frustration that she hadn't been able to best Gorsith. Either way, it sent the mages stumbling back before Tezi reached them.

Rivlen looked back at Gorsith, half-expecting him to intervene, but he'd already jumped back up to the mageship and stood on the deck next to Uthari. She'd been distracted and hadn't sensed their king coming out. Wincing, she stopped her attack, wary about what he would say.

Usually, his face was calm, even when he was delivering threats or punishing a person, but he gazed down at her with a hint of madness in his eyes, something that reminded her of Grunk. When he chuckled into her mind, it only made her warier. She couldn't remember ever hearing him laugh, and Gorsith's words returned to her mind:

He is not himself.

When Uthari eyed her up and down, his gaze lingering on her

chest, the interest from him was so unfamiliar that it alarmed her far more than Gorsith's comment had. Rivlen swallowed. What had Uthari been doing these past couple of days that had convinced his zidarr that he wasn't himself?

You do have power and the potential to learn to harness more, don't you? Uthari purred into her mind. *It would be a shame to do away with you.*

I think so, Your Majesty, she made herself reply neutrally, though his interest continued to worry her.

Come to my suite, Captain. Uthari smiled before turning to walk away from the railing. *As I said, we will discuss this further.*

15

In his cabin, Malek used a damp cloth to wipe the sweat from Jadora's brow and wished he could do more for her. He'd laid her on his bunk, and he sat on the edge, focusing on keeping a barrier around the ship to protect it from water pressure while waiting for her to stir—and wondering what he would do if she didn't.

An hour had passed since she'd summoned a tremendous amount of power to kill the entity that threatened them. Drawing upon so much of one's energy was exhausting, but he doubted that was the reason she'd fainted. It had to do with that damn parasite. Even as she lay immobile, breathing shallowly, the gray was advancing across her skin.

The parasite didn't kill the dragons, so Malek was hopeful that she would wake soon. Maybe her body would grow accustomed to the intruders, and the fever would release her. But it was possible it affected humans differently, and she would suffer a different fate. What if, in her, the parasite was fatal?

Malek closed his eyes, aware of moisture forming in them. He couldn't remember the last time he'd cried, but it might have been when he'd been a boy, when his mother had died. Since then, he hadn't cared about anyone this much.

As a zidarr, he'd always been taught to distance himself, not to grow too attached to others, lest he be swayed by them and make poor decisions. When colleagues had died, he'd regretted it, but it hadn't devastated him. Not the way Jadora's death would.

He'd only recently allowed himself to accept that he loved her. They'd only been together a few times. And now he might lose her. Because Uthari had been attempting to infest Shikari to manipulate—to *control*—Jak.

At the time, Malek had kept his calm, as he'd always been trained to do. He'd gone straight to thinking about rational solutions to the new problem, and he hadn't allowed himself to blame Uthari, Jak, himself, or anyone else for making choices that had led to these events. But now...

As he held Jadora's limp hand, it was hard for him not to resent the people who had caused this. He almost regretted that he'd ever found Jak and Jadora on that beach in the Dragon Perch Islands and captured them and the portal. But if he hadn't, he wouldn't have come to know her. And she was worth knowing.

He brushed her pocket, knowing it held the syringe that she'd intended to use to take a fresh sample of his blood. Not surprisingly, a few empty vials also clinked at his touch, as if she'd thought there would be an opportunity to slip out of the ship and take samples of the thing that had attacked them—she'd probably been aching to do that—and who knew what else.

A lump formed in his throat as he imagined how disappointed her soul would be if she didn't get an opportunity to take those final samples and study them before passing.

If he took a sample of his own blood, would he know what to look for under the microscope? More than once, he'd seen her making drawings and notes. Would perusing them be enough to teach him what to seek?

Malek sensed Jak's approach but didn't stir until he knocked on the door. Though Malek would have preferred not to speak or interact with anyone, Jadora was his mother, and Jak had every right to see her.

Come, Malek said silently as he used one hand to wipe the moisture from his eyes.

Jak stepped inside, his usually amiable and even goofy face so grave that he appeared ten years older than usual.

"Is she awake yet?" he whispered.

Yet, he'd said. As if he was sure she would waken. Malek wished he were, but her breathing was so faint.

"Not yet."

"Oh." Jak bit his lip as he looked at her, his gaze lingering on a gray splotch on her forehead. "I think we're going to need her help."

"I have no doubt." Malek could sense magic in the sea all around them, including more of the entities that had tried to ensnare them. None of the creatures—or their auras—were familiar. They all felt alien and dangerous.

He wondered if dragon-steel weapons or tools had been dumped in this sea long ago and had passed their magic along to the creatures that dwelled in the water. Or maybe dragon steel had been in the city where the orbs were, and when it had flooded, some of the material had been left behind.

"Can you heal her?" Jak turned hopeful eyes toward Malek.

"As far as I can tell, the only thing wrong with her is that the parasite is increasing its numbers within her body, and you know we're all incapable of healing that."

"Yeah," Jak whispered. "But why... It doesn't knock out the dragons."

"We don't know what happens when they're first infested. Perhaps it does render them unconscious while it takes over their bodies, and when they wake again, they're not themselves." Malek shook his head at the thought that Jadora might wake a madwoman with no interest in helping them.

"Not themselves," Jak mouthed, fresh horror filling his eyes. "But we *need* Mother. And we need her to be herself."

"I know, Jak." Malek groped for something to say to the boy—the young man—who'd become his apprentice and more. Some comfort he could give. "She had some ideas the last time I talked to her. We'll continue her research even if she's not able to help us, and we'll find a solution—a cure for her as well as the dragons."

Jak looked at him, a hint of hope returning, replacing some of the horror on his face. He trusted Malek and wanted to believe him.

Malek hoped he was worthy of that trust—and that he was right.

A faint moan came from Jadora. Malek looked intently at her, sensing her rousing, and Jak stepped forward.

"Mother? Are you all right?"

Malek, she spoke into his mind, a hand flexing, coming to rest on his thigh. *You're with me.*

Yes, he replied silently, though her telepathic voice sounded off. Her fingers flexed on his thigh, bringing to mind their earlier interlude in the navigation cabin. Or was *she* bringing that to his mind? A lusty chuckle sounded in his thoughts, and her eyes opened to slits. A smile curved her lips as she watched him through her lashes.

Malek swallowed. He'd expected her to waken weak and wan, not thinking about sex. Was this her? Or the parasite?

Her smile grew wider and her hand slid higher.

"Jak," Malek said, not wanting him to see anything that would disturb him. "There's what feels like some threatening magic ahead of us. Will you go to navigation and see if Vinjo needs help?"

"Uhm, yes, but is Mother all right?" Jak must have noticed the smile, and how out of place it was on her, for he gave her a strange look. "I want to make sure she doesn't need anything."

"She's going to take a sample of my blood to study. She's fine." Malek worried she *wasn't* fine and hated to lie to Jak, but he also felt the urge to protect him, to keep him from seeing his mother become something... other than herself. "Vinjo needs help."

"I don't sense any new magic right ahead of us."

"You will."

Jak hesitated.

Malek made his face stern. "Go. I don't have to tell you all that we're up against."

"No," Jak whispered. "You don't. Did you hear the portal?"

"I heard enough."

"You know we might not be able to leave?"

"We'll figure something out." Malek had to believe they could. He used his power to nudge Jak toward the door.

At first, Jak resisted, but, after another uncertain glance toward Jadora, he stepped out.

With a flick of his power, Malek closed and locked the door.

"Perfect," Jadora whispered as she watched him. She hadn't once looked toward Jak. Her fevered eyes were locked on Malek. She shifted her hips and her shoulders on the bunk, the movements drawing his attention to her body. "We want to join with you."

He caught her hand, grasping it gently, and stopped her from taking more than his thigh in her grip. "*We*?"

"You're not as powerful as a dragon, but you're a strong human. We want you." Jadora sat up, wrapping her free arm around his shoulders and leaning into him, pressing her breasts against his chest.

Fear for her and what she was becoming stole any lust that might have blossomed in him, but he also didn't want to shove her back and risk hurting her. Jadora was still in there somewhere; he was positive.

"It was a mistake before," he said quietly, "and it would doubly be one now."

Uneasy, Malek realized he might not have been making love to Jadora earlier, not fully, but to the parasite within her that wanted to spread, to infest more people. Not random people, apparently, but powerful ones.

"Before, we failed, but this time we won't," she whispered, her lips close to his. "We'll have you. You'll join us."

"If it didn't work before, it's not going to work this time." Malek hoped he was right.

He leaned back as he lifted his hands, intending to extricate himself from her grip, but power surged out of her, locking him in place. He was so startled that he almost didn't get his defenses up. She'd never used her new power against him, and he'd never believed she would.

But this wasn't Jadora. She might be in there, but the parasite had taken over. That scared him. A lot.

Her power tightened around him, pressing against his barrier, diminishing it as few human beings had ever been able to do before. Unlike all the others he'd faced, she didn't want to best him in battle. She wanted to kiss him, to give that parasite another chance to infest him.

Malek shook from the effort of keeping her back, his muscles taut as her lips inched closer, parting.

"Jadora," he whispered, hoping some part of her remained. How would they finish this mission without her? How would they *save* her without her help? "Don't do this. Don't fight me."

Don't *overpower* me, he almost said, but should he admit to the thing inside her that she was strong enough to do so? Maybe it didn't matter. Maybe it already knew.

The ship creaked, and an alarming *snap-hiss* came from the

engine compartment. A muffled curse sounded through the door —Vinjo.

Malek had lost his concentration—no, he'd been forced to focus on defending himself against the parasite—and stopped reinforcing the ship's hull.

"Jadora," he tried again, though he was on the verge of leaping off the bunk and away from her. But they were in a ship sailing along the bottom of a sea and surrounded by water. Where could he go that she couldn't follow? "Please, Jadora. I love you. Stay with me."

Something sparked in her eyes. Recognition? Awareness?

Whatever it was didn't stop her from pressing her lips to his. A harsh blast of power ripped away his defensive barrier, making him wince in pain and leaving nothing between them.

Bleakly, Malek closed his eyes, wondering if he should give in. Maybe the parasite would fail once more to infest him. Maybe that would prove Jadora's hypothesis.

A tingle against his lips startled him, and he jerked back. Surprisingly, he could. Jadora's grip had lessened, and their lips parted a few inches before her magic tightened around him again, holding him in place.

He could see her eyes and a furrow to her brow, and he sensed her fighting herself. No, fighting *it*. The parasite.

Motes of light wafted up from his mouth and around his face. He sprang up, this time escaping her, leaping completely away from the bunk and skittering back until his shoulder blades hit the wall.

The motes lingered, floating in the air in front of her. Another tingle made Malek touch his lips, and one floated up before his eyes.

He spat and blew, trying to get any motes that might remain out of his mouth. Fear coursed through his veins along with the realization that he might not have escaped this time.

If he turned into what Jadora was turning into, Jak and Vinjo would be on their own to complete the mission. Or, worse, Malek and Jadora would be compelled to infest them as well. Then there would be nobody left to visit the Orbs of Wisdom and find a solution.

"Malek," Jadora rasped, her face contorted with distress. "I'm sorry. I—we—no, *I,* damn it."

She gasped and pressed the heels of her palms to her temples, then pitched forward.

Malek surged to the bunk and caught her before she could tumble to the deck.

I'm sorry, she whispered into his mind, pressing her face into his shoulder.

*Are you... * you *now?* Malek held her, but he couldn't keep from watching her warily, afraid more motes would float out of her and into him. But maybe it didn't matter. Maybe they had already succeeded.

Yes, but I can feel them... here. Growing within me. Growing more powerful and trying to take control of my body. When they rose up, I wasn't strong enough to stop them. All that power Zelonsera gave me, and I couldn't stop them. All it meant was that they had access to it too.

Malek was sure it hadn't been the dragon's intent, but she'd effectively turned Jadora into a weapon. A weapon so powerful that even he couldn't overpower her.

Her face twisted in a grimace, as if she was still fighting for control. She probably was. A shudder went through her, and she slumped against him again.

Now I wish I hadn't contemplated that they could be transmitted through sex. Jadora winced and looked apologetically at him.

From what I've seen, they can float over to new hosts at will. Maybe they just like sex.

She snorted. *I doubt it. Sex isn't how parasites reproduce.*

Maybe they like exerting control over their hosts.

That does seem plausible. It's also possible they find it easier to assert their control when their host is distracted by... carnal pleasures. Jadora dropped a shaking hand to her pocket and withdrew her syringe. *Do you mind if we test you while I'm still... somewhat capable of retaining control part of the time?*

We can, but it sounded like the parasites were trying again because they didn't think they succeeded in infesting me last time.

I doubt they're omniscient. We'll check with the microscope.

Now I know *it's you.* Malek rose to his feet and pulled her up. *You want to take samples and examine them.*

As any good scientist would.

He helped her across the corridor toward her laboratory, and Jak and Vinjo peered back through the open door from their seats in navigation.

Jadora winced again but forced a smile and lifted a shaky hand toward her son. Jak wore a worried expression, but he also lifted a hand.

As Malek led Jadora into her lab, he heard Vinjo talking about making a magical device to clean the carbon dioxide from the air so it would be breathable for longer, and saying he could only do it if Jak took over reinforcing the hull.

The number of problems they had to deal with daunted Malek, especially since none of them could be addressed by his sword and main-gauche. He did, however, return his concentration to the hull of the ship, pouring magic into it once more to strengthen it. A weariness seeped into him, the byproduct of using his power continuously on that as well as exerting so much abruptly to try—and fail—to fight off Jadora.

"Sleeve up, please," she said.

Malek almost made a joke about how much more polite she was when she was the one in control of her body, but it would only make her cringe. He also worried that she would lose control again at any moment, so he didn't want to delay.

He shoved his sleeve above his elbow, remembering his own struggle to fight for control against the death-darter bacteria. It hadn't urged him to have sex—though he did recall that crossing his mind once when he'd been close to Jadora. Mostly, it had wanted him to kill everyone.

Jadora's hands trembled as she lifted the needle to his arm, and she paused to close her eyes and take a deep breath.

Malek rested a hand on her shoulder. He doubted power would help her fight the parasite, but he let some of his trickle into her and willed her to feel calm and have the mental strength she needed to retain control.

She took another deep breath. "Thank you."

With steadier hands, she slipped the needle into his vein and drew a blood sample.

"You're welcome." He left his hand on her shoulder as she turned and prepared the slide.

Malek? Jak asked from navigation.

Yes?

I think we're going to need your help with this. We're getting close to that magic you sensed, and I'm worried it's going to be a problem.

Malek had been making up that supposed magic to get Jak to leave, but he wasn't surprised that another threat was out there, something to delay them further and stand between them and the orbs. He stretched out ahead of the ship with his senses and detected… something. A wall? A net?

It was more above them than directly in their path, at least for now, but it stretched for miles.

I'll be there shortly, he said.

Jadora eased her new slide under the microscope and looked. Malek rubbed his lips, the tingle of the motes fresh in his mind. If they'd entered his body, they couldn't have already spread into his blood, he was sure, but it was possible the parasite had been wrong and that it had happened during their earlier joining. What would he do if they'd both been infested?

"I don't see any sign of them," Jadora said, slumping against Malek. "I'll check again later, in case that kiss allowed them a second chance that succeeded, but this is encouraging."

"Yes," he agreed.

"I've been thinking about that protein from the death-darter bacteria. At first, nothing happened, and the parasites never engaged with it in my dish, but… after several hours, they *did* move away from it. It might mean nothing, but…"

Malek raised his eyebrows, encouraged and glad she was still working on their problem. "It might mean they don't like it?"

"Or what it represents, yes." Jadora eyed her backpack on the counter. "If I infect myself with the bacteria—"

"*What?*" Malek gripped her shoulder. "No."

"If we're right, and the protein they left behind is the reason you're now unpalatable to the dragon parasite, then it could be the answer. The parasite could see the protein and believe it means the bacteria are still present. And the two could be natural enemies. Maybe the death-darter bacteria are the stronger of the two, and, once they spread in my body, they'll drive out the dragon parasite."

"Even if that's true, which we don't know if it is, then you'd have *two* terrible things in your body. Having to deal with both could *kill* you. Even if it didn't, you saw what the death-darter bacteria did to me. With the power you now have, you'd be extremely dangerous if you lost your mind and became aggressive. I wouldn't be able to stop you."

"You could sedate me, the same as I did you. Besides, thanks to the power Zelonsera gave me, I know how to and am capable of destroying the death-darter bacteria." Jadora frowned. "But I'd have to wait for a while, I think. It would need to have time to spread in my body and battle the dragon parasite."

"You might not survive that battle."

"If that's true and I die, take samples of my blood, and see which microscopic invader came out on top. I'll leave notes in my journal for you." She reached for her backpack.

"*Jadora*." Malek pressed her hand down to the counter. "At least wait until we're back on our world. We need you here, the knowledge in your head and... We just need you. *I* need you."

"Malek." She met his gaze solemnly. "If I wait, it may be too late. It may *already* be too late. The parasite has a strong foothold." She grimaced. "As you saw."

"Jadora..." He closed his eyes and leaned his forehead against hers.

"I have to do this, Malek. We can't wait. For many reasons. Remember that Uthari is infested too. Right now, he could be spreading it among his fleet."

Malek swore to himself. He hadn't forgotten that Uthari was infested, but he hadn't considered that he might feel compelled to spread it. The thought of him growing sexually aggressive and the parasite prompting him to command all his female officers into his cabin made Malek wince. Hopefully, it wouldn't manifest itself the same way inside him, but... what if it did? Uthari was old, but not too old for such relations. With the parasite guiding him, it might not have mattered even if he was.

Jadora grasped her backpack and pulled it over.

Though Malek wanted to stop her, he didn't. She was right, and if this worked, if the death-darter bacteria could kill the dragon parasite, then she could kill the bacteria afterward. As long as she was still cognizant and capable.

"Wait," he said as she pulled out the glass dishes that held the bacteria. "Can you give me the knowledge of how to kill the death-darter bacteria? Share what Zelonsera shared? In case you're not able to cure yourself?"

Jadora nodded. "That's a good idea. Yes, I should be able to, and here." She opened a drawer to show him four syringes of a clear fluid. "These are the same sedative that I gave to you and the others back on Nargnoth. Not knowing how the parasite would affect me, I prepared amounts suitable for my body mass. When you need to use them, they're here."

Though he didn't want to agree to that—to any of this—Malek made himself nod. "Very well."

"I'm tempted to sedate myself as soon as I inject the death-darter bacteria and let them fight it out in my unconscious body, but..." Jadora frowned over her shoulder in the direction the ship was sailing.

In the direction it *had* been sailing. It had slowed down, and Malek sensed they were close to the magical net.

"You may need my power and Zelonsera's knowledge to reach the orbs," she said.

"I agree." Malek almost mentioned what the portal had said to Jak and that he'd also caught, that the orbs might have been destroyed by another of those vine entities, but she had enough to worry about. "I need to help them with whatever is out there."

"I understand. I'll inject myself, then keep studying." She smiled wanly at him. "Check back on me now and then, will you?"

"I'll check on you *often*."

"And will you do me a favor? Don't tell Jak unless it becomes absolutely necessary. I don't want him to worry."

Malek hesitated, not wanting to make that promise. If something happened to her, Jak would want to know.

"There's nothing he could do," she added, then lowered her voice to a whisper. "And I don't want to risk infesting him. Or having him see me like this." She touched the rough gray splotch on her forehead with fingers that were now equally gray. The spots were growing larger.

Malek sighed and clasped her hands. "Let me know if you need anything or start to feel yourself losing the battle." He was tempted to kiss her on the cheek, but she stiffened and grimaced, having to summon all of her strength to keep the parasite from rising up and taking over again.

He sensed her fighting it and again tried to help, to send calming energy into her, power if she wished to draw upon it.

"I'm fine," she whispered, drawing a shuddering breath and gaining control. "Here."

Jadora poured knowledge into his mind, the intricacies of how she'd destroyed the death-darter bacteria. It hadn't been through brute force but through dragon magic unfamiliar to Malek, something he didn't know if he could replicate. That worried him, but he didn't want to share that worry with her. He knew she wouldn't change her course of action even if he told her.

"But you'd better leave." Jadora stepped away from him. "I'm still attracted to you and stirred by your touch, and when I feel that way, I think that's when the parasite sees an opportunity and tries to take over."

"I understand," he said.

Though Malek didn't want to leave her, he did, heading for the door. He gave her one last long look over his shoulder as she prepared a syringe of the bacteria to inject herself.

16

Rivlen stood outside the door to the suite Uthari had claimed on the *Soaring Eagle*. She'd dried herself after the mercenaries had hit her with water—she knew they'd *meant* to hit Gorsith—but she felt grimy and rumpled after the chaos of the past week.

Not that Uthari had seemed to mind. The contemplative look he'd given her had been disturbing.

It was hard to imagine the white-haired wizard, a man reputed to be three hundred years old, having sexual urges, especially when he'd never before looked at her any differently than he had any of his men, but she didn't think she'd misinterpreted his expression. She hoped that as soon as they had their chat, Uthari and his fleet would continue south to deal with the dragons, and she wouldn't see him again until the war was over, and he'd been cured of his parasitic infection.

Steeling herself, including muscles still wrung out after her punishment, Rivlen lifted a hand to knock, though she knew full well Uthari was aware that she was there.

Come in, Captain.

She tried to decide if he sounded more professional than when he'd been purring into her mind about her power. Unable to tell, she braced herself to expect anything.

Yes, Your Majesty, she replied as the door swung open on a whisper of Uthari's power.

The suite on the *Soaring Eagle* wasn't as large or posh as his quarters on his personal yacht, but she wasn't surprised that he'd chosen a more heavily armed and armored vessel to ride upon. He wasn't heading off for a state dinner in another kingdom but to lead an attack on the dragon fortress.

Uthari was lounging in a reclining chair beside a porthole in an outer room, a stack of extremely old books on a table next to him, the pages yellowed, the weathered covers falling apart. A door was open to an inner room that held a large bed. The covers were turned back, as if he was preparing to visit it soon. It *was* the middle of the night.

Uthari, however, did not appear tired as his gaze locked on to her. His pale blue eyes glinted oddly in the illumination of the lamps around the room, and a smile curved his lips as she walked in.

"I was impressed with how well you took your punishment," he said.

Not sure how to respond to that, Rivlen stopped several paces from him, clasped her hands behind her back, and stood ramrod straight. She wanted to look like a fleet officer to him, a professional mage and fighter, and nothing more. No different from the rest of the officers in his fleet.

"I'm aware of your power, of course—your aura—but it's been some time since I've seen you in battle. I would hope you'd be as quick to defend me as that scruffy druid boy, should five mages—or five dragons—leap upon me."

"Of course, Your Majesty. And I only defended him because I told him I would if he gave me the dagger back. When Gorsith ordered me to set it down, I didn't expect someone to spring forward and grab it." Worried Uthari would think her a fool for having let the druid get it in the first place, Rivlen wanted to make it clear that she never would have let it out of her grip if the zidarr hadn't ordered her to.

"No? It's a fine weapon. An *effective* weapon against those with power. Though I have acquired a dragon-steel blade of my own—" he waved toward the bedroom, "—I contemplated having one of my guards take yours from you before allowing you in to see me."

It took Rivlen a moment to realize what he was implying. "I'm not an assassin, Your Majesty. I'm loyal to you."

Did she need to offer to let him into her mind again? Hadn't he seen everything when Gorsith had torn away her mental defenses and he'd been raking through her thoughts?

Or... was it *because* of something he'd seen in there that he doubted her? Her feelings toward Jak? She'd tried to quash them, to vow that he wouldn't deter her from her duty and her loyalty to her superiors, but maybe she hadn't fully succeeded. Maybe on some subconscious level, she felt loyal to Jak.

Still, with the dagger back on her person, Rivlen shouldn't have to worry about Uthari reading her thoughts now. Unless her face gave something away.

Uthari rose from his chair, agile for such an old man, and walked toward her. A patch of skin at his temple was discolored, a gray that was familiar but that Rivlen couldn't quite place. Had he received some wound that had turned his skin that color?

He came close to her, pausing only when his chest was less than a foot from hers, and Rivlen had to fight the urge to skitter back.

"Some people resent being punished," Uthari said quietly.

"I know I've made mistakes and deserved it."

Uthari lifted a hand to the side of her head, and she again had to fight the urge to spring away. If she was going to be loyal to him, she had to trust him, or at least not let him believe she doubted him and his intentions.

"*Hyslar wis il ee forsarik,*" he whispered, gazing into her eyes.

She'd never heard the words before and didn't know what language they came from, but power emanated from Uthari and seemingly from the words as well. It was as if they were tangible and hung in the air around her head, glowing with magic. Gooseflesh rose on her arms as the cabin grew colder.

"Your thoughts are my thoughts," he whispered, smiling.

"How?" she breathed, though she could feel him in her mind even as his fingers threaded into her hair, his nails against her scalp.

His grip wasn't painful, and she barely noticed it, being far more concerned by his mental presence. Why wasn't the dragon steel keeping his magic from working on her?

With ancient knowledge, I command it, Uthari said, switching to telepathy. *As I learned, attempting to command the portal is dangerous, but the weapons are not infused with the souls of ancient dragons. They have no intelligence to resist compulsions.*

"I see."

You are much more attractive than Gorsith.

Rivlen had no idea what to say to that and didn't want to voice an agreement.

These past few days, I find myself aware of things I'd forgotten or become indifferent to over the years. Uthari shifted his fingers against her scalp, rubbing them through her hair.

A jolt of fear went through her. When Tonovan had died, she'd thought she was done suffering at the hands of superior officers with greater power than she. But if Uthari decided he wanted her, what could she do to stop him? Especially if he could nullify the power of the dragon steel.

I've never shared in his perversions, Uthari said dryly, *and I'd like to think I wouldn't have to force a woman into my bed.* Power trickled from his fingers, magic that curled through her body, promising greater pleasure. *Surely, you'd be intrigued to spend time with someone so experienced, not a boy who can barely find his own equipment.*

"Your Majesty." Rivlen cleared her throat and stepped back even as she anticipated him using his magic to stop her.

For a second, he did, fingers tightening as his power wrapped around her, but he winced and stopped himself. She stepped back, and he let her, his hand falling from her head.

Her heart pounded against her rib cage as she watched his face, afraid he would come after her.

"It's getting harder to resist," he whispered, looking past her shoulder.

"It?"

"*Them.*" Uthari waved at his body with a jerky motion.

Abruptly, Rivlen realized where she'd seen that shade of gray before. She stared at his temple in horror. It was the same color that marked the scales of the brown-and-gray dragons.

Would *all* of him turn that color? Was the same thing happening to Jadora?

"I've been one of the most powerful beings in the world for a long time," Uthari whispered, still looking past her, focusing on the wall instead of her. "Then the dragons came. It was understandable, although not desirable, that they would have more power than a human, no matter how long-lived and experienced, but now... *this.*" He curled his lip as he gestured at his own body again. "Minuscule, microscopic *nothings*, and yet they are magical, and as they advance, their population growing larger and larger within me, I can do nothing to stop them. I've tried using my power, my vast and great power, to destroy them, and I *can't.*"

Finally, he met her gaze again, and such anguish wrenched his face and haunted his eyes that it prompted sympathy from her. Before she remembered that he'd ordered her punished and scraped through her mind, Rivlen caught herself resting a hand on his shoulder. She wasn't the most maternal person, and hardly knew how to comfort others, but she said, "I'm sorry. I'm sure it's awful."

"Don't come too close, Captain," he whispered, though he gripped her hand, and he'd been the one touching her a moment before. "I think they want to spread. I think that's why they've woken within me urges I'd almost forgotten. They've made me crave things that haven't ruled my mind in ages."

Concerned at his talk of the parasite *spreading*, Rivlen pulled her hand from his grasp.

He allowed it, though he chuckled, that hint of madness in his eyes again. "I want you to come with me, Captain."

"Your Majesty?" she blurted.

"You understand the ramifications. I see that in your mind. Gorsith is a good zidarr, but he's not the swiftest. I want you to come along to battle the dragons and destroy their fortress and save the world from that which we've allowed to enter. Which *I've* allowed to enter." His lips twisted with displeasure.

Rivlen licked her lips. Going with him was the *last* thing she wanted, especially if he was losing his mind and body to some parasite that wanted to spread through sex.

"You'll protect others from me and me from myself. You know what must be done, and you'll stand at my side as we do it."

Rivlen kept herself from shaking her head but barely. "I promised Lord Malek that I would defend the portal, Your Majesty. Make sure neither the dragons nor druids take it, so he and the others can get back after they finish their mission. You gave them that mission; you must want them to finish it."

"I do, and they will. I have faith in Malek."

"But if the druids or the dragons get the portal—"

"They won't. I'll send Gorsith down to lead the mages and protect it, and you'll go into battle at my side."

"But Malek said—"

"Gorsith is more than your equal. He'll be as able as you to defend the portal and keep the way open for Malek."

"I know he's more powerful than me, Your Majesty." Rivlen couldn't keep her words from coming out sounding stiff, even though she accepted that he spoke the truth. "That's why he should go into battle with you at the fortress."

"*You* will go into battle at my side, Xeva Rivlen." Uthari held her gaze, power crackling in the air around him and spreading to embrace her.

As unappealing a lover as a three-hundred-year-old man would be, she couldn't help but be aware of his aura, of the way his power tantalized her. It wasn't anything that would send her springing to wrap her arms around him, especially with her new awareness of what the parasite wanted, but it was intriguing.

"And I will reward you," he added, not blinking at all as he watched her. "I'll show you how to use your power more effectively and to draw upon even more, all of that which is within you." He looked at her chest again and started to smile—a lascivious smile—but caught himself, shook his head, and stepped back.

"You're going mad, Your Majesty," she whispered.

"I'm aware. Gorsith is concerned, but he didn't say anything. You, I think, will. I need that. Resisting them will only grow more difficult."

And what was she supposed to do when it reached the point that he *couldn't* resist them any longer? That seemed inevitable. What would he become when he was fully their minion?

"Let us hope a solution is found before we learn that," Uthari whispered, a reminder that he could still read her thoughts. "In the meantime, I will reward you, as I promised. As we fly to the fortress, I'll teach you. And... I'll lend you this."

He turned to walk into the bedroom. Having him move away and take his gaze from her was a relief, as she could feel the spell over her diminishing, but she worried what *this* was waiting for her in his bedroom. What if he slid under the covers and used magic she couldn't resist to compel her to join him?

But he went to a trunk instead of the bed, pushing back the lid, and she sensed another dragon-steel artifact. Maybe the blade he'd mentioned? It wasn't the only dragon steel she sensed in the bedroom—maybe he had some of those ingots that Malek had brought back from Vran—but it had a substantial aura.

He returned with a sword in hand, the blue-black blade unmistakable.

"It's magnificent, isn't it?" he asked.

"Yes, Your Majesty. Where did you get it?"

"Let's just say that I'm learning who my allies are and who my *enemies* are during all this madness." His eyes glinted again, promising the madness was within him as much as it was without. "When I asked other rulers for troops and ships to take to the fortress, King Darekar sent one of his zidarr instead. He wielded two identical swords and attempted to assassinate me during the night. But the zidarr found that my power has not diminished over the years, and I'm a light sleeper." Uthari smiled. "I sent the other sword with Malek. This one, however, needs an appropriate wielder."

Uthari held out the blade, the dark metal absorbing the lantern light instead of reflecting it. He squinted at her, as if he'd forgotten that he'd already searched her thoughts and found no signs of duplicity.

By all the ancient gods, he truly was losing it.

Uthari chuckled. "Yes, you will help keep me in line, Captain. I am certain of it." His eyes blazed with triumph, as if he'd won a prize.

Having no idea how to respond to that, Rivlen asked, "Why do you think King Darekar wouldn't help and picked a fight instead?

All the rulers should know what's at stake by now. The dragons have been wreaking havoc on every continent."

"They have, and the other rulers well know the danger, but they want to see me fail." Uthari lifted his chin. "They resent me for my power, for having acquired the portal, and for all that I am."

Rivlen didn't mention that the mysterious death of Queen Vorsha, while she'd been a guest in his bed, might not have endeared anyone to him either. He must have seen the thought in her mind, for he chuckled again.

"Those who do not help me will not be rewarded in the end, but those who do..." Uthari walked to her and gripped her shoulder, bringing the long blade up between them.

She tensed, nervous at having a deadly weapon so close when he was so unstable, but he turned it so the hilt was toward her.

"Take it. Slay dragons with it and defend this ship while you stand at my side." His eyes burned into hers. "Faithfully, loyally. Once we succeed together, I'll reward you even further. Your father will wonder why he ever doubted you when he sees how powerful you've become and that you've won a king's favor."

Rivlen closed her eyes, knowing he was saying what she wanted to hear to manipulate her. An hour earlier, he'd been casting accusations at her, and she didn't know what had changed. But what choice did she have?

Besides, if Gorsith would be down there, guarding the portal, it would be all right, wouldn't it? He could protect it as effectively as she could. And Rivlen hadn't gotten the sense that Gorsith hated Malek or would secretly work against him, not the way Yidar had.

"Take it," Uthari repeated, squeezing her shoulder, "and have your belongings brought up. I've had the cabin next to mine cleared for you."

"I have no belongings left after the shipwreck."

"Then that'll make the transfer simple." He chuckled. "We'll have our first lesson in the morning. I'll teach you to use your power even more than you already can. Once you fully master your gift, you'll be unstoppable. Nobody—no *man*—will force you against your wishes again."

By Shylezar, he knew exactly what to say, exactly what to offer her. But she'd sworn her loyalty to him long ago and would have obeyed even if he hadn't offered her anything. To obey Uthari was her duty.

She took a shaky breath and wrapped her hand around the hilt of the sword.

"Good," he crooned. "You'll soon forget that boy."

Another wave of tantalizing power flowed from his fingers, her body responding in a way that was a betrayal to her mind. She stepped back, breaking the contact.

"Yes, Your Majesty," she said as she hurried for the door.

His chuckle followed her out.

~

The Thorn Company mercenaries sat around one of the campfires they'd rebuilt, their shoulders hunched as they huddled together. Not for warmth, because the jungle wasn't cold at night, but for support and comfort.

Tezi had appointed the watch duty to herself and listened to them speaking quietly, wondering if there was any way the captain had survived, but she didn't join them. Her axe rested against her leg, the haft within reach, as she leaned against a tree and alternated watching her surroundings and the mageships above. One mageship in particular. The *Soaring Eagle.*

After she'd been tortured, Rivlen had been taken up to that one. Tezi didn't know why, and she worried about Rivlen.

From their previous conversations, Tezi knew Rivlen had believed she would be punished and even that she deserved it, but those long minutes of excruciating pain the zidarr had inflicted on her counted as far more than mere punishment. That had been the kind of agonizing torture that one reserved for one's enemies, not that Tezi believed even enemies should be treated that poorly.

But what if Uthari decided Rivlen had strayed and was no longer his loyal servant? What if, after all that torment, Uthari ordered her killed?

After all she'd endured at the hands of mages, Tezi hadn't thought she would ever befriend one, and she wasn't sure Rivlen would call her a friend, but they'd been through a lot together. Rivlen was the best of the lot, a decent human being most of the time. Tezi didn't want to see her killed.

A shadow stirred beside her, and she dropped her hand to the butt of the axe.

Grunk lifted his open palms and stopped a couple of paces away. Tezi released the axe.

"Thanks for your help distracting the mages earlier," she told him.

She'd tried to get away to help Rivlen when the zidarr had first started torturing her, but it hadn't been until Grunk sneaked in, got the dragon-steel dagger, and attacked the mages restraining her that Tezi had been able to do something.

Thank you for commanding the captain not to let her mages kill me. Grunk grimaced and touched the side of his head—maybe magic or a weapon had clunked him there earlier.

"I think she was going to stop them whether I said anything or not. She's... decent. Honorable." Tezi looked toward Uthari's mage-ship again.

Grunk didn't deny her assessment, but his shrug wasn't a gesture of agreement either. *You are honorable. And strong. Only you among your people haven't given up.*

Tezi frowned over at the campfire, not certain she would say Thorn Company had given up, but they *were* dejected. Yelotta sat apart from the others, her knees drawn up to her chin, as she gazed fearfully up at the ships and into the night.

Shikari was out there somewhere, but he hadn't returned since Rivlen told him to go hunt. Maybe he believed the mages would attack him and try to throw that collar around him if he returned to the area.

Yelotta sighed deeply and rested her face on her knees. Tezi wondered if she could say anything to bolster her, to bolster all of the mercenaries. She also felt the losses keenly—especially that of the captain—but moping around wouldn't do anything. Further, she worried the company would lose its way and come apart if they didn't soon return to their standard routine of exercise and training.

Only you, Grunk repeated.

"You're kind," Tezi said, "but I'm nothing special."

His eyebrows arched. Unlike his dyed-green hair, they were blond, and she was reminded of her northern people, of her lost parents and brother. Her parents were dead, but her brother had been taken to serve in one of the sky cities. Now and then, she wondered if he was still alive.

Nobody calls me that. I'm crazy Grunk, remember? He showed her his filed teeth.

Are you? Or is that an act? Tezi didn't know why someone would pretend to be crazy if he wasn't, but as he stood quietly with her, he seemed almost normal.

Grunk hesitated before answering. *It's not an act. I don't always feel... on edge, but when a lot of people are near me or talking or yelling, I get uncomfortable. I need to push them back before... I don't know. I don't like them close. It makes me tense. Maybe crazy.* He shrugged again.

I get that, I think. Somewhat. I've had some things happen to me, and I don't like anyone touching me, especially when I'm not expecting it. Especially mages and men, she thought but didn't share since he was both. A druid maybe, rather than a mage, but she had a hard time trusting anyone with magical power. She wasn't even sure she liked having him this close to her, but she hadn't caught him giving her speculative looks laden with bedroom nuances. She wondered if he knew why he felt compelled to protect her. Because, as with Tezi and Rivlen, they'd been through battles together? Because he didn't have anyone else?

Tezi, a new voice spoke into her mind. Rivlen.

Tezi looked up and found her at the railing of the mageship. Rivlen wore the same rumpled and travel-stained uniform as before, but she'd gained something new. A long blue-black sword that glowed faintly as she lifted it, as if in a salute.

Yes?

Uthari has ordered me to join the fleet and fly south to the fortress with them.

What? But Malek asked you to guard the portal. And we need you if we're to have a chance at keeping the dragons from getting it. Tezi didn't believe that Shikari's ruse would keep their enemies from coming back, at least not for long.

Uthari is sending Gorsith down to take my place.

The zidarr who tortured you? Tezi didn't try to hide her dismay.

He's more powerful than I am, so he'll be more effective at guarding the portal.

Are you sure? I doubt he cares if Jak, Jadora, Vinjo, or even Malek come back, not like you do. Tezi knew Rivlen would fight hard to keep the way open for them. She would risk her life to do so. Would this Gorsith? Tezi hadn't observed that the zidarr cared much for each other.

I... can't care for Jak anymore.

Tezi was about to ask what *that* meant, but Uthari stepped into view. His gaze skimmed over the camp, though he appeared indifferent to Tezi and the others, and lingered on the cave with the portal. Then he looked to the tall trees to the south. Maybe it was a coincidence, but that was the direction in which Shikari had gone when Rivlen told him to leave the area.

Uthari smiled at Rivlen, which was startling because Tezi had never seen the old wizard smile, then rested a hand on her shoulder. It didn't look like the friendly pat of a colleague or mentor but the possessive grip of a jealous lover. Surely Uthari wasn't that, not at his age.

Or was he? Apparently, he'd been sleeping with Vorsha when she'd been killed. Maybe all the magical concoctions he took kept him virile. Tezi grimaced at the thought and hoped Rivlen wasn't in the same situation she'd been in with Tonovan.

Rivlen shifted uncomfortably, but she didn't attempt to remove Uthari's hand. *We're leaving shortly. Tell your people to obey Gorsith as you would myself or King Uthari.*

Tezi couldn't hide another grimace.

Uthari squinted down at her, his eyes narrowing. Grunk, whom she'd almost forgotten about, moved to stand closer to her.

I'll tell them, Tezi said reluctantly, though a part of her hoped Sasko would reject the idea outright. That was doubtful. They all had to stay here to keep the portal safe in the hope that Jak and the others found a solution. Tezi could only hope Gorsith wasn't too loathsome a leader, but that was hard to imagine after he'd tortured Rivlen.

Once Malek and the others return, you'll all come south to join in the battle at the fortress, Rivlen said. *And to cure those afflicted with the parasite.*

Tezi wondered what would happen if Malek and the others *didn't* find a cure.

Uthari murmured something in Rivlen's ear, squeezed her shoulder again, and walked away. She watched him go. Tezi hoped she was contemplating using that sword to decapitate him, but she doubted it.

Before leaving, Rivlen pulled out her dragon-steel dagger. *Give this to one of your people, another weapon to be used against the dragons if they come.*

Rivlen tossed it so that it landed point first in the earth a few paces in front of Tezi. Grunk's eyes locked on it with longing.

Won't the zidarr want it? Tezi didn't think Gorsith had been carrying dragon-steel weapons. *Or one of Uthari's mages?*

I'm sure, but they have other ways to defend themselves. And if Gorsith gives your people any trouble... Rivlen turned a palm upward.

Is he likely to? From what Tezi had seen, the zidarr were largely indifferent to sex, but there were other ways Gorsith could torment the Thorn Company women.

I don't think he's a menace in general, and he was only obeying Uthari earlier, but if there are disagreements about opening the portal every night or if he questions if it's worth defending...

I understand. And Tezi did. She also understood that Rivlen cared about Jak, no matter what she might have said in front of Uthari. She wanted that portal to stay open so he could come back.

The mageships started moving, heading south. Once more, Rivlen saluted Tezi with the sword, then stepped away from the railing and disappeared from view.

Given how poorly Tezi's last encounter with the dragons at their fortress had gone, she couldn't help but fear she wouldn't see Rivlen alive again. Not unless Uthari had some powerful secret weapon or amazingly brilliant plan.

Tezi was a little surprised he wasn't taking the portal with him, since it could be used to attack the dragons, but he must have wanted to see Malek finish his mission badly.

As the *Soaring Eagle* headed over the trees, leading the fleet, two men on skyboards floated into view and angled toward the cave. One was Gorsith, and the other Tezi didn't recognize at first, but his face was vaguely familiar. Ah, it was the blacksmith who'd worked in the tent with Jadora when she'd been figuring out the acid concoction that allowed one to manipulate dragon steel. Homgor. He carried a huge toolbox and wore a backpack.

As they floated to the ground, Gorsith looked toward Tezi. No, he was looking at the dagger still stuck in the ground in front of her.

She stepped forward and pulled it out. When she looked over at the camp, she found Sasko, Tinder, and a few others watching her and wondered if they'd caught any of Rivlen's telepathic words.

She eyed the dagger, well aware of all the trouble that found someone who wielded such a weapon. It might protect the handler from magic, but since everyone from dragons to colleagues to zidarr coveted dragon steel, it also made that person a target. And whoever carried it would be expected to jump into the middle of battles with dragons, to try to do damage and lower their defenses for others. To give it to someone was as much a curse as a blessing.

Sighing, Tezi turned to Grunk. "You've used one of these before. Do you want to carry this one?"

Grunk had been looking at the dagger the whole time, probably wishing he could replace the one he'd lost, but he didn't immediately reach for it. He raised his eyebrows and asked, *Is there not another among your people that you would rather give it to?*

Tinder, who'd had and lost the other dragon-steel axe, might resent her for her choice, but Tezi shook her head. *You're a good person to wield it. Besides, I think the zidarr would be less likely to try to take it from you than from one of Thorn Company.*

As it was, Tezi worried she would have to guard her axe from Gorsith. If he was anything like Tonovan, he would be certain a terrene human didn't deserve such a gift and that *he* did.

She held the dagger out to Grunk.

I will use it well and attempt to drive it into the eye of a dragon. Grunk bowed over her arm before accepting the weapon.

The blacksmith stepped off his skyboard and headed immediately to the dragon-steel chain, but Gorsith kept watching the dagger, and his eyes narrowed as Grunk sheathed it.

Grunk might have to drive it into the eye of a zidarr before the dragons ever returned.

17

STRANGE STRANDS OF BLUE AND GREEN BIOLUMINESCENT VEGETATION created a net that spanned miles, if not *hundreds* of miles. As the gateship traveled under it, Jak kept peeking up through the porthole, certain there had to be a gap in it somewhere. It seemed to be natural, the weave irregular and reminding him of crystals he'd once looked at under a microscope, but it was easy to imagine it had been formed to thwart their mission.

Using magic, he'd tugged at a few strands, thinking he might be able to create a gap through which the gateship could rise, but the strands had proven less flexible than they appeared. Further, like so much of the vegetation—or whatever was out there—it was infused with magic. The power was nothing like that of a mage or the portal, but it was there and made manipulating the undersea flora difficult.

Malek hadn't appeared that worried when he'd come to look at the net earlier, but that didn't mean that much. It took great danger for him to show any sign of being alarmed.

Vinjo gazed at the ceiling, his eyes glazed. Daydreaming? No, he was drawing upon his power for something. Jak could sense it, as he sensed Malek using his power to reinforce the hull. There had been fewer creaks emanating from it since they'd risen a couple hundred feet, but what would happen when Malek grew weary and needed to sleep?

The last Jak had checked, he was resting on his bunk, but he was also continuing to use his magic, and he wouldn't be able to sleep as long as he needed to do that.

Jak would ask him how to perform that magic—he could tell it wasn't as simple as creating a barrier—but he'd caught himself yawning too. "We'll have to sleep in shifts if it's much farther to this place."

Vinjo, eyes still glazed, didn't answer, but the magic he was drawing upon shifted slightly, as if he were raking something above him.

"What are you doing?" Jak asked.

"Using my power to examine the carbon dioxide in the air and see if the device I built is doing anything to lessen it. Your mother said we should have brought along a bunch of plants instead. Apparently, through their respiration process, they take in carbon dioxide and emit oxygen. I admit I have to take her word for it since I'm an engineer, not a botanist. My interest in plants doesn't go much beyond using them to clean my butt when I'm stuck in a lavatory-scarce jungle. As I informed her. Then she snapped at me."

"My mother *snapped*?" Jak had occasionally stretched the limits of her patience, especially in his youth, but he rarely saw Mother lose her temper.

The parasite, he realized. He'd noticed the signs of her fever, and he'd worried all along that she would grow more aggressive, if not outright mad, like the dragons, so he should have expected... snapping.

"She seems tense," was all Vinjo said, not passing judgment.

"I hear being infested with a malevolent parasite can cause

that." Jak had a feeling Mother wouldn't classify any organism, aside from mages, as malevolent, but he had no qualms about doing so.

"Indeed." Vinjo eyed the net. "We may have to punch a hole through that to go up to the surface and replenish our air supply."

"Are you sure your device isn't doing enough? Is there anything I can do to help?" Since Jak had seen the hazy volcanic air above the surface, he didn't know how viable it would be for replenishing their air supply. At the least, he believed they might have to find a way to filter it.

"I don't—" A huge blue creature with a long proboscis and a maw full of fangs swam past the porthole, and Vinjo squawked in surprise.

An eye on the side of its body focused on them. The creature reminded Jak of a shark, but the fin placement was odd, and numerous squid-like tentacles flowed behind it.

Malek stepped into navigation.

"Is Mother all right?" Jak peeked around him toward the laboratory, but the door was shut.

Malek had come from his cabin, but Jak knew he'd been checking in on Mother often.

Malek hesitated. "She refuses to rest."

"That sounds typical."

"She *needs* to rest."

"I bet she said she'll rest after our mission is over."

"She did, but she's not taking into account..." Malek shook his head.

Jak frowned at him. "What?"

Malek gazed toward the porthole at another tentacled shark up ahead—or had the same one circled around to put itself in their path?

After adjusting their steering to avoid it, Vinjo poked into his tool satchel as he hummed under his breath.

What isn't she taking into account? Jak asked Malek telepathically in case there was something he didn't want Vinjo to overhear.

Malek looked at Jak and shook his head again. *She asked me not to tell you. She doesn't want you to worry.*

I'm going to worry if you don't *tell me.* Jak couldn't help but feel a sense of betrayal that Mother had told *Malek* something important and not him. Jak understood that they were… *close* now, but he was her son. They'd been working side by side on the dragon-portal research for years, and they'd been through a great deal together.

Do you have a sense of how far we are from the orbs? Malek asked.

Jak scowled at his attempt to change the subject. *The overhead view the portal showed me wasn't a map with a legend denoting miles, but if one can gauge based on the size of the volcanos, hours at least. I'm not even sure how fast we're going. Vinjo isn't either. Much slower than through air.*

Jak stepped around Malek, intending to check on Mother for himself, but Malek caught his arm and stopped him.

Since time is crucial, Malek said, gazing toward the ceiling, maybe probing that living net with his senses, *it may behoove us to apply force and break through that mass so we can rise up and fly through the air to our destination and then descend again.*

The last time we broke some vegetation, it didn't go well. Jak tried to pull his arm free.

Malek's grip wasn't hard, but it was implacable, and Jak couldn't tug his arm away.

Stay in navigation, Jak.

I want to check on my mother.

I know, but she doesn't want you to see her.

She lets you see her. Frustrated, Jak yanked harder and attempted to use his magic to give himself more strength. He might as well have been tugging at dragon-steel bars. *Malek. Let me go.* Realizing brute force, even magical brute force, wouldn't work on him, Jak added, *Please. Whatever she's doing, if she's ill—and I know she is—she should have people who care about her with her.*

Malek gazed at him, unmoving, and the word *implacable* came to Jak's mind again. But Malek surprised him by sighing and releasing Jak's arm.

She worries about infesting you. Earlier, she... the parasite tried to infest me. It would *have, but I seem to have some immunity to it.* Malek shared an image of him sitting on his bunk with Mother and some of the motes floating toward his mouth.

Jak shuddered, but the image didn't sway him. *I won't get that close to her. I just want to make sure she's all right and... Malek, what is she doing that you won't tell me about?*

Malek frowned and looked over his shoulder.

Using his senses, Jak checked on Mother through the walls. Did her aura seem weaker than usual? And different?

Malek must have sensed something off as well, for he strode back to the laboratory and tried to open the door. It was locked, as it had been when Jak had checked.

Jadora, Malek said telepathically, allowing Jak to hear, *it's me. Let me in.*

If Mother responded, it was only to Malek. But maybe she didn't say anything, for Malek scowled at the door and drew upon his magic to try to unlock it.

A zidarr would have the power to blast the entire gateship into pieces, but Malek couldn't do that when they were riding inside it. He had to focus on the door, but Mother's magic reinforced it. Mother's dragon-gifted magic that was even greater than what a zidarr possessed.

Judging by his consternated expression, Malek wasn't pleased about that. Again, he drew upon his power and attempted to break the magical lock she'd created.

Jak tried to aid Malek by channeling power into him, but the door didn't budge. Jak wished Shikari were with them, that they'd tried harder to find a way to bring him along. A dragon might be the only one with the power to override Mother's magic—and reenergize the portal.

"I think she's on the deck." Malek knocked on the door, as if that would help.

"Lying on it, you mean?" Jak could sense her aura but couldn't tell if she was standing or sitting—or had collapsed.

That last thought drove fear into him though, and he groped through his repertoire of magic, trying to think of a way to assist in breaking the lock. He could sense that she'd secured not only the hinges and lock mechanism but the entire door and the wall around it.

Mother, Jak tried. *Let us in. We're worried about you.*

Maybe that wasn't the best thing to say. If she didn't want to see him because she might pass the parasites along to him, that wouldn't prompt her to open the door.

There's also a fascinating *miles-long plant that we're sailing under. You should come out and look at it. Maybe Vinjo can help us get a sample. I'm sure you'll be curious about it.*

Malek, who'd heard the words, managed a faint smile, but the worried crease to his brow remained.

"I'm not sure she's conscious," he said. "I'd expect her to answer you if she were, even if it was to tell you to go away."

"I know. How do we get in? From below?"

"No," Malek said. "The hull is right underneath the laboratory—remember when there was a hole in the deck and we could see all the way through?"

"I remember Vinjo complaining vociferously. What about the ceiling?"

Malek probed the area above the lab with his senses. "There's a gap between it and the hull—Vinjo ran the tendrils from the power supply in the engineering room to the navigation cabin and lamps through there."

Jak nodded, sensing the magical tendrils up there.

"She's reinforced this door, this wall, and the walls to either side." Malek touched the wood, Mother's magic turning it into something as impenetrable as diamond. "But not the hull, the deck, or the ceiling. She mustn't have believed we could get in that way."

"Did *she* do it, Malek?" Jak asked quietly. "Or is it possible... Do you think the parasite is influencing her?"

"I *know* it's influencing her." Grim-faced, Malek stepped into the cabin next to the laboratory.

He flicked a finger and busted a hole in the ceiling. Yellow illumination from the power tendrils highlighted how compact an area they were dealing with.

"Boost me up," Jak said. "I might be able to fit. I'm less muscled than you."

"Another time, I'd make you levitate yourself up to practice your magic." Malek clasped his hands together and crouched.

"Another time, I'd be delighted to learn from you." Jak stepped into his grip, and Malek hoisted him up, not bothering with magic.

As Jak scrambled into the tight space, clunking his head against the hull and fighting not to grow tangled in the power tendrils, he sensed Malek continuing to probe the walls and the door, looking for weaknesses.

The hull groaned, perhaps a testament to Malek's distraction. He had to be worried about Mother too.

An ominous creak came from right above Jak, the sound even more alarming now that he was so close to it.

"You're still reinforcing that, right?" he called back as he squirmed toward the laboratory. Belatedly, he wondered if he should have stuck to telepathy so Mother, if she was conscious, wouldn't hear him, but she would have been able to sense him regardless.

Yes, Malek replied, *but Vinjo is cursing softly in navigation, so it's possible there's—*

Something jolted the gateship, and Jak spread his palms on the wood as another creak sounded above him.

—a new problem, Malek finished.

"These shark things are trying to *herd* us," came a muffled call from Vinjo.

Jak continued forward. He had to help Mother. *Then* he could worry about the other problem.

"I'll attempt to discourage them with zaps of energy," Malek called back. "They're not magical; they should be more easily affected than some of the other entities here."

As if Malek needed more things to split his attention. Better him than Jak, though. Malek had far more experience with magic.

Sensing he was above Mother, Jak summoned fire to burn a hole in the laboratory ceiling. He was glad he'd been practicing and could create everything from single flames to fireballs now. Lighting the ship they were in on fire would not be good, so he burned the wood slowly and carefully.

Another jolt rocked the vessel, and his concentration lapsed. Growling, Jak focused and reignited his flames, summoning the heat of a wildfire racing across the mountains on the map of his mind. Smoke tickled his nose as the warmth flared against his skin, but he didn't back away.

The next jolt came from behind, as if one of those sharks had rammed the ship at top speed.

"They're going to do damage if we keep allowing that," Vinjo called.

"I'm extending the barrier around the ship," Malek replied, "but something about the water here is making it more difficult."

"There's magic in it too. I can feel it all around us, and I see more of those huge heart-shaped creatures with their networks of vines down there."

"We haven't descended, have we?" Malek asked.

A rough circle of wood fell free from the ceiling, the edges scorched. Jak caught it with his magic, realizing his mother was right below, and levitated it to the side.

"Mother?" he called softly.

As they'd feared, she lay crumpled on the deck on her side.

"No," Vinjo said. "We're at the same level, I believe, but the ground has risen in this area. That net above us is lowering too. The area available for us to sail through is getting tighter."

Maybe that was where the sharks were herding them to. A spot where the net and the sea floor came together. If they were intelligent, they might want to coerce the strange invader to their waters into a trap.

Grimacing, Jak squeezed through the hole and swung down, careful not to land on his mother. She didn't stir. She didn't even appear to be breathing. Had he not sensed her aura, proof that she lived, he would have worried more, but just because she was alive didn't mean she wasn't in danger. And now that he was closer, he sensed the change to her aura even more keenly. It was almost as if the parasites had their own aura that was mingling with hers. Or irrevocably entwined?

Shuddering, Jak knelt beside her and touched her shoulder, "Mother, are you in there?"

Her eyes remained closed, not the least flicker to her lashes, and sweat bathed her flushed face. Before, he'd seen the patch of gray on her forehead, but it had spread, blotches all over her face and hands. And all over her body?

Jak rubbed the back of his neck with a shaking hand, then touched her cheek to see if she was as fevered as she looked. Was there a thermometer in the first-aid kit? He didn't remember, but so much heat radiated from her skin that he had no doubt her temperature was high.

"Mother," he whispered, tears forming in his eyes, "what do I do? You're the one who's supposed to take care of me. This isn't right." His voice cracked on the last word.

Jak reminded himself that he was growing in power as a mage and a healer—he'd mended arrow and bullet wounds—and that he ought to be able to figure something out. But nobody had yet taught him how to cure diseases. Even if they had, these parasites weren't a disease with a known cure.

Mother released a deep exhale—a sigh. Jak leaned forward, hoping that meant she was rousing.

But glowing motes floated out of her mouth.

Jak jerked back, banging his shoulders on the counter behind him. They floated into the air and straight toward him.

Instinctively, he started to summon magic to destroy them with fire, as he had in the past, but he couldn't create flames right on top of his mother. She was defenseless at the moment.

"Malek," Jak called, scrambling to the side, then jumping to his feet as he raised a barrier around himself.

Would that be enough? Back in Utharika, Shikari had used a barrier to keep the motes from reaching him, but he was a dragon, not a neophyte mage.

Jak backed to the door, but Mother's magic—or the *parasites'* magic—kept it as secured as ever. The only escape from the laboratory was through the hole above, but he would have to run through the motes and leap over Mother to get out that way.

Thuds and scrapes came from above as Malek maneuvered through the tight crawlspace. He must have sensed what was going on, for he formed a barrier around Mother.

Blast them, Jak.

Trusting that Malek would protect Mother, Jak did so. He formed a fireball in the air, centered it on the motes, and made it burn with as much heat and intensity as he could.

Glass shattered on the counter on the far side of the laboratory. Fresh fear rushed into Jak as he worried his heat might break the dishes containing the other samples. He pulled the fire closer to him, his own barrier protecting him from the blaze. He scooted sideways in case the motes were still floating toward him. He couldn't see or sense them through the brilliance of the magical flames and tried not to think about how he, unlike Malek, had no natural immunity to the parasite.

Malek's legs came through the hole, and he dropped down into the middle of the inferno, his barrier around him. Warily, Jak let the flames lessen, hoping he'd taken care of the motes.

But as soon as the fire dwindled, he saw them, glowing golden in the air not four feet from him. They'd stopped their advance, but they hadn't been destroyed. And, as his fire disappeared, they started moving again, floating toward him.

Malek had landed astraddle Mother, but he lunged to the counter, rooting in her backpack. He found an empty sample dish and lid, then sprang for the motes.

One sent a tiny arc of power toward him, almost like miniature lightning, and Jak gaped. They could *attack* now?

Fortunately, Malek's barrier protected him. He swept one mote after another into the dish before smacking the lid down on them.

Jak shook his head, hardly believing that would work, but he sensed Mother's magic imbuing what appeared to be simple glass. Those were the dishes she'd originally made to contain the parasites, so maybe it *could* trap them.

"I forgot fire doesn't work on them anymore." Malek swore. "We had the same experience back on Uthari's yacht."

"So lovely when one's enemies evolve to be *more* powerful." Jak grimaced when his voice came out squeaky, but he doubted Malek would judge him for his fear.

The strain on Malek's face suggested he was too busy maintaining his magic in multiple places to think about it.

After adding more magic to further seal the lid, Malek set the dish on the counter. The motes continued to glow inside, making

Jak uneasy. He remembered how Uthari had broken a dish like that to unleash the parasites back in his throne room.

"I hope *he's* unconscious and on the deck now," Jak muttered.

Malek glanced at him, and Jak didn't clarify who he meant. Though he wanted to return to Mother's side, he dared not get close again. Who knew how many motes those parasites had created within her?

Malek knelt beside her, resting the back of his hand against her cheek. His eyes were haunted, proof of how much he'd come to care about her.

"The parasites don't make the dragons pass out." Jak crouched to look at Mother from a few feet away, as if her unconscious form might respond and offer suggestions—solutions. "Why is this happening to her?"

"It's possible they do at some point in the process—before they take over completely."

Jak scowled.

"But I think this is because of what she did to herself," Malek added.

"What?" Jak stared at him. "You have to tell me. Please."

Malek sighed and stroked Mother's sweaty hair. "She injected herself with the death-darter bacteria."

Jak's jaw dropped.

Before he could ask why, Malek continued. "She believes my past infection from those bacteria are the reason the dragon parasite hasn't been able to get a foothold within me. Either my immune system knows how to fight off what could be similar bacteria or they're natural enemies, and in a battle for a host, the death-darter bacteria come out on top."

Malek opened a cabinet and pulled out a blanket and one of the collapsible cots that Vinjo had made before their trip to Vran.

"She's *hoping* they come out on top," Malek added as he unfolded the cot. "And that it's a solution to killing the dragon parasite, but we don't know what will happen to the host—to *her* —while the two species do battle inside of her."

After gathering Mother in his arms, Malek carried her to the cot. He closed his eyes and held her to his chest for a long moment before settling her down and pulling the blanket over her.

"I'm going to try to get some water into her," Malek said. "Why don't you go back to navigation and see if Vinjo needs help?"

Jak started to shake his head—several minutes had passed since the last jolt, so he hoped that meant the sharks had grown bored or Malek's barrier was sufficiently deterring them—but Malek gave him a steady look that promised it had been an order even if he'd phrased it as a suggestion. He wanted Jak out of the laboratory so the motes couldn't go after him again.

Though it broke his heart to leave his mother like that, Jak didn't want Malek to have to split his attention—his magic—in any more directions.

I need help up here, Vinjo told them, panic in his telepathic tone.

Sharks? Jak jumped for the hole, Malek giving him a magical boost to help him out.

No. Worse.

As Jak crawled away from the laboratory, he hoped that whatever it was, he would be capable enough to help. Once more, he wished Shikari were with them.

A barrier guarded the entrance to the tower Sorath believed held the beam weapon. The single window was more than forty feet up, near the roof, and the smooth dragon-steel walls didn't offer handholds for climbing.

"Pop it?" Ferroki whispered, waving at the dagger in his hand as she watched the sky for enemies.

It had been quiet in the fortress for the last few hours, and they'd hoped that meant the dragons were asleep, but as soon as they'd stepped into the courtyard, they'd spotted a dozen or more flying in the air high above. They alternated wheeling and nipping at each other between throwing magic around.

Practicing at combat, Sorath had realized. Whatever they were doing, they appeared suitably distracted.

"We'll have to." He always worried that popping a barrier alerted whoever had made it, and he'd hoped to have more time to consider that which they wanted to destroy this time, but they had little choice.

The dagger slid into the translucent barrier, a faint buzz in the air the only indicator to his mundane human senses that something had changed. After waving a hand through the air to make sure, he led Ferroki into a tunnel that headed to the tower.

After making a right turn, they almost stepped on a body sprawled on the floor. A *human* body.

Sorath swore and drew his foot back. It was a roamer, one of the men who'd been captured and taken off the druid raft. With his skull crushed, and huge bite marks mangling his torso, there was no doubt that he was dead.

"I think he was in that prison tower with us," Ferroki whispered.

"Yes." Sorath made himself walk around the body, though he was chilled by the reminder that any dragon who chanced across them could easily kill them. He prayed they could accomplish something before they met that fate.

"Maybe he escaped," Ferroki said, "or was sent on an errand and had the same idea as us. Sabotage."

"Or he was just looking for a way out of this place." Sorath deemed that more likely. There were roamer pirates and warriors in the world, but those who'd been along with the druids had largely been fishers.

"He didn't have a dragon-steel weapon," Ferroki said, looking back at the body as they continued toward the tower. "I wonder how he got through the barrier."

"It's possible someone put that one up recently, because of our misadventure in the control cave. It might even be what trapped the man in this part of the fortress." Sorath shrugged, having no way to know what the dragons were thinking.

They entered the tower warily and found themselves in a chamber large enough for a dragon to spread its wings. Something like a ceiling was twenty-five feet above their heads, but it had a hole in the center, a hole wide enough for a dragon to fly through.

The opening allowed them to see the great red sphere hanging from the roof above, streaks in or under the surface swirling about. It was positioned directly in front of the window—poised to send out a beam?

A faint hum reverberated through the tower, originating in the sphere.

"The window is higher than I realized," Ferroki said. "I doubt we're going to be able to climb up and push it out."

No, the dragon-steel walls were as smooth on the inside as the outside of the tower. Sorath didn't even see a way they could reach the next level.

"Do you feel its energy?" Ferroki winced and squinted as she turned her face away from it. "Or does the dagger protect you?"

"I can hear it buzzing." Afraid it was making her uncomfortable with its magic, Sorath rested a hand on her arm to extend the influence of the dagger.

Relief smoothed her face. "That helps. Thank you."

Sorath nodded and looked around the bottom level of the tower. "I don't see a switch or lever or a sign with handy instructions on how to turn it off." Nor had he verified that the sphere *was* the source of the beam weapon. It would be nice to be able to do that.

"Rude of dragons not to include such in their fortresses."

A shadow fell over the window, and Sorath stifled a curse. As a dragon landed in the window, talons curling around the frame, they skittered back to the wall, hoping they hadn't been seen. Doubting they would be that lucky, Sorath crouched, ready to fight, but he couldn't help but think of the body they'd passed.

Hello, servants, came a familiar voice from above.

Sorath sighed, not certain whether to be glad Yoshartov had been the one to find them or not. He would have preferred *not* to be found until after they'd managed to accomplish something.

The spiced and cooked fish was most delightful. Yoshartov hopped through the window and dropped down, landing at the edge of the hole. His head lowered, his long neck allowing him to reach through the gap and peer at them. *Even the queen agreed that it was interesting. I found it most delicious. Dragons never use spices. It was a unique and enjoyable travel experience.*

"I'm glad," Sorath said.

You are not in the correct tower.

"We had to use the latrine and got lost on the way back." Never mind that the dragons didn't *have* latrines, at least not that Sorath had seen. Maybe they flew over the edge to handle their biological needs.

Why does the servant Colonel Sorath keep thinking I am a foolish dragon? You seek to damage our weapon, just as you sought to damage the control devices.

Well, at least Sorath had his verification that this was their weapon.

"How did your date go?" Ferroki asked the dragon.

Date? Yoshartov's head swiveled to look at her. *It was not that but a valiant effort to show the queen my value.*

"So, not horribly but not perfectly?"

Some servants are more perceptive than others. His single yellow eye locked back on Sorath. *The queen has assigned me a quest, a chance to fully prove myself worthy of an exalted position in dragon society.*

"To gather more dragon steel?" Ferroki asked.

To gather the one item we covet that we have not yet been able to acquire.

Sorath slumped. "The portal."

Yes, the gateway to the other worlds. Until we have it, we can neither leave this place nor invite more dragons to join us here.

"It's not that nice a place for dragons," Ferroki said. "Maybe you *shouldn't* invite any more."

But the servants here make the most delightful meals! Yoshartov's tongue came out to run along his scaled lips.

It took Sorath a second to realize Yoshartov meant they'd prepared a delightful meal, not that they *were* a delightful meal.

"Maybe we should have tried to make the fish more dreadful," he muttered.

"It was already a dubious blend of spices and an awkward cooking method," Ferroki said.

"When all you've eaten in your life is raw food, it must not take much to impress."

I must leave to acquire the portal. Perhaps I will also acquire more servants. I could have a whole legion of your kind preparing meals for the queen and me.

Sorath bit down a sarcastic comment as he realized the implications of Yoshartov's assignment. "If you're leaving the fortress, you should take us with you. We can help you get the portal."

He squeezed Ferroki's hand. This could be their chance to escape and rejoin their people.

"Yes," Ferroki said. "Your kind have failed numerous times to acquire it. You need our help."

"Send us to wherever it is, and we'll act as spies and assist you."

Yoshartov looked back and forth between them. Though the

dagger should have protected his thoughts, Sorath did his best to clear his mind of anything duplicitous. He hoped Ferroki could do the same.

If you were loyal servants and would *act as my spies, I would agree to this, but you seek to deceive me. You are faithful to your own kind and will not help even a mighty and deserving dragon such as myself. I see why the queen wishes you dead.*

"Uh," Sorath said.

"She said that?" Ferroki frowned.

Yes, all the dragons here wish my servants dead. It is known that you cause trouble. Yoshartov looked pointedly up at the weapon. *But I have enjoyed our battles together, and you made me most delicious fish. I want you to make me more fish, many more times.*

"We want that too," Ferroki said.

Sorath's mouth twisted at the idea of being a permanent dragon chef, but if it kept Yoshartov from obeying an order to kill them, he couldn't object.

You will stay here in the fortress and plan my next meal. You will not wander, or the other dragons may kill you. Yoshartov's focus returned to Sorath—no, to his hand and the dagger in it.

Sorath hid it behind his back, though it was a pointless gesture. It was too late to put it out of the dragon's mind.

It is unwise to leave you with a weapon capable of thwarting our barriers.

"Don't you want your favorite servant to be able to protect himself if another dragon tries to kill him while you're gone?" Ferroki asked.

I do like it when my servant prongs an arrogant dragon in the nose!

"We all like that," Ferroki said.

You keep it, but you must stay out of trouble. I cannot protect you if all the other dragons decide you must die.

"Is that likely to happen?" she asked.

It could happen. Go back to the cooking tower and stay there.

Yoshartov used his magic to stir a wind to blow them toward the exit.

Sorath could have resisted it—he barely felt it with the dagger in hand—but he and Ferroki went along with it. If Yoshartov had been told to kill them and wasn't doing it, Sorath didn't want to irk the dragon. He did, however, keep trying to convince Yoshartov to take them along, promising to cook for him on the journey and help him get the portal. It was a lie, and he and the dragon both knew it, but he couldn't help but make the attempt. If they didn't get a ride out of the fortress, he doubted they would be alive by the time Yoshartov got back.

I am a clever dragon and will find a way to retrieve the portal on my own. I will return soon, and I will also bring more fish for you to prepare.

Leaving them in their original tower, Yoshartov disappeared from view. Before departing, he put a barrier in place over the exit. Little more than a gesture since Sorath could pop it and the other dragons could too.

"Do you think we'll be safe here without him?" Ferroki asked skeptically.

"No."

18

IT DIDN'T TAKE LONG FOR JAK TO CLIMB DOWN FROM THE crawlspace above the ceiling and join Vinjo in navigation, but by the time he did, the gateship had come to a stop.

"What's wrong?" Instead of sitting, Jak gripped the back of the empty seat and peered out the porthole.

The tentacled sharks were out there, casually swimming about, lit from above by the glow of the ever-present bioluminescent net. Neither sharks nor net seemed to be testing Malek's barrier, so Jak wasn't sure why they'd stopped. Then a green vine wafted up from below, waving in the current in front of the porthole.

"Are they surrounding us again?" Jak leaned across the console to peer down as he checked the sea floor with his senses. It was no longer far below. Several of those entities, with their sprawling vines, grew from the silt a couple dozen feet beneath the ship.

"A forest of vines rose up behind us, but so far none are blocking the way ahead. They and the sharks are bumping us from behind and trying to nudge us in that direction." Vinjo pointed through the porthole. "I've tried to resist, but they, or something else, are fiddling with the currents too, and we've been pushed off course. I've stopped the ship, but we're continuing to float in that direction."

"Isn't that all right?" Jak asked, though the idea of all the flora and fauna having some intelligence and working together toward a common goal made him uneasy. "We're not that far off course, are we? That's roughly the way we want to go."

"I worry that they're trying to direct us to certain doom."

Jak started to ask what kind of *certain doom* they were likely to encounter in a sea, but it wasn't as if this world had been kind to them thus far.

Malek joined them, splinters and chunks of singed wood on his shoulders. "I'm still not able to open the door to the laboratory."

At least Jak and Malek had been able to get in and could presumably return through the ceiling.

"Is Mother still unconscious?" Jak asked.

"I wasn't able to rouse her, but she's started thrashing around and moaning." Malek grimaced and switched to telepathy. *I believe it's a result of the organisms battling in her—or her immune system trying hard to destroy them—which she expected when she injected herself, but I worry she's in pain.*

Jak wished they hadn't had to leave, but as the vines kept batting at the back of the craft and currents pushed them forward, he believed he and Malek might both be needed up here.

I worry that she'll lose the battle, Jak said. *I don't think any of her books mentioned what she's trying.*

No.

"There are the sharks again," Vinjo muttered, his hands tense on the controls. "Even the stuff that looks like seaweed seems to be stirring currents to keep us going forward."

"Even the *seaweed* is intelligent?" Jak asked skeptically.

"I consider it more likely," Malek said aloud, only reserving his concerns about Mother for telepathy, "that something with magic and intelligence is compelling the native flora and fauna to attack rather than that everything here is sapient."

"Oh," Jak mouthed, rocking back.

It seemed obvious, now that he heard it, but he wanted to shy away from the implications. Dealing with uppity magical foliage was less daunting than facing a powerful and dangerous—and intelligent—entity trying to thwart them.

"I've been loath to wantonly destroy things," Malek said, "especially since there were repercussions the first time, but I doubt we want to see where everything is trying to herd us. Jak, work with me, and we'll cut down the vines and use electrical jolts to drive off the sharks. Then we'll slice a hole in the net of tendrils above us, go up, and travel on the surface until we're above the orbs."

"Yes, my lord," Jak said, compelled to formality by the order, though he also lowered his voice to whisper, "I don't know how to create electrical jolts yet."

"I'll show you."

"Wait." Vinjo rose to his feet and squinted at something on the sea floor ahead of them. "That may be the spot. We—"

Magic flared somewhere behind the ship, and a surge of water struck them. They zipped forward, as if Vinjo had commanded the craft to travel at full power, but he hadn't touched anything.

"Strengthen your barrier, my lord," Vinjo whispered. "There's something coming out of the ground. Little bubbles."

Jak and Malek leaned forward together, bumping shoulders. Jak sensed Malek adding more power to the barrier around the gateship.

"It's probably a vent with natural gases coming out," Jak said, though he wished Mother were awake so he could consult her. "Sulfur, water vapor, and hydrogen sulfide and the like. The portal showed me a lot of volcanos in this part of the world."

Once the gateship floated over the vent, the currents stopped pushing them forward.

"Uh." Vinjo looked at Jak. "Are you *sure* about that?"

"No," Jak said.

"I don't sense anything magical about the gas or the vent," Malek said.

"Neither do I," Vinjo said, "but what if it's something corrosive, and that's why they want us over it? Maybe they think it can eat through the hull of the ship."

Jak leaned back. "What if it's the same acid we encountered on Vran? The stuff that can mold dragon steel?"

"My barrier appears to be effective against it so far," Malek said. "Your mother didn't mention if that acid would affect wood. She was keeping it in a glass container, I believe."

"I suppose there's no way to tell from here. She would want us to get a sample though." Jak smiled and glanced toward the corridor, as if he might find her standing there and nodding in agreement.

But a moan came from the laboratory, and he dropped his smile.

"I'm certain she would," Malek said grimly, "but we don't have an easy means of collecting specimens here, and we have more important concerns. Vinjo, get us moving forward again, out of this area and to the ruins."

"I'll try, my lord."

Jak made a note of the vent's location on the mental map he was making. There was nothing to suggest it was the same acid as had been present on Vran; his only reason for believing it significant was that the sea life had brought them to it.

But even if it *was* the acid that could manipulate dragon steel, they didn't need more of it. Mother had mastered the formula for producing it and given it to Uthari's blacksmith. As Jak well knew from the creation of Shikari's collar, the man had effectively made some and used it on dragon steel.

Vinjo frowned at the control lever that moved the ship forward. He'd pressed it all the way toward the porthole, but they'd barely moved and only for a second. Now, they were stopped again, still floating over the vent.

"The water has grown very difficult to navigate through." Vinjo pulled the lever back, then pushed it forward again, before tilting his head and reaching out with his magic. "The engine and power sources are fine. The problem isn't with the ship but with the water."

"Try to go up." Malek gazed toward the ceiling, and Jak sensed him shifting the woven tendrils in the living net above them. This time, he wasn't cutting them, perhaps fearing they would lash out, but he nudged them and changed the way they were woven together to make a gap. He'd once admitted he used crafting imagery as an aid for his magic, so maybe this was natural for him.

Jak wiped his palms on his trousers. It had either grown warm inside, or he was nervous about whatever power was working against them.

He funneled some of his energy into Malek, in case it helped, and watched so he could learn what Malek was doing.

"It's working," Vinjo said. "I can sense a hole growing. It needs to be about three times bigger—especially longer—and I think we can fit up." His voice lowered to a mutter. "*If* we're able to travel in that direction."

Abruptly, Malek gasped and dropped to one knee as he grabbed his head. Jak was close enough to sense something attacking him—some kind of mental attack—but he couldn't tell where it came from.

"Can I help you, Malek?" Jak rested a hand on his shoulder. "Do you want more power funneled into you or something else? Who's attacking you?"

Malek hissed but didn't respond, merely pressing his palm to the side of his head, as if he could drive away the mental attack that way. Jak sensed him using his power, attempting to push away the assault, but he couldn't tell if it did anything. Jak stretched out beyond the ship, hoping to find whatever was doing this to Malek.

He didn't sense anything besides the vines and tendrils. Were they responsible?

"The barrier dropped." Vinjo barely glanced at Malek, instead scowling at his control panel and glancing through the porthole. "Jak, can you help me get it back up?"

"Yes," Jak said, though his first instinct was to help Malek fend off whatever—or whoever—was attacking him. It couldn't be his mother and the parasites, could it?

"It's harder than it should be," Vinjo whispered, his face tense. "I didn't realize he was expending so much energy to keep the water pressure from crushing the hull."

A groan from the framework convinced Jak to release Malek's shoulder and funnel his energy into Vinjo, whom he trusted knew more about reinforcing the hull with magic than he did.

"Oh, Shylezar," Vinjo said, his eyes squinted shut with concentration. "Something really is trying to eat away at the bottom of the ship. Jak, help me reinforce that area."

Jak willed a barrier to form along the bottom of the hull, aware of the link from the dragon-steel chain affixed to it. So much for it proving lucky or protecting them from magic.

Now that he was responsible for protecting the hull, Jak could sense the gas from the vent rising up and burbling against his magic. Whatever the stuff was, it *was* corrosive. Not only against physical materials but against magic. It ate away at the barrier even as he willed his power to build another layer, to thicken the protection around the ship.

If the hull was breached, none of them would make it back to the portal.

Malek roared, surged to his feet, and flung his arms up. Maybe with the effort, he also flung away whatever had been attacking him, for he immediately poured his magic into the barrier, lessening what Jak needed to do. He also gave up on reweaving the tendrils in the net above—in the short time since he'd stopped, they'd changed back to their original placement and made the hole disappear. Instead, he cut through them, slicing them away with huge swaths of his magic.

"Up," Malek snarled, his voice tight with effort.

Before Vinjo touched the controls, it surged up to the hole Malek had made.

As they passed through it, Jak could see the tendrils, some grasping for them as if to capture them. Others were already repairing themselves, reweaving their pattern into a seamless mesh that would close the hole again.

That was fine. Jak and the others could figure out a way back through it when they reached the orbs. As long as they escaped in the first place.

Fortunately, with Malek throwing huge amounts of power at the obstacles and into moving the gateship, they surged upward rapidly. Once more, Jak sensed the water pushing against them, but it didn't matter. Though he grunted and cursed, Malek pushed successfully against it.

The water around them grew lighter, and Jak looked upward, hoping they were nearing the surface. And hoping the surface wouldn't be dominated by deadly unbreathable gases and more things that wanted them dead.

"That's daylight," Vinjo blurted in relief as Jak's ears popped. "He did it. We're escaping."

The gateship rose up so quickly that it burst out of the water and lifted several feet above the waves before splashing back down, sending Vinjo tumbling from his seat. Jak grabbed the other seat to steady himself and reached toward Malek in case he needed help.

But as the gateship settled on the surface, rocking on the waves, Malek's eyes rolled back in his head, and he crumpled to the deck.

Jak stared in horror, not sure if Malek had overexerted himself or if whatever had been attacking him was responsible. Either way, he wasn't moving.

~

Daylight found Sasko yawning and half-heartedly leading Thorn Company in sparring exercises in an open area below the cave. The mages were blasting things with fireballs, also practicing their skills in anticipation of battle. The roamers joined in with Thorn Company, a few still proclaiming that when Colonel Sorath returned, he would lead them to defeat the dragons.

Sasko shook her head, doubting Sorath was alive, but since he'd been with the captain when they'd been lost, she hoped he was, that they both were.

"What's going on there?" Tinder asked during a break. She pointed toward Tezi and Grunk, who'd paired off to spar together with their dragon-steel blades.

Sasko hadn't ordered them to work together, but it made sense, since they both had weapons that could cut through mundane steel.

"Romance?" Tinder added.

Tezi, her face set with determination as she swung and parried with the axe, didn't look like *romance* was on her mind. Her braid swung about behind her as she lunged, trying to behead the druid kid.

Grunk was fast, a more experienced fighter than she, and merely dodged, tapping his new dragon-steel blade against the haft of her axe. Deceptively powerful, the tap drove the axe wide, allowing him time to dart in and punch Tezi under the ribs. He pulled the punch, making only light contact. Tezi cursed but acknowledged the blow and jumped back with her axe up, ready to start again. Grunk must have said something telepathically, for she nodded before they began another round.

"Just training, I think." Sasko wished everyone else in the company appeared as determined. But she struggled to find the enthusiasm to motivate them—or herself. After all they'd endured, she was tired, and she couldn't help but feel they were going through the motions without any real hope of success, as they waited for their inevitable end.

"Romantic training?" Tinder asked.

"I don't know. Don't you have your own renewed romance to keep you busy?"

"I've always got time to muse on the affairs of others." Tinder winked, but her amused expression faded as she looked toward the mouth of the cave.

The zidarr Gorsith had gone in there to sleep, but he was up now, his arms folded over his chest as he watched the camp and its surroundings. He observed Tezi and Grunk more than anyone else.

Sasko hoped he wouldn't try to take their weapons. If he wanted a dragon-steel blade, his blacksmith ought to be able to provide one soon. Though from what Sasko had gathered, the mage was taking apart the chain to craft bullets, not swords or daggers.

He'd brought tools and a tent down from the ship and set up a work area, though the typical anvil and hammer weren't present. It looked more like a chemistry lab, with beakers and burners resting next to bullet molds. When he sprinkled a liquid concoction over the link he'd removed from the end of the chain, plumes of bluish smoke wafted up, wreathing his head. He wore goggles and a mask, but that didn't keep him from reeling back and waving at the smoke.

Gorsith wrinkled his nose as some of it wafted up into the cave. He climbed nimbly down the rocky slope and headed toward the mercenaries.

"Trouble coming," Tinder muttered.

"I see him." Sasko moved to intercept the zidarr since he was heading toward Tezi and Grunk.

"Don't forget to call him my lord and lick his boots," Tinder advised.

Gorsith frowned at Sasko when she stepped in his path.

"My lord," Sasko said, though she refused to tongue his footwear, "I'm Lieutenant Sasko, in charge of Thorn Company until our captain returns. Do you have orders for us?"

"Yes, stay out of the way when the dragons come. You've been no use as far as I've heard."

Sasko almost pointed out that Tezi and her axe had been, but she didn't want to bring attention to the weapon.

"See if any of them have black-powder firearms," the blacksmith called. "Those could shoot dragon-steel bullets without modifications. I can alter the magelock rifles, but it'll be more difficult."

Gorsith squinted at Sasko. "Do you?"

"I'll check," Sasko said, though she knew everyone in the company had magelock rifles and pistols since they were quieter and more powerful than black-powder weapons. The roamers might have the latter. Sorath had always preferred black powder, saying one couldn't depend on magical weapons, and the rest of the roamers held similar beliefs. "Is there anything else?"

"I want nothing from you." Gorsith used his magic to nudge her aside and strode toward Tezi and Grunk.

Scowling, Sasko hurried after him. Against most foes, she

would trust that Tezi, with that weapon in hand, could defend herself, but against a zidarr?

They'd stopped their sparring, and Grunk lowered into a crouch with his new dagger, growling as he faced Gorsith. Tezi stood more normally, but she held her axe in both hands as the zidarr approached.

"I understand that's your axe that you lucked into finding on another world," Gorsith said to Tezi, "but that dagger was Tonovan's."

"Actually," Tezi said, "he stole it from King Temrok after assassinating him and his wife."

Gorsith's eyes narrowed.

"My lord," Tezi added flatly.

"He challenged Temrok in battle and won the blade," Gorsith said.

"No, he killed an injured man and his defenseless wife. *I* was there. You weren't."

Gorsith looked toward her forehead, as if to read her mind, but the axe must have protected her. "That is not what King Uthari said."

"*He* wasn't there either," Tezi said. "And I'm sure he was trying to protect his reputation and that of his awful general, though I can't imagine why. Tonovan was a rapist and a complete asshole."

Gorsith's eyes narrowed. "Do not allow that weapon to make you overly confident in your abilities to defend yourself from those more powerful than you, mercenary. You would be wise to show respect to your superiors."

Grunk growled at him, but Gorsith ignored the druid.

"I'm not that wise," Tezi said, "and Sasko is my superior."

Sasko was busy trying to figure out how she could cause the discussion to end and Gorsith to go away.

Grunk growled at him again, carving a pattern in the air with the dagger. That was enough to draw Gorsith's attention to him.

"Rivlen should have given that weapon to me," Gorsith stated. "I'm the superior magic user and fighter and will be most able to put it to use against a dragon."

"Maybe Rivlen doesn't like you," Tezi muttered.

"You have magic and can fight a dragon without a dragon-steel dagger, my lord," Sasko said. "It's better to spread the weapons that can damage them around so we have more people who can injure the dragons."

A reasonable argument, she thought, but Gorsith didn't look at her. He was bristling at Grunk's swipes through the air with the dagger, though Grunk hadn't yet come within two feet of him.

Maybe he said something telepathically, for Grunk snarled, crouched, and sprang.

Gorsith glided to the side, blocking a swipe toward his face by knocking Grunk's arm wide. He moved so quickly that Sasko almost missed Gorsith's leg sweeping out to trip Grunk, sending the druid toward the ground.

Grunk recovered, turning the fall into a roll, and whirled as he sprang up, landing to face Gorsith.

"If I best you in battle," Gorsith told him, "you'll concede that I'm the proper owner for that blade and give it to me."

Grunk showed him his filed teeth. Tezi stepped toward Gorsith, but Grunk shook his head at her. He pointed his dagger at Gorsith's chest.

Sasko fingered her magelock pistol, but what was she going to do? Attempt to shoot a zidarr? Later, if she had bullets that could breach a mage's defenses, that might be a possibility, one she would fantasize about. For now, only Grunk and Tezi had weapons that could manage that.

Gorsith glanced toward the sky. Grunk used his distraction to lunge in, attacking again, but Gorsith, though he hadn't yet drawn his weapons, was ready for him.

Once more, he blocked and dodged. The second time, Grunk

jumped before the zidarr's foot could come out to trip him, but that proved to be a feint, and Gorsith employed a different strategy, coming in with punches. Grunk scrambled back, blocking them with a fist and the blade.

He defended well, and Sasko thought he might keep Gorsith from overpowering him, but the zidarr was fast and relentless. He pressed Grunk back, finally catching his wrist and twisting it hard enough that Grunk gasped and released the dagger. As it fell to the ground, its power to protect the druid vanishing, Gorsith used his magic to hurl Grunk into the trees.

"No!" Tezi cried as he smashed into a trunk hard.

"Stay out of it," Sasko warned, even as Tezi surged toward Gorsith.

But the zidarr grabbed the dagger before Tezi reached him and spun to face her in a crouch.

"Do you also want to challenge me?" Gorsith asked softly. "And risk giving up your blade if you lose?"

Tezi stopped, but she didn't lower the weapon. She glanced at Grunk as he groaned and pushed himself to his feet.

"No, she doesn't," Sasko said.

"Dragon coming," one of the mages in the camp called.

Sasko cursed and spun in the direction Gorsith had looked during the fight.

"Little dragon," someone amended, relief in her voice.

Shikari flew out of the trees, landed with a thump next to Gorsith, and roared.

The zidarr squinted at him, lifting the dagger. The roar almost made Sasko raise her own weapons, but she hoped they had nothing to fear from Jak's ally.

I am not little, Shikari proclaimed. *And humans should not fight among themselves. We have problems.*

"So many problems," Sasko muttered as Tinder and Basher jogged over to join her.

"Something new?" Tezi asked, though she hadn't lowered her axe or taken her gaze from Gorsith.

Grunk rose to his feet and stepped closer, eyeing the dagger again.

The one-eyed dragon has returned to Zewnath, Shikari said.

Sasko winced. "With friends?"

For now, I sense only him. Shikari pointed his snout toward the southern sky. *He flew near my hiding place last night, and I dared not leave. I tried to camouflage myself from him. There may be more dragons. I cannot sense all the way to the sea or the fortress.*

"This dragon is coming from that direction?" Gorsith pointed south.

Shikari sniffed him. *Who are you?*

"Zidarr Gorsith. I serve Uthari and command here now."

Shikari's yellow eyes closed to slits. *You tortured Jak's mate. He will be angry with you.*

"*Jak* is a wild one who's lucky to be alive," Gorsith said. "I don't know why Malek was permitted to train him, but the boy should have been killed, according to the laws that mages have made over the years."

He is my ghesivalar. *Dragon laws say that he will be protected by dragons.*

Gorsith snorted. "What dragons want to protect him?"

This *dragon does.*

Power emanated from Shikari, such great power that even sense-dead Sasko felt it. Next to her, Tinder and Basher took involuntary steps back.

Will you battle me for that dagger? Shikari must have witnessed the skirmish between Gorsith and Grunk before flying out of the trees.

"What?" Gorsith's eyebrows drew together.

If I defeat you, the prize shall be mine, yes? I need practice fighting against those with power, and I wish Jak's friends to have the dragon-

steel weapons. Shikari showed off his fangs. *You do not sound like a friend of Jak.*

Gorsith considered Shikari, and Sasko wondered if the dragonling was unwise to challenge him. She doubted a zidarr could easily beat a full-grown dragon—though Malek apparently had—but Shikari was still much smaller than his grownup brethren.

"You fight on the side of humans? Mages?" Gorsith asked.

I fight to defeat the dragons afflicted with the parasite. When Jak removes the parasite, and they are fun dragons again, dragons who do not want to turn me into a monster, I will stop fighting against them.

"I will spar with you," Gorsith said, though he didn't look like he'd followed everything. "I could use practice battling winged and tailed foes."

And you will give me the dagger if I win.

"What do I get if I win?"

I will not chew on your boots while you sleep. Shikari sank low on his forelegs, his tail swishing in the air, and eyed Gorsith's footwear.

Gorsith's eyebrows rose. "You were planning on doing that?"

Leather tastes good.

"This is a quirky dragon," Gorsith announced, not the first to do so.

"He's only a few months old," Tezi said.

"And he's a lot better than the other ones." Sasko didn't know how much experience Gorsith had with the other dragons yet, but he must have helped defend his sky city during the last attack.

Shikari growled… at Gorsith's boots.

The zidarr surprised Sasko by snorting and smiling faintly. "Come, dragon." He headed for the open area. "We will do battle."

"What just happened?" Tinder scratched her head.

"I think zidarr like training and fighting so much that Shikari seduced him with his offer." Sasko wondered if Shikari had known that would work to distract Gorsith from Grunk and Tezi. If so, he was a smart dragon. Grunk had still lost his dagger, but there was a chance he might get it back.

As Gorsith and Shikari faced off, murmurs came from the camp. At first, Sasko assumed they were related to the sparring match, but, when she turned, she found the mercenaries and roamers facing a white-haired woman wandering out of the jungle with a staff. The roamer seer Jary.

Saskο hadn't seen her for a while.

"I have had a vision," Jary announced, waving her staff, the tips covered in lesser dragon steel.

Tinder grunted skeptically, but the roamers turned toward the blind woman with rapt eyes.

"Colonel Sorath is alive!" Jary announced.

Stunned silence followed the proclamation, save for the grunts and growls from the dragon-zidarr sparring match. The roamers looked at each other and around before a few raised their arms with a cheer.

"We knew he would survive and lead us to victory over the dragons," one man said.

"Where is he?" Corporal Basher asked skeptically.

"I have seen him surrounded by smooth dark walls," Jary said. "I believe he is a prisoner in the dragon fortress. But in my vision, he was alive."

"The dragon fortress?" People groaned and slumped. "If he's not dead yet, he will be soon."

"No," Jary said. "He is crafty, and he lives. He will find a way to escape. We must travel to the fortress and pick him up so that he may lead our people in battle. He will ride on the back of a dragon!"

"All of the mageships are gone," someone said. "We couldn't go to the fortress even if we wanted to."

"We will ride with the long, narrow ship when it returns," Jary said. "Trust that Colonel Sorath is finding a way to help us, to defeat the dragons, but we must go to assist him. It is too great a task for one man alone. Have faith, people of the sea. We will find him, and we will be victorious."

The cheers were uncertain, but they did come. In the aftermath of her words, the roamers resumed their training, the clangs of weapons ringing over the sounds of the dragon-zidarr skirmish. Thorn Company appeared bolstered as well, and they also resumed their training with more gusto than before.

"Do you think she really had a vision?" Tezi asked quietly.

"You're carrying a dragon-steel blade," Sasko said. "You're more likely to know if visions are possible than I."

"I do get them, but... what if she's trying to bolster people's morale and didn't really see anything?"

Sasko shrugged. "There are worse things."

"I suppose. I just want it to be real."

Sasko did too. "Any chance you saw Captain Ferroki in your vision?" she called over as Jary sat on a log.

"I did not, but the face of Colonel Sorath was determined, not morose."

"What does that mean?"

"His eyes were not the eyes of mourning," Jary clarified.

Sasko's mouth twisted with skepticism. She suspected that even if Sorath were in mourning, his face would be determined. If anything, he would be *more* determined if he wanted to avenge Ferroki's death or make her sacrifice worth it.

But, as Sasko looked around at the camp of people—and a dragon—sparring, she wanted to believe the seer was right. She longed for Sorath *and* Ferroki to be alive and for them all to find a way to be reunited one day.

19

THOUGH MORNING SUNLIGHT STREAMED THROUGH THE PORTHOLE OF the outer room in Uthari's suite, Rivlen's head ached from all the magic she'd been drawing upon, and she already longed for a nap. But Uthari seemed to feel the press of time—and the parasites growing inside of him—for he was relentless in his instruction. Rivlen, not wishing to disappoint him, and also wanting to absorb all that she could in this private time with him, pushed herself to do everything he asked and more.

Thus far, he hadn't shown her anything new, but testing herself against him was good practice. If she one day had to do *more* than practice against him, having this opportunity to familiarize herself with his abilities could be a boon. She was a little surprised he was giving it to her.

Was it because Malek wasn't there and Uthari needed someone capable that he could trust? Or because that uncharacteristic lust that radiated from him made him want to keep an attractive woman close?

She didn't know, but she would learn all she could and endure his glances toward her chest. Besides, he truly seemed to be trying to control that. He often grimaced and looked away, reasserting his own power until the lust diminished. And he never sat close to her for long. Whenever he caught himself drawing near, he stepped away. He kept muttering about not wanting to spread the parasite.

Rivlen did not want that either. It was bad enough that *he* had it.

A knock on the door interrupted their training session.

Uthari's face contorted with anger, and he snapped, "*What?*"

A long pause followed. Rivlen sensed Admiral Nakor outside, the man recently promoted to lead the fleet in General Tonovan's place. She suspected the rest of Uthari's officers weren't any more accustomed to experiencing him being short and angry than she was. She understood the reason but wondered how much, if anything, Uthari had admitted to others. Malek of course knew, but had he confided in anyone else?

When the admiral didn't answer, Uthari growled and waved the door open with a touch of power.

Nakor, a powerful mage with short salt-and-pepper hair and a nose that could have hooked a fish, stepped warily inside. He looked at Rivlen and glanced at the door to Uthari's bedroom before coming to a rigid attention stance in front of their liege.

Rivlen hoped that look didn't mean he'd expected to find her in there, that everyone believed she was attempting to sleep her way to a promotion—or back into good favor. She clenched her jaw, telling herself it didn't matter what the other officers believed, but it was already hard enough to lead those who thought her boobs had gotten her promoted to captain.

"Report, Admiral," Uthari said, his voice calmer, his face smooth, though his left cheek kept ticking.

"We're approximately two hours from the southern shoreline of Zewnath and several more from the dragon fortress, but Admiral Flaron from King Zaruk's fleet has reached out via the dome-jir. He says they've realized we must work together, and he wants to lead a joint fleet against the dragons."

"*He* wants to lead." Uthari surged to his feet, his face losing the battle for calm. "When *I* am here?" Belatedly, he added, "And *you* are fully capable?"

Rivlen wondered if Uthari truly believed that. A number of passing remarks from the king had led her to believe he missed having Tonovan to rely upon. *She* didn't miss him, but she'd been careful not to voice that. She had no desire to remind Uthari about the events that had led to Tonovan's death.

"I told him you would wish to discuss that with him, Your Majesty," Nakor said. "He said the dome-jir is insufficient for such a discussion and suggested you talk about it in person. His fleet is flying toward ours."

"How *large* is his fleet?" Uthari's gaze grew unfocused as he looked toward the porthole. "I see. I sense them now."

Rivlen stretched out with her own senses but couldn't detect other mageships yet. Fortunately, she didn't detect any dragons either. It seemed Shikari's ruse had effectively sent them winging back toward their fortress, worried they needed to defend it.

At the time, she'd considered that good since it had kept them from finding and taking the portal, but now that she sailed on a mageship heading to do battle with that fortress, she wished the dragons were spread out all over the world instead of defending it.

"He said eight ships, Your Majesty," Nakor said.

"I sense twelve," Uthari said. "Is Zaruk's admiral being dishonest, or are you?"

Nakor blinked. "Your Majesty? I wouldn't lie to you. Of course, he is the dishonest one. We can't trust Zaruk's people. We've been at odds with them from the beginning."

Uthari strode toward him and lifted a hand. "Give me your thoughts, Admiral."

Nakor gaped and stepped back, alarm flashing in his eyes. "You want me to lower my mental barriers?"

Uthari narrowed his eyes. "If you have nothing to hide, you won't object."

Nakor looked at Rivlen, as if hoping for help.

What did he think *she* could do? It surprised her that he appeared so worried—she'd thought *she* was the only one who'd made choices that went against her king's wishes. But she didn't know Nakor well and had no idea what his ambitions and secret hopes and desires were.

"You are not lowering your defenses," Uthari whispered. Sweat gleamed on his forehead.

"Your Majesty, are you feeling unwell? Perhaps you should rest." Nakor pointed to the bedroom door.

"*Hyslar wis il ee forsarik*," Uthari whispered, and again Rivlen felt strange ancient power drip from the words.

This time, it wasn't directed at her and didn't tear down her defenses. Nakor was the one to grunt and reel back, having to grab the door frame for support.

Uthari gripped Nakor's head, as he'd done with Rivlen's, but when his fingers dug in, Nakor gasped with pain. Rivlen didn't think she had. When Uthari had done it to her, it hadn't hurt.

Now, she sensed Uthari's aura surging around the admiral, power scouring his mind and tearing ruthlessly into his thoughts.

Surprisingly, Rivlen caught a few of those flying thoughts. A conversation Nakor had engaged in, not with Zaruk's admiral but with the king himself. Nakor admitting that Uthari was sick, maybe dying, the rumors said. Zaruk promising him a great mansion in his city with all the wealth and servants a man could ever wish—and protection from Uthari's loyal zidarr, should Nakor work for him. Nakor, who never would have considered betraying Uthari under normal circumstances, had worried their king was going crazy and leading them on a suicide mission.

The admiral roared and shoved at Uthari with his power, and that was all Rivlen got. Uthari must have been surprised by the response, or maybe his fevered body lacked its usual reflexes, for he stumbled back before getting his own defenses up and halting.

Rivlen lunged for the sword she'd set aside before they started training.

Not noticing her, the admiral yanked out a dagger and summoned what must have been every ounce of his power to throw at Uthari.

Again, Uthari was pushed back, but only a step this time. Nakor must have thought that was his best shot at getting through Uthari's defenses, for he sprang farther into the cabin instead of fleeing, stabbing with the dagger.

Rivlen rushed in with her sword and knocked the dagger aside. She sensed Uthari's defenses hardening like diamond and doubted the blade would have gotten through, but the last thing she wanted was for Uthari to die and Nakor to try to take charge. Judging by his thoughts, he might try to hand the entire fleet over to Zaruk.

Her sword sliced through Nakor's dagger. He dropped the remains of his weapon and whirled toward her, trying to blast her with his power, but the dragon steel protected her. Rivlen lunged in, the sword popping the admiral's defenses, and rested the tip at his throat.

She was about to ask what Uthari wanted done—she wouldn't presume to kill a fellow officer—but Nakor stiffened abruptly, his head jerking back as he gasped.

With the admiral's defenses down, Uthari had no trouble applying his power with crushing force. Nakor's gasp turned into a scream of unadulterated pain, and blood ran from his nostrils and ears. He stumbled back, gripping his temples with both hands before his legs collapsed. By the time he hit the carpet, blood spattering the lush blue wool, he was dead.

An animalistic snarl of triumph—or pleasure?—came from Uthari.

Rivlen, worried that he'd lost control of himself, eyed him warily and kept the sword up.

Drawn by the scream, several young officers with weapons appeared in the corridor. They gaped at the dead admiral and at their king.

"Remove the body of that traitor," Uthari rasped.

The officers glanced at each other in concern, and Rivlen could only imagine the rumors that were floating about when it came to their king.

"Remove it!" Uthari roared.

"Yes, Your Majesty." They hurried inside, picking up the body instead of levitating it, and carried it into the corridor.

The door slammed shut, Uthari's doing, and he looked at Rivlen, pure madness in eyes that had been calm and aloof almost the entire time she'd known him. She swallowed, prepared to defend herself.

"Captain Rivlen," he said, his voice a purr instead of a roar. "This is the second time you've defended me."

Uthari flashed an image into her mind of her standing over him after the portal had attacked him, and as the then-invisible Colonel Sorath had been coming, hoping to finish him off.

"It's my duty to do so, Your Majesty," she whispered, though none of the wariness left her.

"You have developed questionable alliances and been swayed by inappropriate romantic feelings," he said, "but you have not betrayed me."

"No, Your Majesty." At least Rivlen could say that truthfully.

Maybe loyalty to him was something rarer than she'd believed, at least of late, for Uthari smiled and walked toward her. She made herself lower the sword, though that madness in his eyes made her certain she wasn't safe.

Though her steadfastness had never wavered, for the first time, she found herself wondering if the other officers, those who questioned Uthari, were wise and she was the fool for standing with him when he clearly wasn't himself.

Was she being loyal to the king to whom she'd sworn an oath? Or was she being loyal to billions of parasites that would happily take her as a host on their way to conquering the whole human world?

Uthari lifted a finger and pressed the sword aside so he could step closer to her. Again, she fought the urge to skitter back, but maybe she shouldn't have.

"I will continue to teach you," he said softly, "and I will reward your loyalty. Perhaps, if we're victorious against the dragons and I'm able to secure my rule over the world, I'll even let you have the one for whom you've developed those inappropriate romantic feelings."

Rivlen's eyes widened. "Your Majesty?"

He couldn't mean Jak. He *hated* Jak.

Only after that thought settled in did the rest of what he'd said register in her brain. He wanted to secure rule over *the world*? Not only his kingdom?

Of course, she shouldn't be surprised. He'd ordered Tonovan to take over Temril and kill its king.

"Yes, Jak." Uthari's mouth twisted. "He's a thorn in my foot, especially since Malek doesn't want him or his mother dead, but, over the years, I've learned to reward loyalty, not punish it more than necessary."

Though she'd recently endured intense pain at his behest, Rivlen carefully kept her face blank, not wanting any resentment to slip through. She didn't know if he still had the ability to see past her mental barrier and into her mind.

"And when the dragon threat is gone, I won't need to worry as much about one boy with modest power."

Rivlen almost asked *what about his mother and her far-from-modest power?* But she didn't want to remind Uthari of that, not if he was contemplating letting Jak live. And maybe even letting her have a relationship with him?

But would *Jak* consider that? He was so damn wholesome and good-hearted. Would he ever settle down and become the mage he had the power to be if Uthari got what he wanted? Rule over the world? Or would he and his mother keep fighting him?

Rivlen didn't know, but she had suspicions, and she believed Uthari was too smart not to share those suspicions.

It occurred to her that he might be lying to her. She'd already sensed him manipulating her. Why wouldn't he do so again? To ensure she would loyally stand beside him and keep fighting anyone who dared betray him. Or even question him. She glanced at the fresh blood staining the carpet.

Uthari touched her jaw, turning her face toward him again. A tingle of alluring power ran from his fingers and through her.

"Remain at my side," he said, magical compulsion in those words, "and I'll reward you with all that you wish and more."

"Yes, Your Majesty," she said, afraid to say or think anything else as he watched her with his eyes and his senses.

"And you'll protect me as I struggle with this unpleasant internal problem, won't you? I can trust you, Captain. I know I can."

Rivlen swallowed, mesmerized by his magic. "Yes, Your Majesty."

She couldn't help but wonder how much *he* was mesmerized, or at least affected by the parasite growing within him. Once again, she debated if he was choosing her because he trusted her. Or was it whatever ancient lust the thing had stirred within him that wanted him to keep her close, a young and attractive female perhaps more appealing than his balding generals and admirals?

"Good." Uthari smiled and nodded at her, then pointed toward the door. "Let's go out and see how we can wrangle control of Zaruk's fleet from him, shall we? I want more ships to throw at the dragons, and I'd be delighted if they weren't mine. Let Zaruk's people be dragon fodder."

"Yes, Your Majesty." Rivlen trailed him out, though she wished she were off with Jak, someone who dreamed of saving the world instead of conquering it.

Until that day, Rivlen hadn't questioned whether there was anything wrong with pursuing her personal goals and having ambitions, but maybe that was because it had been too inconvenient to do so. Achieving greatness in Uthari's fleet was the only way she knew to get what she'd always craved: her father's respect. But maybe the price for that prize was too great.

A thought she wished she'd had *before* Uthari had swept her up onto his ship, given her the dragon-steel sword, and elicited a promise from her to protect him.

Tezi woke to the roars of a dragon. She grabbed her axe and leaped to her feet, glancing skyward, but the roars came from Shikari. He and Gorsith were sparring again. Or *still* sparring.

But the zidarr was using his own weapons instead of the dragon-steel dagger. Did that mean Shikari had bested him and won it back? Tezi looked around but didn't see Grunk.

A yawn caught her, and she tried to guess the time. They'd all been up late, and few of the mercenaries were stirring, but it was well past dawn, with morning sunlight filtering through the canopy. The cave, the top of the portal visible from the camp below, lay in shadow.

Shikari roared and must have drawn upon his magic, for Gorsith went flying backward through the air. Before he would have smashed into a tree, the zidarr used his own power to halt his flight, doing a somersault to land on his feet and face the dragon again with his weapons up.

"We should be sparring too," Tezi muttered.

After relieving herself and splashing water on her face, she went to Sasko, who was sitting up with Tinder, both chewing on jerky.

"Ma'am, may I lead a training session?" Tezi waved toward the mercenaries lying on the ground, most with eyes open but few appearing interested in doing anything. "In case Sorath and the captain are alive, we should stay in good shape, right?"

"The crazy old seer didn't say the captain was alive," Tinder pointed out.

"She didn't say she *wasn't*," Tezi said.

"Rookies. So optimistic."

"She's a corporal now, remember." Sasko nodded at Tezi. "Round up some victims, Tezi. Tinder and I will join you after we finish our delightful breakfasts." She made a face at her jerky.

"Don't forget to try the mystery fruit." Tinder handed her a large leaf serving as a plate, with unevenly sliced purple-fleshed rings with spiky rinds.

"You could cut yourself on that fruit."

"Only if you eat the pointy side. The inside isn't too bad. Kind of a mix between strawberries and chalk."

"Mm, chalk."

Tezi patted a few mercenaries on the shoulders, including Yelotta.

"I don't want to train," the woman muttered.

"It'll help keep your mind off our problems," Tezi said. "And your losses."

Yelotta looked at her without stirring, and Tezi was about to move on to someone else, but she sighed. "I guess you're right. Moping doesn't help anything."

"I've heard that."

"Is there room out here for more?" Tezi asked, leading her crew into the open area below the cave mouth.

Shikari and Gorsith had churned up the earth, even charring it in places, but it was the only place where trees wouldn't get in the way.

There is room, Shikari replied, *but watch out for flying humans who can't keep up their defenses.*

"My defenses are more than adequate for dealing with a baby dragon," Gorsith replied.

That is why those trees over there have dents that look like your face in them. Shikari swished his tail in the direction of a copse.

"Just as those trees over *there*—" Gorsith pointed in the opposite direction, "—are littered with *your* face dents."

I barely brushed them as I flew past. Had you succeeded in knocking me against them, they would have fallen over.

"Please. You're such a small dragon that the leaves wouldn't have fallen off."

I am growing. Large and mighty. Shikari roared and charged.

As they came together, blades meeting horn and fang, Tinder shook her head. "Are they bonding or trying to kill each other?"

"Yes?" Tezi offered. "Did you see if Shikari won back the dagger?"

"I'm not sure how or when it happened, but it seems so. Grunk took it with him when he went to wash and piss."

"Dragon steel is good company."

Tinder snorted. "All right, kid—Corporal. Let's spar."

Tezi nodded, but she pulled Yelotta aside to work with, waving to indicate that she would join Tinder later. Maybe if someone spent time with Yelotta, she would feel more wanted and important in the unit. Tezi had longed for that when she'd first joined and had been mourning the loss of her family.

An hour into their workout, Shikari and Gorsith parted, with the zidarr wiping sweat from his face, then heading up the slope to the cave. Though Tezi kept practicing her attack combinations with Tinder and Yelotta, she kept an eye on him. It continued to worry her that Rivlen had been replaced by him.

What if he wasn't as dedicated to this mission as she had been? What if he did something to the portal so the others couldn't return?

Tezi knew Shikari would object to anyone attempting to keep Jak from returning, but after their sparring match had ended, he'd flopped down on his side in the shade.

"Should we check on the zidarr?" Tinder tapped Tezi's axe with her sword but didn't take advantage of her distraction.

"I was wondering that," Tezi said.

"I figured. Either that or you were checking out his taut muscular ass, the way Sasko always did with men before she got moony over her engineer."

"I hadn't noticed his ass, and I didn't think you noticed such things on men either."

"I can appreciate tautness in all its forms." Tinder winked, then waved toward the cave. The zidarr had disappeared inside. "I'm not sure he'll appreciate us snooping on him though."

"No." Tezi shivered, remembering the run-ins with zidarr she'd had this past year, but she reminded herself that as long as she held the axe, Gorsith wouldn't be able to read her mind. "But it's not snooping if we go up to check on the portal. Or rub it for luck." She headed for the slope.

"Isn't that what Uthari was doing when it zapped him with a lightning bolt?"

"He was commanding it to do his bidding, not rubbing it."

When they crested the slope and stepped into the cave, they found Gorsith standing beside the portal, his hand next to the device responsible for its hibernation.

"What are you doing?" Tezi blurted, envisioning dragons

coming from all directions if the device were removed and the portal exuded its natural power like a beacon.

Gorsith squinted at her. "You question me, girl?"

"Uh, yes."

"No." Tinder held up a hand, stepping in front of Tezi and shooting her a warning look. "We're not questioning you, my lord. We came up to rub the portal for luck."

Gorsith turned his squint on her. Realizing he would have no trouble reading Tinder's thoughts, Tezi rested a hand on her arm, hoping to spread the axe's influence. To keep him not only from reading Tinder's mind but from lashing out at her with his magic.

"It is not a *luck* charm, and I don't need to read your mind to tell you are lying." Gorsith eyed Tezi's hand.

Regardless, she didn't remove it.

"Return to your unit, and do not question me," Gorsith said. "I'm in charge of this camp, placed here by King Uthari, and I will do as I wish."

"If your wish is removing that, you could get us all killed," Tezi said.

"Those with the power to fight dragons will not die." Gorsith eyed the portal speculatively as he ran a hand over the smooth dragon steel.

"A lot of powerful mages have died fighting dragons," Tezi said. "Did Shikari best you and get the dagger back?"

Gorsith sneered. "He *tricked* me by making believe an attack came from behind."

"Other dragons could trick you too."

"I will not fall for that again, now that I know they employ such tactics."

What, had he thought dragons were dumb? The creatures that had invented and built the portal system?

Gorsith reached for the device, resting his hand on it.

"We're only supposed to remove that at midnight each night," Tezi said, though she was certain Rivlen had passed on that information to him. "If it doesn't stay on, the portal won't remain dormant."

"I am aware of what it does. I have also seen the portal shoot out immensely powerful lightning attacks. Just yesterday, it did so. We should be using its power, not suffocating it. Let it draw dragons to us, and then, while it hurls lightning at our foes, I will attack and *kill* them." Gorsith lifted his chin. "It will be glorious."

"What if *all* the dragons come? And what if you can't convince the portal to attack them? It's only done so willingly for Jak. It likes dragons and wants to help them, not kill them so they can't be cured of their parasitic infections."

Gorsith frowned at her. Tezi couldn't tell if it was because he continued to object to a terrene human questioning him or if he didn't understand. Maybe Rivlen *hadn't* briefed him fully.

"It would be foolish not to attack those dragons and keep them from taking it to their fortress," Gorsith said. "It *will* help us. It will help me, and I will slay dragons and prove myself to my king. He will see that I am as great a zidarr as Malek." Gorsith lowered his voice. "And if Malek doesn't return, I will take his place at my king's side."

"It's not going to happen that way," Tezi said, stepping forward. "You'll only get us all killed. You included. Even a zidarr can't win against a dragon."

"*Malek* won against a dragon." Indignation and fury burned in Gorsith's eyes. "As Uthari reiterated numerous times to me. Lovingly." Gorsith shook his head. "I do not begrudge him his victories, but I will show Uthari that I am as capable."

Was that why Gorsith had wanted to practice with Shikari? So he could better learn to fight dragons? Maybe he hadn't yet had an opportunity to do so, and that was why he was arrogant in his belief that he could slay them. As Tezi well remembered, Malek had barely survived his first battle with a dragon.

"Wonderful," Tinder said. "A zidarr who's out to prove himself. In our camp."

Gorsith scowled and flicked power at Tinder.

Realizing she'd released Tinder when she stepped forward, Tezi cursed and lunged to grab her arm again. But she was too slow. Tinder flew backward, landing on her butt and rolling down the slope amid grunts and curses.

All the mercenaries, mages, and roamers in camp stood, looking from her to the cave.

"Are you all right?" Tezi called, tempted to run after her, but Dr. Fret jogged out of the trees toward Tinder.

Blue light flared behind Tezi and she whirled. Gorsith had removed the device. He smiled and stuck it in his pocket, then slid a hand over the portal again.

"You will defend yourself against the dragons, won't you?" Gorsith crooned to it, as if it were a lover.

If the portal responded in any way, Tezi didn't hear it. But that telltale blue glow was enough to inform her that it had woken.

"I sense your great power," Gorsith whispered. "Together, we'll defeat any dragons that show up. You should be able to bait them and lure them in, not remain hidden in this cave, forced into unnatural slumber."

Tezi licked her lips and stepped forward with her axe raised. "Put the device back on."

Once more, Gorsith's eyes narrowed as he looked at her. "You *dare* give me orders, girl?"

"*Please* put the device back on, my lord." Maybe if Tezi was polite about it...

"If the portal doesn't smite you for your impudence, I will."

Tezi was confident the axe would protect her from smiting, but she was a lot less confident in her ability to best a zidarr in a sparring match. No, in a fight to the death. She had little doubt that Gorsith would kill her for presuming to give him an order.

"You must put the device back on." Tezi attempted to sound reasonable. "It is what your king ordered, isn't it?"

"All he said was to keep the portal open so the others could return. That will be easier for them to do if they don't have to wait until *midnight.* And if we slay any dragons in the area." Gorsith patted the portal. "Strike her down, my friend. Show her the folly of trying to force you into hibernation."

Tezi remembered that Rivlen had been worried the portal wouldn't allow the device to be put on. She'd heard Jak had been too. What if the portal *enjoyed* being awake and free and ended up siding with Gorsith?

"It won't lash out at me," Tezi said, not sure how confident she managed to sound. "It's friends with Jak and Shikari, and they like me."

"*Like* you. A girl with no innate power of your own? Doubtful." Gorsith drew his sword. "But if you keep threatening me and giving me orders, I'll happily punish you. Or perhaps, those more powerful, who deserve that axe more than you, would prefer you cease to exist altogether."

Tezi stepped forward, though she didn't know what she would do if he wouldn't put the device back on. Swing her axe at his head?

Shikari? Though she had no telepathic ability, it was possible the dragonling would hear her. His magic had allowed him to do so often. *I need your help. Jak does.*

Gorsith prowled closer to her, and Tezi doubted Shikari had heard her. After exercising all night, he might be sleeping. Maybe there had been *two* reasons Gorsith had wanted to spar with the dragonling.

Refusing to back down, Tezi crouched, prepared to defend herself.

Blue flared, and the air crackled with electricity. Gorsith whirled toward the portal.

Tezi hoped it would strike him in the chest with lightning, but, beyond the warning flare, it didn't attack. It did, however, reach out telepathically, sharing feelings and imagery.

A vision popped into Tezi's mind, as if her axe were giving her a warning, but she was sure it came from the portal. It showed her and Gorsith standing in the mouth of the cave, shoulder to shoulder, their weapons raised not toward each other but toward the sky. Shikari and the portal were inside behind them, and, as dragons flew to their position—no fewer than ten of them—they braced themselves to work together to protect Shikari.

The dragons roared and leered, their long fangs easily capable of piercing a man straight through. Their eyes were angry—or mad?—as they snapped at the air, then arrowed toward the cave.

Shikari roared at the sky, but the portal conveyed the need to keep the dragons from reaching him, from infesting him with the parasite or killing him outright. He was no match for one, much less a huge group of them.

Though it didn't use words, Tezi had the distinct impression the portal was telling them to knock off their squabbling and focus on what was important. And that was keeping Shikari alive. If it cared whether Tezi and Gorsith lived or died, she couldn't tell, but the portal *did* flash blue at Gorsith when he scowled over at Tezi. She assumed he was receiving the same vision, the same warning, and didn't care for it.

"Will you fight with us, portal?" Gorsith asked it.

The ancient artifact flashed again, then shared a vision of it beaming out glowing particles toward the approaching dragons. Longing and wistfulness emanated from the portal as it wrapped the particles around the dragons, making them glow as well. They turned from mottled brown-and-gray dragons to iridescent-blue-scaled dragons. The fury left their faces, and, instead of arrowing down to attack, they flapped through the air, diving and banking and playing with each other in the sky. More longing came from the portal.

"*That's* what it wants," Tezi said, though she doubted anything the portal could beam at the dragons would change them. Jak and Malek were on a mission because nobody knew how to do that. "And I think that's why it won't help you kill dragons."

"If it won't help me," Gorsith said stiffly, "I will slay them on my own."

He stalked down the slope without looking back.

"You're going to kill ten dragons single-handedly?" Tezi called after him.

Gorsith didn't answer, instead striding into the trees and disappearing. He'd taken the device with him, damn it.

"I don't suppose you can hibernate on your own?" Tezi asked the portal.

It showed her another image of blue dragons frolicking in the sky. Tezi rubbed her face, wondering how Jak had convinced the portal to do anything.

20

MALEK WOKE WITH HIS MOUTH DRY, HIS HEAD POUNDING, AND HIS mind filled with the certainty that he'd called upon far too much of his power. He'd never been drunk and had a hangover, alcohol and other excesses being frowned upon, if not outright forbidden, by the zidarr code, but he imagined it felt similar.

He couldn't remember ever dealing with so much magic working against him that hadn't come from a person—or other intelligent being. All of the natural world had seemed to be trying to trap the gateship beneath the surface, holding it over the strong corrosive gases coming out of that vent.

No, not the natural world. As he'd told Jak, he believed something had been manipulating everything from afar. Near the end, he'd even sensed something out there, though it had been so distant that he hadn't been able to detect the source. He feared that whatever it was had the power of a dragon, or even *more* power than a dragon, if that was possible. He hadn't yet heard of or experienced dragons being able to cast their magic across hundreds of miles and do great damage from a distance.

Though it hurt, Malek reached out with his mind, wanting to

see where the gateship was and what was going on. The deck rocked underneath the cot he found himself on, so he knew they'd reached the surface, but he didn't know how much time had passed or if they were currently in danger.

He sensed Jadora beside him, and that made him pause in surprise. How had he gotten into the laboratory with her? The hole in the ceiling remained, but the door was also open.

Strangely, Malek still sensed her power reinforcing it and the walls around it, but a small magical device attached over the lock hummed softly. It had Vinjo's essence all over it.

Had he used engineering know-how to override Jadora's great magic, magic that Malek hadn't been able to thwart with all his raw power? If so, there was a lesson in zidarr arrogance for him. He should have asked Vinjo's thoughts on the door in the beginning.

Jadora moaned softly. As soon as Malek assured himself there weren't any dangerous magical entities nearby, he rolled off his cot and knelt beside hers.

Her eyes remained closed, but she shifted under the blanket, her hair dampened with sweat. She didn't waken when he touched her fevered cheek and whispered, *Jadora?* into her mind. Pain and discomfort radiated from her. He used his magic in an attempt to soothe her, to boost her immune system to better fight off the bacteria battling within her.

Malek could sense them and, in an angry fit, tried to destroy them using the knowledge she'd shared. But, as he'd feared, it wasn't a magic he was familiar with and couldn't master so quickly. All he could tell was that both the dragon parasite and the death-darter bacteria had multiplied within her.

"Oh, Jadora," he whispered softly and stroked the side of her head, the pain in his skull convincing him to stop using his power. He might need it soon to combat the enemies without.

Clangs came from the engineering room, and he sensed Jak

and Vinjo back there, furiously building something. Soon, Malek would check on them, but it was hard to leave when Jadora was in so much pain.

Her face contorted, her back arching off the cot, and distress filled him as he groped for some way to help. Again, he willed some of his power into her, hoping it would give her the energy she needed to win the battle.

She slumped, an arm flopping off the cot as her muscles went limp. Whether that was a good sign or not, he didn't know. He picked up her arm and laid it across her stomach, then rested his hand on hers, her heated skin worrying him.

I'm sorry I let Uthari do this to you, he spoke softly into her mind, though he doubted she was aware of him. *You've endured great torment, not only now but for these past months, because of him. And... because of me. Because I serve him.*

Malek closed his eyes, realizing Uthari's torment had started even further back. It had been years since Jadora had lost her husband and Jak's father, because Uthari had wanted the portal and had given Tonovan free rein to use whatever means necessary to find it. Back then, Malek hadn't considered fighting and deterring Tonovan. Deterring Uthari. Because it had been his duty to obey without question.

He'd owed Uthari for taking him in as a boy and training him, but after thirty years of service, he'd repaid that debt, surely. Now... to mindlessly obey was wrong. It had led to this.

When we get back, Malek continued, *whether he's willing to release me from my service or not, I will leave him. As long as you survive and will come with me. I need you to survive, otherwise... I don't know.* Would he walk away from Uthari if he had nothing to walk toward?

Yes, he decided. It was because of Uthari that she was in this state. He deserved death for what he'd done—all the cruelties that he'd committed through the years. Maybe Malek deserved death, as well, for mindlessly obeying him.

If he didn't have Jadora, he might not care if that fate found him. Though *she* wouldn't approve of him letting himself be killed, he was sure.

You need to survive, Jadora. I love you. And I want the opportunity to help you find happiness. To make up for all that we've done to you.

He bent his neck, lowering his forehead to rest on her stomach, and wished he'd said all that earlier, when she was awake to hear him. When they weren't in danger of being killed or trapped on this strange world forever.

A soft touch at the back of his head surprised him, and he turned his face to look at Jadora. Her eyes were open, glazed as she stared up at the ceiling, but she'd brought her hand to the back of his head.

You're awake, he said softly, though his senses told him that not much had changed, that the bacteria continued warring within her.

Someone was whispering to me in my dreams, she replied, her fingers threading through his hair. *It seemed polite to wake up and respond.*

That is *polite, yes.* Malek was hesitant to move, lest her hand drop from his head, but her lips were cracked and dry. She needed water badly. *I love you, Jadora*, he said in case she hadn't heard it before.

I love you too, Malek. She closed her eyes.

Wait. Don't sleep. He gently set her hand aside and picked up the canteen, cradling her head in his arm and lifting the water to her lips.

I'm tired.

You can sleep after you drink. Malek frowned when she didn't open her mouth to try.

Are you giving me orders, Malek? Her eyes remained closed, but she smiled.

You know it's my duty as an arrogant zidarr.

I thought you said you would retire from that.

Ah, she *had* heard some of what he'd been saying. Good.

He stroked her cheek. *I can retire from being a zidarr.* He hoped that was true. *I don't think I can retire from being arrogant any more than you can retire from collecting specimens.*

Innate nature?

Yes. Now drink.

Her lips parted and he tipped small amounts of the water in, afraid she would be too weary to swallow. But once she got a taste, she drank deeply.

Your obedience in this matter pleases me, he said, hoping she would appreciate his attempt at humor. The gods knew that making people laugh wasn't a strength of his.

You know how eager I've always been to obey arrogant mages.

You're one of those yourself now, he reminded her.

I'm a modest mage, not an arrogant one.

I believe modest mage is an oxymoron.

How is Jak doing? Is he all right?

Fine. He's working on a project with Vinjo. Malek didn't want her to worry about anything beyond getting better, so he didn't mention that something powerful was out there and didn't want them to live. He did, however, realize she might be curious about the vent, so he shared an image of it with her. *We encountered a corrosive gas wafting out of a fissure in the sea floor. It attempted to eat away at my barrier.* He realized that some of it had gotten *through* his barrier when he'd been under attack. *It may have damaged the hull.*

Later, he would check. On the surface, they didn't have to worry about water pressure crushing the gateship, but if they went back down again, they would need to make sure any damage had been patched. *Well* patched.

Interesting. I'd like a sample.

We've left the area.

If the hull is corroded, scrape off a piece for me, and bring it in, please. It's possible the water won't have entirely washed it away.

You want me to do this now? Malek asked dryly.

Whenever you're done cuddling with me. Though I do enjoy that. Jadora finally had her fill of the water and leaned her head against his chest. *When Zelonsera gave me this power, I didn't want it. I thought it would be more of a curse than a blessing.*

But that's changed?

I'm not sure I could have survived the dragon parasite and the death-darter bacteria both raging in my system without it. They don't seem to care if they destroy their host in their quest to annihilate each other. I feel like a bystander, watching in horror as they sling explosives at each other and waiting to be caught by a stray round.

The thought chilled him. *Do you think you're past the worst of it?*

I don't know. They're both still alive. They may be regrouping before starting the war again.

It was hard for him to imagine microscopic organisms plotting out battles like generals in armies. *I hope the worst is past and that you'll return to yourself soon.*

Malek kissed her forehead before remembering that being that close to her wasn't a good idea. Logically, the parasite ought to be too busy to think about spreading to another host, but if it sensed that Jadora was dying or that it was losing the battle, might it not try to flee and establish a foothold somewhere else?

I hope for that too. Jadora's eyes remained closed, but she lifted her hand, resting it against his chest. *I'm glad you're here with me. And that my execrable state has convinced you to retire from zidarr-ness.*

But not pompousness.

I can live with that.

Good. I need you to live.

I'm trying. If I don't... this won't be much of a solution for the dragon parasite.

Malek didn't point out that Uthari would probably *prefer* it as a solution, one that killed the parasite and the host at the same time. That would leave Torvil free of dragons so wizards could continue to rule, their power unopposed by a greater species. But Uthari himself would also die, so maybe he no longer wished that result.

Malek pushed aside the thoughts. He was tired of worrying about what Uthari wanted. He didn't know if a world full of dragons like Shikari would be better than one without dragons at all, but, for Jadora's sake, he would wish for a solution that didn't kill the host.

You'll survive, he told her firmly. *And you'll find a way to make this work. I am confident in you and your abilities.*

Thank you for that. She patted his hand before slumping down on the cot again, weariness taking her back into the realm of unconsciousness.

~

"We could use Malek's help," Vinjo said as he fiddled with the latest magical device he was making. "And a *lot* more raw materials. Had I known how much I would have to build out here, I would have brought an entire workshop and a warehouse full of supplies."

"You're doing a good job of repurposing things." Jak smiled, attempting to be encouraging, but he was highly aware of time passing, of some entity out there that didn't want them to live. Back home, the fleet might already be engaged with the dragons—and their fortress of death.

Worse, the air in the ship kept getting thinner. His lungs ached, and he had a headache.

They were on the surface, the gateship bobbing in the waves as the engines took them in the direction the portal had pointed Jak, but Vinjo had examined the air outside before opening the hatch and confirmed Jak's suspicion. It was too full of deadly gases and would kill them if they breathed it for long without filtering out the toxins. The device he was working on now, something to stretch across the hatchway and purify the air that came in, *should* allow them to replenish the supply within the gateship—if it worked. Vinjo's curses and scowls weren't encouraging.

From what Jak had sensed of the world outside, all the life was down in the ocean. They weren't that far from land, one of the smoking volcanos the portal had shown him, but there was no hint of birds or insects or anything on the surface. Whatever had happened to this world, it might have made all of the land uninhabitable.

"We need some of Jadora's plants," Vinjo muttered. "I believe they filter toxins as well as taking in carbon dioxide."

"Maybe you can emulate a plant with your filtration system."

"I… hmm."

Jak sensed Malek approaching and looked toward the corridor. As soon as Vinjo had found a way past Mother's magically sealed door, Jak had levitated Malek into the laboratory, figuring they would want to be unconscious together in the same room—true love was like that, wasn't it?

Since then, Jak had been helping Vinjo and sweeping out and down with his senses, hoping none of the entities that had attempted to trap them would follow them to the surface. Thus far, they remained far below. Maybe however they'd evolved to survive at such depths made it difficult for them to live in the light and with less water pressure. He hoped so, though that only gave the gateship a reprieve. Once they dove down again to reach the ruins, they might encounter the same trouble and more.

Malek stepped into the doorway, appearing almost as weary and haggard as Mother. He held what looked like a scalpel and vial in his hand. "Are we floating because we've been damaged and can't fly?"

"We should be able to fly as soon as the ballast tanks finish draining," Vinjo said without looking up from his work. "The water adds a lot of extra weight."

Malek nodded.

"If you're feeling better," Jak told him, "Vinjo would like your power for his new device."

Malek *didn't* look like he was feeling much better, but if they couldn't get clean air into the ship, they would all be doomed.

"Jadora wants a sample of the corrosive acid," Malek said.

Vinjo gaped at him. "You want us to go back to that vent?"

At the same time, Jak blurted, "She woke up?"

"Briefly," Malek said, "and she thinks I can get it off the hull of the ship."

"She woke up from her deathbed to ask for a sample to examine?" Vinjo used a wrench to scratch his head.

"It's not her *deathbed*," Malek said coolly. "It's a cot in a laboratory, the ideal place to examine a sample."

Jak started to smile—he wasn't surprised in the least that his mother, however poorly she felt, wanted to examine that acid—but the gesture faltered as he realized Malek might not be able to go outside.

"The air is bad," Jak said. "Toxic. Until we can create a filtration device, we're stuck with what little we have left to breathe in the ship."

Malek eyed Vinjo's contraption. It looked more like a strainer for a pond than a high-powered magical filtration device.

"I'll create a barrier over the hatch to keep the outside air from coming in," Malek said, "then hold my breath while I swim out to collect her sample."

"Are we sure that should be a priority now?" Vinjo looked at Jak.

"Uhm." Jak didn't think so, but he wouldn't argue with Malek.

"I think we should get this filter working before anything else," Vinjo said.

"But *I* am in command, so we will do what *I* wish," Malek said, then relented to add, "I'll assist you with your device after I collect the sample."

"He's better than most zidarr," Vinjo whispered after Malek headed for the hatch, "but he's still a pompous ass."

Jadora has assured me, Malek told them telepathically as he climbed the ladder, *that she appreciates my pomposity.*

"That's because she's sick and delusional," Vinjo muttered and bent over his work again.

Concerned about Malek's ability to keep the air out while he left the ship, Jak tracked him with his senses. He also checked on his mother, but if she'd been awake earlier, she was sleeping again now.

Malek created a bubble that filled the ladder well, and when he opened the hatch, it kept the air out as he exited. With a flick of his magic, he closed the hatch. Once on the deck, he paused to look around but only for a second. Jak had peered out the portholes and knew there wasn't much to see there except hazy gray air.

Malek dove over the side of the ship and swam quickly down to the bottom, finding the spot on the hull that had been damaged by the gas. From inside, Jak couldn't see that damage, and it wasn't magical so he couldn't sense it, but he didn't doubt that it was there. It didn't take Malek long to take his sample, swim back up, and climb onto the deck of the ship. But when he reached the hatch, he paused.

Something wrong? Jak asked when long seconds passed and Malek didn't move. Jak didn't want him to inhale that noxious air.

More long seconds passed before Malek replied. *Yes.*

He opened the hatch, again using his magic to keep the bad air out, then joined them in engineering, carrying not only vials but a blue-black link of chain.

"That's my luck charm," Vinjo protested. "It's supposed to stay on the hull of the ship. It's... er, is that *corroded*?"

Malek held it up for Vinjo to examine. Large chunks had been eaten out of it, leaving a white residue behind.

"I didn't think that could happen to dragon steel," Vinjo breathed.

"The wood of the hull, even though it's covered in your pitch, is in worse condition. You'll need to patch it before we dive down again." Malek held up a vial with shards of wood inside, but he eyed the chain, as if that were the true find. Maybe it was.

"Fascinating," Vinjo murmured. "The barrier was down so briefly. That is some potent acid. To be able to corrode *magic.* Not just magic, but *dragon steel.*"

"When I was out there," Malek said, "I was able to sense the being that attacked me earlier."

"I'd wondered about that," Jak said as Vinjo examined the link from all angles. "When you, uhm, collapsed, it seemed to be from more than exertion."

Malek narrowed his eyes, as if displeased by the reminder that he'd had a moment of weakness. "It was. Something was attacking me from afar. Something extremely powerful. It was too far away for me to sense at the time, and yet it was still able to affect me."

Affect him? It had incapacitated him. Given how powerful Malek was, Jak found that worrying.

"You're able to sense it now?"

Malek nodded. "It's in the direction we're heading."

"Of course it is," Vinjo muttered.

"I don't know yet what it is, but I believe it's more powerful than a dragon." Malek lifted the vial and chain link. "I'll take these to Jadora, then return to assist with the filter. We may also want to reapply the camouflaging magic to the gateship, as it hasn't been effective here."

"Because I didn't design it to fool *plants*," Vinjo said.

"It didn't fool the sharks either."

"I'm sorry. I'm not perfect."

"Perhaps you should remedy that flaw." Malek smiled faintly—Jak caught it but he didn't think Vinjo did—before heading to the laboratory.

"Is it wrong to hope the super powerful thing out there eats him?" Vinjo asked.

"Yes. We need him."

"Tedious."

"As mages often are," Jak said.

"You're one too now, remember."

"Yes, but I'm a delight."

"Uh huh. Hold my wrench."

As Jak accepted the tool, he grew aware of something in the distance. Though the ship was floating, it was sailing in the direction of the ruins, and he realized he could now sense what Malek had sensed. The powerful entity that had been attempting to thwart their mission, if not outright destroy them, since they'd arrived.

Malek was right: it was located in—or *waiting* in—the place they were going.

21

"He's been gone a long time," Ferroki said.

She sat beside Sorath, her head leaning on his shoulder. Had they been anywhere else, he would have appreciated the intimacy. Even in their current predicament, he managed to appreciate it a little.

"Our people are capable of killing dragons, especially *lone* dragons," he said.

"You think they got him? He's clever, you know."

Sorath grunted. "So he thinks."

He admitted that Yoshartov wasn't dumb—it wasn't as if Sorath had managed to fool him at any point yet. But he was vain, the type of dragon who believed he could single-handedly acquire a well-guarded artifact. To impress his queen, no doubt. She'd probably intentionally sent him to his death to get him out of her hair—her scales.

Sorath didn't know if he'd yet seen that queen—all dragons looked alike to him—but he would cheerfully sink his dagger in her eye if he got a chance.

"I feel like we should try again to do something," Ferroki said.

"We should, but the dragons don't seem to be thinking about us right now, and I'm hesitant to change that when our protector isn't around."

They'd slept through the night and passed half a day and hadn't been disturbed. During the rest period, Sorath had woken often, thinking he'd heard talons on the hard floors. A couple of times, he'd contemplated leaving Ferroki to make another attempt at sabotage by himself. But she would be vulnerable if he didn't stay close enough to extend the influence of the dagger over her.

We have been training hard, but we are out of food, someone announced, a telepathic message sent indiscriminately to everyone in the fortress. There had been a few like that, Sorath and Ferroki able to hear and understand them as well.

Go get some more fish. Or humans.

Sorath exchanged an uneasy look with Ferroki.

There's a dead human that hasn't yet been disposed of.

One must eat one's enemies alive to thoroughly enjoy them. Stale meat is of little interest.

Two remain alive.

Sorath rose to his feet. "This doesn't sound good."

Yes, a dragon practically purred. *Yoshartov's pets. The male is feisty. I would enjoy eating such an enemy.*

"I'm feisty too," Ferroki muttered.

"Don't tell them that." Sorath headed for the exit, the discussion of feisty potential meals propelling him to action. "Let's see if there really *is* an access panel in that control cave."

Maybe they should have done that earlier. Sorath couldn't tell from the telepathic words how close the dragons were, but he suspected they were all in the fortress. The nest in the courtyard near their tower was empty, but that didn't mean the others were.

With Ferroki following, he started at a stride, but they ended up running as the flap of wings drifted down to them. They had to pass through the open courtyard to reach the tunnel and cave system on the far side. As they hurried across, the sun out and shining on them for all to see, Sorath offered his pickaxe arm to Ferroki.

"Grab on," he said, hoping the dragons would use magical instead of physical attacks on them.

Even as she grasped his arm, the first blast of power swept through the courtyard. He sensed it whispering past and ran faster.

They have dragon steel, someone cried.

That fool left them with weapons.

Wings flapped, and Sorath didn't have to look up to know a dragon was diving for them. Sprinting now, he and Ferroki made it to the tunnel entrance on the far side. A dragon thumped to the floor right behind them, and a fireball blasted into the passageway as they raced inside. Though it didn't burn them, flames flaring all around them and scorching the air ahead was alarming.

That won't do anything. Use your fangs to catch them. We're starving.

Unfortunately, the tunnel was wide enough for the dragons to fly into. As Sorath and Ferroki neared the control cave, one of the creatures stepped out of the alcove scant feet beyond it. It was the same dragon that had tried to kill them before, and its eyes lit up with pleasure as it likely imagined chomping them in half.

Cursing, Sorath guided Ferroki into the control cave, then turned, intending to face their enemy, to buy her the time she needed to find the panel. If there *was* a panel. If not, this would be their last stand.

He glanced at the magical machinery, wondering if he should take these last moments to try again to destroy it. After all, he'd only struck a few of the devices. Maybe there was a vulnerable one in there.

More dragons arrived in the tunnel outside.

"Get between the devices," Ferroki called from the back. "It'll be harder for them to reach you without destroying their own machinery."

"Good point." Sorath backed between a floating sphere and a glowing and humming cylinder attached to the floor. The power the devices emitted made his skin itch even with the dagger in his hand, but he scooted in deeper.

Maybe the dragons would be so eager to reach him that they *would* destroy their own machinery. It would be worth his death if that happened, and the fortress crashed.

Three dragons prowled into the control cave. Their bulk filled the front half, but there was enough room for them to stand fully and maneuver. And get closer to Sorath.

One snapped at him, its maw darting between the sphere and cylinder. He swiped at it, the dagger pricking its defensive barrier, but he had to back farther to avoid being caught. Another dragon extended its long neck over the sphere, trying to reach him from above.

Ducking low, Sorath slashed at it as the other tried again to pluck him out.

"I've got something," Ferroki whispered, the words barely audible over the snapping jaws.

"Go down," Sorath called without looking back. He was too busy defending from above and ahead. What if the other dragon was able to come at him from behind?

One of the creatures roared. Sorath spat at it, a completely useless gesture, but he didn't care. A large eye peered down at him, and he was tempted to throw the dagger, but he would be dead the second its protective influence left him.

Jaws slid in again, and he stabbed, fighting to do enough damage to keep his attackers back. Even though he jammed the blade in under the dragon's nostrils and drew blood, the maw kept coming, determined fangs reaching for him. The other dragon's head whipped in from above, lunging for him.

Sorath dropped to his belly and rolled under the sphere. The third dragon came into view, lowering its head to the floor to track his movements.

Frustrated, Sorath jabbed the dagger upward, willing it to pierce the sphere. But as before, even the dragon steel wasn't sufficient to destroy the devices.

"Sorath!" Ferroki called, her voice echoing strangely. "Hurry. Down here."

She'd found a shaft.

Scrambling on hand, pick, and knees under the machinery, Sorath crawled as fast as he could for the back of the cave. Flames bathed the machinery, turning everything brilliant orange.

"Look out!" Sorath cried, knowing Ferroki would be vulnerable to magical fire.

A dragon was targeting him, using its magic out of habit, but she might be caught in the backlash.

When she didn't reply, terror stampeded into Sorath. As he scrambled in her direction, staying under the machinery for cover, he told himself that she would have screamed if she'd been struck. She had to have escaped the fire. She *better* have escaped it.

"Ferroki? Are you all right?" The hole she'd mentioned came into view, an opening with four glowing tendrils disappearing into it. A panel now lay beside it.

But that didn't mean she was alive. The flames could have reached inside, scorching her to death too quickly for her to cry out.

Come to us, human female, one of the dragons crooned as others kept snapping at Sorath around the devices, determined to get him. *Your pitiful life is worth nothing. Give yourself to us, to sustain our great might.*

Ferroki lifted her head through the hole, the light of the tendrils shining on the side of her face, her eyes glazed as if she were hypnotized. No, compelled by dragon magic.

Sorath cleared the devices, rose into a crouch, and ran toward her.

More flames roared into the room, and he dove, reaching for Ferroki, terrified he would be too late, that their power would hold her there while the inferno incinerated her.

The flat of his pickaxe blade rammed into her shoulder just before the flames roiled over them. It wasn't a gentle touch, but it extended the dagger's protection.

"Down, down," Sorath barked as he grabbed her with his fingers, barely maintaining hold of the dagger in his desperation to protect her. He tightened his grip, envisioning dropping the weapon and them both being incinerated.

The flames died down, but shadows moved toward them. The dragons.

Ferroki blinked, coming out of the hypnosis. Eyes widening, she ducked down, grabbing Sorath and pulling him after her.

More flames poured toward them, bathing the back wall of the cave. Sorath squirmed into a shaft hardly more than three feet high and wide, with the tendrils running through it further constricting the space.

He didn't care. With his shoulders jammed against the tendrils and the unyielding wall, he followed Ferroki away from the opening.

More whispers of air streamed past them, the dragons trying to pull them out with their magic. Sorath made sure to maintain contact with her as they moved away.

Do not think you are safe, verminous humans. We built those shafts, and we can un-*build them.*

Sorath didn't answer, but he didn't believe it was a hollow threat. If the dragons wanted them badly enough, he was sure they could get them.

Rivlen stood at Uthari's side on the deck of the *Soaring Eagle*, the dragon-steel sword in her hand. She felt more like a bodyguard than a fleet officer trained for command, but a lot of mages, both on their ship and the others flying nearby, kept shooting dark and uncertain looks toward their king. Rumors about what was happening to him, some true and some not, had spread faster than a virulent pox.

Worse, two fleets of ships floated in the sky ahead, Zaruk's blue-hulled vessels and also King Dy's brown-hulled craft. Hundreds of uniformed officers were out on the decks, preparing for battle. If the world—and all of its mages—were sane, they would be planning to fly with Uthari's fleet into battle, but she knew it wasn't. This looked more like trouble than assistance.

"A message for you on the dome-jir, Your Majesty," a lieutenant called from the communications cabin.

Uthari nodded curtly, his forehead gleaming with sweat and more gray splotches spreading on his skin.

"Come, Rivlen." Uthari headed toward the cabin.

She held back a sigh, though she missed her own ship and the autonomy she'd had as a captain. Oh, she'd followed the fleet's orders, as there was always some superior officer to report to, but for long stretches at a time, she'd been in command. Now...

"Bodyguard," she muttered.

Uthari glanced back, and she bit her tongue. Things would change once he was healed. She hoped he would remember that she'd served him faithfully—even if she'd started to wonder if she *should* be serving him faithfully.

The problem was that if she gave up her career, she gave up everything. And she might be hunted for turning traitor.

Rivlen wished Jak were with her. He would come up with some scheme or another and naively try to convince her that everything would be all right. She wouldn't mind hearing that.

Uthari disappeared into the navigation cabin, but the captain of the mageship stepped into Rivlen's path, blocking her from following him. With her barrier up and the sword in hand, she didn't worry about her safety, but she didn't want to deal with the officer, especially since a sneer rode his lips. Whatever he planned to bring up, she doubted it would be concern for Uthari's health.

"What favors have you done for him that he invites you to trail him into meetings like a faithful hound?" the captain asked.

"I've done my duty, unlike Admiral Nakor and whoever else's loyalty has been faltering since Uthari was infected," Rivlen said, promptly feeling like a hypocrite since she'd been questioning her career and willingness to remain in it not seconds before.

"What happened to Nakor? We heard him scream, but by the time my men got there, he was dead." The captain glanced at her sword. If he'd seen the body, he ought to know magic had killed the admiral, not a blade.

"He tried to sell us out to Zaruk," Rivlen said.

"That doesn't sound like him."

Rivlen shrugged. "I saw his thoughts, as did Uthari. He wasn't hiding them at the end."

"At the end?" the captain mouthed. "You mean after he was tortured and near his death?"

"He wasn't tortured," she snapped, though the admiral's death *had* appeared painful. And Uthari had taken advantage to extract what he wanted to know. "I suggest you remain loyal yourself, Captain. Our king is more than a normal mage."

"What is *that* supposed to mean?"

"That he can read your thoughts, even if you're guarding them."

The captain blanched. Was he someone else who wasn't as faithful in his mind as he outwardly portrayed himself? If so, Rivlen was starting to believe that there was far less loyalty among mage officers than she'd believed. Maybe there was a reason Uthari liked Malek so much. Somehow, she couldn't imagine

Malek entertaining mutinous or traitorous thoughts. She had a feeling that if he decided he no longer wanted to be loyal to Uthari, he would walk away rather than turning on him.

"I doubt that's true," the captain recovered to say. "You're probably inadvertently sharing yours with him. Lovers sometimes do that with each other."

"He's not my lover," she snapped.

"No? Since he's been afflicted with this mystery illness, there's been speculation about who his heir is. He's always been elusive about saying that in public."

Because he never expected to die, Rivlen thought. Even *before* Jadora had created that longevity potion, Uthari had employed methods of extending his life.

"General Tonovan was certain *he* was Uthari's heir," the captain said, "though few believed that. There's speculation that Uthari has children nobody knows about that he's been grooming in secret, but as long-lived as he is, one would think his children would have died of old age by now."

"As fascinating as your speculation is, I'd appreciate it if you would step aside, Captain." Rivlen peered past his shoulder through the open door of the communications cabin. Since he was waiting for her, Uthari hadn't shut it, but the glow of orange light from an active dome-jir warmed his face, promising he was already speaking to someone.

Rivlen marshaled her power and let her barrier expand so the captain would know she would move him aside if need be. He was powerful, but so was she.

His eyes narrowed to slits. "Given your recent toddling along after him, holding his penis, some speculate *you* hope to be named Uthari's heir."

Right. After losing the *Star Flyer*, Rivlen wasn't even certain she would be given command of a ship again, much less a kingdom.

"Know this, *Captain*." He emphasized her rank, probably to

draw her attention to her lack of a ship, then pointed his finger between her eyes. "Even if he did name you as heir to the crown, the fleet would not obey you, and neither would any of the old, retired lords and officers. Even your own father doesn't support you. You'd be ousted by force or assassinated, and a worthy successor to the throne would step in."

"Uthari isn't going to die, and I know I'm not his heir. What ridiculously juvenile mind thought that notion up?" Angry at the words and the interruption, Rivlen drew upon her power to push him aside.

Armored by a barrier of his own, the captain didn't budge, but his jaw did clench as he strained to match her power. She drew upon even more and, with a little jaw-clenching of her own, managed to ram his barrier hard enough to send him stumbling to the side.

Without waiting for a response, she strode into the communications cabin.

The door slammed shut behind her, Uthari's doing. He was listening to someone speak—that looked like King Wortalia's profile floating above the dome-jir—but he gave Rivlen an appreciative smile and looked her up and down, nodding to himself and licking his lips.

Had he seen her use her power and found it… appealing? A chill went through her. That madness still lurked in his eyes—did Wortalia see it as well?

Knowing the parasite was influencing him didn't make Rivlen less uncomfortable. She wondered if Jak had ever felt that way when she'd admitted to him that she found it appealing, even arousing, when he used *his* power.

Rivlen rubbed her face, not enjoying the insight any more than she appreciated Uthari's attention.

"Our fleet will be there within a few hours," Wortalia was

saying. "I'm coming personally to lead my officers. This is important. You're mistaken when you say we don't grasp the significance. We've all endured dragon attacks, and word has gotten out about the fortress. Everyone understands the threat. I've spoken to Zaruk and Dy, and we've all agreed to join forces to deal with the fortress."

"Under my command," Uthari said.

"We'll *jointly* command the fleet. Myself, Zaruk, you, and the rest of the admirals and monarchs that are coming."

"My people have the most experience with the fortress. *I* will lead. Are you aware that the fortress has a powerful weapon capable of obliterating ships protected by a strong barrier? One of my commanders saw it destroy a druid craft in a single blow."

"Druids," Wortalia scoffed.

Uthari crooked a finger for Rivlen to stand by his side. "Tell him."

Rivlen hadn't personally seen the weapon being used, but she'd received the report from Kywatha before the druids had gone down. "It's a great beam that shoots out of the fortress, Your Majesty," she told Wortalia. "There were dozens of druids on their raft defending it, and it still tore through them in a single strike. That was independent of the dragons attacking. We not only need to work together—"

"Under *one* commander," Uthari put in.

"—but we need a plan to destroy that weapon as soon as possible, or it'll pick off all our ships one by one," she finished.

"The druids aren't the equals of mages," Wortalia said.

Rivlen ground her teeth. *He* hadn't been at the pool and battled the druids, and he hadn't been interacting with them these past months. Their training was unorthodox and their methods of using magic different from the mages', but they *were* their equals. And neither mages nor druids were anywhere close to the equals of dragons.

"I'm sure we'll be able to handle it when we arrive," Wortalia added.

"Under my command." Uthari gripped Rivlen's shoulder. "I have an experienced commander who already fought them near their fortress. You would be wise to heed her warnings and follow me."

Rivlen fought the urge to step away from his grip. She didn't want to undermine Uthari's authority in front of another king.

"We will follow you." Wortalia smiled faintly at him. "Under a joint command. What is wrong with you, anyway, Uthari? You don't look well. Did a dragon bite you?"

"Something like that, and I'm fine. Perfectly capable of leading the fleets into battle."

"I'm glad to hear it." Wortalia ended the communication, and the dome-jir went dark.

For long seconds, Uthari scowled at it. A bead of sweat dripped from his temple down the side of his face. In all the years Rivlen had served Uthari and even before she'd started, she'd never seen him anything but clean-shaven, but days' worth of white stubble bristled from his jaw.

"He is scheming." Uthari rubbed her shoulder, though he kept looking at the dark dome-jir.

"Yes, Your Majesty," was all she said, then tried to step away so his hand would drop.

But he tightened his grip and looked at her. "*You* are one of the few who stand at my side, loyal to me. You allowed Tonovan to be killed, and that angered me, but I know why you did it. You wished to take his place and serve under me directly." His eyes glinted, lips parting.

"I…" What could she say? She *had* thought she might one day take Tonovan's position as the commander of the fleet, but it had been a mixture of her own ambition and the fact that she'd detested him and wanted him dead. Serving directly under Uthari

—the possible double meaning of those words unsettled her—hadn't been in her thoughts.

"I understand." Uthari chuckled and pulled her closer.

She summoned her power to defend herself, realizing he meant to kiss her—to kiss her and *more*—and barely resisted whipping the sword she held toward him. Not only was he her king, whom she'd sworn to serve, but he was being affected by the parasite. She couldn't believe he truly wished this.

The blade protected her from magic, but he was physically stronger than he should have been, and she couldn't pull away from him. Further, something protected him from *her* magic, and she couldn't use it to shove him back. He stepped in closer, his lips looming in front of her face.

Her grip tightened on the sword hilt. Maybe if she tapped the blade to his arm, that would stop him without hurting him much.

She was on the verge of trying when a knock at the door made Uthari pause and scowl at it.

"Another fleet has shown up, Your Majesty," an officer called through the door. "Wortalia's people, and a couple of King Temrok's ships that survived the devastation to their kingdom are with them. Their barriers are up, and their weapons are pointed at us, their mages lined up on deck to attack."

"Attack? *Us?*" Uthari released Rivlen and flung the door open. "With a fortress of dragons scant hours away? That's ludicrous."

"Yes, Your Majesty." The lieutenant reporting glanced at Rivlen, frowning briefly at the sword in her hand before returning his gaze to Uthari.

Rivlen, realizing she'd raised the weapon to strike, lowered it before Uthari could look over at her.

"Their intent seems clear. They haven't tried to speak to us yet, but..." The lieutenant pointed toward the railing.

Uthari strode out to look, leaving Rivlen with her sword at her side and her heart pounding. Another two seconds, and she would have struck Uthari. No matter how light her touch, the king would have considered it an attack. A *betrayal.*

But damn it, she wouldn't let him maul her, parasitic infection or not. The problem was that she didn't know how to stop him short of using the sword on him.

She rubbed a shaky hand over her face and stepped outside. Never had she been so relieved to have a fleet of mages attack the ship she rode on.

22

As twilight settled over the jungle, insects buzzed and something Tezi couldn't identify screeched in the distance. She chewed on tart, stringy fruit while she sat in the mouth of the cave, hoping Uthari's fleet, and every other fleet in the world, had reached the fortress by now, and the dragons were too busy to notice the portal. She hadn't seen Gorsith—or the device that was supposed to stay on the portal—since that morning.

Tezi shook her head, wishing Rivlen were with them and that Gorsith had never gotten off his ship. Though the portal had stopped glowing blue, she had little doubt that it was active and emitting an aura. That not only meant the dragons would be able to sense it from afar but creatures from other worlds could fly through. Remembering that awful hundred-foot-long and nearly indestructible flying worm made her shudder.

"Maybe I shouldn't be sitting here with my back to the portal," she said.

Dr. Fret left the camp, where most of the other mercenaries had gathered after their day of training, and headed toward the cave, pausing along the way to peer into a bed of ferns. Shikari lay there, having returned from a hunt that afternoon. As Fret passed, he rolled onto his back with all four legs in the air and his headed flopped to the side. Tezi thought he was changing positions, but then he wriggled in the ferns. Scratching his back?

Fret snorted softly and picked her way up the slope toward Tezi. Tinder had been up and about during the day, so Tezi trusted she hadn't been badly wounded when Gorsith had thrown her from the cave. How would that confrontation have ended if the portal hadn't intervened?

Tezi envisioned her decapitated body on the floor of the cave with Gorsith prancing around, claiming he'd fairly won the axe in a duel.

"Are you all right up here in the dark?" Fret asked. "I notice your druid protector has disappeared."

"I'm fine for now." Tezi hadn't seen Grunk for hours and didn't know where he was, but she didn't mind being alone. "Thanks for checking."

"Of course. It's my job." Fret sat beside her. "There's little else I can do. I lost my knitting needles and yarn in the shipwreck. All the projects I had in progress too. This whole experience of working for wizards and battling dragons has been loathsome."

"Because you lost your yarn?"

"Among other things. I couldn't knit you tassels for your axe handle even if you wanted me to."

"That is tragic." Tezi patted the axe, and it surprised her by sharing a vision.

In it, she and Fret were sitting exactly as they were, but night had fallen fully, shrouding the jungle in a blanket of darkness. Figures clad in fur or woven grass cloaks crept toward the camp. They gripped staffs, had wolves and jaguars and other animal companions at their sides, and wore the determined faces of hunters. No, of druids coming to get the portal.

They stopped, and a familiar green-haired man with tattoos

stepped into the vision, bowing his head and extending his hands toward the lead druids. Grunk.

He hadn't gone to get them, had he? If he had, Tezi couldn't blame him since they were his people, but she couldn't help but feel a twinge of betrayal. She'd thought he'd agreed to work with her.

Then she realized the lead druid was pulling him forward by his hands, as if a magical leash bound him and she were reeling him in. His feet stuttered as he fought it. The druid frowned and appeared to exert more effort. He came all the way to her, bowing his chin to his chest. She rested her hand on his head, then pointed for him to join them. Woodenly, Grunk stepped into the group, his face slack.

Where was the dragon-steel dagger? That should have protected him.

Then she spotted it in the druid leader's grip, a satisfied smile on the woman's face. Maybe she'd called Grunk to them and ordered he give it to her. Or they'd taken it with their superior numbers.

Tezi scowled. Either way, they were controlling him. She was sure of it.

The druid leader pressed a hand to Grunk's head. To forcibly read his mind? Did she believe Grunk would reveal everything about the portal and the mercenaries' and mages' defenses? Or had she summoned him because she feared he would sense them coming and hadn't wanted to risk him warning Tezi and the others?

Cursing, she surged to her feet and peered into the trees, the vision of the future mingling in her eyes with the present.

"Either you've realized the loss of my knitting supplies is more tragic than you first thought, or you heard something." Fret pushed herself to her feet.

"The axe gave me a vision."

At the bottom of the slope, Shikari rose to his feet and sniffed the air.

"Go warn the others, please," Tezi said. "Druids are coming. I think maybe the same ones that captured us after the shipwreck."

"Oh, delightful. I was afraid we wouldn't see them again."

"They may have their local friends too. If you see Gorsith, tell *him*." Tezi was certain the druids had only found them again because the zidarr had removed the device. Or, if not that, they'd only decided the portal was a problem because he'd removed the device. She wouldn't be surprised if they'd known all along where it had gone. This was their land. The trees probably spoke to them.

"Yes, I do enjoy chatting with arrogant zidarr," Fret muttered before heading down the slope.

"Maybe you can befriend him by offering to knit him something."

"I'd rather stick one of my needles in his..." Her words faded as she moved farther away.

Tezi took a deep breath, shook out her arms, and looked back at the portal. "I understand why you don't want to attack dragons, but if you could help us keep the druids from taking you, we'd appreciate it. They want to bury you forever, not just stick something on you that makes you take a nap."

Enemies are attempting to creep up on us, a voice spoke into her mind. Gorsith. He must have sent the message to everyone, for the mercenaries, mages, and roamers all grabbed their weapons and stood up. Fret was also whispering to Tinder and Sasko and pointing into the trees. *Be ready to engage them and protect that which is ours.* Gorsith pointed at the cave—at the portal inside.

Only a zidarr and his master would be so arrogant as to claim that the ancient dragon artifact belonged to them.

Shikari roared into the twilight.

Tezi hoped the sound made the druids pause and worry. The

roars had grown more fearsome of late. *Shikari* had grown more fearsome—when he wasn't rolling in ferns to scratch his back.

The druids might have intended to sneak up on the camp, but by the time they arrived, everyone was ready, many of the mercenaries standing back-to-back in a large circle, facing the trees. Shikari had exited the fern bed and stood at the bottom of the slope, his tail and head erect as he waited. Gorsith stood near him, his blades ready.

Alone in the mouth of the cave, Tezi couldn't help but feel it would be her duty to keep the druids from getting the portal.

She'd no sooner had the thought than Tinder jogged up the side of the slope to join her.

"Sasko said I should keep you from getting killed," she said.

"How are you going to do that?" Tezi whispered.

"Drag you into the back of the cave so you can't run down there and join the fight."

"I don't want to fight druids, but..." Tezi glanced at the portal again. "We can't let them take it."

"I know." Tinder sighed and drew her sword. "Sasko said you're doing a good job, by the way."

"At irking a zidarr and potentially getting myself killed?"

"At keeping the morale up in Thorn Company. If any of us were getting paid, I think she would sign off on a combat bonus for you. Or a perky-young-corporal bonus."

"I didn't know such things existed."

"The captain used to make exceptions." Tinder shook her head. "I hope that seer is right and that she's alive down there."

Tezi didn't point out that the seer hadn't mentioned the captain, only Sorath. She wanted Ferroki back too.

Two druids walked out of the shadows, Kywatha and the female leader from the south. They looked toward Tezi and the cave but picked out Gorsith as the leader and the most dangerous person present, and walked toward him.

Long seconds passed as they engaged in a telepathic exchange in which Tezi wasn't included.

Gorsith lifted his head and opened his mouth. "If you want the portal, you must best me in a duel for it," he told them. "One on one."

"He likes to challenge people to duels, doesn't he?" Tinder muttered.

"Because he thinks he's better than everyone and can win." Tezi wished she'd seen Shikari best him.

"I would be foolish to fight you alone." Kywatha held up her staff. "I have only my magic and a simple weapon with no blade. But I've brought friends."

Numerous figures were visible now in the shadows of the trees, and Tezi suspected even more were out there. The vision had shown her dozens if not hundreds of people approaching.

You did not leave our land, as we told you to, the other druid leader said, sticking with telepathy, but for all to hear, *and you've not taken the portal to a place where it can't be used.*

"Our people do not take orders from druids." Gorsith stalked toward them, his sword and dagger in hand. "If you will not duel me, you will not have it, for we will keep your people away by whatever means necessary, including using the portal itself as a weapon. Your power will be nothing next to its, or next to mine."

A rock clattered somewhere outside the cave.

"I think they're trying to climb up from behind," Tezi whispered. "To take the portal while our leaders are distracted."

A scraping came from behind her, the portal wobbling.

"They're trying to levitate it away," she blurted and ran back.

As the portal shuddered, being tugged from the spot it had claimed in the cave, Tezi planted her hand against its frame, willing the power of the axe to keep magic from affecting it. But would that work? The portal itself was dragon steel and that hadn't kept mages from lifting it and moving it around.

The portal reacted to her touch—or maybe the magic being applied to it—and flared, pale blue light filling the cave. Behind it, wings flapped as an alarmed bat flew out into the night.

A vision blasted into Tezi's head, so forceful that it almost felt like an attack. She managed to stay on her feet, but Tinder gasped and dropped to her knees.

The vision showed the portal in the cave, shining brilliantly and its center glowing with a constellation before the gateship flew out of it. Returning victoriously from its mission?

Tezi didn't know if that was an accurate representation of the future or simply what the portal hoped would happen. Either way, the artifact wanted to wait there until it found out if those events came to pass. Four blue strands of energy shot out of its circular frame, one sizzling past Tezi's eyebrows and making her jerk her head back, and they plunged into the rocky floor of the cave.

They grew taut, like straps anchoring something in place, and Tezi realized that was precisely what the magic was doing. The portal didn't plan to go anywhere, and it was letting them know.

Assuming it was sharing its message with everyone in the camp as well as the druids, Tezi was surprised when the clash of weapons rang out from below.

A four-legged figure sprang into the mouth of the cave, and she hefted her axe. But it was Shikari.

The portal wants me to make them stop fighting, Shikari told them. *It believes greater threats are coming. Dragons.*

"I know, but they didn't listen when it warned them," Tezi said.

Shikari turned, his tail toward the back of the cave, and roared out into the night. A tingle of power seemed to flow from him, though Tezi had a hard time telling when she held the axe. Tinder swore, however, and backed toward the portal.

Human friends of Jak, Shikari called out telepathically.

Tezi snorted, certain the druids didn't know who Jak was. And none of the mages that had served with Rivlen would call him *friend*. She wasn't even sure how many of the Thorn Company women would.

Despite that, the clangs of weapons paused. The portal flared blue, throwing its light past Shikari, highlighting him as he looked from the cave down upon the camp.

From behind him, Tezi couldn't see the others to gauge their reactions, but nobody spoke.

More dragons approach, dragons who want the portal for themselves. I am not like their kind, tainted by a parasite and cruel, but I am gaining in power and wisdom, and I urge you to listen to me.

Tezi hoped the others didn't dismiss him because he'd been rolling around in the ferns earlier.

I will work with you to keep them from getting the portal, Shikari continued, *and I will urge it to help, but you must also help. You must work together instead of fighting among yourselves. It is not...* Shikari looked from left to right, to the stars and down, as if searching for the right word. *It is not grown-up and mature.*

Tinder grunted softly. "Got that right."

Only mature humans and dragons will be victorious, Shikari added.

Even if Tezi agreed with the sentiment, she worried the little speech wouldn't sway anyone. Shikari must have felt the same way, for he exuded more magic, a surge of power that made Tezi tingle even through the protection of the axe. Maybe because it wasn't aggressive or offensive power. A wave of amicable feelings washed over her, a desire to be content with her fellow humans—mercenary, mage, and druid alike—and accept them all as allies, allies she would need to survive the coming battles.

"Is that dragon manipulating us?" Tinder whispered. "I feel warm and gushy feelings toward the druids and the zidarr. That can't be right."

"I think he is, but his goal is a good one, so maybe it's not a bad thing."

Tinder took several steps toward the cave mouth to peer down the slope. Curious, Tezi followed her.

Everyone below had lowered or sheathed their weapons. The druids had come forward, some bowing or extending hands and patting the shoulders of the mages and mercenaries. Gorsith and Kywatha, who might have been squared off in battle before, were doing *more* than hand patting. Tezi gaped as their arms wrapped around each other, and they kissed.

"That's unexpected," Tezi said.

"I'll say," Tinder agreed. "But I did warn you about that zidarr's taut and appealing ass."

"I thought you were pointing it out as something to admire, not as a warning."

"One person's warning is another's—"

Kywatha slid a hand down Gorsith's back to grip the taut subject of discussion.

"Yes, that," Tinder finished.

Shikari sat on his haunches. *I did not mean to encourage them to do this thing with their lips. That is how humans mate, is it not?*

"It's kind of a precursor to mating. Those two won't get naked and frolic horizontally in the middle of camp." Tinder eyed the handsy pair. "Probably."

They must prepare to do battle. I sense a dragon circling the area at a distance. More may be on the way. That is why I had to use my magic and couldn't allow the humans to fight each other.

Tezi grimaced at the promise of a new dragon. "You were wise to use your magic," she assured Shikari.

Should I release them from my urging that they be friendly with each other? Will they go back to battling even if a threat approaches?

"I think the only battling those two are going to do is under the covers." Tinder looked away from Kywatha and Gorsith and waved down at Fret, who was waving back at her. Actually, that was more of a beckoning.

"Maybe you can tone it down a bit," Tezi suggested to Shikari. "We don't want everyone engaged in *mating* activities when the dragons show up."

Grunk, whom she hadn't seen since he'd appeared in the vision, left the druids and trotted up the slope toward her. He shook his head as he ran, as if he were clearing his mind of Shikari's magic—or maybe shaking off the magical hold the druid leader had held over him.

"Here's someone who's probably interested in mating activities," Tinder said. "Better watch out."

"He doesn't have the dagger." Tezi noted the empty sheath among his other blades and trusted the vision had shown her the truth.

When he reached them, Grunk dropped to his knees in front of them—no, in front of Shikari.

You have power over humans but aren't cruel. Grunk looked up at Shikari and opened his palms toward the sky. *You were sent by Shylezar to help mankind. This must be true. Or maybe you are the offspring of the great dragon god.*

"Maybe you're not the one he wants to mate with," Tinder said, watching the admiration in Grunk's eyes.

"Ssh." Tezi elbowed her. "Grunk's a little…"

"Crazy?" Tinder suggested. "This is Jak's baby dragon, not some god or child of a god."

"We don't know who mothered those eggs," Tezi pointed out.

Tinder gave her a scathing look.

I am only a dragon, Shikari said. *Humans don't need a new god, only to work together to protect their world.*

Yes. Grunk nodded firmly, his shaggy hair falling in his eyes. *Shylezar wished this. It must be so.*

Grunk rose to his feet and stood beside Tezi. *We will work together,* he told her.

"I hope so," she murmured. "What happened to you? To your

dagger?"

He scowled and pointed at the druid leader. *She reminded me that I am one of them and called upon me to come give them information on your camp and the new zidarr. I am not a spy and planned to tell her I would not betray you, but several of her warriors surrounded me and demanded I surrender the dagger so that she could read my mind. I told them about the zidarr, but it is fortunate that I didn't know the dragon could force them to be friends.*

More than friends.

Shikari looked back at the portal. Wanting advice from it? Or to have *Jak* return to give him advice? Then he looked at the kissing couple—no, couples, as more had joined together—and dropped to his belly, his tail wrapping around him to drop over his snout and hide his eyes. He no longer appeared to be emanating magic, but perhaps its influence would take a while to wane.

"How long until this new dragon shows up?" Tinder asked.

Tezi shook her head; the axe hadn't shown her that. "I don't know."

"Will the portal fight with us to defend itself from being taken?"

"I don't know that either."

~

When Jadora woke, she found a vial lying on her stomach, small shards of blackened wood inside.

Is this for me? Jadora asked telepathically, sensing Malek in the engineering room with Jak and Vinjo.

A get-well gift, Malek replied.

Some people give flowers or candies.

Do not pretend you would wish such vacuous items over a sample of a strange new acid.

Jadora smiled and held the vial to her chest. *You know me well.*

The item resting on the deck next to your cot is also for you.

She turned her head to find the piece of dragon-steel that Vinjo had brought along, half of it corroded away. *Fascinating.*

Far more so than candies, yes.

You're a good gift-giver.

As zidarr are known to be.

Jadora snorted softly, doubting Malek had given many gifts in his life. That, of course, made the fact that he kept bringing her things all the more special.

Smiling, she gingerly pushed herself into a sitting position. Her heart pounded in her chest, as if the simple exertion were akin to climbing a mountain. Even so, she felt better than she had the last time she'd woken. Her mind was clearer, and for the first time in days, she wasn't sweating and fevered.

As she lifted her canteen for a drink, she used her power to survey herself. She sensed the death-darter bacteria hunkered down, spread throughout her bloodstream to every corner of her body, and she started to grimace but then realized what she *didn't* sense.

"The dragon parasite," she rasped. "It's gone."

Jadora checked again, investigating more slowly and thoroughly. It was indeed gone. The death-darter bacteria had won.

She smiled again and clenched a fist in triumph, but the feeling faded quickly. As she'd told Malek, the experience had very nearly killed her. And she would have to soon gather the power to eradicate the death-darter bacteria, or it would start to affect her in its own way. Remembering the aggressive and half-crazed Malek from Nargnoth, she did *not* want that to happen.

"Do you need help with anything?" Malek asked from the doorway. "Defeating the death-darter bacteria? I'm afraid I didn't grasp enough of what you shared to do it alone, but if I can help you in any way..." He arched his brows, his eyes concerned as he considered her.

"I need to urinate," she said.

Malek hesitated. "I'm not sure if that's a statement of fact or a request for assistance."

"I can probably make it to the head on my own," Jadora said, though she wobbled when she stood, intense weariness gripping every muscle in her body.

Malek strode in and caught her before she could flop back down on the cot.

"Then again," she said, "I might not be able to make it to the door on my own."

"I'll help you with whatever you wish." Malek kissed her on the forehead, then paused and stared at it.

"Are you admiring my natural post-sickness beauty?"

"The gray splotches are receding." He stepped back, gripping her arms as he looked her up and down, his gaze lingering on the backs of her hands—the gray there was also going away. "You did it," he breathed.

"Actually, the death-darter bacteria did it."

"That's excellent. If they healed you, they could heal Uthari. And the dragons."

"I do hope so, though I'm not sure I'd call it *healing* when I was a battleground for a war—and feel like it." She didn't know if this was quite the ideal solution. What if not everyone survived having bacteria warring inside of them?

"You'll recover. I'm certain of it." His face relaxed for the first time in days, and Malek let some of his magic trickle into her, invigorating her with energy and bolstering her body's ability to heal.

She drew upon what he offered and also dredged energy from deep within her, wanting to eradicate the death-darter bacteria before it did more damage to her. Using the techniques she'd learned for targeting the microscopic organisms, she swept through her body, enhancing her immune system and commanding it to destroy the invaders. She felt a little guilty doing so since they'd helped her, but not when she remembered what they'd done to Malek when they'd infected him.

He grasped what she was doing and funneled more energy into her, giving her what she wouldn't have otherwise possessed in her weakened state.

You brought me a sample and *you're strengthening me?* Jadora asked when she was done, relief at having dealt with the problem warming her as much as his lingering magic. *I may swoon.*

That's only because you're in a weakened state.

No, it's because you're amazing.

It does please me that you believe so. Malek smirked at her.

She longed to melt against him and enjoy the moment, but they had much to do before they were safe, and that sample was calling to her. In addition...

I still need to urinate.

Of course. Malek released her, though he kept his hands out in case she wobbled and he needed to steady her.

Fortunately, she remained on her feet and made it to the head by herself. On the way back, she grew aware of a great power somewhere ahead of their ship.

Malek, do you feel... Jadora groped for a word to describe it. Was it a being? A collection of beings? Whatever it was, it had a powerful aura.

Yes. We think it's right over the ruins with the Orbs of Wisdom.

Jadora slumped. *Naturally.*

It's also what attacked me earlier.

You were attacked? Jadora rejoined him in the laboratory and noticed how tired he appeared. Maybe part of what she'd believed relaxation was fatigue.

A painful mental attack that came from afar. If I'd been closer to it, it might have killed me outright. You were unconscious at the time.

She stepped up to him, resting a hand on his chest, and used her senses to examine him, as he had her, to make sure he hadn't suffered lasting ill effects.

"Don't worry about me," Malek said softly and gestured toward her microscope, the sample vial waiting next to it. "Continue to do your research, and I'll worry about getting us to the orbs. I—" He halted, eyes widening with realization. "Wait, if you now know how to destroy the parasite, we don't *need* to visit the orbs, do we? We can turn around and leave this world."

"*Can* we leave it?" Jadora remembered the weakness of the portal, its power drained over the years by that entity.

Jak hadn't said anything to her, but she had a hunch it might not be strong enough to send them home, that they might be stuck on this world unless they could figure out a way to heal or recharge the portal.

Malek opened his mouth, as if to say *of course*, but she shared her thoughts with him, and he closed it again. "I don't know," he said instead.

Jak? Jadora reached out to engineering.

You're awake! he blurted, pleasure coming through with his words.

I am. The death-darter bacteria won the battle inside of me, destroying the dragon parasite.

Then that's the secret, right? All we have to do is infect the dragons with the death-darter bacteria, and let the organisms fight it out? And then go around eradicating the death-darter bacteria from them after they win.

Jadora thought about how ill she'd been, how close to dying she'd felt. *I'm not sure. I need to think about it. I... almost didn't make it.*

But a dragon would make it, surely. They're more powerful than we are.

I don't know if their immune systems are more powerful than ours. I might need to do some experimentation on Shikari, if he'll allow it, when we return.

He might if it's for the good of all dragons. Uhm, about returning...

Yes? This was why she'd reached out to Jak.

I'm not sure if we can unless we can repair the portal.

Jadora sighed. *I was afraid of that.*

Is there any chance you know how to do that? Was there information about the portals in the knowledge that Zelonsera gave you?

Some information, yes, but there aren't any repair manuals in my brain, no. I think it took the power and cooperation of many dragons to originally build the portals.

Then we have to keep going to the Orbs of Wisdom, Jak said. *And hope they have knowledge on how to fix the portals.*

"I think we need to continue on," Jadora told Malek.

"I was afraid of that."

"I didn't think pompous zidarr were afraid of anything." She smiled.

"When I almost lost you," he said seriously, "I feared a great deal."

"I'm sorry I put you through that."

Malek clasped her hands. "It's not your fault. It was Uthari's fault. All of this has been."

Jadora nodded, touched to hear him say it, and encouraged by the condemnation she read in his eyes. Maybe he truly would leave Uthari when they returned. *If* they returned.

No, she resolved. They would find a way and they *would* return. Not only that, but they would also fix the dragons, oust Uthari from power, and change the world for the better. She looked toward the corroded dragon steel and her microscope, eager to examine it in case she learned something helpful.

Malek released her hands. "I won't keep you from your research."

"You're a good man, Malek."

"I'm not," he said softly as she went to the microscope, "but I'm glad you think I am."

23

CHUGS, POPS, AND HISSES CAME FROM THE FILTRATION DEVICE stretched over the open hatch, followed by the whir of a fan.

Standing at the base of the ladder, Jak could see the hazy red air above and imagined the toxic substances swirling about in it. Would Vinjo's device work to make it breathable?

Vinjo stood beside him, also looking upward, watching with his eyes and senses. A whisper of air came down to them, freshly filtered air drawn in from above.

Jak took a couple of experimental sniffs. Vinjo wasn't breathing at all. Because he was too busy concentrating or because he was *afraid* to breathe?

"You're sure this will work, right?" Jak whispered.

Moderately sure, Vinjo replied telepathically, not opening his mouth or taking in air.

"Then why aren't you breathing?"

In case I'm wrong. You'll pass out first, and then I'll know I need to make modifications.

I doubt you can make whatever modifications are needed in the time you can hold your breath. We'll all be doomed if this doesn't work.

I'm an amazing engineer. Didn't Sasko tell you? Vinjo's face grew wistful at the mention of the mercenary.

I remember her describing you more frequently using frustrated words like pain in the ass.

They were fond *words. I am that too, but I'm also amazing.* Vinjo lost the battle with his lungs and drew in a breath.

The air smelled acceptable to Jak. It wasn't brimming with freshness, but it didn't make him want to gag. He'd read about gases that could kill a man without smelling bad, but he had learned to have faith in Vinjo's abilities. Amazing probably *was* an accurate adjective for him.

"I think it's working. It shouldn't take long to replenish our air supply. And then we can descend again." Vinjo held a hand out as he glanced downward. "When we're in the right spot, that is."

They'd taken to the air and were cruising quickly along now, but they hadn't yet reached the ruins.

"It's twenty or thirty more miles," Jak said. "You'd better reapply the camouflage Malek asked for. I know we're getting close to our destination, because I can sense the powerful entity right where the portal suggested the ruins are."

"I was afraid those two things were in the same spot." Vinjo grimaced. "And I already checked the camouflage. It's fine. It should still be working."

"Then why isn't anything on this world having trouble seeing us?"

Vinjo had said he hadn't made the camouflage to fool plants, but if Malek's hypothesis was correct, the entity out there had been controlling the plants, sharks, and everything else that had tried to lead them to their destruction. He supposed it was possible the being had sensed their arrival because it always monitored the portal through the eyes—or other senses—of the flora and fauna in the area, but Jak didn't know.

"I don't know," Vinjo said, "but I'm not sure what else I can do.

I think it knows we're coming anyway. Malek will have to figure out a way to handle it."

Jak shook his head bleakly. How did one *handle* something more powerful than a dragon?

He headed toward navigation, where Malek was watching the route ahead as the gateship flew above the waves. As he passed the laboratory, Mother's murmurs of *fascinating* drifted out. Jak was glad to see her on her feet. He hadn't asked if her surviving the battle of the bacteria meant she knew how to cure the dragon parasite yet, but he hoped so.

In navigation, Malek's eyes were closed, his focus on the entity they were approaching rather than the waves or a volcano island ahead and to the left, the peak half-shrouded in red haze and gray smoke.

"It feels like a dragon," Malek said, not turning at Jak's approach, "but different."

"More powerful?"

"That and... different."

Thus far, all Jak could sense was that the entity had a very pronounced aura. It hadn't attacked *him*, so he didn't have as much familiarity with it.

"I suppose it's pointless to hope that it's enjoying dinner, a swim, and a nap, and is ignoring us." A yawn almost interrupted Jak's words, and he wondered what time it was back home. Or what *day*.

Worry for Mother and their predicament had kept him from resting, though maybe he should have. *Malek* certainly should have, given the attack he'd endured and how much magic he'd used. Jak doubted his bout of unconsciousness counted as sleep.

"I'm surprised it hasn't attacked me again," Malek murmured.

"Well, don't send it an invitation to do so," Jak said, though he was tempted to reach out to it.

If there was any chance it *was* a dragon, a Shikari-like

untainted dragon, maybe it could be talked into working with them instead of against them. Though he admitted it would be more likely to be a tainted dragon, here to guard... what? The ancient city? The Orbs of Wisdom?

"Oh," Jak said, struck by realization.

Malek turned, arching his eyebrows.

"If it *is* a tainted dragon, maybe it believes what Zelonsera believed, that the Orbs of Wisdom could lead to a solution to the parasite problem. And, if it's like all the other tainted dragons, it doesn't want that problem solved." Presumably, neither Zelonsera nor any of the dragons knew that death-darter bacteria could defeat the parasite.

Malek looked toward Mother's laboratory. "It does appear that after the parasite is firmly established, it can exert control over the host."

"Some of the dragons that spoke with me referred to themselves as *we*. At the time, I thought they might mean dragons collectively, but now I wonder if that was the parasite talking." If Mother had been calling herself *we* when she spoke to Malek, Jak was glad he hadn't witnessed that.

He sensed her coming and turned.

She stepped into navigation with a slide in hand, smiling and patting Jak on the shoulder. Though she had to be as weary as the rest of them, her eyes were bright. This time, it seemed a result of enthusiasm rather than fever.

"You're looking less gray." Jak waved to her visible skin. It no longer gleamed with sweat, and the gray splotches had almost disappeared. "And, uhm, gross."

"It's not polite to call your mother gross," she said.

"I said *less* gross. It was a compliment."

"Did you truly woo Rivlen with that tongue?"

Jak blushed and looked at Malek. How had his mother found out about the *wooing*?

Malek only gazed blandly back at him. Jak supposed it wasn't proper to accuse a zidarr of gossiping. Besides, Vinjo would have been more likely to blab. Or Mother had simply *known*. Mothers did seem to have that ability, magical powers or not.

"The acid is fascinating." She held up the vial, thankfully switching topics. "It's water insoluble so there were traces left on the wood of the hull *and* the dragon steel. That it ate through that is amazing."

"It attempted to eat through my magical barrier too," Malek said.

"Attempted to or did?"

"It was successfully doing so. I kept adding layers to thwart it, until the entity attacked me and distracted me." Malek looked out the porthole. Checking to see where that entity was now?

Though the scenery hadn't changed, the aura of the being had grown stronger. Jak had no trouble detecting it.

"Is it the same stuff that we found on Vran?" Jak asked. "That Uthari's smith is using now to turn bars of dragon steel into collars for innocent dragons?"

"It has a similar molecular structure to that acid," Mother said, "but it isn't identical. I also thought it might be, but this acid breaks down and weakens dragon steel, rather than softening it for manipulation. I used my power to do some experiments, and it seems to break down magic itself."

"Huh."

"Could it be used to destroy a dragon-steel fortress?" Malek asked.

"I don't see why not," Mother said, "though you'd need a lot of it, and I don't know how to make it yet. It's possible we don't have the elements at home to do so. I suppose we could go back to that spot and gather more."

"We shouldn't need to destroy the whole fortress," Malek said, "just the magical power supply that keeps it in the sky. And perhaps that beam weapon Rivlen described."

"We have to deal with that entity and get off this world first." Jak pointed to the route ahead.

"Perhaps the acid could be used as a weapon against *it*." Malek looked at Mother.

"Like the bug guts the natives of Nargnoth smear on their spear tips?" Jak asked.

"If you smear this on your weapons, it'll dissolve them." Mother waved to Malek's sword and main-gauche. "You might want to stick to a known effective tool when battling something unknown."

The pensive expression on Malek's face suggested he wanted something *better* than known tools for what they would face. He pointed at her vial. "Is glass impervious to it?"

"It hasn't corroded my vial, so it may be," Mother said.

"So, if I had a glass spear..."

"I don't believe this ship is equipped with an armory," Mother said dryly.

"I ought to be able to fashion something." Malek twitched his fingers. "Or perhaps Vinjo could *engineer* something. I wonder if this ship could be outfitted with harpoon launchers."

"Launchers of *glass* harpoons?" Jak asked.

"Maybe." Malek glanced toward the door, and Vinjo stepped into navigation, looking frazzled, with fresh grease smeared on his cheek.

"A harpoon launcher?" Vinjo had either heard them talking or received the question telepathically from Malek. "I don't think you know how limited my supplies for building things are, my lord. You want the impossible."

"You've done the impossible several times now."

"That's not true, my lord. I've done the *improbable*."

"I'll take improbable weapons."

Vinjo's face twisted skeptically. "Let me see if I can make a glass-tipped spear first, one that isn't too fragile to be practical."

Malek nodded. "You're doing good work, Vinjo. Work that will be necessary if we're going to make it back home again."

"Home," Vinjo mouthed, longing filling his eyes. "I wish *that* were a probability."

"It will be," Jak said. "We'll find a way."

"But Zaruk..." Vinjo looked hopefully at Malek. "Lord Zidarr, is there any chance that if we survive this, you can help me and my family get away from King Zaruk and my zidarr brother? If they're... vengeful?"

"If you need refuge," Malek said, "I'll see that you get it."

"Oh, thank you." Vinjo lurched forward, and Malek lifted a hand, as if to defend himself, but Vinjo flung his arms around him for a hug.

Malek grew stiffer than a dragon-steel sword, and he grimaced, but he didn't fling Vinjo away. Mother smiled at Malek.

"My spear, if you please," Malek said. "The tip to be smeared with acid."

"Of course, my lord." Vinjo released him and stepped back but paused and tilted his head. "Acid?"

"I'll explain while you work." Malek pointed him back toward the engine room and all his tools and started to follow.

"What should we do when we're over the ruins?" Jak pointed at the deck. "We're almost there."

"I know," Malek said. "I can sense the entity and also more magic below."

"The orbs?" Jak asked hopefully, stretching out with his own senses, though he struggled to detect anything else with the blazing aura of the entity blotting out lesser auras.

"It could be. I sense multiple things. None of them are that strong though, nothing like the aura of the portal or other dragon steel." Malek looked gravely at Mother. "This may not be what we expected."

"The orbs don't have to be magically powerful to hold information," Mother said.

"If what the portal showed me is accurate..." Jak realized he hadn't mentioned all that the portal had shown him. He should have.

"Yes?" Mother and Malek asked.

"The orbs may be damaged. I'm hoping it's not too late for us to extract information from them."

"You're saying we've come all this way and might be about to face something more deadly than a dragon, and it could be for nothing?" Malek asked.

Jak winced. "I don't know. I hope not. But Mother's already figured out how to defeat the dragon parasite, right? All we *really* need to know is how to fix the portal so we can go home."

"Let's hope," Mother murmured and exchanged a long look with Malek.

Maybe she *hadn't* figured out how to defeat the dragon parasite. Was there something Jak didn't know? Or was it that she didn't know how they could spread the death-darter bacteria to the dragons? That *would* be difficult. With his sturdy scales, Shikari had been impervious to the death darters that had tried to sting him.

"I have an idea for the spear," Vinjo called from the engine room.

"I'll help him." Jak waved Malek toward the pilot's seat. "We'll need to submerge soon, and if that net plant is spread across miles down there, you'll have to get us through it."

Jak hurried out, worried they still had a lot of problems.

The single dragon flying over the jungle draws closer, Shikari announced, looking at Tezi.

She'd been sparring with Tinder, Yelotta, and a few others, and it took her a moment to realize he was addressing her alone. With Jak and Rivlen gone, had the dragonling decided she was in charge? That was far from being true, as Gorsith—or even Tinder or Sasko—would have been quick to point out.

It is the one-eyed dragon again, Shikari added. *He is relentless in seeking this portal.*

How far away is he? Tezi lowered her axe and waved to the others that she needed a break.

Close. He saw the portal when it first arrived, and he must believe it's still in the area.

He's not wrong.

No, he may be clever. Almost as clever as I.

Tezi smiled and didn't say anything disparaging. *If he's alone, we ought to be able to handle him. We have a zidarr now and several dragon-steel weapons.*

And me.

And you.

The others were fooled by my ruse. Perhaps I shall attempt to fool this one too.

Let me know how that works out. And tell Gorsith about the dragon, please.

Tezi waved for Yelotta to resume sparring with her. She was only defending, since her axe could have cleaved the mercenary's weapon in half if she'd struck with it, but it was good practice for both of them. Nearby, Grunk was sparring with Gorsith, both of them growling and grunting at each other.

Tezi couldn't say that she liked Gorsith, especially after he'd tortured Rivlen, but he was single-minded in his desire to train and would grab his weapons and spar with anyone willing to do so. He spent most of his time exercising instead of stalking around, ordering people to do things and letting the world know how superior he was and how inferior everyone else was. She liked that in a mage.

When they parted for a break, Yelotta pushed sweaty hair out of her eyes. "Thanks for working with me, Tezi."

"You're welcome."

Yelotta had changed since losing the two women she'd originally joined Thorn Company with. Some of it was likely due to being sad and chagrined, but she'd also grown easier to be around. When Tezi had first worked with her, Yelotta and her friends had muttered under their breath, saying Tezi was too young to know anything and had lucked into her axe. They hadn't taken instruction from her without snide comments. Though Tezi wouldn't have wished anyone to lose comrades, Yelotta was a lot more palatable to be around now.

"Can I tell you something?" Yelotta asked.

"Of course."

"When my friends and I asked to join your company, it wasn't because we were being kicked out of Moon Guard or disliked it there. Though I'll admit I didn't *love* it there. Our captain told us to pretend to ally with your people so we could get your axe away from you."

"He's the same one who had three of his people attack me back at the pool, right? When Grunk first showed up?"

Yelotta nodded. "He never stopped wanting it. He said it would be better to steal it than confront you directly, and he said he'd give us a bonus if we got it. But now he's gone, and all of Moon Guard might be gone too." Yelotta paused, her voice tightening, and looked toward the trees as she took a steadying breath. "I also don't want to steal it from you anymore. I didn't want to in the beginning either, but you do what your captain asks. That's how it is. I'm sure you know."

"Yes," was all Tezi said, though she was tempted to add that

Captain Ferroki would never ask her to steal or do anything dishonorable. If anything, Ferroki had questioned Tezi when she'd been tempted to do something morally dubious on her own, even if it had been, as Tezi had believed, for the good of the company.

"I wanted to let you know. You're not what I expected. Thorn Company isn't either. I wish I were back home in Zar, but if I can't be there, I'm glad to be here."

"Good." Even Tezi couldn't say that she was glad to be here.

"I'll be even more glad when we get paid again."

"Me too." Tezi smiled faintly, though she didn't care that much about that, not now. It wasn't as if they had anything to spend money on out here. "Hopefully, when this is all over and we've resolved the dragon problem…" She trailed off, not certain how to finish. The last she'd heard, Thorn Company was still on Uthari's payroll, but would Uthari, now infested with parasites and possibly going crazy, survive to pay them?

"Dragon coming," Gorsith called. "Brace yourselves for battle."

He headed up the slope toward the cave. Intending to talk the portal into helping? Would he succeed?

The haft of the axe warmed in Tezi's hand, and a vision crept over her. She saw herself standing next to Shikari as the one-eyed dragon streaked toward them, talons extended. But instead of fighting it, Shikari, Gorsith, and the rest of the mages and druids combined forces to craft a magical net. They threw it over the dragon, entangling it and causing it to crash to the ground. Then the blacksmith ran over with the remains of the chain and collar and locked it around the dragon's neck.

The vision faded before Tezi could make out why they had captured the dragon instead of killing it. Was it a prediction of the future? Or a recommendation of what they should do? And if the latter, *why*?

"Shikari?" Tezi called to the dragon. "Should we try to kill the dragons or capture them?"

Shikari tilted his head, tail swishing contemplatively in the dirt. *So far, I sense only one dragon.*

That didn't answer her question. She explained the vision, and Shikari gazed at her axe, then up at the portal.

Maybe capturing it would *be a good idea*, he said. *It might even be a most clever idea.*

So we could hold it hostage? Tezi couldn't imagine that the dragons cared enough about each other that they would bargain with humans to save a life.

So Jak and his mother can experiment on it when they return. They go to the Orbs of Wisdom to seek a solution to heal my kind. Shikari jumped up, spinning in the air. *Yes, that makes sense. If they return with ideas, they will need a tainted dragon to implement them on. Show me what the axe showed you.*

Tezi leaned the blade against a tree so Shikari could see into her mind. His mental touch was light and inoffensive.

Ah, a net. Hm, yes. It would take great power to make a net strong enough to hold a full-grown dragon, but perhaps with my help and the mages and druids... Shikari looked toward the cave. *I will speak with Malek's servant.*

Is that Gorsith?

Yes.

Tezi doubted one zidarr could be considered a servant of another—and expected Gorsith would explode if Shikari used that term with him—but he was already trotting up the slope to the cave with his tail swishing in the air behind him.

Blacksmith Homgor came over with four black-powder rifles in his hands. "Who are the best marksmen among your mercenaries?"

Realizing they had to be loaded with the new dragon-steel bullets, Tezi was tempted to volunteer herself to try out the weapons. How many times in battle had she lamented that the dragons weren't flying close enough for her to attack? But she already had a weapon capable of hurting them. It would be better to spread out the dragon steel among the others.

"Sergeant Tinder is a good shot," Tezi said, surprised the blacksmith had come to her to ask. It wasn't as if she was in charge of Thorn Company, though she supposed she'd been taking the lead on a lot of their drills. "And Lieutenant Sasko."

"I'm a fair markswoman," Yelotta said, gazing wistfully at the rifles.

Tezi hadn't seen her shoot but nodded toward her to suggest Homgor give her a weapon. Even if Yelotta wasn't the best shot in the company, it wasn't as if a dragon would be a hard target to hit. The question would be if such small bullets, even if made from dragon steel, would do any damage. It might be like peppering an elephant with slivers.

"We're not going to *capture* the dragon," Gorsith roared from the cave. "We're going to *kill* it. We're going to kill *all* of them if we can."

Tezi ran up the slope in case she could help sway him. What she could say that Shikari hadn't already, she didn't know, but it had been her vision.

Grunk jogged beside her, her self-appointed bodyguard not willing to let her face an angry zidarr alone. Though she thought she would be all right, especially if Shikari was there, she nodded her appreciation toward him. Sometime during the day, he'd gotten his dagger back from the druid woman. Maybe when Shikari had cast his spell of amiability on everyone.

In the cave, Gorsith was fuming as he glared at Shikari, facing him from in front of the portal.

"We need to use every opportunity to kill every dragon we can," Gorsith growled, only glancing at Tezi and Grunk before locking his gaze on Shikari again. "If this one is alone, it's perfect. Picking them off in ones and twos is our only chance to eliminate them all."

Not this one, Shikari said, including Tezi and Grunk in his communication. *The axe has shared a vision, and I see that it makes much sense. When Jak and his mother return, they must have a tainted dragon to try to cure. That is the only way they will know if their solution works.*

Tezi decided not to point out that it was possible Jak and Jadora hadn't found a solution and wouldn't return with anything. Even if they couldn't cure the one-eyed dragon, they might be able to use him to gain an advantage against his kind. If nothing else, he knew about the fortress and maybe if it had weaknesses. Was it possible to interrogate a dragon?

"The *solution* to the dragons is to kill them and make sure no more can come to our world," Gorsith said.

The dragons must be cured, not killed. Shikari bared his fangs at him.

Tezi lifted a hand. "Maybe we should save the arguing for later. I assume that dragon is getting close."

Gorsith glared at her, but before he could reply, the portal flashed blue.

Tezi looked hopefully toward it—maybe Jak and the others were returning—but it didn't remain blue and form stars in the middle, as it would have if a passageway had formed. Instead, it shared a vision with them.

It was so similar to what the axe had shared with Tezi that she wondered if the portal had been responsible for her original vision. In it, they were capturing the dragon, hurling a magical net over it as it swooped in to try to get its prize. Instead of shooting lightning at the dragon, the portal poured energy into the net that the mages and druids had made, enough energy that the one-eyed dragon was flattened to the ground and couldn't escape.

The vision ended, and the portal went dark.

"I think we just received instructions," Tezi said.

Shikari swished his tail and looked smug. *The portal wishes the tainted dragons to be cured, not killed. It will only assist us with capturing that one.*

Gorsith swore and stalked out, his hands wrapped around the hilts of his weapons.

Will he defy us? Grunk asked telepathically, sharing an image with Tezi of the one-eyed dragon captured and under the net, then Gorsith running up to slay him while he was helpless.

"I hope not," Tezi said, though she didn't know the zidarr well enough to predict his actions.

If he tries to kill the dragon, I will bite him, Shikari informed them. *Or I will fill him with amorous thoughts again.*

"Uh." Tezi remembered Gorsith and Kywatha kissing, the dragon's magic coercing them together. "Humans don't like to be manipulated. As strange as it sounds, biting him is probably less likely to cause resentment."

Shikari opened his maw to show off fangs that had grown quite long, then stalked out of the cave with his tail up.

I am glad not to be a zidarr right now, Grunk said.

"Me too," Tezi said.

24

JADORA KNEADED HER HANDS IN HER SKIRT AS MALEK PUSHED THE lever to make the gateship descend. The hatch had been sealed, Vinjo's filtration device removed. Little was going right, but at least they'd been able to replenish their air supply.

Bubbles wafted up all around them as the ballast tanks filled with water so the vessel would sink.

Jadora marveled at how much Vinjo could do with so little—at the moment, she sensed him working with Jak on a spear with a glass head—and smiled at Malek, glad he'd offered Vinjo refuge. Though if Malek ended up butting heads with Uthari and walked away from his duties as the king's zidarr, she didn't know if he would have the power to grant Vinjo anything. They might all end up fleeing hordes of angry mages together and hiding in a remote wilderness. Still, Jadora was touched that he'd offered.

"You've come a long way, Lord Malek," she said softly.

He'd been gazing pensively out the porthole as they descended, the water growing darker, but he managed a gentle smile for her. "I assume you don't refer to this odometer, since it's been broken since Nargnoth." He ticked a gauge on the control panel.

"I didn't even know what that measured. It could have been the number of enemies that want to slay us."

"True. The number looks right for that." His face grew grave again as he met her eyes. "Can you sense the Orbs of Wisdom? If it were possible to communicate with them and get what we need from afar, that would be ideal. We might be able to avoid conflict that way."

"I can sense that the extremely powerful entity is right above the ruins and probably blocking access to them, physically and magically. I don't think we'll be able to avoid it."

Malek sighed, but with his power, he had to be able to sense the same thing. "I know. I've been mulling over ways to divert it while you and Jak get close enough to activate the orbs, but we have nothing we can send out to lure it away. Except me."

Jadora frowned. "You're not a *thing* to be sent out."

"I'm the only one aboard with weapons skills. And I think I could use my magic to keep the water pressure from crushing me, as long as my concentration doesn't lapse."

"Such as might happen when a *dragon tail* smacks you in the head?" She objected highly to his line of thinking. After all they'd been through together, she refused to let him consider sacrificing himself for them.

"It's not a dragon."

"It's dragon*ish*. You can sense that in its aura, the same as I do."

"Yes, but whatever it is, it's more powerful and different."

"I'm hoping it's intelligent and that we'll be able to reason with it."

"You're welcome to try." Malek looked sadly at her, probably not believing for a second that they would have luck with that.

Considering the thing might have been behind everything on this world trying to kill them from the second they'd arrived,

Jadora had a hard time arguing with the sentiment. But she *would* argue against any plan that involved him sacrificing himself.

"I will," she said firmly. "And you need to give me a chance to do so." Jadora leaned over and rested a hand on his thigh, wanting to elicit a promise from him, but as their faces drew closer, a memory popped into her mind.

The events were hazy, and she hadn't been fully herself—no, she'd hardly been herself at all—but she remembered what she, guided by the parasites, had tried to do. She'd tried to use sex to spread the parasites to him. Not once but twice. The first time, neither of them had quite realized what was happening; she'd just been so intensely drawn to him that she hadn't been able to resist. And he hadn't realized he *should* resist. Thank Shylezar he'd been immune. The parasites hadn't realized that the first time. And the second time... they'd stubbornly wanted to try again, wanting to claim, in the absence of dragon options, another powerful human as a host.

"You'll have your chance," Malek said quietly, oblivious to her thoughts. "Soon."

"I'm sorry, Malek," Jadora whispered, half lost back in that moment, in the kiss she'd forced on him, the motes trying to float into his mouth.

He raised his eyebrows. "For what?"

"For what happened before I injected myself with the death-darter bacteria. For what the parasites made me try to do to you. For what I *let* them try to do." Jadora shook her head, disgusted that she hadn't been able to retain control over herself.

Back when he'd been taken over by the death-darter bacteria, he'd managed to keep from hurting her. He'd *protected* her.

Malek smiled at her. It didn't seem like the appropriate response.

"What?" she asked.

"I know it was unpleasant for you, and I accept your apology, even though it wasn't your fault, but I am amused that you're apologizing to me. Usually, you're the proper one, quick to point out how unacceptable my loutish zidarr behavior is."

His eyes crinkled, so she didn't think he was annoyed by that, but it made her hesitate anyway. She hadn't realized she'd lectured him that often.

"Your behavior isn't loutish," Jadora said, "just..."

"Arrogant?"

She shifted her hand to his shoulder. "I struggle with your loyalty to a person and system that has no trouble enslaving most of humanity. You know that. You've read my mind. Frequently. But that doesn't mean I don't appreciate you and love you for the person you are with me. It's hard sometimes because caring for you puts me at odds with what I believe to be fair and right." *Most* of the time, she thought to herself. "I'm sorry if I've been overly critical. I can't help but want you, with all your power and ability, to be a champion for people. *All* people."

"I doubt all people want a zidarr as a champion, but I'll try to be *your* champion." He pulled her into his lap for a hug.

Jadora wrapped her arms around him and buried her face in his neck, resolving to use every iota of power the dragon had given her to protect him if he did insist on being a *distraction*.

"How do you propose to infect the dragons with the death-darter bacteria when we return?" Malek asked as he stroked her hair. "Assuming that's your plan?"

"It is, even if it's a challenging one. I've been mulling over if one could make a vaccine, but it was that unique protein rather than an antibody response that I believe made the parasites leave you alone, and I don't know how to cause that to proliferate in someone without having the actual death-darter bacteria proliferate in them." She shook her head. "My expertise doesn't lie in that field, and vaccines are nascent technology back home, even for those who study microbiology. It might take years to perfect something effective, and we don't have years."

"No."

"I've thought about smearing the bacteria on a dragon-steel blade and having someone try to prong each and every dragon, then hoping for the best. Thanks to all the experiments I did trying to destroy them, I know that exposure to neither air, nor water, nor heat will destroy the bacteria, so they ought to last for a while on a blade."

"As the one who'd end up responsible for the pronging, I feel obliged to point out a method of wide dispersal would be more ideal."

"I know, but I'm not sure one could create an inhalant or lace their water supply. I'm growing more bacteria in my dishes now, but I'll still have a limited amount by the time we get back." She refused to say *if* they got back. "The delivery method will have to be pinpoint. You'll recall the death-darters had those stingers to deliver their venom and the bacteria deep into the bloodstream of their victims."

"I remember," Malek said grimly.

Jadora rubbed the back of his neck where he'd been stung. "Have I mentioned that it was heroic—the act of a champion—when you pushed Zethron out of the way and took the sting intended for him?" She hadn't been there, but she'd gotten the story from Jak.

His eyes crinkled with humor. "You haven't mentioned how heroic I am *nearly* enough."

"No?" She slid her hand up to push through his hair. "That's inconsiderate of me."

"Yes," he agreed and kissed her.

Jadora wished there were no impending danger to worry about so they could have stayed like that for hours, but she sensed Jak coming and broke the kiss. He appeared in the doorway before she'd decided if she should fling herself away from Malek and pretend they hadn't been intimately cuddling.

"Uh, I had a thought on disbursing the death-darter bacteria to all the dragons," Jak said. "Assuming you're not too busy, uhm, snuggling to hear it."

"We're not too busy," Jadora said, "and we're simply comforting each other in this dark and dire time."

"Comforting each other's lips maybe," Jak muttered as Jadora patted Malek on the chest before returning to the empty seat.

Malek looked at Jak, and Jak straightened.

"My thought is that we don't need to infect *all* the dragons ourselves," he said. "If we can cure some of them, then they should be happy with us, join our side, and take over spreading the bacteria to the others. They can claw each other and have the power to tear down their barriers, and they should want to. The old *good* dragons were all against the parasite changing their kind. I know Shikari would help, of course."

"That is a good point," Jadora said, "but we don't know how quickly the dragons will change once the parasite is killed and what shape they'll be in after they do so. We don't even know that what worked on me will work on them. They've been infested for thousands of years. If we *are* successful in removing the parasites, the dragons might die. Remember that Zelonsera only reached her advanced age by hibernating through the centuries. The parasite seems to have granted extra longevity to their hosts."

"Maybe we could get some of Uthari's longevity potion to give them," Jak said. "Do you think it works on dragons?"

"I don't know. Dragons naturally have long lives already."

"Even if your prediction is correct," Malek said to Jak, "and some of the dragons change and are willing to work with us, it's unlikely they'll have an easy time overcoming the defenses of the infested dragons to deliver the bacteria. We'd likely have to infect half of them ourselves in the hope that enough would survive and help remove the parasites from the others."

"Half is better than all, isn't it?" Jak asked.

"It is." Malek looked toward the porthole, the water outside completely dark again, the sun's influence left behind. "We've descended to within a few hundred feet of what we believe are the ruins, but there's another net of tendrils that extends for miles—if not all the way to the other net—in the way. And underneath it..."

Jadora and Jak nodded. She had no trouble sensing the powerful entity waiting below.

"Vinjo has your spear ready," Jak offered.

Malek nodded and stood. "Have him come navigate. I'll break through the net and get ready to go out there." He touched the hilt of his sword.

Such meager weapons to fight the creature emitting the great power that Jadora sensed. Worse, he had to do so underwater.

"How long can you hold your breath?" Jak asked him, worry creasing his brow. "While also keeping the water pressure from crushing your body? And fighting a battle?"

"I haven't timed myself while doing those things simultaneously before," Malek said dryly.

Neither Jadora nor Jak could share in his humor.

"Under normal circumstances, I can hold my breath several minutes longer than the typical human being."

"These are hardly normal circumstances," Jadora said. "Your body will use up its oxygen more quickly if you're active."

"I'm aware." Malek nodded to them both, then headed back into the ship to get the spear and prepare himself.

"Be careful," they heard Vinjo say as he offered the acid-tipped weapon to Malek.

"Would you miss me if I died?" Malek asked, his tone still dry.

"Well, no *other* zidarr has offered me refuge."

"So, you'd be heartbroken."

"Obviously."

"I told him I'd try to communicate with it to see if there's a way it will work with us," Jadora told Jak when they were alone, "but if it's part dragon, or was created by the dragons, you might have better luck."

"I actually already tried." Jak shrugged. "You know I enjoy chatting with anything dragon-related."

"And?"

"It didn't reply or acknowledge me in any way. I did have a sense that it was aware of and watching us."

"Comforting," Jadora said, though it wasn't surprising, not when it had been launching attacks at them all along.

"I'll try again when we're closer."

Jadora nodded and stretched out with her senses, running them along the entwined tendrils below as Vinjo slipped into navigation and slowed the gateship's descent. It was hard to examine the net carefully with the intense power of the creature blazing like an underwater sun, but she believed she could create a hole. The more of Malek's power he could save, the better.

She summoned her magic and pushed the tendrils aside, attempting to create a gap large enough for the gateship without destroying the flora itself. But, as Malek had discovered, the magic inherent in everything here—or being reinforced by that entity—made the task far more difficult than it should have been for someone with her power. Even the water fought against her.

"Be ready to take us down quickly," she whispered, certain the tendril net would close up again immediately.

"I am," Vinjo said.

With an intense burst of energy, she created the hole, tendrils snapping in the process, despite her wishes.

As the gateship descended, the net pushed back at Jadora, attempting to close itself again. Worse, she sensed the entity stirring and had no doubt Jak was right, that it was watching them. It had been watching them since they first came through the portal hundreds of miles away.

"Going down," Vinjo said.

The tendrils grasped at their vessel. Before they'd started descending, Malek had formed the barrier around it again, but that only protected the gateship. It didn't keep things from wrapping around the barrier—and them.

Jadora split her focus, pushing back the tendrils and helping Malek with the barrier. Weakness crept into her body, a reminder that she'd been sick not long ago.

"It's moving," Jak said, his focus on the entity.

He funneled some of his power into Jadora, giving her more strength. She kept the tendrils back until the gateship was out of their reach, then released them.

Vinjo nudged a control, and a beam of yellow light shone ahead of the gateship. A couple of tall columns covered in gray gunk rose up, the tops broken off. In thick silt ahead and below, a broken red orb gleamed, but only the faintest magical signature came from it.

Jadora hoped that wasn't one of the Orbs of Wisdom. In the visions, they were always on pedestals, but those visions might have come from memories of how they'd been long ago, not how they were today.

"We've reached the ruins," Vinjo said. "The, uh, creature isn't coming straight toward us but seems to be swimming toward something in the center."

"The orbs," Jak said with certainty. "I sense something right there."

Yes, Jadora did too, but the magic wasn't much greater than that of the broken sphere below. Were the orbs in a similar state of disrepair?

"Take us to them," she said, aware of Malek standing under the ladder with his weapons, his magic already creating an airlock that would allow him to go out without flooding the ship with water.

They navigated between the columns and toward a pyramid, one of many grime-covered structures resting on the sea floor. Most of what had been buildings were unidentifiable as such anymore, walls and roofs long since crumbled. A set of stairs that led nowhere was covered with gray silt inches thick. What looked like an ancient amphitheater remained largely intact.

"Keep us low to the ground and among the ruins, Vinjo," Jadora said. "Maybe they'll be an obstacle if the creature tries to get us."

"*When* the creature tries to get us." Jak pointed into the gloom ahead.

Jadora sensed it stirring and, for the first time, heading in their direction.

When it came into view, her first thought was that it was more like a giant whale than a dragon, but when the light from a glowing orange slab half-buried in the silt shined on its body, she caught her breath. It had mottled gray-and-brown scales and a tail, limbs, and talons. That was, however, where the similarities to dragons ended. In place of wings, it had fins, including a large triangular-shaped one on the end of its tail. A ridge of spikes ran down its spine, and, where horns might have once been, it had tentacles that quivered as it swam. Its snout was wider and flatter than a dragon's, reminding Jadora of a platypus, though it had teeth—*fangs*—as fearsome as a dragon's. And it was larger, easily twice the size of the dragons they'd encountered.

"What *is* it?" Vinjo breathed, even as he navigated the gateship toward a clump of columns that looked more like stalagmites in a cave than ruins. "Not a dragon."

"I think it might have *been* a dragon," Jak said. "Or evolved from them after this place got flooded."

"That would be a lot of evolution in a relatively short time," Jadora said, "especially for a long-lived species."

"Maybe it wasn't *natural* evolution. Maybe someone wanted a guardian. Or some*thing* wanted one." Jak looked at her, though he also kept an eye on the porthole, dread emanating from him as the great creature lazily swam toward them, not appearing worried in the least by their arrival or their combined power. "Do you think the parasites could have altered it? Changed it into something suitable for guarding this world?"

"Perhaps," Jadora said, though they hadn't seen evidence yet of the parasite doing more than changing the coloring of skin and scales—and personality. "Or maybe the infested dragons did it to one of their own kind themselves."

"Can we discuss it later?" Vinjo asked. "When it's *dead*?"

"Are we trying to kill it?" Jak asked. "Or just get to the orbs?"

"I think we may need to do the former to achieve the latter," Jadora said grimly, "but see if we can get past it."

"Getting past it seems unlikely," Vinjo said.

The huge creature continued toward them, its eyes growing visible. They were yellow and slitted, the reptilian eyes of a dragon, and they were focused on the gateship.

~

Rivlen stood at the railing of the *Soaring Eagle*, helping Uthari and the mages on deck funnel power into the barrier. Pines and fir trees dominated the landscape below, promising they were nearing the more temperate southern coastline of Zewnath, perhaps not far from where she, her crew, and Thorn Company had washed up. That also meant they weren't far from the sea that led to the Glacier Islands and the fortress.

The alert dragons had to know they were close, but Wortalia's fleet was hurling fireballs and magically enhanced cannonballs at

Uthari's fleet. Rivlen hadn't heard any telepathic warnings, but she wouldn't be surprised if the leader was communicating with Uthari telepathically. A frustrated sneer stamped his sweaty face.

In the distance, the other two fleets floated, neither approaching nor raising their barriers. They looked like they were going to wait and see what happened rather than getting involved.

King Wortalia, Uthari boomed telepathically, surprising Rivlen by sharing the words with everyone and not solely the recipient. Did he hope to embarrass the king? Or did he, with his illness affecting his mind, not realize what he was doing? *Why do you foolishly attack my fleet when we have a greater enemy to deal with?*

King Wortalia strode into view on the deck of one of the larger mageships, one flying beside a handful of vessels from the fallen kingdom of Temril. Gray-haired and bearded with the broad shoulders of a gladiator, Wortalia walked to the railing, his fur-trimmed cloak flapping in the breeze. His gaze skimmed over Uthari's fleet before he looked toward the other fleets and nodded. To himself or to someone on one of those ships?

Rivlen had a feeling the other fleets were working together—and hadn't invited Uthari to join the party.

When Wortalia had spoken of a joint command, maybe he'd meant that Uthari's fleet would head in first as cannon fodder—*dragon* fodder—while the rest of the mageship commanders and kings determined how best to take advantage of their enemies' distraction.

We've had this greater enemy that we've needed to join forces to fight for weeks now, and you've been running around, taking advantage of kingdoms being devastated by the dragons. Wortalia also shared his words with everyone. *Did you think nobody would find out about the assassin you sent to Temril?* He spread his arm toward the ships from the island kingdom. *That you had the king and queen killed in cold blood because you wanted fewer monarchs in the world so you could take over their lands? Do you fancy yourself an emperor, Uthari? A leader over all of Torvil?*

I want to get rid of the dragons that afflict our world. Temril was no help in that. The dragons had already destroyed their kingdom when my people arrived.

And you took advantage and obliterated it further. For your own gain. Your time nears its end in our world, no matter what longevity potion you've discovered.

Rivlen raised her eyebrows, surprised the rest of the kings had learned about that so quickly. Did that mean other kingdoms had spies in Utharika?

Do not envy me my long life or what I've discovered in it, Wortalia. Uthari dragged a sleeve across his sweaty forehead. *If anything, you should be agreeing to work with me. Join my fleet to deal with the dragons, and I'll share the secret of long life with you, the recipe for the potion.*

More likely, you'll have me assassinated as soon as my back is turned. Nobody trusts you, Uthari. Prepare to suffer for your greed. Wortalia lifted his arm, and the attack resumed.

"So be it," Uthari whispered. "Captain Jagobar. Attack back. Focus on Wortalia's ship and destroy it. *Completely*. After he's dead and his ship is wrecked, the rest of his fleet shouldn't be so eager to attack us."

"Yes, Your Majesty!"

Rivlen didn't know if that would work. Uthari had made a lot of enemies lately.

He waved for her to join him at the railing.

"As soon as we lower our defenses," he said as fireballs burst against the *Soaring Eagle's* barrier, "send everything you've got at them."

"Yes, Your Majesty," Rivlen said, but she also glanced at the other two fleets hovering in the distance. "What do we do if they join in?"

She counted a total of twenty-eight ships out there to their dozen. If the two fleets stayed out of it, the odds would be more even, but she wasn't confident they would.

"Those cowards won't." Uthari wiped his brow again. "Look at them loitering in the distance like vultures, waiting to pick at what's left after the predators handle all the danger."

A fireball slammed into the barrier directly in front of Uthari. He scowled and lifted his chin. "Prepare to lower the barrier for a counterattack that will utterly destroy them."

Normally, a cheer would go up at the command to return fire—mages across the world loved offense far more than defense—but only a few concerned utterances of, "Yes, Your Majesty," came as a response.

With foreboding hollowing a pit in her stomach, Rivlen braced herself to join in.

After another wave of cannonballs and fire and lightning attacks, Uthari called, "Lower the barrier and return fire now!"

As soon as their defenses dropped, Rivlen blasted a wall of fire toward Wortalia's ship. It sizzled through the air, a great wave of flaming power.

Her frustration with the situation and desire to survive the day allowed her to summon more strength than usual. Though the wall of fire met the barrier of the ship she targeted, its magic repelling hers, it was enough of a threat to force the mages aboard to turn their offense to defense.

She kept the stream going as her fellow officers joined in, sending magical attacks as the *Soaring Eagle's* cannons boomed. Uthari launched streaks of lightning across the sky. They branched when they reached the barrier, striking all around it, seeking a weakness, a place to enter and blast the mages on the deck.

Despite Uthari's order to focus on the lead ship, his officers spread out their attacks, peppering Wortalia's entire fleet. A good idea so the rest of the ships also had to keep barriers up and couldn't fire upon Uthari while he focused on a single vessel.

Rivlen imagined the dragons lounging in their fortress, munching on fish—or humans—and using their magic to watch this from afar, amusement rippling through them as they realized their human opponents were so busy attacking each other that they weren't a threat.

The thought infuriated her because it was true, and it was stupid. Why couldn't these idiots—*all* of them—work together? Maybe Jak and Jadora were right to believe these people didn't deserve to be in charge of the world.

Letting her frustration feed into her magic, and envisioning the power of the dragon-steel blade adding to her own, Rivlen increased the heat and breadth of her wall of fire. Surprisingly, the dragon steel helped, almost as Jak did when he stood beside her, funneling his power into hers. She hadn't been aware the weapons could do that, but she was quick to use the assistance, intensifying her attack once again.

A couple of the mages on Wortalia's ship dropped to one knee under the strain of keeping their barrier up. Their faces gleamed with as much sweat as Uthari's.

Rivlen didn't know how much longer she could throw so much power at their ship, but the indications that Wortalia's mages were growing weaker made her press on, her fire mingling with Uthari's lightning as their magic hammered their enemy.

As magic streamed from his fingers, Uthari looked over at her. *Your power has grown, Xeva.*

His use of her first name, said with a mental caress, disturbed and frustrated her as much as the overall situation. Rivlen willed the sword to help her pour more power into her attack. On Wortalia's ship, another mage on deck dropped to his knees. As Rivlen's fire railed at their barrier, she sensed it weakening.

Uthari's lightning intensified. He must have also felt their victory growing near.

We'll join tonight, he told her, looking over again, a creepy smile on his lips. *Our bodies and our power. You'll know pleasure such as you've never known.*

The dragons might interfere with that. Was it horrible to hope they would?

She would almost be surprised if they didn't use this distraction to swoop in and attack.

We'll see. They might see our great power and decide to leave us alone.

Rivlen doubted that.

Uthari chuckled into her mind, sharing an image of them naked and writhing in bed, then thankfully went back to his primary task. It was hard for Rivlen to focus after that, but she growled, determined not to fail when they were so close to victory. Through the fire, she glimpsed Wortalia, his face contorted with effort as he helped his people reinforce their barrier.

Just as their enemy was on the verge of losing their defenses and being blasted from the sky, a call of, "Incoming!" came from the bow of the *Soaring Eagle*. Fireballs blasted toward them from another direction.

"We have to raise our defenses, Your Majesty!" an officer yelled.

Uthari, lightning still streaking from his fingers, looked toward the new threat. The other two fleets were opening fire on them.

Rivlen halted her attack, legs wobbling in the aftermath of all the power she'd drawn upon, and started to raise a barrier, but Uthari hadn't stopped his attack yet. Envisioning lightning bouncing around inside once the barrier went up, singeing his own people, she ran over and gripped his shoulder.

"Your Majesty, we have to defend ourselves."

"I know that, Captain," he snapped and brushed off her hand.

With a surge of power, he raised the barrier an instant before the first fireballs arrived. Rivlen added her power, as did the other mage officers, and the attacks bounced off, but the sheer number of ships throwing magic at them worried her. Not only were Dy's and Zaruk's fleets flying closer but their mages were launching everything they had. Meanwhile, Wortalia's mages were recovering, and the king bellowed for his people to join in.

"There's another fleet coming!" someone in the stern of the *Soaring Eagle* yelled.

Rivlen groaned, sensing the newcomers before she looked to see a dozen yellow-hulled vessels sailing over the trees. King Darekar's fleet. When she sensed a powerful aura aboard the lead ship, she feared he'd come personally.

"We're outmatched, Your Majesty," she said.

"None of them… are as powerful… as I," Uthari panted.

Whether he was taxed from using his power or from the infection or both, Rivlen didn't know, but Uthari wobbled on his feet. She reached out a hand to steady him. He was still pouring his energy into defending the *Soaring Eagle*, but it wasn't as much as before, and his eyes were glazed, his face flushed. In addition to being bathed in sweat, more than half his skin was that scaly gray now. Rivlen would have recoiled from the idea of sleeping with him even if she hadn't had feelings for Jak and Uthari hadn't been three hundred years old and as wizened as a raisin.

"Together, they're greater than us," Rivlen said. "I wish it weren't true, but it is."

Around them, officers gasped, fighting as hard to maintain their barrier as Wortalia's people had been minutes before. Once the newcomers came within range and joined in, that would be the end for Uthari's fleet.

King Uthari, a new voice bellowed into their minds. That *was* King Darekar. *As much as we would all enjoy seeing you dead, we need you to help against the dragons.*

Screw you, Darekar, Uthari replied, though he was panting and on the verge of dropping to his knees.

Rivlen kept channeling her power into the barrier, but she diverted a small amount to funnel into Uthari, trying to keep him on his feet. They might be in worse trouble if the other kings realized how close he was to collapsing.

An unappealing offer, and one that didn't go well for Queen Vorsha. You deserve to die for that alone, but we must worry about the dragons. Do you surrender to our superior power and agree to obey us in our attack on the fortress?

My people have more experience, Uthari replied, stubborn to the last, *so it's logical for us to lead.*

Yet you will not. You'll tell us everything you know, and you'll go in first with your fleet, taking the brunt of the dragons' ire as we flank them and attack from the sides and behind.

Rivlen scowled. She'd been right. They wanted to use Uthari's fleet for cannon fodder.

She formed an image in her mind, the memory Kywatha had shared with her of the great red beam striking their raft, burning through their barrier and blowing the logs to pieces. Then she did her best to blast it out to all the mageships around them, including those approaching. She tried to convey that the beam would have no problem picking off ships that attempted to *flank* or come in from *behind* the fortress, and that the mages had to all work together to create something capable of destroying that weapon.

That, Darekar said, *is why your people will go in first, Uthari. We will observe what the dragons and their fortress do to you. If you're the wizard you think you are, you will survive. Now, surrender. We are on the verge of destroying your barrier—we all sense it. We'd like to have a wizard with us against the dragons, but if you're too stubborn to cooperate, we will kill you and your crew.*

Uthari swayed again, and Rivlen gripped him more tightly to keep him upright. His tunic was drenched with sweat. The faces of the officers defending the ship all turned to him, fear and hope mingling in their eyes. They knew they were outmatched; what they didn't know was if Uthari would agree to surrender, to save their lives.

Uthari's jaw set with the very stubbornness his rivals had accused him of.

"You need to surrender, Your Majesty," Rivlen whispered. "We can't win against them."

I've never surrendered in my life, and I refuse to do so now, he replied, not only to her but to everyone.

Then you will meet your death, Uthari, Wortalia said. *No potion will save you.*

Rivlen licked her lips, not wanting to die like this. This was utter foolishness. If she was to die, she wanted it to be in a dragon's maw with her sword driving up through its brain.

"Do you want to die when the dragons will live?" she asked. "The dragons that are only here because you ordered that portal erected?"

Maybe accusing him of failures wasn't the best option, but he looked at her with his glazed blue eyes.

"We need to defeat those dragons before we die, either of us," she continued. "If you say you'll work with the other kings, that doesn't mean you can't get back at them later. Maybe you can be clever and figure out a way to get the dragons to destroy them first while *we* survive."

"You're attempting to manipulate me, Rivlen."

"Yes, Your Majesty, I am."

He laughed hoarsely. "I do appreciate honesty."

She didn't think his words indicated that he agreed with her, but he nodded and faced the oncoming ships.

You give me no choice, King Darekar, Uthari said. *I surrender.*

More fireballs and lightning bolts hammered into their barrier, and Rivlen feared they'd waited too long, that Darekar,

Wortalia, and the others had decided they wanted to rid the world of Uthari.

But as Rivlen and her colleagues were on the verge of collapse, their barrier wavering, the attacks halted. She barely had the strength left to remain standing, much less support Uthari, and she used the sword as a cane as she led him to the railing. He slumped against it, his breathing labored.

I'm pleased you see the wisdom of doing so, Darekar said. *Perform any repairs you need to do, and head south. You and your fleet will lead us to the dragon fortress.*

Very well. Uthari took a few more deep breaths, marshaled his strength, and headed for his cabin.

Rivlen hoped he was far too busy recovering and scheming ways to take revenge on his colleagues to remember that promise he'd made about them having sex and mingling their power. That was the last thing she wanted, but if he came to her cabin, she didn't know what she would do.

"Jak," she whispered, looking toward the north, toward where they'd left the portal, "I really need you and your mother to return with a solution for this parasite."

25

Jak joined his mother and Malek in reinforcing the barrier around the gateship. Before, it had only needed to protect the craft from the pressure of the water outside. Now… who knew what the creature swimming toward them could do.

Are you an intelligent being? Jak asked it, though it had thus far ignored his attempts to communicate. Even if it understood him, he doubted he could reason with it, not if it was aligned with the tainted dragons—or had been created by them.

"It's blocking our way." Vinjo manipulated the levers on the control panel. "I'll try to go around."

So far, it hadn't attacked them, but if they were right, it had caused everything else in the sea to attack them.

"Watch out for those plants down there." Mother pointed to the now-familiar heart-shaped entities dotting the ruins, long vines flowing from them. Some of them had ensnared dully glowing artifacts, remnants of the lost civilization.

"Oh, I will," Vinjo said.

Jak glanced through the doorway and down the corridor to where Malek had been waiting, but he'd climbed the ladder and disappeared from view. Jak could only sense him and the magical airlock he'd created.

A current rocked the vessel. Jak, who'd given the co-pilot's seat to his mother, gripped the back of it for support.

Another current swept in from the side, pushing them toward columns rising from the sea floor, vines wrapped around them. Despite Vinjo's efforts to steer them away, the ship, cocooned in its barrier, bumped into them. The vines stirred and grasped at it.

"That wasn't natural," Vinjo said.

"Nothing here is natural," Jak muttered. "I'm talking to it, but it isn't answering."

We apologize if we've invaded your world and territory that you feel is yours, he spoke to the creature, its slitted yellow eyes regarding them through the porthole. *We're explorers, and we'll leave as soon as we figure out how to fix the portal.* No need to mention the orbs. *I don't suppose you'd like to advise us on how to do that?*

Vinjo navigated them away from the columns and attempted to pick a path through the ruins to the orbs, but the creature kept floating into view ahead of them, blocking them.

We know why you have come, a sonorous voice boomed in Jak's mind, *and we will ensure you never leave.*

It was the first response the creature had given, and it didn't bode well.

That's not very polite. Don't you like visitors? You must get bored here with only plants to speak with.

Currents knocked into the gateship from all sides, and the deck tilted wildly. Jak lost his grip on the seat back and tumbled into the corridor. Though their barrier held—the creature hadn't attacked that yet—the ship was pushed backward.

"What are you saying to it?" Mother asked.

"Nothing it likes," Jak said.

"Well, say something it *likes* then," Vinjo said.

"What do you suggest? Recipes for roasted humans that it might enjoy cooking?"

Jak sensed Mother drawing upon her power to make a current to push the *creature* back. Even though she succeeded in bestirring the water, it parted when it reached its wedge-shaped snout, gushing past the creature instead of disturbing it.

Vinjo angled the ship off in another direction and made progress in taking them deeper into the ruins. Until magic rose in front of them. Before he could halt the vessel, it rammed into an invisible wall, bouncing off with a jolt that almost sent Jak tumbling again.

"It's formed a barrier around the core of the ruins where we believe the orbs are," Mother said. "At least a mile across."

"I sense it," Vinjo said. "It just appeared."

Shall I go out and attack it now? Malek asked them. *Since there's a limited amount of time I can hold my breath, I need to do it when we're close to the orbs. Ideally, while you're accessing them and acquiring what you need.*

I don't want you to go out, Mother replied, *but we won't make it any farther if you don't. Also, if you could pop the barrier blocking our way as you go, we'd appreciate that.*

Would you? came Malek's dry reply.

Very much so. I'll kiss you later for your valiant bravery. Despite the words, Mother didn't smile. From the concern in her eyes, Jak knew she worried Malek wouldn't return.

Hoping to lighten her mood, he said, *Others of us are here and listening to you two. Please keep talk of kissing to a minimum.*

Are your young and innocent ears offended by talk of adult relations? Mother asked.

Not mine, but Vinjo may not want to be distracted by it. Jak sensed Malek using his magic, moving through his airlock and opening the hatch.

"Be ready to surge forward as soon as the barrier is down,"

Mother said. "We'll have to hurry so we can get back in time to pick him up."

The look Vinjo gave her suggested he didn't think there would be anyone left alive to pick up, but he didn't voice his belief. All he asked was, "What happens if neither his dragon-steel sword nor the acid-coated spear is enough to pop the barrier?"

"Then we'll have to access the orbs from afar." Mother looked at Jak. "I believe I've located them."

"Oh? I sense so many magical things that I can't tell for certain. I have no idea what kind of aura *Orbs of Wisdom* are supposed to give off."

"I'm taking a guess based on what's precisely at the center of the barrier the creature has raised." Mother shared what she sensed with Jak, guiding him toward one of many magical artifacts in the center of the ruins.

He grimaced because it was one of the weaker auras out there, and he worried the portal's vision of the orbs being damaged would prove true.

"Malek is out," Vinjo said.

Since Malek was above the gateship, they couldn't see him through the porthole, but they sensed him, his aura shining more brightly than usual as he wrapped his power around himself as protection from attacks—and the water.

Propelled by his magic, Malek swam first toward the barrier. He slashed it with both spear and dragon-steel blade. The sword was what popped the barrier, and Mother breathed an audible sigh of relief.

"Hurry through," she urged.

"I am," Vinjo said.

Neither pointed out that the creature could reestablish another barrier. What if it killed Malek and trapped the ship inside?

Its yellow eyes were already focused on him, and it sent a current toward him to impede his swimming.

Mother must have been paying attention when the creature had parted her current, for she used her power to do the same, sending the streams of water past Malek instead of into the front of his barrier. Even so, he struggled to swim quickly toward the creature, the magically heavy water like molasses as he navigated through it.

While their enemy watched him, the gateship continued toward the center of the ruins. Mother must have shared where she thought the orbs were with Vinjo, for he arrowed in that direction.

Though he worried about Malek once he was out of view, Jak made himself reach out to the faint aura of the orb his mother had shown him, examining it and wondering if he could communicate with it the way he did the portals. More likely, they were akin to the dragon-steel weapons, with a hint of sentience but not true intelligence.

It didn't stir with awareness when he brushed it with his mind. He thought about asking Mother to help, but she'd craned her neck, looking to the rear of the gateship, as if she could see through its hull to where they'd left Malek. Jak sensed her using her power to help him in whatever way she could. He also sensed that his aura was next to the creature's, that he'd engaged it in a battle.

Knowing they didn't have much time, Jak made himself focus on the orbs. Vinjo cursed as he guided them around grasping vines. The creature might have shifted its attention to Malek, but that didn't mean it couldn't still manipulate the plants and currents.

The hull of the gateship groaned.

"Malek isn't reinforcing it anymore," Vinjo said. "I'm using my own power, but I'm not as strong as he is."

"I'll try to help," Jak said, though he worried he wouldn't be able to divide his concentration.

"No," Mother said, power surging from her to infuse the hull. "I'll do it. Figure out how to extract our information, Jak."

Easier said than done. He sent imagery of the broken portal to the orbs, asking them how to repair it.

We're friends of the dragons, he added, in case they could understand. *The old, untainted dragons. We want to cure them. If you can help us fix the portal and share anything you know about the parasites that are affecting them, we would greatly appreciate it.* Realizing that last was similar to what his mother had said to Malek, Jak almost added that he'd be willing to kiss the orbs, but he doubted his lips would entice them.

As the gateship rounded a broken wall covered in lumpy gray nodules that reminded Jak of warts, the orbs finally came into view. Three of them rested on separate pedestals, but it was as the portal had promised. One was shattered—the rubble of a fallen column lay all around it. One was intact but dark, and the third glowed so faintly it might have been Jak's imagination. Vines twined up their pedestals, spicules and nubs half hiding the orbs from view.

Jak focused on the faintly glowing orb, sensing the others were destroyed. He repeated what he'd said before, sending more imagery to it, asking it to assist them so they could in turn aid the dragons.

"Malek isn't sure how much longer he can hold his breath," Mother whispered, "and he's been injured. The creature is *very* strong, and even though it doesn't move quickly and he can reach it with his weapons, they're not doing much damage. He's distracting it with his attacks when it tries to come this way, but he's struggling to survive its mental blows and everything it's throwing at him. I'm trying to help from a distance, but..." She gripped the edge of the console, her eyebrows drawing together as she concentrated.

The thought that they might lose Malek made Jak want to command Vinjo to turn the gateship around, to go retrieve him, but he made himself keep trying to access the orb. That was what Malek would want.

It wasn't reacting to his attempts to communicate, but maybe that wasn't what one was supposed to do. They were repositories of knowledge, after all, not intelligent beings.

He envisioned himself standing in the university library back home, flipping through a card catalog, seeking books on portal repair and parasite destruction.

A very faint essence sparked within the orb, and it glowed slightly brighter. It flashed a confused jumble into his mind that he couldn't parse. Was it because it was damaged? Maybe he should have asked for only one thing.

Portal repair, he decided since they already had an idea about how to deal with the parasite.

When he sent the request to the orb, an image of the portal flashed into his mind, followed by schematics of its interior, sophisticated wiring, and diagrams showing which panels to open to access the crucial components. Jak hadn't known there *were* panels or anything but solid dragon steel within its frame. Close-up imagery of one section followed, showing a glowing egg-shaped device with pulsing yellow cords coming from it. Its glow diminished until a blue-scaled dragon landed beside the portal and beamed immense power into the egg. Two more dragons landed beside the first, also channeling power into the egg. It grew brighter again, the panel shut, and the portal flared to life.

"We can recharge it, but we need the power of three dragons to do so?" Jak grimaced.

Mother gasped. "It knocked Malek away, and he's almost out of air. We have to go get him before it's too late."

"Wait," Jak said, though he was as worried about Malek as Mother was. "I haven't asked it about the parasite."

"There's no time," Mother said.

"Can we take it with us?" Vinjo wiped sweat from his face—he'd been focused on keeping the barrier around the ship up—and tried to levitate the orb from its pedestal.

It was either attached or didn't want to be taken, for it resisted his attempt to remove it. Jak tried as well, but he sensed something tethering it to the pedestal. Could he cut it? What if doing so cut the remaining power to the orb and rendered it useless?

"The creature is coming," Mother said. "It cast Malek aside, leaving him for dead, and it's coming. Fast."

"I can't get the orb," Vinjo said.

"Who *cares* about the orb when Malek is dying?" Mother demanded. But with a surge of her power, she snapped the magic tethering the orb to the pedestal.

As Jak had feared, it went dark. He slumped.

Mother levitated it toward the ship as she waved at Vinjo to take them back toward Malek.

"The creature is coming from that direction," Vinjo said, though he turned the gateship around.

"We'll have to go around it," Mother said. "Malek needs us."

Vinjo worked the controls to do as she wished, but he gave Jak a long look over his shoulder. Afraid Mother would get them all killed out of her desperation to save Malek?

Jak wasn't sure Vinjo was wrong, but he only nodded toward the porthole. They had to do their best to get to him—before it was too late.

~

For the fifth time, Sasko checked the ammunition in the rifle she'd been given.

"You can tell from the color that it's dragon steel," Tinder said, leaning against the tree beside her.

She, Yelotta, Basher, and Sasko had accepted the blacksmith's weapons, along with rather obvious instructions to shoot the dragon and not waste ammunition by missing. Sasko felt more nervous than pleased to have been given the rifle. If the special bullets could breach the dragon's defenses and hurt it, they would doubtless *irk* it and probably draw its attention. Visions of herself with her head torn off kept coming to mind.

"Can you tell from the color if they'll pierce dragon scales?" Sasko muttered.

"That's to be determined."

Corporal Basher puffed from her cigar as she examined the rounds in her rifle. "I heard we were capturing the dragon, not trying to kill it."

"That's what they said." Sasko looked toward the cave entrance.

Nobody was guarding it or the portal inside, the better to lure in the solo dragon circling the area, but the druids crouched in the undergrowth to one side of the slope and the mages to the other. Gorsith and Homgor were poised with a hastily made magical net and intended to ensnare their foe. Thus far, Sasko hadn't caught sight of the dragon, and she wondered if it somehow *knew* this was a trap.

"*They* being Jak's dragon and Tezi," Basher said. "I'm not sure when they ended up in charge, but I have some concerns."

"I'd rather take orders from them than a zidarr we barely know," Sasko said.

"I suppose I'd agree with that, but they're not in the chain of command of the person who's paying us."

"If it helps, I'm not that sure Uthari is paying us anymore."

"That does *not* help. Do you know how much I've had to pay to acquire fine smokes in the middle of this jungle?" Basher drew out her cigar to blow a smoke ring. "I need to be paid."

"That looks like it was rolled by monkeys using mud and jungle grass."

Basher examined her lumpy green cigar. "It was rolled by druids, not monkeys, but you may be right on the ingredients. It's got a nice aroma and pleasant kick though."

"It smells like rotting blackberries." Sasko wrinkled her nose as Tinder nodded in agreement.

Tezi jogged out of the trees and pointed at the air above the cave. To indicate the direction the dragon was coming from? According to her vision?

Sasko didn't want to scoff at those visions, given that some of them had come true, but she also wouldn't plan a battle according to them. But the mercenaries apparently appreciated the suggestion of which way to watch and where to point their weapons, for they nodded to Tezi before she trotted back into the trees to take a position beside Gorsith.

He glowered at her. Briefly, she glowered back, then ignored him to focus on the sky.

"Who knew when we got her scrawny arms into the company that she'd turn out to have some grit?" Tinder asked.

"The captain did," Sasko said.

"That's why she's in charge," Basher said. "She's got a grit-detector."

The dragon is nearby but circling the area instead of heading straight in, a voice spoke in their minds. Shikari. *He may suspect a trap.*

"That's what I figured," Sasko whispered.

I will attempt to be clever and lure him in, Shikari continued.

"This should prove interesting." Basher returned her cigar to her mouth.

A great rustling of leaves came from the trees, and something roared. It wasn't a dragon.

"What was that?" Basher pointed her rifle not toward the sky but into the trees. "A panther?"

More roars came from that direction, followed by the howls of wolves. Sasko looked toward the druids, but they were murmuring among themselves and peering into the trees in puzzlement. A great cat screeched.

Something is riling up the predators of the jungle, Kywatha warned everyone.

It's more than that, Gorsith said. *Someone is* rounding *them up.*

I sense no one with magic in that direction, Kywatha said.

The dragon isn't that far away.

Would a dragon—

A roar interrupted the question. More foliage rattled, and branches snapped. Sasko caught the glint of red eyes in the dark and pointed her rifle.

"Don't waste the dragon-steel bullets," Homgor called.

Sasko cursed and patted her ammo pouch, wondering if she had time to load regular rounds.

The dragon is coming closer! Shikari cried into their minds.

Sasko lowered her hand. She dared not change out the ammunition.

It may be coercing the animals into attacking to distract us, Kywatha warned.

She lifted her arms, as did several other druids, and they caused green light to flare between the trees. Their magic didn't make the animals flee; all it did was highlight how many of them there were.

Sasko groaned, spotting dozens, if not hundreds, of wolves, great cats, and furred and fanged creatures she couldn't name. Their eyes were glazed, and she had no trouble believing they were under a magical spell.

"This dragon is craftier than the others," Sasko said.

"Oh, good," Tinder said. "Just what I like in my enemies. Craftiness."

As one, the animals charged. Mercenaries with magelocks and roamers with regular black-powder weapons fired at them. Gorsith, Kywatha, and the others with power launched magical attacks into the trees. A fireball roared toward a pack of wolves, and they sprang aside at the last moment, their fur singed.

The dragon is coming now, Shikari announced, watching the sky instead of the trees and the animals. He crouched low, as if he expected the opportunity to pounce at any second.

And that opportunity came as a dark winged shape flew into view over the cave. A single yellow eye glinted in its face.

"There's our target," Sasko said and fired as the dragon dove.

She aimed for that eye. When she'd loaded the ammunition, the bullets hadn't done anything to indicate they were special, but her first shot flared blue as it streaked toward the dragon. Tinder, Yelotta, and Basher also fired.

The dragon twisted in the air before the bullets struck, and Sasko realized it hadn't meant to dive straight at them but fly into the cave. Her round didn't reach the dragon's eye, but it *did* go through its barrier. All of their bullets did, and Basher let out a whoop.

The blue glow allowed them to see the bullets hitting the target, but it was hard to tell how much they affected the dragon. It didn't cry out or alter its path. Instead, it ignored them, and, as more animals raced into the camp and charged people, it alighted in the mouth of the cave.

Cursing, Sasko and the others fired again. They couldn't let the dragon rush in and get the portal.

Shikari ran up the slope to the cave and launched into the air, wings flapping as he flew at the intruder's back. Ignoring his approach, the dragon strode inside toward the portal.

Sasko cursed as she lost sight of their enemy, and blue light flared within the cave. Shikari flew inside, and she lowered her rifle. Even if she'd been able to see the dragon, she wouldn't have wanted to risk hitting Shikari.

A rattling of leaves and panting to her right made her swing her rifle around. Two red eyes glinted, and something large and black sprang for her. She fired at the same time that Tinder did. Their bullets slammed into the snout and eyes of a charging wolf.

Its momentum carried it forward, and they dove to either side, rolling as it crashed down where they'd been standing. Fortunately, their bullets had halted it.

"Thanks for the help," Sasko said, even as Homgor yelled at them.

"Don't waste those bullets on oversized dogs!"

"Bastard," Basher growled.

Flashes of blue light in the cave drew their attention back to it, and Sasko raised her rifle again, but she still had no target. Both dragons had disappeared inside.

Then the larger one flew out, tumbling through the air as if the portal had punched it. Sasko hoped it had.

The dragon landed hard on the slope and rolled down toward the camp. Sasko and the others fired as several mages and druids combined forces to pull the net of glowing yellow strands of energy over it. As the dragon rolled to a stop, bullets peppering its scaled hide, the net descended over it.

Roaring, the one-eyed creature sprang to its feet, muscles bunching in a spring that would have taken it away from the trap, but a blast of blue energy came out of the cave and struck it in the face.

The magic seemed to stun the dragon, for it halted mid-spring. More rustling and crunching of foliage made Sasko worry that another round of jungle predators was coming, but a jaguar that had been creeping up on their group turned and raced away.

It's lost control of the animals, someone said.

The net tightened, strands of energy crackling as they trapped the dragon.

"Stop firing!" Sasko ordered as Shikari ran down the slope, launching himself into the air and flying toward their enemy. He landed atop the dragon and the net, and either through magic or body weight—or both—bore it to the ground.

Despite her order, Sasko and the others kept their rifles pointed at the larger dragon, waiting to see if the net would be enough to hold it.

Homgor strode from the trees, carrying the collar and chain. He'd only used a couple of the links to create the bullets so most of it remained intact.

Sasko lowered her rifle. "It looks like we've captured a dragon."

Basher grunted, blew another smoke ring, and said, "Just what I always wanted."

26

MALEK HAD GONE ON MISSIONS BEFORE THAT REQUIRED HIM TO SWIM underwater and hold his breath for an extended period of time. That was when he'd discovered he could do so for much longer than a normal human being. But his missions had involved spying on naval vessels or planting magical devices, not engaging in battle. And they hadn't taken place hundreds if not thousands of feet below the surface. Even though the barrier he'd carefully erected around himself—close to the skin so as not to create an air bubble that would make him float upward—was intact, he could feel the immense pressure from the weight of the water above him.

For the third or fourth time, he swam after the finned dragon-creature as it headed toward Jadora and the others. It kept using currents to knock him into the ruins and get him out of the way. It hardly seemed to care if he lived or died, though it had nearly knocked him senseless with some of its crushing magical blows. Its priority was to make sure the gateship didn't reach the orbs.

Though he used great magic to propel himself through the dense water, he struggled to catch up with the creature. He was on the verge of releasing the spear since it was awkward to swim with weapons in both hands and the glass tip hadn't pierced its thick hide when he'd stabbed it. Abruptly, the creature spun about and charged toward him, riding a wave of its own magic.

Had something changed? Maybe the gateship had reached the orbs, and Jadora and Jak had gotten what they needed.

Dodging underwater was a challenge, and Malek had to use his power to push himself to the side faster than he could stroke. He wanted to kill the creature, not evade it, but he'd already found out what happened if it made contact.

Barely missing a bite from its fanged snout, Malek paddled behind a column. Lifting his weapons, he intended to slash the creature as it went around the obstacle, but it swam right into it.

The column broke into pieces, the topmost crumbling toward Malek. Propelled by his magic, he swam out of the way and managed to get a slash in at his hulking assailant.

Expecting gravity to take the pieces of column to the sea floor, he kept his attention on the creature, glad when the sword cut through thick rubbery scales and drew blood. His foe unleashed an unearthly moan in Malek's mind and cast its magic, not toward him but toward the broken column. As the creature turned, bringing fangs to bear, a hunk of stone rose up. It slammed into Malek's barrier.

It didn't go through, but the force knocked him away, like a bubble batted by the wind. Malek tumbled into the ruins, his barrier bumping against more columns and piles of stones.

Again using his magic, he managed to slow and right himself, only to realize the creature was swimming away from him again. At first, he thought the cut from the sword might have been worse than he'd believed, but it was once again heading toward the others.

Cursing silently, Malek swam after it. His lungs ached for air. His zidarr enhancements might have allowed him to stay underwater longer than a normal human, but even he couldn't survive down there indefinitely.

The creature came into view ahead of him. He sensed Jadora and Jak using their power, shielding the mageship, but their hulking foe wrapped its fins around it and applied tremendous pressure.

Malek swam faster. The ship was already vulnerable to the pressure of the water, and he could sense the creature using its magic to tear away Jak and Jadora's.

Its back was to him, and he pointed his sword straight out ahead of him, summoning his magic to send him into their foe like a battering ram. It must have sensed his approach, but it was either unconcerned about him or so driven to stop Jak and Jadora that it risked injury to focus on crushing the mageship.

The dragon-steel blade destroyed the creature's barrier, then sank deep into its scales. It stiffened, head pulling back and fins releasing the mageship.

Malek tugged at the sword to pull it out, but a burst of enemy magic fused it into place. The creature whirled, a fin nearly knocking him in the head. He ducked, refusing to release the sword, lest he never get it back. A wave of water crashed into him from behind and knocked him into the creature. Its maw opened, fangs snapping toward his skull.

Malek, look out! Jadora told him. *We're trying to help. Give us a moment.*

He didn't have a moment.

Due to the wave mashing him forward, he couldn't maneuver beyond pointing the spear he hadn't cast away upward. With the current fighting him, Malek managed to jam it into the roof of the creature's mouth and keep its jaws from snapping around his head.

But he couldn't get away, and several objects—more broken pieces of ruins—arrowed in from the sides to pummel his defenses. A vine from one of those cursed plants reached up, gliding through his barrier with magic that defeated his, and wrapped around his leg.

Furious, he summoned all of his physical and magical strength to finally yank his sword free. With the spear still jammed in the creature's mouth, he sliced through the vine. As he swung, his powerful foe snapped the spear in half.

Malek hurried to bring the sword up, but he wasn't fast enough. A fang sank into his shoulder, and he couldn't keep from releasing his air in a grunt of sheer pain. His deprived lungs wanted to gulp for fresh air, and, as he slashed at the maw with his sword, trying to drive the creature away, he almost inhaled water.

Knowing it might be his last action, Malek summoned all of his magic and, ignoring the fangs biting into his shoulder, drove the sword upward, under his enemy's jaw. The blade sank deep, and he had the satisfaction of hearing another groan of pain in his mind.

The creature released him, and he sensed its aura weakening. Hoping he'd made a killing blow, he tried to swim back to the hatch, aware that he had to get inside, had to *breathe*, but his air-starved brain could no longer function. Blackness swept over his vision, and he lost consciousness.

~

"How did he make the airlock thing?" Jak blurted, surging up the ladder.

Jadora stood under him, concentrating on pulling Malek's unconscious body to the hatch, struggling for calm though she knew his lungs had filled with water. When she'd sensed him losing consciousness, she'd wrapped a barrier around him, aware that his would fail, but she hadn't known how to drive all the water away from him first. All she'd been focused on was keeping the pressure from crushing his defenseless body.

Terrified that she hadn't done enough, she was tempted to fling the hatch open, yank him inside, and they could figure out how to get the water out of the ship later, but they also had to worry about the pressure, not only flooding.

"I've got it," Vinjo said, face twisting with concentration.

"I feel it!" Jak rose up, Vinjo's barrier morphing around him to allow it, and opened the hatch, a bubble of air above it, though that bubble trembled under the water pressure pushing against it.

Jadora had moved Malek's body close, so all Jak had to do was grab him, making sure to also snatch the dragon-steel sword that was slipping from his fingers. They tumbled down the ladder, and Jadora used her power to slow their fall. The unconscious Malek didn't react. Vinjo waved a hand, and the hatch slammed shut.

"I'm reinforcing the hull," he said, "but is that monster dead? Because if it's not dead, it's going to try to crush us again."

Jadora spread Malek on the corridor deck, not wanting to waste time carrying him into the laboratory. She knew physical methods of expelling water from one's lungs but opted for magic, finding the knowledge of how to do so among the information Zelonsera had given her.

"It swam away wounded." Jak crouched near Malek but gave Jadora room. "Mother was doing something to lessen its defenses so the dragon steel could more easily get through, and Malek landed a good blow." A hint of fear crept into his voice as he added, "Is he going to be all right?"

Pushed by Jadora's magic, water spewed out of Malek's lungs, through his trachea, and out his mouth and onto Jak's legs.

"I hope that means *yes*." Jak scooted back as much as he could in the cramped corridor.

Coughing followed, though Malek's eyes didn't open. His body spasmed of its own accord, sputtering out the last of the water.

Jadora hoped the creature hadn't knocked him out with a mental attack, and that it was only his exertion and the lack of oxygen that had caused him to black out. She also hoped he hadn't been without air long enough to have brain damage. Or any other kind of damage.

A tremble went through her as she imagined that happening, but she told herself the enhanced zidarr were far sturdier than normal human beings.

"I hope that's true in this case," she whispered.

"What?" Jak looked at her.

"Nothing. Will you two head us back to the portal, please? If you got what you needed?" Jadora glanced at a dark gunk-covered orb resting on the deck, not sure who'd brought it in or when. She'd been too focused on Malek.

"I think I did, but..." Jak shared an image with her of a panel open in the portal and three blue-scaled dragons combining their power to repair something inside. "Fixing it might not be easy."

"I see." Jadora levitated Malek into the laboratory and onto a cot. "We'll figure it out."

They had to.

Vinjo and Jak ran into navigation to get the ship moving again. As she entered the lab, she heard them discussing the possibility of stopping back at the vent to collect more acid.

"It didn't do any good against that monster, did it?" Vinjo asked.

"I don't know, but we've *seen* it corrode dragon steel," Jak said, "and we need to battle an entire fortress made of the stuff."

Jadora sat on the edge of the cot with Malek, her hand on his chest, and she closed her eyes so she could examine him with her senses and heal him. His barrier appeared to have protected him from physical blows as well as the water pressure, and she didn't see anything wrong with his body. But the mind was harder to know, even with magic. She *did* find dead brain cells, a result of the lack of oxygen, and the words *cerebral hypoxia* floated into her thoughts.

"Oh, Malek," she whispered, afraid he hadn't simply been knocked out but was in a coma.

How had he managed to keep fighting right up until the end? It might have been one of the creature's mental attacks that had done him in, not simply a shortage of air.

"Let's see if dragons knew how to build new brain cells," she murmured, rooting through Zelonsera's memories. After all, the old dragon had known about expelling water from the lungs. Maybe dragons were as capable of drowning as humans. "There we go," she murmured, finding what she hoped would work, though dragon brains were, not surprisingly, more similar to lizard brains than mammal brains.

Letting her chin droop to her chest, she assumed a meditative state as she wove her magic into Malek, making use of his body's ability to regenerate more effectively than a normal human could.

How long she sat like that, she didn't know, but hours might have passed. Jak called back a few times with updates. Once was about collecting more acid, but it didn't sound like they needed her help, so she didn't stir. He passed through, gathering some of her empty glass containers, and she kept working on Malek.

By the time she came out of her meditation, she was tired and hungry. Malek hadn't woken, and she bit her lip, worried that even with Zelonsera's knowledge, she hadn't been able to do enough. Maybe the creature had done something to him that she couldn't sense.

"We're almost to the portal," Jak called back.

I'll come up in a bit, she replied, though she didn't want to leave Malek's side.

"Please wake up, my arrogant zidarr," she whispered, touching her hand to the side of his face. "We're going to need you. Jak says it takes three dragons to recharge the portal. We need you to use your great and powerful magic to have a chance."

She feared that even with all four of them, they wouldn't possess the necessary power, but their odds would be better with Malek beside them. More than that, *her* odds of living and being happy would go down drastically without him at her side.

Her chest tight with emotion, Jadora groped for something else she could do to help him. Maybe he would recover on his own, but what if he didn't? What if this whole trip had been a waste of time?

She looked at the dark orb that Jak or Vinjo must have brought in from the corridor, her laboratory equipment shoved aside to make room for it. Maybe they would be able to repair it, and it would contain more knowledge, the kind that would benefit all of humanity. They had to find something that would make all this worth it. Yes, Jak had learned how to recharge the portal, much like one put new charges in a magelock rifle, but they wouldn't have needed to know how to do that if they hadn't come to this world and been stranded.

Jadora shifted her focus back to Malek. "I've had some thoughts about the dragon parasite and the death-darter bacteria," she said, as if speaking to him might rouse him.

Maybe his unconscious mind would hear her voice and be curious enough about what she had to say that it would wake him.

"As I said before, I think it would be beyond my knowledge to make a vaccine and that it might not work in this case regardless. I believe we'll have to infect the dragons the same way I was infected. Well, not *exactly* the same way. I'm positive my needles would break off if we tried to stick them between their scales." Jadora stroked the side of Malek's head as she spoke. "But before we left, I overheard Rivlen and Tezi talking about making dragon-steel bullets. If those were fired with sufficient force, such as from a black-powder rifle, they might make it through magical defenses and scales. They *should*, based on what we've seen from the bladed weapons, right? Well, what if I make a concoction that contains the death-darter bacteria and smear it onto as many bullets as Uthari's blacksmith can make? And we shoot them into all the dragons we encounter?"

She paused, as if Malek might respond, but he remained still, his breathing shallow.

"Yes, thank you. It *is* a good idea." She smiled faintly. "Of course, we don't know if the death-darter bacteria will work the same way in dragons. Ideally, we'd find one to experiment on. Not Shikari, of course. But maybe we can capture another."

That wasn't at all a daunting prospect. But they'd been undertaking nothing but daunting activities of late, so what was one more?

"I've also been thinking about the new corrosive acid," she continued. "Vinjo and Jak stopped to gather some more. Not enough that it could take down a whole fortress, but if someone were to sneak in and find some crucial system, the acid might be sufficient to sabotage it. Or at least take out that weapon."

"Mother?" Jak called again. "We're going to need you soon."

"I know," she replied. "I see the problem."

Her senses told her not only that the portal was still weak, lacking the power to send them home, but that the heart-shaped plant had regenerated and extended its vines again, wrapping the ancient artifact in a lover's embrace.

"More like a power sucker's embrace." Jadora patted Malek on the chest before rising. "I need to go. I'll be back to check on you soon. In the meantime, you can ponder our plan and how we might accomplish it."

After rubbing her eyes and straightening her dress, Jadora joined Jak and Vinjo in the navigation cabin.

"Any luck fixing the orb?" Jak asked her.

"I've been concentrating on fixing *Malek*," Jadora said.

"Well, I do approve of that, but he's hardy. He'll be all right, assuming no more creatures waylay us. *That,* however, is our most pressing problem." Jak pointed through the water ahead, to the dark shape of the portal, only the faintest magical signature emanating from it. The heart-shaped plant was pulsing, its vines wrapped tightly about it, as it fed eagerly off it. Maybe it needed more power to heal the damage they'd done earlier.

"It's only one of our pressing problems," Vinjo said. "We lost some air when Malek went in and out. I think we're going to be experiencing headaches again soon."

"We can go up to get more air if we need to," Jak said.

Vinjo's face twisted with skepticism, and he waved upward.

Jadora sensed the net of entwined plants up there, their magic alerting her to their presence, and she realized that some of the inhospitable—and obstacle-like—plant life might have had nothing to do with the creature.

"I can make a hole again, if we need to, but if we repair the portal, the rest won't matter." Jadora nodded toward it. "As for the orb, I'll look at it when we get back. Or Vinjo can. He's the engineer among us, after all."

"I do have gifted hands." Vinjo caressed the air above his control panel. "Orbs like that almost as much as women do."

"Ew," Jak said.

"If Jadora can talk about kisses with a zidarr, then you can't object to me discussing giving pleasure to the ladies."

"Yes, I can," Jak said. "And the only lady who's shown any interest in you would probably pound you if you suggested other lovers."

"She's not a violent lady, but she is firm. I miss her and her fearsome muscles." Vinjo sighed toward the portal, then looked hopefully toward Jadora. "Do you have any ideas?"

"First, let me see if I can convince the plant to remove itself."

"There's a panel we need to open," Jak told Vinjo. "And a

power device inside. The orb shared the image with me, sort of like slipping a few pages of a technical manual into my brain. I hope I can remember everything."

"You were given a technical manual?" This time, Vinjo's sigh was envious and full of longing.

Instead of focusing on the vines, Jadora examined the source this time. Much as magical power had tethered the orb to the pedestal, it anchored the heart-shaped core of the plant to the ground. It had the equivalent of roots as well, but it was the power that would be difficult to slice through. She summoned her energy and with one swift motion, formed it into a blade and cut at the tether, willing the plant to be cut from the earth.

The first hack didn't do anything. She narrowed her magical blade to make it finer and swept in again. It nibbled a tiny chunk out of the tether.

"If Malek were awake, I would send him out there with that sword." Jadora chopped again, willing more power into her efforts.

Surprisingly, another source of power came from behind her, mingling with hers to reinforce the magical blade she'd created. Each chop grew stronger, and it made progress on the plant's roots and tether, like a logger applying an axe to a great oak.

Malek, he spoke into her mind from his cot, *might object to being sent out like a zidarr lumberjack.*

Malek! Jadora blurted in pleasure.

He was alive, conscious, and sounded like himself.

My lungs still ache from my last adventure outside of the ship.

I healed your lungs. They should be fine.

His *brain* had been more troublesome.

It's metaphorical aching.

Together, they hacked through the base of the plant, severing its connection from the sea floor. As it floated upward, the vines writhing, Jadora summoned a great current, as the creature had done, and blasted it into the plant. It would have sailed away from the gateship and portal, but it was still attached via its vines. Malek handled those, slicing through them until they'd all been severed or they detached of their own accord. Once he finished, Jadora's current whisked the plant away.

The portal remained dark with no change in its aura.

"One thing at a time," she murmured, turning as she sensed Malek approaching.

He stepped into navigation, leaning a hand against the door frame. She wrapped her arms around him and kissed him soundly.

Though he partially leaned against the frame for support, his arms came around her, and he returned her kiss.

"They're making out like teenagers," Vinjo said, "and you complained about me simply talking of my skilled hands?"

Jak turned his back to them, probably not wanting to see his mother kissing anyone. "I complained because you were waving your hands in the air as if you were groping some poor girl's boobs," he grumbled.

"I was pantomiming groping an *orb*, not boobs."

"Unless there were two orbs, I don't believe you. And orbs probably don't like being groped either."

"You know so little about women, young man," Vinjo said.

"You know more about wrenches than women. I'm positive Sasko would agree."

Jadora reluctantly broke the kiss, though she couldn't release Malek fully, instead basking in having his arms around her.

Thank you for your help with the creature, he said telepathically. *I wouldn't have survived without you.*

We *wouldn't have survived without* you. *And you're welcome. I love you. Stop trying to die.*

I love you as well, and I'll attempt to live. For your sake.

Good. Jadora decided to wait until later to repeat her plan about someone having to get close to the dragon fortress to sabotage it, while shooting a few dozen dragons along the way, instead turning in his arms so she could look out the porthole.

"You received information from the orb, Jak?" Malek asked.

"Yes. There's a panel on the side of the portal that we need to open. There are a lot of panels, actually, but the one with the power supply behind it is about there." Jak pointed and nodded for Vinjo to take them closer.

"Panels?" Vinjo asked. "Interesting. During my examinations, the portal appeared seamless."

"If I recall correctly," Jak said, "your last examination was interrupted by you plucking leeches off your legs."

"That's not untrue, but such a small thing as leeches wouldn't keep me from noticing gaps indicating panels."

"Show me what you saw," Malek told Jak. "I tried accessing the orb in the laboratory, but it was unresponsive."

"I know," he said. "I'm not sure we should have removed it, but we had to hurry."

Malek grimaced. "To come help me. I regret that I wasn't able to give you more time."

Jadora gripped his arm, amazed by the amount of time he *had* been able to give them. "Even zidarr weren't designed to fight long battles underwater."

"No," Malek agreed. "A deficit I'll make sure to mention to Uthari. Perhaps he has some ancient magic that can correct that flaw."

"It's not a flaw, and I'm sure he's busy with other things right now." Jadora frowned, realizing he was still enduring the parasitic infestation and that his symptoms had had more time to progress. She hoped he wasn't making life miserable for his crew—and anyone who came into his path. She thought of Thorn Company and Rivlen.

"Yes." Malek's voice was grim. Maybe he was also thinking

about how much Uthari might be deteriorating. "Another reason to get back quickly. Jak?"

"I already showed some of this to Mother, but I'll try to share what I learned with all of you. I wish I'd thought to find paper and drawn it down as soon as the orb shared it with me. My memory isn't perfect."

Images of the inside of the portal came to Jadora. Despite his uncertainty about his memory, they came through crisply. Since Jak had an eye for detail and a knack for remembering maps, she wasn't surprised.

"Fascinating," Vinjo breathed.

"The part about needing three dragons is more alarming than fascinating," Malek said.

"We'll find a way," Jak assured them. "Vinjo and his gifted hands are on our side. That has to be better than a dragon."

"Better than three dragons?" Malek asked.

Vinjo turned his hands over, his expression growing dubious as he examined them.

"We'll see," Jadora said.

"It's hard to sense anything through the dragon steel." Vinjo stopped the gateship in front of the portal as he contemplated it. "I can't hold my breath as long as a zidarr, so I need to think about how to remove them and do the repairs from inside our ship."

Jak nodded. "I noticed that the images showed dragons repairing a portal that wasn't underwater."

"It was probably general instruction meant to apply to all portals." Vinjo closed his eyes. "It's our bad luck that ours happens to be submerged."

Jadora could feel Jak and Vinjo using their senses to examine the artifact and groped for a way to help, but Zelonsera hadn't shared any knowledge on the inner workings of the portals. It was specialized knowledge, something that dragon engineers passed down among each other.

She smiled faintly, imagining the dragon equivalent of Vinjo wandering around with a wrench and screwdriver in its maw. "Let me know if there's any way I can help."

Long minutes passed, Vinjo's and Jak's faces tense with concentration. Behind her, Malek seemed to be using his senses to survey the water around them, watching for threats—or returning plants with grabby vines. She leaned back into his arms to mull over her plan with the bacteria, though she ended up yawning and longing for sleep rather than to return to their world and leap into another battle. Unless one counted her time unconscious as parasites and bacteria battled within her, she'd barely rested since they'd left Torvil. None of them had.

It's not far from midnight, Malek spoke softly into her mind.

It took her a moment to grasp the significance, and then she stiffened with alarm. She'd forgotten that he'd ordered Rivlen to keep the nullifying device on the portal and only remove it at midnight each night. If they missed that fifteen-minute window, even if they got the portal working, they wouldn't be able to travel to their world for another day. Or more. It was also possible Rivlen had failed to keep the druids or dragons from taking it.

The thought of being stuck in this underwater realm indefinitely made her shudder.

If we're not able to access our portal, Malek said, *we can return to another world.*

True. She only relaxed an iota. She wanted to go home and fix their world, not flee to another. Their people needed them.

Even though she knew it would horrify Malek, Jadora wondered if Uthari's officers would turn on him if he grew too aggressive and cruel. Maybe they would have done so by the time they returned. Maybe he was already dead.

Unfortunately, whoever took his place would likely be as bad. Besides, she knew Malek would prefer to earn the freedom he'd spoken of, the retirement Uthari had promised him if he and Jadora dealt with the dragon threat.

She looked over her shoulder at him, wanting him to be content and not feel that he'd failed his king, his master of thirty years. She smiled gently at him.

Malek arched his eyebrows. *I hope that fond expression on your face is for me, and you're not imagining visiting that archaeologist on Vran.*

It is for you, though I'm amused you viewed Zethron as a rival.

Because you had fond feelings for him.

Just because he reminded me of someone.

Your late husband.

Yes. She'd told Malek about that before—or he'd seen it in her mind—so there was no point in denying it.

Do you still miss him much?

Sometimes. I'll forever regret that he was killed for his research, that he's gone at all. He was a good father to Jak and a good husband. Jadora rested her hand on Malek's chest, hoping he wouldn't feel she cared for him less because she would forever miss the man who'd been her first love.

I understand, he said and rested his hand on hers.

"Ah ha!" Vinjo stood up and leaned closer to the porthole.

"Ah ha?" Jak asked. "Nothing happened."

"I loosened a panel."

"Is it the right panel?"

"Depends on how accurate of a schematic you shared with me." Vinjo flexed his fingers toward the portal. "It's hard to budge."

"If we can't open the panel, we're going to have a hard time repairing the portal," Malek said dryly and channeled power into Vinjo to help.

The promised panel popped open, then glided upward to hover over an egg-shaped hole.

"Dragons must not care much for squares." Jak pointed. "Look past those cords and cables. See that faint glow? That's the power source. We need to use our own power to recharge it. I assume that's what the dragons did."

"There's usually a transformation that needs to take place," Vinjo said, "converting magical energy to an equivalent amount of amperage. We need to make sure our power is even and steady as it flows in and exactly what the device requires."

"How do we know that?" Jak glanced at Jadora and Malek.

"Run your power through me, hopefully without knocking me on my ass—" Vinjo also glanced at them, his expression wary, "—and I'll handle the conversion." He shook out his arms, flexed his fingers, bent his knees and bounced up and down, then cracked his neck as he tilted his head from side to side. "I'm ready."

"I'll start," Jak said.

Jadora nodded, letting him go first so she could watch with her senses and figure out how much power to share. As he'd done often in battles, Jak funneled power into Vinjo. What came out of Vinjo was altered, and she wasn't sure how he did it, as this again went beyond Zelonsera's knowledge. As long as one of them knew what they were doing...

Vinjo's beam of energy flowed through the water and into the egg-shaped device nestled among the wiring inside the portal. Seconds passed with little appearing to happen. The device absorbed the energy, but it didn't react by glowing more brightly or flashing or doing anything else Jadora had seen magical power sources do. Nor did the portal emit a stronger aura.

"We're going to need more power," Vinjo said, his eyes closed. "Malek next."

"Not me?" Jadora knew she had the greatest amount.

"We'll save you for last."

Energy crackled in the air around Malek as he also channeled power into Vinjo, who gasped and gripped the control console.

"Are you sure you can handle all this?" Jadora asked quietly.

"I have to," Vinjo said through clenched jaws. "Though I can't recommend being a conduit for magic as a career path for anyone who wants a long life."

The amount of energy flowing out of him and into the portal increased as he transformed Malek's power as well as Jak's. Did the egg-shaped device grow a touch brighter, or was it Jadora's imagination?

"Yours now," Vinjo told her after another minute.

"This is taxing," Jak admitted, slumping back in his seat.

Emulating him and Malek, Jadora funneled energy into Vinjo. He gasped again, his knees buckling, but he caught himself in his seat, fingers still gripping the console. As he grew accustomed to the addition of her power, and poured more into the device, she increased the amount she was sending him, drawing it from the depths of her core, realizing they would have to provide a great deal for this to work.

The device grew brighter, and Jadora tingled from the power everyone in the ship was providing.

"It's not enough," Vinjo said, sweat beading on his forehead. "All together, we might be almost the equivalent of *one* dragon, but if it takes three…"

"You don't think one or two were simply there to advise and hold the panel?" Jak asked, an attempt at levity though he was sweating as much as Vinjo and breathing heavily.

Vinjo shook his head. "I don't know how much longer we can maintain this—how much longer *I* can maintain it."

"Is there a way to tell if we're close to achieving the goal? Replenishing its energy?" Jadora had no idea how much power it took to allow the portals to connect with each other on different worlds but wasn't surprised that it was a lot.

Malek released her and gripped the door frame for support.

He was also breathing heavily. Jadora drew upon her reserves, sending more power into Vinjo.

He writhed and squirmed under everyone's contributions, and Jadora worried he would be wounded or pass out, but he found a way to pour everything forth into the portal.

"It's too bad we don't have any magical vehicles," Jak said.

"What?" Vinjo glanced at him.

"On Vran, I used a vehicle's power supply to charge skyboards."

Vinjo gazed at him for a long moment, then looked past Malek toward the engine room. "I can try to pull more power from the ship's devices."

"Doesn't the ship need those?" Jadora asked. "To get us home?"

"Maybe we don't need all of it," Malek said.

"We're close enough that we could climb out and swim through," Jadora said.

"And abandon my ship here?" Vinjo blurted.

The notion must have distracted him, for the power going into the device wavered, and its growing light dimmed. Cursing, he turned and refocused on it.

"You'd be crushed if you went out in the water without a barrier protecting you," Malek said. "And it's possible none of us will have the energy left in the end to build them. A few more minutes, and I might not have the strength left to keep the ship from being crushed." He slumped fully against the doorjamb.

Jadora rested a hand on his shoulder.

"I have to do it," Vinjo whispered, and Jadora sensed him drawing from the devices that powered the vessel. "We're not getting home if we can't give it more power. Keep sharing yours."

Jadora did. They all did.

The lighting in the gateship flickered, then went out. As Vinjo pulled power from the engine room, Jadora sensed the ship's magical signature diminishing. Had it been a person or dragon, it would have been as if it were dying.

The device in the panel glowed brighter, and she sensed it sending power through the cords inside the portal.

"I think it's working," Jak blurted. "Keep going, Vinjo. We've got to be close."

Vinjo groaned and pitched to the deck unconscious.

27

Tezi gripped her chin as she considered the dragon under the magical net. Its single eye was closed, and it was either growling or snoring or both.

Shikari sat on his haunches atop their prisoner, his tail swishing back and forth, the net occasionally sending a yellow spark into the air at his touch. Less than half its size, Shikari didn't appear large enough to keep the other dragon pinned if it regained consciousness.

"Are that net and the dragon-steel collar going to keep it from using its magic if it wakes up before the others get back?" Sasko asked dubiously from Tezi's side.

"I think they just physically restrain it, ma'am."

"So, it can level the camp with powerful magical attacks."

"Let's hope the others get back soon," Tezi said.

"That doesn't sound like much of a plan."

Tezi thought about pointing out that Sasko was in charge, at least of Thorn Company, but it wasn't as if the mercenaries had been tasked to do much except shoot dragon-steel bullets into their scaled captive. Numerous holes in its side wept blood, proving that they'd all hit it a few times, but Tezi didn't know if they were what had knocked the dragon out or if the mages, druids, and Shikari had been responsible. The dragon had crashed hard when it landed.

"Maybe you can make suggestions to the zidarr," Tezi said.

Sasko's expression promised she would rather suck on, chew, or maybe swallow a lemon whole than approach Gorsith. "I guess if it stays pinned, you can always run up and smash it in the head if it starts using its magic." She waved to Tezi's weapon.

"The portal and my axe want the dragon kept as a prisoner."

"The *portal and the axe* are impervious to the jaguars, wolves, and other jungle creatures it was trying to shoo into our camp."

"If it helps," Tezi said, "I think the dragon will attack more directly if it's trying to escape."

"That does not help."

One of the wingtips under the net twitched, and the growl-snores stopped.

Tezi stepped back and hefted her axe. Sasko raised her rifle, more dragon-steel bullets loaded inside.

Our prisoner has awakened, Shikari announced to the camp, rising to all fours on its flank. *I will do my best to keep him subdued.*

The dragon's single eye opened. *Who dares imprison a great and mighty dragon?*

"I believe that question is for you," Sasko told Tezi.

Gorsith and Kywatha strode into view, and Tezi pointed her axe at them. "They're in charge."

The dragon roared. *I am the great Yoshartov, and I* take *prisoners. I do not become one.*

He shifted under the netting, muscles flexing. Though it wasn't physically staked down, the net's magic held the dragon in place, and the chain from the collar around his neck ran through it on its way to a stout tree.

Tezi, not sure if the bullets loaded in Sasko's rifle would be enough to protect her from magical attacks, gripped her arm. And none too soon. A wave of magic roiled off the dragon, knocking people over, batting down lean-tos, and ripping slender trees out of the ground.

What is this? Yoshartov shrieked into their minds, jerking his body to reach a forelimb up to his neck, a talon curling over the edge of the collar. *You leash me like one of your domesticated hounds?*

"Mages, druids," Gorsith called, "form a barrier around the dragon to keep its attacks from getting out. Mercenaries be prepared to shoot it again."

Under the net, wings heaved as Yoshartov tried to unfurl them and clamber to his feet. *The indignity! I will not take any of you presumptuous humans for servants. I will guide the rest of my kind here to slay you all.*

"Who knew dragons woke up in such a snit?" Sasko muttered, her cheek against the stock of her rifle and her finger on the trigger.

"I'm not surprised," Tezi said.

"We've got a barrier up," one of the mages reported, "but it's fighting us. And it's a strong bastard."

Yoshartov must have sent out more magical attacks, for several mages gasped from the struggle of keeping a barrier around the dragon to thwart him.

"We may have to kill it," Gorsith said. "We won't be able to hold it like this forever."

"No," Tezi said. "Just maintain that barrier. Jak and the others will be back soon. I know it."

Gorsith squinted at her. "Did you see that in a vision?"

"Yes," she answered without hesitation. "They'll be back tonight. Soon!"

As Yoshartov writhed and cast more magical attacks, Gorsith growled and ordered his people to focus harder and keep the barrier up.

"Did you really get a vision that showed them coming back tonight?" Sasko asked quietly.

Tezi hesitated. "No."

"What happens if they don't?"

"I don't know."

All power was gone from the gateship, and the remaining air in the ballast tanks released, bubbles wafting up. The craft sank slowly and landed on the sea floor a hundred yards from the portal. Jak could barely make it out, only a faint blue light emanating from it and illuminating its surroundings. Then silt rose up, clouding the water in front of the porthole, and shrouding them in darkness.

Mother knelt beside the unconscious Vinjo. Jak made himself focus on the portal, relying on his senses rather than his eyes to gauge whether they'd succeeded in recharging it. With Vinjo's power no longer flowing into it, the panel that had risen to float above the access point for the wiring and power supply automatically closed, leaving no evidence that it had ever existed.

Portal? Jak asked it, hoping they'd done enough.

As they'd channeled power into it, the device had gotten brighter, the aura from the portal stronger, but would it be able to create a passageway back home? Even if they'd repaired it, had it been in time?

Jak glanced at a chronometer built into the control console, and his stomach twisted. It was past midnight. They might have missed their window.

Portal? Are you aware? We need a ride home, and I really hope you can provide it. Jak touched his hat, the medallion nestled in its band. A couple of times, he'd convinced a portal to open the passageway without the key, but if this one wasn't back up to full operation, it might need the personal touch. The *physical* touch.

A sense of grogginess emanated from the portal. Before Jak could get his hopes up that it was back to its usual self, that grogginess turned to suspicion.

Who are you that carries the vile parasite within? the portal demanded, surprising him by using words.

Jak's first thought was that it sensed that Mother had been infested, but he realized it could refer to the specimens she had in magically sealed dishes.

We've been experimenting on it in order to find a way to cure the dragons, and we believe we have a solution. Jak shared what they'd learned as well as images of Shikari and Zelonsera, hoping to convince it in a short time that they were friends, that the portal should help them.

Suspicion continued to emanate from it. Jak grimaced at the thought that they might have recharged it only for it to use that power to destroy them.

Please open the way to Torvil, he said. *Our world is in danger from the tainted dragons, and we want to rid them of the parasite.*

We have a plan, Mother added, looking up from the deck, and she shared something Jak hadn't yet been privy to, someone flying over the fortress and dropping vials of acid and shooting bacteria-laden bullets into dragons.

"Who gets *that* job?" Jak wondered, especially since he feared they had destroyed the gateship in order to power the portal.

"I know a crazy zidarr who will volunteer for anything dangerous," Mother whispered, glancing at Malek.

"The zidarr isn't crazy," Malek said. "He's loyal and noble."

"Yes, he is." She smiled but only briefly before a loud *snap* came from the rear of the ship.

Malek grimaced and summoned the dredges of his power to keep the hull from caving in, but Jak could sense his weariness.

They were *all* weary. If the portal ignored them and other threats arrived, he didn't know how they would fight them off.

Abruptly, a wave of energy came from the portal, flowing through the hull of the gateship to grasp Jak. Startled, he didn't have time to get a barrier up or defend himself in any way.

The portal scraped through his thoughts, reminding him unpleasantly of Uthari's interrogation when Jak had been on his knees in front of the cruel wizard. The portal wasn't cruel, but it wasn't kind either, and he tumbled from his seat, gripping his head as he sank down beside Vinjo.

"Jak?" Mother touched him, and he sensed her trying to push away the magical grip.

But they'd given all their power and more to the portal. The sapient artifact hunted through Jak's mind, learning everything about him, its magical touch rough in the way the other portals hadn't been.

As he panted on the deck, palms pressed to his temples, Jak resisted the urge to fight. Instead, he let it see whatever it wanted, hoping it would find the truth and realize he was trying to help.

"What's it doing to him?" Malek demanded. "Do I attack it?"

"Wait," Mother said. "Give it a minute. So far, the portals have all liked him."

"This one may be cranky after millennia of having plants feed off it."

No kidding. Cranky, suspicious, and angry.

Just as Jak thought he couldn't take any more of the forceful ripping through his thoughts and memories, the portal released him. He collapsed next to Vinjo, grabbing his chest. His heart felt like it was trying to pound its way out from his rib cage.

You are an ally to dragonkind, the portal spoke into his mind, the suspicion waning.

Yes.

If you heal the dragons, we will carry you anywhere you wish whenever you wish.

Jak didn't know if that meant the portals would open passageways for him, or if the dragons would let him ride them, but he hoped for the latter. Though there was only one dragon he wished to fly with, and he dearly hoped Shikari was doing all right without him.

Reminded of the midnight deadline, he sat up. *Please, we need to return to Torvil quickly. There's great danger there.*

Yes, the portal agreed. *Go.*

The silt had settled so that when the portal brightened, beaming its blue light into the water all around it, Jak saw it clearly. He pulled himself into his seat and managed a grunt of satisfaction as the familiar stars swirled inside, forming the Dragon's Tail constellation. Then he realized they had a problem. Their engineer was unconscious on the deck, and they'd drained all the power from the ship.

A *crack-pop* came from the rear of the vessel, and he worried the hull had finally been breached. They might not have much time.

"Malek?" Jak turned, intending to ask Malek or his mother for help, but they both appeared too weary to levitate a pencil, much less the entire ship. "Never mind."

He could do this. Jak closed his eyes and drew upon his geyser imagery, imagining the ship rising on it. Not too far, though. He wanted to propel the craft forward, not send it hurtling to the surface.

The ship wobbled but resisted his efforts. It felt as if it had gotten stuck in the grime coating the sea floor.

Grimacing, he tried to draw on more power, but he was as drained as Mother and Malek. They knew what he was trying to accomplish, though, and added their magic to his. The ship wobbled again, then rose free with a sucking sensation.

Another crack reverberated through the craft, followed by the sound of water gushing inside.

"Hurry," Jak whispered, afraid the entire vessel would implode in a few more minutes. Or seconds.

On the deck, as the ship inched toward the glowing portal, Vinjo groaned and muttered, "Repairs, need to do repairs." He looked around blearily, heard the water rushing in, and stared toward the rear of the ship. "Will Sasko miss me if I die?"

Jak, Malek, and Mother, all concentrating on levitating the ship toward the portal, didn't respond. The vessel moved so sluggishly that Jak feared they wouldn't make it. It felt heavier than steel and the water thicker than molasses. What if the portal winked out before they reached it?

Then a fourth source of power joined theirs, grasping the ship and propelling it forward. The portal itself was helping, sending the vessel swiftly toward its center with even greater speed than it had possessed when it operated.

Do not forget the eggs, it spoke into Jak's mind. *They are the future, and when the universe is safe for them, they must be allowed to hatch, and they must be taught the ways of the dragon.*

I won't forget, Jak promised as the ship hurtled through the stars back to their world.

~

Sorath lay on his side, facing Ferroki, a glowing yellow tendril on the floor of the shaft highlighting their faces.

"I used to dream of spending more time with you," he said, wondering how long they'd been trapped under the floor of the fortress. Also wondering if the dragons would do as they'd threatened and tear apart the bottom of the structure to get to them.

It had been a while since they'd said anything that Sorath and Ferroki could hear, and he had a feeling they might have gone off to find other humans to dine on. He was also beginning to suspect that Yoshartov had been killed, that nobody would return to help them.

"Has our forced proximity made that dream fade?" Ferroki smiled wearily at him, though they were both hungry, thirsty, and ill in the mood for humor.

"No, but I've refined it to include a tropical island, bounteous water, food, octli, and a dearth of dragons in the sky."

"You should have wished for that from the beginning."

"Clearly. A fool am I for not having specific dreams." Sorath shifted so he could bring a hand up to stroke her face. Since he couldn't hold anything with his pick, he had to put the dagger in his mouth to do so. He might have sheathed it, but it was awkward to pull it out again when his shoulders were smashed against the top and bottom of the shaft, and he didn't trust that there wasn't a dragon poised above them, waiting to take advantage if he dropped the weapon for even a second.

"I used to think I would one day have to face you in battle," Ferroki said, not mentioning if she'd ever dreamed about him.

His dreams had involved them doing things far different from fighting.

"Instead of in a shaft in a dragon fortress?" he asked.

"Yes. Having to go into battle against you wouldn't have been pleasant."

"Is this pleasant?"

"I'm not sure about pleasant, but I am feeling better since I relieved myself in that last shaft."

They shared a smile that was more of a grimace, both acknowledging how awkward it was down there, especially since they needed to remain in contact to share the dagger's protection.

"Nothing makes a man's caress better than having recently pissed in an enemy fortress," he said.

"I could think of a few things that would improve it, though if I have to be here, I'm glad it's with you."

Sorath nodded. "Will you ever retire from leading your company? Assuming we survive this, and you have the option."

"I built Thorn Company from scratch. It would be hard to let it go, though I'll get too old eventually for this life." She looked up and down the shaft, then winced as she tried to find a more comfortable position. "It's possible I'm *already* too old for this life."

"I'm older than you."

"You're too old for this too, then."

"Since my shoulder is currently jammed in my ear, I can't argue."

"I might consider retiring in a few years," Ferroki said, "if I could hand off the company to someone competent who would keep it going and make sure everyone was well cared for."

"You have someone in mind?" Sorath assumed it was her second-in-command Lieutenant Sasko.

Ferroki hesitated. "I do."

"Good. I'd be happy to stick around and fight with you for a couple more years if eventually we could retire together." He hoped she wouldn't mind his implication that he would stick around *with her* and her company. It wasn't as if he was the right sex for it.

"That's not an unappealing idea," she said.

"I'm glad."

"I don't have a lot of money squirreled away for retirement though. I have some, assuming our headquarters back in Zar is still there, but I always assumed I would die to an enemy blade before I needed to consider such things."

"I used to have more before my shop and home were blown up in Perchver," Sorath said. "But Uthari ought to owe Thorn Company a few million oroni by now. We just need to get rid of the dragons and convince him to pay up."

"The contract wasn't for *that* much," she said.

"Well, there should be combat bonuses. A *lot* of combat bonuses."

"What should happen and what actually happens are rarely the same thing when dealing with wizards."

Sorath sighed. "I know."

Dragons to the towers, one of their enemies called. *The human fleets come!*

Sorath lifted his head, as if he might hear the sounds of cannons, but the dragons had likely sensed the mageships from miles away. A hint of hope brightened Ferroki's eyes. Sorath felt it too.

Until another dragon said, *Ready the weapon!*

"Damn," Sorath whispered. "I wish we'd found a way to take that out."

"Maybe we can still find a shaft that leads in that direction."

"Let's try."

Sorath didn't know if they would have any success, but with allies coming, they had a new reason to try. It renewed his determination, and he hoped that humankind would somehow succeed against the dragons. He wanted to retire with Ferroki, damn it.

28

THE GATESHIP RETURNED TO TORVIL AT A SPEED THAT WOULD HAVE been perfect for a vessel capable of flying of its own accord, but with the power supply dead and the engines inoperable, its momentum carried it only so far. It sailed out of the portal, out of the cave, and then plummeted.

Jak gasped, tumbling from his seat and onto Vinjo as the ship struck the rocky ground, bounced twice, then rolled down the slope like a malformed barrel.

Mother screamed. Malek cursed. They all slammed into each other, then the ceiling, and then the deck. Jak ended up falling into the corridor, his shoulder, then head cracking against a wall as he landed. Water that had come in through their leak washed over him.

He flopped down into it and groaned as pain pulsed from all over his battered body. With his energy drained, all he wanted was to lie there, breathe the fresh air of home, and rest for a couple of weeks.

That was not to be. As the ship settled into a resting spot on its side, lodged against a tree halfway down the slope, an indignant telepathic cry boomed into Jak's mind. *You dare pepper me with these tiny insects? I will flay you! And slay you! And not allow you to serve me as others do.*

"That's not Shikari," Jak mumbled, the sounds of a battle permeating the hull.

It was dark, no light streaming in through the porthole, but it sounded like everyone in the camp was awake. Everyone he expected and more.

He sensed a dragon—the source of the booming words—and a lot of mages and druids. And there was Shikari, off to one side of the slope. Wait. Where was Rivlen? Jak sensed a powerful mage—a zidarr?—but he didn't sense her.

Fear made him claw his way into a standing position, heedless of the pain, to crouch on what had been the wall next to the laboratory and was now acting as a floor. Dear Shylezar, what if Rivlen had been killed?

Jak has returned! Shikari cried into his mind. *We shall hunt and fly together soon!*

Happy to do so, and good to see you again, but where's Rivlen? Jak glanced toward navigation and saw Malek, Vinjo, and Mother stirring but not quickly enough for him. He scrambled through water toward the exit.

Since the hatch was on the side of the ship now, he had to crawl sideways along the ladder well to reach it.

Your king took her and left a snooty warrior mage behind. I battled him to practice fighting such foes, but I did not enjoy it. He is arrogant.

Was that the zidarr Jak had sensed? He shook his head, hardly caring. *Uthari took Rivlen? Why? To punish her? To* kill *her?*

Reminded that Uthari was still afflicted with the parasite and might be crazy by now, Jak shoved at the hatch with even more fear for Rivlen surging through his veins. Expecting the hatch to open, he clunked his head against it when it didn't. It had warped in the crash and didn't budge.

"Damn it," he snarled, too tired to summon enough magic to force it open. "Malek, I need help, please."

My kind will come for me, came another announcement from the adult dragon. *You will regret this great insolence. You shall all die. I will chomp you to pieces myself. You'll never know the honor of serving a mighty dragon such as myself.*

"That dragon sounds mad," Malek said, crouching at the bottom of the ladder well.

Though he had to be as weary as Jak, Malek found reserves and used his magic to blow the hatch open, ripping it from its hinges. It clattered as it landed on the rocky slope ten feet away. Fresh jungle air thick with the scents of flowers and black-powder smoke washed over Jak as he scrambled out.

With so little strength left, he didn't know how he could help —he wasn't even armed—but he forced himself to his feet, prepared to do so anyway.

But the sounds of battle had died. A faint click floated up from the bottom of the slope, and Jak gaped at the large dragon lying prone with Shikari standing on top of him. A zidarr he recognized from Uthari's castle—Gorsith—stood nearby with Kywatha and Tezi and Sasko.

A net with glowing tendrils smothered the dragon, a one-eyed mottled creature that Jak had seen in battles before. He bled from dozens of small wounds. Insects, he'd said, but it looked more like he'd been shot. With dragon-steel bullets?

Look at me, Jak! Shikari turned a half circle, talons digging into the defeated dragon with each step, and swished his tail in the air. *I have grown mighty and have defeated a much larger dragon.*

All by yourself? Impressive.

I had a small amount of help from the human mercenaries with their noisy weapons.

Rifles.

Yes. But I was instrumental in the defeat of the one-eyed dragon.

Said one-eyed dragon roared with fury, or maybe indignation, his own tail thrashing about in the undergrowth. Jak didn't know how instrumental Shikari truly had been, but his magic mingled with that of the net to pin down the dragon, so maybe he had played a pivotal role.

Two dozen roamers and mercenaries with rifles stood lined up to the side, their weapons pointed at the dragon. Jak suspected they'd been at least as crucial.

"Do we shoot it again?" Sergeant Tinder asked.

"I think we've got it subdued again, and our vision has come true." Tezi gave the most heartfelt smile to Jak that he'd ever seen.

Once, he would have been overjoyed to receive such a smile from her, but he had a feeling it was an I-really-hope-you-know-what-to-do-with-this-captured-dragon smile. It probably should have gone to his mother, but she hadn't climbed out yet.

"Does that mean we'll be safe from it?" Sasko asked.

The dragon's long neck whipped about, and he snapped at Gorsith.

"Probably not," Tezi said.

Gorsith glared at the dragon but didn't step back, his barrier and the net protecting him from the deadly fangs. "I still think we should kill it."

No! Shikari said, power riding the single telepathic word. *I saw a vision of the future, and now it is coming true. Jak and the mother of Jak have arrived. They must have a tainted dragon to experiment on, and this one has volunteered himself.*

Volunteered? The one-eyed dragon snapped at Gorsith again, then twisted his neck and tried to reach Shikari with his jaws. Shikari, however, also had a barrier up. In his weakened state, the one-eyed dragon couldn't thwart his power. *I only sought to get what rightfully belongs to my people. A baby dragon and a bunch of humans are not the rightful owners of the gateway. We shall take it to our fortress, my servants shall polish it, and we mighty dragons shall use it once more to travel to other worlds and bring more of our kind here to fully conquer this world.*

"Are you *sure* we can't shoot it?" Tinder grumbled.

"He's mad from the parasite," Mother said.

She and Malek had climbed out, then helped Vinjo to the ground. He looked around blearily, focused on the mercenaries, then spotted Sasko and waved to her. She held her position, her rifle trained on the dragon, but her eyes filled with sympathy for his battered state and she nodded back to him.

"If he's alone, he'll be the perfect dragon to experiment on." Mother glanced toward the sky. "I don't sense any others around."

The others are defending the fortress, Shikari said. *The fleets of humans have reached it and are going to engage in battle with it.*

The fleets of humans?

There's more than one fleet? Jak asked.

Yes. According to this dragon, many are approaching the fortress. Your king and his fleet of black ships are among them, but this dragon does not think they are leading.

Because Uthari had gone crazy and was incapable of leading? Because the other fleet commanders had refused to let him do so? Jak bent and gripped his knees, exhausted and more worried than ever about Rivlen.

Mother crawled back into the ship and headed to her laboratory, and Jak tried to focus on the current situation. If she could infect this dragon with the death-darter bacteria, and they drove away the parasite within him, maybe they could gain an ally. At the least, they would find out if what had worked on her would work on the dragons. And Uthari.

Can you tell if Rivlen is still alive? Jak asked Shikari.

The fleets are too far away for me to sense. I cannot know this. But your mate is strong and survives much. It is likely she is alive.

His mate. Jak managed a lopsided smile as he imagined how Rivlen would react to that description. *I hope so.*

Mother returned with a couple of syringes. "I'll inject him in one of the spots where he was wounded." She nodded toward the bullet holes dripping blood down the mottled gray-and-brown scales. "Much easier than finding an exposed vein."

Malek nodded and walked down the slope with her. Jak sensed him adding his magic to Shikari's, further pinning down the dragon so that not even his head or tail could move.

Their prisoner howled and railed at them telepathically, issuing threats and promises of a painful demise for all of them. He kept mentioning how they wouldn't be permitted to be servants for dragons.

Do you have human servants? Jak asked, curious but also hoping to distract the dragon while Mother worked.

I am the great dragon Yoshartov! Of course I have servants. They made me fancy fish in the human way.

"That's the dragon that Colonel Sorath will one day ride," a woman said from the trees behind the mercenaries.

It was the blind seer, Jary.

"I have seen it in a vision. The dragon will turn blue, and then Sorath will ride him."

Her people, as well as the roamers and the Thorn Company mercenaries, gave her pitying looks, as if they'd heard tell of this vision numerous times and knew it wouldn't come true.

But Jak realized it could. If the death-darter bacteria worked to kill the parasite, and the dragon turned back to what he had once been…

The colonel Sorath, yes, the dragon said, panting and straining against Shikari's and Malek's magic. *He does not ride me; he* serves *me. He and his female made me fish.*

"His female?" Sasko had been picking her way up the slope, giving the dragon a wide berth as she headed toward Vinjo, but she paused. "Do you mean Captain Ferroki?"

I do not know the female servant's name, but she is wise and knew that feeding a dragon excellent fare would be better than fighting him. I am a mighty dragon. I must be properly served! He—Yoshartov—strained again against the magic, his sides heaving as he panted, but he finally ran out of energy and gave up, his tongue lolling between his fangs to lie in the dirt.

"If there's a chance Captain Ferroki and Colonel Sorath are alive in that fortress, we have to try to rescue them." Sasko looked toward Gorsith, who scowled and shook his head, probably indifferent to the mercenaries. She turned toward Malek, Mother, and even Jak with her eyebrows raised in hope.

Jak would happily try to retrieve the colonel and captain if they could, but he glanced at the crashed gateship, not certain how they would rescue anyone. Unless there was another mage-ship around, and he didn't sense one, they wouldn't even be able to leave the area.

"Do you think the dome-jir still works?" Jak asked Vinjo, who wobbled, as if he would flop down on the ground, but Sasko's approach kept him on his feet.

"Hmm?" Vinjo smiled broadly at her, spreading his arms wide, and staggered down the slope.

Though Sasko looked like she hoped one of the leaders would answer her and agree with her sentiment, she did climb the last few yards to reach him. "You look awful."

"But I feel so delightful now that I've seen your brave and beautiful face." Vinjo wrapped his arms around her and kissed her.

Still holding her rifle, Sasko clunked him in the head with it when she returned his embrace, but he didn't notice.

Deciding he wouldn't get an answer from Vinjo for a while, Jak climbed back inside to check for himself. The dome-jir had its own built-in power supply and worked independently of the ship, so if it had survived the crash, it ought to still work. He hoped.

If Rivlen was on Uthari's ship, he didn't know if he would be able to contact her directly, but it would be worth enduring speaking with the king to find out if she was still alive. But would Uthari tell him? Or did he hate Jak so much that he wouldn't share any information?

With so little magic remaining active in the ship, Jak's senses led him toward the area with the dome-jir. It was in the navigation cabin, in one of the drawers, though they were so warped from the crash that he struggled to open it. The thought of having to call Malek to help him with a drawer, as he had with the hatch, disgruntled him. Irritated, Jak dredged up vestiges of his power, though it added a headache to his other pains, and used it to yank open the drawer.

The sphere-shaped dome-jir lay inside, dark with a hairline crack along its surface. Jak groaned. Would it still work?

He sensed its magic, so he hoped so. Pulling it out, he sat on the floor—a wall—and rested it in front of him. As he was trying to muster the courage to reach out to Rivlen, knowing he might get Uthari instead, Malek returned to the ship.

"That's the same thing I intended to do," Malek said.

"Find out if Rivlen is all right?"

"Report in to Uthari," Malek said dryly.

"Shikari said she's with him. I'm worried about her."

"I know. Let me contact Uthari." Malek hesitated, concern darkening his eyes, and Jak had a feeling he'd been thinking about the parasite and about how advanced Uthari's condition might be. "Among other things, I need to warn him of something."

Though Jak was curious, Malek didn't explain further.

"Go help your mother," Malek said.

Jak frowned, wanting to stay until he learned about Rivlen's fate.

"I'll let you know what I find out, but seeing you may infuriate Uthari if he's... being affected by the parasite."

Jak sensed there was something else, something about that

warning Malek wanted to share, that Malek didn't want him to know about, but he didn't pry further. He trusted Malek would ask about Rivlen. Jak longed to talk to her himself, but that would have to wait.

"All right. Thank you." Jak left Malek to make contact and climbed down the slope to see if his mother needed assistance.

As Shikari and the others used their power to keep Yoshartov still, Mother knelt near the dragon's belly. She slid a needle into a bullet hole and delivered the bacteria.

The dragon yowled and roared at her. *The indignity! The pain! You thrust your vile needle into me to experiment on me like a mouse in a laboratory. When my kind free me, we shall slay you most ruthlessly.*

"He's been shot two dozen times," Jak said, "and he's complaining about a needle?"

"This dragon has a flair for the dramatic," Mother said. "I'm going to give him a second syringe full to make sure it has a chance to take. He has a big body."

"Will there be enough to infect the rest of the dragons? Assuming this works?"

Jak didn't know if he should assume that. All along, his mother had suggested that if they found a cure, it might be too late to return the tainted dragons to their normal states, that after thousands of years of coexisting with the parasite, they might be too irrevocably bound together. It was possible they would die themselves if the parasite died.

The thought saddened Jak, as he knew Shikari dreamed of having playmates, other goodly dragons with whom to frolic. As the portal had reminded him, those eggs were still waiting on the first world they'd visited, and they could presumably be freed from the ice and hatched once the parasite threat was gone. But they needed mothers and fathers to teach and guide them. It wasn't as if Jak could raise them all. Even trying to guide Shikari properly had been a challenge.

He smiled, remembering his first days with him, trying to figure out what a dragonling could eat. And Shikari hunting flies.

"The bacteria have grown quickly in my dishes," Mother said, kneeling back after she finished with the needles, "so I do have a decent amount to use, but not enough to shoot at all forty dragons individually."

"We've managed to kill a few. They might be down to thirty."

"Let's hope."

"So we need to get to the fortress? It sounds like most of them are there guarding it."

Mother nodded. "I think that's our best bet."

"Any idea how we're going to get there?" Jak wondered if Malek would request that Uthari send a ship back for them. If Uthari wasn't in command, he might not have that option.

Mother looked back to where Vinjo and Sasko were still embracing, though they were leaning wearily against each other now, forehead to forehead, instead of kissing.

"Let's also hope our miracle worker of an engineer can get the gateship airworthy again," Mother said.

"And if he can't?"

Her gaze turned back to the dragon. "We'll have to find another way."

~

Deep in the night, the four fleets sailed southward, leaving the continent of Zewnath behind as they flew toward the Glacier Islands. Toward what might be an indestructible dragon fortress.

That wasn't even Rivlen's primary concern at the moment. Maybe it was foolish to worry about such little things, but, as she sat alone in the communications cabin in front of the dome-jir, she worried Uthari would call her to his cabin. If he did, she hadn't decided yet what she would do.

Attack him? The dragon-steel sword leaned against the table the dome-jir rested on, its hilt within easy reach. Tell him *no* and hope he understood?

That was her current plan, but she worried it wouldn't be enough, that he would be even more splotched with gray since the last time she'd seen him and even more under the parasites' grasp.

If Rivlen killed him—which she didn't know if she could do, even with the dragon-steel blade—the other officers wouldn't accept her as their leader or his replacement. Captain Jagobar had made that clear. Not that she expected to kill Uthari and take his place. Kings always laid out succession lines. Uthari hadn't publicized his, but she had no doubt he had left documents in Utharika that would be revealed upon his death.

Instead of following her, the other mages would kill her for her crime. Which was ridiculous since they all knew Uthari was sick and they were making plans for what would happen if he died.

Despite all that had happened, Rivlen didn't *want* him to die. She wanted him cured. If another ruler got the best of him and he didn't survive, fine, but dying because some microscopic parasite had taken over one's body was a crummy way to go.

"Maybe he won't pester me tonight," she murmured to the dark dome-jir.

The afternoon's battle had exhausted her, and she hoped it had exhausted Uthari as well, that he would sleep through the night. He would wake in the morning, the fleet having arrived at the fortress, and there would be no time to do anything except prepare for the impending battle.

But hope wasn't a plan.

Every few minutes, Rivlen envisioned Malek's face, using her magic to order the dome-jir to reach out to the dome-jir on the gateship. If it was on this world.

Midnight had passed, and Gorsith should have detached the device from the portal. If Jak, Malek, and the others had completed their mission, they would have flown through and come home. If they hadn't, if another full day passed before they returned, it might be too late.

How long did Uthari have until the parasite completely took him over? He didn't seem to be fighting it as much anymore. And could the fleets survive more than a few minutes against that fortress? They had a lot of ships now, but she didn't know. What they needed was for Jak and Jadora to have found a solution, one that would destroy the parasites and alter the dragons, either killing them or changing them so they no longer saw humans as lowly beings to prey upon.

Either solution would work, though Rivlen found Shikari cute and fun, and, if all the other dragons became amenable souls, she wouldn't mind them in the universe. Maybe not the *world*, as she didn't know if they would interfere with humanity's systems for governing itself, but they could exist elsewhere and visit. Shikari, she decided, could stay. Jak ought to get his dream of being able to ride him.

Despite her requests for the dome-jir to connect with the one on the gateship, it remained dark. She wasn't surprised that their magic didn't allow them to communicate between worlds, but she assumed that once the gateship returned, she would be able to make contact. She hoped.

Rivlen sensed Uthari's aura on the deck outside and sighed. He wasn't sleeping. Damn it.

He stopped to speak with whichever officer was on watch before heading toward the communications cabin. Rivlen eyed the sword, making sure she could reach it, and took a deep breath, standing as the door opened.

Uthari walked in, shaven, bathed, and in fresh clothes. His face wasn't gleaming with sweat, but the gray had advanced even further, covering most of his face, neck, and the backs of his hands. Maybe his whole body?

She had to fight to keep her lip from curling as she imagined him tearing off his clothes to reveal scaly gray skin all over his penis.

But maybe she didn't need to worry about that. Perhaps the fact that he'd cleaned up and wasn't oozing sweat meant he was feeling better. More like himself? Was it possible his immune system could have overcome the parasite?

The door thumped shut behind Uthari, and he considered her speculatively. That mad glint was still in his eyes, and her belly knotted with trepidation.

"What are you doing in here?" he asked. "I expected you in my cabin hours ago."

Rivlen met his gaze. "I won't have sex with you, Your Majesty. I'm not interested."

His eyes narrowed with displeasure. "Because of another?"

"No, because we're on an important mission, and it's not the time for this. You're supposed to be scheming a way to ensure we survive and the other fleets take the brunt of the dragons' attack, remember?"

"Who were you trying to communicate with?" Uthari asked softly, dangerously. "The boy?"

The boy? Jak? Uthari ought to be delighted if Jak and Jadora came back.

"I'm trying to reach Lord Malek on the gateship," Rivlen said. "If Gorsith removed the device, and they were able to return, maybe they've got a solution to your problem."

"My *problem* isn't any of your concern." Uthari stepped forward, slapping his hand down on the dome-jir.

Rivlen jumped back, reaching for the sword, though she didn't grab the hilt. Her palm hovered over it.

Uthari didn't appear to notice. His eyes were locked on hers. "You will not contact anyone without my permission. Especially not anyone you wish to have sex with."

Since she assumed he meant Jak, she was startled when he thrust an image of Malek into her mind. She almost objected to that but remembered she'd been attracted to him once. Embarrassment warmed her cheeks as she realized Uthari, whom she hadn't thought paid any attention to her, beyond looking over her record, might have known about that.

"I want you to get better, Your Majesty," Rivlen said steadily. It was the truth. It wasn't as if the old Uthari had been a delight, but he'd been rational and predictable and hadn't so much as glanced at her breasts. "That's all."

He held her gaze as he muttered something, the same words that had allowed him to read her mind earlier. By Thanok and Shylezar, what would he find in there this time?

"You do want that, don't you?" Uthari said softly, the anger fading from his face. "My loyal Xeva."

"I prefer Captain Rivlen," she said quietly, though she was glad he'd lost the irritated edge.

"Is that what you ask the boy to call you?" Uthari took her hand, the one hovering above her sword hilt, and clasped it in his. His skin was clammy now instead of sweaty. "Does he drop to his knees and obediently do all you wish? I can't imagine him having much of a spine."

"Let's talk about how we're going to survive the dragon fortress and ensure the other fleets take the brunt of their attacks." Rivlen tugged at her hand, but he didn't release it, his magic curling about his fingers, making his grip stronger than it otherwise would have been.

"We'll worry about that in the morning." He eased closer, emanating power and desire.

"I won't have sex with you tonight or ever." She lifted her chin, trying not to remember that she'd once said the same words to Tonovan. But he'd been too powerful, and she hadn't been able to stop him. Just as Uthari was too powerful for her to stop. Unless she used the sword.

"Your independent spirit is admirable," he rasped, pulling her toward him, "but we insist on being with you."

"We?" That chill returned to her spine—her entire body. Was she even talking to Uthari anymore?

"*We*," he growled and leaned in, pressing his clammy lips to her.

Disgusted, she tried to shove him away, but his power wrapped around her, holding her in place, plastering her to him, her mouth to his.

"Get off me," she tried to snarl, drawing upon her own power.

She wasn't able to push him away, but she did succeed in pulling her hand free and grabbing the sword. As she lifted it, hoping all she had to do was strike him with the flat of the blade to break his hold on her, something tingled in her mouth, flicking over her tongue and gums.

Horrified and afraid, she swung the sword.

Uthari sprang back, drawing a dragon-steel dagger with lightning speed that such an old wizard shouldn't have possessed. He parried her strike without looking at her. As their weapons hung crossed in the air, glowing motes floated between their faces. And in her *mouth*?

Rivlen spat and backed away, holding the sword before her to keep him back. Had he—*they*—tried to infest her?

She spat again and again, almost gagging in her terrified haste to get them out of her body before they could spread, before they could turn her into him.

Uthari merely stood and smiled, his eyes gleaming. By the gods, had he wanted to have sex or only to spread the parasites? Was *that* why they'd driven him to kiss her?

"You'll start to feel the effects in a day or so," he said, still smiling. "We prefer powerful hosts, and even if humans aren't dragons, some of you aren't too bad. We'll grant you longevity and greater power. You'll be thankful to have been chosen. Not many were. The rest of these—" Uthari waved to indicate the mages on the ship—or in the entire fleet? "—won't survive."

Rivlen wanted to throw up all over his feet. And gargle with alcohol. Douse her whole body in alcohol. Whatever it took to make sure the parasites weren't able to establish a hold over her.

The dome-jir glowed orange, startling both of them.

Uthari rested a hand on it, accepting the request to open communications.

Malek's face formed in the air.

Rivlen wanted to feel relief—they'd made it back!—but the overwhelming fear about her own problem made it hard.

"Lord Malek." The way Uthari squinted at Malek didn't suggest relief or pleasure. "Were you successful?"

A flash of insight came to Rivlen. The parasites didn't want Malek to succeed. If he said yes, Uthari might try to do something to make sure the gateship crashed and Malek and Jak and Jadora were never able to rejoin the fleet.

"Don't tell him," Rivlen blurted as Malek opened his mouth.

She lunged into his view. "The parasite has taken over, and he's not—"

Uthari whirled toward her, the dagger up. Instinctively, she whipped the sword across, parrying the blade. Whether he'd meant to silence her and hold it to her throat or thrust it into her heart, Rivlen didn't know, but she knew with certainty that parrying had been wise.

"Fight it, Your Majesty," Malek urged. "Fight the parasite. Jadora was able to when it tried to take her over."

Uthari didn't look at him. He was glaring at Rivlen, as if he resented her for defending herself.

Too bad.

"You can fight if off, Your Majesty," Malek repeated. "I know you're still in there. Don't harm Rivlen. She's loyal to you, as am I."

"But *not* loyal to parasites," Rivlen said, not daring to take her gaze from Uthari.

"I know it's easier to give in than not, but we need you, Your Majesty. Uthari." Malek lifted a hand, as if he could reach out to Uthari through the dome-jir. "Find the strength to sublimate them. Not for long. We'll be there as soon as we can, and we have a plan. One that will defeat the dragons and leave you free again to rule. To rule as yourself, not some puppet for parasites."

Uthari's face contorted, and his body shook.

Rivlen expected him to tell Malek to shut up or maybe break the dome-jir to end the communication. His hand tightened on the dagger hilt, his knuckles white through his gray skin. His entire body quaked.

"Fight it, Uthari," Malek urged. "Realize they're manipulating you, just as they did Jadora. She tried to infest *me* because they made her. Don't let them take you over; you've never allowed anyone to manipulate you in your life."

Chest heaving, Uthari tore his gaze from Rivlen and met Malek's eyes. He shook all over, but he listened as Malek continued to urge him, to give advice.

Rivlen barely heard it. His words *tried to infest me* rang in her mind. Had Jadora leaped on Malek and kissed him? With those damn motes on her tongue?

Uthari threw his head back and roared like a dragon.

Rivlen sensed mages on the deck stopping and turning in their direction. She hoped they didn't think he was in the middle of having sex with her.

A spasm went through Uthari's body, and he slumped forward, dropping the dagger. He gripped the edge of the table as his body swayed.

"Malek," he whispered, grimacing and pressing the heel of his palm to his forehead. "It's hard. It's so hard."

"I understand, Your Majesty," Malek said. "I endured something similar on Nargnoth."

"I don't know how long I can fight them off. We're in trouble here. Did you succeed? Do you have an antidote?"

"Of a sort."

What did *that* mean?

"We're enacting a plan, but it'll take a little time. Don't attack the fortress yet. And hold on longer. Once we reach you, we have a way to help you. I promise."

"I trust you, Malek," Uthari whispered.

"Good." Malek looked at Rivlen, as if to give her some separate instruction. What? To protect Uthari? She'd been *trying,* but this was an assignment from the depths of the Slavemasters' hell.

"How did you keep Jadora from infesting you?" Rivlen asked.

"I was immune, and the parasite wasn't able to take hold. Not for lack of trying."

Rivlen stared bleakly at him, certain *she* didn't have immunity. "Lord Malek, will you tell Jak..." What did she want Jak to know? That she cared for him? Loved him? Wanted him to be happy if she never saw him again? She couldn't imagine having any of those words relayed through Malek's mouth. "Let him know I'm fine and look forward to seeing him again."

She looked warily at Uthari, hoping he wouldn't rage again about *the boy*, but he was either busy trying to keep control over himself or exhausted by the effort he'd had to expend to do so.

"I will tell him," Malek said. "We're heading your way."

"Good," Rivlen said. "But we're in trouble here. The other fleets have taken charge, and they intend to throw us at the fortress as a distraction. I don't suppose you learned how to disable their big weapon."

"We do have some thoughts on that."

"I hope they're good thoughts."

Malek nodded. "Take care of Uthari, please."

She'd never heard a zidarr say *please*. Too bad it was at the end of such an impossible request. She had little faith that Uthari would be able to retain control for hours much less the days it might take Malek and the gateship to join them.

"Don't take too long, my lord." Rivlen rested her hand on the dome-jir to close the communication, then faced Uthari.

The dagger lay at his feet. She backed up a few steps, her sword in hand, and waited to see how he would act with Malek's voice no longer filling his ears.

Uthari picked up the weapon, his movements jerky, and it took him three attempts to sheath it.

He turned to face Rivlen, muscles ticking in his jaw and cheek. He glanced at the sword between them. "I apologize for my behavior, Captain Rivlen."

Her first thought was to reject the apology—he'd infested her with that parasite, damn it—but unless he was fooling them all, he hadn't been acting of his own accord.

While keeping her face carefully neutral and without judgment, Rivlen made herself say, "I accept your apology, Your Majesty."

"As soon as I'm able, I will reward you for standing with me." After a jerky bow toward her, he headed for the door. Telepathically, he added, *And I'll do my best to stay away from you until Malek has healed me.*

It would far more likely be *Jadora* who healed him, but Rivlen didn't say that. Uthari seemed to want to pretend neither Jak nor Jadora was a part of his world at all.

With luck, they won't be as interested in you now, Uthari added as he stepped outside, disappearing from view.

Yeah, because they'd gotten what they wanted. A faint tingle against the roof of her mouth made her certain those motes had slipped their awful load into her bloodstream.

29

As dawn crept over the jungle, Malek sat in the mouth of the cave with Jadora, her head on his shoulder as he watched the camp, their dragon prisoner, and the gateship. Vinjo had gotten the latter turned right side up, supported by a framework of logs the druids and mercenaries had helped him cut and place, but now he was snoring inside, promising he could only perform miracles after a proper night's sleep.

Though Malek was worried about Uthari and wanted to get the ship repaired immediately so they could catch up with the fleet, they had to wait regardless until they saw if the bacteria would affect Yoshartov. Besides, Malek was tired too, having slept only fitfully during the few hours between their arrival and dawn. Reluctantly, he'd accepted that they all needed rest. After spending so much energy on repairing the portal on the water world and escaping, they needed to replenish their reserves before heading into another battle.

Jadora roused and lifted her head from his shoulder. She'd been dozing, using him for a pillow. He hadn't minded, and he wrapped his arm around her now, hoping she would stay beside him. His empty belly rumbled, requesting breakfast, but he preferred being up here with her instead of down in the camp, surrounded by people. And Gorsith.

Malek didn't know why Uthari had replaced Rivlen with him and taken her along, but he worried Uthari might have hurt her. When Malek had spoken with him the night before, he'd seemed on the verge of losing himself, losing the war for his body to the parasite. And Rivlen had been stuck at his side enduring it.

He sensed Jadora using her magic to check on the dragon. The chain from the collar around Yoshartov's neck was attached to a stout tree, and the magical net covered him, but Malek didn't know if the items would be sufficient to keep him prisoner once he recovered from his injuries.

When he'd imprisoned Shikari with the collar, it had been attached to a heavy weight, one that had been too much for the dragonling to fly with at the time. But an adult dragon would have the physical power to uproot a tree, even if the dragon steel touching it kept him from using his magic on it.

For now, their adult dragon was sleeping and hadn't tried to rip up the tree. After injecting the bacteria, Jadora had also given Yoshartov a sedative, seeming surprised but pleased that the substance had worked on a dragon. At least it *appeared* to work. Malek wouldn't put it past that dragon to fool them with a ruse.

Shikari must have believed similarly, for he'd checked on Yoshartov often during the night. He'd finally succumbed to sleep an hour before dawn. Now, partway up the slope, Shikari dozed on his back, his legs crooked up and his tail curled to provide a pillow for Jak. Amusingly, Jak was in a similar position, on his back with his mouth dangling open as he slept with his face toward the waning stars.

"Can you tell if the death-darter bacteria are spreading within him?" Malek nodded toward the dragon.

"They are. The bacteria and the parasites are both magical,

and now that I know what to look for, I can sense the difference and identify both within him."

"It didn't take that long after you injected yourself for the bacteria to grow strong enough to wage a war on the parasite."

"Something like that, yes." Jadora grimaced at the memory. "When the dragon wakes up, he might not feel well."

"The bullet wounds have already healed, though I can sense bits of dragon steel embedded within him. That was a good idea to make bullets from the material." Malek looked toward the blacksmith's tent.

"Jak mentioned it was Rivlen and Tezi's idea."

"Yes."

"He's worried about her. Rivlen. Did you find out if she's all right when you spoke to Uthari?"

"She's with him and alive." Malek had already told Jak that, but he had omitted his concerns that Uthari was on the verge of losing his humanity and might become dangerous to her. It probably hadn't been necessary. Jak's eyes had been haunted with worry. He'd probably already considered the effect the parasite was having on Uthari.

Malek wished there were a way he could transport himself across the continent and onto Uthari's ship so he could inject the king with the death-darter bacteria immediately. But he also needed to reach the fortress as soon as possible to take out the weapon and enact Jadora's plan of using bacteria-laced bullets to shoot the dragons.

Would he have to choose between helping his king and helping the world? All that needed to be done weighed on him, and waiting in the camp made him antsy.

His gaze drifted to the gateship. In a few more minutes, he would rouse the engineer and get him to work.

"I'm glad Rivlen is alive," Jadora said softly, "but Jak is also worried that she's in danger from Uthari. I heard from the mercenaries that he had her punished. By Gorsith."

Malek hadn't spoken to the mercenaries and hadn't been aware of that, but he wasn't surprised.

"If he did that right after we left, then it would have been *before* the parasite was having a large influence on him," Jadora said, anger creeping into her tone.

Malek sighed. "What do you want me to say, Jadora?"

He'd already promised her—and himself—that when this was all resolved, one way or another, he would leave Uthari and his position as the king's zidarr.

"I don't know." She slumped against him. "I'm angry on her behalf. She's been helping us, helping Jak, and he cares about her."

"For Uthari, that's part of the problem."

"Because he's an ass who doesn't understand love or loyalty. People can hold both in their heart at the same time, you know, for separate individuals."

"I do know that."

"I'm sad for Rivlen. She doesn't deserve punishment. She's tried so hard to be a good fleet officer, and just because she cares for my son..." Her voice had grown tight, and he wasn't surprised when she didn't continue.

Malek rubbed her back through her dress, then kissed her, though he wasn't certain it was what she desired. It had been easier when he'd been able to read her feelings and knew exactly what she wanted. Back then, though, he hadn't dared give in to her wishes—or his.

Jadora returned his kiss, infusing it with warmth, gratitude, and a certainty that *he* wouldn't have tortured Rivlen if Uthari had asked. Malek didn't deny the sentiment, but if Uthari had pressed him to punish her, would he have? No, he decided. He would not hurt Rivlen. Even if Malek didn't have any strong feelings for her, he did care for Jak and Jadora, and he wouldn't hurt someone close to them.

He didn't reply to Jadora's thoughts with words, only sharing a sense of agreement with her. She responded with contentment and warmth as she brushed her fingers through his hair.

A great thrashing came from the bottom of the slope, startling them apart. The dragon was stirring.

More than stirring. Yoshartov rolled onto his back and howled loudly enough to be heard for miles, if not all the way to his fortress.

Mercenaries and roamers with rifles loaded with dragon-steel bullets jumped to their feet. The druids came warily out of the trees, raising their hands and readying their power. A scowling Gorsith strode out of the blacksmith's tent, his weapons in hand. Jak rolled to his feet, crouching beside Shikari, who also rose to face the adult dragon. The seer Jary peered blindly toward Yoshartov, her staff in hand.

They crawl through me. Diseased organisms assail me from snout to tail. The dragon thrashed that tail in the undergrowth and howled again. *You have done this to me, horrible humans. This is why your kind will all die. You do not respect your superiors. You do not live to serve dragons, as is the way.*

"If the seer's vision is accurate," Jadora murmured, "and Sorath is supposed to ride that dragon, he's going to have his hands full."

"That man likes challenges. Though Yoshartov doesn't refer to himself as *we* very often. Maybe he's less under the control of the parasites than his kin."

"Or maybe he's more self-centered than the others and has a bigger ego."

"That's possible." Though Malek thought *all* dragon egos were large.

The dragon yowled again, head swinging on his long neck until he spotted Jadora. *You have done this to me. Scientist human, you are experimenting on me. You have put organisms in me that should never have made it past a dragon's defenses. I will slay you.*

Jadora wrapped her defenses around herself, her power so intense it was almost startling, and Malek drew his weapons. If the dragon had recovered during the night and regained his full strength, he might be able to escape and attack them.

As if he had exactly that in mind, Yoshartov rose to his feet, his slitted yellow eye locked on Jadora. But he only took two steps before the chain grew taut, keeping him from advancing farther. The net glowed a more intense yellow and crackled with energy.

Yoshartov roared toward the sky, then whipped his head around to snap at the chain. Fangs clinked against the dragon-steel leash, but it held, not dented by even those mighty teeth. Yoshartov roared again, then flung himself on his back, legs and tail thrashing.

Is that what the human expression temper tantrum *means?* Shikari didn't appear that concerned by the dragon's antics, so maybe Yoshartov's odds of escaping in his current state were poor.

Yes, Jak replied, sharing his response with them all, *that's about right.*

You once accused me of having a temper tantrum. Shikari eyed him.

You remember that? You were only a month old.

It was not long ago.

You were being cranky about your food.

Because you brought it to me dead. A dragon mother would know to feed her offspring live tarantulas.

I don't know if you noticed, but I'm not a dragon mother.

Shikari looked Jak up and down. *I noticed. You would be a funny dragon.*

I'm kind of a funny human.

I noticed that too. Shikari swatted Jak in the back with his tail.

As large as he'd grown, he could have sent Jak flying down the slope, but it wasn't a hard strike.

Even though Yoshartov continued to flop and flail and moan melodramatically, Malek lowered his weapons.

"I don't think he's going to escape," he said.

"He might be able to if he focused on the chain and tree," Jadora said, "but I think he's distracted by the battle playing out inside his body. Much as I was. It was unpleasant."

"I could tell. I'm sorry you had to endure it." Though Malek was in a hurry to get going, that didn't keep him from sliding his arm around her waist and resting his head against hers.

Gorsith, after glowering at the thrashing dragon for a few minutes, strode up the slope toward them. Malek thought about releasing Jadora, since Gorsith was a reminder of the oath he'd sworn to abide by as a zidarr, including a refusal to engage in romantic attachments, but he found himself caring less and less about the Code. Now that he'd decided to retire and seek a new career, what did it matter if another zidarr saw him with a woman?

Not just *a* woman. Jadora. The woman he loved. Malek lifted his chin as Gorsith approached.

"I need to speak with you, Malek." Gorsith glanced at Jadora but didn't otherwise acknowledge her. If he noticed Malek's arm around her waist, he didn't acknowledge that either.

"Yes?"

"Have you been in communication with King Uthari?" Gorsith eyed the gateship—checking for a dome-jir?

"I have." Malek relayed what he'd learned, wishing he'd been able to gather more intelligence, not simply urge Uthari to get ahold of himself.

"Are we going to join him for that battle? We *have* to. I came here to fight dragons. All I got to do was help knock that one down so the squirt could sit on it."

"The squirt?" Jadora murmured.

Gorsith waved toward Shikari.

"I need to prove myself," Gorsith said. "I've barely had a chance to battle any dragons."

"You assisted me in Utharika," Malek said.

"Assisted you." Gorsith curled his lip. "Malek, your shadow is large, and I don't want to be hidden in it. I want to prove myself independent of you. Also... if any rumors about... *things* get back to Uthari, will you let him know it wasn't my choice to engage in... *things*?"

"I don't follow you." Malek wanted to shoo him away. Later, he might challenge Gorsith to a sparring match to limber his muscles and prepare himself for the next battle, but he would prefer to spend his last quiet minutes before they left with Jadora.

"There's this attractive druid woman." Gorsith waved vaguely toward their camp. "When her people showed up, I was about to engage in battle with her to keep them from getting the portal. Up until that point, I hadn't noticed her breasts or even thought about her having them."

Jadora blinked. Malek only stared. What was Gorsith talking about?

"And then the squirt decided to use his extremely powerful dragon magic to encourage..." Gorsith waved his arm in the air in a flowing gesture that Malek struggled to interpret.

"Anyway, it was because of the dragon's magic. He *forced* us to get, er, friendly with each other. Otherwise I wouldn't have ever looked at a druid that way. Even though, uh..." Gorsith gazed down the slope toward their camp and lowered his voice. Seeming to mumble to himself more than Malek, he continued, "It was the most incredible thing I've ever experienced. Her magic is different from mage magic. Unique. Stimulating. And she was *amazing*." Gorsith jerked his attention back to Malek. "But I don't have any *feelings* for her, and it won't happen again. It wasn't any different from the girls back home. I'm not *attached*.

And it was only on account of the dragon magic. I wasn't—er, we weren't—the only ones who succumbed either. Homgor had *two* druid women in his tent. What they possibly could have wanted with him, I don't know, but he's not a zidarr, so *he* won't be in trouble."

It finally dawned on Malek why Gorsith was telling him all this. Jadora must have figured it out earlier, for her eyes were glinting with mirth.

"I was hoping," Gorsith said, "that if Uthari heard and was angry with me because he believed I'd violated the Zidarr Code if you would let him know about the dragon magic. And that the sex meant nothing to me." Despite his words, the longing look he sent toward the druid camp—was that Kywatha that he kept looking at?—suggested he wanted to have sex with her again. "It's all right for us to have meaningless encounters, after all, right? We just can't fall in love. No romance. No children. That sort of thing."

"That is what the Zidarr Code says," Malek murmured, thinking about finding a private spot to spend an hour with Jadora.

"Yeah. Tell him, please. You're his favorite. You always have been. He'll believe you."

"I suspect he's preoccupied with other matters right now and wouldn't worry about it," Malek said, bemused that Gorsith was making this request of him while he had his arm around Jadora.

"That's true. Who would even tell him, right? The druids? If the squirt used his magic to coerce us together again, Uthari probably wouldn't even hear about it. He's got a war to fight, after all." Gorsith sent the most intense look of longing at Shikari that a dragon had likely ever received.

But Jak and Shikari were talking, pointing and speculating about the thrashing Yoshartov. Whatever had driven Shikari to compel the druids and mages together seemed to have passed.

"I bet he wouldn't hear about it even if there *wasn't* dragon magic compelling us." Gorsith bit his lip and raised his eyebrows toward Malek. "Right?"

"I will not speak of it," Malek said.

He couldn't imagine having tattled on one of his fellow zidarr even before he'd decided to retire. Though he'd always followed the Code himself, he'd trusted others to obey it—or not—of their own accord. He might have made a comment if he noticed an impressionable young man going astray, but he wouldn't have blathered to Uthari. Besides, Uthari had always had ways of finding things out on his own. Though, in this case, Malek truly believed Uthari was too busy to worry about Gorsith's wayward urges.

"Thank you, Malek. Yidar was wrong. You're not a sanctimonious ass."

Malek snorted as Gorsith walked away.

"Is it just me," Jadora said as Gorsith's gait took him toward the druid camp, "or did he not realize you were cupping my butt and thinking lustful and inappropriate-for-a-zidarr thoughts while he was talking to you?"

By Shylezar, *Malek* hadn't even realized he was cupping her butt, but it was an appealing place to let his hand linger. As for the rest... "I'm certain my mental barriers kept you from knowing what I was thinking about when he was talking."

"You'd be amazed how much butt caresses can convey without need for telepathy."

"I'd like to convey even more to you, but I suppose it'll have to wait until our mission is over."

"It does seem that such should be our focus, though we do have some time to kill." Jadora rested a hand on his chest and looked toward Jak. "But first, I want to know why Shikari was compelling people to have sex with each other. I'm not sure we want our ally dragons to force us to do things."

"I don't know that Gorsith felt that affronted by that coercion."

If anything, he'd been hoping for more of it. As Gorsith approached the druid camp, Kywatha smiled at him, thrusting her chest out and brushing her green hair away from her face. Malek suspected she hadn't detested their joining either.

"Still, the precedent could be disturbing."

Jak looked back in response to her telepathic contact, then raised his eyebrows toward Shikari.

Shikari had been sitting up on his haunches, but he dropped to his belly, rested his head on the ground, and covered his eyes with his tail. Malek had never seen a dragon assume such a chagrined position.

"Ah," Jadora said after a moment. "It was an accidental coercing."

"He accidentally used his magic to make people have sex?" Malek asked.

"Sex wasn't on his mind. He's a little young to fully understand mating practices. The druids and the mages were about to battle each other, and Shikari knew another threat was coming. *That* threat specifically." Jadora pointed at Yoshartov, the dragon writhing and groaning on the ground as people had breakfast and filled their canteens from a stream. "He was afraid the one-eyed dragon would sneak in and get the portal while humans were fighting with each other, so he used his power to coerce them to be friends. Apparently, he magically oozed the desire for them to have an amicable relationship with each other. And it worked better than he had in mind. He feels contrite and apologizes."

"I see."

"I guess we can continue to allow him to be our ally," Jadora said.

"Jak should appreciate that."

"I believe so."

"I should wake Vinjo and get him to work." Malek looked toward the gateship.

"He may need more rest, and nothing has been resolved with our dragon captive yet." Jadora clasped his hand. "Why don't we rest a little more ourselves?"

"Rest?" He arched his eyebrows, letting his hand drift to her backside again.

"It could be *active* rest."

"That sounds agreeable."

~

Jak filled a canteen with water and headed toward Yoshartov, the dragon continuing to groan and thrash, radiating distress and discomfort as the bacteria and parasites battled within him. Malek and Mother had disappeared into the cave—Jak was choosing to believe they were guarding the portal in case anything came through and nothing else that required privacy—so he and Shikari had taken it upon themselves to keep an eye on their dragon prisoner.

After the first couple of hours, most of the people in the camp had started ignoring Yoshartov's thrashing, but Jak couldn't help but pity the dragon and think someone ought to take care of him. After all, Malek had been there to care for Mother when she'd been enduring this. They'd even broken through the ceiling in the gateship to do so.

Be careful if you go close to him, Shikari warned.

I will be, but I'd be obliged if you'd use your power to keep him from smashing me with his tail. Jak didn't know if the dragon, who'd stopped cursing Mother and every other human in the world for his execrable state, would be cognizant enough to drink the water Jak offered or even be aware of him, but he would try.

I will do so. Did you see me on top of him last night? Did you see how powerful and strong I'm growing?

I did see. You're turning into a fearsome adult dragon.

Yes! Shikari stood on all fours and waved his tail in the air as he made thrusting motions with his head, as if he were ramming his horns into an enemy.

I think you grew in the short time I was away.

My wings have increased in size. Shikari spread them to demonstrate. *I might be able to fly with you on my back now.*

Jak had been about to venture close to Yoshartov's head with the canteen, but he paused to look at Shikari, the old dream of riding on a dragon's back coming to mind. *Do you think so? You know I would love to fly. Skyboards and mageships are nice, and something I'd never experienced a year ago, but...*

Very boring compared to flying with a dragon.

I have no doubt.

Good. Maybe we should try now while there is time. If it works well, we could fly into battle together. Shikari shared an image of Jak on his back as they soared toward the dragon fortress, flying between the mageships to slip in and attack with fireballs.

What if it doesn't work well?

Then we both may end up stranded in a tree. The next image from Shikari showed them dangling from branches a hundred feet above the ground, coconuts rattled by their crash falling on their heads.

You have more of a sense of humor than I thought dragons would have.

That's because you've only known pompous tainted dragons. Are you truly going to give that one water?

He's sick and needs it. Protect me, please.

Of course.

Bolstered by the idea of getting to fly with Shikari as his reward, Jak approached Yoshartov's head. The dragon had switched from roaring and howling to groaning with his eye closed.

Not wanting to startle him, Jak asked, *Do you need some water, dragon?* before he crept closer to the head.

All the creature would have to do was turn his head sideways, and he might cut off one of Jak's limbs with those sharp fangs.

Jak could keep a barrier around himself, but he would have to lower it to pour water into Yoshartov's maw. Currently, the dragon didn't appear well enough to cut anything off anyone, not with his tongue lolling out between his fangs and onto the dirt, but that could change quickly.

Dragon! came an indignant protest, the single yellow eye opening. *I am Yoshartov, slayer of enemies, winner of races, more magnificent than the stars!*

Right now, you look like Yoshartov, the dehydrated.

I am thirsty. You appear to be a good servant. Bring me the refreshing nectar of the jungle.

I have water.

That will do.

Jak inched closer, holding the canteen out in front of him. *Did you say Sorath and Ferroki are alive in your fortress?* he asked, hoping for information. *Where are they being kept? Is there a dungeon?*

A dungeon! They are my servants. They are being kept in a luxurious suite so they may better serve me. Yoshartov shared an image of a circular room in a tower with charred bones all over the dragon-steel floor. It looked like the kind of place one dumped bodies for incineration.

Jak shivered. *Luxurious?*

For a servant, yes.

At least that seemed to be a confirmation that Sorath and Ferroki lived, or had the last time Yoshartov had seen them.

Jak tilted the canteen to pour water into Yoshartov's mouth.

Ahhhh, yes, the dragon crooned as glugging noises came from his throat.

It is good of you to care for a dragon, Shikari said. *Even a tainted one.*

The jaws started to shut, startling Jak. He released the canteen and jerked his arm back, raising a barrier around himself as Shikari also enrobed him in protective magic.

But Yoshartov's target was the canteen, not Jak's arm. He chomped it into pieces, sucked down the water it held, then spat out the pieces to land at Jak's feet.

Delicious. Yoshartov's tongue slid over his teeth.

Very good of me, Jak told Shikari.

Yes, Shikari agreed.

What is wrong with me, human servant? Yoshartov's head tilted sideways, and his eye focused on Jak.

You're sick.

Dragons do not get sick! *What did the female do to me?*

It's complicated. I'll explain it when I get back. Or ideally after the parasite within Yoshartov had died off. *There's a dragon who wants to give me a ride.*

A ride! Servants do not ride their masters.

We're friends. Nobody's a master.

Friends with puny insignificant beings that infest this world like termites?

Then again, maybe Jak wouldn't explain anything to the dragon. Yoshartov let his head and wings flop back to groan pitifully toward the sky.

"Sorath is going to have his hands full if what the seer said is true," Jak said as he approached Shikari.

I look forward to the other dragons one day being less pompous. Shikari looked Jak up and down. *Let's go up to the top of the cave so I can spring off from an elevated perch.*

Jak envisioned Shikari springing with him on his back, only to land hard and tumble down the rocky slope as the gateship had the night before. It would be Jak's second crash in less than a day. He gingerly touched a bruise on his hip.

I will not crash. Shikari trundled up the slope, then hopped into the air and flew to a perch above the cave.

Jak was positive he hadn't been sharing his thoughts, but maybe his grimace and bruise touching had been self-explanatory.

If my wings are not sufficient to hold up your weight, I will use magic.

That seems reasonable. Jak had once believed magic was a part of dragon flight regardless. Their wings weren't small but had never seemed large enough to propel their great muscular bodies through the air.

I am a reasonable dragon. Unlike some. Shikari sniffed and pointed his snout at Yoshartov.

He's sick. A certain amount of grouchiness and, ah, unreasonableness is to be expected. Jak climbed the rocks to the side of the cave entrance.

What are you doing, Jak? his mother's words came from inside.

Not coming in to disturb you two. Don't worry. Jak made a face at the rocks, attempting to convince himself that his mother and Malek were doing nothing more scandalous than reciting poetry to each other in the cave. Zidarr, of course, being known for appreciating the arts. *Shikari is going to give me a ride. He thought it would go better if he launched himself from an elevated perch.* He didn't think he shared the image he'd had of them crashing down the slope, but maybe Mother had the thought independently.

You don't think the thumps and cries of my son crashing would disturb us? she asked dryly.

We'll try to crash quietly.

Be careful.

Jak rolled his eyes. Only a mother would stop her... poetry time with someone to tell her son to be careful.

Yes, Mother.

Jak reached the top of the cave and picked his way to Shikari. Yoshartov's dramatic wails drifted up to them.

It's going to be a challenge to keep the fleets from taking advantage of dragons in a state like that if we succeed in infecting them with the bacteria while we're at the fortress, Jak pointed out.

It wouldn't be honorable to attack an enemy in such a pitiful condition. Shikari tucked his wings in and lowered himself to his belly.

Considering how many dragons attacked and killed humans who lacked the power to fight them off, I think they'll feel justified in doing so. You may have to act as an ambassador and try to establish a peace treaty on their behalf. Remembering that Shikari was only a few months old, Jak felt silly suggesting that, but he was the only untainted dragon available for it. Besides, he already had the intelligence of an adult and the memories of his kind that Zelonsera had shared with him. It wasn't as if *Yoshartov* would make a suitable ambassador, a thought that was punctuated by another wail and more tail thrashing.

Tezi, who appeared to have been assigned by the mercenaries to keep an eye on the dragon, watched Jak curiously from their camp, her druid companion at her side. When Shikari levitated Jak onto his back, her eyes widened in surprise, but she lifted a hand to give an encouraging wave.

You're in charge if we crash, Jak told her.

In charge? There are about twenty mercenaries here who outrank me, not to mention two zidarr, dozens of mage officers, and a bunch of druids.

I meant in charge of giving the dragon water. Jak winked at her.

Tezi eyed the broken pieces of canteen next to Yoshartov's head. *Can I decline that duty?*

Maybe your druid friend will do it. He looks hardy.

Tezi turned to Grunk, asked a question, and Grunk shook his head.

He also declines, she said.

I guess I'll have to survive the ride then.

A good idea.

Once settled on Shikari's back, his legs pulled up so they wouldn't get in the way of his wings, Jak pushed his hat low on his head and leaned forward to rest his palms on Shikari's smooth scales. Those scales didn't offer the least handhold. Without a saddle and saddle horn, the only thing Jak might have grabbed were the twin horns that jutted from Shikari's head. But he would have to scoot onto his neck for that, and he doubted Shikari would appreciate someone riding his neck.

Guess I'll use my magic to stay on, Jak said, though he wasn't sure what map imagery could aid him in that.

I won't let you fall, Shikari promised. *Are you ready?*

Yes. Jak bit his lip, anticipation flowing through his veins.

Shikari crouched, swished his tail a few times, then sprang into the air and flapped his wings.

With nothing to grab onto, Jak wobbled, slipping backward on the smooth scales as soon as Shikari's head was higher than his back half, but gentle magic grasped him and held him in place. The wings beat fast, and a few grunts of exertion came from Shikari as he struggled to rise higher than the cave. Jak sensed him applying his magic to himself, and they gained elevation.

Jak grinned down at the mercenaries, mages, and roamers looking up at them, many of their mouths opening in surprise. Gorsith and Kywatha walked out of the trees, their clothing askew, and Gorsith frowned up at them.

Jak hardly cared. His young dragon friend was flying, and *he* was along for the ride.

Once they were above the trees, Shikari leveled their flight, and his wingbeats smoothed out, a combination of their effort and magic keeping them aloft. Birds squawked in surprise and fled their perches as Shikari flew past above them. Jak looked around in wonder at the sun gleaming on the lush green leaves in the treetops. A monkey hooted at them, then fled down a trunk to hide in the branches.

The wildlife know a mighty predator flies above them, Shikari said. *And a mighty mage.*

I'm not that mighty yet, but thank you.

You are improving. So am I. Together, we will be very mighty. More than our enemies can handle.

I hope so, Jak replied, well aware of what they would soon face.

He worried that Rivlen and the fleet might already be at the fortress and engaged in battle while they dawdled here, waiting to see if the bacteria could change Yoshartov back to the dragon he was meant to be.

Shikari banked and dipped low to fly over a river, a fish jumping in the water below.

This is even better than being on a skyboard. Jak vowed to enjoy the flight and worry about the rest later.

Naturally. Shikari soared over a waterfall, then flew upward again, weaving between the trees, barely missing their branches.

More than once, Jak had to duck or lean left or right, but he only grinned, delighted by the journey and the wind whipping past them. Shikari flapped his wings hard again to fly up several hundred feet before sailing over a marshy area where few trees grew. Below, a couple of animals that looked like giant toads leaped from log to log.

Hang on. Shikari tucked his wings in close to dive toward them.

As the wind whistling past intensified, threatening to steal Jak's hat, he smashed it to his head and bent lower, pressing his chest to Shikari's back. Exhilaration filled him as they dove faster than gravity would have taken them down. Even though he trusted Shikari, Jak's heart pounded in his chest.

One of the giant toads saw them coming and leaped into the water, disappearing under a log. The other was too slow. It leaped, but Shikari's jaws snapped around it as his wings came out, halting their descent so quickly that Jak would have tumbled off if not for magic. Shikari's talons skimmed the marshy water before he flew upward again, chomping his prize along the way.

I didn't know you would stop for lunch in the middle of our flight, Jak admitted, sitting up as they leveled out. He patted Shikari's scaled shoulder.

It is more effort to fly with a rider. I needed food to replenish my reserves.

Understandable.

We can go back for the other toad if you're hungry.

Jak imagined eating a giant amphibian raw—and still alive. *No, thank you. I'm not the one doing the work.*

True. I do not sense any other dragons nearby. This is good.

For their sake, it was, but Jak feared what that meant, that the rest of them were all in their fortress, waiting to attack or already attacking the fleet.

30

"I THINK THAT LEADS TO THE COURTYARD AND THE WEAPONS tower." Sorath pointed down one of three shafts at an intersection he and Ferroki had reached.

Since the dragon leader had ordered its kind to prepare for battle and ready the weapon, they'd felt compelled to continue through the crawlspaces underneath the fortress, hoping to reach a crucial piece of infrastructure that they could sabotage.

"I don't know how you're not completely lost," Ferroki said, "but if you think so, let's try it."

Sorath hoped he wasn't lost. Usually, he had a good sense of direction, but they'd wound around a lot, the shafts not always going in a straight line and several of them coming to dead ends.

He crawled forward. They would find out soon if this was another dead end.

A *thwump* reverberated through the fortress. Sorath grimaced. Was that the beam weapon firing?

He crawled faster, but a draft of fresh air coming in from a side shaft made him pause. Thus far, they hadn't come to many places where they could have climbed out of the passageways if they wished. Maybe the draft indicated an open panel or door. With the dragons readying for battle, they shouldn't be searching for Sorath and Ferroki, so it might be safe to crawl out.

"I want to check something." He turned down the shaft and crawled toward the salty cool air brushing his cheeks.

"The sanity of our captors?" Ferroki grunted but continued after him.

"We already know *that* is long gone." Spotting daylight ahead, he hurried. He clunked his head on the low ceiling but didn't care.

Expecting to find a way up to the floor of the fortress, Sorath grimaced when bars came into view at the end of the shaft. If they couldn't cut their way through them, this would be another dead end. As pleasant as the cool air felt after hours—or maybe days—trapped in the shafts, they wouldn't be able to escape out into it.

"Is that a grate?" Ferroki asked, forced to peer past his bulky form to see ahead.

"Yes."

"Made of dragon steel, I suppose."

"It looks like it." Sorath reached the vertical and horizontal bars and didn't have to touch them to know they were indeed dragon steel. Almost everything in the fortress was, so he couldn't claim to be surprised. There was little point in trying the dagger on it. As they'd learned, dragon steel couldn't destroy dragon steel.

"Ships," Ferroki whispered, squeezing in beside him and peering past the grate instead of at it. "Black-hulled ships mostly. Uthari's people."

Sorath looked at her grave face before focusing on the approaching vessels. Twelve armed and armored mageships flew toward the fortress, large crews on deck, readying their magic and their artillery weapons.

"I'm sure Thorn Company isn't with them," Sorath said, though he wasn't sure of that at all. The worry in Ferroki's eyes made him want to say something comforting.

"I doubt they've managed to escape their contract. *Our* contract that I agreed to."

"That you had no choice but to agree to."

Ferroki might have said more, but another *thwump* coursed through the fortress, and the red beam lanced out from above them. The air sizzled with its power, and they were close enough that Sorath's skin tingled in response. Even the dragon-steel dagger couldn't keep him from feeling all that power.

The beam slammed into one of the ships, ripping through its barrier as if it didn't exist. Without mercy, it blew the vessel into pieces.

Sorath swore. "Just like with the druid raft."

"Why did they come without more of a plan?" Ferroki whispered as the beam fired again.

Some of the ships attacked as they flew erratically—trying to present difficult targets? It didn't matter. The fortress was protected, and Sorath didn't feel the impact of any of the fireballs, lightning, or cannonballs the mage crews sent toward it. Meanwhile, the beam weapon tracked their vessels without trouble, firing again and again.

Not once did it miss, and each shot blew a ship to pieces, screams floating over the icy sea as the crews tumbled toward their deaths. Some of them slowed their falls by levitating themselves, but it didn't matter. Dragons flew out of the fortress to catch them, killing them outright or taking them prisoner.

"We *have* to disable that weapon," Sorath said, backing away from the grate.

"I don't think we can, Sorath," Ferroki said, but she followed him.

"If we can't, our people are doomed. All of humanity may be doomed."

Clangs, clunks, and curses emanated from the gateship, its repairs in progress. Vinjo had pressed a few mercenaries and mages into helping him, or at least holding his tools for him.

Jadora looked to the sky as she and Malek left the cave to find something to eat and to check on Yoshartov. She sensed Shikari and Jak several miles away and assumed the flying was going well. There hadn't been a crash, at least not at the takeoff, either noisy or quiet. She smiled, glad Jak had finally gotten his chance to ride a dragon.

"He's stopped moaning." Malek nodded to Yoshartov, flies buzzing around his belly.

The dragon lay on his back, completely still, wings limp. If Jadora hadn't been able to sense his aura, she would have believed him dead. He seemed to be unconscious—in the final stages of the battle between bacteria and parasites? With the mercenaries and roamers practicing with their weapons nearby, the clangs ringing from the trees, it was hard to imagine anyone sleeping.

"He looks half-dead," Malek said.

"Didn't I look similar when I was going through this?" Jadora asked.

"You were a lot more attractive when you were unconscious."

"I saw my gray-splotched face in a mirror and know that isn't true, but I appreciate you saying that." Jadora spotted something on Yoshartov's flank and halted mid-step. "Is that..."

She switched from a walk to a run. Halfway to the dragon, she sensed Malek wrapping a protective barrier around her. Wise, she supposed, but the scientist in her was far more moved by curiosity than self-preservation.

She stopped at the dragon's side and touched a scale that was no longer the same mottled gray-and-brown as the others. A hint of blue tinged one side. It was a tiny spot on a large dragon, but she couldn't help but grin.

"It's *working*." Jadora looked back at Malek.

"Careful." He'd stopped several paces away and pointed at Yoshartov's head.

His yellow eye had opened halfway.

Human, what did you do to me? A dragon's telepathic voice usually boomed in her head, but his was weak, a whisper.

We're healing you.

I was not ill.

You were tainted by a parasite living in your body, turning you into something that you weren't meant to be. Maybe she shouldn't have said *were.* It was early to assume all the parasites were dead inside and that he'd reverted to the dragon he'd once been. *Also, my name is Jadora.*

I am Yoshartov, slayer of enemies, winner of races, more magnificent than the stars.

His name and list of accolades hadn't changed, but maybe he would claim all that even if he were normal. It wasn't as if Shikari was modest.

I know. We've met.

Have we? It's... fuzzy. His eyelid came down in a slow blink.

Is it? Interesting. Jadora remembered everything from the time she'd been infested with the parasite, but it hadn't been that long for her. For the dragons, it had been thousands of years.

Wait, I was *ill. When I woke, I found strange organisms inside of me. I had to obliterate them.*

Her first thought was that he meant the parasite, but he had to be referring to the death-darter bacteria. If he had the same knowledge of them as Zelonsera, then he would have known how to eradicate them.

That made her nibble uneasily on her lip. What if he'd noticed them and destroyed them too soon? Before they'd destroyed the parasite?

Where are my servants? Yoshartov asked. *I want fish. Seasoned like humans season it.*

Colonel Sorath and Captain Ferroki? They're mercenary officers, not servants to a dragon. You imprisoned them in your fortress against their will.

Jadora hoped the dragons wouldn't be eager to call humans *servants*—or imprison them—after the parasite was gone, but she couldn't truly know what their relationships had been like all those millennia ago. The legends were such a mix, some praising dragons and calling them benevolent and kind, some making them into gods, and some painting them as monsters to be feared. It was hard to know if those old tales had all originated from a time before the parasites or not.

They make good fish. Very tasty.

Hm, that wasn't exactly agreement that Sorath and Ferroki weren't servants.

They might be willing to make you more fish if you help us rescue them from the fortress.

Be careful what you say, Malek spoke into her mind, pinpointing his telepathy to her alone. *If he knows of our plans and still considers himself allied to the tainted dragons, he'll be able to warn them from afar.*

Jadora nodded. As much as she hoped this worked and that Yoshartov would be willing to help them when he recovered, she couldn't know for certain that he would feel benevolence toward them. After all, they had him chained to a tree in their camp.

I'm trying to convince him he wants to rescue Sorath and Ferroki, Jadora told Malek.

Isn't he the one we think put them there?

Yes. It's a chance for him to nobly make amends for past crimes.

Water, Yoshartov wailed into their minds, the earlier weakness gone. *I must have water and fish. I am chained and so very weak.*

I don't think he's changed much yet, Malek said dryly.

Please, Jadora told the dragon.

What?

Humans will gladly help dragons if they're polite.

Malek snorted softly, no doubt remembering the times she'd encouraged *him* to say *please.*

Yoshartov blinked slowly a few more times. *Please bring this weak and sick and parched dragon water and food, human. Jadora human.*

Huh.

I'll do so. Jadora headed off to find a canteen, Malek falling in at her side.

"He learns more quickly than a zidarr," she said.

"Really."

"Maybe dragons are less stubborn."

"That seems unlikely. It could be a ruse."

Yoshartov crooned pitifully. It almost sounded like a song. A song of lament. *A dragon has great thirst but must lie weakly in the dirt. When will his needs be met by those who put him there?*

"Was that.... poetry?" Jadora asked. "Song lyrics?"

Malek grunted skeptically.

It rhymes in the dragon tongue, Yoshartov said. *Our language is so very beautiful. We love music.* He issued more croons.

They reminded Jadora of someone stepping on a fireplace bellows.

"I'm not sure *this* is the dragon we should have captured." Malek grabbed a couple of canteens from camp, and they filled them together.

"This is the only dragon that presented himself."

"Because he was more interested in sneaking in and stealing the portal than defending his outpost. He could be a coward."

"He could be seeking glory out of a desire for his people to deem him important."

Yoshartov crooned.

"He's starting to make me appreciate Shikari more," Malek said.

They headed back with the canteens, and Yoshartov lolled his maw open. He gurgled contentedly as Jadora poured water down his gullet.

Yes, most delicious, Jadora human. And human mate of Jadora.

"It's Malek," he said, his tone dry again.

Jadora decided not to ask why the dragon believed they were mates, though her cheeks warmed as she considered the possibility that Yoshartov might have heard them enjoying each other's company in the cave earlier. She looked around the camp, hoping human hearing wasn't as keen.

Will you free me, Jadora human? Yoshartov lifted his head, the chain rattling. He looked toward the tree where it was attached.

As soon as he grew stronger, he would be able to free himself, especially if Shikari hadn't returned by then to help keep him down.

Jadora raised her eyebrows toward Malek, and he shook his head and frowned at the idea. But they couldn't keep Yoshartov here indefinitely. They themselves needed to leave as soon as the gateship was repaired.

We would like to free you, but we're worried that you will be in danger if you leave this area.

In danger? The dragon's head swiveled toward her.

From the others of your kind. They may realize that you're not one of them anymore. Jadora held her breath, waiting to see if Yoshartov would deny that. She also touched the half-blue scale on his flank.

He twisted his head to look at the altered scale, his neck bending impressively so he could examine the spot up close. He sniffed it, then licked it, then turned his head sideways to examine it from different angles.

Malek arched his eyebrows. *This is an odd dragon.*

I think Sorath gave that assessment of him before.

I thought he might change when the parasite was gone.

I'll cheerfully take odd over threatening to eat or enslave humans. He hasn't done that since he woke up.

Not yet, but this could all be a ruse. Can you test him? Malek pantomimed jabbing a needle in the dragon's side.

Yoshartov? Jadora asked. *Will you let me take a sample of your blood? You were very ill, and I want to see if you've recovered.*

I feel better. Stronger. Hungrier.

If you let me take a blood sample, I'll bring you some of our ration bars. She wondered how much the dried and pulverized meat would appeal to a dragon accustomed to eating food raw and freshly killed. He *had* mentioned enjoying fish prepared by humans, but the ration bars weren't culinary delights.

Are these bars tasty?

No, but they provide nourishment.

Yoshartov's nostrils wrinkled. *I will try them.*

Jadora sensed Jak flying with Shikari a couple of miles away and reached out to him. *Our dragon friend is awake and hungry. Is there any chance Shikari can bring him something to eat? He doesn't sound excited about our ration bars, and it would probably take fifty to fill him up.*

Is he a friend now? Jak replied.

I'm not sure. I'm trying to get him to let me test his blood. The bullet wounds have sealed up, so I'm going to have to find a new place to draw a sample.

Malek won't mind stabbing him with his dagger, I'm sure.

I want him to consider us allies.

While he's chained to a tree? Jak asked.

I'm working on explaining that. Jadora switched her attention to Yoshartov, who was eyeing his chain again as he lifted a talon to the collar to probe it. *We can remove that as soon as we've confirmed that you're no longer ill. Food is on the way.* Jadora jogged to her battered laboratory in the gateship—it was upright again, with some of her equipment back on the counters—and retrieved one of her kits with vials and tools. *I need a sample of your blood,* she said when she returned. *I suppose saliva might work. When I tested people and dragons for sign of the, uhm, illness, that was sufficient.*

Saliva?

Yes. May I swab your mouth?

Are you experimenting on me again, Jadora human? I remember this now. His eyelid descended halfway. *You used needles to put things in me.*

Yes, I did. To heal you. We want dragons to be as they were meant to be, not cruel and aggressive and ugly mottled gray-and-brown monsters. She attempted to share one of the visions Jak had given her, of frolicking dragons playing around the jungle pool where the portal had been set up.

My scales are *ugly and mottled,* Yoshartov said. *Once they were beautiful and blue and glinted in the sun like shimmering rainbows. I remember this.* He scraped his talons over his scaled sides, bobbed his head, and let out another distressed moan.

"Apparently it's his vanity you need to appeal to," Malek said, "not his interest in being cruel or not."

"I guess so."

As Yoshartov moved more, the chain impeded him, and he frowned at it. *I must be free, Jadora human.*

Swab first. She held it up.

He squinted at her, then it, and finally lowered his snout to sniff the implement.

Very well. He opened his maw.

As always, it was hard not to step back in alarm at having those long, sharp fangs so close, but she leaned in and rubbed the swab inside his maw.

That tickles. I thought it would hurt.

She withdrew it. *We don't want to hurt you. We would prefer to be friends with you. I'll be right back.*

After nodding to Malek, she returned to the gateship. Vinjo

was speaking animatedly to someone, likely Sasko, though he was so busy talking to her about their adventure and repairing the portal that she wasn't able to get a word in.

During the crash, the orb they'd brought back had fallen on the floor in the laboratory, and Jadora winced, feeling they weren't respecting it properly. Perhaps it was nothing more than a broken husk now, but after all they'd gone through to find it, she hated to believe that. She picked it up and found a place where it wouldn't fall if—*when*—the ship ran into trouble again.

That done, Jadora prepared a slide with the swabbed saliva and placed it under her microscope. Outside, Shikari and Jak arrived, landing near Malek and the dragon.

Her first examination didn't reveal any sign of the parasite, and hope rose within her. She made herself shift the slide around, looking more carefully. She did spot the protein that indicated the death-darter bacteria had been within him. As he'd promised, he'd destroyed the actual bacteria, for there was no sign of the living organism.

A negative slide didn't prove conclusively that the parasites were no longer in his body, but he'd used her name and acted somewhat agreeable. More than he had before. "Let's hope Malek's suggestion that it could be a trick is wrong."

"Jadora?" Sasko stuck her head through the doorway.

"Yes?"

"Vinjo says to tell you he's almost done, that you ought to be able to fly the ship again by nightfall."

"Thank you. Will you ask him to come see if he can repair this orb once we're underway?"

"He looks like he needs a nap, not more work," Sasko said.

"We all do. Ask him anyway, please."

"Yes, ma'am."

Once Jadora was back outside, she found Yoshartov sitting up and polishing off the remains of whatever animal Shikari and Jak had brought him. Only tufts of brown fur on the ground under his jaws hinted at what it might have been.

The raw flesh of freshly caught prey is acceptable, Yoshartov said, *but it is not as wondrous as spiced fish prepared by humans.*

Jak arched his eyebrows. "One wonders what *spices* Sorath and Ferroki have access to in the middle of the dragon fortress."

I brought them many spices. Yoshartov shared an image of himself carrying a vendor's cart from Port Toh-drom all the way to the Glacier Islands, with twists of dried leaves and bottles of peppercorns occasionally falling out to be lost in the jungle below. *Will you free me now*? He looked at Jadora and rose to all fours, his tail in the air. *Did I pass the tests?*

You did. Jadora looked to Shikari, wondering if he could tell if Yoshartov was likely to be an ally now. Aside from the single blue scale, the rest remained brown and gray.

Shikari sniffed him as he used his magic to examine the adult dragon, but he only tilted his head, as if he couldn't tell.

Will you help us rescue Sorath and Ferroki? Jadora asked Yoshartov. *So they can, ah, make more spiced fish for you*?

She trusted that Sorath, however he might gripe, would be willing to prepare a few fish in exchange for his freedom.

Of course I will rescue him. Humans who do nice things for dragons must be rewarded. But— Yoshartov's tail drooped. *Oh.*

Oh?

Ooooooh. He slumped, belly and tail dropping to the ground, as if he'd had a great epiphany.

Jadora hoped he had and that it was the one they all wanted him to have.

He is deep in the fortress that we made. The other dragons want to eat him. All of them. Many of the humans have already been eaten. They do not even taste good, but the other dragons believe it's appealing to consume their enemies.

"I don't want to know *how* he knows humans don't taste good," Jak muttered.

Will you help us get them out? Jadora asked.

I can't fight the others. There are too many, and they're mean.

"No kidding," Jadora murmured.

"What if we don't fight them?" Jak asked. "What if you help us sneak in, we rescue them, and sneak back out before the fighting starts?"

Jadora met his gaze. Yes, that might work, especially if they acted quickly, before more of Yoshartov's scales turned back to their original color.

As far as the other dragons knew, he was one of them. They shouldn't object to his presence or him bringing in new slaves. She envisioned her and Jak riding into the fortress on Yoshartov's back. Or maybe it would be better to take Malek, in case they had to fight. And if, while they were there, they got a few chances to shoot bacteria-doused bullets at the dragons, all the better. She would have to gather what remained from the mercenaries.

I can't. They will kill me. They will kill us all. Yoshartov dropped his jaw to the ground. *They are mean.*

Jadora rubbed her face. How were they going to convince him to help?

31

"I'M AMAZED YOU'RE ABLE TO GET THIS THING RUNNING AGAIN EVERY time it's broken." Sasko handed Vinjo a screwdriver.

"*This thing* is a sleek, magnificent ship built with the latest technology and all the knowledge this engineer has in his head," Vinjo said. "You should worship it appropriately."

"You know there are weird bits of gray seaweed and blue vines stuck all over the hull, right? I don't know what you did on that underwater world, but your magnificent ship looks like you dug it out of a garbage heap."

"Not for long. I'll clean the outside on the way to rejoin the fleet." Vinjo made a face as he twisted something.

She didn't know if the expression was for the vines or the thought of rejoining the fleet. Sasko wanted to rescue the captain, but she couldn't muster any enthusiasm for the thought of heading into more battles with dragons—or back into close proximity to Uthari and all those overbearing mage officers. She wished they could take Vinjo's ship and sail off to some distant land where nobody was at war with anybody else.

"Me too," Vinjo said with a sigh.

"Are you reading my thoughts again, Vinjo?"

"Not intentionally, but you're oozing them all over me." He set down the tools, rested his palms on a new power supply he was shaping, and gazed at her. "I would *love* to sail off with you, Sasko. Would you really leave the mercenary life for me?"

"I'd be leaving it for me, but it would be nice to have company as I sought out a new career."

"I'd leave the fleet life for you."

"Something that would mean more if all your people didn't want you dead."

Vinjo winced, and she lifted a hand in apology.

"Sorry. I meant to make a joke, but I realize that wasn't funny."

"No. But technically, it's probably only King Zaruk who wants me dead."

"King Zaruk who commands all of your people?"

Vinjo sighed again. "Yes."

"In the past, I haven't seriously considered leaving Thorn Company, and especially not since the captain disappeared, leaving me in charge, but if we can somehow reach her, and she's all right and can return to commanding the company… Oh, I don't know. I'm still her second-in-command. I'd have to talk to her, see if maybe she has someone else in mind. For all we know, she may want to disband the company altogether after losing so many people. Maybe she's dreaming of sailing off to a distant land with Sorath."

Vinjo wrinkled his nose. "What for?"

"Passionate and frequent sex, I'd guess."

Vinjo dropped his screwdriver. "With *Sorath*? He's a big brute."

"Not sexy like you, huh?" Sasko plucked at the rope waistband of his homemade grass trousers.

"Not in the least. And he doesn't have any magic or even both hands. How could he, you know, pleasure a woman?"

Sasko rolled her eyes. "I'm sure they can find ways to satisfy each other. Besides, they're old. How much pleasuring could they need?"

Sasko smiled, imagining the captain tartly informing her that fifty-something wasn't that old. She wished Ferroki were there now to do so.

"That is true." Vinjo retrieved his wrench. "So, if I've got this right, we have to rescue them, and then you'll sail off with me?"

"Something like that. Better make sure the camouflage on this ship is reapplied."

"Oh, I will. It didn't work well on the other world—I wonder if the water itself was able to sense us moving through it and relay to the other creatures our presence. There was a lot of magic there."

Sasko was glad he'd made it back, that they all had. "We may also have to help with the dragon problem before we can sail anywhere together."

"I'm hoping that dragon chained to the tree out there is part of that."

"Do you think there's a plan that involves him?"

"Jadora's coming," Vinjo said. "You can ask her."

Sasko peered into the corridor as Jadora stepped off the ladder. She headed straight to her laboratory.

"Do you need any help with anything, Professor?" Sasko asked, though Jadora appeared to be on a mission.

"Not unless you can convince a dragon to turn brave and assist with a rescue." Jadora tilted her thumb in the direction of their captive.

"I wouldn't know how to do that, no. I've found you can convince engineers to do brave things by kissing them." Sasko smiled at Vinjo, though his tongue was between his teeth as he concentrated on something, and he gave no indication that he'd heard her.

"You're welcome to kiss the dragon. The parasite seems to be gone, so it's likely safe."

"Parasites wouldn't be the only concern I'd have about kissing a dragon." Sasko wrinkled her nose. "Will the rescue be of the captain and colonel?"

Jadora paused in the doorway to her lab. "We're trying to arrange their rescue, yes, but that's going to depend on the dragon."

"How so?"

"He can fly straight into the fortress. We can't, not without being seen and obliterated."

Sasko almost mentioned Vinjo's camouflage, but that hadn't proven entirely reliable. The last she'd heard, the druids had camouflaged their raft, and the dragons had still detected and destroyed it.

"What will *we* do?" Sasko asked.

"Malek is in charge, but I'm guessing he'll want to take the portal and rejoin the fleet."

Sasko grimaced. She'd been afraid of that. And the fleet might well be off on a suicide mission. How were she and Vinjo supposed to sail off together if they got sent on that?

"Pardon me," Jadora said, "but I need to smear bacteria on bullets."

"Of course," Sasko murmured, though she didn't know what Jadora was talking about. She stepped inside with Vinjo again, then rested a hand on his shoulder. "I hope we can escape this, Vinjo."

"Escape what?" he asked absently.

"Never mind." She kissed him on the cheek.

~

You are a powerful grownup dragon, Shikari spoke to Yoshartov while Jak mulled over their options, pondering what they would do if they couldn't convince their captive to help.

He was largely mulling by himself since, after a challenge from Gorsith, Malek and the zidarr were sparring shirtless nearby while Vinjo finished repairs to the ship.

You must be brave and help free the others, Shikari continued. *They are living awful, tainted lives when they should know the joyous existence of being dragons free of parasitic infection.*

It is because I know exactly what they are and how they live that I fear them, Yoshartov replied, sitting and listening, though he kept eyeing the tree his chain was attached to. *And you are a young whelp. What do you know?*

Jak didn't know how much longer they would be able to keep Yoshartov there against his wishes. His aura had grown stronger, indicating he was recovering from his illness, but Jak couldn't help but hope Shikari would get through to him. Two more of Yoshartov's scales had turned blue. Jak hoped they would all be that hue soon and that he would turn into a magnificent ally dragon willing to fly through the skies alongside the human fleets.

Even though I'm a dragonling, I am not afraid to fight tainted dragons.

You should be.

Look, Jak said. *You won't have to fight them if we do this according to our plan. You, Yoshartov, since you're a trusted resident of that fortress, who single-handedly brought in a lot of the dragon steel that went into making it...* Jak well remembered that. *You'll be able to fly in unquestioned, and if you bring a human or two and say they're your servants, the other dragons will believe that, right? You did it before. If you want, you can drop us off and leave.*

Jak couldn't warm to the idea of being stranded in a lair full of angry dragons, but someone had to go there to deliver Mother's bacterial concoction, retrieve Sorath and Ferroki, and sabotage the fortress. Hopefully, with the fleet attacking, the dragons would be too busy to notice someone sprinkling acid all over the place.

I can leave? You wish me to take you there and leave?

It would be braver to stay, Shikari announced. *Grownup dragons are supposed to be brave.*

Yoshartov ignored him in favor of studying Jak. *If I agree to do this, you will remove this collar from my neck?*

We'd need you to fly us to the fortress before you left, but... Jak worried an ally who felt manipulated into helping wouldn't be a good ally. Yoshartov might abandon them halfway to the fortress, leaving them dangling in a tree. *You don't deserve to be a prisoner.*

I believe I've been saying that.

We only captured you so we could heal you. We knew the parasite might not wish it and would fight us. I will release you.

Jak left his barrier down as he unfurled the magical net from Yoshartov's back, then walked slowly toward the dragon's neck. He was putting a lot of faith in the three blue scales among the hundreds if not thousands on the great creature, but how could he ask Yoshartov to risk his life on their behalf without offering some trust? Perhaps in showing vulnerability, Jak could win *his* trust as well.

What are you doing? Shikari asked.

Trusting him.

Why?

Not answering, Jak slid his hand along the collar, looking for the hidden fastening mechanism he'd seen Malek activate when Shikari had worn it. There. He thumbed it open and stepped back.

The collar thumped to the ground. Yoshartov sprang back, then shook his head, neck, and body, like a dog flinging water from its coat. Then he rolled onto his back, wings tucked in as he kicked his taloned feet in the air and thrashed all about.

Is he ill again? Shikari asked.

Just happy to be free, Jak said. *You did something similar.*

Shikari sniffed.

Yoshartov was covered in dirt by the time he rose to his feet again. A chunk of moss hung from one of his horns. Everyone's assessment that this was an odd dragon was possibly correct.

He lowered his head to look at Jak. *Thank you, human.*

Jak.

Human Jak.

Yes.

I will carry two of your people to the fortress so that you may rescue the colonel and his mate.

Thank you. Though I don't think we'll be ready to go until... Jak trailed off, sensing Mother climbing out of the gateship.

She wore the magical backpack Malek had given her and clanked as she climbed to the ground. She also carried several ammo pouches and a black-powder rifle. One that could fire dragon-steel bullets? He assumed so, since he'd seen her gather the ammunition from the mercenaries, but...

Mother didn't think *she* was going, did she? He'd envisioned Malek and himself on the mission. Jak wished they could take more people, but there was a limit to how much weight a dragon could carry over hundreds of miles. If they succeeded in finding Sorath and Ferroki, they would have to figure out an alternate way to get them out of the fortress. They might *all* have to find an alternate way out since Yoshartov hadn't said he would stick around.

Malek finished his sparring match with Gorsith, grabbed his shirt, and jogged over with his weapons in hand.

"Yoshartov has agreed to take two people to the fortress," Jak said.

Malek and Mother looked at each other and nodded.

"I'm ready," she told him, tilting her thumb toward her pack and offering him the rifle.

"As am I." Malek accepted it and the ammo pouches.

"Uhm." Jak raised a finger. "While I don't necessarily object to being left out of this rescue mission, as I'd like to take some of that bacteria to jab in Uthari and make sure Rivlen is all right… I don't think *Mother* is the right person to take."

"What's wrong with *Mother*?" she asked, eyebrows arching.

"You're not a warrior and slayer of dragons, and you're…" Jak spread his palm toward the sky and looked to Malek for help. Surely, if he cared for her, he wouldn't want to take her into such immense danger. What were the odds that their plan would work? That Sorath and Ferroki were alive? That the fortress would be vulnerable to that acid? And that they could manage to mass-infect dozens of dragons by shooting them?

"She's the strongest mage we have," Malek said. "And I'm a trained warrior, so I can fulfill that role, though if we need to fight in the middle of a bunch of dragons, we'll have already failed and be doomed."

"I don't want my mother to be doomed. She should stay here and guard the portal. We need someone strong to guard it, don't we?"

"You're going to need to take it with you when you go to join the fleet," Mother told him. "So it can help against the dragons. Our plan is only going to have a chance at working if they're distracted by mageships attacking them."

"Those mageships might all be destroyed already," Jak argued, though he didn't want that to be true, not when Rivlen was on one of them. But he wanted to convince his mother not to go. "What if you arrive and there's nothing but wreckage?"

"The fortress needs to be destroyed," Malek said.

"And the dragons altered." Mother clasped his hand.

Jak stared at them, abruptly reminded of the way his mother and father had once joined hands to inform him of their plans. Usually, those plans had involved such things as Jak going to camp in the summer or not being allowed to skip weeks of school to go with his father on one of his archaeological trips. Nothing to do with storming deadly fortresses. But once they'd stood like that, they'd been implacable, no amount of rational convincing—or boyhood whining or crying—able to change their minds.

It was strange seeing Mother and Malek like that, a unified front. A team. But he supposed he was glad they'd found each other and realized they wanted to be on the same side.

"All right," Jak said quietly, reluctantly. "Be careful."

He stepped forward to hug them, blinking back tears as he tried not to think about what would happen if he lost them both.

"You be careful as well." Mother squeezed him hard, then pulled something out of an outside pocket in her pack. A couple of syringes with a dubious liquid inside. "You may have the more daunting task. One of these needs to be injected into Uthari. It doesn't have to go into a vein. The muscle is fine. Both syringes are the same. I'm sending along an extra in case one breaks. But be careful with them."

Jak, remembering how Uthari had intentionally tried to infest Shikari with the parasite, gingerly accepted the syringes. "I will be, but, uhm, I'm not Uthari's favorite person. Depending on how far gone he is, he might not let me inject him."

Might not? Jak couldn't imagine any scenario and any state of mind that Uthari could be in that he would allow Jak to inject him. Unless he were sleeping or unconscious…

Malek waved to someone. "I've briefed Gorsith. He's going to be in charge of the gateship. You'll take the portal and as many mages as you can fit on it."

Gorsith, who'd drawn Kywatha's attention with his shirtless sparring, said a few words to her before heading over. She walked at his side.

"What about the mercenaries? And roamers?" Jak asked. "We can't leave them here in the middle of the jungle."

"Take Tezi and Grunk since they have dragon-steel weapons," Malek said. "As for the rest, the druids can care for them until we're done with this. Assuming we're successful, we can pick them up on the way back. If we're not... I'm sure they'll find a way back to civilization."

"We have a civilization here," Kywatha pointed out.

"That a bunch of mercenaries and roamers would wish to join?" Malek asked.

She lifted a shoulder. "It's not so bad here."

"Their magic is intriguing," Gorsith put in, sharing a smile with her.

She smiled back at him.

Only then did Jak realize how close they were standing to each other. They couldn't still be under the influence of Shikari's coercion, could they? Jak had thought that had been a temporary spell applied to keep them from fighting.

I'm not doing anything to them, Shikari promised when Jak looked at him. *That was very temporary and wore off the same night. Before they'd even finished mating the first time. The copious other matings were not influenced by my magic.*

"Copious?" Jak mouthed.

Shikari swished his tail. Jak decided that was the dragon equivalent of a shrug.

Blacksmith Homgor walked up to listen to the planning, as did Sergeant Tinder and Tezi. The last Jak had seen, Sasko was with Vinjo in the gateship, helping with the repairs.

Mother looked toward the north. Jak frowned, hoping she hadn't sensed dragons coming. If they could capture one, they could possibly do to it what they'd done to Yoshartov, but if numerous dragons were approaching, that would be far more difficult.

"There's a ship coming," she said.

Kywatha smiled and nodded. "That's what I came over to tell you. I was distracted by the insult to our civilization." She eyed Malek.

He gazed back blandly.

"Our people have crafted another vessel. We weren't sure we would join your fleet again as that didn't go well last time—" Kywatha frowned and touched the side of her head, "—but we've seen what's happening to this dragon, and we believe you may be right about why the dragons grew evil and how they could be saved." She pointed at Yoshartov, who was nipping under his armpit like a dog with a flea.

Another blue scale had appeared there. Maybe they itched when they turned back to normal.

Jak sensed the ship that his mother had, the aura of the devices that powered it. Though they wouldn't be able to see it for a while, he assumed it was another log raft.

"We'll take the roamers and mercenaries and whoever else can't fit on your small ship." Kywatha took a deep breath, as if bracing herself. "And we'll go with you to help destroy the fortress."

After being shipwrecked and hitting her head and losing her memory, that had to be the last thing she wanted to do.

Gorsith squeezed her hand.

She forced a smile and nodded at him. "We'll even take this cocky zidarr if he wishes to travel with us."

"Are you inviting me to share a cabin with you?" Gorsith asked.

"Cabin?" Kywatha looked blankly at him.

Jak snorted. "I'm guessing Lord Gorsith hasn't seen a druid vessel yet."

"She might share a log with you," Malek told him, not commenting on his fellow zidarr's interest in spending time with a woman.

Jak wondered if all these romantic urges going around meant that Uthari would find himself without any zidarr left soon. He fervently hoped so.

"Gorsith, you will ride on the gateship and lead our people to reunite with the rest of the fleet. At that point, Uthari or his admiral will tell you how to best assist in the battle. Jak, you'll go with him, under Gorsith's command."

Jak eyed the zidarr, not pleased at the idea of taking orders from someone he'd never interacted with before—and who probably agreed with Uthari that he was a pain in the ass if not someone they'd like to see dead. Gorsith eyed him back with an equal lack of enthusiasm.

"Isn't he the one who was responsible for Tonovan's death?" Gorsith gestured in the air with his hands—it looked like he was pantomiming jail bars to imply Jak should be incarcerated somewhere.

"He played a role," Malek said, "but he's useful. And he'll make sure Uthari receives what he needs to be cured of his parasitic infection. Don't interfere with that, Gorsith. We all want Uthari to get better." Malek switched to telepathy to tell Jak, *Get Rivlen to help you with injecting him. Depending on how far gone he is —how much the parasites have taken him over—he may fight the needle.*

Jak had already decided Uthari would fight a needle that Jak waved in front of him, regardless of whether he'd been taken over or not. Would the old wizard trust Rivlen? Jak didn't know. The last he'd heard from her, Rivlen had felt she'd made a number of mistakes and was out of favor with him.

"I'm tempted to go with you to help him," Malek said quietly, "but..." He looked toward Mother, and determination kindled in his eyes. "The dragon problem has to be the priority."

I'll do my best to help him, but what if Gorsith hinders me? Jak asked silently.

I understand your dragon can fly with you on his back now. That offers you a modicum of independence.

Jak didn't know how *far* Shikari could fly while carrying his weight, but maybe it would be enough. He imagined sneaking up behind Uthari, stabbing him in the neck with the needle, then running and leaping onto Shikari's back before the crew could catch him.

Let's hope something so dramatic won't be necessary, Malek said dryly, and Jak realized he'd shared the image. *And I trust you'll do your best to help Uthari.* Malek held his gaze.

Jak swallowed. He hated Uthari and wanted to see him and every other wizard ruler removed from power, but this wasn't the time to put an end to his reign. Besides, he wasn't an assassin. And he hoped he wouldn't need to be. Once they healed the dragons, they would help fix the world. He still had faith in that.

I will. He nodded firmly at Malek.

Thank you, Malek said solemnly.

I am ready to fly and take my new servants to the fortress, Yoshartov announced, flexing his wings.

Gorsith raised his eyebrows and pointed to the firearm and Malek's sword. "If you're supposed to be going as servants, won't the other dragons find it suspicious that he's bringing you to their fortress armed?"

"I'm hoping they'll be too busy to look us over thoroughly," Malek said.

Dragons have little concern for human weapons, Yoshartov said. *Only those made from our steel are of any interest at all, and since we've been collecting it, they should believe I would bring more. But if necessary, I can carry the weapons*. He opened his maw to suggest where he would carry them.

Malek eyed the long fangs. "I'll keep them for now."

Jak doubted he would willingly give them up at any point.

Vinjo clambered out of the gateship, his hair sticking up in spicules, his face and hands smeared with even more grease than usual. "I have more repairs to do, and I haven't had a chance to look at the orb yet, but our vessel is operational, my lord."

Malek nodded. "Good. Gorsith will be riding with you and in charge."

"Gorsith?" Vinjo mouthed, disappointment darkening his eyes. "Not you, my lord?"

"Jadora and I have arranged alternative transportation." Malek extended a hand toward Yoshartov.

Vinjo curled his lip, either at the thought of flying on a dragon over a mageship or because Gorsith would be in charge. He'd made friends, in a manner of speaking, with Malek, and, like Jak, Vinjo probably worried about working with a new zidarr, one who might find out that he'd also played a role in Tonovan's death, or at least in teaching Jak how to build the kerzor that had been responsible.

"That dragon's back is a sharp, scaly ridge," Vinjo said. "It doesn't look nearly as comfortable as the seats I built in the navigation cabin. Nor does the dragon come with bunks for sleeping."

"I don't think any of us will be sleeping again until we've seen this through and found a resolution." Malek gazed toward the southern sky, his jaw set with determination. "One way or another."

32

MALEK SHIFTED AS MUCH AS HE COULD WHILE CLUTCHED IN SHARP talons, the wind whipping at his eyes as they flew over the sea far below, icebergs dotting the surface. When he'd envisioned being taken to the fortress as Yoshartov's prisoner, he'd imagined Jadora and himself flying on the dragon's back, the way Jak had ridden Shikari. That hadn't been what *Yoshartov* had in mind.

This is how I carried Sorath and his mate to the fortress, he'd informed them. *No tainted dragon would allow a servant to ride on his back, as if he were a human's domesticated equine.*

Would an untainted *dragon allow it*? Jadora had asked.

Perhaps if it were a very favored servant. Yoshartov had sniffed, clasped them in his grip, and taken off.

Hours later, with talons digging into him through his clothes, Malek looked forward to reaching the fortress, if only to have his feet under him again.

Are you all right? He looked over at Jadora. He'd already asked several times on the journey, but he kept questioning whether he'd made the right choice in allowing her to come. Not that he could have stopped her if she'd used her magic and insisted, but he'd understood Jak's reaction perfectly. Malek would far prefer Jadora stay back and away from the fighting than thrust herself into the middle of it. But if something went wrong with the acid or the bacteria, she needed to be there to hopefully correct the problem.

Yes. It's exhilarating flying over the treetops like this. Jadora smiled at him.

She appeared more comfortable than he, and he realized she was using her magic to create cushions of air between her body and the talons. It was as if she were flying atop a mattress instead of dangling from sharp hooks. He snorted softly, approving of her ingenuity and deciding she was the best person to have along.

I am a little concerned, Jadora admitted, eyeing Yoshartov's smooth belly, *that more of our dragon's scales are turning blue.*

Malek followed her gaze. When they'd left, only a handful of them had been visible among the mottled gray-and-brown, but with each passing hour more scales shifted to blue. Not a dull and unnoticeable blue but a vibrant iridescent hue that gleamed when the sun hit it. They were still sparse in the field of gray-and-brown, but if another dragon looked closely...

It'll be night soon. Malek nodded toward the sun sinking toward the horizon. *Let's hope the other dragons won't notice in the dark.*

His aura seems a little different too. Less... crazy.

I wasn't aware that a being could have a crazy aura. Malek cocked his eyebrows. He allowed that Jadora might be able to sense things with greater distinction than he could now, but he'd never heard any mage, wizard, or zidarr mention being able to sense a person's—or dragon's—personality in their aura. He also wasn't certain he would agree that untainted Yoshartov was less crazy than tainted Yoshartov.

That's not quite the word I want, but he feels different to me than when we first encountered him.

That's because he's not spouting unbalanced nonsense in your mind.

She managed a smile, though it appeared forced. *Perhaps you're right.*

As she looked to the south, her smile faded. Did she sense the fortress and the Glacier Islands?

Malek believed they had a couple hundred miles to go, but it was possible she could already detect the great aura that so much dragon steel in one place had to emit.

He reached out himself, hoping to sense the fleet more than the fortress. The worry that they were too late plagued him. When he'd communicated with Uthari, he and the fleet hadn't been that far from the fortress. What if they'd already reached it, attacked, and all their mageships had been obliterated? That would leave Jadora and Malek heading into enemy territory, with the small gateship and whatever log raft the druids were bringing as the only vessels coming to back them up.

I can sense the fortress and many, many dragons, Jadora told him.

What about our fleet? And the others?

Jadora hesitated. *The mages and mageships don't have as strong of auras as the dragons and their fortress. It's possible they're there, and I can't detect them yet.*

Malek decided not to share his fear that Uthari's fleet had arrived earlier and already been destroyed. If that had happened... nothing would change for the two of them, he realized. Zelonsera had given Jadora the duty of healing the dragons, and she'd promised to do her best. And Malek, even if the world hadn't been in peril, would have supported her in her efforts to do so. They had to do this. It would just be harder without the fleet attacking simultaneously.

My kind have sensed me, Yoshartov said. *Surprisingly, they are not as pleased to see me as I would have expected. After all, I am magnificent and a delight.*

Can they sense that you've changed? Jadora asked.

Not from this far away, no.

He hadn't, Malek noted, said that sensing such a change wouldn't be possible. Malek frowned, afraid Jadora was right, that untainted dragons had auras different from tainted ones, and that they could tell.

They are not pleased because I said I'm bringing more servants. It seems my last *servants have been causing trouble.* Yoshartov sounded more proud than irritated, and he shared an image with them of Sorath and Ferroki facing him with their weapons in hand. *They are very spirited servants.*

Whom, now that you are untainted, you consider friends, right? Jadora asked.

Untainted dragons may have human servants, Yoshartov informed them, *but we would not force humans to be such. Long ago, it was only because they revered us that some wished to serve dragons.*

I don't think Sorath is going to revere you, Jadora said.

No? He and his mate made me excellent fish. The spices were so flavorful!

He might agree to cook for you again without being a servant or revering you.

Malek cleared his throat, caring little about Sorath's dragon-servant status or ability to wield spices like a broadsword. *Will your kin allow you to enter the fortress with us?*

They did not wish to, but I told them I have more dragon steel and have also tricked humans into bringing the portal to them.

Unease hollowed out Malek's gut, because their allies *were* bringing the portal. When he and Jadora had left, Vinjo and Gorsith had been levitating it out of the cave and onto the gateship.

They are skeptical, but they will see, Yoshartov informed them cheerfully.

I suppose they will. Jadora shared a dubious look with Malek. *Does that mean they'll allow you to land with us?*

Yes. I'm heading straight for the fortress now.

Can you sense any of our people flying in mageships near it, Yoshartov? Malek asked, thinking the more powerful dragon might detect the fleets sooner.

Ah. One moment. It is more difficult to sense those with lesser auras.

Even though Malek had now encountered numerous beings, and even other humans, with auras greater than his and Uthari's, he couldn't help but scowl at being considered *lesser.*

Is your zidarr pride prompting that dyspeptic expression? Jadora asked him.

You've come to know me well.

Your pride isn't that difficult to know. She smiled and lifted a hand toward him though they were too far away to touch.

He managed a faint return smile and used his magic to caress her cheek, wishing they were riding closer together, especially since they might both die before the sun rose again.

Yes, yes, Yoshartov proclaimed. *I sense some of your flying ships, and some of my kind also say they have picked off human targets that presumed to come close to the fortress.*

Picked off? That sense of unease returned to Malek's gut.

Yes. Their defenses were not great, especially against the giloknozar.

The what?

You do not know that word? It is the weapon we built into the fortress to protect ourselves and the portal we knew we would soon acquire.

The beam Rivlen and the druids had described. The weapon that had burned through the collective defenses of dozens of druids and blasted their raft to pieces in seconds.

Yoshartov shared an image of the beam at work, blowing through the black hull of a mageship that had flown within range of the fortress. The vessel snapped in half, as if a giant had gripped both ends and dropped the ship over its knee. Mages on the deck tumbled off, dropping into the sea far below, ahead of the two halves of the ship.

At first, Malek thought it was an example, not something that was happening, but other ships were visible in the distance. More of Uthari's black-hulled vessels. Even farther back, yellow and brown hulls were visible. Lurking in the rear while Uthari's fleet went in first.

Malek clenched his fist. This was what was actually happening. Or had it already happened?

It is unwise of them to get so close, to attack at all. As the beam paused to find its next target, Yoshartov shifted the imagery he was sharing to focus on the fortress instead of the fleet.

More than two dozen dragons were visible, lounging in nests perched atop towers. One yawned as the beam lanced out again, blasting into another ship that had flown within its range. The dragons weren't concerned in the least. Only a couple were even in the air, flying out to finish off the humans that survived the weapon.

Malek wanted to rail at whoever had taken command of the fleets, though he didn't know what he would recommend. If the collective power of the mage crews wasn't enough to keep a barrier up against that beam, what could any of them do?

If all the ships attacked at once, they might be able to get close enough to do some damage before the beam focused on them, but what good could they truly do against a fortress made from dragon steel? They needed Jadora's acid.

The imagery Yoshartov was sharing shifted again, this time showing the sea and the jagged white contours of the glacier island below the fortress. Malek swallowed, realizing the fleet *had* attempted to send in several ships to attack at once. Several black-hulled vessels were wrecked on the ice or in the water below. Here and there, dead humans in Uthari's red uniforms were visible, their bodies broken on the ice.

Was Uthari among them? If his enemies had forced him to accede to their leadership, they might also have been able to force him and his ship to go in first.

Malek reached out with his mind, hoping he could contact Uthari telepathically from a distance. He'd done so numerous times before, though it had been when he'd been meditating in the quiet of his cabin, not while dangling from a dragon's talons. Also, Uthari had been easily locatable in his city, not close to a fortress and dragons with auras that dwarfed his.

My liege, Malek asked. *Are you there?*

Of course we are here, Uthari replied. *Where else would we be except attempting to unite with our own kind?*

Malek closed his eyes. That *we* wasn't entirely unexpected, since he'd heard the dragons refer to themselves that way, but he worried it meant his ruler was completely buried within his own body and there was no way to reach him.

From what I've seen, your own kind are trying to destroy you, Malek said.

To destroy the humans that infest this world.

Of which you are one.

Not for long. As soon as we are able, we will abandon this mediocre husk and be borne again inside a dragon.

Deciding he would get nowhere speaking with the parasite, Malek attempted to push deeper into Uthari's mind, to find him in there somewhere. The last time they'd spoken, Uthari had managed to rise up and regain control.

Uthari, my mentor and friend, Malek said. *Are you still there?*

He has been subsumed, came the cool reply.

Malek had been afraid of that. *Once you reunite with a dragon, will you leave him behind? Allow him to live as he once did without your influence?*

Once we are again with a dragon, this host will die. We have been irrevocably linked. Without us, he will perish.

Distress filled Malek, and he hoped the parasite was lying to him.

Just as you will perish, it added. *Since you were foolish enough to reach out to us, we will pass along your location and your intent to the collective.*

The collective already knows where I am, Malek replied, though the statement shook him. It hadn't occurred to him that Uthari, the parasite controlling Uthari, would pass along intelligence to the tainted dragons or the parasites controlling them. He tried to remember what of their plan he'd shared with Uthari during their communication via the dome-jir. Nothing, he hoped. At the time, Jadora hadn't yet healed Yoshartov.

Good, the parasite crooned into his mind. *The fewer humans with power and dragon-steel weapons that remain, the easier it will be to destroy the rest, to take this bountiful world for our own.*

Malek released contact, drawing back into his own mind.

I'm afraid I've given Jak a very difficult task, he admitted to Jadora.

She turned her worried eyes toward him. *He's good at finding ways to succeed.* She sounded like she was trying to convince herself as much as him. *He'll go to Rivlen first, get her to help and give him information, and they'll work together to reach Uthari with the bacteria.*

I hope you're right. Malek didn't share his concern that Rivlen might already be dead. The lust-filled look Uthari had given her came to mind, as well as the fact that she'd been right at his side when he spoke on the dome-jir. As if he'd taken her to be his trusted right-hand officer. Or maybe his mate.

Malek had never known Uthari to care about such things, but the being he'd communicated with today and the day before... wasn't Uthari.

They'll find a way, Jadora repeated and nodded firmly.

Struggling not to feel bleak and defeated, Malek took a deep breath and told himself there was still hope. Uthari, no matter how greatly the parasites were affecting him, was still alive. If he and Jadora could accomplish their mission, he and the rest of the fleet might be able to *stay* alive.

Do you know where that weapon—the giloknozar*—is located in your fortress, Yoshartov?* Malek asked.

Of course, the dragon replied brightly. *I helped build it.*

Malek might have scowled at that, but Yoshartov showed them a tower where the device was mounted inside, near the roof. A dragon nested on that roof, its tail dangling cheekily down the side, scant feet from the huge eyehole that the beam lanced from. Yoshartov also showed them the device inside the tower, a massive red sphere with swirling inner workings that might have confused even Vinjo.

His first impression of the weapon daunted Malek and made him wish they'd found a way to bring the engineer along, but they didn't have to know how it operated to destroy it.

Jadora and I would like you to deposit us there. Malek nodded at her.

She must have followed his reason for asking Yoshartov about the location, for she nodded gravely back. Before they worried about distributing the bacteria, they would have to take out that weapon.

~

The setting sun shone red on the waves below, the fortress visible scant miles ahead of the fleets. They had passed the place where Rivlen and the *Star Flyer* had been attacked before. Attacked and defeated and shipwrecked. Now, as she watched helplessly, it was all happening again.

Before the fortress had come into view, King Zaruk had ordered some mageships to go ahead. To scout, he'd said, but one didn't send ten ships to scout. And it hadn't missed Rivlen's or the crew's notice that he'd mostly sent *Uthari's* ships.

She was surprised he hadn't ordered the *Soaring Eagle* to go, but maybe the other rulers wanted to keep Uthari alive for the time being, believing they would need his power when they finally attacked en masse. The rest of his people they cared less about. And now they were dying.

From miles back, Rivlen hadn't been able to see the great beam shoot out of the fortress, but she'd sensed the weapon, and she'd heard the telepathic cries of hundreds of mages dying as it lanced into their vessels, burrowing through their barriers to tear their ships in half.

As the destroyed mageships had plummeted toward the iceberg-filled sea, some of the mages had levitated themselves to keep from plunging to their deaths, but it hadn't mattered. Either the beam itself had shot out again, blasting people out of the sky, or the dragons had lazily flown forth from their fortress, killing the mages as easily as if they were powerless terrene humans.

Not all of the mages had been killed. Some had been captured and carried back to the fortress, but Rivlen doubted their enemies had pleasant fates planned for them.

It hadn't taken long for the dragons and their giant beam weapon to destroy all ten scout ships. If any of those vessels, some of which had managed to attack with magic and cannons before being targeted themselves, had found weaknesses that the fleets could exploit, Rivlen hadn't heard about it.

"Idiotic plan," she grumbled as she wiped sweat from her forehead.

As she stood at the railing, breathing in the chilly, salty air, Rivlen tried not to think about the parasite growing inside of her. She hadn't seen Uthari for hours and was glad. He—or his parasites—had lost interest in her once she'd been infested.

That had been their plan all along, she'd realized, the reason they'd tried to coerce Uthari to have sex with her. Not that it had taken sex. Only one disgusting kiss.

Rivlen wiped her brow again, wondering how much longer she would retain her sanity. She also wondered if, as the parasite grew and spread within her, it would try to coerce *her* to fling herself at people in an attempt to infect them through locked lips.

A couple of young officers stepped up to the railing not far from her. They didn't speak aloud, but she caught them pointing at the sea below and at a lifeboat on the deck. Wondering if they could slip away before being forced within range of that beam weapon?

Normally, Rivlen would have hated the idea of cowardice and fleeing from a battle, but in this case, she had a hard time faulting them. The *Soaring Eagle* and other ships might be out of range of the weapon for now, but the dragons knew exactly where they were, and there were a lot of them.

The majority of the fleet was holding position, a number of the kings, admirals, and high-ranking officers convening to try to figure out what they could do against such a foe. Rivlen would have been bitter that she hadn't been invited, but they hadn't invited Uthari either. Possibly because he'd last been heard singing about the end of the world and the death of mankind and how it was something he could drink to. Rivlen didn't need to see his eyes to know the madness gleaming in them had grown stronger.

How long until that happened to her?

She swept her senses back toward Zewnath, wondering if Jak, Malek, and the others were heading this way yet. *Hoping* they were. And that they had a plan.

Rather than detecting their auras, she sensed a dragon approaching and scowled. It was coming from the direction of Zewnath. Had the myriad dragons at the fortress sent it to attack the fleet from behind?

She was about to warn the officer in charge when she recognized the dragon's aura. It was one she'd encountered before. That one-eyed dragon that kept singling out Colonel Sorath and who'd fled when she and the druids had taken down its buddy.

There was something else familiar about it. No, *someone*.

"Professor Freedar?" Rivlen wondered, detecting her substantial aura right next to the dragon's.

At first, she thought the gateship might be sailing alongside the dragon, and that she simply couldn't detect the less substantial auras of Vinjo and the others yet, but Jadora appeared to be *on* the dragon, not next to it.

"Riding it?" Rivlen couldn't imagine how that had come to pass, but then she realized the more likely scenario. It had captured her and was taking her back to the fortress.

But why? To interrogate her? And find out what she knew about the parasite?

Rivlen reached out to her. *Professor Freedar, can you hear me?*

Yes, Captain Rivlen.

Are you a prisoner?

Ostensibly.

What did *that* mean? Rivlen was about to ask for clarification when she sensed a second familiar aura. Lord Malek. He appeared to be right next to Jadora—and the dragon.

Rivlen frowned north into the darkening sky, though they weren't close enough to see yet. *What's going on? Is Jak there too?*

He's not. Jadora hesitated. *Are you with King Uthari?*

Not right now.

Malek said he spoke to Uthari, and he's... not himself.

Yes, he hasn't been himself for a while. Rivlen debated whether to mention that he'd managed to infest her with the parasite and she no longer felt like herself either. Even though she doubted Jadora would judge her for it, the way it had happened embarrassed her. She should have been able to stop him. "It would have been better to have him throw a vial of glass at my feet," she grumbled. From what she'd heard, that was how Uthari had gotten himself—and Jadora—infested.

I was afraid of that. Jak and the others are coming to help you with that situation.

Rivlen frowned, about to ask why Jadora was being vague. As much as Rivlen wanted to see Jak again, she didn't know how he might remedy what seemed a hopeless situation. She also didn't want to see him and the gateship be propelled by the other fleets into a suicidal attack on the fortress.

Then she realized the reason for Jadora's vagueness. *Are you worried Uthari can read my mind?*

Yes. Can he?

Rivlen slumped. *He has gotten past my mental defenses, yes. I'm not a neophyte, and he shouldn't have been able to, but he's dredged up some more ancient magic. He's capable of more than the typical mage.*

"There's a statement of the obvious," she whispered to herself.

In that case, Malek and I are indeed prisoners, caught by a dragon we couldn't defeat, and being taken to the fortress against our wishes.

Rivlen arched her eyebrows, an inkling of hope touching her for the first time in days, if not weeks. She wanted to ask for details, certain Jadora and Malek were up to something—had they somehow taken control of that dragon?—but she dared not. As much as she hated to admit it, Uthari could come out any time and read her thoughts.

Jak will be along soon, Jadora continued.

His face formed in her mind, and a surprising blast of lust flushed her already heated body. Damn, did the parasite want *him* as a host? For her to kiss him so it could spread further?

Please help him in his quest, Jadora said.

Rivlen did her best to squelch the lust, though images of Jak joining her on the ship and them joining each *other* in a cabin flashed through her mind. *I will.*

Good. Thank you.

"There's a dragon flying this way," someone shouted. "Get ready to shoot at it."

Irritation surged up within Rivlen, and she almost drew upon her magic to lash out at the officer. Frowning, she tamped down the response, surprised by its intensity. Maybe the parasite was starting to get to her.

"No," she called out. "It has Lord Malek. If we attack it, it might kill him."

The officer swore, as did several others. "I *do* sense him. And that woman who was gifted all that power for free." He sneered, as if how Jadora had acquired her power mattered one whit right then.

"Let the dragon pass," Rivlen ordered. "Maybe Lord Malek will be able to do something from inside the fortress."

"Not if he's a prisoner."

"Just do what I say," she snapped, the fury rising up again.

The officer narrowed his eyes. "You are not in charge of this ship, Captain."

Rivlen clenched her jaw and wiped sweat out of her eyes. Heat as well as anger flushed her body. It *was* that damn parasite.

The question of attacking the dragon ended up being moot, for the one-eyed creature flew around the fleet, staying out of range, before heading toward the fortress. Rivlen barely caught sight of it, though her stomach knotted when she did. Jadora and Malek were clutched in the dragon's talons, not riding on its back, as she'd originally envisioned. They genuinely did look like prisoners.

How far behind is Jak? Rivlen asked Jadora.

It shouldn't be more than a couple of hours. They'd gotten the gate-ship repaired by the time we left, but I believe this dragon flies more quickly than it does, for we've outpaced them.

Rivlen hoped that the parasite within her couldn't progress

that much in a couple of hours. *There's something I need to tell you,* she added, worried that she might not be able to help Jak as much as she wanted, especially if more than two hours passed. *Uthari also infested me with that parasite.* Rivlen really hoped Jadora wouldn't ask how. *I'm starting to feel its effects.*

A long moment passed, and Rivlen wiped her brow again, grimacing at the heat under her skin and the damned sweat.

I sent two syringes with Jak, Jadora finally said. *Let him use one on you.*

Two syringes of what?

I'd best not go into detail, but trust him, please. You know you can.

Rivlen knew she could trust Jak not to hurt her. She was less positive that he wouldn't take advantage of the situation to cut down Uthari if he could. And she had, for good or ill, promised to protect Uthari.

Trust him, Jadora repeated. *We're going to need all our people working together at their full capacity if we're going to have a chance at this.*

This? Rivlen asked before remembering Jadora wouldn't tell her everything.

Saving the world.

33

You may want to stop using your magic, Yoshartov spoke into Jadora's mind.

For most of the trip, she'd been forming a cushion around herself to keep the dragon's talons from digging painfully into her. Malek, with his honed and hardened zidarr body, hadn't seemed to notice the discomfort, but riding dangling from talons was not an experience that Jadora would recommend.

Now that they neared the fortress, with the dark blue sea passing far below, she allowed her cushion of air to fade. *Because servants wouldn't use magic to better serve their dragon master?* Jadora asked, glancing at Malek.

It will be better if my kind believe you helpless, Yoshartov said.

They will sense our auras, even if we're not using magic, Malek pointed out.

Yes, but your auras are puny and insignificant to dragons. They will think nothing of them if you are not actively doing something. Perhaps you could hang more limply and appear unconscious. And injured. Clearly, we would have had to do battle together before I captured you.

Your dragon has this all worked out, Malek said to Jadora.

My *dragon?* She touched her chest. *Didn't we agree that this one has bonded with Sorath?*

If by bonded with, *you mean locked him in a tower in a fortress overrun by dragons, I suppose so.*

Colonel Sorath was my first servant! Yoshartov said, pleased. *I defeated him in battle before capturing him. That is what the other dragons will expect.*

Jadora sighed and attempted to hang limply while appearing injured. Whatever kept the other dragons from questioning Yoshartov. Though she was more worried about them noticing that he was turning blue. Every time she looked, more of his scales had transitioned.

Malek gazed behind his shoulder and off to the left. They'd passed the fleets, and she didn't know what discussions, if any, he'd had with Uthari.

Hers with Rivlen had been unsettling, and she worried that Jak, even with Tezi and Shikari to help him, would be outmatched. What if Uthari and Rivlen were beyond reason and wouldn't let him inject them with the bacteria? When she'd parted ways with Jak, she'd assumed that Rivlen would be an ally, not another potential foe.

After we finish in the fortress, we'll join them, Malek told her, perhaps thinking along similar lines.

He was likely more worried about Uthari than Rivlen, but Jadora believed he was also worried about Jak.

Yes. Wreckage floating on the sea below drew her eye. It had once been a mageship. She grimaced.

With its hull broken and strewn across the waves, its magic had been destroyed, and it gave off no aura. Nor did she detect anyone alive down there. At first, she believed the officers might have been taken prisoner, but no. She glimpsed bodies floating in the water. If the dragons' great weapon had not only destroyed the ship but also obliterated the crew, the druids who'd survived when their raft had been blasted had been fortunate.

Were she and Malek delusional to believe they could sneak in without being discovered? And could they know for certain that Yoshartov was on their side? What if he was still under the parasites' influence and delivering them to his kin, to ensure the bacteria could never be put to use?

Ahead, the great blue-black fortress came into view, spires and towers rising up from its mile-wide floating platform. A single slinky long appendage dangled below it from the center, the tip spiked, as if it were itself a dragon tail.

Even if she hadn't sensed two dozen or more dragons inside, the fortress alone would have been ominous, dark and full of spikes that made her think of talons and fangs. She spotted a tall tower with an oval window near the top that reminded her of an eye. Was that where the weapon was located? Where the beam erupted from? She sensed great energy within the tower and feared the weapon wouldn't be easily destroyed.

And yet the questions Malek had asked Yoshartov suggested he wanted to stop there first. He wanted to help the fleets.

Jadora reluctantly agreed, though she wished they could prioritize curing the dragons. The problem was that as soon as they started shooting the creatures, they would know she and Malek weren't *servants* and attack back.

Malek?

Yes? He gazed solemnly over at her.

In case we don't make it... I love you.

I love you whether we make it or not. He smiled.

You know what I mean.

Yes.

Please take care of Jak if anything happens to me.

It won't, but I will. Malek stretched a hand toward her, frustrated that they were too far apart to touch, and he lowered it, his eyes sad.

We may have a problem, Yoshartov said.

Three dragons sprang from nests perched atop towers.

That most definitely looks like a problem, Jadora said.

Malek didn't draw upon his magic, other than to create a barrier around himself, but his hands dropped to his weapons. He hadn't yet removed the rifle strapped to his back, but his fingers twitched toward it.

Jadora touched the pocket in her pack that held the vials of acid from the water world. It might be able to eat through a dragon's barrier, as it had eaten through the barrier around the gateship, but she lowered her hand. She had to save it for the fortress and hope it could destroy that weapon.

Are they speaking with you? Jadora asked Yoshartov.

Yes. These are the same dragons who questioned me before. They say I feel odd to them.

Another time, Jadora might have joked that Yoshartov *was* an odd dragon, but the words worried her too much. If the others knew he'd changed, they wouldn't welcome him as an ally. She grew more certain they'd already made up their minds that he was an enemy as they flew straight toward him, their talons flexing.

Can you get us to the fortress and drop us inside? Malek asked. *Then lead them off?*

More dragons wait inside. They will sense you. Even as he spoke, Yoshartov dove, then flapped his wings hard to veer away from the approaching dragons.

Try to drop us by that tower, Malek said. *I'm sure flying will be easier if you're not carrying us.*

That's a truth.

Malek looked at Jadora. *I'll do my best to camouflage us when we land.*

She didn't think that would work, not with two dozen dragons searching for them, but she made herself smile and nod. What choice did they have?

You are not the Yoshartov we know! one of the dragons cried as all three gave chase.

One hurled a magical attack at him.

Jadora drew upon her power and attempted to reinforce the barrier Yoshartov automatically erected around himself, but the sheer power of the attack made her feel puny and insignificant.

As Yoshartov banked, wheeled, and dove, Malek focused on the fortress. Other dragons had risen up in their nests to watch. Jadora shook her head as queasiness assailed her stomach. With so many watching, she didn't see how she and Malek could sneak inside.

A fireball the size of a sun roared toward Yoshartov. *You have been turned! You are no longer one of us! The humans did this!*

Right on all accounts...

You are foolish, Yoshartov replied. *I am the same mighty dragon I've always been.*

You are no longer one of us. We'll not allow you near the fortress. They were indeed cutting him off, keeping Yoshartov from getting close enough to drop off Malek and Jadora.

Several times, he attempted to fly toward the tower, but the defenders kept cutting him off. Fireballs came not only from the three dragons in the sky but from those inside the fortress.

A red glow started up behind the window in the tower.

Jadora pointed. *If that beam strikes us, all three of us will be dead.*

I cannot get close, humans, Yoshartov said. *What do you want me to do?*

Release us as close to the fortress as you can, Malek said.

Please, Jadora added. *You've been a very good dragon to help us.*

A fireball slammed into Yoshartov's barrier, orange light flaring all around them. A mental attack must have gripped his mind, for he screamed in pain, his wingbeats faltering.

He flew in the direction of the fortress, but he was losing altitude. He careened not toward the dragon lair but toward the icy glacier island below.

Yoshartov roared and shook his head, trying to shake off the mental attack. Fireballs followed him until they were under the fortress. At that point, it acted as a shield, and the only dragons able to attack them were the three chasing them. Unfortunately, those three had no problem keeping up and casting more attacks. Fire and waves of sheer devastating energy rained down upon Yoshartov.

Jadora kept adding her energy to his, helping to reinforce his barrier so it wouldn't fail. So focused on that was she that it startled her when Yoshartov let go of her. She couldn't keep from crying out.

Malek plummeted beside her. As they tumbled toward the glacier, Yoshartov wheeled in the sky and flew back toward the three dragons, beating his wings to sail through the fire they kept launching at him.

Malek's power wrapped around Jadora, and he slowed their descent. Yoshartov roared and launched fire of his own, a great wall of flames that filled the air and hid the other three dragons from Jadora's view. And—she realized—hid her and Malek from *their* view.

Take us up, not down, Malek. She pointed toward the bottom of the fortress, protrusions jutting down from the platform and that dragon-steel tail dangling from the center.

He understood immediately and used his magic to levitate them upward.

Jadora eyed the glacier below as it receded, spotted more wreckage and dead mages on the icy white ground, and forced her gaze back toward the fortress.

Deliberately trying to mask their presence, Yoshartov launched more walls of fire at his fellow dragons. But he was in pain. Jadora could sense it. He was running out of the energy to fly and protect himself from their attacks.

Go back to the gateship and Shikari and Jak, Jadora urged him as Malek swept them closer to the bottom of the fortress. *Please don't sacrifice yourself for us. We didn't mean for you to be killed.*

Yoshartov was too busy fighting and flying to respond. All three dragons stayed on his tail, seemingly furious at him for changing back and attempting to sneak in. Yoshartov flew away from the island and the fortress, as if to obey Jadora and head back toward Zewnath, but too many attacks pummeled him. Relentless, the other dragons tore away his defenses and kept blasting him with their power.

For a final time, Yoshartov's wingbeats faltered, then halted completely. Wings limp, he plummeted toward the sea, then splashed into it, disappearing under the surface. The other three dragons pulled up scant feet above the waves. Yoshartov's aura disappeared from Jadora's awareness.

"Damn it," she whispered, as Malek guided them to the dangling tail. She'd succeeded at curing one of the dragons only to see him die in front of her eyes.

"Grab hold," Malek whispered, gripping the tail.

She did, the dragon steel like ice under their palms, and looked up. A hundred feet above loomed the ominous platform of the fortress. If there was a door or any way in from the bottom, she couldn't see or sense it.

A whisper of power wrapped around her, Malek attempting to camouflage them. And not a moment too soon. Two of the dragons, apparently convinced that Yoshartov was dead, headed back toward their nests in the fortress, but the third flew toward the island below. Looking for them.

Jadora held utterly still, though the cold metal burned her palms with its icy touch. As the dragon flew down to the glacier below, searching among the wreckage and sniffing at a few of the bodies, she didn't use her magic and barely dared to breathe. Malek's eyes were closed as he concentrated on camouflaging them, diminishing their auras and making them appear to be nothing more than part of the fortress structure.

Had it not been made from dragon steel itself, its aura helping to drown out their own magical signatures, it might not have worked. But the dragon seemed to believe they'd landed below, not levitated themselves upward. Maybe it didn't realize humans could do that. Eventually, after flicking a few corpses over, it flew back to the top of the fortress without looking their way.

Jadora exhaled slowly. She wouldn't presume to believe they were safe, especially when their only ally capable of standing up to dragons had died, but they at least had a minute to figure out what to do next.

Or, perhaps they didn't, for Malek immediately started climbing. She gaped as he scaled the tail, pulling himself up easily, though there were no handholds.

Do you think there's a door up there? Jadora asked.

Malek glanced down at her. *I think I know someone with acid capable of eating through dragon steel.*

You want me to waste my acid trying to burrow a hole in the floor of a fortress? I don't have an unlimited amount.

The alternative is to levitate up past all the dragons perched in the towers and on the walls. My meager attempts at camouflage will be insufficient to escape their notice. I'm hoping, however, that they're not monitoring the floor.

I may be able to spare a little acid.

Excellent.

Using her magic as an aid, Jadora followed him up the tail, doing her best not to look at the long drop below. She reminded herself that she could levitate back up if she slipped, but that knowledge didn't keep her heart from pounding in her chest.

Human instincts about the horrors of falling refused to be quelled even by powerful magic.

Malek paused ten feet below the bottom and waited for her to catch up. As they faced each other, the icy blue-black tail between them, he smiled slightly. *You're clinking.*

Are the vials and syringes in my pockets disturbing your attempt to camouflage us?

I believe I can compensate for them. Malek touched her cheek, his fingers icy from gripping the cold dragon steel, and continued to the top.

As they'd guessed, there wasn't anything so handy as a door or access panel.

This won't be easy, she said as she maneuvered open a flap on her backpack, a chill wind whipping at her braid.

I'd like to tell you that you have plenty of time. Malek looked toward the north, then upward, as if he could see through the fortress toward the dragons.

But?

The dragons are moving about. They may know we weren't killed.

Jadora sensed the same and frowned. *I'll do my best to hurry. Here. Hold my vials.*

Always.

~

Jak paced on the deck of the gateship, circling around and around the portal, which was once more balanced with magical straps holding it in place as they sailed south. Shikari alternated between flying and perching in the bow of the ship. Behind them, a couple of miles back, came the druid vessel, another raft. Once again, it carried roamers and mercenaries as well as druids. A few of the Thorn Company mercenaries were also on the gateship, though Jak had wished most of the women—most of *everyone*—had stayed behind. Only those with dragon-steel weapons would be able to help, and his mother had requisitioned most of the bullets for her mission.

They've arrived at the fortress, Shikari told him.

Not that long ago, the gateship had passed over the southern coastline of Zewnath, and they were flying toward the Glacier Islands.

They? Jak asked. *Mother and Malek?*

Yes. Something happened. Shikari hesitated. *I think Yoshartov might be dead.*

Dead? Jak jerked to a stop.

They attacked him.

What about Mother and Malek?

I can't sense them, but it may only be because they're close to the fortress, and its aura is overpowering.

Jak sank into a squat. It could also be because they were dead. If the dragon hadn't made it, how could they have?

They are clever, Shikari told him. *Certainly cleverer than that haughty dragon who is overly obsessed with servants and fish. They have likely survived.*

I hope so. Jak rose, walked to Shikari's side, and gave him a pat. *Thank you for keeping me apprised. You're a good dragon.*

Yes, and far cleverer than Yoshartov.

Undoubtedly.

Jak caught Gorsith glowering at him from the hatchway. He'd been doing a lot of that since Malek and Mother had left, and Jak worried he wouldn't be the ally to him that Malek had believed.

He didn't know what Uthari had told Gorsith, or what rumors had reached his ears, but even if it had been nothing but the truth... the truth was a good reason for a zidarr to despise and distrust Jak. He wished he had another kerzor with him. Just in case.

I sense your mate, Shikari said.

She's still alive? Bolstered by hope, Jak searched the sky ahead for mageships as he swept out with his senses. He couldn't yet see the fleet, but he did sense the fortress and smaller auras between it and the gateship. A lot of smaller auras.

"How many mageships have gathered for the battle?" he wondered.

It felt like a lot more than had left Utharika with Uthari.

There are close to a hundred in the sky, Shikari said. *And about ten have been wrecked on the island and in the waves below.*

Jak scowled. *Are the rest fighting now?*

They are waiting outside the range of the fortress's large weapon. The dragons are not leaving their fortress to attack them. Both sides appear to be assessing each other or waiting for something.

Like the arrival of the portal? Jak eyed it looming on the deck beside them.

The portal had objected when he'd suggested they should put Vinjo's hibernation device back on it, showing Jak images of it casting lightning bolts and helping defend the ship.

He'd been reluctant to openly fly south with it, its aura shining through the camouflaging magic on the gateship, but it had occurred to him that it would be better for the dragons to focus on them than Mother and Malek. As much as Jak hated to admit it, what he and Shikari and the mercenaries and druids could do in this battle would be of secondary importance. It would be up to Mother and Malek to make a difference.

"We are here to be distracting," he murmured, though he also wanted to find Rivlen.

Jabbing Uthari with a syringe full of death-darter bacteria could wait until after the dragons were defeated, but Jak continued to worry about her safety. The sooner he saw her and could make sure Uthari wasn't hurting her, the better.

Since Shikari had sensed Rivlen, Jak searched through the auras on the mageships until he located hers.

A smile split his lips. Yes, she *was* alive. But—his smile faltered—she stood at the railing on the same mageship as Uthari. And Uthari wasn't that far from her.

What if he was threatening her? Or controlling her?

Jak double-checked to make sure the syringes of death-darter bacteria were in his pocket. He envisioned himself springing onto the mageship, pulling Rivlen from Uthari's grip, and jabbing a needle into him. Unfortunately, as noble as the vision was, it wouldn't work unless he caught Uthari by surprise. Even if the parasites had taken him over, he would still be powerful. For all Jak knew, he might be *more* powerful than he had been before.

And what of his crew? Dozens of officers patrolled the deck and would be quick to aid their king.

Jak glanced at the portal, wondering if it would help him. He was about to ask when Rivlen reached out to him.

Jak, she purred into his mind, her telepathic tone coming across as sultry.

Rivlen, are you all right? As much as he appreciated sultry, especially from her, this was hardly the time for bedroom thoughts. *Has Uthari done anything to you?*

He's done much, but it was unsatisfactory. She shared an image of Uthari grabbing her head and kissing her, trying to shove his tongue in her mouth.

Jak rocked back in shock. He had no trouble imagining mages wanting sex with her, but Uthari? He was three *hundred* years old. Jak had never even seen him look at a woman.

He tried to force you to... Jak trailed off, struggling to get the words out.

I drove him off with my new sword. Rivlen shared an image of a dragon-steel blade with him.

Where did you get it?

Uthari.

Is he, uh, trying to seduce you?

If he was, it wouldn't matter. I want you. She purred the words into his mind. *Come to me, Jak.*

He stared in the direction of the ships he couldn't yet see. Even though she was a straightforward woman and not shy about expressing her desires, she didn't sound like herself.

I am coming to you, he replied, *but we have a few issues to resolve first.*

Of course. I want you at my side in this battle.

I want that too.

Come to me, she ordered again.

Yes, ma'am.

Jak mulled over the odd conversation, then searched for his mother's and Malek's auras, wanting their guidance. But if Shikari hadn't been able to sense them, he wouldn't either.

Mother? Jak tried, projecting his thoughts broadly toward the fortress and hoping no dragons cared enough to intercept his message. *Are you alive in there?*

Ssh, came her soft response from the center of the fortress's huge aura.

He sagged in relief that she was alive. At least something was going right.

We're still alive, she said, *but we haven't been able to implement our plan yet.*

What happened? Jak attempted to pinpoint his telepathy based on where her voice came from. If she was hiding, he didn't want to lead the dragons to her.

They recognized that Yoshartov was no longer one of them and attacked. He dropped Malek and me, and we're hiding in the bowels of the fortress.

I can't distinguish your auras from the dragon steel.

Unfortunately, the dragons have keener senses.

Jak's stomach knotted. *They've captured you?*

Not yet, but we may not have much time. We're going to try to reach the weapon to destroy it, but it's guarded.

Can't you start sprinkling acid around and shooting dragons with your special bullets?

We have a limited amount of both things, and neither would be effective from our current location. She sent him an image of a dark tunnel—or maybe a shaft under the floor. It wasn't tall enough to stand in, and only a power tendril running through it provided light. Malek was crawling ahead of Mother, his sword in hand. *If we can get to the tower and up in it, that may work.*

Be careful.

We're attempting to be so, but using telepathy might make it easier for them to find us.

Sorry. I just... I've been in contact with Rivlen, and she doesn't seem like herself.

I spoke to her earlier. She admitted she's been infested with the parasite.

What? How? The image of Uthari forcing a kiss on Rivlen came unbidden—and unwelcome—to Jak's mind. Had he done that to spread the parasite? *Never mind.*

It should have occurred to me earlier that he might have spread it to others. I regret not giving you more syringes, though I hadn't had long to grow more of the death-darter bacteria. Until our trip, I had no idea that I would need so much more.

It's all right. I'll figure out a way to inject both of them. Jak looked at Shikari, hoping the dragon could help him stand up to Uthari's power. He doubted he could talk Gorsith into levitating over to the mageship at his side.

Be careful.

Didn't I just give that command to you?

Yes, but I think it applies to both our situations.

Unfortunately, yes.

Your fleets are not far from the fortress. Shikari pointed his snout toward ships now visible ahead, their running lights standing out against the darkening sky.

The fortress itself had no lights, since dragons could see in the dark, but Jak sensed that it wasn't much farther; it floated a couple of miles beyond the fleet.

We need to get over to the ship with Rivlen on it, Jak told Shikari. *Can you fly me to it?*

If the gateship got close, he might be able to levitate himself over, but if he arrived on a dragon, the officers might think twice about attacking him.

Will this vessel not go there? Shikari asked.

I don't know, but I— Jak paused.

Gorsith left the hatch and walked toward Jak.

Jak tensed. "My lord," he said as politely as he could, though he couldn't keep from frowning.

When Gorsith had started wandering around hand-in-hand with Kywatha, Jak had hoped he would want to ride on the druid raft, but Malek had ordered him to fly on the gateship and protect the portal.

Gorsith speared Jak with his eyes. "Uthari has spoken to me."

Jak almost said that *Rivlen* had spoken to *him*, and that was a far more appealing person to communicate with, but he doubted the zidarr would appreciate his wit.

"Oh?" he asked warily.

"He wants me to bring you to him, preferably with my hand wrapped tightly around your neck."

"I'm prepared to go see him," Jak made himself say, though he wished there were a way he could get to Rivlen and inject her with the bacteria first. He told himself that it didn't matter, that even after she was injected, it would take hours, if not days, for her body to fight off the parasite, but that didn't keep him from wanting to help her get it out of her body as soon as possible. Uthari... Jak wished Uthari and his parasite-ridden body would simply fall over the railing of his mageship, never to be seen again. "A strangulation hold won't be required."

"He said it would be appreciated, not required," Gorsith said dryly, though his brow furrowed. "He sounded very odd though. He kept growling into my mind and saying *we* instead of *I*."

"That's because the parasites have control of him."

Gorsith eyed Jak skeptically. "Uthari is a great and powerful wizard. Nothing so insubstantial could affect him."

"You're wrong. The insubstantial parasites have been affecting the dragons—dragons that are lot more powerful and greater than Uthari—for millennia. You can tell, because they talk like that, saying *we* instead of *I*. They think of themselves as a collective rather than individuals."

"An intelligent, talking parasite?"

"They're what's altered the personalities of the dragons. I don't know if their intelligence comes from their hosts or how exactly it works, but it doesn't matter. All that matters is that they have control." Jak shrugged, not wanting to discuss it further with him, not when Uthari's mageship was in view. And there. As he'd sensed, there was Rivlen at the railing, her dark hair down around her shoulders.

That would have alerted Jak to something wrong even if her earlier words hadn't. She *always* wore her hair in a bun when she was in uniform, which she was, with a dragon-steel sword hanging from the belt of her trousers.

Gorsith also looked toward the ship, but his gaze locked onto someone else at the railing. Uthari.

He stood ten feet away from Rivlen, his fingers gripping the railing as he gazed hungrily at the portal.

The dragons had made it clear from the beginning that they wanted it. Or had it been the *parasites* that wished to have it? So they could control who came from and went to this world?

Uthari's blue eyes gleamed across the distance, his enraptured face making Jak shiver. He hadn't liked Uthari before, but the wizard worried him even more now. He wished he hadn't told Malek he would do his best to cure Uthari. If he'd forced a kiss on Rivlen and intentionally infested her… he ought to die. Jak wanted to kill him, not cure him.

Look out, Shikari said.

Sensing Gorsith's approach, Jak ducked and skittered back.

"What are you doing?" Jak blurted.

"Taking you to my king." Gorsith lifted an open hand, making it clear he intended to obey that order literally and wrap his fingers around Jak's neck.

Jak sprang to put the portal between them, though he had little doubt that a zidarr could catch him.

You have been a tick for months, boy, Uthari spoke into his mind. *We will now take your life, while Malek is away and won't know what happened.*

Why do some parasites care about me or my life? Jak replied, though he didn't take his focus from Gorsith—and stayed out of his reach.

Unfortunately, Gorsith didn't need to reach him to hurt him. He flicked a finger and ripped Jak's barrier from him, painfully tearing it away as if it were Jak's own skin.

Jak gasped and stumbled back, struggling to reapply his defenses, to protect himself. He tugged his hat low on his head, willing the dragon-steel medallion to protect him from magic, but it never had in the past. He could only assume there wasn't enough dragon steel in it so it didn't have the power of the weapons.

Gorsith drew a knife and leaped through the portal toward him.

Shikari roared and rushed in, putting himself between Gorsith and Jak. Though his eyes widened, Gorsith didn't draw back in fear.

He swiped at Shikari and barked, "Get out of the way, little dragon. I have my orders."

Shikari roared at him as he telepathically told Jak, *Get on.*

Uhm?

We must go rescue your mate!

Not to mention escaping the determined zidarr...

As Shikari roared again at Gorsith, using his magic to push him farther away, Jak was able to climb onto his back. Since he'd been considering riding him over to start with, he couldn't object.

It wasn't until he was astride, with Shikari springing over the railing and into the sky, that Jak realized they wouldn't be able to retrieve Rivlen without the help of a lot of magic. At Shikari's size, the thought of two full-grown humans riding him was silly. And where could they go to hide from Uthari's wrath?

But Shikari arrowed straight toward the *Soaring Eagle*, as if he had a plan, leaving Gorsith shouting orders for them to come back.

You will grab your mate, Shikari said. *I will keep the wizard from harming us.*

And what if the crazy parasite-ridden wizard was too much for Shikari to handle? Or Rivlen didn't want to join them? And where would they go after they had her? Back to the gateship and Gorsith's waiting weapons?

This might not work, Jak said.

It will. We are mighty!

Jak could only shake his head and hang on as Shikari flew toward Rivlen—and Uthari.

34

GORSITH'S SHOUTS PERMEATED THROUGH THE SHIP FROM THE DECK above. Tezi didn't know what was happening but assumed they'd reached the fortress and the battle.

She grabbed her axe and shouted, "Come on, Lieutenant," to Sasko, who'd been in navigation with Vinjo. On the way to the hatch, she spotted Yelotta, Tinder, and Basher and also told them it was time for battle. She almost called Grunk before remembering that Kywatha and the other druids had requested he join them on the raft. He'd been reluctant to leave Tezi, but she'd assured him that she and Thorn Company could handle themselves. She hoped she was right.

"Are corporals supposed to be that perky?" Tinder asked as Tezi ran for the ladder.

"Not in the least," Basher said. "Especially not when heading into a hopeless battle."

"Maybe she's broken," Tinder said. "Like one of Vinjo's gadgets."

"Vinjo's gadgets don't break," Sasko said. "He's a brilliant engineer."

Someone made gagging sounds, but Tezi was already opening the hatch and surging outside, so she didn't know who. It didn't matter. All that mattered was that the others followed and they shot some dragons with their new bullets. Jadora had taken a lot of them, but Tezi and the other mercenaries still had some left. She hoped it would be enough.

A chilly sea breeze smacked her in the face as she climbed out on deck, expecting to find Jak and Shikari there, guarding the portal. Hadn't they said they were doing that?

The only one there was Gorsith, who stood at the railing with the stock of a magelock rifle pressed into his shoulder. No, that was one of the black-powder rifles loaded with dragon-steel ammunition.

As Tezi jogged toward him, she peered into the twilight sky, looking for his target. He fired, the round blazing blue as it sped away. Sped away and almost smacked into the back of a half-sized dragon that she was certain was on *their* side.

Yes, Jak was riding on the back, holding his hat on with one hand as Shikari dipped and zigzagged. Trying to be an erratic target because Gorsith was *shooting* at him.

"What are you doing?" Tezi rushed up and grabbed for the firearm.

Her first urge was to use her axe to slice it in half, but Gorsith saw her coming and jumped back, raising the weapon, as if to parry a blow. She doubted the rifle could stand up to her axe simply because dragon steel rounds were chambered inside, but she didn't want to fight a zidarr.

"Stay out of it," Gorsith barked, glancing at Shikari.

He and Jak were still bobbing and dodging, expecting more bullets, but they were also flying toward another mageship. One of *many* mageships. They'd caught up with the fleet. *Multiple* fleets, but Jak was heading for one of Uthari's black-hulled vessels.

"Why are you shooting at our allies?" Tezi asked Gorsith.

Uthari is telling him to, Jak spoke into her mind. *Distract him, please. We need to help Uthari and Rivlen—whether they want our help or not.*

Tezi didn't fully understand—all she could imagine was that Uthari and Rivlen were in danger because of the other fleets' mages—but she didn't need to understand to know it was a problem when Gorsith turned back to the railing with his rifle raised. His target was unmistakable.

"No," Tezi growled, lunging toward him with her axe raised.

She would aim for the rifle, not the zidarr, but she wouldn't let him shoot her friends.

Gorsith got a shot off, then had to deal with her. He snarled, yanking the rifle aside so her blade didn't strike it, and launched a side kick toward her stomach. Tezi whipped the axe in to defend herself from the flying foot, and he didn't complete the kick, not with the risk of cutting himself on the wicked blade. She tried to knock his leg aside, hoping to make him lose his balance, but he was too fast for that. He sprang back, landing in a crouch and drawing a sword made from lesser dragon steel.

"You mercenaries stay out of this," he growled, glancing toward Sasko, Tinder, Basher, and Yelotta, all up on deck now. "You don't even know what's going on."

"I don't think you do either," Tezi said as a gout of orange fire came from the mageship ahead of Shikari and Jak.

It flew from Uthari's fingers and headed toward them as surely as Gorsith's bullets had. A barrier around Shikari protected him and Jak, and the fire parted as it struck it.

Ten feet away from Uthari, Rivlen crouched with a dragon-steel sword raised. Tezi expected her to run and strike, or at least try to stop, Uthari. But he glanced at her with a savage sneer and must have given a telepathic order, for she didn't move from her position. Uthari spread his fingers and launched more gouts of fire at Jak and Shikari.

The dragonling's wingbeats faltered. He was trying to get to the mageship, but he seemed to struggle to carry Jak, fly, and keep his barrier up all at the same time.

Jak rested his hands on his scales, his body rigid with concentration, and Shikari's wingbeats strengthened again. Just in time, for mages on the ship, responding to Uthari's orders, started throwing fireballs at them.

"Rivlen!" Jak cried.

Her hand twitched upward, and Tezi thought she would launch one of her walls of fire at Uthari, orders be damned, but her hand froze in midair. Was she torn? Between Jak and her king?

Why, damn it? Jak was her lover, and he cared about her a lot more than Uthari did. Tezi was sure of that.

Shikari flew under the mageship so he would have a reprieve from the fireballs. But Uthari barked an order toward a mageship flying near his, one that could target Jak and Shikari below them. Several officers lined up at the railing, readying their firepower.

Gorsith raised his rifle again, his movements jerky, as if he was half under someone else's control. Maybe he was. He'd already admitted Uthari was commanding him.

"Help them, Rivlen!" Tezi yelled, knowing nobody else on that ship would.

Rivlen's face contorted, and she shook her head.

Indignation flared within Tezi—how could Rivlen care about Jak and not help defend him? When she spotted Gorsith turning his firearm toward Shikari again, she snarled and sprang. She didn't have the power to stop Uthari from a distance, but she could stop Gorsith.

Tezi leaped in, swinging for the firearm again, but he anticipated her, and jumped into the air. With his zidarr-enhanced muscles, he flew up and landed on top of the portal.

"Stay out of this, mercenary," he growled down at her, "or I'll shoot you next."

Tezi ground her teeth, wanting to deny that it was a valid threat, but it was. Unless her axe took control of her reflexes to dodge his shots, she wouldn't have a defense against dragon-steel bullets.

A rifle fired, startling her. It wasn't the one in Gorsith's hands. The noise came from near the hatch, and the round clanged off the top of the portal near the zidarr's boot.

"If you shoot our corporal," Tinder said, readying a second shot. "We'll shoot you."

Sasko, Basher, and Yelotta stood at her side, ready to put the other firearms with dragon-steel bullets to use.

"That's right," Basher said. "And we'll *like* it."

"Don't waste the dragon-steel bullets, you fools," Gorsith yelled, not appearing daunted.

"You mean like you're wasting them on our ally?" Tezi asked.

"I'm following orders."

"Well, we're following orders too." Basher aimed her rifle at his chest.

Gorsith glared down at her from the top of the portal, then crouched low and aimed his rifle at her. Basher fired, but he must have anticipated the shot, for he rolled off before it zipped through the air where he'd been.

After landing, Gorsith sprinted at them, sword and rifle in hand.

Tezi lunged around the portal, intending to help, but it flared a much brighter blue than the bullets had, and a single branch of red lightning struck Gorsith in the back. He cried out and flew forward, his entire body spasming as electricity flowed through him. He landed on the deck on his stomach, managing to keep his sword, but the rifle flew from his grip and skidded toward the hatch.

Sasko picked it up and tossed it to Tezi. Though she preferred her axe, she accepted it without hesitating, knowing she needed a ranged weapon to help Jak.

Another branch of red lightning shot from the portal, this time heading toward the other mageship. It split and arced toward two officers trying to incinerate Jak and Shikari. They saw it coming and flung themselves to the deck, but the lightning found them nonetheless.

Jak roared, as if he were a dragon, and cast fireballs at the mages who'd been hurling magic at Shikari. Maybe he'd figured out how to attack while the dragon kept defending them. However he was doing it, he managed to get off a number of withering strikes. Thanks to the magical blows, and the mages' blatant fear of the portal, those who'd been attacking Jak backed away from the railing.

Tezi looked for Uthari, her heart thundering as she imagined taking advantage of the chaos to fire at *him*, but he'd moved close to Rivlen and grabbed her arm. Wanting that dragon-steel sword for himself? As protection from the portal?

Maybe, but as Shikari and Jak reappeared on the opposite side of his mageship, Shikari's fangs on display and Jak's eyes full of rage, Tezi realized Uthari might want protection from *them*.

~

Jadora crawled through a horizontal shaft, with her head brushing the low ceiling and a glowing yellow energy conduit humming beside them. The experience brought to mind her and Jak's attempt to escape from Utharika months earlier, running through the tunnels under the sky city, afraid Malek would catch up with them. It was such a strange series of events that had caused her to be here with him, allies instead of enemies. *Lovers* instead of enemies.

She shook her head as he led the way around a bend and

willed herself to focus. Malek continued to use his magic in an attempt to camouflage them, but they'd left a hole in the bottom of the fortress near that tail. Jadora sensed dragons flying about, above the mile-wide structure as well as over the glacier below, and believed Malek was right, that they were looking for their intruders. Intruders that they knew carried a way to cure them, something the parasites in control definitely did not want.

This reminds me of Utharika and other sky cities, Malek whispered into her mind.

I noticed. I'm going to guess that our mages originally learned the magic and technology required to build them from dragons.

Does that fascinate you? He smiled back at her, though his eyes were haunted, as he no doubt worried about Uthari.

Jadora was as worried about Jak, but she returned his smile, preferring to keep her mind off those concerns. *Obviously.*

I thought so.

Malek led her down another shaft, attempting to take them toward the tower and the weapon. Thanks to her senses, she knew where it was, but she also knew where the dragons were. They'd stopped examining the wreckage on the island below, and she had a feeling they'd figured out that Yoshartov's supposed prisoners weren't among the dead humans down there. One was flying up toward the tail—to examine the bottom of the fortress?

From a distance, the new hole might not be that noticeable, especially since the interior of the fortress was made from the same dark dragon steel as the exterior, but she had little doubt that a close-up inspection would reveal where they'd entered.

Malek halted and lifted a hand.

She stretched her senses ahead of him but didn't detect anything except the magic of the conduit and the pervasive dragon steel.

We're not alone, Malek told her.

Uhm? She checked on the dragon below the fortress again and cursed under her breath. He'd flown closer, and she worried he'd seen the hole.

Not answering, Malek continued forward, his sword in hand. What enemy did he think they would find inside the shaft? She didn't sense any dragons ahead waiting to pounce.

A male voice groaned and said, "I would have rather run into a dragon."

"Colonel Sorath," Malek replied coolly.

"No fighting," Jadora whispered, though she didn't believe they would spring for each other's throats when they were surrounded by dragons. "We came to rescue them, remember."

She tried to peer around Malek in the tight shaft, hoping Captain Ferroki was with Sorath.

"We didn't think anyone knew we were alive," came her voice from behind Sorath. "We've been trapped in here for days."

Jadora slumped against the side of the shaft. Thank Shylezar. "We didn't know you were alive until recently. First, the seer saw you in a vision, and then Yoshartov verified that he'd brought you here."

"You talked to that crazy bastard?" Sorath asked.

"Yes," Jadora said. "He brought us here, but... I think he's dead. The other dragons attacked him."

"Why?" Sorath asked. "Besides the obvious that he's a loon."

"He was reverting into one of the untainted dragons."

An angry and suspicious screech came from below the fortress, echoing up into their shaft, and Jadora shut her mouth.

Intruders! a dragon cried telepathically, its powerful voice thundering painfully in her mind. *The humans have infested our fortress like termites!*

Sorath groaned. "You led them to us?"

"We need to get to the tower with the beam weapon in it," Malek whispered, ignoring the accusation. "Can you lead us to it?"

"Yes, but I don't think you can destroy it. We've tried to sabotage a bunch of stuff, and dragon steel doesn't work." Grunts sounded as Sorath turned around in the shaft, struggling in the tight space.

"We have a way," Malek said.

Another screech sounded, and Jadora sensed more dragons flying toward the hole she'd made. They wouldn't be able to fit through, but if they wanted to, they could tear another hole right under their shaft and pull them out.

As Sorath and Ferroki led her and Malek forward, Jadora reached out, hoping Jak had reached Rivlen and Uthari. Thanks to his earlier communication, she knew he was in the area, but she also knew he had his hands full.

Jak? Can you hear me?

After a pause, he replied. *Yes, but I'm in a little trouble right now.*

Jadora winced. *So are we. If there's any chance you can talk Uthari into leading the fleet to attack, we could use a distraction.*

He shared an image with her of him and Shikari battling Uthari and more mage officers than she could count. *I'll try to convince him of that, but he's not acting rationally right now. I think he wants the dragons—the parasites—to win.*

I'm afraid that may be true.

"I think we're on our own," Jadora said when Malek glanced back.

Another screech came from below along with a surge of power and the wrenching of metal. The bottom of the shaft shook.

"I was afraid of that," Malek said.

~

Jak's plans to swoop in, grab Rivlen, and take her from the clutches of Uthari and every other officer on the mageship were dashed when the old wizard grabbed her arm. The influence of her dragon-steel sword protected him from the lightning strikes the portal was launching and any magic Jak would have sent his way.

Uthari's eyes narrowed as he lifted a hand to target him.

Brace yourself, Shikari, Jak warned.

They'd been working together, Shikari lowering his barrier for split seconds, just long enough for Jak to cast fireballs, then raising it again before enemy attacks could strike them.

I am braced. Clever dragons know when they are being targeted, and they make plans.

As Shikari flew toward Uthari and Rivlen, Jak only had time to ask, *What plan?*

To rescue your mate.

They arrowed toward Rivlen, fireballs bouncing off Shikari's barrier. Jak couldn't tell from the anguished expression on her face if she wanted to be rescued. She looked like she was in pain. Or fighting off a mental compulsion? Unfortunately, she didn't—or couldn't—jerk away from Uthari's grip. It would be hard to grab her without taking him as well.

Shikari roared at him. Uthari flexed his fingers and cast a fireball at his snout.

Jak winced as the flames scorched the air all around, but Shikari strengthened his defenses, and the fire didn't touch them. They landed on the deck, Shikari knocking people over with his tail while using his magic to keep the other mages back.

Rivlen, Jak spoke into her mind. *Get on Shikari's back with me. We need to get out of here and... figure things out.* He feared she wouldn't come if he said he wanted to jab a needle into her.

Uthari opened his mouth and spouted what sounded like gibberish. At first, Jak thought he might have gone mad, the parasite affecting his mind, but Shikari yelped in pain and shook his head.

He attacks me through my barrier! Shikari shook his head even more, as if something had burrowed into one of his ears. His entire body convulsed.

Jak launched a fireball at Uthari.

The old wizard smiled icily at him and didn't so much as blink. His proximity to Rivlen's sword protected him, though Jak's magic probably couldn't have reached him, regardless.

Uthari chanted more gibberish—or were they words from some ancient language? Jak could sense the power in them, even if he didn't understand them.

Shikari yelped in pain.

"Stop!" Jak bellowed and sprang from Shikari's back.

Other mages on the deck raised their hands, no doubt targeting him, but he hardly cared. He raised his own barrier as he focused on Uthari, on getting him to stop hurting Shikari.

He will be one of us soon, Uthari whispered into his mind, smiling. *And you will be dead.*

No, I won't. Jak dipped a hand into his pocket, felt the outline of the syringe, and looked at Rivlen. *Help me, Rivlen. For just a second. Can you—*

Great power ripped into Jak from all sides, halting him in his tracks as it tore down his defenses.

Behind him, Shikari cried out again, in too much pain to help. The portal launched red lightning at the ship, but the mages aboard had combined their forces to create a barrier to protect against it. The zigzagging bolts flashed, turning the night sky red, but they couldn't get through.

Uthari's power slammed into Jak, pummeling him to the deck and mashing his cheek against the wood. He barely kept from landing on the syringe. If it broke, he wouldn't be able to inject Uthari—or Rivlen. The one he cared about.

Muscles straining, Jak managed to lift his head even as the pain intensified. He tried to catch her gaze, to think of something he could say to convince her to leave Uthari's side and help him. It would be for her own good. He wanted to cure her!

"Stop," Rivlen whispered, the word barely audible over the pain roaring in Jak's mind. "We are not— *I* am not—"

"Yes, you are." Uthari released her, took the dragon-steel sword from her grip, and stepped forward. He focused all his power on Jak and Shikari. *You've promised us your loyalty, and you are one of us.* The words were for Rivlen, but Jak heard them as Uthari kept assaulting him with his power, boring into him, channeling his anger at having lost Malek's loyalty.

Shikari, Jak thought, hoping the dragon could escape while Uthari was focused on him, hoping he could do something. *I need to inject them with these syringes. Please, can you—*

A dragon's screech of agony came from behind him.

No, Shikari couldn't help. He didn't have the power to overcome whatever magic Uthari had found this time, or that the parasites had *helped* him find.

You've been a thorn in my foot since this began, Uthari snarled into Jak's mind as he strode closer.

Jak panted, trying to get his barrier back up, to concentrate through the pain, but it was too much. Nobody except the portal was trying to help him, and even it couldn't get through. As long as Uthari had that sword, magic wouldn't be able to touch him.

Rivlen, he gasped into her mind. *Please. I need your help.*

The syringe was in his hand, his shaking hand, but he couldn't do anything with it.

Inject him with this. Jak summoned all of his energy and his magic to move his arm, to fling the syringe across the deck toward her. *To save his life. To save all our lives.*

He looked up, hoping she wasn't too far gone, but she'd let Uthari take the sword, so he didn't know. Maybe the parasites had stolen her humanity. Or maybe she'd never cared more for him than for her career and her duty to her king.

Uthari was too busy pouring his tormenting power into Jak to notice the syringe. It bumped against Rivlen's boot. She looked down at it.

More pain ripped into Jak, worse than anything he'd ever felt. He curled onto his side in a ball, unable to focus on Rivlen or anything except the terrible agony.

You took my general from me, Uthari said, using me instead of we, and Jak sensed that, no matter that the parasite was in there and affecting him, this was the wizard himself, the hatred that Uthari felt for him coming out. *And you took Malek, stole his loyalty. You and your whore of a mother. Did you think I would forgive that? That I would let you live? That I would let him leave me after all I've done for him? I* made *him. He's* my *zidarr, boy. And you are nothing.*

Uthari stood over Jak and raised the sword for a killing blow.

Jak tried to roll away, but his body was convulsing with the pain and wouldn't obey him.

"Your Majesty," Rivlen whispered, startlingly close to him. When had she moved? "You don't want it to be over so quickly, do you? Look." She pointed down at Jak as she stepped even closer to Uthari. "He wishes to beg for his life."

Uthari squinted down at Jak. "He *should* beg, but I don't—"

She jabbed the syringe into his neck.

Uthari screamed and whirled, lifting the sword to strike at her. Jak rolled toward Uthari's legs, determined to distract him, to keep him from striking Rivlen.

She ducked the sword blow and tackled him to the deck. They landed on Jak, and an elbow slammed into his side. Something clattered near his head. The dragon-steel sword.

Footsteps thundered as several of the mages ran toward it, but Jak grabbed it first, wrapping a shaking hand around the hilt.

"You disloyal traitor," Uthari snarled at Rivlen. "We'll *kill* you."

He poured his magic into Rivlen, ripping apart her barrier and dropping her to the deck. Jak stumbled to his feet, using the sword for support. After enduring Uthari's torment, weakness afflicted every muscle in his body, but he had to help Rivlen. Ignoring the mages running toward him, he swung the blade at Uthari.

The wizard spun toward him, raising a barrier and preparing to attack, but the sword cut through his defenses—and the side of his neck. Uthari sprang back before the blade severed an artery, but he stumbled into Shikari, the dragon rushing over after being released from his own torture. He leaped on Uthari's back and bit him in the top of the head, fangs crunching through bone.

Once more, Jak lunged in with the sword, jamming it into the old wizard's chest, into his heart.

Uthari stared at him in shock and disbelief, not voicing a cry or even a gasp.

"You," he mouthed, but that was all he got out before he wobbled, then fell.

As Uthari crumpled to the deck, Jak sensed more than a dozen mages on the deck approaching, and dozens more on the nearby ships taking aim at him. He planted one hand on Shikari, wanting to protect him with the power of the blade, but doubted they would be able to survive against so many.

"Look out!" someone barked.

Wary, Jak lifted the blade.

Red lightning streaked out of the night and struck the speaker in the chest. He flew backward, skidding across the deck into another mage. The portal had gotten through the mages' defenses; or maybe they'd been so shocked when Uthari had fallen that they'd forgotten to concentrate on the barrier.

Get on my back, Shikari ordered, though he sounded as weary as Jak. *They're not happy with you.*

No kidding. Jak worried about Shikari flying after all that, but he pulled himself onto his back, then reached out toward Rivlen, vowing to levitate her if he needed to. He couldn't leave her there to suffer retribution from the other mages. Besides, she'd injected Uthari but not herself.

I'll carry your mate too, Shikari promised.

But Rivlen wasn't looking at them. She was staring at Uthari's body as his blood flowed out of fatal wounds, the madness leaving his glazed eyes. Horror and chagrin filled her own eyes, as if she believed she'd failed.

Did she think that by saving Jak she'd made a mistake? He prayed that wasn't so. He didn't want her to regret this, but there was no time to question the events now. The dragons and the fortress remained, and, somewhere inside, Mother and Malek might be fighting for their lives.

Rivlen, Jak urged. *Come with us.*

He couldn't leave her.

More lightning strikes struck the mages on the ship, keeping them from attacking Shikari. Jak glanced toward the portal, wanting to thank it, but what he saw made him wince. Several ships from the other fleets were flying closer to it, and Tezi and the other mercenaries were facing off against Gorsith.

Rivlen, come, Jak commanded, not wanting to use compulsion but he had to try whatever it took to get her to join him.

She wrenched her gaze from Uthari's dead body and met his, then lifted her head. She sprang onto Shikari's back behind him and wrapped an arm around his waist.

They were too much of a burden for a half-sized dragon, but Shikari leaped into the air regardless. He wrapped his own power around himself to aid his flight. They flew over the railing and away from the mageship to head back toward the gateship.

Uniformed mages on other vessels stared at them, and Jak had a feeling they all knew Uthari was dead. And that he'd been responsible. Would they call him a murdering wild one and gang up to kill him?

"I'm sorry," Rivlen rasped. "I kept having to fight Uthari and—

the thing growing inside me, making me want to work with him and kill you instead of helping you. You have—" Her grip tightened, and she gasped, as if she were *still* fighting the parasite. "They know what you have, what you want to do." Her voice turned to a snarl, and her arm tightened around his waist. "They'll stop you. *We'll* stop you."

He sensed her warring with the parasites, as she'd done when he'd thrown her the syringe, and groped for something to say, for a way to help. "You're stronger than they are. You're the strongest woman I know. You won't succumb."

She pressed her forehead against his shoulder, her entire body shaking.

Jak twisted so that he could wrap an arm around her. With the other, he delved into his pocket for the second syringe. Tension radiated from her taut body, and he knew she was still fighting the parasites. Afraid they would stop him if they realized what he wanted to do, he whispered soothing words to Rivlen while stroking her hair.

I love you, Rivlen, Jak whispered into her mind and, without warning her, he slid the needle into her.

She stiffened but surprised him by not jerking back, not trying to stop him. *I know. Thanks for coming for me.*

You're welcome.

Shikari lurched under them, and they broke apart. Jak thought they'd been attacked, but he'd landed on the gateship. Gorsith faced them, rage contorting his face, and Jak had no doubt that he knew who had killed his king.

And what would Malek say when he found out? He had asked Jak to cure Uthari, not slay him.

Other ships were flying closer, dozens of them with angry uniformed mages glaring at Jak from all sides.

"I think we're still in trouble," Jak whispered.

Rivlen sighed and gripped his shoulder. "We are."

35

WITH DOZENS IF NOT HUNDREDS OF ANGRY MAGES GLARING AT JAK, he wanted nothing more than to hide under Shikari's belly until they all went away. But Malek and his mother needed a distraction if they were to accomplish their mission in the fortress. And there was nobody here to provide that distraction except the mages who'd come for that purpose. Unfortunately, they seemed more interested in fighting among themselves—and perhaps killing him for his audacity in defending himself against Uthari—than in tackling the dragons.

Back me up, please, Jak told Rivlen and Shikari.

He handed the dragon-steel sword to Rivlen, then slid off Shikari's back. He gave the glowering Gorsith a wide berth—the zidarr might have already sprung at him, but the mercenaries were pointing rifles at him—and levitated himself to the top of the portal. From the higher position, Jak spread his arms, hoping it would keep protecting him, and used his magic to amplify his voice.

"Listen to me, honored mages of the world," he called as

politely as he could, projecting his voice telepathically as well as aloud. "An enemy capable of destroying every human life on Torvil is poised not two miles away." He pointed toward the fortress, the dragons now circling it instead of waiting in their nests. "We can't fight among ourselves."

You cut down a king, you snotty bastard, and you say we can't fight among ourselves? An admiral in a yellow uniform, his aura as powerful as Tonovan's had been, lifted an arm and summoned an immense crackling fireball to hurl at Jak.

Jak raised his barrier, hoping it would be enough, but worried he would need help. *Your assistance, please,* he whispered to Rivlen and Shikari.

They were already funneling their power into his barrier, but the greatest assistance came from the portal under his feet. Four branches of red lightning shot from its frame, all streaking toward the admiral.

The officer halted his attack and raised a barrier, and other mages on deck with him combined forces to make a shield around their ship, but the lightning all struck in one spot with tremendous power. It tunneled a hole through their defenses.

Perhaps seeing his fate, the admiral flung himself to the deck and rolled away from the raw energy. It sizzled over his head and blew the aftcastle to pieces, leaving nothing but smoldering wood and smoke. The lightning halted, and Jak suspected the portal had been making a point, not trying to kill anyone.

Thank you, he told it, glad it understood that they would need every mage they could gather to assault the fortress. Assuming Jak could convince them to try.

Swearing, the admiral climbed to his feet, and he shot a scathing look toward the gateship, but he didn't attack again.

We have allies inside, working to take out that beam weapon, Jak said. *If we all go in and attack now, and distract the dragons from hunting them down, they'll be able to succeed. Then we'll only have to deal with the dragons and not the weapon they've made.*

Only, someone scoffed into his mind from their own ship. Gorsith.

You said you wanted to kill dragons, Shikari told him. *To engage them in noble battle and win.*

Not twenty at a time.

If we have allies inside, another officer called to Jak, *then let them take out that weapon* before *we commit our troops. We already tried to attack the weapons tower and take it out of action. You can see the wreckage of those ten ships below.*

I understand your reticence, Jak replied, *but they need our help to succeed. It is not an easy weapon to destroy, and the dragons are hunting for them as we speak. They need our help.*

What allies are in there? another officer asked. *Are you sure they even live?*

Jak hesitated, not wanting to draw attention to his mother, nor believing anyone outside of Uthari's fleet would have heard of her or know about her power. But everyone knew Malek, and many feared him. Maybe knowing he was inside would sway them.

Lord Malek, the zidarr, is inside, poised to destroy the weapon as soon as we provide him a moment free of dragon attention so he can reach it. Jak took a deep breath. *I will lead the fleets to the fortress. The brunt of their attack will come toward this vessel.* He didn't know if that was true, but he prayed to Shylezar that the portal would somehow be able to defend the gateship from that weapon. It might be a vain hope, given that nobody else's combined efforts had been sufficient. He hated the idea that he'd pulled Rivlen from Uthari's people only to have her die because she was standing at his side. *I only ask that you help attack and distract the dragons.*

You will lead us? Someone else scoffed into his mind. *A boy who was a wild one scant months ago? A boy who presumed to take advan-*

tage of a sick and weakened king to slay him? Why would we be so foolish as to follow you?

Jak, his body still aching from the pain Uthari had inflicted upon him, wanted to protest the idea that Uthari had been sick *or* weakened by the parasite, but that wasn't what mattered now.

You will follow me because I can draw upon the power of the portal. You've seen it assist me against enemies before, and it will assist me now. Jak raised his chin and attempted to radiate confidence, even as he feared he was overstepping his bounds and presuming too much from the ancient artifact. It wasn't as if he truly controlled it.

Shikari flapped his wings and flew up to join him, talons clinking against dragon steel as he landed. *Jak is favored by the portal and all untainted dragons,* he announced to everyone listening. *He is the one we foresaw coming to save our people, so we follow him. We will follow no other human.*

Jak rested a hand on Shikari's scales, appreciating the support even if they both knew—and likely everyone listening knew—that he was the *only* untainted dragon around. Jak didn't even sense Yoshartov in the area and worried he'd been cut down and killed by his kin for presuming to bring humans to the fortress, or simply for having allowed himself to be changed back.

If you wish to save your world and your people, you will follow Jak, just as the portal and I will. Shikari finished with a roar that floated to the ears of everyone in the combined fleets.

Even though it was a booming sound these days, the reedy roar of Shikari's youth long past, Jak expected more scoffing, or for someone to point out that he was half a dragon at best, and that his contribution would matter little against so many adult dragons.

But as Shikari gazed from ship to ship, he projected confidence and... was he trying to use magical coercion again? It was subtle, but Jak detected him sending out his power.

"It didn't go well the last time you tried to do that," Jak whispered to him.

I'm letting them know how wise it would be to follow us. That's all. Nobody will kiss anyone else. We don't have time for that.

A comment punctuated by four dragons leaving the fortress and heading toward the fleets.

You will follow Jak's mighty lead, and we shall attack! Shikari boomed into everyone's mind, then whapped Jak on the back with his tail. *Make this airboat go.*

People might question the mightiness of my lead if my own dragon companion smacks me.

It was an affectional nudge. Had it been a smack, you would have fallen off the portal. Perhaps off the ship.

Good to know. With the dragons coming, Jak reached down to Vinjo in the navigation cabin. *Take us toward the fortress.*

I was afraid you were going to say that, kid, came Vinjo's grim reply.

Between Shikari tail-whacking him and Vinjo calling him kid, Jak didn't know how many people would agree to his leadership, but as the gateship headed for the fortress—and the dragons flew out to intercept it—he willed every mage and every vessel to follow his lead.

~

Rivlen gazed up at Jak on the portal as the gateship flew toward the fortress, as powerful a barrier as he, she, and Gorsith could conjure protecting their vessel. She would have believed it a futile effort, that even with a zidarr's assistance, they wouldn't have been able to keep it up against the beam or even one dragon, but Jak had gotten Shikari and the portal to help.

Even before Shikari had claimed they would follow Jak's lead, she'd known it to be the truth. She'd been proud of him as he stood up there, speaking fearlessly to all the curmudgeonly captains and admirals on the other ships.

"Just need to support him so they all believe we can win," Rivlen muttered, glancing back.

Thus far, none of the ships were following them. If they had to face four dragons alone—not to mention the beam weapon and the rest of the dragons in the fortress—that would be a lot to ask of even the portal.

"I can't believe you helped that kid kill Uthari," Gorsith growled to her.

The mercenaries had shifted their rifles from aiming at him to the dragons, and he'd walked over to glower at her and up at Jak.

"We tried to *heal* him," Rivlen said, though she didn't have any idea what she'd jabbed into Uthari's neck or what she'd let Jak inject into her. She could still feel the parasite within her, struggling to take over her conscious mind and force her to act against her wishes. She'd barely managed to help Jak against Uthari, and, even now, the parasites were trying to compel her to knock him from the portal and tell the oncoming dragons everything she knew about who was inside the fortress. Whatever had been in that syringe, it wasn't fast-acting. "If Uthari hadn't tried to kill Jak, I wouldn't have raised a hand against him."

It was the truth—even when Uthari had forced that kiss on her and infested her, she hadn't attacked him—but Gorsith's face twisted with skepticism. Protesting or acting innocent wouldn't sway him. He would more likely respond to power and confidence.

"You'd best work with us if you want to survive the day," she said, pouring more of her power into the barrier as the dragons tested it with their magic. "Until you know who Uthari's heir is, you better not rock any boats."

Gorsith looked sharply at her, though he was also concentrating on their defenses. "Do *you* know who it is?"

She had no idea, but she only gave him a cool gaze, as if she was aware of vastly more than she was. "Focus on the battle, and we will all live to find out."

He growled, but he did as she'd suggested.

As the dragons threw fire as well as attacking the gateship physically, she and Gorsith stood side by side, protecting it as they sailed closer to the fortress. Atop the portal, Jak and Shikari did the same, channeling their own power into the barrier.

Since the other ships hadn't joined them, all four dragons focused on them. And was it her imagination, or did she sense that weapon powering up? Preparing to shoot one of those deadly beams at them?

"We need to take one dragon down!" Rivlen called up to Jak. "To convince the fleets that we're strong enough to follow, that they have a chance of winning if they stand with us."

"I'm amenable to that if you tell me how we're going to do that while keeping our defenses up," Jak called back, then looked toward the weapons tower. Maybe he also sensed it powering up. If so, they dared not lower their defenses.

The portal glowed blue, but it likely couldn't attack while their barrier was up any more than the mages could.

"You've got to do *something* to convince them," Rivlen said, then mentally kicked herself for stating the obvious. He'd already tried, and it hadn't worked. What more could he do?

But Jak exchanged a long look—and a telepathic conversation? —with Shikari. As one, they peered at the ship with the admiral who'd attacked Jak earlier.

Instead of speaking to the man, he narrowed his eyes and met the admiral's gaze across the distance as dragons swooped in, clawing at the gateship's barrier.

"Enter the battle," Jak mouthed, as he used his magic to compel the admiral to do so.

Rivlen held her breath, wondering if it would work. That admiral was a lot more powerful than the mage officer Jak had once compelled into helping him defeat Tonovan. But he drew upon power even greater than she'd known he possessed and repeated the words, eyes locked on the admiral. The officer's mouth opened, his own eyes glazing as if he were mesmerized.

Shikari added his power to Jak's. That pushed the officer over the edge. He called to his navigator and ordered the ship to sail into battle.

"All of them," Jak mouthed, likely sending the same message telepathically.

Every ship, join us, the admiral relayed to everyone.

Jak turned toward the officer in charge of Zaruk's fleet, a captain squinting suspiciously over at the admiral. He repeated the command, using his magic to compel the officer. Without Shikari's help, it wouldn't have worked, but as the portal glowed, working on keeping a barrier up around the gateship, Jak compelled officers to join them.

I hate doing it this way, Jak said, looking sadly down at Rivlen. *Using power to bully others, to take away their free will... It is everything I hate about mages.*

You can self-flagellate over your vileness later. Get the rest of them to join us.

You're so practical.

Damn straight, I am. Her cheek twitched as she fought another attempt from the parasites to rise up and take control of her body. They wanted her to leap onto the portal and strangle Jak, to end the threat to their kind.

No, she snarled to herself, tightening her grip on the sword. She would take her own life before ending his.

Are you all right? Jak must have seen her tendons flexing and her face contorting.

Just waiting for whatever you stabbed me with to take effect. Her legs moved of their own accord, carrying her several steps closer to the portal. She half-drew the sword before she snarled and, with all of her willpower, sublimated the parasite-driven urges.

Oh, of course. It will take a while, I'm afraid. And you'll get very sick first.

That wasn't what she'd wanted to hear.

Jak hesitated as a dragon battered at the barrier behind him. With his eyes full of concern for her, he barely noticed. *If you want, my mother might have some syringes full of a sedative in her laboratory. I could... knock you out.*

I will not *sleep through this battle,* she said, though her anger was for the parasites, not him. *I will maintain control over them. I did before, and I will continue to do so.*

Rivlen hoped she was right, but it was hard not to doubt. Uthari, with all his power and experience, hadn't been able to in the end.

I believe you, he said earnestly and smiled at her.

Perhaps sensing Jak was succeeding at gathering allies, one dragon attempted to blast the gateship with a mental attack, one Rivlen recognized from the battle where the *Star Flyer* had been shipwrecked. She tightened her hand around the hilt of the dragon-steel sword and gripped Gorsith's forearm with her other hand. Hopefully, the portal would protect Jak and Shikari.

To her side, several of the mercenaries gasped and dropped to their knees. Tezi with her axe was unaffected, but the dragon-steel bullets in the mundane rifles weren't enough to protect the others. They dropped their firearms and grabbed their temples.

Sensing the barrier weakening, Rivlen pushed down the compulsions coming from the parasites and poured more of her power into it. Tezi gathered the mercenaries and touched them to extend her axe's protection, but cries of pain emanated from belowdecks. Vinjo had no dragon steel to protect him.

"Maybe we should drop the defenses so we can attack them," Tezi called up to Jak as she jerked her chin toward one of the rifles.

Sasko, with Tezi's protection allowing her to shrug off the pain, picked it up.

"They could rip us apart in seconds if we did." Jak looked toward the weapons tower.

It could rip them apart in *less* than seconds. Rivlen was surprised it hadn't already fired. How much time could they have?

36

A WRENCHING OF METAL CAME FROM FEWER THAN TEN FEET BEHIND Jadora. She flinched, her backpack scraping on the top of the shaft.

She was last in line as their group maneuvered through the maze under the fortress floor, so she had an unimpeded view when she looked back. Dragon talons, magic giving them the power to destroy dragon steel, tore open a hole in the shaft.

Wind ripped through the opening as the creature gripped more steel to widen the gap. To tear the entire floor out?

The shaft quaked under Jadora and the others. She used her power, attempting to stabilize the structure, but she had little experience with using magic to reinforce materials, and the dragon succeeded in ripping out another chunk.

"Go," Malek whispered, gripping her shoulder to ease her aside so he could take the rear position. And attack the dragon? "Take this." He thrust the rifle toward her. "Sorath says we're almost there."

Malek squeezed past her, not waiting for an answer.

"Malek," she whispered and reached for him.

"I'll buy you time." He leveled a determined stare over his shoulder at her but didn't slow down. "Go."

He didn't use magic to add compulsion to the word. He didn't need to. Jadora understood what he was doing and why. She hated it and was terrified he wouldn't be able to stop the dragon and catch back up again, but Ferroki touched her shoulder from the other side.

"We have to keep going," she whispered.

"Are we truly close?" Jadora whispered back.

"I don't know."

Jadora frowned.

"The fortress isn't *that* large," Ferroki said, "so we have to be."

Except that the under-floor infrastructure had been a labyrinth, and Jadora wasn't convinced they weren't going in circles.

"We're not far," Sorath said firmly from his spot in the lead. He didn't comment on Malek leaving the group. "Come."

Jadora wrenched her gaze from Malek as he crawled toward the talons widening that hole. He had a dragon-steel sword. She hoped it would be enough.

After spinning back around, the rifle in her grip, Jadora followed Ferroki and Sorath as quickly as she could. Quicker than they. As the shaft slanted upward, she kept clunking the stock of the rifle against Ferroki's boots and wanted to shout, "Hurry!"

Light appeared ahead, and Jadora spotted a grate beyond Sorath. A roar echoed through it. Were there dragons waiting for them to come out?

She sensed them in the area but not right in front of the grate.

"Damn, I was hoping this exit wouldn't be blocked." Sorath stopped at the bars. "As I've learned these past two days, dragon steel can't cut dragon steel." He eyed the glowing tendril flowing out of the shaft, between the bars, and into the wall of a nearby tower, one of many framing an open courtyard. "Would cutting *it* do anything?"

"Blow us to pieces, maybe," Ferroki said.

Shadows created by dragons flying in front of the moon danced in the courtyard, and Jadora had a feeling their enemies knew exactly where they were.

The clacks of talons striking metal echoed through the shaft from behind, and she winced, aware of Malek engaging with the dragon. She longed to go back and help him but instead dug into her backpack.

"The weapons tower is across that courtyard." Sorath pointed through the bars. "There's the entrance that leads to it. You take a right, then go through a short corridor, and you can enter the tower. But I don't know how to get through *this*." Sorath gripped a bar with a snarl of frustration. "We didn't go this way the last time we were in there."

"I have something that can eat through the steel. Scoot over." Jadora winced as a cry of pain came from behind them, followed by a battle roar. Both noises came from Malek. She sensed him using his power as well as stabbing at the talons with his sword, but she made herself dig into her pack for vials of acid instead of looking back to check on him.

"Do you have a lot of it?" Sorath asked. "We also know where the power devices are that keep the fortress aloft."

"No, I don't. Weapon first, and we'll see about the rest. The others need it out of operation to approach the fortress." Jadora could sense Jak and the gateship in the vicinity and hoped they weren't close enough for the beam to strike.

Horrified at the thought, she hurried to smear her acid on the bars, ignoring the toxic fumes that wafted up, bringing tears to her eyes.

"If we can destroy the fortress ourselves," Sorath said, "and make it crash on the ice below, the mageships won't *have* to approach it."

"I'm afraid they're already on their way. And they would still have to face the dragons."

"True."

Jadora blew on the acid, as if that might make it eat through the bars more quickly. More winged shadows flew through the courtyard.

"The fortress shouldn't be a threat without the weapon, right?" Ferroki asked.

"I wouldn't bet on that," Sorath grumbled.

"Have you seen evidence of another weapon?" There hadn't been much time for chitchat since they'd reunited, but Jadora knew they'd had time to explore in the days they'd been trapped inside.

"No, but the whole fortress is *dragon steel*," he said. "It has powers we don't understand, and we've seen the portal lash out with lightning. What if the fortress can too?"

He gripped a bar above where she'd smeared the acid and shook it. The affected metal cracked, and the grate shuddered.

"After we take care of the weapon, you can lead us to the engineering room or its equivalent," Jadora said.

Sorath nodded. "Step back."

Jadora and Ferroki scooted back on hands and knees.

The screech of a dragon came from behind them. She hoped that meant Malek had landed a painful blow. If nothing else, she hadn't heard any more metal wrenching. He was keeping it from further tearing open the shaft.

Sorath pulled on the damaged bar, bending it back far enough for them to pass through. Jadora sensed dragons gathering above the courtyard. Though she couldn't see them, she suspected they were looking down, watching her and the others, and would pounce as soon as they came out of the shaft.

Sorath started to scoot out, but Jadora grabbed his belt.

"We can't go out there without a plan, without a distraction," she said.

"I thought the mages were going to attack and provide that," he grumbled.

Jadora checked on Jak again and frowned, sensing that the gateship was heading toward the fortress by itself. Had Uthari or one of the other leaders forced them to go alone as a decoy? To make matters worse, four dragons were flying out to meet it.

"Never mind," Jadora said, fresh urgency flowing through her veins. "We'll have to disable the weapon whether there's a distraction or not. Here. You two will have to keep them busy. Please." She pulled the rifle up and handed it to Ferroki, trusting the experienced mercenary would be a better shot than she. Jadora didn't know how many bullets Ferroki could fire before the dragons descended on them and tore them to pieces, but there weren't any other choices.

"I'll do it," came Malek's voice from behind them.

Distracted, Jadora hadn't sensed his approach. She spun, spotting blood weeping from a gouge on his cheek, and wanted to fling her arms around him for a hug.

But, as grim-faced as ever, he squeezed past her and rose to a crouch in the low shaft, maneuvering his sword so it was in front of him. "I'll run out into the courtyard. The rest of you sneak around the edge to the tower."

"I'll go with you." Sorath lifted his dagger.

Their eyes met, two men who were enemies, who'd wanted to kill each other for months. Malek nodded at Sorath.

As one, they surged out of the shaft. Shouting battle cries, they ran across the courtyard toward a cave opposite the entrance that Sorath had pointed out.

The shadows moved as the dragons flew toward the men with their talons outstretched.

Though terrified, Jadora propelled herself into the courtyard. She and Ferroki ran along the wall toward the tower, though Ferroki kept glancing at their allies and looked like she wanted to stop and put that rifle to use.

"I need you to stick with me," Jadora said, though she also wanted to help Malek and Sorath. "If there are dragons between us and the weapon..."

"I understand," Ferroki said.

That didn't keep Jadora from casting an anguished look back at Malek as she ran for the entrance. Malek and Sorath had split apart, putting their backs to walls for protection, and they parried as talons and jaws slashed and snapped for them.

Malek's blade clanked off a fang that came inches from driving through his shoulder. He summoned his power to punch the dragon in the snout as it withdrew its head for another strike, but if his magic bothered his foe, it didn't show it.

Another creature landed, joining the first two, and Jadora knew there were too many. As fast as Malek was, he and Sorath would never be able to keep that many deadly foes at bay.

She summoned all of the power within her and cast it at the dragons, a great wall of raw energy ramming into their sides. Two of them glanced in her direction, but her power did no more to harm them than Malek's had. Only the blades had a chance.

Was it possible the acid could also harm them? She was tempted to veer toward the battle and hurl a vial, but she didn't have enough to throw around. With her son vulnerable, she had to prioritize reaching the weapon. Reaching it and *destroying* it.

Jadora made herself turn and sprint after Ferroki.

Following Sorath's directions, they ran right and then into a tower, but there were no stairs to carry them up to the second level. Jadora swept air under them and levitated them toward a hole in the center of the ceiling.

As they rose toward the weapon, she could sense it, but she

could also sense a dragon above it. The one nesting on the roof. It hadn't left its perch.

"Of course not," she muttered. "It's there to guard the weapon."

Ferroki glanced at her.

"Just grousing to myself," Jadora whispered and fell silent, wincing every time weapons clanged against talon or fang in the courtyard.

When they passed through the hole, Jadora directed them onto the floor beside it. They were in the chamber that held the weapon, but it was up near the ceiling, a great red sphere with dark whorls of power writhing behind what appeared to be a glass surface. She had no doubt it was made from a material far stronger than glass.

The weapon fired, a huge beam that filled the great oval window as it shot out.

"Jak!" Jadora blurted, certain the beam was surging straight at the gateship. "Watch my back, Ferroki." She pointed at the rifle as she used her magic to propel herself upward toward the weapon.

The air crackled with its energy, electricity dancing around her. It was painful as it flicked at her skin. Even with her barrier raised, she felt it. Red light gleamed on the walls as the beam surged out, continuing to fire in one long blast.

Jadora was so worried that it was blowing the gateship to pieces that her hands shook as she grabbed her vial. Since the beam filled the window, she couldn't see where it went, but she sensed it. To her surprise, she also sensed the portal on the gateship. Great power emanated from it, and she grew aware of it sending out a thick band of lightning.

For an alarmed instant, she thought it was targeting the tower, that she was about to be blown up, but the lightning hit the beam, the two energies crashing together. They met in the sky like two fists pressing against each other, each halting the progress of the other.

Mother? Jak spoke into her mind. *You're in the tower, right?*

Yes. She uncapped the vial and floated closer to the swirling surface of the sphere, fighting the pain its great power caused. Grimly, she realized she would have to lower her barrier to sprinkle on the acid.

The weapon is stronger than the portal, Jak said. *It showed me... It can't hold out for long. The other ships are coming, but I don't think the weapon cares.*

A screech came from above the sphere, from the roof. The dragon up there had realized its weapon had company.

Doing my best. Jadora levitated herself closer as she dropped her barrier. Right away, intense agony smothered her, and she once again almost dropped the vial. Instead she flung it at the top of the sphere, willing the substance to land and spread all over it.

A surge of even greater power came from the weapon. She didn't know if it was a reaction to her acid or if one of the dragons had commanded it to intensify its attack on the gateship, but the backlash knocked her away. She got her barrier up right before she would have struck a wall.

A yell of pain echoed up from the courtyard. Sorath.

Jadora wanted to let herself descend, but the beam was still lancing out. With the red sphere glowing brighter, she couldn't tell if enough of her acid had made it through to make a difference. Was it doing anything? Or was the weapon somehow impervious to it as well?

A thunderous crack came from the sphere. A tsunami of power struck Jadora, blowing away her barrier and hurling her into the wall. Her head struck, and she tumbled downward as her senses reeled.

Above, red light flared so bright it scorched her eyes as she fell. She struggled to find her magic, to wrap it protectively around herself, but she hit the floor with a painful thud that knocked her breath from her. Blackness crept into her vision, and she growled, willing it to go away. She couldn't lose consciousness *now*.

"Look out," Ferroki called and flung herself over Jadora.

With another great crack, the sphere split in half, and the two huge pieces tumbled down. One headed for the hole, but the other fell straight toward them.

With the last of her power, Jadora formed a barrier above her and Ferroki. The piece of shattered sphere struck it and bounced sideways, falling through the hole and crashing onto the other half.

The beam was gone, the weapon destroyed. But before Jadora could feel any relief, a dragon's roar sounded outside the tower wall, and two sets of talons gripped the window. The last calculation she managed before falling unconscious was to figure out that the opening was large enough to admit a dragon to their tower.

~

Malek would have sensed the huge surge from the weapon being destroyed even if a red flash hadn't lit up the courtyard. The two dragons Malek had been facing, able to do little more than parry their fangs and talons as Sorath did the same against his foe next to him, halted in surprise and looked toward the tower.

Taking advantage, Malek sprang in and plunged his sword into one of his foes' taloned feet.

Jadora? Are you all right? His senses had told him she'd been close when the weapon exploded, and now her aura was diminished. Worse, the dragon on top of the tower had flown down and alighted on the side of it. It stuck its head in the window through which the weapon had been firing.

The dragon Malek stabbed screeched, the harsh noise making his eardrums reverberate, and yanked its foot back. Not without leaving a chunk of scale and flesh on the sword. There was no time for satisfaction. The dragon opened its maw and snapped for Malek.

He rolled to the side, guarding himself with the blade as he evaded the attack. It was good that he kept the sword up, for the other dragon tried to cut him off. A great taloned foot came down, attempting to pin him.

Mustering all the speed he could, Malek crouched and sprang fast enough to whip his sword up and greet it, the tip of the blade sinking in as the sharp talons flexed toward him. The dragon hurled fire at him. Even though it had to know the attack wouldn't work, it reflexively poured an inferno onto Malek.

He felt some of the heat as it splashed against the courtyard wall, but his barrier and the sword protected him. He plunged the weapon deeper into the foot, debating between yanking it out and trying to climb up the limb to the dragon's back, where he might reach more vital targets. But an alarmed gasp came from his ally.

"That dragon went in," Sorath shouted, jabbing his dagger toward the tower. "We have to help Ferroki."

Malek was more concerned about *Jadora*, but he grunted an agreement.

Sorath dodged an attack and ran for the entrance, but one of the dragons chased him. Malek used his magic to emulate the red flash that had come from the tower, hoping that a repeat would make the dragons think something was happening with the weapon and pause again.

Whether it fooled them, he didn't know, but they did pause, their eyelids narrowing under the assault of light. Malek sprinted after Sorath—and the dragon chasing him.

It roared, its head snapping toward Sorath's back. He was out in the open and too far from the entrance to the tower. He wouldn't make it.

Malek lunged and caught up to the tail flowing behind the dragon. He growled and swung for the tip, resenting that it was all he could reach. The sword sliced through, cleaving the last few inches off.

The dragon had been about to bite into Sorath's back—or maybe his head—but it screeched and reared back as the piece of tail flopped to the ground. Sorath made it to the entrance and leaped inside.

Malek ran through the dragon's legs as it stamped about, trying to take revenge for the insult to its tail. Malek threw a half-hearted swipe toward its belly as he sprinted under, but fear for Jadora drove him to get to her instead of worrying about finishing the battle. Besides, they hadn't managed to seriously wound any of the dragons. They were too resilient and too powerful for a couple of humans. Unfortunately.

Cursing came from a round chamber ahead—the bottom of the tower. Sorath had reached it and was looking up to a hole in the center of the ceiling. A dragon had landed on the ledge next to it.

"There are no stairs." Sorath eyed the smooth dragon-steel walls, as if he might climb them.

"Give me your dagger for a second," Malek said. "I'll levitate us up."

Sorath whirled toward him, that dagger in his single hand and suspicion leaping into his eyes. Did he think Malek cared enough about past differences to attack him then?

Malek crouched, intending to go without Sorath if he didn't comply, but Sorath must have decided he trusted Malek enough to relinquish the blade. Malek took it and levitated them both up. He intended to give it back as soon as they landed on the floor above, for they would need weapons to face the dragon together, but when he saw the creature prowling toward Jadora, Ferroki kneeling protectively over her limp form, fear and rage drove rational thoughts from Malek's mind.

With both weapons in hand, he charged the dragon, hurling a

blast of magic at its head to ensure it didn't bite the women before he reached it. The creature started to turn toward him, but Ferroki, a rifle in hand, fired at it.

The bullet flashed blue as it pierced the dragon's barrier and then scale and flesh. The projectile was too small, however, to bother their foe. The dragon roared and snapped for Malek.

He rolled under its jaws and sprang up, bunching his muscles to leap up to its throat. The dragon started to pull its head back, but the confines of the tower made it hard for such a large creature to maneuver. One of its horns clipped the wall, and it paused long enough for Malek to reach the underside of its long neck. He slashed with both weapons, dagger and sword slicing into scales before he dropped back to the ground.

As soon as his feet touched, he jumped again, using muscle and magic to reach the dragon's back. He drove both blades between its scales, sinking them in deep.

Roaring, the dragon spun around as its jaws snapped at him. Malek ducked, but the creature was as fast as he, and a fang grazed him in the shoulder, knocking him off its back. As he fell, he slashed again, cutting a gouge in its flank.

He expected to land on the ledge, but he came down where the hole was and fell past Sorath, Jadora, and the others.

"Bring my dagger back, you ugly, arrogant zidarr thug!" Sorath shouted.

Another rifle shot fired, Ferroki sinking another bullet in.

As soon as Malek landed, his zidarr muscles absorbing the fall, he sprang back up again. He came down on the ledge, ready to keep fighting, but the dragon must have had enough. It screeched one more time, blood dripping from its neck and flank, and leaped up to the window. It flew out, leaving the tower empty of enemies, at least for the moment.

Malek was surprised the others hadn't come in to help it, but when he reached out with his senses, he detected the mageships approaching. *All* of them. Someone had finally convinced all the ships to attack, and the dragons must have deemed them the greater threat.

Malek handed the dagger hilt-first to Sorath, though his gaze locked onto Jadora. "Ugly?"

"Hideous." Sorath accepted the weapon.

"He's a *beautiful* zidarr thug," Jadora whispered, opening her eyes as she turned her head toward Malek.

With emotions forming a tight knot in his chest, he ran to crouch at her side. When he'd first seen her crumpled on the floor, he'd feared he was too late.

"Beautiful?" Ferroki sounded skeptical.

"Mage taste is beyond dubious," Sorath said.

Ignoring them, Malek touched Jadora's cheek. *I love you,* he whispered telepathically. Out loud, he said, "I noticed you didn't object to his other adjective."

He used his senses to examine her for wounds.

"Arrogant? Certainly not." Jadora smiled at him. "You know that one is entirely accurate."

"It is," he agreed, then, not finding any deadly wounds, gathered her in his arms. There was a lump already swelling on the back of her head, and her eyes didn't focus entirely as she looked at him, but he could heal such wounds later.

"Are we going somewhere?" she murmured muzzily.

"I'm going to carry you around this fortress, and you're going to sprinkle acid everywhere."

"We should only need to destroy the magical devices in the control cave," Sorath said.

"Lead us there," Malek said.

"*Please,*" Sorath grumbled.

Malek gave him a frosty look. Why was the damn mercenary worrying about *politeness* now?

Sorath rolled his eyes. "Arrogant," he muttered, then climbed through the hole to jump down.

"Shoot every dragon you see with that, please," Jadora told Ferroki, lifting a finger toward the rifle.

"It didn't seem effective in wounding the one that was trying to kill us." Ferroki shook her head with disappointment.

"Trust me," Jadora said. "It did what it was meant to do. In a day or two, should we live that long, I believe we'll see the result."

Ferroki's brow furrowed, but she nodded.

With Jadora in his arms, Malek leaped down, landing as lightly as he could. Roars and shrieks came from all around the fortress. He didn't know what had happened, how Jak had convinced the rest of the mages to join him, but the entire fleet was swarming the structure now, throwing magical attacks by the hundreds. Red lightning from the portal flashed in the night sky above.

"What happens if they destroy this place while we're inside it?" Sorath took off at a jog, but he kept glancing warily upward. Ferroki ran at his side.

"We crash along with it," Malek said, carrying Jadora as he ran.

"After all we've survived—" Sorath glanced at Ferroki, "—I was hoping to make it out of this alive."

As more dragons than Malek had realized were on Torvil swarmed the mageships, he had to admit the odds were still against them. He hoped Jadora had enough of the acid left and that the loss of the fortress would dishearten the dragons, for the bacteria wouldn't work quickly enough to make a difference. He, Jadora, and all the other mages might be dead by the time the dragons returned to their normal selves.

37

"THE BEAM WEAPON STOPPED FIRING!" ONE OF THE MERCENARIES cried.

Rivlen, busy funneling her energy into the barrier protecting the gateship, glanced toward the fortress.

"I don't sense it anymore," Jak said from the deck beside her, the portal at their backs. "I think they succeeded in destroying it."

She didn't sense it either. Dragons still filled the sky, and the fortress itself appeared undamaged, but if the cursed weapon was gone, that was something.

Jak smiled broadly around at everyone on the deck, holding Rivlen's gaze the longest.

She nodded back at him, proud of how he'd taken charge. If Malek and Jadora had destroyed the weapon, the fleets had a chance against the dragons. It was hard for her to manage a smile, however. The parasites seethed inside of her, fighting to rise up and take control of her. They wanted her to drive her sword through Jak's heart to prevent humanity's victory.

As they stood side by side on deck, with Shikari, Gorsith, Tezi, and the mercenaries nearby, Rivlen struggled to sublimate those urges and keep helping with the battle. During a moment when no dragons were attacking them, she and the others lowered their barrier and cast fire and lightning. Rivlen channeled the aggression and rage the parasites were evoking within her and used it to make her magical attacks stronger, but she worried she would lose control. The enemies inside her were worse than the enemies outside.

She looked toward the railing, tempted to levitate over to another ship so she wouldn't be as close to Jak. After all they'd been through, after how much she'd come to care for him, the last thing she wanted was to hurt him. Or worse. If she were to attack him, he wouldn't see it coming. He might not realize he needed to defend himself until it was too late.

Slavemasters in hell, maybe she should throw herself over the railing and to her death. But that would hurt him as well, in another way.

"Jak," she rasped as the portal lashed out, lightning forking to attack two dragons. Their barriers protected them, and the mercenaries had run out of bullets, but the mage officers had learned that the lightning weakened their enemies' defenses. With their combined might, they could sometimes get through to the dragons if they attacked at the same time.

"Yes?" Jak glanced at her as he channeled his power into Gorsith, helping the zidarr create an inferno of a fireball to blast at one of the dragons.

"Keep your defenses up around me, all right?"

His brow furrowed. "They've been up except when we're attacking."

"And when you're doing that." Rivlen waved curtly to indicate him channeling power into others.

"Why—"

"Because I'm struggling to keep control of myself," she

snapped, then closed her eyes and took a deep breath. She didn't want to be short with him. She loved him, damn it.

"Oh," Jak mouthed, then offered a forced smile. "And here I thought I only had to worry about dragons killing me, Shikari hitting me with his tail, and what I'm going to tell Malek about..." He waved toward Uthari's mageship—what had *been* Uthari's mageship.

"We both have to worry about that." Rivlen grimaced. She'd been trying to save the old wizard; they both had. But would Malek believe that? What if he thought they'd colluded to take him out so they could take over his kingdom or something idiotic like that? What if she'd survived these past few weeks only to die at the hands of a vengeful zidarr who should have been her ally? What if she and Jak *both* died that way?

"Yeah. Sorry." Jak touched her shoulder but quickly pulled his hand back. "Is that all right? Or are you... about to boil over?"

Shikari, who sat beside Jak as he added his power to the portal's attacks, looked at them but didn't say anything. He peered toward the dragons circling the ship, leaving the human problems for them to deal with.

And Rivlen *would* deal with them. She took another deep breath, though it didn't help to calm her—or that which lived within her. "It would be better if we weren't close. I think the parasite specifically wants you dead because you're a threat to its survival."

"That's more my mother, but I don't want it targeting her either. Who targets a middle-aged university professor?" He gave her another strained smile. "It's not right."

"This isn't a joke, Jak. I—"

A wave of fury so strong that it hurt surged up within her. Blackness edged her vision, and her hand dropped to her sword hilt of its own accord. Propelled by a power—an entity—that lived within her and feared its end was near, she drew the blade and lifted it.

Rivlen tried to step back, to fling herself away from Jak—from the ship entirely if need be—but the parasite drove her arms to swing.

Eyes round, Jak ducked as he skittered back, but Shikari's tail was behind him, and his heel caught on it.

Shikari sprang away and used his magic to catch Jak and keep him from falling, but it did nothing to halt Rivlen's attack. It couldn't, not when she wielded dragon steel.

She managed to divert the blow enough that it didn't take off Jak's head, but it clipped the top of his ear. Blood poured from the wound as he yelled and grabbed the side of his head. Satisfaction and eagerness flowed from the parasites, and they urged her to strike again, to take off his head this time.

"No!" she roared, forcing her legs back, trying to use her magic to squelch their power.

Shikari leaped protectively in front of Jak and tried to push Rivlen back with magic. When that didn't work, he bowled her over with his body, knocking her to the deck and leaping on her.

Talons dug into her arms and legs, and the pain distracted her from the parasites' presence. She welcomed it.

Gorsith ran up beside Shikari, pointing his sword at Rivlen, though confusion creased his brow. "What are you doing, Captain?"

"It's all right." Jak straightened and lowered his hand, though blood streamed from his ear. "She's not in control of herself."

"Then why is she standing here with us in the middle of a battle?" Gorsith flung his arm toward the dragons all around the fleet.

Why indeed. Panting, Rivlen stared up at the sky. She should have jumped, sacrificed herself so she couldn't hurt anyone else.

"Because we need everyone." Jak knelt beside Rivlen and lifted a hand toward Shikari, as if to tell him to get off her, but he lowered it again without giving that command.

Good. If Rivlen couldn't control herself, it was better that she be imprisoned. Even now, the parasites roiled inside of her, making her want to knock Shikari aside so she could attack Jak again.

"Are you all right?" he asked.

"*I'm* fine," she rasped. "Your ear is..." She shook her head, staring at the flat bloody top where the curved tip of his ear should have been.

"So I gathered."

"I'm sorry."

"I forgive you. It wasn't even you." He squeezed her shoulder. "Don't worry. You'll recover from this."

"I can't believe you want to touch me right now."

Jak smiled lopsidedly, ignoring the lightning flying through the sky above his head and the dozens of mages attacking dragons as they defended their ships from counterattacks. "I always want to touch you."

"I'd kiss you if I weren't crazy right now." Not to mention pinned by his dragon.

"I'd let you kiss me, even if you are crazy."

"I know you would. You're crazy too."

"Yeah."

"Here." With the dragonling pinning her, Rivlen couldn't lift her arm, but she opened her grip and released the dragon-steel sword. "You better hold that for now."

She felt like an idiot for not giving it to him earlier. Such a blade was a difficult prize to relinquish, but if she hadn't been holding it, Shikari could have used his magic to knock her back before she'd landed her blow.

"Maybe forever," she finished with a whisper.

"Nah." Jak did slide the sword away from her hand. "You deserve it."

She didn't feel like she deserved anything.

Maybe that sentiment showed on her face for Jak leaned closer and whispered, "Uthari would have killed me. You saved my life."

Smiling again—not a forced smile this time—he kissed her. A brief kiss, for he didn't want to tempt the parasite by too close a proximity. Rivlen hoped that one day it would be safe for them to share a longer one again.

He released her shoulder, knelt back, and looked at Shikari, probably telling him to keep an eye on her. An order she couldn't disagree with at that moment. Afterward, he turned to the railing and waved for Gorsith to join him in continuing the attack.

Rivlen closed her eyes, hoping Jak was right, that she would recover, that this insanity wasn't forever.

~

"You can put me down now." Jadora ignored her wooziness and the pain in her skull, certain she could stand, and squeezed Malek's shoulders.

She appreciated his help, but he was carrying her and her pack *and* worrying about the dragons. Though their winged enemies appeared to be fully engaged with the fleets now, all it would take was one noticing them skulking through the fortress to fly down and obliterate them. She was surprised the one Ferroki and Malek had attacked hadn't already sounded the alarm. Maybe the dragons were more worried about the hordes of mages and the portal's lightning. The red streaks of electricity kept crackling through the air above, wrapping around the dragons' barriers and trying to slip past their defenses.

"I enjoy carrying you." Malek leaped over a pile of rubble in the wide corridor they were running through, no ceiling above hiding them from aerial view.

Jadora eyed that rubble, at first wondering how some of the nearly impervious dragon steel had been destroyed. Then she realized the wreckage had come from a mageship.

She reached out with her mind, sweeping across the battlefield in search of her son. With so many ships swooping around out there, it took her a few seconds to locate him, and it was the portal's great aura she first sensed. He'd been standing on it earlier, but now he was down on the deck of the gateship. Still alive—thank Shylezar, Thanok, and all of the forgotten gods of ages past—but she sensed that he was in pain.

Regretting that she'd been too busy to check in with him again, Jadora asked, *Jak? Are you... Is the battle going as well as can be expected?*

It's not her fault, he blurted.

She blinked. *What?*

Don't blame her, all right? Next time you see her. It was the parasite.

Using her senses, Jadora checked him again, but all she could tell from a distance was that he was in pain. *You're not gravely wounded, are you?*

She wished Sorath weren't leading them in the direction opposite Jak and the gateship, and that there weren't work yet to do.

"You're supposed to say that you enjoy being carried by me," Malek said as he followed Sorath and Ferroki around a corner.

"I thought you knew that."

"It's still nice to hear."

Malek slowed as Sorath and Ferroki came to an abrupt halt.

Thank you for destroying the weapon, Jak said. *We* all *appreciate that, but the portal especially does. If it had lips, it might kiss you.*

Jadora eyed red lightning streaking past above. *Just have it keep stray bolts from hitting us, and that'll be good enough.*

I'll try.

Sorath swore. "The control room is up there in that series of caves, but that's too far to jump."

Jump? Jadora tried to see around his and Ferroki's backs.

"Give me your dagger again," Malek said, coming up beside Sorath and juggling Jadora in his arms so he could hold out his palm.

She started to ask why but saw a gaping hole torn in the floor of their corridor, a broken power tendril visible below and the white ice of a glacier far, *far* below. They'd crossed back over the shafts they'd been crawling through earlier. That dragon had done a lot of damage trying to get to them.

"The rifle too," Malek said. "There's only a little dragon steel in those bullets, but they might keep me from lifting you."

Sorath and Ferroki frowned but handed him the weapons. Jadora sensed Malek using his magic to lighten her so he could grab everything at once before he floated Sorath and Ferroki across.

"You really can put me down," Jadora said.

Malek shook his head, crouched, and sprang, using raw zidarr muscle to carry them across.

Through the hole, Jadora spotted a dark shadow. A *winged* shadow.

Surprisingly, she barely sensed the dragon making that shadow, but there was no mistaking that shape. She hoped it was heading for the battle and hadn't spotted them. No matter how distracted the creatures were, as soon as they figured out what Jadora and the others were up to, they would break away and come after them.

As Malek landed on the far side, and Ferroki and Sorath took back their weapons, Jadora's senses twanged, alerting her to a dragon arrowing down from above. She blurted a warning and pointed as it brought its wings in tight to land in front of the cave entrance. *Blocking* the cave entrance.

It roared at them, sending power that would have blasted them back and dropped them through that hole, but Malek held Jadora, protecting her with his dragon-steel sword, and Sorath grabbed Ferroki before the magic struck. It whispered past them without affecting them.

Ferroki lifted her rifle, aimed at the dragon's eye, and fired. It turned its head, though it didn't seem to believe the bullet would reach it and shrieked in surprise when it lodged in its scaled cheek.

Presumptuous human vermin! It ran at them, the walls of the corridor not leaving room for them to slip past.

Sorath charged it with a roar. Malek only took long enough to set down Jadora before rushing to join him, facing an enemy side by side with Sorath once more.

Ferroki lifted the rifle to fire again, but Jadora gripped her arm and pushed it down.

"I have to help them," Ferroki blurted, her eyes wide as the dragon snapped at Sorath's head.

"I know, and we will, but we need to plant one of those bullets in *each* dragon instead of wasting them by lodging multiple rounds in one. It's how we're going to cure them."

Another angry roar nearly drowned out her words. Sorath ducked, barely evading the snapping jaws, as Malek leaped in and cut into the creature's maw.

Though Jadora wobbled, still dizzy after the head trauma, she reached within herself for magic to use to distract their foe. But a roar from behind them—from underneath that hole—made her falter. The other dragon was coming.

"Look out." Jadora pulled Ferroki to the side, envisioning the creature arrowing toward their backs, its talons stretched out to stab them.

The dragon flew through the hole, but it landed beside it and didn't attack them. It looked at them with its single yellow eye, but its gaze soon focused on the other dragon.

You! The dragon attacking Malek and Sorath paused to glare behind the human party.

Yes! I! Yoshartov, slayer of enemies, winner of races, more magnificent than the stars!

You brought the human infestation into our lair. And you're supposed to be dead!

I live. And I shall keep you from killing my loyal servants. Yoshartov leaped over Jadora and Ferroki and barreled into the other dragon.

"I'd been wondering what happened to him," Ferroki said.

"He crashed after flying us here." Jadora caught a glimpse of Yoshartov's body as he sailed overhead and spotted more blue scales than had been there the last time she'd seen him. But she was puzzled about his appearance since she'd last *seen* him sinking into the ocean, dead. Or apparently dead. "We thought he'd died."

Sorath and Malek paused, their weapons hanging in midair, as surprised to see Yoshartov as Jadora, but they recovered quickly and rushed in to help him. With the enemy dragon focused on defending against the larger threat—who *was* scorched and gouged from his earlier battle—they could easily find openings.

They leaped in, cutting into whatever part of their enemy they could reach, then leaped back out again before they were battered with a wing or talon. With the two dragons wrestling, it was almost as dangerous to be close as when the group had been facing their enemy alone.

Screeches and roars filled the corridor, making Jadora wince and glance up, certain the fracas would draw more enemies. All she could do was keep a barrier around herself and Ferroki and hope it would be enough if the wrestling creatures rolled toward them.

Assailed from three sides, the enemy dragon gave a final roar of fury and launched itself into the air. It hissed at them, tongue flicking out, before flying out of view.

"I didn't know dragons could hiss," Ferroki observed.

"That one was particularly irked." Jadora hurried up to check on Malek and Sorath, but neither was gravely injured from the skirmish. Yoshartov had appeared in time.

But *why* and *how* had Yoshartov appeared?

He shook himself like a dog, water and blood hitting the walls, then folded in his wings and settled on his haunches in the corridor. *Did you miss me, Colonel Sorath, cooker of fish and fearless battler of dragons?*

"Terribly," Sorath said.

"We thought you were dead," Jadora said.

I was only playing *dead.*

Jadora had never seen a dragon wink, but Yoshartov's single eyelid flickered in an approximation.

When it grew clear that I couldn't survive being chased and attacked by so many, I flew down and appeared *to crash into the ocean. I dove down and under a ledge in the glacier that makes up this island, then used magic to slow my heart and body's metabolic process so I wouldn't need air for a while—and so the other dragons would not believe me alive. I also camouflaged myself the best I could.* Yoshartov preened under a wing, nipping at a blue scale. An itchy blue scale? *I am a most clever dragon.*

"You're an odd dragon," Sorath said. "And I'm not your servant. Especially now that you're…" He waved to the blue scales appearing among the brown and gray. "Molting."

I am changing back to my glorious former self. Like a butterfly emerging from a cocoon after having been a larval nothing for thousands of years. Yoshartov lifted his head and tilted it. *Of course, for that analogy to be proper, I would have had to be a butterfly, then turned into a larva, and then turned back into a butterfly.*

The booms of cannons rang in the distance, a reminder that the battle was far from over.

Malek pointed past Yoshartov. "We have to sabotage the workings of the fortress. Will you..." He looked at Jadora, as if she might have a better idea what they should ask a dragon to do for them.

That was more her son's purview. Given that they'd only finagled a ride to the fortress for their original deal, she didn't know how much they could expect from the dragon.

"We appreciate you flying up to help us," Jadora told Yoshartov. "Will you let us know if more trouble is coming? I'm certain that if you're willing to continue fighting nobly alongside us, Colonel Sorath will be impressed by your magnificence, and he and the captain will want to cook for you again."

Sorath stared at her.

"He was taken by some fish that you made him," Jadora explained. "He's mentioned it numerous times."

Ferroki snorted softly.

Malek waved for Jadora to follow and headed past the dragon toward the cave.

I do wish to have more fish spiced and cooked for me, Yoshartov said. *I will aid you in your endeavor.*

"Thank you," Jadora said as she hurried past. "If our plan works, we may also need you to carry Sorath and Ferroki to safety."

Plan? Yoshartov turned to watch them enter the cave.

"You'll see," Sorath said as he ran after them.

Dragon power sources will prove impervious to your human weapons, Yoshartov called after them, perhaps reading their intent in Ferroki's mind, her thoughts not guarded by a dragon-steel weapon.

"As impervious as the great beam weapon was?" Sorath called back.

Yes, exactly so. Great dragon engineering prowess goes into creating such devices.

"Check on that weapon and get back to us."

Glowing yellow and orange light came from a chamber ahead of them, drawing them past alcoves occupied by nests. Fortunately, those nests were all empty.

Malek stopped in the mouth of the chamber, the back half filled with glowing devices. Power tendrils trailed across the floor and disappeared through holes to what had to be more shafts below the floor.

Jadora frowned. Not only were the devices huge, but there were far more of them than she had expected. As she slung off her backpack to pull out the remaining vials of acid, she wished Vinjo were there to help her guess which were the most crucial to the operation of the fortress.

"Do you have enough acid?" Malek took up a defensive stance in the mouth of the chamber as Sorath and Ferroki also entered.

"I hope so. I also hope..." Jadora trailed off, not wanting him to worry, though *she* worried that when she applied the acid, the devices might blow up as spectacularly as the weapon had. The shockwave from that had nearly killed her.

Despite her intention not to worry Malek, she must have shared the memory with him.

"Can you levitate the vials over to the devices and use your magic to break them above them?" he asked.

"That's a good idea." Jadora didn't know if that would have worked with the weapon, but she admitted she hadn't thought to try it. Solving problems with power was still a new experience for her and not something she automatically fell back on.

"Zidarr are occasionally smart," Malek said, his eyes crinkling.

"I've heard that."

As Jadora levitated a vial toward one of the more important-looking devices, she said, "You may want to wait outside," to Sorath and Ferroki.

Sorath shook his head to object, but Ferroki took his arm and pulled him out of the chamber. "Trust her. It's a good idea for those of us without magic to protect ourselves."

"I have a dragon-steel blade," Sorath said, though he let her pull him away.

"I don't know if that's enough to protect you from explosions."

"You don't think *I* should wait outside?" Malek smiled at Jadora when they were alone.

"I'd happily shove you out there with them to keep you safe, but you would resist me."

"I would. Someone has to protect *you*."

Jadora nodded and took a deep breath as the vial hovered over the cylindrical-shaped pump she'd chosen. "Brace yourself."

With a nudge of power, she cracked the glass, and the acid dribbled onto the cylinder. As before, nothing happened immediately. It would take time for it to eat through the outer layer. She sent two more vials out over the equipment, selecting devices with power tendrils flowing out of them.

Dragons come, Yoshartov announced. *I will attempt to lead them away.*

Wait, Jadora blurted. *If this works, the fortress will crash. We may need help getting out before it hits the ground.* As she cracked open the two new vials, she shared an image of Sorath and Ferroki riding away on the dragon's back. Ideally, she and Malek would be able to levitate the group to safety, but if they were separated or if she were injured...

Then I will... Yoshartov hesitated. *Make a valiant and noble stand.*

Thank you.

Hm. He didn't sound that enamored with the decision.

When Jadora sensed how many dragons had abandoned the battle with the mageships and were flying toward them at top speed, she understood why. They must have realized they had saboteurs in their control area.

"Two dragons just landed in the tunnel out here," Ferroki yelled.

Smoke wafted up from all three devices, filling the air with a pungent scent reminiscent of magma.

"Keep them distracted if you can," Jadora yelled back.

Malek crouched nearby, his weapons in hand as he alternately looked at the smoke and toward the tunnel. Above them, Yoshartov sprang into the air, flying to meet the other dragons heading toward him.

Gunshots boomed in the tunnel. Ferroki. Sorath roared and sprang to meet the threat.

"Come on, come on," Jadora whispered, reaching for her last vial of the acid. More than two dozen devices occupied the chamber. What if the ones she'd selected didn't do anything crucial? Or what if the acid didn't work?

As more shots rang out, Malek turned. "I'd better help—"

Magic swelled in the chamber, and a thunderous boom erupted as the cylindrical device exploded. Even though Jadora had a barrier up, it hurled her into Malek. She bounced off *his* barrier as they tumbled into the tunnel, thrown by the shockwave of power.

Someone screamed in pain as Jadora hit the ground, but more explosions boomed, filling the air with blue smoke, and she couldn't get her bearings. The ground, walls, and ceiling trembled, and the world tilted sideways.

"We're falling!" Sorath cried, then broke into coughs. "Ferroki!"

Another explosion went off, and Jadora couldn't find her balance to rise to her feet. Malek reached for her, but her barrier kept him from making contact. She was afraid to let down her defenses. More devices had blown up than she'd sabotaged, and shockwave after shockwave rolled out of the chamber, the sheer magical power dwarfing what she could command.

Dread filled her as she realized she'd set off a chain reaction, and they might not be able to get out in time.

~

The collapse of the fortress was so abrupt that it startled everyone, and utter silence fell for several seconds as it plummeted out of the sky and landed on the glacier island below. The white ground shook, and the glacier calved, sending huge chunks of ice sliding down the slopes and into the sea. Despite the fall, the fortress itself remained intact, the dragon steel impervious to the end. But its aura diminished slightly, and it didn't look like it would rise into the air again soon.

A familiar one-eyed dragon soared out of the structure with two riders on his back. At first, Jak thought they were Malek and Mother, but he soon recognized Sorath and Ferroki.

Fear gripped him until he reached out with his senses and detected Malek's and Mother's auras. They were alive.

"Thank Shylezar," he whispered, slumping against the railing of the gateship.

They appeared from behind the fortress, levitating toward what remained of the fleet.

More than a dozen ships had fallen, crashing into the sea below after being struck by the beam, in addition to those that had been destroyed before Jak and the gateship arrived. Dozens more remained. Survivors.

In the battle, few dragons had been slain, but they stopped their attack after the fortress crashed. They flew away from the ships and gathered in the distance to confer in the air, with several shooting dirty looks toward the one-eyed dragon.

Yoshartov, Jak reminded himself.

The dragon flew with his head high, his tail swishing back and forth, as if he were quite proud of himself for the role he'd played. Maybe he was.

Something about him reminds me of you, Jak told Shikari, glancing back to check on his companion.

He'd climbed off poor Rivlen's chest and sat beside her. Her eyes were glazed, and she hadn't tried to get up. Jak suspected she was starting to feel the effects of the bacteria fighting against the parasite within her body. That made him want to find a damp cloth to rest on her forehead, but he didn't know if the battle was over. Those dragons might resume their attack.

Was it wrong of Jak to wish they would? He didn't want any more humans—or dragons—to be hurt, but he dreaded the aftermath and having to face Malek.

Did Malek know yet that Uthari had fallen? It was possible he'd been too busy in the fortress to sense his king dying. Or, if he did know, did he assume a dragon had been responsible? Not an ally? Not Jak.

He is not as clever as I am, Shikari replied.

Jak wrenched his mind back to his conversation with Shikari and tried to smile.

Are you sure? He was playing dead earlier, I think, and confused the other dragons. Jak hadn't spoken with his mother enough during the battle to catch the whole story, but he'd gotten the gist. *It must have worked because they left him in the sea.*

A simple ruse. When I am his age, I will come up with masterfully clever schemes to vex and befuddle my enemies. Shikari spun in a circle and made a stabbing motion with his tail, as if it were a spear.

I hope we won't need any masterfully clever schemes in the years to come.

It is foolish to hope for a future without any enemies at all, Jak. Shikari gazed into his eyes. *Did your mother not teach you this?*

Well, I like to be an optimist. Sometimes, your dreams can come true. After all, I always longed to ride a dragon, and now I have.

You are a human of simple dreams.

For a long time, it was an impossible dream, not a simple one.

All you had to do was find a dragon egg to hatch.

Yes, and people do that all *the time.* Jak hoped that all the dragons in the world—in the *worlds*—would be cured of the parasite and that it would be safe to return to the frozen world to remove the rest of the eggs from the ice. To bring many more young dragons into the world.

I hope for that too.

I wonder how many dragons my mother was able to infect with the death-darter bacteria. Jak would be able to find out soon. She and Malek were floating closer, giving the dragons a wide berth.

Afraid they would be easy targets if the dragons decided to take revenge for their fallen fortress, Jak watched the congregation intently. Sorath and Ferroki, riding the one-eyed Yoshartov, did *more* than watch them. They sailed toward the milling dragons, Sorath waving a dagger and Ferroki aiming a rifle at them.

Portal master! an excited voice cried in Jak's mind. *You must help my servants.*

Ah, Yoshartov?

Of course it is I! How many dragons converse with you?

More than you'd think. What do you need, and why are you on a suicide run with, uhm, they're not your servants. That's Captain Ferroki and Colonel Sorath. Jak looked to Mother and Malek again—were they going to levitate over there too?

Yes, they are great warriors who have promised to spice and cook more fish for me if we survive this. You must bid the portal to help. The firestick of bacteria-laced bullets must pierce the hides of as many dragons as possible.

Ah, Jak repeated, this time in understanding. They must not have had a chance to shoot many dragons when they'd been in the fortress. Jak rested a hand on the side of the portal. *Have you the power left to distract more dragons with your lightning?* He attempted to share what he understood of the bacteria and how the bullets could infect the dragons with it.

The portal pulsed blue, the frame warming under his hand. It conveyed agreement and perhaps indignation that Jak had implied it might be out of power.

Lightning sprang forth, and dragons who'd been preparing to attack Yoshartov were forced to raise their barriers. He turned so Ferroki could fire easily at her winged targets. The glowing blue bullets streaked toward the dragons as lightning branched and struck their barriers. The bullets sliced through their defenses, lodging in the scaled hides.

A few ragged cheers went up on the druid raft, roamers waving their arms. The seer with the staff was over there. She pointed it at Yoshartov—or maybe Sorath—as if to proclaim that her vision had been right.

The roamers chanted Sorath's name, which made Ferroki give him a wry—or maybe perturbed—look. He rode in front of her, but *she* was the one shooting the dragons.

If the tiny projectiles hurt the great creatures, Jak couldn't tell. It was more the lightning that seemed to disturb them, and perhaps the loss of their fortress. Amid screeches of displeasure, they turned to the north, flying off toward Zewnath.

We will regroup and return, vile humans! one cried.

Roars of agreement came from the throats of the dragons, but they didn't look back.

"Let's hope what they're really going to do is spend the next couple of days sick in the jungle before waking up to decide that humans aren't that bad, after all." Jak looked toward Rivlen, regretting that she would also have to spend the next couple of days sick before waking up feeling like herself again.

Sensing Mother and Malek's approach, Jak stepped away from the portal and took a deep breath.

To his surprise, Rivlen found the strength to rise, and she came over to stand beside him to face them. No, to face *Malek.* Mother wouldn't care a whit that Uthari had died. Malek was the one who would see Jak's hand in the king's death as a betrayal.

Jak drew a second breath, this one shuddery. Emotion tightened his throat and made his chest ache. He couldn't help but feel that he *had* betrayed Malek. Even if he believed the world would be better off without Uthari, he hadn't wanted to be the one to kill the wizard, especially not after Malek had specifically asked Jak to cure him.

By now, Gorsith, Tezi, Sasko, and the rest of the mercenaries had heard about Uthari's death, and they also watched Malek warily as he landed on the deck. Unlike Rivlen, they didn't come over to stand beside Jak. They looked like they didn't want anything to do with telling Malek what had happened.

Jak couldn't blame them, but he was glad for Rivlen's support, especially since her face was flushed with a fever, her lips cracked with dehydration, and her beautiful eyes plagued by dark bags under them. He clasped her hand.

Mother hurried up to him, lifting her arms for a hug, though she noticed the blood drying on the side of his face and halted, horror dropping her jaw. "What happened to your ear?"

"A little accident." Jak saw Rivlen wince in his peripheral vision. "It's not a big deal."

It stung as if someone were holding a burning brand to the tip of his ear, but given that others had suffered far worse fates, he couldn't complain.

"Oh, Jak." Mother hugged him, careful not to bump his ear. "Let me rest for a moment, and I'll heal that."

He patted her, relieved she'd made it out of the fortress, but the impending discussion he needed to have with Malek made it a distracted pat. Maybe she sensed some of what was on his mind, for she stepped back and to the side, though not before giving Rivlen a concerned look.

"Lord Malek," Jak said, compelled to formality.

Malek was looking toward the mageship that Uthari had ridden aboard. An officer stood at the railing, returning his look. And giving a telepathic report?

"I need to tell you something." Jak wanted to speak before someone else relayed their version of events, a version that might not flatter him—that might not be the truth.

Graveness hooded Malek's eyes, and Jak knew he'd already heard about Uthari's death.

"We tried to get the bacteria into him," Jak said. "Rivlen helped me. But he was… extremely displeased to see me. He attacked me—or maybe it was the parasites that made him do it. I don't know, but he or they seemed pleased to flatten me to the deck and—Well, that's not important, but it was self-defense. I promise. We genuinely *tried* to help him."

Rivlen nodded. "I got the needle in his neck and injected the concoction."

Malek gazed at Jak and didn't seem to hear Rivlen. Nor did he respond to Jak. Was that mage still speaking telepathically to him?

Jak didn't know if the disappointment he thought he saw in Malek's eyes was truly there or if it was a reflection of his own fears. He didn't *want* to disappoint the man who had become a mentor to him, who'd even become like a father to him. But he knew that Uthari had filled that role for Malek for thirty years. Maybe he wouldn't be able to forgive Jak for taking that person from him.

"I'm sorry," Jak whispered. "If you don't trust… I mean, if you want to see what happened, I'll lower my mental defenses for you."

As if Malek couldn't rip away Jak's modest defenses if he

wanted to see into his mind. Still, maybe the offer would mean something to him. Maybe Malek would prefer not to use force.

Malek kept gazing at him without speaking. Jak blinked away moisture in his eyes, not wanting to cry in front of him, his mentor, the last person he wanted to disappoint. To betray.

"No," Malek finally said with a soft sigh. "That's not necessary."

Malek dropped his chin to his chest, then walked to the hatch and descended into the gateship.

Jak stared at the hatch after he was gone. "What does that mean?"

He'd expected anger, disbelief, disappointment, accusations, and more. He had no idea how to interpret the abrupt departure.

Mother rested a hand on Jak's shoulder. "That he's devastated, I think. And probably that he trusts you."

"I don't see how he can in this case. He's got to question…" Jak looked at Rivlen.

She spread her hands, then went to the hatch herself, probably needing to lie down on a bunk.

"Do you think he'll forgive me?" Jak asked.

"I hope so. If it was self-defense or an accident, it wouldn't be logical for him to blame you or hold a grudge."

Jak shook his head bleakly. "Human beings aren't known for being logical."

Not when it came to feelings. He remembered how he'd railed at the world when his father had died, how he'd blamed everyone, even his mother, and how she'd taken up Father's work only because he'd guilted her into it. Logic had been far, far from his mind.

"He's a special man," Mother said, looking toward the departing dragons. They appeared as dots in the distance, only visible because dawn had come, brightening the sky.

Yoshartov was returning, flying Sorath and Ferroki toward the gateship.

"Do you think it'll work in the dragons?" Jak asked. "That there was enough of the new bacteria on those bullets to drive out the parasite?"

"I hope so. I don't want to have to fight this war all over again."

Jak didn't either.

"How many do you think Ferroki shot?" he asked. And would it be enough?

"Quite a few, I believe. And, as you suggested, those who are cured should want to cure the rest. We'll tell them about the death-darter bacteria, and they can figure out how to infect the rest of their brethren."

"Do you think they'll be able to? They need to not only get the dragons here on Torvil but across all the worlds in the portal network."

Mother nodded. "I know. But if I'm right, if it works the same way with dragons as with humans, once they've been infected with the death-darter bacteria, they won't be able to be reinfected by the parasites."

"I hope that's true."

"As do I." She squeezed his shoulder, then headed for the hatch. "I'm going to see if Malek wants company."

He might not. Jak didn't point out that Malek might see her as an extension of him and partially blame her. Was Malek really as logical or *special* as Mother believed?

If he doesn't, I can entertain myself in my lab. She patted a pocket, and it clinked.

You haven't changed much. Despite all the magical power.

I should hope not.

38

If the seasons had changed since the last time Malek visited the frozen land that held the secret stash of dragon eggs, he couldn't tell. If anything, it had grown colder. Icy air formed crystals in his eyelashes and froze the hairs in his nostrils with each breath.

I'm going to have siblings! Shikari danced about in the glacial cavern, his tail smacking the walls and leaving gouges in the ice. *Siblings to fly and frolic with me.*

Jadora smiled gently. Malek couldn't manage to duplicate the gesture. With Uthari's death so recent, he was struggling to feel anything but numbness. Numbness and the belief that he'd failed. Sending Jak to his mageship had been a mistake; Malek should have had the foresight to know that. *He* should have gone.

But that would have left Jadora sneaking into the dragon fortress without someone who could properly defend her from the inhabitants. And he would have been an equal failure if she'd died. Malek had to reluctantly admit that he would have missed her a lot more than he was going to miss Uthari. It felt like a betrayal to his mentor to admit that, even silently and only to himself, but… it was what it was.

"They're not going home with you," Jak said as he carefully used his magic to melt the ice around the eggs nearest the surface. Despite the cold, sweat beaded on his forehead from the effort. Melting ice wasn't difficult, but he had to use great care not to damage the eggs.

Malek sensed dozens and dozens of them buried within the glacier and, for the sake of Torvil, was glad they were to be taken back to Nargnoth. Before coming here, the group had visited Zelonsera, her guardians rousing her from hibernation so Jak and Jadora could report their success to her. Back on Torvil, the dragons Ferroki had shot were coming out of their illness with their scales turning blue.

Yoshartov had already completed the transformation, and he shimmered iridescently as he flew through the sky with Sorath on his back. Malek didn't know how the surly colonel had ended up with a dragon loyal to him, but the pair were inseparable now. Yoshartov continued to refer to Sorath as his servant and Sorath continued to inform him that he most certainly wasn't a servant, but that didn't keep them from flying around together, with Captain Ferroki also a frequent passenger. When Malek, Jak, and Jadora had left, dragon and riders and Thorn Company had been accompanying Uthari's fleet back to Utharika, everyone remaining on high alert until they knew all of the dragons had been turned.

Before departing, Malek had ordered the highest-ranking admiral remaining to make sure Thorn Company got paid for the last few months of work. In truth, Malek didn't know if he'd had the authority to do so, as the fate of Utharika and all of the Kingdom of Uth was undetermined. Someone back in Uthari's court would have to dig up his will and see who he'd named as his heir.

Malek hoped it was someone who could take charge quickly

and decisively. Otherwise, an opportunistic enemy would challenge that heir and attempt to usurp the kingdom. Just because Jak had convinced the fleets to work together against the dragons didn't mean there was an alliance or any love between the rulers who remained alive.

He supposed it was also possible the dragons would intervene in the way humans governed themselves. That was what Jadora and Jak had always desired. Malek couldn't bring himself to hope for that, as it would likely lead to another war, for no king would willingly give up his throne simply because a dragon wished it.

I will visit them often as they grow, Shikari announced.

"Maybe." Jak looked back at Malek. "We'll have to see if the portal is going to remain open. A lot of unfriendly things came through it in addition to tainted dragons, and I know the druids don't want that to happen again in their land."

"Zelonsera spoke of altering the portals so that only dragons can travel through them," Mother said. "For the protection of humans on all the worlds. Torvil isn't the only world that's struggled to defend itself against the great magical predators capable of operating it."

"I hadn't realized you'd had a conversation with her," Malek said.

They hadn't stayed on Nargnoth for long. Malek had wanted to accompany Jak and Jadora through the portal to protect them, but he also felt compelled to make the trip quickly, so he could get back to Utharika to defend the city, if need be, and help keep order. Threats might come not only from enemy kingdoms but from ambitious mages within its own walls. The face of Rivlen's father came to mind.

"Yes," Jadora said quietly as Jak freed another egg and rested it on the ground beside the growing collection. "I asked her to take her power back."

Malek blinked. "Why would you do that? To have magic is useful, even in academic studies. Surely, you've seen that."

"I have found it useful, but I'm not sure it'll ever feel natural to me. And I don't care for how arrogant male mages all want to have sex and offspring with me now." She wrinkled her nose.

"Great power is alluring. Though *some* arrogant male mages must be tolerable to you."

"Just one." She clasped his hand, making him wish they weren't wearing gloves, but it was too cold to leave flesh exposed. "And only because I've trained him to say *please* and *thank you* with me."

"Trained?" Malek quirked an eyebrow.

"Trained." She patted his chest with her other hand.

He clasped it and held it there. "What did Zelonsera say? I can't help but notice you continue to radiate immense power. Alluringly."

That prompted another nose wrinkle, but he sensed she didn't mind romantic interest from *him*.

"She said my body has integrated with the power within it and may depend on it to some extent now and that it might harm me if she removes it. And also that I may find it useful going forward, so I shouldn't be eager to cast it aside."

"She's not wrong," Malek said. "I know I talked about retiring and going off with you to visit archaeological digs or hunt for alchemically interesting plants, but the world will be in upheaval after this. I owe it to Uthari not to let his kingdom fall apart or be conquered by an opportunistic neighbor. If you stay with me, you might be a target for those who would want a handle on me. You'll be much better able to protect yourself if you keep that power. And protect Jak as well." Malek tilted his head toward him, knowing that argument would sway Jadora more than one about the importance of her own safety.

Jadora sighed and leaned against him. "I'd hoped that if we cured the dragons, the world could fix itself without our help."

"I don't know what the future holds, but I haven't noticed that human beings are good at *fixing themselves* without tremendous external influences forcing change."

"Dragons are tremendous external influences."

"But we don't know what they wish. Jak's fantasy is likely unrealistic." Malek didn't want to offend her, so he didn't point out that it was also *her* fantasy. He doubted that had changed for her since the days when he'd been able to read her mind. "They'll be too busy rebuilding their own society and raising their young to interfere with human civilization."

"We'll see." Jadora looked at him. "Have you heard anything from Vinjo about the orb? I've wondered what other information it might hold and if anything might be useful to people trying to bring more fairness and equality to the world."

Malek arched his eyebrows but didn't comment on her dreams. "You think he confides in me?"

"You did offer him refuge."

"Which practically makes us brothers," Malek said dryly.

"I'll take that to mean you haven't heard anything."

"I believe he *was* trying to repair it as the fleet flew north. I don't know if he'll be successful."

"I regret that my brusque manner broke it," Jadora murmured.

"Weren't you hurrying so you could come back to help me?"

"I was."

"I hope you don't regret *that*."

"No." She squeezed his hand through their gloves.

Shikari danced among the eggs, sniffing them as he investigated each new one. He galloped past Jak, whapping him in the back. *We will play later.*

"Of course," Jak said.

"We know what *some* dragons wish," Malek murmured.

Shikari paused in front of another egg. *This one is a female. Perhaps she will one day be my mate.*

Jak gaped back at him. "Aren't you a little young to want a *mate*?"

Of course not. I am growing large and maturing quickly. I sense that these eggs are from several clutches, so we are not all related. That is good for the purposes of mating.

"Do you even know what mates do with each other?"

They have fun and frolic together. Shikari shared an image with all of them of two dragons chasing each other in the sky, then plunging into the sea and swimming and floating on the surface on their backs. One dove under the waves and came up with a fish in its mouth and shared it with the other dragon.

"I guess that's accurate," Jak said dryly.

Shikari shifted the image to show Jak and Rivlen swimming in the ocean and *Jak* diving down and coming up with a fish in his mouth. He waved for Rivlen to paddle over to share it with him.

"Uh, that's less accurate," Jak said. "I believe she likes her fish cooked first."

In the image, fire scorched the air in front of Jak's face, roasting the fish without roasting him. Rivlen came over and shared it with him.

"I'll be sure to suggest that activity to her when we get back." Jak wiped his brow and turned back to the eggs.

"I'll give him a break." Jadora kissed Malek on the cheek and went to change places with her son.

Malek thought about assisting her, but she had the power to handle the task herself, and the wary look Jak gave him as he walked over made Malek certain they should have a discussion about Uthari's death. He'd heard various versions of what had happened from the officers that had been aboard the *Soaring Eagle* —officers who'd been quick to point out that Jak should be put to death, per the ancient ways. But Malek trusted Jak's version the most. Maybe it was strange that he did, when he knew Jak had long wanted to see Uthari ousted from power, if not killed, but he'd come to know him and that he was honorable. Rivlen was too, and Malek doubted she would have stood at Jak's side and faced him if they'd been telling anything but the truth.

I am not angry with you, he told Jak.

Jak glanced at him. *I'm relieved. You know I hated him, but I also didn't want to make you mad or disappoint you. I—we—really did try to help him.*

I believe you. It's not your fault. Again, Malek couldn't help but feel that he was the one responsible because he'd made the choice to send Jak. Whether he'd fully realized the ramifications at the time or not, he'd chosen to go with Jadora instead of going to Uthari. He had to accept the consequences.

What will happen to us now? Jak touched his chest, then pointed at his mother. After hesitating, he also pointed at Shikari. *My grandfather back home too. Do you know who's in charge of Uth? Will we be able to go home, or are we still...* His mouth twisted. *Prisoners?*

It's hard to imprison someone who has a dragon at his side.

Maybe, but all the mages who saw Rivlen and me kill Uthari really hate me. They or you—or whoever comes after Uthari—could keep us from living in Sprungtown, keep me from going back to the university to finish my studies.

After all this, is that what you wish to do?

Yes. Shikari said he would be happy to fly Rivlen and me to the different worlds so I can map them. I can create the first atlas on Torvil of all the worlds in the portal network.

I don't know who will end up in charge, but I'll attempt to use my influence to make sure you and your dragon can attend the university. Though I don't think any of the desks there are large enough for him.

He can sun himself by the pond while I'm in class.

More likely, he'll be fishing and denuding your pond of its inhabitants.

That's possibly true. Jak bit his lip and looked toward the egg extraction instead of at Malek. *I was also hoping you might stay around and continue to teach me sometimes. You're a good instructor, and I hope you don't go back to being the next king's... zidarr.*

Malek could no longer read Jak's mind, but he was positive the word that had first come to his mind had been *assassin*. Malek hadn't mentioned his plan to retire from being a zidarr to anyone but Jadora, and now that the future was in flux, he didn't bring it up. He did say, *I am a different person than I was thirty years ago when I swore an oath to Uthari. I wouldn't be quick to promise to be a loyal zidarr to anyone else.* He smiled faintly. *Except perhaps your mother.*

He almost expected a nose wrinkle from Jak. Though he hadn't objected at any point to Malek's relationship with Jadora, it had to be strange for him to see his mother with a man who wasn't his father.

Well, she *won't make you do anything onerous,* Jak said.

You don't think so? She makes me say please *and* thank you.

Jak snorted. *That's because she's a good influence on you, not a bad one. Mages have a lot to learn.*

Malek didn't point out that Jak was a mage himself these days.

The dragons will teach them, Jak said firmly.

Malek arched his brows, though he believed he was right, that the dragons would be too busy rebuilding their society to worry about what the humans of Torvil were up to.

We'll see, was all he said.

~

Rivlen walked beside Tezi and Sasko through the courtyard of Uthari's castle and into the corridor that would take them up to the treasury. Numerous guards also accompanied them, mages who'd once been unflappable and certain about their duties but who were sharing uneasy glances with each other as they wondered what would become of them now that their king was dead. As of yet, nothing akin to anarchy had descended upon the city, but since Uthari had never made his heir public knowledge, a lot hinged on the reading of the will. The anarchy might come after that.

If so, Rivlen was prepared to help get her family out of the city, though her father was a fit and virile mage and might insist on staying and throwing his support behind his favorite candidate. Her mother, though, would need protection. She was a crafter, not a battle mage.

Not that Rivlen had yet gone to check on them. She told herself it was because she'd been sick, the vestiges of the illness leaving her fatigued, and the fleet had only arrived home the night before. There simply hadn't been time. Besides, it wasn't as if her father had come to the docks to visit *her*. All he'd done was send a telepathic message that he wanted to see her and hear firsthand what had happened to Uthari. He'd said nothing about being glad she was alive; he was probably worried that she'd brought shame to the family.

She shook her head and imagined Jak smiling at her and telling her she deserved a dragon-steel weapon and more. That, she decided, was enough. She was done worrying about what her father thought of her. If her family needed help, she would give it, but if her father didn't approve of her, so be it. It had taken her twenty-five years to figure it out, but she was enough without him.

"Do you really think we'll get paid, ma'am?" Tezi whispered to Sasko as they walked.

"I hope so," Sasko said. "I have plans."

"To find recruits, buy new gear, and fully outfit the company for future battles?"

"I have a feeling *you'll* be doing more of that than me."

"Ma'am?" Tezi cocked her head.

"She's leaving you to go off with her sexy engineer," Rivlen said, having no trouble picking up the lieutenant's thoughts.

Sasko was so distracted by said thoughts that she'd almost walked into a column earlier. They danced from images of her and Vinjo in bed to them traveling all over the world on the gateship together, the vessel modified to be one large engineering workshop. Thoughts of them together in a house with toddlers running about occasionally popped into her mind as well.

Rivlen couldn't imagine fantasizing about Vinjo, but to each her own. After all, she'd had a few fantasies of what she and Jak would do when he returned. Now that she could no longer infest anyone with parasites through kisses, she looked forward to pursuing that activity. Frequently.

"Leaving the company?" Tezi gaped at Sasko. "That's not true, is it, ma'am?"

"I won't leave right away, but I did talk to the captain about it," Sasko said. "She said she'll forgive me for leaving her. Possibly because of her new infatuation with her strapping colonel, she wasn't even that distressed when I brought it up."

More likely, Ferroki had seen it coming. She had to be used to occasionally losing people from her command when they fell in love and decided to start families.

"I gather Sorath will help Ferroki out with training and running things until my replacement is a little more seasoned."

"Your replacement?" Tezi asked. "Who will *that* be? Sergeant Tinder?"

"No." Sasko gave her a sidelong look. "That's not who she has in mind."

Tezi might have inquired further, but they reached the heavy gilded door of the treasury, magic and a huge wheel and locking mechanism securing it from possible robbers. The castle steward applied intricate magic to it before it swung open, but he paused before going in to re-read the paper in his hand.

Ferroki had tabulated what she believed the company was owed. Rivlen didn't think it an extravagant amount, especially given how many people she'd lost while Thorn Company had been forced to work for Uthari, but the steward wrinkled his nose with distaste. Lord Malek had signed the paper, but zidarr didn't usually have anything to do with treasury requests.

"This should wait until Uthari's heir has been declared," he said, looking at Rivlen.

As if she had anything to do with the agreement Uthari had made with the mercenaries. She'd only come along because she'd worried the steward would balk. He'd only been swayed to head to the treasury in the first place by the large one-eyed dragon perched on the ship that had brought Thorn Company back north. Yoshartov was only ferocious until he spoke, but he'd fortunately done little of that while looming intimidatingly over the man.

"Depending on what happens with that, the mercenaries might need to be called again to fight and help defend the city," Rivlen said. "It's a good idea to pay people for the last job before trying to recruit them for a new one."

Sasko curled a lip, her thoughts proclaiming that she didn't want Thorn Company to be called upon by mages ever again.

"I just don't know if a zidarr's authorization is sufficient in this matter," the steward said. "I could be in trouble if the next ruler wants—"

"Get their money," Rivlen said tersely, using her power to add compulsion to the words. "Or the girl with the big dragon-steel axe will get crotchety and lop your head off."

Since Rivlen still carried the dragon-steel sword that Uthari had lent her, she could have threatened head-lopping of her own, but the axe had a larger and more menacing blade.

The steward eyed Tezi, who lifted her chin and folded her arms across her chest, the axe haft poking over her shoulder from its carrier on her back. "I've heard that thing has killed some dragons."

"It has," Tezi said.

"Think about how much less scaled and armored you are than a dragon," Rivlen said, "and then decide if you want to keep dawdling."

The steward grimaced, but he walked into the vault, muttering about how alarmed his wife would be if he developed scales. Coins clinked inside as he counted out the amount.

Sasko elbowed Tezi. "Congratulations, Corporal. You're officially menacing. I know you worried it would never happen."

Tezi smiled slightly. "I think it's the *axe* that is menacing."

"Nah, you've got scars now, and your arms aren't as spindly as they used to be. You look like a soldier instead of a whore."

Rivlen raised her eyebrows, debating whether that was a compliment or not. The mercenaries had crass humor.

Fortunately, Tezi appeared pleased by the dubious accolade. "Thank you, ma'am."

The steward returned and deposited a bag of coins in Sasko's hand. "I hope we won't need your services again."

"Trust me. We hope the same thing." Sasko hefted the bag a few times, then turned around to leave. "Come on, Tezi. The captain wants to see you."

"About what, ma'am?"

"You'll find out."

As Rivlen watched them go, she wondered how long it would be until Tezi realized she was being groomed as Sasko's replacement. Or maybe, through her actions and determination to keep the mercenaries motivated through all this, she'd been grooming herself.

Rivlen started to follow them out of the castle but slowed down as she grew aware of a few familiar auras approaching the city from the south. First she sensed Shikari, then Jadora, then finally Malek and Jak.

She smiled as she reached out, eager to see him again. *Did you return with a few hundred dragon eggs?*

Jak beamed pleasure into her mind and shared an image of them falling into bed naked together, though he hastily pulled it back, and she had a feeling it had been an inadvertent sharing of his fantasy. She didn't mind. She'd been having a similar one.

No, the eggs went to Nargnoth. Zelonsera and her guardians are going to start raising them. She doesn't think she'll live much longer, so she didn't want to wait until they were certain all of the tainted dragons had been cured before hatching them. She did, however, ask Mother to prepare more of the death-darter bacteria, so they can be infected prophylactically. If that's done with all dragonlings when they hatch, they shouldn't have to worry about any dragons being tainted for a long time.

Rivlen winced at the memory of being ill as the parasites and bacteria battled within her body. *I suppose being sick is better than being taken over by a parasite.*

Yes, but they shouldn't get that sick if the bacteria are injected before the parasite ever finds them. They only need to have them spread through the body for a bit, and then they can eradicate them. The dragons know how to do that. We're lucky the ones Ferroki shot were too busy battling us to realize what had happened. Since most of them have already turned, we're assuming they didn't figure out until later that they'd been infected with something they could kill. Fortunately. If the future tainted dragons figure that out early, they may have to be sedated while the bacteria battle the parasite. Jak shrugged into her mind. *The blue dragons can handle it. We've cured enough of them now for them to be in charge of fixing the rest of their kind.*

Maybe you can smear bacteria on Shikari's tail, and he can go around whapping them all with it.

He is an effective whapper.

I'm imagining you rubbing the bruises on your back, Rivlen said.

Oh? I was hoping you were imagining me naked and under the covers with you, satisfying your womanly needs.

I woke up imagining that and was distraught that you weren't in bed with me.

Really? Jak did the mental equivalent of clearing his throat. *I mean, of course you were, as I am manly and extremely desirable in bed.*

You're even more desirable when you don't say stupid things like that.

Hm, maybe I shouldn't talk when we meet later?

Probably wise. She sent her own image of them in bed, one in which his mouth was far too busy for talking.

He returned such warmth and affection for her that it nearly stole her breath. It *did* make her wish she was somewhere in private, not walking down a corridor with the steward and the castle guards.

Later, she told herself. Later, she and Jak would find privacy and have a wonderful time together. Let the world figure out how it would go forward. They had done enough.

~

Tezi parried the knife thrust without giving ground, then swept her axe toward her assailant. He leaped back, pulling in his belly, but recovered quickly, seeming to melt around the big blade to get in close enough to swat her on the forearm with the flat of his dagger. She grunted, yanking her weapon back into a defensive position.

"Just when I think I'm improving," she muttered.

You are *improving.* Grunk stepped back and saluted her with the dagger. *Knife fighters are fast and shifty.*

"You are shifty," she agreed.

Grunk smiled, showing off his sharpened teeth. Somewhere

along the way, she'd stopped seeing them as alarming, and the mad glint in his eyes wasn't as off-putting anymore. At least to her. Tezi didn't know if the druids fully understood him. After the battle, he'd joined Thorn Company to fly north with them. As far as she knew, he hadn't asked if he could; he'd simply shown up, and, in the aftermath of the dragon chaos, nobody had seemed to notice that there was a druid roaming about. Tezi had a feeling Lieutenant Sasko or the captain would say something sooner or later. Now that they'd been paid, the company would leave for its next mission, and Grunk... Where would he go?

Needing a break from their sparring match, Tezi lowered her axe. "Are there other druids up here in the north? Will you return to them?"

Grunk hesitated, then shook his head. *Too broken. They are kindly people. Sane people. Don't need a fighter who has nightmares all the time and wakes up—* Grunk spun and lashed at the air behind him.

"Plagued by memories of the past?" she asked.

Facing her again, Grunk shrugged. *Plagued by much. Warriors understand.* He waved at the mercenaries, though after all Thorn Company had been through, most were taking the opportunity to relax, lounging on the grassy lawn outside the city wall. Numerous mageships, including the gateship they'd ridden back north, were docked nearby.

"They do." Tezi still had nightmares of her own that plagued her. She'd hoped that getting the axe and better learning to defend herself would change that, but maybe the past never completely left one's mind.

Maybe I can stay with your people. Grunk shrugged again, but he looked at her intently, with hope in his eyes. *Like the engineer.*

"As far as I know, Vinjo hasn't been invited into Thorn Company." Nor would Tezi, a mere corporal, have the power to recruit new soldiers, especially male soldiers, into the all-female mercenary unit. She was about to say she would ask the captain, but Grunk pointed at Vinjo and Sasko.

Are you sure?

Sasko was leaning against Vinjo as he gestured at the gateship with one hand. His other hand was quite firmly on her butt.

Tezi snorted. "I think Sasko might be leaving rather than Vinjo joining." It had taken her a while to parse the lieutenant's earlier words, but when Tezi had seen them holding hands and making plans for renovations to the gateship, which Vinjo seemed to think he was going to be allowed to take when they departed, it had dawned on her.

Captain Ferroki caught Tezi's eye and walked over.

"Good afternoon, ma'am," Tezi said.

"Tezi. Grunk." Ferroki nodded to them. She'd received a few new scars during her time trapped in the dragon fortress, or perhaps in the battle when she'd been captured, but the wounds had largely healed, and she didn't appear too traumatized. If anything, Tezi had noticed her smiling more, especially when Sorath was around.

Sorath and his dragon. It boggled Tezi's mind that the roamer seer had been right and that Sorath had ended up with a dragon to ride.

"Will we be leaving soon? Or waiting to see, uhm?" Tezi waved in the direction of Uthari's castle. She'd heard the old wizard's will would be read and an heir announced. There was speculation that fights might break out in the aftermath, if he'd chosen someone the populace didn't approve of. Or if he hadn't chosen anyone at all. Then the city—the entire kingdom—would be up for grabs by whomever had the power to claim it. "If we're needed," she finished.

"Even if we are needed, I'm disinclined to volunteer our services in another battle involving mages and dragons." Ferroki frowned, a reminder that they hadn't *volunteered* for any of the previous battles, not since first leaving Zar. "I've been having a powerful urge to go back to the desert and break up bandit camps along the highway."

"I'm ready for whatever's next, ma'am."

Ferroki smiled. "Like the hungry fox in the thicket. I believe you are."

"I was wondering something though." Tezi glanced at Grunk. "Is there a rule that says absolutely no men can join the company?"

"It's traditionally been all women."

"But could there be exceptions? Grunk's a good fighter, and he… doesn't have anywhere else to go." Tezi hoped he didn't mind her pointing that out to others. She didn't think he'd told it to her in strict confidence.

"I suppose if you vouched for him, I might allow it," Ferroki said.

"Oh?" Tezi hadn't realized her word would have much sway.

"Assuming you're planning to stick around for a while."

"Oh, I am, ma'am. I don't have anywhere else to go either." Tezi had, now that she had a dragon-steel blade and could handle herself in most situations, thought about going back to her homeland to see if she could find her brother, but the idea of hunting for him alone in a city of mages daunted her. Maybe if Grunk joined the company, they could one day take leave together, and he would join her for the trip.

"That's the story for most of our troops. Per Sasko's recommendation, one I agree with, I'd like you to think about doing some extra training with the thought of one day becoming an officer."

"An officer, ma'am? I thought you and Sasko were the only ones."

"We are currently, but we've had more in the past, when the company was larger. And Sasko wants to retire, if you can believe that. I'll need to replace her eventually with someone who would be willing to accept the responsibility of being second-in-command of the company. Maybe even *all* the way in command one day."

Tezi's jaw sagged open as she realized what Ferroki was suggesting. "But there are so many who are older and more experienced."

"There are, but not everyone has the desire, personality, and mental fortitude for leadership. Also, I'm not talking about you taking over Sasko's or my position tomorrow. I just want you to think about it, and if you're interested in becoming an officer, we'll talk more." She nodded to them and headed back to the grassy lawn as a dragon flew into view.

Shikari. And Jak was riding him. Appearing a natural, as if he'd been born riding dragons, he smiled and waved down at them.

A second dragon flew into view, Yoshartov with Sorath on his back.

There was nothing natural about the way Sorath gripped the one-eyed dragon's back, legs clenched against his scaled flanks. His bronze skin looked far paler—or maybe *greener*—than usual, and the reason became apparent when Yoshartov and Shikari flew into sinuous somersaults and rolls, magic keeping their riders on their backs without harnesses or even saddles.

Jak laughed and lifted his arms in the air, the wind whipping through his hair, as if the experience was the greatest ever. Sorath's cheeks puckered, as if he was trying not to throw up.

I came on Lord Malek's behalf, Jak said telepathically to Tezi, *to let you know that Uthari's will is to be read this evening in the castle's audience chamber.*

Is there something in it that concerns mercenaries? Tezi didn't know if that had been an invitation or a warning.

I haven't the faintest idea what's in it. I'm only relaying the informa-

tion. Malek thinks trouble may break out afterward, and if your people don't want to be caught up in it, they should leave beforehand.

We've been discussing that possibility, but unless one of these mage-ships wants to fly us to our desert homeland, we're stuck here.

I'll ask Malek if he can arrange transport for you before... Well, he doesn't know if he'll have any power once the new ruler is announced.

Ask him soon then, please.

I will.

Isn't it possible that you will also be in trouble? Tezi pointed at Jak. *And your mother?*

Oh, highly possible. Most of the mage officers in the fleet now glare at me as they rub their daggers. Malek said he'd keep an eye out for me, but it's possible Mother and I will have to disappear too.

I hope that's not the case. You both did so much. They should see you as heroes.

I'd settle for being able to go back to school and not having mage assassins come after me. Jak looked toward Vinjo and Sasko. *Vinjo is asking me if he can have the gateship. I don't know if he realizes I don't have any power in this city or influence over anyone.*

He seems a touch oblivious to such things.

I've noticed.

Shikari banked and flew over the city wall, and Jak disappeared from view.

"We should pack up and prepare to go," Tezi said.

Go where? Grunk asked.

"The next adventure." She smiled at him and went to talk to the others.

39

"How nervous should I be?" Jak whispered, wiping his palms on his trousers, then tugging his hat lower on his head, as if he might escape notice.

Given that everyone in the castle's audience chamber was a mage, that was unlikely. Jak eyed Uthari's vacant throne, remembering the last time they'd been gathered here, when the king had hurled a dish of parasites at Shikari's feet. He couldn't help but worry that Uthari would find a way to torment him from his grave.

"You?" Rivlen asked from his side, her uniform crisp and clean, her dark hair swept back in a tidy bun. "You have a *dragon* beside you to ensure nobody pesters you."

"Technically, he's above me." Jak pointed toward the roof where Shikari was perched. "He doesn't fit through doors anymore."

"I'm sure he'll *make* a door if he needs to help you. You have less to worry about than I do. I..." Her expression grew bleak as she eyed the stiff-faced officers in the chamber, all there to hear the reading of Uthari's will, and she didn't finish.

Yes, Rivlen had been at Jak's side and helped him kill Uthari.

Depending on who ended up in charge, they could both be in danger of retribution. Unlike with Thorn Company, Jak couldn't tell Rivlen to vacate the area. Not only was Utharika her home and where her family lived, but, unless she was told otherwise, she was a captain in the fleet, an officer who'd sworn to always serve and obey the crown.

Jak had overheard speculation about who Uthari might have named his heir, and he'd been surprised to catch a few officers glaring at Rivlen and accusing her of sidling up to the old wizard in the end because she'd been angling to be named his successor. He shook his head, irritated that those idiots refused to accept the truth, that Uthari, acting under that parasite's influence, had sidled up to *her*.

"If anyone tries to pester you," Jak said, "Shikari will roar at them, and I'll glare in a fierce and manly manner."

"What will that do?"

"Terrify them. Have you heard Shikari's roar lately? This morning, he made a ferocious guard dog in front of a vendor's stall clench its tail and tinkle down its leg."

"I meant *your* glare. I know dragons are ferocious, but you..." She cocked an eyebrow at him. "You look wholesome even when you glare."

"It's a good thing some women like that."

Her face softened, though the worry remained in her eyes.

"Some women do," she agreed. "Thanks for coming for me on the mageship, especially given that I was..."

"Forceful and demanding?" Jak winked at her. "Some men like that."

"Good." Rivlen clasped his hand.

Aware of his mother standing on the other side of Malek, Jak glanced at her. He didn't *think* she objected to Rivlen, especially after all they'd been through, but she hadn't specifically said that she approved of their match.

She, however, was clasping hands with Malek and gazing at *him*. She'd never asked if Jak approved of their match, so he supposed it was all right if he spent time with Rivlen without asking for a parental blessing. Though, as he caught the dark glower of a man entering the chamber and Rivlen stiffened at his side, Jak was tempted to release her hand. It was Admiral Dayum. And Rivlen's father had made it clear that *he* didn't approve of Jak.

I've decided to stop caring what he thinks, but I do wonder what he's heard. Rivlen sighed into Jak's mind, squeezing his hand instead of releasing it.

Probably about my ferocity and how we worked flawlessly together to defeat the dragons. Jak smiled at her and didn't mention the incident with his ear. His mother had stopped the bleeding and sealed the wound, but there wasn't anything to be done about the missing tip. At least he didn't need it to draw maps or use his power.

Those who went into the fortress did most of the dragon defeating, Rivlen pointed out.

We played an important role too.

You were paramount in assisting our people, Shikari informed Jak from the rooftop.

Are you reading my mind even through my mental defenses? Jak asked, though he wasn't offended.

We are linked now as dragon and rider. It's typical for us to know each other's thoughts.

Is it? Our literature didn't mention that.

Your literature is old and incomplete. Have no fear. I will stay out of your mind when you undergo human mating rituals.

Uh, I appreciate that. I'll do the same for you when you meet attractive female dragons—or rather when they grow old enough for you to meet. Jak didn't know how fast dragons matured—they certainly *grew* quickly—but he had a feeling it would be some years before he had to worry about Shikari taking a mate.

Excellent.

Rivlen sighed. Her father was still looking at her, his face dark. Had they argued telepathically? She released Jak's hand, lifted her chin, and turned her back toward the retired admiral.

Dayum's eyebrows flew up. For a second, he looked like he would charge across the chamber and grab her, but he merely set his jaw and took up a position on the other side, facing the empty throne.

"Everything all right?" Jak asked softly.

I told him that if the family needed my help, I would offer it, but that I was done caring what he thinks, and I will find my own way in the world. He will no longer influence my decisions.

Ah. Jak didn't know what else to say—he didn't want to risk coming across as flippant—so he offered his hand and magically and emotionally attempted to share his support.

She clasped his hand again and looked toward the front of the chamber. Soft murmurs in the crowd suggested the time had come.

Several musical instruments played, and the castle steward, dressed in gold-trimmed blue, strode in and headed toward the throne. An older man that Jak hadn't seen before walked beside him, carrying an ivory box on a velvet cushion. Magic protected it, and Jak envisioned the steward being zapped across the audience chamber when he opened it.

It has already been opened, Shikari said. *I sense that the seal is broken.*

Can you also sense what's inside?

Slender sheets of wood pulp.

We call that paper.

Shikari sent the telepathic equivalent of a yawn.

The music fell silent, as did the conversations in the audience chamber, though people continued to nod and share glances, so telepathic communication likely continued.

Jak noticed Malek looking at him and asked, *There's not any chance that the will has been updated recently, is there? With a request for the castle mages to slay Mother and me?*

Nobody will slay you, Malek said.

Jak nodded, though he couldn't help but wonder what he was doing in the chamber. After all, he'd *killed* the man whose will was about to be read. But he had to learn what his and his mother's fates would be and trusted Malek to protect them.

"Nothing to be nervous about," he whispered.

A throat cleared at the front of the chamber, the steward ready to announce the contents of the will. More music played as he shook out voluminous sleeves, unrolled a piece of parchment from within the ivory box, and held it up.

"There is a list of items to be bequeathed to allies," the steward said. "There's also a list of enemies to receive vitriol and poison daggers. What you, however, are all curious about is who is King Uthari's heir, the future ruler of this kingdom and guardian over the sky city and those who reside in it. I'm sure it will be to nobody's surprise that King Uthari wished his successor to be Lord Malek zem Uthari."

Judging by the startled expression on Malek's face, it was to *his* surprise.

Jak let out a relieved exhale. His mother didn't look pleased, probably because they'd been talking about Malek retiring and the two of them going on adventures together. Rivlen nodded, as if she had expected Uthari to leave his kingdom to his favorite zidarr.

Most of the mages in the chamber nodded as well, some coming forward to bow to Malek and congratulate him. A few praised him profusely, promptly taking the opportunity to curry favor. Though he masked the shocked expression on his face, Malek stood still, saying little and looking numb at the crowd surging around him.

Nobody jostled Mother, not with her powerful aura intimidating them, but she stepped back regardless. Jak did too, wondering what this would mean for them—and for Malek. Would he actually *accept* the job? The *kingdom*? Would he feel he had to do as his old mentor had wished?

I guess we didn't need to worry about sending the mercenaries away, Jak told his mother. Though he had no doubt mages could smile, shake hands, and scheme and plot all at the same time, nobody was objecting openly to Malek as heir. Quite a few even looked relieved at the choice.

No, Mother agreed. *Maybe we should have sent* Malek *away.*

You don't think he wants this?

Mother shook her head sadly. *No.*

Do you think he'll accept it?

She hesitated. *I don't know.*

Servants filed into the chamber carrying trays of food and beverages. Slavebands gleamed on their heads, their eyes glazed as they wordlessly distributed the libations.

Mother's eyes narrowed as she watched them. *Though if he's willing, he could be the change we've hoped for all along.*

I think we have a better chance of getting the dragons to help mold a new future.

I don't know. He's already changed a lot in the time we've known him. And he's...

Special? Jak asked, their earlier conversation coming to mind.

She smiled. *He is.*

You're special too, you know. I guess if anyone can nudge him to be more of a humanitarian, you can.

You can't change anyone who doesn't want to change, but I hope that he's starting to see the world as we do.

If not, you can probably bribe him with bedroom favors.

He'd meant it as a joke and wasn't surprised when Mother gave him a scandalized look. *Really, Jak.*

Though she'd backed away from the mages earlier, Malek looked over his shoulder at her and lifted a hand. Because he wanted her at his side? Or because he needed support? Either way, she stepped forward and clasped his hand.

What did you say to your mother? Rivlen came up to Jak's side, her shoulder brushing his. *She looked scandalized.*

I may have suggested that bedroom favors can get a man to change and be a lenient ruler.

Really, Rivlen thought dryly. *Would simple pleasures of the body change* you?

It would depend on who was giving them and what changes she wanted.

She tilted her head toward a back corridor leading out of the chamber.

Are we going somewhere to do something interesting? Jak asked, happy to let her lead him away.

Oh, yes.

Will it involve you changing me through bedroom favors?

Rivlen gave him an arch look over her shoulder. *I've* already *changed you.*

That may be true, but I think I've changed you a bit too.

Of that I have no doubt. She squeezed his hand as they walked out together.

Dawn found Jadora and Malek snuggled in his small bed in his room in Utharika. The night before, Malek hadn't presumed to claim Uthari's suite, so they were in his sparsely furnished and even more sparsely decorated room in the castle. At least it was well lit with a large window letting in the early-morning light.

Jadora sensed that Malek was awake, but, despite his arm around her, he was subdued and distant. Lost in thoughts? She couldn't blame him, and she didn't prompt him to speak, simply waiting in case he decided he wanted to. She was, however, curious to learn what he would decide. To stay and rule over Uth? Or find someone else with more desire for the job? Even if he wanted to do that, would he? Or, after thirty years of service, would he feel compelled to obey Uthari's wishes one final time?

She stared bleakly at the wall, fearing he would. Her gaze snagged on a sign that held the five tenets of the Zidarr Code, the words barely visible in the wan light.

Integrity, duty, courage, austerity, honor.

Even if he retired from being zidarr, she doubted he would retire from upholding those values.

"I was, I believe, coming to terms with the ramifications of the choice I made," Malek said quietly, "when that will was read."

"And that changed things for you?" she asked.

"It made it worse. I... feel that I turned my back on him, and he still left me his legacy. To me, it's a burden rather than a reward, but I'm sure he didn't see it that way." After a reflective moment, Malek snorted softly. "Or maybe he knew exactly how I'd feel about it but also knew I would be compelled to protect his people and not let everything he built fall apart."

"I think so." Jadora didn't point out that she believed Uthari had been manipulating him to the last.

Malek was too smart not to realize for himself that it was at least a possibility. But even if he knew Uthari had manipulated him, that didn't mean the old wizard hadn't cared for him in some way. And Malek had certainly cared for Uthari. It didn't surprise her that he would feel duty bound to see the old wizard's desires carried out. Even if it meant committing the rest of his life to doing so.

"I think he knew before I did," Malek said slowly, "that he'd lost me. That I would one day have to choose between him and you. As much as we'd like to think otherwise, two things can't hold equal importance in your heart. The tyranny of time ensures that one will always have to be prioritized over the other."

He drew a deep breath and lifted a hand to his face. Jadora glimpsed moisture in his eyes before he wiped them. He started to look away, as if he didn't want her to see, but sighed instead and leaned his face against her shoulder.

She stroked his hair and waited a time before speaking again. When she did, she was tentative, wanting to respect his feelings. "Is it possible you could fulfill his final wishes without chaining yourself to his throne for the rest of your life?"

"I don't know." He lifted his gaze to hers. "How?"

"You know I'm biased in what I believe and what I want for humanity, so take that into consideration, but maybe you could keep Uth safe while also spearheading the creation of a new government. Maybe it's time for terrene and mage humans to both have a say in who leads them, to vote democratically for their rulers and to write founding documents that mandate that people of all persuasions be treated fairly. Nobody should be enslaved and forced to work for the ease of others. Everyone should have the opportunity to live life to its fullest, whether they have magical power or not."

After she finished, she held her breath, hoping he wouldn't be disappointed that she was bringing this up now, when he was dealing with his grief. But if she waited, he might be embroiled in his new position, locked into a future that she didn't think he wanted.

Malek brushed her cheek. "I am not surprised that pillow talk with you involves such topics."

His tone was light, and that gave her hope that she hadn't offended him.

"I should hope not. You've known me a while now."

"Yes. I am not opposed to giving the slaves their freedom—"

"And taxing regular, working, terrene humans less onerously," she put in.

He cleared his throat, and she bit her tongue. She ought to only ask for one thing at a time....

"Yes. But our entire system is built on free or cheap labor, and that would disappear if we changed everything. None of the mages would approve, and I'd find myself ousted from power, if not assassinated by the end of the first month of my reign. *You* might even be a target."

"Because those mages would actually have to work for themselves, they'd kill us?"

"Because they'd have to do what they consider *menial* work. They aren't trained or educated for any of it either. They'd probably starve."

"You can feel the pity oozing out of me."

"I believe that's sarcasm you're oozing," Malek said.

"Maybe."

"I'm open to discussing how things could be restructured slowly over years, but it's the work of a lifetime. And we are only one kingdom in a world of many."

"It's possible for one kingdom, one *person*, to lead by example."

"Hm."

Jadora shifted in his arms to face him and ran her fingers along his jaw and down to his chest. "I know I hope for a lot. I appreciate that you're open to considering some changes."

"*I* appreciate that you fondle me with almost as much interest as you do your microscope."

"*More* interest." She scooted closer and kissed him. "I rarely put my lips on the microscope."

"Only on special occasions?"

"Indeed."

Malek threaded his fingers through her hair and pulled her

close for a long kiss. Before it went beyond that, they sensed the auras of dragons. *Several* dragons.

Malek glanced toward his weapons, but Jadora held up a hand, sensing they were cured dragons, and they exuded... contentment. Was that the word? Whatever it was, they seemed to be in a good mood as they winged toward the city.

A knock sounded at the door. "Lord—er, Your Majesty Malek?" came the castle steward's voice.

"Just Malek is fine."

The steward hesitated. "I don't think that's proper, Sire, but I need to ask about the dragons that are approaching. Do you know if we're in danger? Do you want me to order the city defenses up?

Malek looked at Jadora and raised his eyebrows. She checked on the dragons again, picking out their emotions in their auras. They seemed like they were on an amiable mission, not a belligerent one. She shook her head.

"Not yet," Malek called, "but have the troops at the ready."

"Yoshartov is with them," Jadora said. "I wonder what they want."

"*He* likely wants spiced fish."

"That is possible, though Sorath is his purveyor for that."

"I can't tell if he's with them." Malek looked toward the window. "They don't seem to be carrying anyone who has dragon steel."

"It's early in the morning. I'm guessing Sorath is with *Ferroki* instead of a dragon."

"You think he prefers her company to a scaled creature that calls him a servant?"

"It's just a hunch."

Jadora sensed the dragons splitting, with several landing in the courtyard and Yoshartov and a large female flying toward their part of the castle. *Precisely* toward their part. She looked at the ceiling as the scratching of talons on the tile roof reached their ears. A dislodged square of terra cotta tumbled past the window and shattered on the walk below.

Oops, Yoshartov spoke into their minds.

"That dragon continues to be odd," Malek said.

"Based on what we've seen from him and Shikari, I'm beginning to believe their personalities may represent the norm and not a deviation from the mean."

They hadn't spoken yet with many of the dragons who'd recovered, but the handful she'd seen wheeling and diving in the distance had also seemed a touch eccentric.

"Shikari is young," Malek said. "He has a reason to be quirky."

"Were you quirky when you were young?" Jadora had a hard time imagining Malek ever being playful, though she was sure he must have been as a boy, before he'd lost his mother.

"I was regal and stately as befitting a future zidarr."

"Oh, I'm sure."

"There's skepticism in your voice."

"Is there? Strange."

"*You* probably spent your youth fondling microscopes."

"Looking at cells of plants was of interest to me at a young age."

"I knew it."

A large shadow fell over the window, blotting out the morning light. As one, they frowned over at the upside-down dragon head looking through the glass at them.

Malek made a disgusted noise and pulled up the blanket to cover Jadora's bare shoulders, though she highly doubted dragons were interested in such things.

What can we do for you, Yoshartov? she asked calmly, as if a dragon hanging from the gutters and peering in the window was a normal thing. The female dragon merely perched on the roof, surveying their surroundings.

The queen and I have come to inform you about what the Dragon

Council has decided regarding humans and their treatment of each other on this and other worlds.

Malek's expression switched from contentment to wary concern. "I thought they'd be far too busy with their own affairs to worry about us. When did they have time to form a council?"

Go ahead, Jadora said, curious about their verdict, though she hadn't realized the dragons were debating the fate of humanity. Had Jak spoken to them? She wouldn't be surprised if he had, but, like Malek, she *was* surprised that they'd already decided to do something.

We deem you an honorable leader, so we will not object to you ruling over this land, Yoshartov said.

"Wonderful," Malek muttered.

We have observed the inequality between those humans with power and those without, Yoshartov continued, *and this distresses us. It is because of dragons and the tools we gifted mankind long ago that some humans developed magical powers, powers that they've used to enslave others.*

Malek's jaw tightened, and Jadora worried this might lead to a lot more *restructuring* a lot more quickly than he'd envisioned. Though if the dragons were behind it, and they enforced change in the other kingdoms as well, maybe the mage populace wouldn't blame Malek and send assassins.

What are you going to do to change that? Jadora wondered if the dragons would decide to take magic from all humans, to put people back on level ground. Was that possible? When she'd asked Zelonsera to take *her* magic, the dragon hadn't been willing to do so, but she also hadn't said it was impossible.

It will take some time, but we will give everyone magic who wishes it.

Everyone? Malek asked. *All humans? That's a lot of people.*

Yes. As I said, it will take time. Yoshartov rubbed his snout on the glass, as if he had an itch. *Those who serve us delightfully seasoned fishes and meats might be moved to the front of the line.*

And those who agree that they're servants to dragons? Malek frowned.

Yoshartov showed off his fangs in a toothy dragon smile. *Only Colonel Sorath is a servant, because I defeated him many times in battle, and because calling him one irks him.*

You're intentionally irking the human you allow to ride you? Jadora asked.

Oh, yes. It's delightful. He irks me too. Last night, he called me a giant scaled slug. Can you imagine? When I'm so clearly gleaming with dragonly magnificence? Yoshartov flung himself from the gutter, knocking several more roof tiles off as he spun a somersault and flapped his wings to take to the air.

Get to the point, Yoshartov, the female said. *We have many human rulers to speak with today.*

Had Yoshartov been elected the liaison between humans and dragons? If so, what an interesting choice.

Yes, my most magnificent queen. Once more, Yoshartov perched on the roof and directed his words toward Malek and Jadora. *It may not be possible to make all humans have precisely the same amount of power, so they are equal, and some will always excel at battle or sport or academics and such, and they will continue to have advantages over others. We will, however, destroy the magical bands that enslave many humans. We will also help anyone leave their world and travel to another through the portal if they feel oppressed.* His telepathic voice grew stern. *We do hope, however, that there will not be* oppression, *King Malek. We will give this message to the other rulers as well.*

"I wasn't planning to oppress anyone," Malek muttered.

"Will you say *please* and *thank you* to people?" Jadora stroked his cheek.

"*All* people?"

"All people," she said firmly.

"You're the oppressing tyrant here, not me."

"Any chance you find that appealing in a woman?" Jadora smiled.

"Fortunately for you, I *do* find it appealing. Are you going to assist me with the changes it looks like we'll be forced to implement far more quickly than any sane person would have dictated?" He raised his eyebrows as the dragons launched themselves into the air, presumably heading off to land on the rooftop of the next ruler's bedchamber.

"It's not quite the retirement I imagined for you or the return to my career that I envisioned, but I'll stand at your side. Some things are more important than a single person's desires."

"They are," he agreed. "And I'll permit you to continue your studies."

"You'll *permit* me, will you?" She ran a hand over his shoulder, using her magic to tease his senses and remind him of her power.

"I will. I intend to be a magnanimous king."

"So you won't mind if I have microscopes and texts brought to our room today? I haven't studied that acid as much as I'd like, nor the other specimens I brought back from the water world."

"I won't object, as long as you make time to fondle me as often as you fondle your equipment."

"I think I can manage that." She wrapped her arms around him for a kiss.

EPILOGUE

One year later...

Jak whistled cheerfully as he copied onto large sheets of parchment the maps being projected into his mind by the softly glowing orb mounted on the desk beside him.

This is wonderful, Shikari, he spoke telepathically to the dragon soaring alongside the rebuilt *Star Flyer*, the new mageship under Captain Rivlen's command. *There's so much information in here. I knew there would be. The challenge was prying it out of Vinjo's hands. He's been hogging it all year, which is impressive since he's not even a subject of our kingdom.*

Admittedly, Vinjo had spent far more of the year in Uth than Zar. Malek had given him a workspace in the castle and kept calling him the court engineer. Vinjo seemed content to spend most of his time there while he waited for Sasko to retire from the mercenary life.

Is he not doing important work crucial in maintaining your civiliza-

tion's infrastructure now that the enslaved humans have been freed? Shikari asked.

He is, and I've been busy with school, but he still could have come by to visit and shown me some of the information in the orb. Jak patted the artifact fondly.

It had taken a while for Vinjo to get it working again, but once he'd accessed the knowledge inside, he'd rarely let it out of his sight. Just as Jak was now using it to make maps of other worlds, Vinjo had used it to make all manner of magical machinery. Some was for mining, some for farming, some for transportation, and some for tasks Jak hadn't heard about yet.

All he knew, from what Vinjo had said and what Jak had witnessed, was that the machines were far more advanced than anything Torvil had previously known. Tiny bits of dragon steel in each made them quasi-intelligent, enough to perform the mind-numbing tasks that slaves had once performed. Now, the freed slaves could pursue education and other interests, and Malek and the other rulers didn't have to worry about their people starving for want of food.

He might consider the work he's doing more important than cartography, Shikari said.

They're of equal *importance, I assure you.* Jak gave the orb another pat as a new map floated into his mind. *Of course, I intend to spend this voyage confirming and updating everything on these maps as we go through the portal to explore various realms. I'm sure the flooded world isn't the only one that's changed in ten thousand years. It's going to be such an amazing summer!*

Because you'll make maps?

Yes. You should be excited too, since Nargnoth is our first stop. Jak smiled, remembering how much Shikari had enjoyed their visit to see the other young dragons that spring. Dozens and dozens had hatched from those eggs, and they'd been learning to swim and fly and catch fish in between wrestling and chasing each other all over the swamp. *Are you going to seek a mate among the other young dragons?*

He didn't know if Shikari was interested in such things yet, but over the past months, he had reached his full adult size, so it was possible. It was also possible he just wanted more dragons his age to play with. He'd succeeded in getting Yoshartov to frolic with him, but most of the adult dragons, according to Shikari, mostly wanted to *educate* him. The queen had accused him of being overly ebullient and rambunctious.

More than once, Jak had asked if he wanted to leave Torvil and go be raised alongside the other hatchlings, but Shikari always said that he was *so* much older and more experienced than they that it wasn't necessary. Jak liked to think that Shikari considered this world his home and that he would miss Jak if he left.

I have not had mating urges yet, Shikari said, *but we will hunt and play together. I look forward to this.*

Me too.

Jak? Rivlen spoke into his mind from the forecastle above. *We're flying over Zewnath and getting close to the portal.*

I'll be right up. Do you want to see my maps?

Would you be crushed and heartbroken if I said that's not necessary until we reach a new world and have need of one?

Yes.

Then of course I want to see them.

Why don't I believe you?

Because I already have my favorite map. Rivlen shared an image of her holding up the sphere he'd made for her the year before. *All the maps in it are originals now, thanks to your diligent updates, and not simply reproductions from some uptight sphere.*

Uptight? This is an Orb of Wisdom! Made by the dragons of eld.

It wouldn't show me anything when I touched it and asked it questions.

Because you didn't phrase your inquiries correctly.

As an uptight artifact demands.

Yes. Jak smiled and left his work in the large cabin he'd been given, the space meant for an admiral or important guest rather than a cartographer, but Rivlen was spoiling him. Either she knew he needed a lot of space for his maps or she wanted him to have a large bed, suitable for two. *That* might be a fantasy, since she hadn't visited his quarters yet on the journey, but he hoped she still wanted to be with him.

Since Malek had restructured the fleet and reinstated her as a ship's captain, she'd been away on missions often, and Jak hadn't seen her as much as he would have wished. But this new exploratory mission that they were jointly leading was a chance for them to be together again, and he was almost as excited about that as he was about making maps.

Almost? Rivlen asked into his mind, and he blushed, realizing he might have shared his meandering thoughts.

Equally?

I suppose that's acceptable. Malek warned me that dating an academic can be tricky.

He and my mother are more *than dating now. Did you hear? They're going to get married. My grandfather is going to officiate to ensure the mages don't get it all wrong—his words. I think that means he approves of their union. Possibly because when they visited him to share the news, Malek said Thanok was wise and much could be learned from The Teachings.*

Malek said that? I didn't think he was religious.

Well, Grandfather *said that, and Malek didn't object. He's too smart to irk his future father-in-law.*

Hm. Does this mean I need to find a wedding gift for them while we're exploring other worlds? What does one get for a king and— I guess your mother will be a queen now. They ought to be able to get anything for themselves that they wish.

My mother would appreciate vials full of interesting specimens.

Oh? And what would Malek appreciate?

For my mother to have vials full of interesting specimens.

He's going to make a good mate.

Yeah. Kind of funny, isn't it? Zidarr aren't known for that.

Kings either.

My mother says he's special.

Undoubtedly.

Jak pushed open the door and stepped on deck and into the humid jungle heat. Monkeys hooted, and birds screeched in the trees below.

Little had changed in Zewnath since his last visit, though he sensed a number of dragons up ahead in addition to the portal, which had been returned to its preferred perch beside the pool with the waterfall, a spot that seemed to hold some special meaning to it. Or maybe the dragons simply liked it because of the amenities. When it came into view, Jak spotted four of them flying about, diving into the pool, and floating on the surface as the sun beamed on their iridescent blue bellies.

Shikari squawked and flew ahead to join them, his tail swishing from side to side behind him.

"I see that our dragons are guarding the portal assiduously," Rivlen said dryly as Jak joined her in the forecastle. Her dark hair was in a bun, her uniform clean and pressed, and a new dragon-steel sword was belted at her waist. The twin blades that Uthari had purloined from another kingdom had been returned, but the blacksmith Homgor, when he hadn't been busy crafting the pieces for Vinjo's machinery, had made more weapons in the past year. Though the various kingdoms had ceased hostilities in the aftermath of the battle at the fortress, few believed peace would last forever.

"All they agreed to," Jak said, "was to keep an eye on things and not let any powerful man-eating creatures through."

"Do you think they find it hard to do that while they're floating on their asses with their eyes closed?"

"Of course not. They're *dragons*. And they don't really have asses."

Shikari plummeted toward the pool, somersaulted in the air, then plunged tail-first into the water. It sprayed everywhere, and the floating dragons flickered irritated eyelids at him. Jak needed to get his boisterous companion to Nargnoth so he could play with the others his age.

"Are you sure?" Rivlen asked. "Your dragon just went ass-first into the water."

Shikari came up with a fish in his mouth, chomping happily as he paddled around the dragons trying to get back to their relaxing floats.

"That was tail-first."

"The tail is ass-adjacent." Rivlen elbowed him, then dug out the map device she'd shown him earlier. "Can this be updated to contain maps of the other worlds?"

Jak gazed thoughtfully at it. "Yes, I should be able to do that."

"Good. I'm sure your giant pieces of parchment are handy for libraries, but a ship's captain prefers something more compact." She slid the sphere back into her pocket.

"I'm touched that you've kept it."

"It's useful."

"*I'm* kind of useful too." He smiled at her, though he knew she wouldn't kiss him or even hold his hand when she was on duty, with several of her officers out on deck. After all those stupid rumors had gone around about her sidling up to Uthari to gain favors, she was still working on establishing a reputation of supreme professionalism and competence. Jak was relieved Malek had reinstated her in the fleet, as well as making it clear that neither she nor Jak had been at fault for Uthari's death. Jak didn't know if everyone believed that, but Malek had also made it clear there would be repercussions if anyone attacked them, and nothing had diminished *his* reputation.

"You're all right," Rivlen said, smiling back at him.

"So all right that you'll want to visit me tonight?"

"I don't know. Have you sprouted any more chest hairs while you've been finishing your studies at the university?"

"Oh, tons. There's practically a rug on there now." Jak patted his chest.

"I see you've still got a poet's tongue."

"Drawing is usually how I woo women."

"So if I come by tonight, you'll capture my likeness on one of those sheets of parchment?"

"I'll capture anything you like." He wriggled his eyebrows at her.

"You're a good mate too, Jak."

"And you like that, right?"

She clasped his hand, not worrying about the rest of her officers. "I do."

THE END

AFTERWORD

Thank you for completing my Dragon Gate series!

I hope you enjoyed spending time in this world and with these characters. If you have time to post a review online, I would appreciate it.

If you would like to try more of my high fantasy, please check out my Emperor's Edge or Dragon Blood series. They're some of my earlier works, but they're both fan favorites.

- The Emperor's Edge (Emperor's Edge, Book 1)
- Balanced on the Blade's Edge (Dragon Blood, Book 1)

Whatever you read next, I hope you enjoy it and have a great rest of the year! Thanks for the support!

Printed in Great Britain
by Amazon

42287098R00381